PI                    R'S

"Fast-paced."                                              —*People*

"A good storyteller . . . Coulter always keeps the pace brisk."
                                        —*Fort Worth Star-Telegram*

"With possible blackmail, intra-judiciary rivalries, and personal peccadil-loes, there's more than enough intrigue—and suspects—for full-court stand-ing in this snappy page-turner . . . A zesty read."          —*BookPage*

"Twisted villains . . . intriguing escapism . . . The latest in the series featur-ing likable . . . FBI agents Lacey Sherlock and Dillon Savich."
                                        —*Lansing (MI) State Journal*

"Coulter takes readers on a chilling and suspenseful ride . . . taut, fast-paced, hard to put down."                    —*Cedar Rapids Gazette*

"The perfect suspense thriller, loaded with plenty of action."
                                        —*The Best Reviews*

"The newest installment in Coulter's FBI series delivers . . . a fast-moving investigation, a mind-bending mystery . . . The mystery at the heart . . . is intriguing and the pacing is brisk."              —*Publishers Weekly*

"Fast-paced . . . Coulter gets better and more cinematic with each of her suspenseful FBI adventures."                    —*Booklist*

# TWICE DEAD

## CATHERINE COULTER

BERKLEY BOOKS, NEW YORK

**THE BERKLEY PUBLISHING GROUP**
**Published by the Penguin Group**
**Penguin Group (USA) Inc.**
**375 Hudson Street, New York, New York 10014, USA**
Penguin Group (Canada), 90 Eglinton Avenue East, Suite 700, Toronto, Ontario M4P 2Y3, Canada
(a division of Pearson Penguin Canada Inc.)
Penguin Books Ltd., 80 Strand, London WC2R 0RL, England
Penguin Group Ireland, 25 St. Stephen's Green, Dublin 2, Ireland (a division of Penguin Books Ltd.)
Penguin Group (Australia), 250 Camberwell Road, Camberwell, Victoria 3124, Australia
(a division of Pearson Australia Group Pty. Ltd.)
Penguin Books India Pvt. Ltd., 11 Community Centre, Panchsheel Park, New Delhi—110 017, India
Penguin Group (NZ), 67 Apollo Drive, Rosedale, North Shore 0632, New Zealand
(a division of Pearson New Zealand Ltd.)
Penguin Books (South Africa) (Pty.) Ltd., 24 Sturdee Avenue, Rosebank, Johannesburg 2196,
South Africa

Penguin Books Ltd., Registered Offices: 80 Strand, London WC2R 0RL, England

PRINTING HISTORY
Berkley trade paperback edition / February 2011

Library of Congress Cataloging-in-Publication Data

Coulter, Catherine.
    [Riptide]
    Twice dead / Catherine Coulter.—Berkley trade pbk. ed.
        p.   cm.
    ISBN 978-0-425-24003-8
    1. United States. Federal Bureau of Investigation—Fiction.    2. Suspense fiction, American.
I. Coulter, Catherine. Hemlock Bay.    II. Title.
    PS3553.O843R5    2011
    813'.54—dc22
                                2010039460

PRINTED IN THE UNITED STATES OF AMERICA

10   9   8   7   6   5   4   3   2   1

# CONTENTS

# RIPTIDE

*My ongoing love and thanks to Iris Johansen and Kay Hooper, and a big special hug to Linda Howard for a terrific twist.*

—CC

# ONE

*New York City*
*June 15*
*Present*

Becca was watching an afternoon soap opera she'd seen off and on since she was a kid. She found herself wondering if she would ever have a child who needed a heart transplant one month and a new kidney the next, or a husband who wouldn't be faithful to her for longer than it took a new woman to look in his direction.

Then the phone rang.

She jumped to her feet, then stopped dead still and stared over at the phone. She heard a guy on TV whining about how life wasn't fair.

He didn't know what fair was.

She made no move to answer the phone. She stood there and listened, watching it as it rang three more times. Then, finally, because her mother was lying in a coma in Lenox Hill Hospital, because she plain couldn't stand the ringing ringing ringing, she watched her hand reach out and pick up the receiver.

She forced her mouth to form the single word. "Hello?"

"Hi, Rebecca. It's your boyfriend. I've got you so scared you have to force yourself to pick up the phone. Isn't that right?"

She closed her eyes as that hated voice, low and deep, swept over her, into her, making her so afraid she was shaking. No hint of an Atlanta drawl, no sharp New York vowels, no dropped R's from Boston. A voice that was well educated, with smooth, clear diction, perhaps even a touch of the Brit in it. Old? Young? She didn't know, couldn't tell. She had to keep it together. She had to listen carefully, to remember how he spoke, what he said. *You can do it. Keep it together. Make him talk, make him say something, you never know what will pop out.* That was what the police psychologist in Albany had told her to do when the man had first started calling her. Listen carefully. Don't let him scare you. Take control. You guide him, not the other way around. Becca licked her lips, chapped from the hot, dry air in Manhattan that week, an anomaly, the weather forecaster had said. And so Becca repeated her litany of questions, trying to keep her voice calm, cool, in charge, yes, that was her. "Won't you tell me who you are? I really want to know. Maybe we can talk about why you keep calling me. Can we do that?"

"Can't you come up with some new questions, Rebecca? After all, I've called you a good dozen times now. And you always say the same things. Ah, they're from a shrink, aren't they? They told you to ask those questions, to try to distract me, to get me to spill my guts to you. Sorry, it won't work."

She'd never really thought it would work, that stratagem. No, this guy knew what he was doing, and he knew how to do it. She wanted to plead with him to leave her alone, but she didn't. Instead, she snapped. She simply lost it, the long-buried anger cutting through her bone-grinding fear. She gripped the phone, knuckles white, and yelled, "Listen to me, you little prick. Stop saying you're my boyfriend. You're nothing but a sick jerk. Now, how about this for a question? Why don't you go to hell where you belong? Why don't you go kill yourself, you're sure not worth anything to the human race. Don't call me anymore, you pathetic jerk. The cops are on to you. The phone is tapped, do you hear me? They're going to get you and fry you."

She'd caught him off guard, she knew it, and an adrenaline rush sent her sky-high, but only for a moment. After a slight pause, he recovered. In a calm, reasonable voice, he said, "Now, Rebecca, sweetheart, you know as well as I do that the cops now don't believe you're being stalked, that some weird guy is calling you at all hours, trying to scare you. You had the phone tap put in yourself because you couldn't get them to do it. And I'll never talk long enough for that old, low-tech equipment of yours to get a trace. Oh yes, Rebecca, because you insulted me, you'll have to pay for it, big-time."

She slammed down the receiver. She held it there, hard, as if trying to stanch the bleeding of a wound, as if holding it down would keep him from dialing her again, keep him away from her. Slowly, finally, she backed away from the phone. She heard a wife on the TV soap plead with her husband not to leave her for her younger sister. She walked out onto her small balcony and looked over Central Park, then turned a bit to the right to look at the Metropolitan Museum. Hordes of people, most in shorts, most of them tourists, sat on the steps, reading, laughing, talking, eating hot dogs from the vendor Teodolpho, some of them probably smoking dope, picking pockets. There were two cops on horseback nearby, their horses' heads pumping up and down, nervous for some reason. The sun blazed down. It was only mid-June, yet the unseasonable heat wave continued unabated. Inside the apartment it was twenty-five degrees cooler. Too cold, at least for her, but she couldn't get the thermostat to move either up or down.

The phone rang again. She heard it clearly through the half-closed glass door.

She jerked around and nearly fell over the railing. Not that it was unexpected. No, never that, it was just so incongruous set against the normalcy of the scene outside.

She forced herself to look back into her mother's lovely pastel living room, to the glass table beside the sofa, at the white phone that sat atop that table, ringing, ringing.

She let it ring six more times. Then she knew she had to answer it. It might be about her mother, her very sick mother, who might be dying. But of course she knew it was him. It didn't matter. Did he know why she even had the phone turned on in the first place? He seemed to know everything else, but he hadn't said anything about her mother. She knew she had no choice at all. She picked it up on the tenth ring.

"Rebecca, I want you to go out onto your balcony again. Look to where those cops are sitting on their horses. Do it now, Rebecca."

She laid down the receiver and walked back out onto the balcony, leaving the glass door open behind her. She looked down at the cops. She kept looking. She knew something horrible was going to happen, she knew it, and there was nothing she could do about it but watch and wait. She waited for three minutes. Just when she was beginning to convince herself that the man was trying new and different ways to terrorize her, there was a loud explosion.

She watched both horses rear up wildly. One of the cops went flying. He landed in a bush as thick smoke billowed up, obscuring the scene.

When the smoke cleared a bit, she saw an old bag lady lying on the sidewalk, her market cart in twisted pieces beside her, her few belongings strewn around her. Pieces of paper fluttered down to the sidewalk, now rutted with deep pockmarks. A large bottle of ginger ale was broken, liquid flowing over the old woman's sneakers. Time seemed to have stopped, then suddenly there was chaos as everyone in view exploded into action. Some people who'd been loitering on the steps of the museum ran toward the old lady.

The cops got there first; the one who'd been thrown from his horse was limping as he ran. They were yelling, waving their arms—at the carnage or the onrushing people, Becca didn't know. She saw the horses throwing their heads from side to side, their eyes rolling at the smoke, the smell of the explosive. Becca stood there frozen, watching. The old woman didn't move.

Becca knew she was dead. Her stalker had detonated a bomb and killed that poor old woman. Why? To terrorize her more? She was already so terrified she could hardly function. What did he want now? She'd left Albany, left the governor's staff with no warning, hadn't even called to check in.

She walked slowly back inside the living room, firmly closing the glass door behind her. She looked at the phone, heard him saying her name, over and over. *Rebecca, Rebecca.* Very slowly, she hung up. She fell to her knees and jerked the connector out of the wall jack. The phone in the bedroom rang, and kept ringing.

She pressed herself close to the wall, her palms slammed against her ears. She had to do something. She had to talk to the cops. Again. Surely now that someone was dead, they would believe that some maniac was terrorizing her, stalking her, murdering someone to show her he meant business.

This time they had to believe her.


*Six Days Later*
*Riptide, Maine*


She pulled into the Texaco gas station, waved to the guy inside the small glass booth, then pumped some regular into her gas tank. She was on the outskirts of Riptide, a quaint town that sprawled north to south, hugging a small harbor filled with sailboats, motorboats, and many fishing boats. Lobster, she thought, and breathed in deeply, air redolent of brine, seaweed, and fish, plus a faint hint of wildflowers, their sweetness riding lightly on the breeze from the sea.

Riptide, Maine.

She was in the sticks, the boondocks, a place nobody knew about, except for a few tourists in the summer. She was sixty-four miles north of Christmas Cove, a beautiful small coastal town she'd visited once as a child, with her mother.

For the first time in two and a half weeks, she felt safe. She felt the salty air tingling on her skin, let the warm breeze flutter her hair against her cheek.

She was in control of her life again.

But what about Governor Bledsoe? He would be all right, he had to be. He had cops everywhere, brushing his teeth for him, sleeping under his bed—no matter who he was sleeping with—hiding in his washroom off his big square office with its huge mahogany power desk. He would be all right. The crazy guy who had terrorized her until six days ago wouldn't be able to get near him.

The main street in Riptide was West Hemlock. There wasn't an East Hemlock unless someone wanted to drive into the ocean. She drove nearly to the end of the street to an old Victorian bed-and-breakfast called Errol Flynn's Hammock. There was a widow's walk on top, railed in black. She counted at least five colors on the exterior. It was perfect.

"I like the name," she said to the old man behind the rich mahogany counter.

"Yep," he said, and pushed the guest book toward her. "I like it, too. Been Scottie all my life. Sign in and I'll beam you right up."

She smiled and signed Becca Powell. She'd always admired Colin Powell. Surely he wouldn't mind if she borrowed his name for a while. For a while, Becca Matlock would cease to exist.

She was safe.

But why, she wondered yet again, why hadn't the police believed her? Still, they were providing the governor extra protection, so that was something.

Why?

# TWO

They had Becca sit in an uncomfortable chair with uneven legs. She laid one hand on the scarred table, looking at the woman and two men, and knew they thought she was a nut or, very likely, something far worse.

There were three other men in the room, lined up against the wall next to the door. No one introduced them. She wondered if they were FBI. Probably, since she'd reported the threat on the governor, and they were dressed in dark suits, white shirts, blue ties. She'd never seen so many wing tips in one room before.

Detective Morales, slight, black-eyed, handsome, said quietly, "Ms. Matlock, we are trying to understand this. You say he blew up this old woman to get your attention? For what reason? Why you? What does he want? Who is he?"

She repeated it all again, more slowly this time, nearly word for word. Finally, seeing their stone faces, she tried yet again, leaning forward, clasping her hands on the wooden table, avoiding the clump of long-ago-dried food. "Listen, I have no idea who he is. I know it's a man, but I can't tell if he's old or if he's young. I told you that I've heard him many times on the phone. He started calling me in Albany and then he followed me here to New York. I never saw him in Albany, but I've seen him here, stalking me, not close enough to identify, but I'm sure it was him I saw three different times. I reported this eight days ago to you, Detective Morales."

"Yes," said Detective McDonnell, a man who looked like he sliced and diced criminal suspects for breakfast. His body was long and thin, his suit rumpled and loose, his voice cold. "We know all about it. We acted on it. I spoke to the police in Albany when we didn't see anything of him here in New York. We all compared notes, discussed everything thoroughly."

"What else can I tell you?"

"You said he calls you Rebecca, never shortens your name."

"Yes, Detective Morales. He always says Rebecca and he always identifies himself as my boyfriend."

A look went between the two men. Did they think it was a vengeful ex-boyfriend?

"I've told you that I don't recognize his voice. I have never known this man, never. I'm certain of it."

Detective Letitia Gordon, the only other woman in the room, was tall, wide-mouthed, with hair cut very short, and she carried a big chip on her shoulder. She said in a voice colder than McDonnell's, "You could try for the truth. I'm tired of all this crap. You're a liar, Ms. Matlock. Sure, Hector did everything he could. We all tried to believe you, at first, but there wasn't anyone around you. Not a soul. We wasted three days tagging you, and all for nothing. We spent another two days following up on everything you told us, but again, nothing.

"What is it with you? Are you on coke?" She tapped the side of her head with two long fingers. "You need attention? Daddy didn't give you enough when you were a little girl? That's why you have this made-up guy call himself your boyfriend?"

Becca wanted to punch out Detective Gordon. She imagined the woman could pulverize her, so that wouldn't be smart. She had to be calm, logical. She had to be the sane adult here. She cocked her head at the woman and said, "Why are you angry at me? I haven't done anything. I'm just trying to get some help. Now he's killed this old woman. You've got to stop him. Don't you?"

The two male detectives again darted glances back and forth. The woman shook her head in disgust. Then she pushed back her chair and rose. She leaned over and splayed her hands on the wooden tabletop, right next to the clump of dried food. Her face was right in Becca's. Her breath smelled of fresh oranges. "You made it all up, didn't you? There wasn't any guy calling you and telling you to look outside your window. When that bag lady got blown up by some nutcase, you just pulled in your fantasy guy again to be responsible for the bomb. No more. We want you to see our psychiatrist, Ms. Matlock. Right now. You've had your fifteen minutes of fame, now it's time to give it up."

"Of course I won't see any shrink, that's—"

"You either see the psychiatrist or we arrest you."

A *nightmare,* she thought. *Here I am at the police station, telling them everything I know, and they think I'm crazy.* She said slowly, staring right at Detective Gordon, "For what?"

"You're a public nuisance. You're filing false complaints, telling lies that waste manpower. I don't like you, Ms. Matlock. I'd like to throw you in jail for all the grief you've dished out, but I won't if you go see our shrink. Maybe he can straighten you out, someone needs to."

Becca rose slowly to her feet. She looked at each of them in turn. "I have told you the truth. There is a madman out there and I don't know who he is. I've told you everything I can think of. He has threatened the governor. He murdered that poor old woman in front of the museum. I'm not making anything up. I'm not nuts and I'm not on drugs."

It did no good. They didn't believe her.

The three men lined up along the wall of the interrogation room didn't say a word. One of them simply nodded to Detective Gordon as Becca walked out of the room.

THIRTY minutes later, Becca Matlock was seated in a very comfortable chair in a small office that had only two narrow windows that looked across at two other narrow windows. Across the desk sat Dr. Burnett, a man somewhere in his forties, nearly bald, wearing designer glasses. He looked intense and tired.

"What I don't understand," Becca said, sitting forward, "is why the police won't believe me."

"We'll get to that. Now, you didn't want to speak with me?"

"I'm sure you're a very nice man, but no, I don't need to speak to you, at least not professionally."

"The police officers aren't certain about that, Ms. Matlock. Now, why don't you tell me, in your own words, a bit about yourself and exactly when this stalker first came to your attention."

Yet again, she thought. Her voice was flat because she'd said the same words so many times. Hard to feel anything saying them now. "I'm a senior speechwriter for Governor Bledsoe. I live in a very nice condominium on Oak Street in Albany. Two and a half weeks ago, I got the first phone call. No heavy breathing, no profanity, nothing like that. He said he'd seen me running in the park, and he wanted to get to know me. He wouldn't tell me who he was. He said I would come to know him very well. He said he wanted to be my boyfriend. I told him to leave me alone and hung up."

"Did you tell any friends or the governor about the call?"

"Not until after he called me another two times. That's when he told me to stop sleeping with the governor. He said he was my boyfriend, and I wasn't going to sleep with any other man. In a very calm voice, he said that if I didn't stop sleeping with the governor, he'd have to kill him. Naturally, when I told the governor about this, everyone licensed to carry a gun within a ten-mile radius was on it."

He didn't even crack a smile; kept staring at her.

Becca found she really didn't care. She said, "They tapped my phone immediately, but somehow he knew they had. They couldn't find him. They said he was using some sort of electronic scrambler that kept giving out fake locations."

"And are you sleeping with Governor Bledsoe, Ms. Matlock?"

She'd heard that question a good dozen times, too, over and over, especially from Detective Gordon. She even managed a smile. "Actually, no. I don't suppose you've noticed, but he is old enough to be my father."

"We had a president old enough to be your father and a woman even younger than you are and neither of them had a problem with that concept."

She wondered if Governor Bledsoe could ever survive a Monica and almost smiled. She shrugged.

"So, Ms. Matlock, are you sleeping with the governor?"

She'd discovered that at the mention of sex, everyone—media folk, cops, friends—homed right in on it. It still offended her, but she had answered the question so often the edge was off now. She shrugged again, seeing that it bothered him, and said, "No, I haven't slept with Governor Bledsoe. I have never wanted to sleep with Governor Bledsoe. I write speeches for him, really fine speeches. I don't sleep with him. I even occasionally write speeches for Mrs. Bledsoe. I don't sleep with her, either.

"Now, I have no clue why the man believes that I am having sex with the governor. I have no clue why he would care if I were. Why did he pull the governor, of all people, out of the hat? Because I spend time with him? Because he's powerful? I don't know. The Albany police haven't found out anything about this man yet. However, they didn't think I was a liar, not like the police here in New York. I even met with a police psychologist, who gave me advice on how to handle him when he called."

"Actually, Ms. Matlock, the Albany police do believe you are a liar. At first they didn't, but that's what they believe now. But do go on."

Just like that? He said everyone believed she was a liar and she was just to go on? "What do you mean?" she said slowly. "They never gave me that impression."

"That's why our detectives finally sent you to me. They spoke to their counterparts in Albany. No one could discover any stalker. They believed you were disturbed about something. Perhaps you had a crush on the governor and this was your way of getting him to acknowledge you."

"Ah, I see. I have, perhaps, a fatal attraction."

"No, certainly not. You shouldn't have referred to it like that. It's much too soon."

"Too soon for what? I'm still trying to get the hang of it?"

Anger flashed in his eyes. It made her feel good. "Go on, Ms. Matlock. No, don't argue with me yet. First tell me more. I need to understand. Then we can determine what's going on, together."

In his dreams, she thought. A crush on the governor? Yeah, right. What a joke that was. Bledsoe was a man who would sleep with a nun if he could get under her habit. He made Bill Clinton look as upstanding as Eisenhower, or had Ike had a mistress, too? Men and power—the two always seemed to go with illicit sex. As for Bledsoe, he'd been very lucky thus far, he hadn't yet run into an intern as voracious as Monica, one who wouldn't fade into the woodwork when he was done with her.

"Very well," she said. "I came to New York to escape that maniac. I was—I am—terrified of him and what he'll do. Also, my mother lives here and she's very ill. I wanted to be with her."

"You're staying in her apartment, is that right?"

"Yes. She's in Lenox Hill Hospital."

"What's wrong with her?"

Becca looked at him and tried to say the words. They wouldn't come out. She cleared her throat and finally managed to say, "She's dying of uterine cancer."

"I'm sorry. You say this man followed you here to New York?"

Becca nodded. "I saw him here for the first time the day after I arrived in New York, on Madison near Fiftieth, weaving in and out of people to my right. He was wearing a blue windbreaker and a baseball cap. How do I know it was him? I can't be specific about that. Deep down, I recognized that it was him. He knew I saw him, I'm sure of that.

Unfortunately I couldn't see him clearly enough to give more than a general impression of what he looks like."

"And that is?"

"He's tall, slender. Is he young? I don't know. The baseball cap covered his hair and he was wearing aviator glasses, very dark, opaque. He was wearing generic jeans and that blue windbreaker that was very loose." She paused a moment. "I've told the police all of this, many times. Why do you care?"

His look said it all. He wanted to see how specific, how detailed her descriptions were, how much she'd embellished her fantasy man. And all of the marvelous particulars were from her imagination, her very sick imagination.

She kept it together. When he hesitated, she said mildly, "He ducked away when I turned toward him. Then the phone calls started again. I know he's keeping close tabs on me. He seems to know exactly where I am and what I'm doing. I can feel him, you know?"

"You told the officers that he wouldn't tell you what he wanted."

"No, not really, other than to tell me if I didn't stop having sex with the governor, he would kill him. I asked him why he'd do that and he just said he didn't want me to have sex with any other man, that he was my boyfriend. But it sounded funny, like it was just something he was saying, not something he really meant. So why is he doing this, really? I don't know. I will be frank with you, Dr. Burnett. I'm not crazy, I'm terrified. If that's his aim, he's certainly succeeded. I simply don't understand why the police think I'm the bad guy here, that I'm making all of this up for some crazy reason. Perhaps you could believe me now?"

He was a shrink; he hedged well. "Tell me why you believe this man is stalking you and making these phone calls to you, why you don't believe that he wants to be your boyfriend, that it really all boils down to an obsession and his possession of you?"

She closed her eyes. She'd thought and thought about why, but there wasn't anything. Nothing at all. He'd targeted her, but why? She shook her head. "At first he said he wanted to know me. What does that mean? If he wanted that, why wouldn't he come over and introduce himself? If the cops wanted a nutcase to send to you, they should find him. What does he really want? I don't know. If I even had a supposition about it, I'd throw it out there, believe me. But the boyfriend thing? No, I don't believe that."

He sat forward, his fingertips pressed together, studying her. What did he see? What was he thinking? Did she sound insane? Evidently so, because when he said very quietly, gently even, "You and I need to talk about you, Ms. Matlock," she knew he didn't believe her, probably hadn't believed her for a minute. He continued in that same gentle voice, "There's a big problem here. Without intervention, it will continue to get bigger and that worries me. Perhaps you're already seeing a psychiatrist?"

She had a big problem? She rose slowly and placed her hands on his desktop. "You're right about that, Doctor. I do have a big problem. You just don't know where the problem really is. That, or you refuse to recognize it. That makes it easier, I guess."

She grabbed up her purse and walked toward the door. He called after her, "You need me, Ms. Matlock. You need my help. I don't like the direction you're going. Come back and let me talk to you."

She said over her shoulder, "You're a fool, sir," and kept walking. "As for your objectivity, perhaps you should consult your ethics about that, Doctor."

She heard him coming after her. She slammed the door and took off running down the long, dingy hallway.

# THREE

Becca kept walking, her head down, out the front doors, staring at her Bally flats. From the corner of her eye, she saw a man turn away from her, quickly, too quickly. She was at One Police Plaza. There were a million people, all of them hurrying, like all New Yorkers, focused on where they were going, wasting not an instant. But this man, he was watching her, she knew it. It was him, it had to be. If only she could get close enough, she could describe him. Where was he now?

Over there, by a city trash can. He was wearing sunglasses, the same opaque aviator glasses, and a red Braves baseball cap, this time backward. He was the bad guy in all of this, not her. Something hit her hard at that moment, and she felt pure rage pump through her. She yelled, "Wait! Don't you run away from me, you coward!" Then she started pushing her way through the crowds of people to where she'd last seen him. Over there, by that building, wearing a sweatshirt, dark blue, long-sleeved, no windbreaker this time. She headed that way. She was cursed, someone elbowed her, but she didn't care. She would become an instant New Yorker—utterly focused, rude if anyone dared to get in her way. She made it to the corner of the building, but she didn't see any dark blue sweatshirt. No baseball cap. She stood there panting.

Why didn't the cops believe her? What had she ever done to make them believe she was a liar? What had made the Albany cops believe she'd lied? And now, he'd murdered that poor old woman by the museum. She wasn't some crazy figment in her mind, she was very real and in the morgue.

She stopped. She'd lost him. She stood there a long time, breathing hard, feeling scores of people part and go around her on either side. Two steps beyond her, the seas closed again.

Forty-five minutes later, Becca was at Lenox Hill Hospital, sitting beside her mother's bed. Her mother, who was now in a near-coma, was so drugged she didn't recognize her daughter. Becca sat there, holding her hand, not speaking about the stalker, but talking about the speech she'd written for the governor on gun control, something she wasn't so certain about now. "In all five boroughs, handgun laws are the same and are very strict. Do you know that one gun store owner told me that 'to buy a gun in New York City, you have to stand in a corner on one leg and beg'?"

She paused a moment. For the first time in her life, she desperately wanted a handgun. But there was no way she could get one in time to help. She'd need a permit, have to wait fifteen days after she'd bought the gun, and then hang around for probably another six months for them to do a background check on her. And then stand on one leg and beg. She said to her silent mother, "I've never before even thought about owning a gun, Mom, but who knows? Crime is everywhere." Yes, she wanted to buy a gun, but if she did finally manage to get one, the stalker would have long since killed her. She felt like a victim waiting to happen and there was nothing she could do about it. No one would help her. She was all she had, and in terms of getting a hold of a gun, she'd have to go to the street. And the thought of going up to street guys and asking them to sell her a gun scared her to her toes.

"It was a great speech, Mom. I had to let the governor straddle the fence, no way around that, but I did have him say that he didn't want guns forbidden, just didn't want them in the hands of criminals. I did pros and cons on whether the proposed federal one-handgun-a-month law will work. You know, the NRA's opinions, then the HCI's—they're Handgun Control, Inc."

She kept talking, patting her mother's hands, lightly stroking her fingers over her forearm, careful not to hit any of the IV lines.

"So many of your friends have been here. All of them are very worried. They all love you."

Her mother was dying, she knew it as a god-awful fact, as something that couldn't be changed, but she couldn't accept it down deep inside her where her mother had always been from her earliest memories, always there for her, always. She thought of the years ahead without her, but she simply couldn't see it at all. Tears stung her eyes and she sniffed them back. "Mom," she said, and laid her cheek against her mother's arm. "I don't want you to die, but I know the cancer is bad and you couldn't bear the pain if you stayed with me." There, she'd said the words aloud. She slowly raised her head. "I love you, Mom. I love you more than you can imagine. If you can somehow hear me, somehow understand, please know that you have always been the most important person in my life. Thank you for being my mother." She had no more words. She sat there another half hour, looking at her mother's beloved face, so full of life just a few weeks ago, a face made for myriad expressions, each of which Becca knew. It was almost over, and there was simply nothing she could do. She said then, "I'll be back soon, Mom. Please rest and don't feel any pain. I love you."

She knew that she should run, that this man, whoever he was, would end up killing her and there was nothing she could do to stop him. If she stayed here. Certainly the police weren't going to do anything. But no, she wasn't about to leave her mother.

She rose, leaned down, and kissed her mother's soft, pale cheek. She lightly patted her mother's hair, so very thin now, her scalp showing here and there. It was the drugs, a nurse had told her. It happened. Such a beautiful woman, her mother had been, tall and fair, her hair that unusual pale blond that had no other colors in it. Her mother was still beautiful, but she was so still now, almost as if she were already gone. No, Becca wouldn't leave her. The guy would have to kill her to make her leave her mother.

She didn't realize she was crying again until a nurse pressed a Kleenex into her hand. "Thank you," she said, not looking away from her mother.

"Go home and get some sleep, Becca," the nurse said, her voice quiet and calm. "I'll keep watch. Go get some sleep."

*There's no one else in the world for me,* Becca thought, as she walked away from Lenox Hill Hospital. *I'll be alone when Mom dies.*

Her mother died that night. She just drifted away, the doctor told her, no pain, no awareness of death. An easy passing. Ten minutes after the call, the phone rang again.

This time she didn't pick it up. She put her mother's apartment on the market the following day, spent the night in a hotel under an assumed name, and made all the funeral arrangements from there. She called her mother's friends to invite them to the small, private service.

A day and a half later, Becca threw the first clot of rich, dark earth over her mother's coffin. She watched as the black dirt mixed with the deep red roses on top of the coffin. She didn't cry, but all of her mother's friends were quietly weeping. She accepted a hug from each of them. It was still very hot in New York, too hot for the middle of June.

When she returned to her hotel room the phone was ringing. Without thinking, she picked it up.

"You tried to get away from me, Rebecca. I don't like that."

She'd had it. She'd been pushed too hard. Her mother was dead, there was nothing to stay her hand. "I nearly caught you the other day, at One Police Plaza, you pathetic coward. You jerk, did you wonder what I was doing there? I was blowing the whistle on you, you murderer. Yeah, I saw you, all right. You had on that ridiculous baseball cap and that dark blue sweatshirt. Next time I'll get you and then I'll shoot you right between your crazy eyes."

"It's you the cops think is crazy. I'm not even a blip on their radar. Hey, I don't even exist." His voice grew deeper, harder. "Stop sleeping with the governor or I'll kill him like I did that stupid old bag lady. I've told you that over and over but you haven't listened to me. I know he's visited you in New York. Everyone knows it. Stop sleeping with him."

She started laughing and couldn't seem to stop. She did only when he began yelling at her, calling her a whore, a stupid bitch, and more curses, some of them extraordinarily vicious.

She hiccuped. "Sleep with the governor? Are you nuts? He's married. He has three children, two of them older than I am." And then, because it no longer mattered, because he might not really exist anyway, she said, "The governor sleeps with every woman he can talk into that private room off his office. I'd have to take a number. You want them all to stop sleeping with him? It'll keep you busy until the next century and that's a very long time away."

"It's you, Rebecca. You've got to stop sleeping with him."

"Listen to me, you stupid jerk. I would only sleep with the governor if world peace were in the balance. Even then it would be a very close call."

The creep actually sighed. "Don't lie, Rebecca. Stop, do you hear me?"

"I can't stop something I've never even done."

"It's a shame," he said, and for the first time, he hung up on her.

That night the governor was shot through the neck outside the Hilton Hotel, where he was attending a fund-raiser for cancer research. He was lucky. There were more than a hundred doctors around. They managed to save his life. It was reported that the bullet was fired from a great distance, by a marksman with remarkable skill. They had no leads as yet.

When she heard that, she said to the Superman cartoon character playing soundlessly on the television, "He was supposed to go to a fund-raiser on endangered species."

That's when she ran. Her mother was dead and there was nothing more holding her here.

To Maine, to find sanctuary.

*Riptide, Maine*
*June 22*

Becca said, "I'll take it."

The real estate broker, Rachel Ryan, beamed at her, then almost immediately backpedaled. "Perhaps you're making this decision too quickly, Ms. Powell. Would you like to think about this for a bit? I will have everything cleaned, but the house is old and that includes all the appliances and the bathrooms. It's furnished, of course, but the furniture isn't all that remarkable. The house has been empty for four years, since Mr. Marley's death."

"You told me all that, Mrs. Ryan. I see it's an old house. I still like it, it's charming. And it's quite large. I like a lot of space. Also it's here at the end of the lane all by itself. I do like my privacy." Now, that was an understatement but nonetheless the truth. "A Mr. Marley lived here?"

"Mr. Jacob Marley. Yes, the same name as in *A Christmas Carol*. He was eighty-seven years old when he passed away in his sleep. He kept to himself for the last thirty years or so of his life. His daddy started the town back in 1907, after several of his businesses in Boston were burned to the ground one hot summer night. It was said his enemies were responsible. Mr. Marley Senior wasn't a popular man. He was one of those infamous robber barons. But he wasn't stupid. He decided it was healthier to leave Boston and so he did, and came here. There was already a small fishing village here, and he took it over and renamed it."

Becca patted the woman's shoulder. "It's all right. I've thought about it, Mrs. Ryan. I'll give you a money order since I don't have a bank account here. Could it be cleaned today so I can move in tomorrow afternoon?"

"It will be ready if I have to clean it myself. Actually, since it's summer, I can round up a dozen high schoolers and get them right over here. Don't you worry about a thing. Oh yes, there's the most adorable little boy who lives not far from here, over on Gum Shoe Lane. I'm not really his aunt but that's what he calls me. His name is Sam and I watched him come into this world. His mother was my best friend and I—"

Becca raised her brow, listening politely, but evidently Rachel Ryan was through talking.

"All right, Ms. Powell, I will see you in a couple of days. Call me if there are any problems."

And it was done. Becca was the proud renter of a very old Victorian jewel that featured eight bedrooms, three spacious bathrooms, a kitchen that surely must have been a showplace before 1910, and a total of ten fireplaces. And as she'd told Rachel Ryan, she liked that it was very private, at the end of Belladonna Drive, no prying neighbors anywhere near, and that's what she wanted. The nearest house was a good half mile away. The property was bordered on three sides by thick maple and pine trees, and the view of the ocean from the widow's walk was spectacular.

She hummed when she moved in on Thursday afternoon. She even managed to work up a sweat. Even though she wouldn't use them, she cleaned the bedrooms just because she wanted to. She wallowed in all the space. She never wanted to live in an apartment again.

She'd bought a gun from a guy she met in a restaurant in Rockland, Maine. She'd taken a big chance, but it had worked out. The gun was a beauty—a Coonan .357 Magnum automatic, and the guy had taken her next door, where there was a sports shop with an indoor range, and taught her how to shoot. He'd then asked her to go to a motel with him. He was child's play to deal with after the maniac in New York. All she'd had to do was say no very firmly. No need to draw her new gun on the guy.

She gently laid the Coonan in the top drawer of her bedside table, a very old mahogany piece with rusted hinges. As she closed the drawer she realized that she hadn't cried when her mother died. She hadn't cried at her funeral. But now, as she gently placed a photograph of her mother on top of the bedside table, she felt the tears roll down her cheeks. She stood there staring down at her mother's picture, taken nearly twenty years before, showing a beautiful young woman, so fair and fine-boned, laughing, hugging Becca against her side. Becca couldn't remember where they were, maybe in upstate New York. They'd stayed up there for a while when Becca was six and seven years old. "Oh, Mom, I'm so sorry. If only you hadn't locked your heart away with a dead man, maybe there could have been another man to love, couldn't there? You had so much to offer, so much love to give. I miss you so much."

She lay down on the bed, held a pillow against her chest, and cried until there were no more tears. She got up and wiped the light sheen of dust off the photo, then carefully set it down again. "I'm safe now, Mom. I don't know what's going on, but at least I'm safe for the time being. That man won't find me here. How could he? I know no one followed me."

She realized, as she was speaking to her mother's photo, that she also ached for the father she'd never known, Thomas Matlock, shot and killed in Vietnam after the war was over, so long ago, when she was just a baby. He was still a war hero. But her mother hadn't forgotten, ever. And it was his name that her mother had whispered before she'd fallen into the drug-induced coma. "Thomas, Thomas."

He'd been dead for over twenty-five years. So long ago. A different world, but the people were the same—both good and evil, as always—mauling one another to get the lion's share of the spoils. He'd seen her before he'd gone, her mother had told her, seen her and hugged her and loved her. But Becca couldn't remember him.

She finished hanging up her clothes and arranging her toiletries in the old-fashioned bathroom with its claw-footed bathtub. The teenagers had even scrubbed between the claws. Good job.

There was a knock on the door. Becca dropped the towel she was holding and froze.

Another knock.

It wasn't him. He had no idea where she was. There was no way he could find her. It was probably the guy to check the one air-conditioning unit in the living room window. Or the garbage man, or—

"Don't be paranoid," she said aloud to the blue towel as she picked it up and hung it on the very old wooden bar. "Do you also realize you've been talking out loud a whole lot recently? Another thing, you don't sound particularly bright." But who cared if she sang to the towel rack, she thought, as she walked down the old creaking stairs to the front entrance hall.

She could only stare at the tall man who stood in the doorway. It was Tyler, the boy she'd known in college. She'd been one of his few friends. He'd been a geek loner and hadn't managed to make more than a few non-geek friends. Only he wasn't a geek anymore. No more heavy-rimmed glasses and pen protector on his shirt pocket. No more stooped shoulders and pants worn too high, his ankles showing his white socks. He was wearing tight jeans that fit him very well indeed, his hair was long, and his shoulders were wide enough to make a woman blink. He was buff, in very good shape. Yes, he was a good-looking man. It was amazing. She had to blink at him a couple of times to get her bearings.

"Tyler? Tyler McBride? Is it really you? I'm sorry I'm gawking. You look so very different, but it's still you. Actually, to be perfectly honest about this, you're very sexy."

He gave her a huge grin and gripped her hands between his. "Becca Matlock, it's good to see you. I came over to see my new neighbor, never dreaming it could be you. Is Powell your married name? I can't imagine why you're here of all places, the end of the world. But whatever. Welcome to Riptide."

# FOUR

She laughed and squeezed his hands and said, "Goodness, you're not a nerd anymore. Listen, Tyler, it's because of you that I'm here. I would have called you. I just haven't gotten to it yet. Can I really be so lucky to have you for a neighbor?"

He gave her a very nice smile and stood there, waiting. Had he had braces? She couldn't remember. It didn't matter, he had gorgeous teeth now. What a difference. Incredible.

"Oh, yes, everyone's a neighbor in Riptide, but yes, I live just one street over, on Gum Shoe Lane."

She let go of his hands although she didn't want to, and stepped back. "Do come in. Everything, including the furnishings, is ancient, but there aren't any springs sticking up in the sofa, and it's fairly comfortable. Mrs. Ryan sent an army of teenagers here to clean the place. They did a pretty decent job. Come in, Tyler, come in."

She managed to make two cups of tea on the ancient stove while Tyler sat at the kitchen table watching her. "What do you mean you came here because of me?"

She dipped a tea bag in and out of the cups of hot water. "I remembered your talking about your hometown, Riptide. You called it your haven." She paused a moment and stared down into her teacup. "I'll never forget your saying that Riptide was in the boondocks, near nothing at all, so private you nearly forgot you were even here. Out on the edge of the world, nearly falling into the ocean, and nobody knew where it was, or cared. You also said Riptide was the place where the sun first rose in the U.S. You said for those moments, the sky was an orange ball and the water was a cauldron of fire."

"I said that? I didn't know I was such a poet."

"That's nearly word for word, and, as I told you, that's why I came. Goodness, I can't get over how you've changed, Tyler."

"Everyone changes, Becca. Even you. You're prettier now than you were back in college." He frowned a moment, as if trying to remember. "Your hair's darker and I don't remember you having brown eyes or wearing glasses, but otherwise, I'd know you anywhere." Well damn, she thought, that wasn't good. She pushed the glasses higher on her nose.

He accepted the cup of tea, not speaking until she sat down at the table across from him. Then he smiled at her and said, "Why do you need a haven?"

What to tell him?

That the governor had been shot in the neck because of her? No, no, she couldn't feel responsible. That madman shot the governor. She stalled.

He backed off and said, "You went to New York, didn't you? You were a writer, I remember. What were you doing in New York?"

"I was writing speeches," she said easily, "for bigwigs in various companies. I can't believe you remember that I went to New York."

"I remember nearly everything about people I like. Why do you need a haven? No, wait, if it isn't any of my business, forget it. It's just that I'm worried about you."

She wasn't a very good liar, but she had to try. "No, it's okay. I'm getting away from a very bad relationship."

"Your husband?"

No choice. "Yes, my husband. He's very possessive. I wanted out and he didn't want to let me go. I thought of Riptide and what you'd said." She didn't want to tell him about her mother dying. To mix that with a lie was just too much. She managed to shrug and raise her teacup to click it against his. "Thanks, Tyler, for being at Dartmouth and talking about your hometown to me."

"I'm glad you're here," he said, his eyes serious upon her face. "If your husband is after you, how do you know he didn't follow you to the airport? I know New York traffic is nuts, but it's not all that hard to follow someone, if you really want to."

"It's a good thing I've read a lot of spy novels and seen lots of police shows." She told him how she'd changed taxis three times on the way to Kennedy. "When I got out at the United terminal, I was sure no one had followed me. My last driver was one of a vanishing breed—a native New Yorker cabbie. He knew Queens as well as he knew his ex-wife's lover, he told me. No one followed me, he was sure of it. I flew to Boston, then on to Portland, and bought myself a used Toyota from Big Frank's. I drove up here to your haven, and he'll never find me."

She had no idea whether or not he believed her. Well, all that about her escape from New York was the truth. She'd only lied about who she was running from.

"I sure hope you're right. But I plan to keep an eye on you, Becca Powell."

She managed to get him to talk about himself. He told her he was a computer consultant, a troubleshooter of sorts, and he designed software programs for major accounting and brokerage firms, "to track clients and money and how the two come together. I'm successful, Becca, and it feels good. You know, you were the only girl in college who didn't look at me and giggle at what a jerk I was. You called me a nerd and a geek, but that was okay, it was the truth. Do you know we've got a gym in Riptide? I'm there three days a week. I find that if I don't work out regularly, I get all skinny again, lose my energy, and want to wear a pocket protector."

"You're sure not skinny now, Tyler."

"No," he said, grinning at her, "I'm not."

When she showed him out some fifteen minutes later, she wondered again if he'd believed her reason for coming to Riptide. He was a nice guy; she'd hated to lie to him. She was glad he was here. She wasn't completely alone. She watched him get into his Jeep. He looked up and waved at her, then executed a sharp U-turn. He lived one street over, on Gum Shoe Lane, but it was a good distance away.

Her house. That felt good. She slowly closed the front door and turned to look at her ancient furnishings. Her mother, the antiques nut, would have shuddered. When Marley Senior had furnished this house, she wondered if he'd ordered anything out of the turn-of-the-century Sears catalogue.

Now that she was settled in, her two suitcases emptied and tucked in the back of her bedroom closet, she decided to explore the town. She locked up the house, got into her car and drove down West Hemlock past one of Riptide's half-dozen white-spired churches. It was a charming town, isolated, and unspoiled. Just being in such a quaint village made her feel safe.

When she turned her Toyota onto Poison Oak Circle ten minutes later, she spotted the Food Fort. Everyone there was friendly, including the produce woman, who handed her the best head of romaine lettuce in the bin. Since it was a fishing town, there was lots of fresh fish available, mainly lobster. Becca was eager to give everything a try.

Her evening was peaceful. She spent the twilight time leaning over the railing of the widow's walk, staring out at the ocean. The water was calm; waves crested gently against pine-covered rocks that she could barely make out from where she stood. But Marley Senior had named the town Riptide. Was there a vicious tide that pulled people out to sea? She'd have to ask. It was a scary thought. She'd been caught in a riptide once when she was about ten years old. A lifeguard the size of Godzilla had managed to save her, telling her you had to swim parallel to shore until you were free of the strong current.

She wasn't being sucked out now, dragged under to die a horrible death. She'd escaped, as she had when she was ten. Only this time she'd saved herself. Like the ocean on this beautiful evening, her life was calm again. She was safe.

She looked to the left at the dozen or so fishing boats coming back into the harbor. Since it was summer, some tourists were out in their white-sailed boats, enjoying the last bit of the day. The deep scent of brine settled around her. She quite liked it. Yes, she was going to be safe here.

The phone installers were coming the next day. She'd changed her mind at least a dozen times as to whether or not she would even have a phone. In the end, she'd decided in favor of getting connected, perhaps as a gesture of confidence that her stalker would fail to track her down. Still, she wasn't about to get another cell phone, not until the monster was gone.

The next morning after nine o'clock, Tyler appeared again at her door, a little boy at his side, holding his hand.

"Hi, Becca. This is my son, Sam."

His son? Becca looked down at the solemn little face looking up at her. He didn't look a thing like Tyler. He was sturdy, compact, with a head of very dark hair and eyes a beautiful light blue. Sort of like hers, she thought, and smiled. He looked all boy. He didn't seem happy to be there. She opened the screen door and stood back. "Do come in, Tyler, Sam."

He was so wary, she thought. Distrustful. Or was it more than that? Was there something wrong with this precious little boy? Was this Rachel Ryan's Sam, the little boy she obviously adored? She smiled down at him, then slowly came down on her knees. "I'm Becca. It's a pleasure to meet you, Sam." She held out her hand.

"Sam, say hello to Becca."

There was a slight edge to his voice. Why was that? She said quickly, "It's all right, Tyler. Sam can do what he wants. I don't think I was all that talkative, either, when I was his age."

"It's not that," Tyler said, frowning down at his son.

The child stared up at her, unmoving, so very still. She didn't stop smiling. "Would you like a glass of lemonade, Sam? Mine's just about the best east of the Rockies."

"All right." His voice was small and wary. Thank goodness she'd bought some cookies. Even wary little boys had to like cookies.

She sat him at the kitchen table, saying, "Do you have an aunt Rachel, Sam?"

"Rachel," Sam repeated, and he gave her a huge smile. "My aunt Rachel."

Sam said nothing more after that, but he ate three cookies and drank nearly two glasses of lemonade. Then he wiped the back of his hand over his mouth. All boy, she thought, but what was wrong? Why didn't he speak? And he looked so blank, as if his mind wasn't focused on the here and now.

"Do come back, Sam. I'll make sure there are always cookies here for you."

"When?" Sam said.

"Tomorrow," she said, giving him a big grin. "I'll be here all morning."

"What are you doing tomorrow afternoon?" Tyler said as he took his son's small hand.

"I'm going to *The Riptide Independent* to see if they need a reporter."

"Then you'll be seeing Bernie Bradstreet, he's the owner and the main contributor. A really nice older guy who has his finger in every pie in this town. He'll probably be very impressed with you. Hey, it seems like you're going to stay for a while."

"Yes, I just might."

"Ah, maybe I'll see you later when Sam's with his aunt Rachel. She's not really his aunt, she's just a really good friend and his babysitter."

# FIVE

Becca pulled the brush through her brown hair. It was long now, to her shoulders. She pulled it back in a ponytail, then stared at herself in the mirror. She hadn't worn a ponytail since she was thirteen years old. Then she hadn't known what evil was. *No, don't think about him.* He would never find her. She looked back at herself. The glasses changed her looks quite a bit, as did her darkened eyebrows.

She looked over at her small portable television and knew that during the news they'd soon show another photo of her. They did. It was from her driver's license. She was grateful they hadn't gotten a more up-to-date shot. She didn't much resemble that photo, except maybe on an excruciatingly bad day. With the slight alterations she'd made to her looks before coming to Riptide, she felt reasonably sure that none of the townspeople would find her out. Only Tyler would make the connection, and she felt she could trust him. Now that her story was being flashed on FOX, she'd have to tell him the truth. She should have told him right away, but she couldn't, simply couldn't, not then, not at first. Now there was no choice.

But Tyler beat her to the punch. Not fifteen minutes after her story aired, her doorbell rang.

"You lied to me." It was Tyler. He stood on the front porch, stiff all over, so angry he nearly stuttered.

"Yes, I know. I'm sorry, Tyler. Please come in. I need to throw myself on your mercy."

She told him the whole story, and was amazed at how relieved she was to confide in him. "I still don't know why the cops didn't believe me. But I'm not hiding because of them. I'm hiding because of the madman who's been terrorizing me. Maybe he wants to kill me now, I don't know." She kept shaking her head, saying over and over, "I can't believe he actually shot the governor. He really shot him."

"The cops could protect you." Tyler wasn't standing so stiffly now, thank God, and his eyes had calmed. Just a minute before they'd been flat and very dark.

"Yes, probably, but they would have to believe I was in danger first. They would have to believe there really was a stalker. There's the rub."

Tyler fell silent. He pulled a small wooden carving of a pyramid out of his pants pocket and began fiddling with it. "This isn't good, Becca."

"No. Is that Ramses the Second's tomb?"

"What? Oh this. No, I won it in a geometry competition when I was a senior in high school. You changed your name to Powell."

"Yes. You're the only one who knows the truth, about everything. Do you think you can keep it quiet?"

"You're not married, then?"

She shook her head. "No. Also, I would have run sooner but I couldn't leave my mother. She was dying of cancer. After she died, there was nothing holding me back."

"I'm very sorry, Becca. My mom died when I was sixteen. I remember what it was like."

"Thank you." She wasn't going to cry, she wasn't. She looked toward an ancient humidor that sat in the corner and jumped to her feet. She'd just realized what she'd done. "I can't believe this. I'm a jerk. This is a big mistake. Listen, Tyler, you've got to forget all of this. I don't know what's going to happen. I don't want you in harm's way. And Sam, I can't take a chance on anything happening to him. It's too risky. Whoever this maniac is, he'll do anything, I'm convinced of it. Then there's the cops. I don't want them to arrest you for keeping quiet about me. I'll go somewhere else that isn't on the map. I'm so sorry I spilled my guts to you."

He stood, taller than she by a good five inches. No more anger in him, only determination. It calmed her. "Forget it. It's a done deal. I'm now up to my neck in this with you. Don't worry, Becca. I don't think they'll ever find you." He paused a moment and looked down at the pyramid lying in the palm of his left hand. "Actually, I've already told a few folks in town that my old college friend Becca Powell has come to live here. Even if someone thinks you look like this Rebecca Matlock they saw on TV, they won't make the connection. I've already vouched for you, and that makes a difference. Also those glasses really alter your looks. You don't wear them usually, do you? And your eyes aren't really brown."

"You're right on both counts. I'm wearing brown contacts. The glasses are window dressing; they're not prescription, just plain glass. I also darkened my hair and my eyebrows."

He nodded, then suddenly he grinned. "Yeah. I remember you as a blonde. All the guys wanted to go out with you, but you weren't really interested."

"I was only a freshman, too young to know what I wanted, particularly in guys."

"I remember there were some bets in the frat houses on who would get you in the sack first."

"I never heard about that." She shook her head, wanting to laugh and surprised by it. "Guys are immensely focused, aren't they?"

"Oh, yeah. I was, too, only it never did me any good, at least not then. I remember wishing somehow that it would be me you'd go out with, but I was too chicken ever to ask. Now, we'll get through this, Becca. You're not alone anymore."

She couldn't believe he'd do this for her. She threw her arms around him and hugged him tight. "Thank you, Tyler. Thank you very much." She felt his arms tighten around her back. She felt safe for the first time in a very long time. No, not safe. She didn't feel alone anymore. That was it.

When she finally stepped back, he said, "It might even help if you go out with me, be seen with me around town. You know, lull any suspicions, if there are any. You'll fit in if you're seen with me, since I'm a native. I'll always call you Becca, too. That's a very different name from Rebecca. I believe that's the only name the media has used."

"To the best of my knowledge it is."

Tyler slid the wooden pyramid back into his jeans pocket and hugged her once more. He said against her left ear, "I wish you'd trusted me right away, but I understand. I think it'll be over soon. A three-day news hit and then it's gone."

As she pulled away from him, she devoutly prayed he was right. But how could it be? The man had tried to murder the governor of New York. He was still at large. They couldn't forget about it. The thing was, there was simply nothing more she could tell the authorities. What if she called Detective Morales and told him she didn't know anything more, that she'd already told them everything? Immediately after Tyler left, she went back into the living room and picked up the phone before she could second-guess herself. She had to try to make him believe her. She didn't know the sophistication of their tracing equipment. Well, she'd have to get it over with, quickly, before they could get a lock on her location. She got through very quickly to Morales, which had to be a miracle in itself. "Detective Morales, this is Becca Matlock. I want you to listen to me now. I'm well hidden. No one's going to find me, nor is there any reason for anyone to find me. I'm not hiding from you, I'm hiding from the stalker who terrorized me and then shot the governor. You do believe me now, don't you? After all, I'm sure not the one who shot him."

"Look, Ms. Matlock, why don't you come in and let's talk about it? Nothing's for sure right now, but we need you here. We have a lead you could help us with—"

She unclenched her teeth and spoke very slowly. "I can't tell you anything more than I already did. I told you the truth. I still don't have any idea why none of you ever believed me, but it was the truth, all of it. I can't help you with any so-called lead. Oh, that's a lie, isn't it? Anything to get me back. But why?" She paused for a moment. Time was passing, he didn't answer her. She said, "Listen, you still don't believe me, do you? You believe I shot the governor?"

"Not you yourself, no. Ms. Matlock—Rebecca—let's talk about it. We can all sit down and work this out. If you don't want to come back to New York, I can come wherever you are to talk."

"I don't think so. Now, I don't want you to be able to trace this call. I will say it once more: The madman who shot the governor is out there and I've told you everything I know about him. Everything. I never lied to you. Never. Good-bye."

"Ms. Matlock, wait—"

She hung up the phone, aware that her heart was pounding deep and hard. She'd done her duty. There was nothing more she could do to help them.

Why didn't they believe her?

She had dinner that night with Tyler McBride at Pollyanna's Restaurant nearly at the end of West Hemlock, on a small curved cul-de-sac called Black Cabbage Court.

She said over their appetizer, "What's with the names in this town?"

He laughed as he speared a cold shrimp, dipped it in horseradish, and forked it into his mouth. "Are you ready for this? Okay, there was this rumor that began floating around in 1912 that Jacob Marley Senior found out his wife was sleeping with the local dry-goods merchant. He was so upset that he poisoned her, and that's why he renamed all the central streets after plants that are toxic."

"That's amazing. Any proof of it?"

"Nope, but hey, it makes for a good tale. Maybe he was a closet Borgia, who knows? I think my favorite is Foxglove Avenue. It runs parallel to West Hemlock."

"What are some more?"

"There's Venus Fly Trap Boulevard, which runs parallel to West Hemlock to the north, Night Shade Alley, that's where my gym is, and Poison Ivy Lane, to the south of us."

"Wait, isn't the Food Fort on Poison Oak Circle?"

"Yes. Since I live outside the center of town, it's Gum Shoe Lane for the likes of me. However, since you're in Marley's house, you get his pièce de résistance—Belladonna Drive. Even better, you're not in a big house next to all the peasants, no, you're out there all by yourself, surrounded by all those beautiful trees and only that narrow driveway to get to you."

She was laughing as she said, "Why did he name his own street Belladonna Way?"

"That's supposedly what Marley Senior used to poison his unfaithful wife. Pollyanna's Restaurant is on Black Cabbage Court. That's the name for this plant in Indonesia that'll kill you with a single lick. It evidently has this sugary-sweet smell and taste, and that's how it gets its victims."

She was laughing when a man came up to their table and said, "Hello, Tyler. Who's this?"

Becca looked up at the older man, who had lots of white hair, a good-sized belly, and a big smile. He said, frowning down at her, "Hey, you look familiar, you—"

"I've known Becca for nearly ten years, Bernie. We were at Dartmouth together. She got tired of the rat race in New York City and decided to move here. She's a journalist. You want to hire her for the *Independent*?"

She hadn't gone to see Bernie Bradstreet for the simple reason that it had dawned on her that she didn't have any legitimate ID and now her face was plastered all over TV. She sat there, smiling stupidly, not knowing what to say. She'd forgotten to say anything to Tyler. She was a fool.

Very sharp gray eyes focused on her. He held out his hand, with large, blunt fingers. "I'm Bernie Bradstreet."

"Becca Powell."

"You write what? Crime coverage? Weddings? Local charities? Obits?"

"None of those things. I mainly write human interest articles about strange and wonderful things that are all around us. I try to amuse people and perhaps give them a different perspective on things. I'm a luxury for a newspaper, Mr. Bradstreet, not a necessity. I'm the last sort of frill a small newspaper needs."

She'd whetted his appetite. Great. He said, a brow arched, "Like what, Ms. Powell?"

"Why feta cheese and glazed pecans taste so delicious in a spinach salad."

"I suppose you went into all sorts of folklore, nutrition information, stuff like that?"

"That's right. For example, with the feta, pecans, and spinach, it all has to do with a chemical reaction that zings the taste buds."

Bernie Bradstreet looked too interested. She drew back, lowered her eyes to the napkin Tyler had tossed beside his plate.

Tyler said, "Dessert, Becca?"

She said, grinning up at Mr. Bradstreet, "Yep, that's what I am, dessert for a newspaper. I'm low on a priority list, very low."

"No," Tyler said. "I mean real dessert. Coffee and dessert for you, Bernie?"

Bernie couldn't stay. His wife was at the far table with one of their grandkids. "They make special hot dogs for kids here," he said; then, "Why don't you drop by with some of the articles you've written, Ms. Powell? Actually, bring me the feta cheese article."

"I didn't bring any of them with me, sir, sorry."

Tyler gave her a look but didn't say anything. But his eyes had widened just a bit. He'd finally realized that this was the last thing she needed. Good, she thought, she was out of it. But no, he ruminated awhile, looking at her, then said, "All right, write me up one—whatever topic you like—not over five hundred words, and we'll see."

She nodded, wishing the guy was more hard-nosed. She watched him walk back to his table, stopping at three more tables on the way. She looked at Tyler and raised her hand to stop him. "No, I can't work for him. I don't have any ID I can use. I doubt he'd want to pay me in cash."

He said, "I didn't think of that. I finally realized that the more he saw you, he might put you together with the Rebecca on TV."

"It's okay. I'll write up an article or two and give them to him, tell him to see how the readers like them, then we can talk. He shouldn't get suspicious then. I don't need the money. I'm not going to starve. It's just that I do need something to keep my mind busy."

"Are you any good with computers?"

"I guess I'm what you'd call a functional genius, but a technological moron."

"Too bad. Since I'm a small-time consultant, I don't need any frills, either."

The night was clear and warm, with a slight breeze off the Atlantic. The stars were brilliant overhead. Becca stood by Tyler's Jeep, staring up at the sky. "Nothing like this in New York City. I could get used to this real fast, Tyler. Too bad you can barely hear the ocean from here. The briny smell is fainter, too."

"Yeah, I found I missed it so much I had to move back, and so I did a couple of years after I finished my master's degree. But you know, more and more young people leave and stay gone. I wonder if Riptide will still be here in another twenty years or so."

"There are lots of tourists to boost the economy, aren't there?"

"Yes, but the entire flavor of the town has changed over the past twenty, thirty years. I guess that's progress, huh?" He paused a moment, staring up at the Milky Way. "After Ann went away, I thought I wanted to leave Riptide and never come back—you know, all the memories—but I realized that all of Sam's friends are here, all the people who knew Ann are here, and memories aren't bad. I can work anywhere, and so I stayed. I haven't regretted it. I'm glad you're here, Becca. Things will work out, you'll see. The only thing is winter. It's not much fun here in January."

"It's not much fun in New York, either. We'll see what's happening by January. I don't understand about your wife, Tyler. Did she die?"

She wanted to take it back at the look of pain that etched lines around his mouth, made his eyes look blank and dead. "I'm sorry, I shouldn't have asked."

"No, it's all right. Of course you're curious. Everyone else in town is."

"What do you mean?"

"My wife didn't die. She just up and left me. She was here one day, gone the next. No word, no message, nothing at all. That was fifteen months, two weeks, and three days ago. She's listed as a Missing Person."

"I'm very sorry, Tyler."

"Yeah, so am I. So is her son." He shrugged. "We're getting by. It gets better as time passes."

What an odd way to put it. Wasn't Sam his son, too?

"The townspeople are like folk everywhere. They don't want to believe that Ann just up and left Riptide. They'd rather think I did her in."

"That's ridiculous."

"I agree. Now, Becca, don't worry. Things will get better. I'm an expert at things eventually getting better, particularly when they can't possibly get any worse."

She sure hoped he was right. They made a date to go to the gym together the following day. His wife had walked out—on him and on her own little boy? That had to be incredibly tough for both of them. Why did folks want to believe he'd kill her?

Three nights later, on June 26, Becca was watching TV, not to see if she was still a footnote in Governor Bledsoe's ongoing story, but to check in on the weather again. The most violent storm to hit the Maine coast in nearly fifteen years was surging relentlessly toward them, bringing with it forecasts of fifty-mile-per-hour winds, torrential rains, and the probability of heavy property damage. Everyone was warned to go to shelters, which Becca considered doing for about three minutes. No, she wasn't about to leave. Being with other people up close and personal as one would be in a shelter would put her at greater risk of being recognized. She didn't think many of the Mainers would even consider leaving their homes. They were incredibly tough, only nodding philosophically when discussing the incoming storm.

Becca paced the widow's walk as the storm approached, watching the skies, the now disappearing stars as clouds blanketed them, the boats in the harbor, bobbing about in the rising waves. Then the winds suddenly increased and tore through the trees. The air turned as cold as a morning in January. When the rain finally hit, crashing down hard and fast, she was driven inside. It was just before ten o'clock at night.

The lights flickered. Becca had bought candles and matches and she set them on her bedside table. She paused to listen as the storm bludgeoned the shoreline. She heard a newscaster predict great destruction of lobster boats and pleasure craft if they hadn't been thoroughly secured. She could imagine what the harbor looked like now, waves frothing high, whipping against the sides of the boats, probably sending water crashing over the sides.

She shivered as she pulled on a sweater and snuggled down into her bed. She kept the TV on nonstop weather coverage and looked at the light show outside her bedroom window. The thunder was deafening. The house rattled with the force of it.

The meteorologist on channel 7 said that the winds were strengthening, nearly up to sixty miles per hour now. He said people should go to official shelters away from the coast for protection. Oddly, he sounded excited. Becca still had no intention of leaving. This old house had doubtless seen its share of comparably violent storms in its hundred-year history just as the Piper Lighthouse had up the road. Both had survived. Both would survive another storm, she didn't doubt that, although she couldn't help but cringe as the house groaned and creaked.

Suddenly, with no warning, thunder boomed, lightning streaked through the sky, and the lights went out.

# SIX

It wasn't dark for long. The lightning and thunder kept the sky lit up for a good five minutes, without a break. She could easily read her clock. It was just after one in the morning. She finally couldn't stand it any longer and reached for the phone, to call Tyler, but the line was dead. She stared at the receiver, then looked out her bedroom window as a huge streak of lightning lit up the sky. She felt the thunder deep in her eardrums as it boomed, almost simultaneous with the flash. It would be all right. It was only a storm. Storms in Maine were just another part of life, like the hordes of mosquitoes that occasionally blanketed a town. This was nothing to get alarmed about.

As Becca lay in the darkness, looking out the bedroom window, she swore that the winds were growing even stronger as they ravaged the land. She felt the house literally shudder around her. It shook so hard, she briefly worried that it would pull free of its foundation. A loud wrenching sound had her bolt upright in bed. No, it wasn't anything, really. Had she come here just to be killed in a ferocious summer storm? She had wished earlier that she was closer to the ocean, listening to the waves hurling themselves against the high cliffs covered with pine trees bowed and bent from the winter winds, or beating against the clustering speared black rocks that lined the narrow cluttered beach at the end of Black Lane, a narrow, snaking little dirt road that went all the way to the ocean.

But not now. It was just as well that crashing angry waves weren't added to the mix. She watched the lightning continue to tear through the sky, making it bright as day for long moments at a time. She felt the scoring of the thunder to her toes. It was impressive, utterly dramatic, and she was getting scared.

Finally she couldn't stand it any longer. She lit the three precious candles, stuck them in the bottom of coffee mugs, and picked up the Steve Martini thriller she'd been reading until the storm had really gotten serious.

Was the storm easing up? She read a few words, then realized that she couldn't remember the story line. This wasn't good. She put the novel back on her nightstand and picked up the *New York Times*, carried only by a small tobacco shop off Poison Ivy Lane. She didn't want to read about the attempted assassination, but she did, naturally. Page after page was devoted to the governor's attempted murder. She was mentioned too many times.

Thunder rolled loud and deep over the house as she read: *There is a manhunt for Rebecca Matlock, former speechwriter for the governor, who, the FBI says, has information about the attempt on the governor's life.*

*Former* speechwriter now, was she? Well, since she'd left without a word or any warning, she supposed that was fair enough.

It was nearly two o'clock in the morning.

Suddenly, with no warning at all, the wind gave a howl that made the hair bristle on the back of her neck and set her teeth on edge. A flash of lightning exploded, filling the sky with a bluish light, and a crack of thunder seemed to lift the house right into the air. She nearly bit her tongue as she stared out her bedroom window. She watched the proud hemlock weave once, then heard a loud snap. The old tree wavered a moment, then went crashing to the ground. It didn't hit the house, thank God, but some upper branches crashed into the window, loud and so scary that she leapt from the bed and ran to the closet. She crouched between a yellow knit top and a pair of blue jeans, waiting, waiting, but there was nothing more. What had happened was over with. She walked slowly back into the bedroom. Tree branches were still quivering as they settled just above a pale blue rag rug on the floor. The window was shattered, rain slithered in around the beautiful green leaves, dripping onto the floor. She stood there, staring at the huge tree branch in her bedroom, listening to another loud belt of thunder, and thought enough is enough. She didn't want to be alone, not anymore.

She dressed and ran downstairs. She had to find something to block up the window. But there wasn't anything except half a dozen dish towels with lighthouses on them. She ended up stuffing all her pillows around the tree branch. It worked.

She closed the front door behind her and stepped into the howling wind. She was wet clear through before she'd taken three breaths. No hope for it. She ran through the heavy rain to the Toyota and fumbled with the lock even as her hair was plastered to her head. Finally she got the door open and climbed in behind the wheel. When she turned the key in the ignition, the car growled at her, then stopped. She didn't want to flood it so she didn't turn the ignition again. No, give it a rest for a moment. Again, finally, she turned the key, and Lord be praised, the engine turned over, started. Tyler's house was a half mile down the road, the first street to the right, Gum Shoe Lane.

At a loud crack of thunder, she looked back at Jacob Marley's house. It looked like an old Gothic manor in the English countryside, hunkered down in the rain, filled with lost and ancient spirits. It looked menacing even without billowing fog to shadow it in more gloom. A sharp lightning flash streaked down like a silver knife. The house seemed to shudder, as if from a mortal wound. It looked like the gods wanted to rip it apart. She was very glad she was leaving. Maybe Jacob Marley Senior really had poisoned his wife and God was just now getting around to some punishment. "Thanks a lot for waiting until I was here," she yelled. She waved her fist heavenward.

The huge hemlock that could have so easily smashed right into the side of the house lay on its side nearly parallel to the west wall. That one very full and long branch that had crashed through her bedroom window looked like a hand that had managed to reach into the house. She shuddered at the image. Everything suddenly seemed alive and malevolent, closing in on her, like the man who had called her and stalked her and murdered that old woman and shot the governor. He was near, she felt him.

*Stop it.* She drove very slowly down the long narrow drive, no choice there. Debris filled the road, wind bent trees nearly to the ground. The boughs glanced off her windshield. Branches whipped toward her, rain hammered against the windshield, pounded against the car, making her wonder if she'd come to Maine only to be done in by a wretched storm. She had to get out of the car twice to pull fallen branches out of the way. The wind and rain slammed hard into her, making it impossible to stand straight and nearly impossible to walk. She knew there had to be dents in the car fenders. The insurance company was going to love this. Oh dear, she'd forgotten, she didn't have any insurance. That required being a real person with real ID.

Suddenly headlights cut through the thick, swirling sheets of rain, not twenty feet from her. They were coming toward her, fast, too fast. Damnation, to get killed on Belladonna Way. There had to be some irony in that, but she couldn't appreciate it right then. She'd come to hide herself and be safe, a tree branch came into her bedroom, and now she was going to die because she couldn't bear to stay in that old house, knowing it would collapse on her, swallow her alive. She smashed down on the horn, jerked the steering wheel to the left, but these headlights kept coming inexorably, relentlessly toward her, so fast, so very fast. She threw the car into reverse but knew that was no good. There was so much debris behind her that it was bound to stall her out. She slammed on the brakes and turned off the engine. She jumped out of the car and ran to the side of the road, feeling those damned headlights crawl over her, so close she wondered if the stalker hadn't found her and was now going to kill her. Why had she ever left the house? So there was a tree branch in her bedroom dripping on a rag rug. It was still safe, but not out here, in the middle of a wind that was whirling around her like a mad dervish, ready to hurl her into the air, and a car that was coming after her, a madman at the wheel.

Then, suddenly, miraculously, the headlights stopped about eight feet from her car. Rain and lightning battered down, blurring the headlights, turning them a sickly yellow. She stood there, the wind beating at her, breathing in hard, soaked to her bones, waiting. Who was going to get out of that car? Could he see her, huddled next to some trees that were nearly folding themselves around her from the force of the wind? Did he want to kill her with his own hands? Why? Why?

It was Tyler McBride and he was yelling, "Becca! Is that you?" He had a flashlight and he pinned her with it, the light diffused from all the rain, pale, blue-rimmed, and it was right in her eyes. She brought up her hand.

She opened her mouth to yell back at him and nearly drowned. She ran to him and clutched his arms. "It's me," she said, "it's me. I was coming to your house. A tree branch crashed through the bedroom window and it sounded like the house was going to collapse."

If he wanted to smack her because she was teetering on the edge of hysteria, he didn't let on, just gripped her shoulders in his big wet hands and said very slowly, very calmly, "I thought I saw some car lights but I couldn't be sure. All I thought about was getting to you. It's okay. That old house won't fall down. There's nothing to be afraid of. Now, follow me back home. I left Sam alone. He's asleep but I can't count on him staying that way. I don't want him to wake up and be scared."

She got herself together. She wasn't helpless, not like Sam was. The wind tore at their clothes, the rain was coming down so hard it hurt where it struck. Her jeans felt stiff and hard and heavy. But she didn't care. She wasn't alone. Tyler wasn't the crazy man from New York. She took a deep breath and watched as he drove at a snail's pace back to his house on Gum Shoe Lane. It took another ten minutes to get to the small clapboard house that sat back in a lovely lawn that was planted heavily with spruce and hemlock. She jumped out of the car and yelled as she ran to the front door, "Gum Shoe, what a wonderful name." She began to laugh. "Gum Shoe Lane!"

"It's okay, Becca, we're home now. We made it. This is one of the worst storms I can remember. As bad as the one back in '78, they said on the radio. I remember that one, I was a little kid and it scared me spitless. I've got to say that your timing is wild, Becca, coming to Riptide just before this mother of all storms hits." He gave her another look, then added, slowly, his voice calm and low, "It's sort of like the Mancini virus that came along last year and crashed every computer in this small software company called Tiffany's. They called me in to fix it. That was a job, I'll tell you."

Becca stood dripping in the small entrance hall, staring at him. He was trying to talk her down and doing a good job of it. "Computer humor," she said, and laughed after him when he fetched some towels from the bathroom. A slash of lightning came through the window and lit up the pile of newspapers on the floor beside the sofa. "I'm okay," she said when Tyler began to lightly rub his palm over her wet back. He drew back, smiling down at her. "I know. You're tough."

Sam was still asleep, curled on his side, his left hand under his cheek. The world was exploding not ten feet away and Sam was probably dreaming about his morning cartoons. She pulled the blanket over him, paused a moment, and said quietly to Tyler, who was standing behind her, "He's precious."

"Yes," he said.

She wanted to ask him why Sam didn't talk much, was so very wary, but she heard something in his voice that made her go still and keep her question to herself. There was anger there, bitterness. Because his wife had left him? Walked away without a word? With not a single regret? Well, it made sense to her. Her own mother had left her, and she felt sick with rage at being left alone. Not her mother's fault, of course, but the pain of it. She looked down at Sam one last time, then turned and left the small bedroom, Tyler on her heels. He gave her one of his wife's robes, pink and thick and on the tatty side, well worn, and she wondered what sort of woman Ann McBride had been. Why hadn't she taken her robe? She couldn't ask Tyler now. The robe fit her very well. It was warm, comfy. She and Ann McBride were of a size.

They drank coffee heated on a Coleman stove Tyler got out of the basement. It was the best coffee she'd ever tasted and she told him so. She fell asleep on the old chintz sofa, wrapped in blankets.

The sun was harshly bright, too bright, as if the storm had scrubbed off a thick layer of dust from all the trees and streets and houses, even given the sky a thorough shower. Becca's jeans were soft, hot from the drier, and so tight she had barely been able to zip them up when Tyler had tossed them to her.

Sam said, his small voice unexpected, startling her, "Did you bring cookies, Becca?"

An entire sentence. Maybe he was just very frightened and wary of strangers. Maybe he didn't think of her as a stranger anymore. She hoped so. She smiled at him. "Sorry, kiddo, no cookies this time." She'd awakened with a start, frightened, tingling, to see Sam standing beside the sofa, holding a blanket against his side, his thumb in his mouth, just staring at her, saying nothing at all.

Sam said now, "Haunted house."

Tyler was pouring cereal into a small bowl for his son. He looked over at Becca.

She said, "You could be right, Sam. It was a bad storm and that old house shook and groaned. I was scared to my toes."

Sam began eating his Cap'n Crunch cereal his father put in front of him.

Tyler said, "Sam's too young to be scared."

Sam didn't look up from his cereal bowl.

It was nearly ten o'clock that morning when Becca started up her banged-up car and coaxed it back to Jacob Marley's house. It no longer looked frightening and menacing. It looked bedraggled, very clean, and the hemlock with its branch sticking through her second-floor window no longer looked like a ghostly apparition, but like a tree that was dead now, nothing more. She smiled as she walked around the house, assessing damage. Not much, really, only the branch in the window. They'd have to haul the tree away.

She called the real estate agent, Mrs. Ryan, from a working public phone in front of Food Fort, who told Becca she would notify the insurance company and the tree-removal people and not to worry about a thing, everything was covered.

Becca went back to the house and toured for the next twenty minutes, not seeing any damage anywhere inside. The electricity flickered on, then off again. Finally, when it was nearly noon, the lights came on strong and bright. The refrigerator hummed loudly. Everything was back to normal. Then, with no warning, the hall and living room lights went off. The circuit breaker, she thought, and wondered where the devil the box would be. The basement, that was the most likely place. She had to check down there anyway. She lit one of her candles and unlatched the basement door, which was at the back of the kitchen. Steep wooden stairs disappeared into the darkness. *Great,* she thought, *now to top it all off, maybe I can fall and break my neck on these rickety stairs.* They were wide and felt sturdy and strong, not so dangerous after all, a relief. There were a dozen steps. The floor was uneven, cold and damp concrete. She raised the candle and looked around. There was a string hanging down and she gave it a pull. The bulb switch clicked but nothing happened. *This light must be on the same circuit.* She began at the right of the stairs, lifting the candle to light up the wall. It was dank down there, and she smelled mildew. Her toes sloshed in a bit of water. Yep, leaks from the storm. On the wall facing the stairs she finally found the circuit breaker box. Beside it were stacks of old cartons, everything dirty and damp. She flipped the downed circuit breaker switch and the bulb overhead blossomed into one-hundred-watt light. Stacks of old furniture, most of it from the forties, perhaps some even earlier, were piled against the far wall. So many boxes, all of them very large, labeled with faded and smeared spidery handwriting.

She started forward to look at the writing on one of the labels when there was a low rumbling noise. She stopped cold, fear spiking through her. Where was it coming from? Where? All the nightmares from the night before tore through her. Sam's words—"haunted house." Shadows, the damned basement was filled with shadows and damp and rot.

She whipped around at the crash not thirty feet away from her, in the far corner of the basement. She watched as the wall heaved and groaned and spewed brick outward onto the basement floor, leaving a jagged black hole.

She stood there a moment longer, staring at the hole in the wall. She was surprised. The house was very old, sturdy. Why, suddenly, would this happen? The storms over the years must have gradually weakened this particular wall and now, finally, the one last night was the final blow. Perhaps all the damp contributed, as well.

She walked to the corner, dodging crates and a huge steamer trunk that looked to be from the 1920s. The light didn't reach quite that far. She raised her candle high and looked into the black hole.

And screamed.

# SEVEN

That black gash in the basement wall had vomited out a skeleton mixed with shards of cement, whole and broken bricks, and thick dust that flew through the air to settle slowly, thickly, on the basement floor.

The skeleton's outstretched hand nearly touched her foot. She dropped the candle and jumped back, wrapping her arms around herself. She stared at that thing not more than three feet from her. A dead person, long dead. It—no, it wasn't an it, it was a woman and she couldn't hurt anybody. Not now.

White jeans and a skimpy pink tank top covered the bones, many of which would have been flung all over the basement floor were it not for the once-tight jeans holding them together. One sneaker was hanging off her left foot, the white sock damp and moldy. The left arm was still attached, but barely. The head had broken off and rolled about six inches from the neck.

Becca stood there, staring down at that thing, knowing that at one time, whoever she was, she'd breathed and laughed and wondered what the future would bring. She was young, Becca realized. Who was she? What was she doing inside a wall in Jacob Marley's basement?

Someone had put her there, on purpose, to hide her forever. And now she was just shattered bones, some of them covered with moldy white jeans and a pink tank top.

Slowly Becca walked back upstairs, covered with dust, her heart still pounding. In her mind's eye the skeleton's skull was still vivid, would probably remain terrifyingly vivid for the rest of her life. Those eye sockets were so empty. Becca knew she had no choice. She phoned the sheriff's office on West Hemlock and asked to speak with the sheriff.

"This is Mrs. Ella," came a voice that was deep as a man's, and harsh—a smoker's voice. "Tell me who you are and what you want and I'll tell you whether or not you need Edgar."

Becca stared at the phone. It certainly wasn't New York City.

She cleared her throat. "Actually, my name is Becca Powell and I moved into Jacob Marley's house about a week ago."

"I know all about you, Miss Powell. I saw you at the Pollyanna with Tyler McBride. What'd you do with little Sam while you two were gallivanting around, enjoying yourselves at one of Riptide's finest restaurants?"

Becca laughed, she couldn't help herself, but it soon dissolved into a hiccup. She felt tears pool in her eyes. This was crazy. Still, she said only, "We left him with Mrs. Ryan. He's very fond of her."

"Well, that's all right, then. Rachel and Ann—she's the dead Mrs. McBride—well, they were best friends, now weren't they? And Sam dearly loves Rachel, and she him, thank God, since his mama is dead, now isn't she?"

"I thought that Ann McBride disappeared, that she just walked away from her family and from Riptide."

"So he says, but nobody believes that. What do you want, Miss Powell? Be alert now, and concise, no more going off on tangents or feeding me gossip. This is an official office of the law."

"There's a skeleton in my basement."

For the first time in this very strange conversation, Mrs. Ella was silent, but not for long. "This skeleton you're telling me is in your basement, how did it get there?"

"It fell out of the wall in the middle of a whole lot of rubble when the wall collapsed a while ago, probably weakened by the big storm last night."

"I believe I will transfer you to Edgar now. That's Sheriff Gaffney to you. He's been very busy, a lot of storm damage, you know, a lot of people demanding his time, but a skeleton can't be put off until tomorrow, now can it?"

"You're right about that," Becca said, and had an insane desire to laugh her head off. She wiped the tears out of her eyes. She realized she was shaking. It was the oddest thing.

A man came on the line and said, "Ella tells me you've got a skeleton in the basement. This don't happen every day. Are you sure it's a skeleton?"

"Yes, quite sure, although, to be honest, I've never seen one before, at least lying at my feet on the basement floor."

"I'll be right there, then. You stay put, ma'am."

Becca was staring down at the phone when Mrs. Ella came back. "Edgar said I was to keep talking to you, not let you go all hysterical. Edgar tends to get tetchy around women who are crying and wailing and carrying on. I'm surprised you fell apart on him, given the way you were talking to me about this and that."

"I appreciate that, Mrs. Ella. I'm not really hysterical, at least not yet, but how could the sheriff have possibly known that I was wavering on the edge? I never said a word to him."

"Edgar just knows these things," Mrs. Ella said comfortably. "He's very intuitive, now isn't he? That's why I'll keep talking to you until he gets there, Miss Powell. I'm to help you keep your wits together."

Becca didn't mind a bit. For the next ten minutes, she heard how Ann McBride disappeared between one day and the next, no explanation at all, just as Tyler had told her. She learned that Tyler wasn't Sam's father but his stepfather. Sam's real father had just up and disappeared from one day to the next, too. Odd, now wasn't it, the both of them, just up and out of here? Of course, Sam's father had been a rotter, whining and bitching about how hard life was, and he didn't want to stay here, so his leaving made some sense, now didn't it? But not Ann's, no, she couldn't have just up and left, not without Sam.

Then Mrs. Ella began with all her pets, and there were a bunch of them since she was sixty-five years old. Finally, Becca heard a car pull up.

"The sheriff just arrived, Mrs. Ella. I promise I won't fall apart." She hung up the phone before Mrs. Ella could give her own mother's tried-and-true recipe for stretched nerves. And she wouldn't fall apart, either, because by Mrs. Ella's fifth dog, a terrier named Butch, there were no more tears in her eyes and the bubbling, liquid laughter was long dried up.

Sheriff Gaffney had seen the Powell girl around town, but he hadn't met her. She looked harmless enough, he thought, remembering how she was squeezing a cantaloupe in the produce department at Food Fort when he first saw her. She was pretty enough, but right then, she was as white as his shirtfront last night before he'd eaten spaghetti. She'd opened the front door of the old Marley place and stood there staring at him.

"I'm the law," he said, and took his sheriff's hat off. There was something odd about her, something that wasn't quite right, and it wasn't her too-pale face. Well, finding a skeleton could put a person off in a whole lot of ways. He wished she'd stop gaping at him like she didn't have a brain or, God forbid, was hysterical. He was afraid she would burst into tears and he was ready to do about anything to prevent that. He threw back his shoulders and stuck out a huge hand. "Sheriff Gaffney, ma'am. What's this about a skeleton in your basement?"

"It's a woman, Sheriff."

He shook her hand, pleased and relieved that now she appeared reasonably under control and her lower lip wasn't trembling. Her eyes looked perfectly dry to him, from what he could tell through her glasses. "Show me this skeleton who you believe with your untrained eye is a woman, ma'am," he said, "and we'll see if you're guessing right."

*I'm in never-never land,* Becca thought as she showed Sheriff Gaffney down to Jacob Marley's basement.

She walked behind him. He was nearing sixty years old, and was a walking heart attack. He was a good thirty pounds overweight, the buttons of his sheriff shirt gaping over his belly. The wide black leather belt tight beneath his belly carried a gun holster and a billy club, and nearly disappeared in the front because his stomach was so big. He had a circle of gray hair around his head and very light gray eyes. She nearly ran into him when he suddenly stopped on the bottom step, stood there, and sniffed.

"That's good, Ms. Powell. No smell. Gotta be old."

She nearly gagged.

She kept back when he went down on his knees to examine the bones.

"I thought it was a woman, maybe even a girl, since she's wearing a pink tank top."

"A good deduction, ma'am. Yep, the remains look pretty old, or maybe not. I read that a dead person can become a skeleton in as little as two weeks or it can take as long as ten years depending on where the body's put. It's a shame that it wasn't airtight, you know, a vacuum back behind that wall. If it had been, then maybe something would have been left of her. But critters can get in most places and they were looking at a whole bunch of really good meals with her. Lookee here, the person who put her down here hit her on the head." He looked up at her, expecting her to see what he'd found. Becca forced herself to look at the skull that had snapped, probably during the upheaval, and rolled away from the neck.

Sheriff Gaffney picked up the skull and slowly turned it in his hands. "Look at this. Someone bashed her but good, not in the back of the head but in the front. Now, that's mean, really vicious. Yep, violent, real violent. Whoever did this was mad as hell, hit her as hard as he could, right in the face. I wonder who she was, poor thing. First thing is to see if any of our own young people went missing a while ago. Thing is, I've been here nearly all my life and I don't remember a single kid disappearing. But I'll ask around. Folk don't forget that. Well, we'll find out soon enough. I think she was probably a runaway. Old Jacob didn't like strangers—male, female, it didn't matter. Probably found her poking around in the garage or maybe even trying to break in, and he didn't ask any questions, just whacked her head. Actually, he didn't like people who weren't strangers, either."

"You said the blow looks violent, and it's in the front. Why would Jacob Marley be enraged if she was a runaway, or a local kid, hanging around his property?"

"I don't know. Maybe she back-mouthed him. Old Jacob hated back talk."

"The white jeans are Calvin Klein, Sheriff."

"You're saying this is a guy now?"

"No, that's the designer. The jeans are expensive. I don't think they'd go real well on a runaway."

"You know, ma'am, many runaways are middle-class," Sheriff Gaffney said, and heaved himself to his feet. "Strange how most folk don't know that. Very few of 'em are poor, you know. Yep, the storm must have knocked something loose," he said, bending over to examine the wall closely. "Looks like old Jacob stuffed her in there pretty good. Not such a good job with the concrete and bricks, though. It shouldn't have collapsed like that, nothing else in here did."

"Old Jacob was a homicidal maniac?"

"Eh?" He spun around. "Oh, no, Ms. Powell. He simply didn't like nobody hanging around his place. He was a real loner, once Miranda up and died on him."

"Who was Miranda? His wife?"

"Oh, no. She was his golden retriever. He buried his wife so long ago I can't even remember her. Yep, she lived to be thirteen, keeled over one day."

"His wife was only thirteen?"

"No, his golden retriever, Miranda. She just up and died. Old Jacob was never the same after that. Losing someone you love, so I hear, can be real hard on a man. My Maude promised me a long time ago that she'd outlive me, so I'd never have to know what it's like."

Becca followed the sheriff back up the basement stairs. She looked back once at the ghastly pile of white bones wearing Calvin Klein jeans and a sexy pink tank top. Poor girl. She thought of the Edgar Allan Poe tale *The Cask of Amontillado* and prayed that this girl had been dead before she was stuffed in that wall.

Sheriff Gaffney had laid the skull on top of the skeleton's chest.

An hour and a half later, Tyler stood next to her, off to the side of the front porch. Dr. Baines, shorter than Becca, whiplash thin, big glasses, came out nearly at a run, followed by two young men in white coats carrying the skeleton carefully on a gurney.

"I never thought Mr. Marley could murder anyone," Dr. Baines said, his voice fast and low. "Funny how things happen, isn't it? All this time, no one knew, no one even guessed." He pushed his glasses up on his nose, nodded to Becca and to Tyler, then spoke briefly to the men as they gently lifted the gurney into the back of the van.

The unmarked white van pulled away, followed by Dr. Baines's car. "Dr. Baines is our local physician. He got on the phone to the medical examiner in Augusta after I called him about the skeleton. The ME told him what to do, which is kind of dumb, since he's a doctor and I'm an officer of the law, and of course I'd be really careful around the skeleton and take pictures from all angles and be careful not to mess up the crime scene."

Becca remembered him carefully setting the skull on the skeleton's chest. But he was right, with a skeleton, who cared?

Sheriff Gaffney said on a shrug, "In any case, Dr. Baines will take the skeleton into Augusta to the medical examiner and then we'll see."

Sheriff Gaffney looked out at the two dozen people who were hovering about and shook his head and waved them away. Of course no one moved. They continued talking, pointing at the house, maybe even at her.

Sheriff Gaffney said, "They'll go on home in a bit. Natural human curiosity, that's all. Now, Ms. Powell, I know you're upset and all, being a female with fine sensibilities, just like my Maude, but I ask that you keep yourself calm for a while longer."

He had to be about the same age as her father would have been had he lived, Becca thought, and smiled at him then, because he meant well. "I'll try, Sheriff. You don't have any daughters, do you?"

"No, ma'am, just a bunch of boys, all hard-noses, always back-talking me, and covered with mud and sweat half the time. Not at all the same thing for little girls. My Maude would have given anything for a little girl, but God didn't send us one, just all them dirty boys.

"Now, Ms. Powell, Dr. Baines will be talking to the folk in the medical examiner's office in Augusta—that's our capital, you know—once he gets there. They'll do an autopsy, or whatever it is they do on a mess of bones. The folk up there have lots of formal training, so they'll know what they're doing. Like I told you, they'll document that old Jacob or somebody hit her right in the forehead, smashed her head in. They'll determine that it was real mean, that blow. In the meantime we gotta find out who she is. There wasn't any ID on her. You got any more ideas about it?"

"Calvin Klein jeans have been popular since the early to mid-eighties. That means that she wasn't murdered and sealed behind that wall before 1980."

Sheriff Gaffney carefully wrote that down. He hummed softly while he wrote. He looked up then and stared at her. "You sure do look familiar, Ms. Powell."

"Maybe you saw me in a fashion magazine, Sheriff. No, don't even consider that, I'm joking with you. I'm not a model. I'm sure I would have remembered you, sir, if I'd ever met you before."

"Well, that's likely enough," he said, nodding. "Tyler, you got any thoughts about this?"

Tyler shook his head.

Sheriff Gaffney looked as if he would say something else, then he shut his mouth. However, he gave Tyler another long look. "I'll be in touch," he said, snapped out a sharp salute, and walked to his car, a brown Ford with a light bar over the top. At the last moment, he looked back at them, and he was frowning. Then he managed to squeeze his bulk into the driver's side. He hadn't been interested in her background, a blessing. Evidently, he realized that she could have had nothing to do with this and so who she was, where she was from, and what she did for a living simply did not matter.

"He's amazing," Becca said as he drove away. "Too bad he didn't have a daughter to go with all those dirty boys."

She looked to see that Tyler was staring down at his feet. She lightly touched her fingers to his arm. "What's wrong? You're afraid I really am going to be hysterical about finding that poor girl?"

"No, it's not that. You saw the sheriff. Even though he didn't really say anything, it was clear enough what he was thinking."

"I don't know what you mean. What's wrong, Tyler?"

"I realize it occurred to him that the skeleton might well be Ann."

Becca looked at him blankly, slowly shaking her head back and forth.

"My wife. She wore Calvin Klein jeans."

# EIGHT

Becca walked into the Riptide Pharmacy in the middle of Foxglove Avenue the next morning and found, to her horror, that she was the center of attention. For someone who wanted to fade into the woodwork, she wasn't doing it very well. Everywhere she went, she was stared at, questioned, introduced to relatives. She was the girl who'd found the skeleton. She was even given special treatment at the Union 76 gas station at the end of Poison Oak Circle. The Food Fort manager, Mrs. Dobbs, wanted her autograph. Three people told her she looked familiar.

It was too late to dye her hair black. She went home and stayed there. She got at least twenty phone calls that day. She didn't see Tyler, but he'd been right about what the sheriff had thought, because everybody else was thinking it, too, and was talking about it over coffee, to their neighbors, and not all that quietly. Tyler knew it, too, of course, but he didn't say anything when he came over later that evening. He looked stoic. She had wanted to yell at everyone that they were wrong, that Tyler was an excellent man, that no way could he have hurt anyone, much less his wife, but she knew she couldn't take the chance, couldn't call attention to herself anymore. It was too dangerous for her, and so she listened to everyone talk about Ann, Tyler's wife and Sam's mother, who had supposedly disappeared fifteen months before without a word to anybody, not her husband, not her son. Ann had had a mother until two years before, but Mildred Kendred had died and left Ann all alone with Tyler. She'd had no other relatives to hassle Tyler about where his wife had supposedly gone. And look at poor little Sam, so quiet, so withdrawn, he'd probably seen something, everyone was sure of that. That he wasn't at all afraid of his stepfather meant that the poor little boy had blocked the worst of it out.

Oh, yes, it all made sense now to everyone. Tyler had bashed his wife on the head—she probably wanted to leave him, that was it—and then he'd bricked her in the wall in Jacob Marley's basement. And little Sam knew something, because he'd changed right after his mother disappeared.

Tyler remained stoic during the following days, saying nothing about all the speculation, ignoring the sidelong looks from people who were supposedly his friends. He went about his business, seemingly oblivious of the stares.

He was in misery, Becca knew that, but there was nothing she could do except say over and over, "Tyler, I know it isn't Ann. They'll prove it was someone else, you'll see."

"How?"

"If they can't figure out who she was, then they'll check for runaways. There are DNA tests. They'll find out. Then there are going to be a whole lot of folk apologizing to you on their hands and knees."

He looked at her and said nothing at all.

Becca went shopping at Food Fort at eight o'clock the next night, hoping the store would be nearly empty. She moved quickly down the aisles. The last item on her list was peanut butter, crunchy. She found it and picked up a small jar, saw that it had a web of mirrored cracks in it, and started to call out to one of the clerks, only to have it break apart in her hands. She yelped and dropped it. It splattered all over jars of jams and jellies before smashing onto the floor at her feet. She stood there staring down at the mess.

"I see you buy natural, not sugar-added. That's the only kind I'll eat."

She whirled around so fast she slid on the peanut butter and nearly careened into the soup. The man caught her arm and pulled her upright.

"Sorry, I didn't mean to startle you. Let me get you another jar. Here comes a young fellow with a mop. Better let him wipe off the bottom of your sneaker."

"Yes, of course." The man not two feet from her was a stranger, which didn't mean all that much since she hadn't met everyone in town. He was wearing a black windbreaker, dark jeans, and scuffed black boots. He was careful not to step into the peanut butter. Her first impression was that he was big and he looked really hard and his hair was on the long side, and as dark as his eyes.

"The only thing," he continued after a moment, "it's a real pain to have to stir the peanut butter before you put it in the refrigerator. The oil always spills over the sides and on your hands." He smiled, but his eyes still looked hard, as if he looked at people and saw all the bad things they were trying to hide, and was used to it, maybe even philosophical about it. She didn't want him looking at her that way, seeing deep into her. She didn't want to talk to him. She wanted to get out of there.

"Yes, I know," she said, and took a step back.

"Once I got used to it, though, I found I couldn't eat the other peanut butter, too much sugar."

"That's true." She took another step away from him. Who was he? Why was he trying to be so nice?

"Miss Powell, I'm Young Jeff. Ah, Old Jeff is my pop, he's the assistant manager. Hold still and I'll clean off your sneaker." He picked up her foot, nearly sending her over backward. The man held her up while Young Jeff wiped a wet paper towel over the bottom of her sneaker. He was very strong, she could feel it since his hands were in her armpits. "I'm sure glad you're here, ma'am. I wanted to know if that poor dead skeleton was Mrs. McBride. Everyone is talking about how it can't be anybody else, what with Mrs. McBride up and disappearing like she did not all that long ago. Everyone says you know it's Mrs. McBride, too, that you were sure, but how could you be? Did you meet Mrs. McBride?"

He finally released her foot. She pulled away from Young Jeff and the man, a good two feet. She felt cold, very cold. She rubbed her hands over her crossed arms. "No, Jeff, I never met Ann McBride. I didn't know anything about her. No one said a single word to me about her. Also, everybody is being premature. Now, I'll bet we'll be hearing very soon that the poor woman I found can't be Ann McBride. You tell everyone I said that."

"I will, Miss Powell, but that's not what Mrs. Ella says. She thinks it's Ann McBride, too."

"Believe me, Jeff, I was there, and I saw the skeleton; Mrs. Ella didn't. Hey, I'm sorry about the mess. Thanks for cleaning off my shoe."

The man stuck out his arm and helped her over the shards of glass. "Young Jeff is a teenage boy with raging hormones," he said, very aware that she had pulled away from him again. "I'm afraid you're now the object of his affection."

She shuddered. "No, I'm the object of everyone's curiosity, nothing more, including poor Young Jeff." She stopped. The man couldn't help it that she was spooked. She drew a deep breath, gave him a nice big smile, and said, "I've got a few more things to buy, Mr.—?"

"Carruthers. Adam Carruthers." He stuck out his hand and she automatically shook it. Big hand, hard, just like the rest of him. She'd bet the last dime in the bottom of her purse that even the soles of his feet were hard. She knew without being told that he was very disciplined, very focused, like soldiers or bad guys were focused, and that made her so afraid she nearly ran out right that minute. Which was silly. Only one thing she really knew for sure—she didn't ever want to have to tangle with him. Actually, if she never saw him again, it would be fine by her. "I haven't seen you around town before, Mr. Carruthers."

"No, I got here yesterday. The first thing I heard about was your finding that skeleton. The second thing I heard was it was the missing wife of your neighbor, Tyler McBride, and that you were seeing him and now wasn't that interesting?"

A reporter, she thought. Oh God, maybe he was a reporter or a paparazzo, and they'd found her. Her brave new world in the boondocks was going to be over just as it was beginning. It wasn't fair. She began backing away from him.

"Are you all right?"

"Yes, of course. I'm very busy. It was a pleasure to meet you. Goodbye." And she was nearly running down the aisle lined with different kinds of breads, hamburger buns, and English muffins.

He stared after her. She was taller than he'd expected, and too thin. Well, he'd be skinny, too, if he'd been under as much pressure as she was. What mattered was that he had found her. Amateurs, he thought, even very smart ones, couldn't easily disappear. He thought about how he had managed to misdirect the FBI, and grinned at the jars of low-fat jams and jellies. They had more procedures, more requirements, more delays built into the system, a system that could have been designed by a criminal to give himself the best shot at escaping. Another thing they didn't have was *his* contacts. He was whistling when he carried his can of French roast drip coffee to the checkout counter. He watched her climb into her dark green Toyota and drive out of the parking lot.

He went back to his second-floor corner room at Errol Flynn's Hammock, booted up his laptop, and wrote a quick e-mail:

*I met her over a broken jar of peanut butter in Food Fort. She's fine, but nervous. Understandable. You won't believe this, but now she's embroiled in a mess here in Riptide. A skeleton fell out of her base-*

*ment wall. Everyone in town believes it's a neighbor's wife who dis-*
*appeared over a year ago. Who knows? Will keep you informed.*
*Adam*

He sat back in his chair and smelled the coffee perking in the Mr.
Coffee machine he'd bought at Goose's Hardware when he'd gotten into
town.

She was wary of him, maybe even afraid. Well, he couldn't blame her,
a big guy trying to pick her up in Food Fort after she'd found a skeleton
in her basement, while already on the run from the FBI, the NYPD, and a
murderous madman. He didn't think she'd been amused by his peanut
butter wit, which meant she wasn't a dolt.

He poured a cup of coffee, sipped it, and sighed with bone-deep satisfaction. He leaned back in the dark brown nubby chair, which was
surprisingly comfortable. The TV played quietly on its stand against a far
wall, providing background noise. He closed his eyes, seeing Becca Matlock again.

No, now she was Becca Powell. Under that name she'd quickly rented
the Jacob Marley place and promptly had a skeleton fall out of her basement wall after that incredible storm that had battered the Maine coast.

The woman had pretty sucky luck.

Now all he had to do was make her come to trust him.

Then, just maybe, he would have a very big surprise for her.

But first he had some reconnaissance to do. It never paid to rush into
things.

So Adam kept his distance the next day, watched her house during the
morning and saw Tyler McBride and his little boy, Sam, pay her a visit
around eleven o'clock. The kid was really cute, but he didn't yell and jump
around like other kids his age. Was everyone right? Had the son witnessed
McBride killing his mother, or was it just talk?

Adam wondered what was going on between Tyler McBride and
Becca Matlock/Powell. He watched Sheriff Gaffney pay her a visit, even
overheard the sheriff speaking to her outside the front door, on the big
wraparound porch. He heard them clearly.

"Nothing yet from the medical examiner's office, Sheriff?"

"They say hopefully tomorrow. I wanted to go over the basement
again, see what I could sniff out. My boys didn't find any fingerprints,
but maybe there's something there we all missed. Oh, and another thing,

Rachel Ryan asked me to tell you that some boys would be arriving to remove the tree and fix the window for you."

The sheriff left after an hour, a chocolate chip cookie in his hand. Adam knew it was chocolate chip. He could smell the chocolate from twenty yards and was salivating.

He sent an e-mail after lunch and within an hour knew all about how Becca Matlock had met Tyler McBride at Dartmouth College. Had the two of them been college sweethearts? Lovers? Perhaps. It was interesting. And now everyone believed the skeleton was Tyler McBride's missing wife, Ann. He'd find out everything he could about Tyler McBride. He supposed there was a certain possible irony at play here. What if she'd managed to get away from one stalker only to stumble upon a man who'd done away with his wife?

Yep, her luck sucked, big-time.

He still wasn't ready to approach her, she was too spooked. So he kept an eye on her that evening as well. She didn't leave the house. Since it stayed light so late in Maine during the summer months, five guys, all armed with chain saws, came to take care of the old fallen hemlock that lay along the west side of the house. They pulled the limb out of the upstairs window and sawed it up. They cut off and sawed up the branches from the tree, then wrapped thick chains around the trunk and dragged the tree away.

Through all of this, Becca read outside on the wraparound porch, sitting in an old glider, rocking back and forth until he was nearly nauseated watching that slow back and forth, that never-ending back and forth, and hearing the small creaking sounds that went with every movement in between the loud grating bursts from the chain saws.

She went to bed early.

AROUND noon the next day, Becca was thanking the windowpane guy for replacing the glass in her bedroom window. Not half an hour later, Tyler and Sam were there, eating tuna fish sandwiches at her kitchen table. She said, "We should be hearing from Sheriff Gaffney soon, Tyler. It should be today, that's what he said when he came yesterday. They're sure taking their time. Then all this nonsense will be over."

He was silent for the longest time, chewing his sandwich, helping Sam eat his, then said finally, some anger in his voice, which surprised her, "You're quite the optimist, Becca."

But she wasn't thinking about the skeleton at that moment. She was wondering why that man—Adam Carruthers—was watching her house. He was standing motionless in amongst the spruce trees, not twenty feet away. He wasn't the stalker. It wasn't his voice, she was sure of that. The stalker's voice was not old, not young, but unnervingly smooth. She knew she would recognize that voice anywhere. Carruthers's voice was different. But who was he? And why was he so interested in her?

ADAM stretched. He went through a few relaxing tae kwon do moves to ease his muscles. He was in the process of slowly raising his left leg, his left arm extended fully, when she said from behind him, "Your arm is a bit too high. Lower your elbow at least an inch and extend your wrist, yeah, and pull your fingers back a bit more. That's better. Now, don't even twitch or I'll shoot your head off."

He was faster than she could have imagined. She was a good six feet behind him. She had her Coonan .357 Magnum automatic, chambered with seven bullets, aimed right at him, and in the very next instant, his whole body was in motion, moving so fast it was a blur, at least until his right foot lightly and gracefully clipped the gun from her hand, and his left hand smacked her hard enough in the shoulder to send her flying backward. She landed on her back.

Becca grabbed the gun, on the ground not two feet to her left, and brought it up only to have him kick it out of her hand again. Her wrist stung for a moment, then went numb.

"Sorry," he said, standing over her now. "I don't react well to folks holding guns on me. I hope I didn't hurt you." He actually had the gall to reach out his hand to help her up. She was breathing hard, her shoulder was aching and her wrist was useless. She scooted backward, turned, and tried to run. She wasn't fast enough. He grabbed her and hauled her back against him. "No, hold it a minute. I'm not going to hurt you."

She stopped cold and became very, very still. Her head fell forward and he knew in that moment that she had simply given up.

He knew her shoulder had to hurt, that her wrist was now probably hanging numb. "It'll be all right. You'll get feeling back in your wrist soon. It'll burn a bit but then it'll be okay again."

Still drawn in on herself, she said, "I didn't think he could be you—your voice is all wrong, I would have sworn to that—but I obviously was wrong."

She thought he was the stalker, the man who had murdered that poor old woman in front of the museum, and then shot Governor Bledsoe. Automatically, he let her go. "Look, I'm sorry—" He was speaking to the back of her head. She'd taken off the second he'd let her go. She was off at a dead run, through the spruce trees, back toward her house.

He caught her within ten yards, grabbed her left arm, and jerked her around. She moved quickly. Her fist hit him solidly on the jaw. His head snapped back with the force of her sharp-knuckled blow. She was strong. He grabbed both her arms, only to feel her knee come up. His fast reflexes saved him. Her knee got him in the thigh. It still hurt, but not as bad as if she'd gotten him in the crotch. That would have sent him to the ground, sobbing his guts out. He whirled her around and brought her back against his chest. He clamped her arms at her sides and simply held her against him. She was breathing hard, her muscles tensing, relaxing, then tensing again. She was very afraid, but he knew she'd act again if he gave her the opening. He was impressed. But now he had her.

"I don't know how you found me," she said, still panting. "I did everything I could think of to hide my trail. How did you track me down?"

"It did take me two and a half days to track you to Portland, actually longer than I'd expected."

She twisted her head to look at him. "Let me go."

"Not yet. I want to hang on to my body parts. Hey, you didn't do too badly for an amateur."

"Let me go."

"Will you stop with the violence? I can't stand violence. It makes me nervous."

Her look was incredulous as she chewed her bottom lip. Finally, she nodded. "All right."

He let her go and took a quick step back, his eyes on her right knee.

She was off and running in a flash. This time, he let her go. She was fast, but he knew that from her dossier. She'd spotted him watching her house. It amazed him. He was always so very careful, so patient, as still as one of the spruce trees. In the past, his life had depended on it more times than he cared to remember. But she'd cottoned on to the fact that someone was out there, with her in his sights.

Well, the stalker had been after her for more than three weeks in New York. That had sharpened her senses, kept her alert. There was no doubt she was afraid, but it hadn't mattered. She'd come out and confronted him anyway. He whistled as he walked over and bent down to pick up her Coonan automatic. It was a nice gun. It had a closed breech that gave it very high velocity. His brother had one of these babies, was always bragging about it. It was steady, reliable, deadly, and not all that common. He wondered how she handled the recoil. He dumped the seven rimmed cartridges into his hand, then dropped them into his pocket. He paused a moment, wondering if he shouldn't leave the gun in her mailbox or slip it just inside her front door.

He imagined she wouldn't feel safe without it.

He saw Tyler McBride and his son leave about ten minutes later. He saw her wave from the front porch. He saw her looking over toward where he quietly stood, surely not visible through the trees. She went back into the house after Tyler McBride and his son drove off. He waited.

Not three minutes later she was back, standing on the front porch, looking toward him. He saw her thinking, weighing, assessing. Finally, she trotted toward him.

She had guts.

He didn't move, just waited, watching her. He realized when she was only about ten feet from him that she had a big kitchen butcher knife clutched in her hand.

He smiled. She was her father's daughter.

# NINE

Slowly, he pulled her gun out of his pants pocket and aimed it in her general direction. "Even that big honker knife can't compete with this Coonan you managed to get off that guy you met at the restaurant in Rockland. He was, however, pissed that you wouldn't go to bed with him." He grinned at her. "Hey, you got what you needed. You did good."

"How did you know about that? Oh, never mind. My knife can certainly compete with the Coonan now. I watched you take the bullets out."

He grinned at her again, he couldn't help it, and held the automatic out to her, butt first.

"What good is it? You've got the bullets. Give them to me now."

He scooped the seven bullets out of his pocket and handed them and the automatic to her.

She eyed the gun and the bullets, then backed up another step. "No, you want me to come a bit closer and then you can kick my knife away. You're fast, too fast. I'm not stupid."

"All right," Adam said, and he thought, Smart woman. He laid the bullets and the gun down on the ground and took a good half dozen steps back.

He said easily, "It's an effective weapon, that Coonan, but if I have to carry one of those things, I prefer my Colt Delta Elite."

"It sounds like some western debutante."

He laughed. "Aren't you going to pick up the gun?"

She shook her head at him and didn't move. She was holding the butcher knife like a mad killer in a slasher movie, her arm pulled back, the point out and arched. The sucker looked really sharp. He could get it from her, but one of them could easily get sliced up. He stayed put. Besides, he wanted to see what she'd do.

"Tell me what you're doing here. Why did you come up to me at Food Fort? Why are you watching me?"

"I'd really rather not tell you yet. I hadn't expected you to see me. When I've wanted to stay hidden in the past, I've managed it quite well." He suddenly looked pissed off, not at her but at himself. She almost smiled, then tightened her grip on the knife.

"Tell me, now."

"All right, then. I'm here to do research on why women dye their hair."

She very nearly ran at him with the knife. She was so mad she nearly forgot the bone-grinding fear. "All right, you jerk, I want you to lie on the ground and fold your hands underneath you. Do it now."

"No," he said. "The windbreaker is new. It looks good on me, hey, maybe it even looks dangerous and sexy. What do you think? Women like black, I've heard. Nope, I don't want it to get dirty."

"I called Sheriff Gaffney. He should be here any minute."

"Nah, you can't bluff me on that. The last person you want here is the sheriff. If I spilled the beans, he'd have to call the New York cops and the FBI."

She was so pale he thought she'd pass out. Her hand trembled a bit, but then she got ahold of herself. "So you know," she said. "I don't think you're the stalker—your voice is all wrong and you're too big—but you know all about him, don't you?"

"Yes. Now listen to me, Becca. I'm not here to hurt you. I'm here to— Hey, think of me as your own personal guardian angel."

"You're so dark, you look more like the devil, but you're taller than I think the devil is. What's more, unlike the devil, I'll bet you don't have a lick of charm. The last thing you are is a guardian angel. You're a reporter or a paparazzo, aren't you?"

"Now you've offended me." She nearly laughed. But she had to remember he was dangerous, fast and dangerous. She couldn't afford to forget that, not for an instant. She would still have laughed if her gut hadn't been frozen with fear for nearly as long as she could remember. He was trying to disarm her, at least figuratively this time. Thank goodness he didn't have use of her gun. And he was too far away to kick out at her. But he was fast. He had long legs. She took another step back, as insurance.

She waved the knife at him. "I've had it. Tell me who you are. Tell me now or I might have to hurt you. Don't underestimate me, I'm strong. No, it's more than that. I'm beyond frightened. I've got nothing to lose now."

He looked at her—too pale, her flesh drawn tightly over her bones, too thin, so stressed out he could nearly see her insides quivering. He said slowly, his voice as unthreatening as he could make it, "To hurt me you'd have to come closer. You know better than to do that. Yeah, you're strong, maybe I wouldn't even want to run into you in a dark alley. But there's a big something you're wrong about. Everyone has something to lose, including you. Things have just gotten a bit out of hand for you, that's all."

"A bit out of hand," she repeated slowly, then laughed, an ugly, raw sound. "You have no idea what you're talking about." She waited, just stood there, the knife up and arched, her hand starting to cramp, her muscles starting to protest, staring at him, wondering what to do, wondering if she could believe him and knowing she'd be a fool even to consider it.

He said, "Actually, I do. What I wanted to say was that the media and the press are after you in full force, that's a fact, but you should be safe here."

"You found me."

"Yeah, but I'm so good I occasionally even surprise myself."

She raised the knife even higher. She felt the sun warm between her shoulder blades. It was a beautiful day and everything was a mess. He was her guardian angel? Her arm muscles were burning.

He started to say something more, then stopped. It was the look on her face that kept him quiet. It was like they were both frozen in time and place. Then she surprised the hell out of him. She dropped the knife to the ground and walked straight up to him. She stopped a foot short, looked up at him thoughtfully, then stuck out her hand. He shook hers, bemused, as she said, "If you're my guardian angel, then get on the phone to the medical examiner's office in Augusta and find out how long that poor woman who fell out of my basement wall was buried in there."

He didn't release her hand. She was tall. He didn't have to look down that far. "All right."

She snapped her fingers in front of his nose. "Just like that? You're so powerful you can find out something just that fast?"

"In this case, yes, I can. You don't look much like your mother."

The hand stiffened, but she didn't jerk free. She said calmly, "No, I don't. Mom always told me that I'm the picture of my dad. My dad—his name was Thomas—he died after the Vietnam war was over. It was very unfair. He was still a hero. My mother loved him very much, probably too much."

"Yes," he said. "I know all about that."

"How?"

"It's not important right now. Believe me."

She didn't, of course, but she was willing to put it on hold for the moment because she said then, "I saw a really old snapshot of him. He looked so young, so happy. He was very handsome, so tall and straight." She paused a moment, and he heard the hitch in her voice. "I was too young to remember him when he died, but my mom said he'd seen me born, held me and loved me. And then he left and didn't come back."

"I know."

She cocked her head to one side, and again she let it go, saying, "When I first saw you in Food Fort, I thought you looked hard, like you didn't smile very often, like you ate nails and hot salsa for snacks. I thought you could be mean if you had to, maybe even cruel. You still look mean. I can sense that you're dangerous; actually, I know it, so don't even bother trying to deny it. Who are you, really?"

"I'm Adam Carruthers. I told you that at Food Fort. That really is my name. Now, take me to your house and I'll get on the phone. We won't find out who the skeleton is, but we'll find out at least how long she was in that wall. They'll have to do DNA tests; that takes a while. First things first."

He watched her pick up her Coonan and stuff the bullets in her jeans pocket. He picked up her kitchen knife and followed her back to Jacob Marley's house.

It took him eleven minutes and two phone calls. When he shut down his cell phone the second time, he looked over at her and smiled. "It shouldn't take long." In no more than three seconds, the cell began playing jazz. He motioned her away and picked it up. "Carruthers here."

He listened, wrote something down on a sheet of paper. "Thanks a lot, Jarvis, I owe you. Yeah, yeah, you know I always pay up. It just might not be tomorrow. You know how to reach me. Okay, thanks. Bye."

He put his cell in his shirt pocket. "It isn't Ann McBride, if that's what you're worried about."

"No, of course it's not Tyler's missing wife. I never thought it was.

I've known him since I was eighteen. I've never met a more decent man. Really." But she was nearly shaking with relief, and he saw it. However, it was his turn to let it go.

But then she said, "I couldn't have stood it if Tyler had been a monster instead of a really nice guy. I guess I would have hung it up."

"Yeah, your boyfriend's off the hook. The skeleton was buried inside that wall for at least ten years, possibly more. She was probably in her late teens when she was killed by a hard blow right in the face, the forehead actually. Whoever did it was really pissed, enraged, totally out of control. Jarvis said it was a vicious blow, killed her instantly."

"It looks like Jacob Marley really might have killed her, then."

He shrugged. "Who knows? It's not our problem."

"It's certainly mine, since she tumbled out of the wall onto my basement floor. I can't believe anyone would kill a teenager for wandering across his yard, and with such viciousness."

A second later the phone rang. It was Bernie Bradstreet, owner of *The Riptide Independent,* wanting to know what she could tell him. "I know the sheriff wants to keep a lid on this, but—"

She told him everything, omitting only what Adam Carruthers had found out from the medical examiner's office. She didn't think the sheriff would like to be cut out of that particular loop. Then Bernie Bradstreet asked her to dinner, with his wife, he hastened to add when she didn't say anything. She put him off. When she hung up the phone, Adam said, "Newspaper? You handled it well. Now you need to call the sheriff. Don't tell him you already know the answers. Encourage him to call the medical examiner's office. Jarvis told me they're not ready to release the information yet, but if the sheriff calls, he might be able to pry it out of them. Oh, yeah, when the sheriff comes, tell him I'm your cousin from Baltimore here to visit. Okay?"

"Cousins? We don't look anything alike."

He gave her a crooked grin. "Thank heaven for that."

SHERIFF Gaffney didn't like the news from Augusta. He liked tidy conclusions, puzzles where all the pieces finally locked cleanly into place, not this: an old skeleton, identity unknown, that had been bricked inside Jacob Marley's basement wall after her gruesome murder. He didn't really want Ann McBride to be dead, but it would have made things so much cleaner, so nice and straightforward. He glanced at Tyler McBride. The

guy looked calm, but relieved? He couldn't tell. Tyler had always managed to keep what he was feeling close to his vest. He was good at poker,
nobody liked to play against him. Funny thing, though, the sheriff would
have sworn that Tyler had killed his wife. He still kept his eye on Tyler,
hoping to see him do something strange, like visit an unmarked grave or
something. Well, he'd been wrong before. He guessed maybe he was
wrong again. He hated it, it wasn't pleasant, but sometimes it happened,
even to a man like him.

Sheriff Gaffney looked over at Ms. Powell's cousin, a big, tough-
looking guy who looked like he could take care of himself. His body was
hard and in good shape. He seemed like a man who could be patient, as
if he was used to waiting in the shadows, like a predator stalking its prey.
Gaffney shook his head. He had to stop reading those suspense novels he
liked so much.

He looked at Becca Powell, a nice young woman who wasn't so
pale now, or on the verge of hysteria. Hopefully her cousin would keep
her that way. After finding that skeleton, maybe she would be glad to
have him around for a while. He found himself studying Carruthers
again. The guy was dark, from his black hair—too long, in the sheriff's
opinion—to his eyes, nearly black in the dim late-afternoon light in Jacob
Marley's living room. He had big feet in scuffed black boots, soft-looking
boots that looked like he'd worn them for a good long time and waited
in the shadows with those boots on his feet, not making a whisper of
a sound. He wondered what the man did for a living. Nothing normal
and expected, he'd bet his next meal on that. Maybe he didn't want to
know.

The sheriff looked around the living room. The place looked like a
museum or a tomb. It felt old and musty, although it smelled like lemons,
just like at home.

He knew, of course, that everyone was looking at him, waiting. He
liked that. It built suspense. He was holding them in the palm of his
hand. Only thing was, they didn't look all that scared or worried or ready
to gnaw off their fingernails. A real cool bunch.

Becca said finally, "Sheriff, won't you be seated? Now, you have news
for us?"

He took the old chair she was waving at, eased down slowly, then
cleared his throat. He was ready to make his big announcement. "Well
now, it does appear that this skeleton isn't your wife, Tyler."

There was a sharp moment of silence, but not the surprise he'd expected, that he'd wanted, truth be told.

"Thank you for telling me so quickly, Sheriff. I'm pleased that it wasn't, because that would have meant that someone had killed her and it wasn't me. I hope that wherever Ann is, she's very much alive and well and happy."

Tyler hadn't acted surprised. He acted like he already knew. Well, if Tyler hadn't killed Ann, then he would certainly know that the skeleton wasn't her, or if it was, then someone else had put her there. That logic made the sheriff's head ache. "Humph, I wouldn't know about that. I've contacted all the local authorities and they're going to check on runaways from between ten and fifteen years ago. There's a good chance we'll find out who she is. She was young, probably late teens. That makes it even more likely that she was a runaway. She was murdered, though. That makes it a big problem, my big problem."

"It's not possible it's a local teenager, Sheriff?" Becca asked.

The sheriff shook his head. "Nobody up and disappeared in the town's memory, Ms. Powell. Something like that, folk wouldn't forget. Nope, it's got to be a runaway."

Adam Carruthers sat forward, his hands clasped between his knees. "You think this old man, Jacob Marley, did it?" He was sitting in a deep leather chair that old Jacob had liked. He looked like he was the one in charge and that burned the sheriff a bit. Fellow was too young to be in charge, not much beyond thirty, about the same age as Maude's nephew, Frank, who was currently in prison out in Folsom, California, for writing bad checks. Frank had always had soggy morals, even as a boy. Maybe the fellow was shiftless, like Frank. No, the last thing this guy looked was shiftless.

"Sheriff?"

"Yeah? Oh, it's possible. Like I told Ms. Powell here, old Jacob didn't like people poking around. He had a mean streak in him and no patience to speak of. He could have bashed her."

Adam said, a dark eyebrow raised a bit, "Mean streak or not, you believe he actually bashed a young girl in the face with a blunt instrument and walled her in his basement because he was angry at her trotting across his backyard?"

Sheriff Gaffney said, "A blunt instrument, you say. Well, the ME didn't know what the murderer struck her with, maybe a heavy pot, maybe a bookend, something like that. Did Jacob do it? We'll have to see about that."

"Nothing else makes much sense," Tyler said, jumping to his feet. He began pacing the room. His whole body was vibrating with tension. He had good muscle tone, the sheriff thought, remembering his own buffed self the ladies had stared at when he was that young. Tyler whirled around, came to a stop, nearly knocking over a floor lamp. "Don't you see? Whoever killed her had to have access to Jacob's basement. Surely Jacob would have heard someone knocking away bricks, then putting them back up. The killer had to have cement to do that. Also, he had to haul the body into the house and down the basement steps. That would be quite an undertaking. It had to be Jacob. Nothing else makes sense."

Adam said, leaning back in that old leather chair now, his legs crossed at his ankles, his fingers steepled, the tips lightly tapping together, "Now, wait a minute. You're saying that Jacob Marley never left his house?"

"Not that I remember," Tyler said. "He even had his groceries delivered. Of course, I was gone four years when I was in college. Maybe he used to be different, went out more."

"Two things were always true about old Jacob," Sheriff Gaffney said slowly. "Two things you could always count on. He was here and he was mean." He heaved himself from his seat. He froze when the button right above his wide leather belt up and popped off. He watched, paralyzed, as the damned button rolled across the polished oak floor to stop at the big toe of Carruthers's right boot. He sucked in his belly, but he still felt that wide leather belt of his continue to cut him something fierce. He didn't say anything, just held out his hand.

Adam Carruthers tossed him the button. He didn't smile. The sheriff clutched that damned button close. Maybe he should think about that diet Maude was always nagging him about.

Becca pretended not to see anything. She rose and stuck out her hand to the sheriff. "Thank you for coming and telling us in person. Please let us know when you find out who that poor girl is."

"Was, ma'am, was. I will. I'm glad I called them. I had to worm it out of them, but I finally got to speak to the main guy, a hardnose named Jarvis, and he finally coughed up the info." He nodded to Tyler McBride, who looked hollow-cheeked, as if he'd been put through a wringer, and then to Adam Carruthers, a cocky bastard who hadn't laughed when his button had popped off.

"I'll see you out, Sheriff," Becca said and walked beside him out of the living room.

Adam said to Tyler, "Becca told me what was going on. I'm glad I was nearby and could get here to help."

Tyler eyed the man. There hadn't been time to question him before the sheriff had arrived. He said slowly, suspicion a sharp thread in his voice, "I didn't know Becca had a cousin. Who are you?"

# TEN

Adam said easily, "Becca's mom was my aunt. She died of cancer, you know, very recently. My mom lives in Baltimore with my stepdad. A great guy, loves to fish for bass."

Thank God she heard that before she came back into the living room. The man was quick and smooth. He was a very good liar. She would have believed him herself if she hadn't known better. Actually, her mother was an only child, both her parents long dead. Her father had been an only child as well. His parents were also dead. Who was Adam, anyway?

Tyler turned toward Becca and said in a voice that was far too intimate, "Well, maybe Sam can have a stepmom, like you got yourself a stepdad, Adam."

Becca felt a jolt that landed a lump in her throat. She couldn't breathe for a minute. Tyler was looking at her like that? A future stepmom for Sam? She cleared her throat twice before she could speak. Well, she'd known him forever and he hadn't killed his wife, but he was a friend, nothing more than a very good friend, which was quite enough, given what her life was right now. "It's getting late. Adam, how about—"

He interrupted her smoothly, standing, stretching a bit. "I know, Becca. I'll be back over in a little while. I've got to get my stuff from Errol Flynn's Hammock. It's a great B-and-B. That guy Scottie is a hoot. You want to eat out tonight?"

"Becca and I were going to go to Errol Flynn's Barbecue this evening," Tyler said, and now he was standing perfectly still, his shoulders back, his chin up, ready for a fight, Adam thought, like a cock ready to defend the henhouse against the fox.

Adam grinned. "Sounds good to me. I like barbecue. You bringing Sam? I'd like to meet him."

"Of course Sam's coming," Becca said, her voice firm as that of a den mother faced with a dozen ten-year-olds. "What street is Errol Flynn's Barbecue on, Tyler?"

"Foxglove Avenue, across from Sherry's Lingerie Boutique. I hear Mrs. Ella loves Sherry's lingerie, always in there on her lunch hour." He shook his head. "It's rather a scary thought."

"I haven't met Mrs. Ella yet," Becca said, then to Adam, "She's the sheriff's dispatcher, assistant, protector, screener, whatever—but I know about every one of her pets for the last fifty years. Her job was to save me from hysteria while I was waiting for the sheriff to come."

"Did it work?" Adam said.

"Yes, it did. All I could think about was the beagle named Turnip who died by running right off a cliff when he missed the corner chasing a car."

Both men laughed, and the male pissing contest that had nearly made her take a kitchen knife to both of them was out of sight, at least for the moment. She would have to speak to Tyler if it turned out he was getting the wrong idea, and evidently he was. But didn't he realize that being her first cousin meant that Adam was no threat? She didn't need this. She could eat barbecue with them, she supposed. Thank goodness Sam would be there.

Sam didn't have much testosterone yet.

IT was after midnight. Tyler McBride was still hanging about at the front door, and Sam was asleep in the car, his bright blue T-shirt and black kid jeans covered with the sauce from the pork barbecue spareribs. The kid hadn't said much—shy, Adam supposed—but he'd eaten his share. He'd finally said Adam's name when he'd taken a big bite of potato salad, then nothing more.

Would the guy never give it up and leave? Adam took a step closer to get him out of there when he overheard Tyler saying quietly to Becca at the front door, "I don't like him staying here with you, alone. I don't trust him."

And then Becca's voice, calm and soothing, and he could practically see her lightly touch her fingers to Tyler's arm as she said, "He's my first cousin, Tyler. I never did like him growing up. He was a bully and a know-it-all, always pushing me around because I was a girl. He's grown up into a real sexist. But hey, he's here and he is big. He's also had some training, something like army special forces, I think, so he'd be useful if someone came around."

"I still don't like it."

"Look, if something happens, he's an extra pair of hands. He's harmless. Hey, I heard from his stepdad that he's probably gay."

Adam nearly lost it then. The laughter bubbled up. He practically had to slap his hand over his mouth to contain it. The laughter dried up in less than a second. He wanted to leap on her, close his hands around her skinny neck, and perhaps strangle her.

"Yeah, right, sure," Tyler said. "A guy like that? Gay? I don't believe it for a minute. You should stay with me and Sam, to be on the safe side."

She said very gently, "No, you know I couldn't do that, Tyler."

Even after that, it took her another couple of minutes to get Tyler out of the house. She was locking the door when he said from behind her, "I'm not a sexist."

She turned around to grin at him. "Aha! So you were eavesdropping. I thought you were probably lurking back there. I was afraid you were going to try to throw Tyler out of the house."

"Maybe I would have if you hadn't finally gotten a grip and pushed him out. I wasn't a bully or a know-it-all, either, when I was growing up. I never tortured you."

"Don't become part of your own script, Adam. I can also write whatever I want to on that script, since it involves me."

"I'm not gay, either."

She laughed at him.

He grabbed her by the shoulders, jerked her against him, and kissed her fast and hard. He said against her mouth, "I'm not gay."

She pulled away from him, stood stock-still, and stared at him. She wiped the back of her hand over her mouth.

He streaked his fingers through his hair, standing it on end. "I'm sorry. I don't know why I did that. I didn't mean to do that. I'm not gay."

She started shaking her head, then, as suddenly, unexpectedly, she threw back her head and laughed and laughed, wrapping her arms around herself.

It was a nice sound. He bet she hadn't laughed much lately. She hiccuped. "You're forgiven for trying to enforce your manhood. Got you on that one, hmmm?"

He realized he'd leapt for the bait. How could that have happened? He looked down at his fingernails, then buffed them lightly against his shirtsleeve. "Actually, what I should have said is I'm not at all certain yet that I'm gay. I'm still thinking about it. Kissing you was a test. Yeah, I'm still not certain one way or the other. You didn't give me much data." Not much of a return hit, but it was something.

She walked past him into the kitchen. She started measuring out coffee. When she finished, she turned the machine on and stood there, staring at the coffee dripping into the pot. Finally she turned and said, "I want to know who you are. Now. Don't lie to me. I can't take any more lies. Really, I just can't."

"All right. Pour me that coffee and I'll tell you who I am and what I'm doing here."

While she poured, he said, leaning back in his chair, balancing it on its two back legs, "Because you're an amateur I looked at the problem very differently. But like I already told you, you didn't do badly. Your only really big mistake was your try at misdirection with the flight from Dulles to Boston, then another flight on to Portland. Another thing: I reviewed all your credit card invoices. The only airline you use is United. Since you're an amateur, it wouldn't occur to you to change."

She said, "Trying another airline flicked through my brain, but I wanted out as fast as I could get out and I feel comfortable dealing with United. I never thought, never realized—"

"I know. It makes excellent sense, just not in this sort of situation. I didn't even bother checking any of the other airlines."

"However did you get ahold of my credit card invoices?"

"No problem. Access to any private records is a piece of cake, for anyone. Thankfully, law enforcement has to convince judges to get warrants and that takes time, a good thing for you. Also, I've got a dynamite staff who are so fast and creative I have to give them raises too often.

"No, don't stiffen up like a poker. We're talking absolute discretion here. Now, there were only sixty-eight tickets issued to women traveling alone within six hours of the flight you took to Washington, D.C. I believed it would be three hours, but we all wanted to be thorough. It turned out you called the airline to make reservations only two hours and fifty-four minutes before the flight, as a matter of fact. You moved very quickly once you made up your mind to get the hell out of Dodge. Then you had to buy a ticket to Boston, then on to Portland, Maine, when you arrived at Dulles in Washington, D.C. You didn't want to buy it in New York, for obvious reasons. You ran up to the ticket counter, knowing full well that the next flight to Boston was in a scant twelve minutes. You wanted out of the line of fire and to get where you were going as quickly as you could. There was a flight from Dulles to Boston leaving only forty-five minutes after you landed in Dulles, but you turned it down. You didn't have any checked luggage, too big a risk with that, which was smart of you. The woman at the check-in counter recognized your photo, said she realized you might miss that plane, what with security and all, but you insisted even though she tried to talk you out of it. She didn't understand at the time, since there was another flight so soon. She told you the chances were very high that you'd miss the first plane to Boston."

"I nearly did miss it. I had to run like mad to catch it. They were ready to close the gate and I slipped right through."

"I know. I spoke to the flight attendant who greeted you at the door when you came rushing onto the plane. She said you looked somewhat desperate."

She sighed, but didn't say anything, crossed her arms over her chest and stared at him, still as a stone. "Come on, let's hear the rest of it."

"It didn't take long to find you on that flight to Portland. Your fake ID was pretty good. Good enough to fool security. At least you were smart enough not to use that driver's license again to get yourself a rental car. You waited an hour for a flight from Boston to Portland, then you took a taxi into Portland—yes, one of my people found the driver and verified that it was you—and went to Big Frank's Previously Owned Cars on Blake Street. You wanted your own car. That told me you had a definite destination in mind, a place where you were going to burrow in for the long haul. I got all the particulars out of Big Frank, including your license plate number, the make, model, and color of your Toyota. I called a friend in the Portland PD to put out an APB on you and it didn't take more than a day to net you. Remember when you got gas at the Union 76 station when you were first coming into town?"

She'd paid cash. No trail. No record. "I didn't make any mistakes."

"No, but it turns out the guy who pumped your gas is a police radio buff with an excellent memory for numbers. He heard the APB, remembered your car and license plate, and phoned it in. It got to me really fast. Don't worry, I canceled the APB. Needless to say, I owe a good-sized favor to Chief Aronson of the Portland PD. Also I spoke to the kid who pumped your gas, told him it had all been a mistake, thanked him, and slipped him a fifty. Oh yes, I got a good laugh over the name on the fake ID—Martha Bush—a nice mix of presidential names."

"I did, too," Becca said, wondering why she'd bothered at all.

"At least Martha was young and had blondish hair. Did you buy it off a street kid in New York?"

"Yes. I had to try six of them before I could find an ID that looked anything remotely like me. I liked the name. When did you get here to Riptide?"

"Two days ago. I went immediately to the only bed-and-breakfast in town and of course you had stayed there for one night. Scottie told me you'd taken the old Marley place." He splayed his fingers. "Nothing to it."

"Why didn't you come to see me right away?"

"I wanted to get the lay of the land, watch you awhile, see what was happening, who you spoke to, things like that. It's an approach I've always used. I've never believed in rushing into things, if I have a choice."

"It was so easy for you." She sighed, her arms still crossed over her chest. "That means that the FBI should be ringing the doorbell at any minute."

"Nah, they're not as smart as I am."

She threw her empty coffee cup at him.

He snagged the cup out of the air and set it back on the table. His reflexes were good. He was very fast. She said, "I'm awfully glad I didn't come any nearer to you. You could have nailed me in a flash, couldn't you?"

"Probably, but that's not the point. I'm not here to hurt you. I'm here to protect you."

"My guardian angel."

"That's right."

"Why don't you think the cops and FBI will be here any moment?"

"They have to follow all sorts of legal procedures to get to the goodies. Also, they tend to use a shovel when a scalpel would work best." He paused a moment, grinning at her. "And I also sent them on a wild-goose chase. I'll tell you about it later."

"All right. Let's cut to the chase. If you're not a cop, then who are you and who hired you to help me?"

He shook his head. "For the time being I'm not at liberty to tell you that. But someone wants me to clean up this mess you've gotten yourself into."

"I didn't do anything at all. It's that demented man stalking me who's responsible. Oh, maybe like the cops in New York and Albany, you don't believe me, either?"

"I believe you. Would you like to know why the cops in New York and Albany didn't believe you? Thought you were a screwed-up fruitcake?"

She nearly fell out of her chair. "I don't believe this. You know something the cops don't? They thought I was crazy or malicious or infatuated with the governor. Come on, what do you know?"

"They believed you were a fake because someone close to the governor told them that it was all a sick sexual fantasy. When the cops called from New York, that's what the Albany police told them. However, the threat to the governor was quite real, no question about that, since someone shot him. They had to refocus, think things over again."

"Who in the governor's office said that about me? Don't you dare sit there staring at me. Damn you, I deserve to know who betrayed me."

"Of course you do. I'm sorry, Becca. It was Dick McCallum, the governor's senior aide."

She nearly fell over in shock. "Oh, no, not Dick McCallum. Oh, no, it doesn't make any sense. Not Dick." She looked stricken and he was sorry for it.

She was shaking her head at him, not wanting to believe him but afraid not to. "But why? Dick has never said anything mean to me or acted like he had it in for me. He never asked me out, so there wouldn't be any sort of rejection involved. I didn't threaten him in any way. I was sure he liked me. I wrote most of the governor's speeches, for heaven's sake. I didn't head up strategy sessions or conduct policy meetings or have anything to do with spin or scheduling or anything that would be in his bailiwick. Why would he do it?"

"That I don't know yet. But to be realistic about it, it will probably come down to money. Someone paid him a lot of money to do it. Now, one of the cops in Albany told me he'd come to them, supposedly feeling all sorts of guilty, but swearing he had no choice because he was afraid you'd go after the governor. I promise you I will find out why he did it. He's got to be the key to this." Actually, he thought, Thomas Matlock was going over everything in McCallum's background, including where he got the small knife tattoo on the back of his right shoulder blade.

She said slowly, thinking aloud really, "If Dick McCallum said those things about me, then he must know about the stalker, maybe even who he is and why he picked me to terrorize. Maybe Dick even knows who is trying to kill the governor."

"Yes, all of that is possible. We'll see."

"Do you mean 'we' as in you and me?"

"No."

"Let me call the cops again. I'll tell them I know about what Dick McCallum told them. I can tell them he's lying. Won't they have to question him more thoroughly?"

"No, Becca, it's too late. I'm really sorry about this."

"What do you mean, it's too late? I know I can get ahold of Detective Morales."

"We'll have to go another route to find out why Dick McCallum did what he did, and who probably paid him a whole lot of money to do it."

She became very still. She shook her head. He said very gently, "I'm sorry, Becca, but someone ran Dick McCallum down in front of his apartment building in Albany. He's dead."

There wasn't a single thought in her mind, just numbing horror.

"They think you could be involved. Everyone's gone nuts. Actually, they were nuts the moment the governor was shot. No one could believe the distance on that shot. Now they're very serious about finding you and finding out what you know, if you're involved in any way. I planted information for them to find and got them off on a wrong track, so you're safe for a while."

He sat back in his chair and cradled his head against his arms. He gave her a big fat smile. "They're not going to find you anytime soon, trust me on that."

# ELEVEN

She could only stare at him. "All right, you're the greatest. Now, tell me how you fooled them."

"Thank you. Actually, I had nearly everything in place before Dick McCallum was killed. To be very precise, I did it right after the governor was shot. I had to shut the spigot off before they had the chance to really turn it on.

"They immediately mounted quite a manhunt. FBI offices all over the country are on the lookout for you. They were just beginning to track you from New York, just like I did, but then—a wonderful thing happened. They became convinced you'd climbed on a Greyhound bus and had gone all the way down to North Carolina, probably disguised in a black wig, maybe even brown contacts. All they had to work on was your driver's license and that was pretty scary. They searched your mom's apartment, but you'd cleaned it out really well. They're still looking for a storage facility for more information about you, photos and stuff like that. I assume you rented a storage locker. Where?"

"In the Bronx. Under an assumed name. To be honest, I didn't have time to go through my mother's stuff. I piled everything into boxes and hauled the stuff to the Bronx. Now, Adam, where would they come up with the idea that I'd be in North Carolina?"

He smiled sweetly at her. "Fiddling. I enjoy it and I'm good at it."

"By 'fiddling' you mean you scammed them?"

"Right. Sometimes con men use it when they get something over on their marks. Ah, sometimes law enforcement uses it, too."

She shook her head at him. "I don't want to know which you are.

You're kidding about this, right? You yourself didn't feed them that information, did you?"

"No. I got one of their best snitches to feed it to them. That way they wouldn't have any doubts at all. I even planted some evidence in your apartment in Albany to show that you knew all about North Carolina, that you'd even vacationed on the Outer Banks, your favorite town, Duck. Agents were swarming all over Duck within four hours of the FBI getting the information."

"I have been to Duck. I've stayed at the Sanderling Inn."

"I know, that's why I selected it."

"But I don't think I kept any souvenirs or books or anything like that."

"Oh yeah, sure you had souvenirs. There were a couple of T-shirts, some shells with 'Duck' etched on them, a couple of Duck pens, and a cute little candy dish showing ducks marching. Now the Feebs will scour the Outer Banks all the way down to Ocracoke. Did you hear about the Cape Hatteras lighthouse being moved?"

"Yes. Do you want more coffee?"

"Please. Oh, yes, Becca, give me the name of the storage locker and the assumed name. I'll get all your stuff out of there and to a safe place."

She snapped her fingers at him. "You can get things accomplished just like that?"

"I can but try." He tried to look modest, maybe even humble, but he couldn't pull it off. "What's the name you used and what's the storage locker name?"

"P and F Storage in the Bronx, and the name is Connie Pearl."

"I don't think I want to know where you got that name."

He watched her walk to the sink with the empty coffeepot and rinse it out. When she turned to reach for the coffee, her head slanted in a certain way. He blinked. He knew that certain set of the head very well. He'd seen her father do that not six days before. He watched her closely and saw that her movements were economical, graceful. He liked the way she moved. She'd inherited that from her father, too, one of the smoothest, most elegant men Adam had ever known. He clasped his hands behind his head, closed his eyes for a moment, picturing Thomas Matlock clearly in his mind's eye, and thought back to that meeting between the two of them on June 24.

"She still believes you're dead."

He nodded. "Of course. Even when Allison knew she was dying, we decided not to tell Becca about me, it was too dangerous."

At least, Adam thought, Thomas had been in close contact with his wife since e-mail had come along. They were online every night, until his wife had gone into the hospital. Adam said, "I don't agree with that, Thomas. You should have contacted her when her mother fell into a coma. She needed you then, and the good Lord knows, she needs you now."

"You know it's still too risky. I haven't known where Krimakov is since right after I shot his wife. I realized soon enough that I would have to kill him to protect my family, but he simply disappeared, with the help of the KGB, no doubt. No, I can't take the risk that Krimakov could find out about her. He would slit her throat and laugh and then call me and laugh some more. No. I've been dead to her for twenty-four years. It stays that way. Allison agreed with me that until I know for certain that Krimakov is dead, I stay dead to my daughter." Thomas sighed deeply. "It was very hard for both of us, I'll be honest with you. I think if Allison hadn't slipped into that drugged coma, she might have told Becca, so that she'd know she wasn't really alone."

The pain in his voice made Adam silent for a long time. Then he said, all practical again, "You can't stay dead to her now and you know it. Or haven't you been watching FOX?"

"That's why you're here. Stop frowning down at me. Pour yourself a cup of coffee and sit down. I've done a lot of thinking. I've got a favor to ask."

Adam Carruthers poured himself some coffee so strong it could bring down a rhino. He stretched out in the chair opposite the huge mahogany desk. A computer, a printer, a fax, and a big leather desk pad sat in their designated spots on top of the desk. No free papers stacked anywhere, no slips or notes, only technology. He knew that on this specific computer, there were no deep, dark secrets, just camouflage. Even he would have a hard time getting through all the safeguards installed to protect any hidden files on the machine, if there had been any, which there weren't. Thomas Matlock had stayed at the top of his game by being careful and smart.

Adam said, "The governor of New York was shot in the neck two nights ago. The man was lucky to be surrounded by doctors and that he'd promised more big state bucks for cancer research, otherwise they might have let him bleed to death."

"You're cynical."

"Yeah, well, you've known that for ten years, haven't you?" Adam took a drink of the high-test coffee and felt a jolt all the way to his feet. "Everyone is after her now, particularly the Feebs. She's gone to ground. They've pulled out all the stops, but no sign of her yet. Smart girl. To fool everyone isn't easy. She's your daughter, all right. Cunning and sneakiness are in her genes."

Thomas Matlock opened a desk drawer and pulled out a 5x7 color photo set in a simple silver frame. "There are only three people alive who know she's my daughter, and you're one of them. Now, her mother got this to me eight months ago. Her name's Becca, as you know, short for Rebecca—that was my mother's name. She's about five feet eight inches tall, and she's on the lean side, not more than one hundred twenty pounds. You can see that she's in good shape. She's athletic, a whiz at tennis and racquetball. Her mother told me she loves football, not college but professional. She'd kill for the Giants, even in their worst season.

"You've got to find her, Adam. I don't know if Krimakov will connect her to me. It's very probable he's known all along that I had a wife and a daughter, no way to bury that, and we didn't want to do the witness protection program. But you know something? I still don't have a clue where he is or what he's been doing the past twenty years. I've got tentacles all over the world but no definite leads on his whereabouts. Now I've upped the ante, but still nothing.

"But you know he's on top of American news, all of it. The instant he hears the name 'Matlock,' he'll go *en pointe*. She's in deep trouble. She doesn't even realize how deep, that the cops and the FBI are the least of her worries."

"Don't worry, Thomas. I'll find her and I'll protect her, from both the stalker and Krimakov, if either of them shows up."

"That's just it." Thomas sighed. "This stalker bothers me. What are the odds that a stalker would go after Becca? Too great, I think. What I'm thinking is that maybe Krimakov already found her, maybe he's the stalker."

Adam said, "I guess it's possible, but unlikely, I think. If he's the stalker, then that means he found her even before your wife died."

"Yes, it scares me to my toes."

"But there's no proof at all that it's Krimakov. Now, first things first. I've got to get the locals and the Feds off her trail once and for all."

"You've already begun to track her, then?"

"Sure. The minute I heard her name, I got all my people working on it. What would you expect? You're the one who always has to look at the big picture. I don't. Let me make a phone call right now, let Hatch know you've approved everything, get all my people on this."

"And if I hadn't called you?"

"I'd have taken care of her anyway." Adam turned to pick up the phone. "She's your daughter."

Adam knew that Thomas Matlock was looking at him as he lifted the receiver of the black phone and punched in some numbers. He knew, too, that Thomas had worried and worried, tried to figure out the odds, determine the best thing to do, but Adam had simply stepped in and begun protecting his daughter from a stalker who could be, truth be told, Krimakov, although to Adam the odds were that Krimakov was long dead. But it was a lead. It was something, the only thing they had.

Thomas should have known that he didn't have to even ask. Adam also imagined that Thomas Matlock felt a goodly amount of relief.

As he spoke quietly on the phone, he saw the jolt of pain cross Thomas Matlock's face, and he knew it was because Thomas would never again see Allison. And more than that. Thomas Matlock hadn't been with his wife when she died. He'd wanted to be, but Becca was there, always there, and he couldn't take the chance. The pain and guilt of that had to be tearing him up inside.

Oh yeah, he'd try to save Thomas's daughter.

Only one mistake in the late seventies, and Thomas Matlock had lost any chance at the promising life he'd begun. He'd had to hold himself private. He'd kept his position in the intelligence community so he would know if Krimakov ever surfaced. But he'd had to remain alone.

*Jacob Marley's House*

Adam slowly opened his eyes. He was in the same room with Allison and Thomas Matlock's daughter, and she was looking at him with an odd combination of helplessness and wariness. She looked so very much like her father. He couldn't tell her yet. No, not yet. He said on a yawn, "I'm sorry, I guess I just sort of flashed out for a while."

"It's late. You're probably exhausted what with all your skulking around spying on me. I'm going to bed. There's a guest room at the end of the hall upstairs. The bed might be awful, I don't know. Come on and I'll help you make it up."

The bed was hard as a rock, which was fine with Adam. His feet didn't hang off the end, another nice thing. He watched her trail off down the hall, pause for just a moment, and look back at him. She raised her hand. Then he watched her close the door to her bedroom.

He'd wondered about Becca Matlock for a very long time, wondered what she was like, how much she'd inherited from her father, wondered if she was happy, maybe even in love with a guy and ready to get married. He discovered he was still wondering about her as he lay on his back and stared up at the black ceiling. All he knew for sure was that someone had put her in the center of his game and was doing his best to bring her down. Kill her? He didn't know.

Was it Vasili Krimakov? He didn't know that either, but maybe it was time to consider anything that put a shadow on the radar.

He woke up at about four a.m. and couldn't go back to sleep. Finally, he booted up his laptop and wrote an e-mail:

> *I told her about McCallum. She really doesn't know anything. I don't either, yet. You know, maybe you're right. Maybe Krimakov is the stalker and the one who shot the governor.*

He turned off the laptop and stretched out again, pillowing his head on his arms. To him, Krimakov was like the bogeyman, a monster trotted out to scare children. To Adam, the man had never had any substance, even though he'd seen classified material about him, been briefed about his kills. But that was over twenty-five years ago. Nothing, not even a whiff of the man since then.

Twenty-five years since Thomas Matlock had accidentally killed his wife. So long ago and in a place that was no longer even part of the So- viet Union—Belarus, the smallest of the Slavic republics, independent since 1991.

He knew the story because once, once, Thomas Matlock had gotten drunk—it was his anniversary—and told him about how he'd been playing cat and mouse back in the seventies with a Russian agent, Vasili Krimakov, and in the midst of a firefight that never should have happened, he'd accidentally shot Krimakov's wife. They'd been on the top of Dzerzhinskaya Mountain, not much of a mountain at all, but the highest peak Belarus had to offer. And she'd died and Krimakov had sworn he would kill him, kill his wife, kill anyone he loved, and he'd cursed him to hell and beyond. And Thomas Matlock knew he meant it.

The next morning, Thomas Matlock had simply looked at Adam and said, "Only two other people in the world know the whole of it, and one of them is my wife." If there was more to the tale, Thomas Matlock hadn't told him.

Adam had always wondered who the other person was who knew the whole story, but he hadn't asked. He wondered now what Thomas Matlock was doing at this precise moment, if he, like Adam, was lying awake, wondering what was going on.

*Chevy Chase, Maryland*

It was raining deep in the night, a slow, warm rain that would soak into the ground and be good for all the summer flowers. There was no moon to speak of to shine in through the window of the dimly lit study. Thomas Matlock was hunched over his computer, aware of the soft sounds of the rain but not really hearing it. He had just gotten an e-mail from a former double agent, now living in Istanbul, telling him he'd picked it up from a Greek smuggler that Vasili Krimakov had died in an auto accident near Agios Nikolaos, a small fishing village on the northeast coast of Crete.

Krimakov had lived all this time in Crete? Since Thomas had found out about his daughter's stalker, after the man had murdered that old bag lady, he'd put everyone on finding Krimakov. Scour the world for him, Thomas had said. He's got to be somewhere. Hell, he's probably right here.

Now after all this time, all these bloody years, he'd finally found him? Only he was dead. It was hard to accept. His implacable enemy, finally dead. Gone, only it was too late, because Allison was dead, too. Far too late.

Was it really an accident?

Thomas knew that Krimakov had to have enemies. He'd had years to make them, just as Thomas had. He'd gotten messages from Krimakov back in the early years, telling him he would never forget, never. Telling him he would find his wife and daughter—yes, he knew all about them and he would find them, no matter how well Thomas had hidden them. And then it would be judgment day.

Thomas had been terrified. And he'd done something unconscionable. He escorted a very pretty young woman, one of the assistants in his office, to an Italian embassy function, then to a Smithsonian exhibit. The third time he was with her, he was simply walking her to her car from the office because the skies had suddenly opened up and rain was pouring down and he had a big umbrella.

A man had jumped out of an alley and shot her between the eyes, not more than six feet away. Thomas hadn't caught him. He knew it was Krimakov even before he'd received that letter written in Vasili's stark, elegant hand: "Your mistress is dead. Enjoy yourself. When I discover your wife and child, they will be next."

That had been seventeen years before.

Thomas had considered seeing Allison that weekend. He had canceled, and she'd known why, of course. He sat back in his chair, pillowing his head on his arms. He read the e-mail from Adam. *Consider Krimakov.*

But Krimakov was finally dead. The irony of it didn't escape him. Krimakov was gone, out of his life, forever. It was all over. He could have finally been with Allison. But it was too late, too late. But now someone was terrorizing Becca. He didn't understand what was going on. He wished he could learn about Dick McCallum, but as of yet, no one had seen anything out of the ordinary. No big deposits, no new accounts, no big expenditures on his credit cards, no strangers reported near him, nothing suspicious or unexpected in his apartment. Simply nothing.

Thomas remembered telling Adam how there were only two other people—besides Adam—who knew the real story. His wife and Buck Savich, both dead now. Buck had died of a heart attack some six years before. But there was Buck's son, and he was very much alive, and Thomas realized now that he needed him, needed him very much.

The man knew all about monsters. He knew how to find them.

*Georgetown*
*Washington, D.C.*

Dillon Savich, head of the Criminal Apprehension Unit of the FBI, booted up his laptop MAX and saw there was an e-mail from someone he didn't know. He shifted his six-month-old son, Sean, to his other shoulder and punched up the message.

Sean burped. "Good one," Savich said, and rubbed his son's back in slow circles. He heard him begin to suck his fingers, felt his small body relax into his shoulder. He read:

> *Your father was an excellent friend and a fine man. I trusted him implicitly. He believed you would change the course of criminal investigations. He was very proud of you. I desperately need your help. Thomas Matlock.*

Sean reared back suddenly and patted his father's whiskered cheek with his wet fingers. Savich stroked his son's small fingers and dried them on his cotton shirt. "We've got a neat mystery here, Sean. Who is Thomas Matlock? How did he know my father? He was an excellent friend? I don't remember ever hearing my father mention his name.

"MAX, let me get you started on this. Find out about this man for me." He punched in a series of keys, then sat back, Sean bouncing from foot to foot on his stomach, watching MAX do his thing.

Savich reached up and flicked the drool off Sean's chin. "You're teething, champ. It's not going to be a pretty sight for the next several months, so that book says. You don't seem like you're feeling any pain. Believe me, that's a relief for both of us."

Sean gurgled very close to Savich's ear.

He held his son back and smiled into that beloved little face that looked more like him than Sherlock. Sean had his dark hair, not Sherlock's curly red hair. As for his eyes, they were as dark as his father's, not that sweet, soft blue of his mother's. "You want to know something? It's four o'clock in the morning and here we are wide awake. Your mama's going to think we're both nuts."

Sean yawned then and stuck three fingers into his mouth. Savich kissed his forehead and stood, gently laying his son over his shoulder. "Let's see if you're ready to pack it in again."

He went to his son's room and dimmed the light. He laid him on his back and pulled a yellow baby blanket over his light diaper shirt.

"You go to sleep now, hear? I'm even going to sing you one of my favorite songs. Your mama always laughs her head off when I sing her this one." He sang a country-and-western song about a man who loved his Chevy truck so much that he was buried with the engine and all four hubcaps, special edition, all silver. Sean looked mesmerized by his father's deep, rich voice. He was out after just two verses. One good thing about country-and-western music—there was always another verse. Savich paused a moment, smiled down at the precious human being that still jolted him when he realized that Sean was, indeed, his very own child, part of him. Just as Savich had been his father's child. He felt a sharp pull somewhere in the region of his heart. He missed his dad, always would.

Who was this Thomas Matlock, who claimed to have known his father?

He went back to his study.

MAX beeped as he walked in. "Good for you," Savich said, sitting back down. "What have we got on this Thomas Matlock guy?"

# TWELVE

Adam said, "You mean they're giving up trying to find her on the Outer Banks?"

Adam knew that Hatch, his right hand, was sitting crouched behind a car somewhere, calling on his cell phone, his dark sunglasses pressed so close to his eyes that his eyelashes got tangled, got into his eyes, and sometimes caused eye infections. "Yeah, boss. Since they have no leads at all, they're counting on Becca knowing something, maybe even knowing this guy who shot the governor. That's why they're searching high and low for her. Agent Ezra John is the SAC running the show down there. I hear he's cursing up a blue streak, wondering where she could have hidden herself. Says they looked everywhere for her and she ain't anywhere, like smoke, he says, and the others grin behind their hands. Oh yeah, you'll love this, boss. Old Ezra believes Ms. Matlock is a lot smarter than anyone gave her credit for, keeping out of sight like she is. If he knew it was you who duped him, he'd want to put your head on a pike and find some bridge to stick it on."

"Thanks for sharing that, Hatch."

"Knew you'd like it. You and old Ezra go back a long ways, don't you?"

That wasn't the half of it, Adam thought, and said only, "Something like that. Okay now. In other words, Ezra's finally come to the conclusion that she conned him? That she isn't anywhere near the Outer Banks?"

"That's it."

"I don't think I need to fiddle them anymore. Too much time has passed for them to find her now. I think we're home free—well, at least for the moment."

Silence.

"Hatch, I know you're lighting a cigarette. Put it out right now or I'll fire you."

Silence.

"Is it out?"

"Yeah, boss. I swear it's out. I didn't even get one decent puff."

"Swell news for your lungs. Now, what about the NYPD?"

"They're talking to their counterparts all over the country, just like the Feebs are. But hey—nothing, nada, zippo. This Detective Morales is a wreck, probably hasn't slept for three days. All he can talk about is how she called him, repeated to him that she'd told him everything, and he wasn't able to talk her in. There's this other detective, a woman name of Letitia Gordon, who evidently hates Ms. Matlock's guts. Claims she's a liar, a nutcase, and probably a murderer. Old Letitia really wants to bring her down. She's pushing everyone to charge Ms. Matlock with the murder of that old bag lady outside the Metropolitan Museum. You know, the murder Ms. Matlock reported? The one the stalker did to get her attention?"

"Yeah, I know."

"Well, they told Detective Gordon to pull her head out of her armpit and try for a bit of objectivity. The woman's really got it in for our gal."

Adam made a rude noise. "Let Detective Gordon get hives over it for all we care. Neither Thomas nor I ever believed they were going to charge her with murder. But a material witness? That's possible. And you know as well as I do that the cops couldn't protect her from this stalker. Nope, that's our job. Now, what do you have on McCallum?"

Adam wasn't expecting anything, so he wasn't disappointed when Hatch sighed and said, "Not a thing as of yet. A real pro spearheaded this operation, boss, like you thought."

"Unfortunately, it can't be Krimakov because Thomas finally got him tracked down. He was living on Crete, and as of a week ago, he's dead. I'm not sure of the exact date. But it was before McCallum was run down in Albany. I guess Krimakov could have been involved, but he certainly wasn't running the show, and that's not his MO. Anything Krimakov was involved in, he was the Big Leader. Thomas is willing to bet his ascot on that. But if Krimakov was somehow involved, it means he knew about Becca being Matlock's daughter. It's making me crazy."

"Nah, the guy's dead. This is a new nutcase, fresh out of the woodwork, and he's picked Becca."

Adam scratched his head and added, "No, I don't think so, Hatch. It's got to be some sort of conspiracy, there's no other answer. Lots of folk involved. But why did they focus on Ms. Matlock? Why put her in the middle? I keep coming back to Krimakov, but I know, logically, that it can't be. Someone, something else, is driving this. How's the governor?"

"I hear his neck is a bit sore, but he'll live. He doesn't know a thing, that's what he claims. He's very upset about McCallum."

Adam sat there and thought and thought. The same questions over and over again. No answers.

Silence.

"Put out the cigarette, Hatch. I know about your girlfriend. She loves silk lingerie and expensive steaks. You can't afford to lose your job."

"Okay, boss."

Adam heard some papers shuffling, heard some mild curses, and smiled. "Anything else?"

"Yeah. Of course there's no positive ID on that skeleton that popped out of Ms. Matlock's basement wall. For sure it was a teenage girl who got her head bashed in some ten or more years ago. I did find out something sort of neat, though."

"Yeah?"

"It turns out there was an eighteen-year-old girl who leaves Riptide, supposedly eloping. Nobody knows who the boyfriend was though. Now ain't that a neat coincidence?"

"I'll say. When?"

"Twelve years ago."

"No one's heard from her since?"

"I'm not completely sure about that. If she's still unaccounted for and they decide she's a good bet, then they'll do DNA tests on the bones."

Adam said, "They'll need something from her—like hair on a brush, an old envelope that would have her saliva, barring that, then a family member would have to give up some blood."

"Thing is, though, it wouldn't be admissible in court if it ever came to it. It'll take some time, a couple of weeks. No one sees any big rush on it."

"I don't like the feel of this, Hatch. We've got this other mess and now this skeleton falling out of Becca's basement wall. It's enough to make a man give up football."

"Nah, you've always told me that God created the fall for football.

You'll be watching football when you throw that last pigskin into the end zone in the sky, if they still have the sport that many aeons from now. You'll probably lobby God to have pro football in Heaven. Stop whining, boss. You'll figure everything out. You usually do. Hey, I hear that Maine's one beautiful place. That true?"

Adam stared at his cell for a moment. He had been whining. He said, "Yeah. I just wish I had some time to enjoy it." He suddenly yelled into the receiver, "No smoking, Hatch. If you even think about it, I'll know it. Now, call me tomorrow at this same time."

"You got it, boss."

"No smoking."

Silence.

BECCA said very quietly, "Who is Krimakov?"

Adam turned around very slowly to face her. She was standing in the doorway of the moldy-smelling guest room where he'd spent his first night in Jacob Marley's house. She'd opened the door and he hadn't heard a thing. He was losing it.

"Who is Krimakov?"

He said easily, "He's a drug dealer who used to be involved with the Medellin cartel in Colombia. He's dead now."

"What does this Krimakov have to do with all this craziness?"

"I don't know. Why did you open the door without knocking, Becca?"

"I heard you on the phone. I wanted to know what was going on. I knew you wouldn't tell me. I also came up to get you for breakfast. It's ready downstairs. You're still lying. This doesn't have anything to do with drug dealing."

He had the gall to shrug.

"If I had my kitchen knife, I'd run at you, right this minute."

"And what? Slice me up? Come on, Becca, why can't you accept that I'm here to do a job and that job is to make sure that you don't get wiped out? Get off your high horse."

He stood up then and she backed up a step. She was afraid of him still. After seeing him all civilized that entire evening with four-year-old Sam, it surprised him. "I told you I wouldn't hurt you," he said patiently. He realized at that moment that he didn't have a shirt on. She was afraid he might attack her? Well, after his teenage attempt last night to prove to her he wasn't gay, he supposed he couldn't blame her. He moved slowly, deliberately, and picked up his shirt from where it was hanging over a chair back, then turned his back to put it on. He faced her again as he buttoned it up.

"Who are you?"

He sighed, tucked in his shirt. Then he flipped the sheet and blanket over the bed. He straightened the single too-soft pillow that smelled, unexpectedly, of violets.

When he finally turned to face her again, she was gone. She'd heard Krimakov's name. It didn't matter. She'd never hear it again. The bastard was dead. Finally dead, and Thomas Matlock was free. To come and finally meet his daughter. Why hadn't Thomas said anything about that? He combed his hair, brushed his teeth, and headed downstairs.

She fed him pancakes with blueberry syrup and crispy bacon, just the way he liked it. The coffee was strong, black as Hatch's fantasies, the fresh cantaloupe she'd sliced, ripe and sweet.

Neither of them said a word. She ate a slice of dry toast and had a cup of tea. It looked like she was having trouble getting that much down.

He said, a dark eyebrow arched, his mouth full of bacon, "What is this? No questions right in my face? No bitching at me? I don't believe it—you're sulking."

That got her, just as he hoped it would.

"How would you like that nice sticky syrup down the back of your neck?"

He grinned at her and saluted with his coffee cup. "I wouldn't like that at all. At least you're speaking to me again. Look, Becca, I'm trying to find out what's going on. Everyone is floating a lot of ideas, a lot of names. Now we have this skeleton."

He was so slippery, she'd bet if he were a pig in a greased pig contest, no one could hold him down, but she was tenacious.

"Who were you telling not to smoke?"

"Hatch. He's my main assistant. He has more contacts than a centipede has legs, speaks six languages, and is real smart except when it comes to cigarettes and loose women. That's the way I can control his smoking. I pay him very well and threaten to fire him if he lights up."

"But I heard you tell him to put out the cigarette. Obviously he's still smoking. And he knew you were on the other end of the line."

"It's more a game now than anything else. He lights up to hear me blow."

"Did he find out anything about the skeleton? What's this about DNA testing? They think they know who that poor girl was?"

He stretched, drank down the last of his coffee, carefully set the cup on the table, then stood up.

She was on her feet in the next instant. Two fast steps and she was in his face. She was fast, he'd give her that, and she was mad. He was grinning down at her when she slammed her fist in his belly. Becca felt her face turning red. "You will not treat me like a cipher, like I'm a moron who isn't even important enough to talk to. Who are you?"

He grabbed her wrist. "That was a good shot. No, don't hit me again or I'll have to do something. I want to keep those pancakes happy."

"Yeah, what?" She didn't care anymore. She smashed her other fist into his left kidney.

He held both her wrists now. He knew she'd bring up her knee next so he jerked her around so her back was pressed against his chest. He held her arms pressed to her sides. "You'd look better as a blonde. Usually a woman's roots are darker than her hair. In your case, you've got all this baby-light hair at the roots."

She kicked back, grazing his shin. He grunted. He sat back down on the chair, holding her on his lap. She was pinned against him and couldn't move. "Now," he said, "I'm sorry we're playing only by my rules, but that's the way it's got to be unless I'm told otherwise."

"You need to shave. You look like a convict."

"How do you know? You've got the back of your head to me."

"You've got as much hair on your face as you do on your chest."

"Oh yeah? Well, you did get an eyeful in the bedroom."

"Bite me."

Adam's cell phone rang. "Will you let me answer this without attacking me again?"

"Actually, I don't want to be anywhere near you."

"Good." He dropped his arms and she jumped off his lap.

He flipped open the small narrow phone. "Carruthers here."

"Adam, it's Thomas Matlock. Is Becca there with you?"

"As a matter of fact, yes."

"All right, then, just listen. I sent an e-mail to Dillon Savich, a computer expert here at FBI headquarters in Washington. I knew his father very well. Actually, Buck Savich was the only other person who knew about all the mess with Krimakov. He's been dead for a while. I e-mailed his son for help. His job is finding maniacs using computer programs. He's good. He managed to track me down before I could even get back to him. That's beyond good. He's agreed to a meeting. I'm going to see him. We need all the help we can get."

"I think that's a mistake," Adam said, thinking of the logistics. "I don't think we need anyone else in on this. I'm worried about maintaining control here."

"Trust me on this, Adam. We do need him. He's got lots of contacts and is very, very smart. Don't worry that he'll talk and expose Becca's whereabouts if he comes on board. He won't. Have you learned anything more of value?"

"There's nothing at all to be found in any of McCallum's records. The governor says he doesn't know a thing. I assume you've come up dry as well?"

"Yes, but I think that Dillon Savich will be able to help us there as well. Word is he's magic with a computer and gathering information."

Adam said, "We don't need anyone else, Thomas." The instant the name was out of his mouth, Adam jerked his head up. Becca was looking at him, her eyes narrowed, intent. He cleared his throat. "We don't want more hands stirring this pot. It's too dangerous. Too much chance of cracks and leaks. It could lead to Becca."

"You slipped, Adam. Is she listening?"

"No, it's okay." At least he hoped it was. She was now simply looking wary and interested, both at the same time.

Adam said again, "Maybe you could have this guy do some specific searches for you."

"That, too, but he's a specialist like you are. All right. We'll see. I'm meeting with him to see what he has to say. Maybe he won't want to join up with us, or maybe he won't have the time. I just wanted you to know. Keep her safe, Adam."

"Yeah."

Becca shook her head at him when he closed his cell phone. She knew there'd be downright lies or at the very least evasions out of his mouth. She was furious, frustrated, but, surprisingly, she felt safer than she had in weeks. When he looked like he would say something, she smiled at him and said, "No, don't bother."

*The Egret Bar & Grill*
*Washington, D.C.*

Thomas Matlock rose very slowly from his chair. He didn't know what to say but he didn't like what he saw. Savich wasn't alone.

Savich smiled at the man he'd never heard of before receiving the e-mail at four A.M. that morning. He extended his hand. "Mr. Matlock?"

"Yes. Thomas Matlock."

"This is my wife and my partner, Lacey Sherlock Savich, but everyone calls her Sherlock. She's also FBI and one of the best."

Thomas found himself shaking the hand of a very pretty young woman, tall, slim with thick, curling red hair, the sweetest smile he'd ever seen, and he knew in his gut, knew without even hearing her speak or act or argue, she was tough, probably as tough as her hard-faced husband, a man about Adam's age, who looked stronger than a bull. Meaner, too. He didn't look like a computer nerd. Whatever that was supposed to mean nowadays.

"So," Thomas said, "you're Buck's son."

"Yes," Savich said and grinned. "I know what you're thinking. My dad was all blond and fair, a regular aristocrat with a thin straight nose and high cheekbones. I look like my mom. You can bet my dad wasn't happy about that. I never had my dad's smart mouth, either."

"Your dad could charm the widow's peak off a fascist general and outwit a Mafia don. He was an excellent man and friend," Thomas said, eyeing the man. "I wasn't expecting you to bring anyone else." He found himself clearing his throat when Savich didn't immediately respond. "This is all rather confidential, Mr. Savich. Actually, it's all extremely confidential, there's a life at stake and—"

Savich said easily, "Where I go Sherlock goes, sir. We're a package deal. Shall we continue or would you like to call this off?"

The young woman didn't say a word. She didn't even change expressions. She just cocked her head to one side and waited, very quietly, silent. A professional to her toes, Thomas thought, like her husband.

Thomas said then, "Is your name really Sherlock?"

She laughed. "Yes. My father's a federal judge in San Francisco. Can you imagine what the crooks are feeling when they're hauled in front of him—Judge Sherlock?"

"Please sit down, both of you. I'm grateful that you came, Mr. Savich."

"Savich will do fine."

"All right. I understand you head up the CAU—the Criminal Apprehension Unit—at the FBI. I know you use computers and protocols you yourself designed and programmed. And with some success. Naturally, I really don't fully understand what it is that happens."

Savich ordered iced tea from the hovering waiter, waited for the others to order as well, then leaned forward. "Like the Behavioral Sciences Unit, we also deal with local agencies who think an outside eye might see something they missed on a local crime. Normally murder cases. Also like the BSU, we only go in when we're asked.

"Unlike the Behavioral Sciences, we're entirely computer-based. We use special programs to help us look at crimes from many different angles. The programs correlate all the data from two or more crimes that seem to have been committed by the same person. We call the main program PAP, the Predictive Analogue Program. Of course, what an agent feeds into the program will determine what comes out. Nothing new in that at all."

Sherlock said, "All of it is Dillon's brainchild. He worked on all the protocols. It's amazing how the computer can turn up patterns, weird correlations, ways of looking at things that we wouldn't have considered. Of course, like Dillon said, we have to put the data in there in order to get the patterns, the correlations, the anomalies that can point a finger in the right direction.

"Then we look at the possible outcomes and alternatives the computer gives us, act on many of them. You said Buck Savich was an excellent friend. How did you know my father, sir?"

"Thank you for the explanation. It's fascinating, and about time, I say. Technology should catch crooks, not let the crooks diddle society with the technology. Yes, Buck Savich was an incredible man. I knew him professionally. Tough, smart, fearless. The practical jokes he used to pull had the higher-ups in the Bureau screaming and laughing at the same time. I was very sorry to hear about his death."

Savich nodded, waiting.

Thomas Matlock sipped his iced tea. He needed to know more about these two. He said easily, "I remember the String Killer case. That was an amazing bit of work."

"It wasn't at all typical," Savich said. "We got the guy. He's dead. It's over." Then he looked at his wife, and Thomas saw something that suddenly made him aware of the extraordinary bond between them.

There was a flash of incredible fear in Savich's eyes, followed by a wash of relief and so much gratitude that it went all the way to Thomas's gut. He should have had that bond with Allison, but one stray bullet in a woman's head had put an end to that possibility forever.

Thomas cleared his throat, his mind made up. These two were bright, young, dedicated. He needed them. "Thank you for explaining more about your unit. I guess there's nothing more to do except tell you exactly what's going on. My only favor—and I must have your agreement on this—is if you don't choose to help me, you will not inform your colleagues about any of this conversation. It all remains right here, in this booth."

"Is it illegal?"

"No, Savich. I've always believed that being a crook requires too much work and energy. I'd rather race my sailboat on the Chesapeake than worry about evading the cops. The FBI is, however, involved, and that does make for some conflict of interest."

Savich said slowly, "You're a very powerful man, Mr. Matlock. It took MAX nearly fourteen minutes to even find out that you're a very well-protected high-ranking member of the intelligence community. It took him another hour and two phone calls from me to discover that you are one of the Shadow Men. I don't trust you."

Sherlock cocked her head to the side and said, "What are the Shadow Men?"

Thomas said, "It's a name coined back in the early seventies by the CIA for those of us who have high security clearance, work very quietly, very discreetly, always out of sight, always in the background, and frankly, do things that aren't sanctioned or publicized or even recognized. Results are seen, but not any of us."

"You mean like the 'Mission Impossible' team?"

"Nothing so perfectly orchestrated as all that. No, I've never burned a tape in my life." He smiled then and it was an attractive smile, Sherlock thought. He was a handsome man, well built, took care of himself. Younger than her father, maybe six, eight years. Ah, but his eyes. They were filled with bleak, dark shadows, with secrets huddled deep, and there was pain there as well, pain there for so very long that it was now a part of him, burrowed deep. He was a complex man, but most important, he was alone, so very alone—now she saw that clearly—and he was afraid of something that went as deep as his soul. She didn't think that being a Shadow Man was the reason for all that bleakness in his eyes.

She said, "It sounds like cloak-and-dagger stuff, sir, like it should have gone out of business when the Cold War ended."

Thomas looked off over Sherlock's left shoulder, seeing into the past, into the future, a future she prayed didn't bear the terrorist threat they carried today. Then he said quietly, "There are always failures, mistakes, lives lost needlessly. But we try, Mrs. Savich. The world has changed, the rules have changed. For the most part we're not allowed to be nice people, so your husband is smart not to trust me. However, this is something entirely different. This isn't business. This is entirely personal. I need help badly."

She lowered her head and began weaving a packet of Equal through her fingers. Finally, she looked straight at him, picked up her iced tea glass, raised it toward him, and said, "Why don't you call me Sherlock."

Thomas clicked his glass to hers. Somehow, he knew, she and her husband had communicated, had agreed to hear him out. "Sherlock. It is a charming name. It goes very well with Savich."

Savich sat forward then. "Let's cut to the chase, Mr. Matlock. We give you our word that nothing you tell us today will go beyond this booth. We will accept the possibility of a conflict of interest, at least for the moment."

Thomas felt the same sort of loosening in his gut that he'd felt when Adam had told him he'd already begun to protect Becca. He smiled at the two of them and said, "Why don't you call me Thomas."

# THIRTEEN

*Riptide, Maine*

Sheriff Gaffney said, "Well now, what we got was an anonymous tip, Mr. Carruthers."

"That's rather odd, don't you think, Sheriff?" Adam had his arms folded over his chest and was leaning against Jacob Marley's screened front porch. Sheriff Gaffney looked tired, he thought, a bit pasty in the face. He wanted to tell the sheriff to lose fifty pounds and start walking the treadmill.

"No, sir, not odd at all. Folk don't like to get involved. They'd rather tattle in secret than come smartly forward and tell you what they know. Sometimes, truth be told, folk are disappointing, Mr. Carruthers."

That was true enough, Adam thought. "You said the girl's name is Melissa Katzen?"

"That's right. It was a woman with a real whispery voice who said it was Melissa. She didn't want to tell who she was. She said everyone believed at the time that Melissa was going to elope right after high school graduation. So when she up and was gone, everyone figured she'd done it. But she thinks now, what with the skeleton, that Melissa didn't go anywhere."

"Who was the boyfriend?" Adam asked.

"No one knew, since Melissa wouldn't tell anyone. Her folks didn't know what to think after she was gone. They didn't know about any elopement talk, came as a shock to them when all their daughters' friends told them it was true. I'm thinking that maybe one of Melissa's family called in this tip, or a friend and that friend is afraid she's in danger if she tells us who she is. Now, if that skeleton is Melissa Katzen, then she didn't elope. She stayed right here and got herself murdered."

"Maybe," Becca said, "she decided she didn't want to elope after all and the boy killed her."

"Could be," said Sheriff Gaffney, shaking his head. "A bad way to end up."

He got no argument.

The sheriff adjusted his thick leather belt that was digging into his belly and said on a sigh, "As the years passed, most folk forgot about her, figured she was in another state with six kids now. And maybe she is. We'll find out. We're talking to all the people who remember her, went to school with her, things like that."

"You don't have any idea who called this in, Sheriff?"

"Nope. Mrs. Ella took the call, said it sounded like someone with a doughnut in her mouth. Mrs. Ella believes it's a relative, or a chicken-heart friend."

"You'll do DNA tests now?"

"As soon as we can locate Melissa's parents and see if they have anything of hers we could use to get her DNA to match against what they have in the bones. It's going to take a while. Science—all this newfangled stuff—it's all iffy as far as I'm concerned. Look at how poor O.J. was nearly sent away because of all that flaky so-called DNA evidence. But the jury was smart. They didn't believe any of that stuff for a minute. Well, it's something to do. We'll know in a couple of weeks."

"Sheriff," Becca said mildly, "DNA is the most scientifically solid tool that law enforcement has going for it today. It's not flaky at all. It will clear innocent people and, hopefully, in most cases, put monsters in jail."

"So you think, Ms. Powell, but you force me to tell you that yours is an Uninformed Opinion. Mrs. Ella doesn't like all this fancy stuff, either. But she thinks it's real possible that the skeleton is poor little Melissa, even though she remembers Melissa as being all sorts of shy and sweet and so quiet you'd have thought her a little ghost. Who'd want to kill a sweet kid like that? Even old Jacob Marley, who didn't like anybody."

Adam shook his head. "I don't know, Sheriff. I go for the boyfriend. Hey, at least there's something to go on now. Won't you come in?"

"Nah. I just wanted to fill in you and Ms. Powell. I gotta go talk to the power company, hear they accidentally cut a sewage pipe. That'd be no good. You pray the wind doesn't blow in this direction. Now, Mr. Carruthers, you going to hang around with Ms. Powell much longer?"

"Oh yeah," Adam said easily, looking over at Becca, who hadn't said a single word since Sheriff Gaffney, button sewn back on, bemoaned poor O.J.'s treatment. "She's still real jittery, Sheriff, jumps whenever there's a sound in this old house. You know how women are—so sensitive it makes a man want to coddle them until the sun's shining again."

"That was well said, Mr. Carruthers. We got us one of our perfect summer days. Smell the air. All salty ocean and wildflowers, and that sun smell. Nothing like it.

"Ah, here's Tyler and little Sam. Good morning. Just running down possibilities on Ms. Powell's skeleton. Could have been Melissa Katzen. Don't suppose you disguised your voice like a woman's and called in the tip?"

"Not me, Sheriff," Tyler said, raising an eyebrow. "Who did you say? Melissa Katzen?"

"Yep, that's right. You remember her, Tyler? Didn't you go to school with her? Your ages are about right."

Tyler slowly lowered Sam to the porch and watched him wander over to a low table that held a stack of books, some of them very old indeed.

"Melissa Katzen." Tyler frowned. "Yes, I remember her. A real sweet kid. I think she might have been in my high school class, or maybe a year behind me. I'm not sure. She wasn't really pretty, but she was nice, never said a bad thing about anybody, as I remember. You really think she could be the skeleton?"

"Don't know. Got an anonymous call about her."

Tyler frowned a bit. "I think I remember hearing that she was going to elope, yeah, that was it. She eloped and no one ever heard from her again."

Sheriff Gaffney said, "Yep, that's the story. Now DNA will tell us, at least if what those labs claim is true. Well, it's time for me to see the power company. Then I'll call that Jarvis guy in Augusta, see what they're doing."

Sam was holding a small, thick paperback in his hands.

Adam dropped down to his knees and looked at the little book with a fancy attack helicopter on the cover. He said, "It's *Jane's Aircraft Recognition Guide.* I wonder what Jacob Marley was doing with one of Jane's publications?"

"Jane?" Sam said.

"Yeah, I know, that's a girl's name. Hey, they're Brits, Sam. You've got to expect them to do weird things."

Becca said, "Hey, Sam, you want a glass of lemonade? I made some this morning."

Sam looked up at her, didn't say anything, but finally nodded.

Tyler said, his chin up, a hint of the aggressor in his voice, "Sam loves Becca's lemonade."

"I do, too," Adam said. "Now, I'm out of here. I'll be back tonight, Becca."

She wanted to ask him where he was going, who he was going to talk to, but she couldn't say a blasted thing in front of Tyler. "Take care," she called out after him. She saw Adam pause just a moment, but he didn't turn back.

"I don't like him, Becca," Tyler said in a low voice a few minutes later in the kitchen, one eye on Sam, who was drinking his lemonade and looking for the goody in the box of Cracker Jack Becca had handed him.

"He's harmless," she said easily. "Really harmless. I'm sure he's gay. So you knew this Melissa Katzen?"

Tyler nodded and took another drink of his lemonade. "Like I told the sheriff, she was a nice kid. Not real popular, not real smart, but nice. She also played soccer. I remember once she beat me in poker." Tyler grinned at some memory. "Yeah, it was strip poker. I think I was the first guy she'd ever seen in boxer shorts."

"Rachel makes good lemonade," Sam said, and both adults looked at him with admiration. He'd said four whole words, strung them all together.

Becca patted his face. "I'll bet Rachel does lots of really good things. She rented me this house, you know."

Sam nodded and drank more lemonade.

After they'd left ten minutes later to go grocery shopping, Becca cleaned up the kitchen and headed upstairs. She made her bed and straightened the bedroom. She didn't want to have anything to do with Adam Carruthers, but she sighed and walked down to his bedroom. The bed was neatly made. Nothing was out in plain sight. She walked over to the dresser and pulled out the top drawer. Underwear, T-shirts, and a couple of folded cotton shirts. Nothing else. She pulled his dark blue carryall out from under the bed. She lifted it on top of the bed and slowly started to pull back the long zipper.

The phone rang. She nearly leapt three feet in the air. The phone rang again.

She had to run downstairs, as that was the only phone in the house. She'd started using her cell phone again but it had run out of power and was recharging. She picked it up on the sixth ring. "Hello."

Breathing. Slow, deep breathing.

"Hello? Who's there?"

"Hello, Rebecca. It's your boyfriend."

Her brain nearly shut down. She stared at the phone, not believing, not wanting to believe, but it was him, the stalker, the man who murdered that poor old woman, the man who shot the governor in the neck.

He'd found her. Somehow he'd found her. She said, "The governor's alive. You're not so great after all, are you? You didn't kill him. You were so ill informed, you didn't even know there would be a bunch of doctors around him."

"Maybe I didn't want to kill him."

"Yeah, right."

"All right, so the bastard is still breathing. At least he won't be climbing into your bed anytime soon. Hear he's having a tough time talking and eating. He needed to lose a few pounds anyway."

"You killed Dick McCallum. You made him tell those lies about me and then you killed him. How much did you pay him? Or did you threaten to kill him if he didn't do as you asked?"

"Where did you get all this information, Becca?"

"It's true."

Silence.

"Nobody could have found me. The FBI, the NYPD, nobody. How did you find me?"

He laughed, a rich, mellow laugh that made her want to vomit. How old was he? She couldn't tell. Think, she told herself, listen and think. Keep him talking. Use your brain. Is he young or old? Accent? Listen for clues. Make him admit to murdering Dick.

"I'll tell you when I see you, Becca."

She said very deliberately, very slowly, "I don't want to see you. I want you to go someplace and die. That or turn yourself in to the cops. They'll fry you. That's what you deserve. Why did you run down Dick McCallum?"

"And just what do you think you deserve?"

"Not this bullshit from you. Are you going to try to kill the governor again?"

"I haven't made up my mind yet. I know now that he isn't sleeping with you, but only because he doesn't know where you are. An old man like that. You should be ashamed of yourself, Rebecca. Remember Rockefeller croaking when he was with his mistress? That could be you and the governor. Best not do him again. But you're a little slut, aren't you? Yeah, you'll probably call him so he can come sleep with you some more."

Why hadn't she had the phone tapped? Because neither she nor Adam dreamed he'd find her here in Riptide and call her.

"You murdered Dick McCallum, didn't you? Why?"

"You're all confident again, aren't you? You've been away from me for only a couple of weeks, but you're all pissy again. Too confident, Rebecca. I'm coming for you very soon now."

"Listen, you come anywhere near me and I'll blow your head off."

He laughed, throaty, deep laughter, indulgent laughter. Was he young? Maybe, but she couldn't be sure. "You can try, certainly. It'll add some spice to the chase. I'll see to you soon. Real soon, count on it."

He hung up before she could say anything more. She stood there, staring blankly at the old-fashioned black phone, staring and knowing, knowing deep inside her that it was all over. Or it soon would be. How could anyone protect her from a madman? She'd done the best she could and yet he'd found her, nearly as easily as Adam had.

How had he found her? Did he have as many contacts as Adam? Evidently so. No, she wasn't going to give up and let him come to kill her. No, she would fight.

She laid the phone into the cradle and walked slowly from the living room. She was tired, infinitely tired. She couldn't stand there in the middle of Jacob Marley's house, she couldn't. She felt itchy from the inside out, and cold, very cold. Nearly numb.

She loaded her Coonan .357 Magnum automatic, slipped it in the pocket of her jacket, and walked to the woods where she'd confronted Adam two days before. Had it really been only two days? She sat down in front of the tree where he'd been doing his tae kwon do exercise. She looked at the spot where she'd stood, pointing her gun at him, so afraid she'd thought she'd choke on it. But she hadn't had time to shoot or to choke. He'd kicked the gun out of her hand before she could draw two breaths. She closed her eyes and leaned back against the tree. Would the stalker have as easy a time with her as Adam? Probably so.

She closed her eyes and let her mind shut down. She saw her mother, laughing down at her—she couldn't have been more than seven years old and she was trying to do a cheerleading chant. Then her mom had showed her how to do it and it had been so wonderful, so perfect. Her mother's laughter, so sweet, filling her, making her warm and happy. She rubbed her wrist where Adam had kicked the gun out of her hand. It didn't hurt, but there was memory of the cold numbness that had lasted for a good five minutes. Where was he? Why had he left?

Adam was back at Jacob Marley's house and he was so scared for a moment he couldn't think. She was gone. The door was open but she was gone. There were even two lights on but she was gone. The stalker had gotten her. No, no, that was ridiculous. He was the only one who had found her.

He searched every room in the house. He saw his carryall lying on top of his bed. It looked like she'd started unzipping it and then, for whatever reason, had walked out of the room, leaving it there for him to see.

Why? Where had she gone? Her car was in the driveway, so she couldn't have gone far . . . unless someone took her.

*Don't panic.* She'd gotten a call, something of an emergency. She'd gone to Tyler's house. It had to do with Sam. The kid was sick, yeah, that was it.

But she wasn't there, no one was home. He drove by the Food Fort, the gas station, the hospital but he didn't see her, he could drive all over this town and not find her.

He drove slowly back to the house. He cut the engine and sat in his black Jeep, his forehead against the leather-wrapped steering wheel.

*Where are you, Becca?*

He didn't know why he raised his head and twisted around to look toward the woods. And in that instant he knew she was there. But why? It took him three minutes to find her.

She was asleep. He came up on her very quietly. She didn't stir. She was leaning against the tree trunk, her right hand in her lap. She was holding the Coonan, its polished silver stock gleaming from the slashes of sun through the tree branches.

Had he seen that flash of silver? He didn't know how he could have, yet he'd known she was there. Why couldn't he have had this marvelous intuition before he'd scared himself spitless?

He came down on his haunches. He looked at her, wondering what had made her come out here. He saw dried tear streaks down her cheeks. Everything had gotten to be too much for her, and no wonder. She looked pale, too thin. He looked at her fingers curled around the trigger of the Coonan, at her nails, short and ragged. He touched his fingertips to her cheek. Her flesh was soft to the touch. He lightly stroked her cheek. Then, slowly, he shook her shoulder.

"Becca. Come on, wake up."

She came awake instantly at the sound of a man's voice, the Coonan up and ready to fire. She heard him curse, then felt the gun fly out of her hand. Her wrist was instantly numb. "Not again."

"You nearly shot me."

It was Adam. She looked up at him and smiled. "I thought it was him. Sorry."

His heart began to slow. He eased down beside her. "What's up?"

"What time is it?"

"Nearly four o'clock in the afternoon. I couldn't find you and I nearly lost my mind trying to figure out where you were. You scared me, Becca. I thought he'd taken you."

"No, I'm here. I'm sorry. I didn't think. So how'd you find me?"

He shrugged. He didn't want to tell her that he knew very suddenly exactly where she was. He would sound nuts. She didn't need anyone else around her sounding nuts.

"How long will my wrist be numb this time?"

"Not more than five minutes. Don't whine. Did you expect me to let you shoot me?"

"No, I guess not."

"You look tired. Better if you'd taken a nap in your bed than come out here to snore beneath the tree. It might not be all that safe." That was one of the best understatements out of his mouth yet.

"Why? The only one who was ever lurking outside here was you, and you're not lurking out here anymore. You've moved right into the house." She sighed. "I don't know why I came out here. I couldn't stand to stay in the house alone anymore."

He said again, "You scared me, Becca. Please don't take off again without leaving me a note."

She looked up at him, her face so pale now it was nearly as white as winter sleet, and said in a dead voice, "He's found me. He called."

"He?" But he knew. Oh yeah, the stalker had found her and he hated it, had dreaded it, but he'd known it would happen. This guy was good. Too good. He had contacts. Whoever he was, he knew people, knew how to use them to get what he wanted. Adam was sure he'd been on her the minute she'd left New York. Still, it surprised him. More than that it scared him to his soul. He hated that surge of fear, deep and corroding. He could almost smell the flames. The fire was coming closer.

"All right, so he called. Get a grip." He stopped, grinned at her. "Oh yeah, I'm talking to myself, not you. Now, what did he say? Did he tell you how he found you? Did he say anything that would help us pinpoint him?"

He'd said "us." She had felt utterly frozen inside, then he'd said "us." Slowly, she began to feel a shift deep inside her. She wasn't alone anymore.

She looked up at him and smiled. "I'm glad you're here, Adam."

"Yeah," he said. "Me, too."

"Even though you're gay?"

He looked at her mouth, then jumped fast to his feet. A man did better when temptation wasn't one inch from his face. He looked down at her, then offered his hand. "Yeah, right. Now come on back to the house. I want you to write down everything you can remember him saying. Okay?"

She got a look on her face that was hard and cold and determined. Good, he thought, she wasn't going to lie down and let this guy kick her like a dog.

"Let's do it, Adam."

They walked side by side up the steps to the veranda. They were nearly to the front door, and he was thinking that he needed to show her again that he wasn't gay, when a shot rang out, and a knife-sharp chunk of wood flew off the door frame not two inches from Becca's head and slammed into Adam's bare arm.

# FOURTEEN

Adam twisted the doorknob, pushed the door in, and shoved Becca into the entrance hall in an instant, and still it seemed too slow. Another bullet struck the lintel right over his head, spewing splinters in all directions. None struck him this time. He slammed the front door, then grabbed Becca's arm and dragged her out of the line of fire.

He came down on his knees beside her. "Sorry to throw you around. Are you okay?"

"Yeah, I'm okay. He's a monster, crazy. It's got to stop, Adam. It's got to." He watched her jerk her Coonan out of her jacket pocket and crawl to one of the front windows. He was right behind her. "Becca, no, wait a minute. I want you to stay down. This is my job."

"He's after me, not you," she said calmly and, slowly, very cautiously, leaned up to look out of the corner of the window. He thought he'd collapse of fright right then.

Another two shots came at heart level through the front door, spewing shards of wood into the entrance hall. Another shot. Becca saw the flash of light. She didn't hesitate, fired off all seven rounds. He heard the *click click click* when there were no more bullets in the magazine.

There was dead silence. Adam was on his knees right behind her, furious with himself because his Delta Elite was in his carryall in the guest bedroom. "Becca? I want you to stay right here. Don't move. I've got to get my gun. Stay down."

She gave him a quick look. "Go ahead and don't worry. We're not helpless. I hit him, I know it, Adam."

"Stay down."

"It's okay." He watched her pull another magazine out of her jacket pocket. He stared at her as she slowly, calmly shoved it into the Coonan.

"Go get your gun," she said, looking out the window, her back to him. "If I didn't hit him, I can at least keep him away from the house."

He couldn't think of anything else to say. He was up the stairs and to the bedroom in three seconds flat. When he came back downstairs, his pistol in his hand, Becca hadn't moved. "I haven't seen a thing," she called out. "Do you think maybe I was lucky enough to hit him?"

"I plan to find out. Keep a sharp lookout. And don't shoot me."

And then he was gone before she could draw a breath. She heard him walk quickly through the kitchen, then the back door opened and closed very quietly. She prayed she'd hit him. Maybe right in his throat, where he'd hit the governor. Or in the gut. He deserved that for killing that poor old bag lady. She waited, waited, not moving, watching for Adam, for his shadow, anything to show her he was all right.

Time passed so slowly she thought it would become night before anything more happened. Suddenly, she heard a shout.

"Come on out, Becca!"

Adam. It was Adam and he sounded all right. She was through the front door like a shot, her hair tangling in her face, realizing only then that she was sweating and cold at the same time, and laughing. Yes, she was laughing because they were safe. They'd beaten the monster. This time.

Adam was standing at the edge of the woods, waving toward her. It was in the exact same direction where she'd fired off all seven rounds. He waited until she was right in front of him. He smiled down at her, then wrapped his arms around her and squeezed her hard. "You got him, Becca. Come take a look."

Blood on fallen leaves. Like Christmas decorations—rich dark red on deep green.

"I got him," she whispered. "I really got him."

"You sure did. I've looked but I can't find a trail because once he realized he was out of the game, he stanched the wound and carefully brushed ground cover over his tracks so he wouldn't leave any kind of a trail."

"I got him," she said again, and she was smiling. "Oh Adam, no!"

"What is it?"

"Your arm." She dropped her Coonan back into her jacket pocket and grabbed his hand. "Don't move. Look, this splinter of wood is stuck in you like a knife. Come back to the house and let me get it out. Does it hurt bad?"

He looked down at the shard of wood sticking like a crude knife out of his upper arm. He hadn't even felt it. "It didn't hurt before I knew about it. Now it hurts like fire."

Thirty minutes later, they were arguing. "No, I'm not going to a doctor. The first thing the doctor would do is call Sheriff Gaffney. You don't want that, Becca. I'm fine. You've disinfected me and bandaged me up. You did a great job. No problem. Let it go. You even pushed three aspirin down my gullet. Now, how about a big jigger of brandy and I'll be ready to sing opera."

She thought of Sheriff Gaffney coming here and asking questions about a guy who shot at them. *"My my, who'd want to do that, folks?"*

She gave him another aspirin for good measure, and since she had no brandy, she gave him a diet Dr Pepper.

"Close," he said and downed a huge drink.

They both froze when there was a knock on the front door.

Then they heard the front door slam open, voices low and muffled.

Becca grabbed her Coonan and crept toward the kitchen door. "Stay put, Adam. I don't want you to get hurt again."

"Becca, I'll be all right. Hold it a second." Adam was right on her heels, his voice low, his hand on her gun arm.

"Who is it?" he called out.

A man yelled, "You guys all right? This door looks like an army tried to shoot its way in."

"I don't know who it is," Adam said. "Do you recognize his voice?"

She shook her head.

"Who is out there? What are your names? Tell me or I'll blow your heads off. We're a bit on the cautious side here."

"I'm Savich."

"I'm Sherlock. Thomas sent us. He said we needed to meet Adam and Becca, talk to them, get all the facts straight and together. Then maybe we can nail this stalker."

"I told him not to," Adam said, laid his gun on the kitchen table, and walked out into the hallway. A big man stood there, a 9mm SIG pistol held snug in his hand. A woman stood behind him, as if shoved there for protection. She stepped around the man and said, "Don't be alarmed. We're the good guys. As Dillon said, Thomas sent us. I'm Sherlock and this is my husband, Dillon Savich. We're FBI."

It was the man Thomas wanted to save his daughter's butt. His friend's son, the computer hotshot at the Bureau. Adam didn't like it, any of it. He stood there frowning at the two of them. A man brought his wife to a possible dangerous situation? What kind of an idiot was he?

Becca stepped forward. "You've got a neat name, Sherlock. You're Mr. Savich? Hello. Now, I don't know who this Thomas is, but he's probably Adam's boss, only Adam refuses to tell me anything about who hired him and why. I'm Becca Matlock. The man who's been stalking me and who shot the governor was just here. He called me and then he tried to kill us. I hit him, I know it. Adam found some blood, but he's gone, covered his trail, and I had to bandage Adam up and so—"

"Now we understand everything," Sherlock said and smiled at the young woman facing her. Sherlock thought she was pretty, but she looked like she'd been ground under for a long time now. She'd been pushed over the line. She said to the big man, Adam, who was standing beside Becca, "Dillon here is great with wounds. Do you want to have him look at your arm?"

Adam was mad and he felt like a jerk for feeling mad. If the guy really was a genius with computer tracking programs, or whatever it was he did, maybe it could help. He shook his head. "No, I'm fine. I hope to heaven the sheriff doesn't show up here, what with all that gunfire."

"This place is set way back from its neighbors," Savich said. "And all those thick trees, it's doubtful anyone heard the shots unless he was real close."

Becca blinked up at him, then said, "I hope you're right. This is Adam Carruthers. He's here as my cousin. He's here to help clean up this mess, and to protect me. As I said, I guess he works for this Thomas character. I told the guy down the street that he's gay because I'm afraid he's jealous of Adam, but he's really not."

Sherlock said, "He's really not jealous?"

"No, Adam really isn't gay."

Savich, that big guy who'd been standing very still until this instant, looking solemn and mean, began to laugh. And laugh.

The woman with the beautiful bright red curly hair looked up at him, cocked her head to one side, sending all that hair to bouncing around her head, and began laughing herself.

"I'm glad you're not gay," Savich said. "What? You really think this other guy is jealous of Adam here?"

Becca nodded. "Yes, and it's so stupid really. This is a life-and-death situation. Who would ever think of jealousy or sex at a time like this? That's just nuts."

"That's right," Sherlock said. "No one would. Right, Dillon?"

"That's exactly what I would have said," Savich said.

Adam watched Savich slip the SIG back into his belt. All right, maybe the two of them could help. He'd wait and see what they did before he said anything more.

Becca said, "Adam is drinking a diet Dr Pepper since I don't have any brandy to help him get over the shock of being wounded. Ice or lime in yours?"

Savich grinned at her. "Give me a goodly amount of lime and then Sherlock and I will go out and buy some brandy." He then looked long at her. He wanted to tell her that her father was worried sick about her, that she looked a lot like him, that, when this was all over, he would come into her life for the very first time. But for now, Savich couldn't say anything at all. They'd promised Thomas Matlock that they'd keep him in the shadows until the mess was all cleared up. Thomas had said, "Until I can be certain that Krimakov is really dead, I can't take the chance. And for me to believe that, really believe it all the way to my gut, I've got to see a photo of him lying on a slab in a Greek morgue."

Sherlock had said, "But if he's not dead, sir, and he is orchestrating all this, then he already knows about Becca and is trying to terrorize her with the ultimate goal of getting to you through her."

Thomas had said, "I know only enough to scare myself spitless, Sherlock. I want to keep a lid on all of this until I'm certain. In the meantime, I want to keep her hidden from all the cops and the FBI because I'm certain they can't protect her from this stalker."

Becca said over her shoulder as she led them into the kitchen, "Before anyone comes over, you've got to tell me who you are and why you're here. As I told you, Adam's cover is that he's my gay cousin."

Adam said as he cocked the soda can at Savich, "You want to be her other gay cousin?"

"Then what would that make me?" Sherlock said. "I can't keep my hands off him. That would blow the cover right off."

"Maybe we'll be your friends, Adam. I know quite a bit about you and your background. You and I went to school together, how about that?" Savich said.

"Then what are you doing in Riptide, Maine?"

Sherlock took a glass of soda from Becca, sipped it, and said, "We're here because of that skeleton that fell out of your basement wall, Becca. You guys wanted some help, and since we live in Portsmouth, it wasn't tough for us to get up here."

"How do you know where I went to school?" Adam said, his eyes dark and hard on Savich's face.

"MAX gave me most of your particulars. It took him a while longer to find out about all your other activities. You went to Yale. No problem. Did we crew?"

Well, damn, Adam thought, it was a good idea. "Yeah," he said. "We did crew. We also beat Harvard, that bunch of pissy little wimps."

Sherlock wondered why Adam Carruthers didn't want her or Dillon there. Didn't he realize that they could help? The stalker was here in Riptide, he'd tried to kill them.

Sherlock gave Adam a sunny smile. "Why don't we go look in the woods and try to uncover a trail for this guy?"

"Yeah," Savich said, rising. "Then we need to figure out why he would want to kill Becca like this. It doesn't make sense. He's into terrorizing her. Why shoot her and end it all? He'd have no more fun."

"Good question," Becca said. "We haven't had time to think about anything since it happened. Me, I don't think he wanted to kill either of us, just scare us real bad, just announce that he was here and ready to play again."

Becca sucked in her breath. "Oh dear, we need to get the front door repaired before our neighbor, Tyler McBride, or the sheriff come to visit. I don't want to try to explain bullet holes in the door."

"Let's check for a trail first," Sherlock said. "Then, Becca, you can tell us what the stalker said to you this time while we all repair the door."

"You're good," Savich said some thirty minutes later to Adam. "You said there was no trail and there isn't."

Adam grunted. "Let's go out a bit farther. Maybe we'll see some tire tracks."

"No way," Sherlock said. "The stalker is a pro, which means that he isn't really a stalker. That's just a cover. A misdirection."

Savich nodded. "I agree. He isn't a stalker."

Becca said, "What do you mean, exactly?"

Adam said, as he slowly lifted leaves some ten feet away, "It doesn't make sense, Becca. Usually stalkers are sick guys who, for whatever strange reason, latch on to someone. It's an obsession. They're not pros. This guy's a pro. This was well thought out."

And Savich thought: *If Krimakov is alive, then it's a terror campaign, and Becca's the means to the end. Thomas Matlock is right to be afraid.* And the ending Krimakov planned wasn't good for either father or daughter.

Becca was shaking her head. "But he sounds nuts whenever he's called me. He called a couple of hours ago. He said much of the same things. He sounded all sorts of excited, very pleased with himself, like he couldn't wait. I know he's toying with me, getting a real kick out of my fear, my anger, my helplessness." She stopped a moment, looked at Adam, and added, "The thing is, I can't help but feel that inside, he's dead."

Sherlock said, "Maybe he's dead on the inside, but it's the outside we've got to worry about. One thing we know for sure is that he's clever; he knows what he needs to do and he does it. He found you, didn't he? Now, could we go back to the house and Becca can tell us everything? You said he called you again. Tell us exactly what he said. Then we can put all our brainpower together and solve this mess."

"Another thing," Savich said as he brushed his black slacks off, "I don't want us out in the open like this. It isn't smart."

And Sherlock, her brilliant red hair shining brightly in the fading afternoon light, led them back to Jacob Marley's house.

They found caulk, an electric sander that worked, and some wood stain in the basement, on some shelves near the hole in the brick wall.

They took the front door off its hinges and brought it inside. While Savich sanded it down and Adam caulked in the bullet holes, Becca and Sherlock kept watch, their guns in their hands, watchful. Very soon, Sherlock had Becca talking and talking. ". . . and when he called me a while ago, he said the same sorts of things, like I would contact the governor as soon as he was well enough again and have him come to me."

"You know," Adam said, "he doesn't believe you've slept with the governor. It's part of a script. He needed something so that he could claim you needed punishment."

"You're right," Sherlock said, giving Adam his first look of approval, for which he didn't know whether to be pleased or snarl. "Yes, you're perfectly right. Go ahead, Becca, what else did he say?"

"When I asked him about Dick McCallum, he wouldn't admit that he killed him, but I know that he did. He said I'd gotten all pissy, that I'd gotten too confident, that he was coming for me soon. I tell you, when I hung up, I was ready to throw in the towel. He calls himself my boyfriend. It's beyond creepy."

"Yeah," Adam said, raising his head to look at her, "she was ready to throw in the towel for about three minutes." Then he said toward Savich, "Then she put her Coonan in her pocket and went out into the woods. Why'd you go out there, Becca? It wasn't real smart, you know."

She looked inward for a moment, all of them saw it—and the sanding and caulking stopped. Not one of them was surprised when she shrugged. "I don't know, really. I wanted to go there, alone, and sit under the sunlight against that tree. Jacob Marley's house was getting to me. There are ghosts here, the air is filled with remnants of the people who lived here, residue, maybe, not all of it good."

"Before I finally found her, I nearly croaked," Adam said, realizing he was grinning at Savich. Well, why not? He was here and he did seem competent, at least so far. Maybe he'd still fall flat on his face.

"Listen, I've got to contact my men," Adam said. "The stalker—or whatever he is—is here. He tried to kill us, or maybe he was after me— that's more likely. We've got to close this town down. And we need to finish with this door before he just walks right up and shoots us."

"He won't even get close," Becca said and raised her Coonan.

"Agreed," Savich said. He winked at Sherlock. "You want to tell Adam about how we've got everything covered?"

"Yep. A half dozen guys from Thomas are on their way here." She looked down at her wristwatch. "In about an hour, I'd estimate. And here we were worried that there wouldn't be enough for them to do. We were really wrong on that one."

"The timing's perfect," Savich said as he wiped all the sawdust off his hands. "Don't anyone fret that they'll all be piling into town and staying at Errol Flynn's Hammock. Nope, they won't stick out at all, but they'll have this place well covered. Now, we need to get busy as soon as we're done with this door. We need to bug the phone. He'll probably call again, soon. Also, we need protection around the house. The guys will be calling in and we'll set up a guard rotation. Also, Adam, you can show them where the blood is and they can get it analyzed. We'll at least verify that it's human."

"I know I hit him."

Savich nodded to Becca. "Yes, I'm sure you did. We'll see if anything interesting shows up in the blood work. Now, it would probably be a smart thing if you stayed inside, Becca."

Sherlock said, "If he was trying to kill Adam, to make things easier for him, then that makes all of us open season. It would be wise if this Tyler McBride kept himself and his kid away from here. It isn't safe."

And Adam thought, *Where's my brain? I should have thought and said all of that.*

Becca said, looking Sherlock straight in the eye, "No, I don't want Tyler or Sam in any danger, either. Now, who's this Thomas?"

"He's Adam's boss," Savich said, well aware that Adam was on full alert, "or he used to be. Now Adam is on his own. Actually, as I understand it, Adam is doing Thomas a favor. Hey, don't worry about it, Becca, you don't know him. Adam, you did a good job of filling in all the holes. A bit of stain and the door will look perfect again."

Becca jumped up. "I left it in the kitchen."

"I'll go with you," Sherlock said. "I think I'd like to look at that gash in the basement wall again."

"Of course he was after you," Savich said easily, once Becca was out of hearing. "He wanted you out of the way, wounded or dead, it didn't matter to him. It still doesn't."

"Yeah, I know."

"He wants her. He wants to take her so he figured he'd have to knock you out of the way."

"That's what I figure."

# FIFTEEN

Becca held the can of stain in front of her.

Adam, instead of taking the can, found himself standing there staring down at the too thin, formerly pale young woman who was now flushed red to her eyebrows.

"I'm really mad now," she said, and he believed her, and smiled. "He shot up Jacob Marley's door. That's beyond the line." He couldn't cut off his smile, because her eyes were glowing. Her soft blue eyes were hard and pulsing with rage. Her dyed hair was nearly standing on end. "I heard the two of you talking. He tried to kill you, Adam, to get to me. That's beyond the line, too." She was panting now. She was major-league pissed, and she wanted to protect him. He took her face between his big hands. His mouth was nearly touching hers. He immediately straightened and took the can of stain. He didn't want this, but he couldn't help it. An enraged Becca Matlock who still wanted to protect him did something to him, something strange and wonderful that seared him to the soles of his scuffed boots.

He looked at her mouth again, but instead of kissing her, he started to laugh. And he kept on laughing, he wanted to kiss her that bad.

She blinked at him and then took a step back. "Don't get stain on your clothes. I'm not going to wash them for you."

"When it's necessary, I'll wash my own clothes," Adam said, then added on a grin, "if you'll show me how to work the washing machine."

"Mechanical things defeat you, do they? No, don't say it, only mechanical things that involve work could defeat a guy."

Adam eyed Savich's outstretched hand, grunted, and handed him the stain. His arm burned and ached and Savich knew it. He said to Savich, "You know something? I'd really like to rearrange your pretty face when this is all over."

Savich stared at him, then laughed. "If you think my face is pretty, then you've got a big problem, because that's what I think about yours."

"Bull."

Savich shook his head. "You want to play at the gym? Fine by me."

Becca stood by the front window as Savich stained the front door, her Coonan held loosely in her right hand, looking all around, like a pro. After a bit, Adam couldn't stand it and took the brush from Savich.

Savich grinned at him. Sherlock said, "I love to see a real macho guy in action."

Adam brushed on the stain, slowly, carefully, gritting his teeth because his arm hurt. But he wasn't about to whine. He whistled low, between his teeth, hoping Savich heard it.

Tyler showed up with Sam an hour later. "Hey, what's that smell? Who are these people?"

Becca went blank for a moment, then said, "I didn't like the stain on the front door. It was looking tatty and old. I just finished re-staining it." She waited to see if Tyler would say anything about hearing bullets, but he didn't.

Sam stared up at her, sniffing, but as usual he didn't say anything.

"Smells weird, huh, Sam? Hey, here are some friends of Adam's. This is Sherlock and her husband, Savich."

Sherlock went down on her knees in front of the little boy. She made no move at all toward him, and said after he'd studied her for a bit, "Hi, do you like my name?"

Sam didn't step back, but he did lean his head back a bit. He gave Sherlock a bit of a smile and eyed her hair. He reached out two fingers and patted the top of her head.

Savich came down beside her. "We've got a little kid, Sam, a lot younger than you are. His name is Sean and he's only six months old. He can't pat the top of his mama's head yet. He doesn't even talk yet. But he is growing teeth."

"Teeth are good," Sherlock said, "but all that drool is a pain."

That drew Adam up really fast. These two had a kid? Well, why was he so surprised? Most men his age were married and had children. He'd been married once, and he'd wanted a kid, lots of them as a matter of fact, but Vivie hadn't been ready yet. A long time ago now, five years, nearly long enough to forget her name, if it hadn't sounded like a song out of *Cabaret*.

Becca said easily, "Sam doesn't talk much, Sherlock. I think it's because he's always thinking so hard."

"I like a kid who thinks a lot," Savich said. "Do you want to come to the kitchen with me and we'll find you a goody to eat?"

Sam didn't hesitate, lifted his arms. Savich scooped him up and carried him away on his shoulders. "I don't think I'll even have to burp you, Sam. I'm really good at that. Sean likes to burp a lot."

Sam grabbed Savich's hair, and Becca saw the smile on his face. Then he turned his head and looked at Adam, at his bandaged arm. He shook his head, frowning, looking confused, then afraid.

Adam said, "It's okay, Sam. I didn't hurt my arm bad, only a little bit. Becca fixed me right up."

"Yep, and I did a good job, Sam, don't worry." Then Sam and Savich were gone, and Tyler said, "What happened here? No, Becca, don't try to lie to me."

She thought of Tyler and Sam and the two of them accidentally being in the line of that madman's fire, and said, "The stalker found me. He fired at me and Adam. I shot him, but he got away. We're okay, but I'm worried about you and Sam coming here. It's not a good idea, Tyler."

He shook his head at her and said, "He shot the door?"

"He fired through it a couple of times, really messed it up. I don't want the sheriff to see it. He'd ask too many questions."

"Don't worry, Mr. McBride," Sherlock said. "Things will be under control, but you know Becca's right. It's best if you keep Sam away from here until we bring this guy down. It could be dangerous until we catch him."

Tyler looked both angry and determined. "Yeah, I'll go but I want Becca to come with me and Sam, either to my house or away, maybe to California. I want her kept safe."

"No, Tyler," Becca said, lightly touching her fingertips to his arm. "We've got to clean it up. There are lots of people here now to help me."

Tyler turned to Adam. "Who are you, really? And you?" he added to Sherlock.

"Dillon and I are FBI, Mr. McBride. Adam here is on special assignment to protect Becca." That sounded like he was with the Bureau as well, Adam thought, which was probably for the best. An independent security consultant didn't sound like he'd know what to do with a madman. FBI did.

"You never told me," Tyler said to Becca, his voice low. "You didn't trust me. You let me think he was your cousin. Why did you do that?"

Becca couldn't think of a thing to say that wouldn't make everything worse. She hadn't meant to hurt him, to keep him in the dark, to make him feel unimportant to her, but—

"Get over it, Tyler," Adam said. "This isn't fun and games. It's serious business. You're not trained to do this sort of thing. We are. Besides, you've got Sam. He's got to be your first priority."

Tyler said, his hands fisted at his sides, "You're not gay, are you?"

"No, not any more than you are."

"You want to seduce her, to take advantage of her. She's scared and you just want her to depend only on you. You're afraid to have me here."

"Look, McBride—"

But Adam didn't have time to calm the man down. Tyler leapt at him, knocking him over on his back in the entryway. Adam landed on his hurt arm, grunted, then bounded back up. He wasn't seeing red this time, he was seeing a very sharp and clear target—right in the middle of Tyler's kidney. No, he couldn't. It wouldn't be fair. Tyler, breathing hard, out of control, was about to jump at him again when Sherlock calmly tapped him lightly on the shoulder, and when he turned, distracted, she clipped his jaw. His head flew back and he stumbled. He regained his balance and stood there, feeling his jaw. He looked at her, stupefied, as Sherlock said, "I'm sorry, Mr. McBride, but that's enough. Listen to me. Becca's life is what's important, not your wounded feelings. Adam didn't even know Becca until a couple of days ago. He's here to protect her. Now, get a grip on yourself or I'll flip you over my shoulder and lay you out."

Tyler looked like he didn't doubt her for an instant. He turned slowly to face Becca. "I'm sorry," he said. "I didn't mean to hit him, well, I did, but I'm so scared for you, and this guy shows up pretending to be your cousin and I knew he wasn't. I didn't know what to do. I'm worried about you, Becca, real worried—"

Becca walked to Tyler and slowly stepped against him, clasping her arms loosely around his back. "I know, Tyler, I know. I really appreciate you being here for me, but these folk are all pros. They know what they're doing and there are even more people coming now. We've got to catch this maniac. Now that he's here I can't pick up and run. We've got to get him. He found me, how, I don't know, but don't you see? If I run, he'll find me again. I've got people here to help me now. Please, Tyler, tell me you understand why I kept quiet about Adam."

He was pressing his cheek against her hair, squeezing her so tightly

Adam thought he'd crush her ribs. Adam wanted to pull him off and give him one good shot in the jaw.

Becca slowly pulled away. He was afraid for her, she knew that, and she didn't want to hurt him. Her voice was very gentle when she said, "You do understand, don't you, Tyler?"

"Yeah, I do, but I want to help." Then he lightly traced his fingertips over her cheek. "I've known you for a long time, Becca. I want to help. This is a real creepy business."

"You're telling me." She managed something of a laugh, which was closer to a cry, really.

Tyler said when Savich came back to the entryway, "Thank you for taking care of Sam." He lifted Sam into his arms and squeezed him nearly as hard as he'd squeezed Becca. "Sam, I'm sorry I lost my temper with Adam. I didn't mean to frighten you. You okay?"

Sam nodded. "I heard you yelling."

"I know," Tyler said, kissing Sam's temple. "You're not used to that, are you? Everyone loses his temper sometimes. I'm sorry I did it and sorry you were close by. Now, you and I need to go over to Goose's Hardware and get some washers for the bathroom faucet. Would you like to do that?"

Sam nodded. He looked relieved. Tyler hugged him again.

"What's the name of the street Goose's Hardware is on?" Savich asked as he looked at his wife rubbing her knuckles, an eyebrow arched.

"West Hemlock," Tyler said. "It's the main street."

When Tyler McBride finally left, Adam turned to see Sherlock and Savich speaking quietly. Adam said, "Are you guys going to stay here?"

"That's probably best," Savich said. "First thing, we're going to put a tap on this phone. Sherlock said we should bring our goodies. She's right a lot of the time." Savich picked up what looked like a very small aluminum suitcase. "This is a dual redundant tape. We're going to set it right beside the phone recorder. Now, I'm going to patch it into the phone line via the recorder starting switch. Okay, now let's plug that puppy in between the phone and the outlet in the wall."

"Goodness," Becca said. "That's quite a gadget."

"Yeah," Adam said. "You can get it at RadioShack for about twenty bucks."

"The recorder will start when the phone rings," Savich said.

"Now for the slammer," Sherlock said. She pulled out a small case that looked about the size of a laptop. "See this, Becca? It's an LED—

light-emitting diode. When our boy calls this number, the name and address of the person who's registered as the phone owner will appear here on this green screen. It's like the automatic phone display for 911."

"All done, Sherlock?" Savich said, then nodded when she pressed a couple of buttons. "Good. Now I'm going to go meet with the guys, set up a surveillance schedule, tell them about the tap and the trace."

"Fine," said Adam. "I'm coming with you. I want to meet them. I don't want anyone shot by accident. Also, we need to start tracking down our boy. He's somewhere close."

"Three of the guys are already on that. They're checking all the gas stations within fifty miles, all the bed-and-breakfasts, motels, inns. They've already gotten a list of every single guy between the ages of twenty and fifty who arrived in Bangor and Portland within the past three days."

Sherlock yawned. "Becca and I will guard the fort. You guys be careful. Hey, a nap sounds good, what with all the excitement. Is there another usable bedroom in this grandiose monstrosity?"

The men got back to Jacob Marley's house two hours later. It was dark, nearly nine o'clock in the evening. The house was lit up from top to bottom, all the outdoor lights on as well. The newly stained front door both looked and smelled great.

Sherlock was drinking coffee in the living room, studying a file she'd brought with her from Washington. The shades were drawn tight, which was smart. Becca wasn't anywhere around. They'd already checked with Perkins. There had been no phone calls.

Adam found Becca in her bedroom. She was lying flat on her back in the middle of the bed, her hands crossed over her stomach. Her eyes were closed but he knew she wasn't asleep. Her shoulders were locked stiff.

"Becca? You okay?"

"Yeah."

She felt the bed give when he sat down beside her. "What do you want? Go away. I don't want to have to look at your pretty face. Has anyone seen him?"

"I don't have a pretty face. It's Savich who's got the pretty face. No, there's no sign of him yet, just that blood in the woods we found. The guys took samples to be analyzed."

She cracked her left eye open. "Did everything go all right? Were all the men there? Have they found anything out yet?"

"Yes, all six of them are here, each of them well trained. I know four of them, even worked with a couple of them in the past, so that's good. They're all top-notch. It's just a matter of time until we track him down. All of us have favors owed. We'll call them all in if necessary. You know, the reason I was here was to protect you from the cops and the Feebs because we knew they couldn't protect you from the stalker. But things have changed now. The guy's here and there's no choice. We've got to get him or you'll never be safe."

"Who is this Thomas, Adam? He must be very powerful to be able to have all this guy power up here for one insignificant person, namely me."

"You're not insignificant." He sounded too harsh, too intense, and he clamped his teeth together. "Look, don't worry about Thomas. He's doing what he's got to do. Now, why are you up here, lying down?" He paused a moment. She was dull-eyed, pale again, and it worried him. He looked at his fingernails and said, "But first things first. I'm getting hungry. Any ideas for dinner? It's nearly nine o'clock. It's nearly time to go to bed. Oh yeah, that was a good idea to have all the lights on."

She opened both eyes then and stared up at him. "Sherlock did that. Now let me get this straight. You're worried about food? Now?"

He nodded. He'd distracted her. Her eyes were narrowed on his face, her lips were seamed into a thin line. Good.

"Of course I'm hungry. What about dinner?"

"Well then," she said, rolling to the other side of the bed to stand and streaking her hands through her hair, "let me get my little self downstairs and see what I can whip together."

She stalked out of the bedroom, Adam on her heels, grinning at the back of her head. She was keeping it together. Being pissed was good. He was pleased and inordinately relieved. He was afraid, though, that being a jerk was a bit too easy for him. He noticed again that the tilt of her head was like her father's.

"So," Sherlock said some thirty minutes later at the kitchen table after she'd chewed a bite of tuna salad Savich had whipped up, "this Tyler McBride seems hung up on you, Becca, and he's wildly jealous of Adam. Could he be a problem?"

"He already is a problem," Adam said, waving a dill pickle. "The guy attacked me. I wasn't doing a single thing and he attacked me."

"You held back from hurting him," Sherlock said. "That was smart. Mr. McBride is not only very afraid for Becca, he also feels threatened because another male showed up. It's strange. Here he knows Becca's in trouble. You'd think the more folks to help, the better."

It was the way he should have felt the entire time, Adam thought. Bottom line, like Tyler, he'd felt threatened. And the women knew it.

"I'm glad you didn't hit Savich," Sherlock said, seeing quite clearly what he was thinking. "I would have done more than clip you on the jaw if you had, Adam." She then gave him a sunny smile, raised the plate, and said, "Anyone want another tuna sandwich?"

Becca said, "Or would you prefer raw meat?"

"That's really quite enough, Becca," Adam said, finally annoyed. "I'm going to take another sandwich and go talk to the guys, see how they're doing. The moon's nearly full tonight. It's quiet. Don't worry about the boyfriend being out there to shoot me. I'll take my gun. Oh yeah, if I had attacked Savich, I would have coldcocked him before you could have hurt me, Sherlock."

He left the kitchen.

Sherlock couldn't help herself; she laughed. Savich looked back and forth between the two women, stood slowly, nabbed a sandwich, then said, "I think it's a little thick in here. See you later, Sherlock. I'm going to go give my mom a call and see how she's faring with our boy."

"Call me when you've got him on the phone," Sherlock said, then took a big bite out of an apple.

Savich walked to the living room, and pulled out his cell phone. He heard Adam whistling outside.

He hated to lie to his mom when she asked him exactly what he and Sherlock were doing, but he did, and cleanly. "It's a background check on someone very important who's being considered for the Supreme Court. All very hush-hush and that's why Jimmy Maitland asked me and Sherlock to take care of it. Don't worry, Mom, we'll be back in a couple of days. I met a really cute little boy today. It seems his mother abandoned him and his father over a year ago and he hasn't said much since then. Is that Sean gurgling in the background? I'd sure like to speak to him, Mom."

# SIXTEEN

The phone in the living room rang sharply at midnight. Everyone heard it, but Becca was the fastest. She was on her feet, running down the front stairs to the living room by the second ring.

It was him, she knew it, and she wanted to talk to him. There wasn't the need to keep him on for any specified length of time. The slammer was instantaneous, the identification there in a flash.

Her hand shook as she picked up the phone. "Hello?"

"I don't know if I want to be your boyfriend anymore. You shot my dog, Rebecca."

*Shot his dog?* "That's a lie and you know it. Besides, no animal would have anything to do with you. You're too crazy and sick."

"His name was Gleason. He was very fat and you shot and killed him. I'm really upset, Becca. I'm coming to get you now. Not long. Hey, honey, you want to send flowers to poor Gleason's funeral?"

"Why don't you bury yourself with him, you murdering psycho?"

Adam heard his hitching breath, the flutter of rage. She'd gotten to him. Good.

He saw Savich write down the name and address from the slammer and sit down on the sofa, opening his laptop. He pressed close to Becca.

"You got that big guy there with you, Becca? Listening to me?"

"Yeah, I'm here listening to you, you pathetic piece of crap. Cheer up, you killed the front door, but we're so good we even brought it back to life. It probably looks better than you do."

Becca could feel the black fury in the silence that flooded over the phone line. She could nearly feel the stench of it—hot and rancid, that fury. "I'll kill you for that."

"You already tried, didn't you? Not much good, are you?"

"You're a dead man, Carruthers. Soon. Very soon now."

"Hey, where are you holding Gleason's wake? I wanna come. You want me to bring a priest? Or isn't your kind of crazy into religion?"

The breathing speeded up, rough and harsh. "I'm not crazy. I'll have Rebecca watch you die. I promise you that. I see you got two more people there with you. I also know they're FBI. You think they're going to do anything to help? No one can catch me. No one. Hey, Rebecca, the governor call you yet?"

Adam gave her a cool nod, a thumbs-up sign. She said, "Yeah, he called me. He wants to see me. He told me he loves me, that he wants to sleep with me again. He said his wife doesn't understand him, and he wants to leave her for me. The dear man, do you think he's well enough yet for me to tell him where I am?"

Cold, dead silence, then, very gently, they heard the phone line disconnect.

She stared at the phone. The slammer was showing "501-4867, Orlando Cartwright, Rural Route 1456, Blaylock" in black letters on a bright-green screen.

Sherlock said, "It's a land line, not a cell phone. Good. Everyone stay still for a moment. Savich will have all the information in a moment. He sounded healthy enough, didn't he?"

"Yeah," Adam said.

"Then it was only a flesh wound, more's the pity," Sherlock said, and scratched behind her left ear. Her curling red hair was all over her head. She was wearing a sleep shirt that said across the front: I BRAKE FOR ASTEROIDS. Savich had pulled on a pair of jeans. He was bare the rest of the way up. So was Adam.

"That dog bit," Adam said, "it was an excellent ploy on his part. All right, let's head out of here and go get him. You got our directions, Savich?"

"In a second," Savich said.

Adam took Becca in his arms. "You did great, Becca, really great. You rattled him. Now, let's get dressed and go nail him."

"We're all going," Becca said.

Savich looked up and grinned. "It's a farmhouse some six miles northwest of here, outside a small town called Blaylock. Let me call Tommy the Pipe." He got him quickly on his cell phone.

"Yeah, Tommy, call all the others and head on out there, but don't go in. This guy is very dangerous. Keep him under wraps until we get there. I'll find out everything I can on the way there. Yeah, on MAX."

In the backseat of Adam's Jeep, Savich kept up a running commentary. "Here we go. The farmhouse belonged to Orlando Cartwright, bought the place back in 1954. He's dead now. Oh yeah, that's good, MAX. He had one daughter, she was with him until he died three weeks ago at Blue Hills Community Hospital. Lung cancer, Alzheimer's. Oh, no, she's still there, alone."

"Not good," Adam said.

"What's her name?" Becca asked, turning in the seat to look at him.

"Linda Cartwright. Just a minute here, okay, good hunting, MAX. She's never been married, age thirty-three, really pretty, even on her DL photo. She's a legal secretary for the Billson Manners law firm in Bangor, been there for eight years. Hold on a second, let me get into her personnel file. Yes, she's got very good evaluations—in 1998 she complained about sexual harassment. Hmmm, the guy was eventually fired. Her work record is clean. Her mother died back in 1987, a drunk driver killed both her and Linda's younger sister. No, MAX, there's no need to go into police files, probably a waste of time."

"She's single and she's alone," Sherlock said. "Not good at all. Hurry, Adam."

"She's alone," Becca said. "She's alone, like I was."

At one o'clock in the morning, beneath a nearly full, brilliant summer moon, Adam pulled his black Jeep next to a dark blue Ford Taurus parked on the side of a two-lane blacktop road. They were some fifty yards from the old farmhouse with its peeling white shutters and sagging narrow front porch.

There was no need for introductions.

Two men, both in their thirties, fit, one wearing glasses, the other smoking a pipe, were leaning against the side of the car. Savich said, "The guy in there?"

"The lights are still on, but we haven't seen any movement at all. No one left since we got here. Chuck and Dave are around the back." He took out his walkie-talkie. "You guys see anything?"

The answer was clear and loud. "He hasn't come out this way, Tommy. You and Rollo haven't seen anything?"

"Nothing."

Dave said, "There's no movement in the house that we can see. Chuck wants to go up close and look through the windows."

"Tell Chuck and Dave to stay put," Adam said. "Here's Savich, he'll give you the rundown on what we're facing."

Savich was concise, his voice clipped.

"I don't like this," Tommy said and puffed frantically on his pipe. "A woman living way out here, all alone, no neighbors for a couple of miles. I'll bet he scoped her out really fast and that he's been here with her. This doesn't look good. We've seen nothing of either of them. Maybe she's not here. Maybe MAX is wrong and she was never here."

"Yeah, right, Tommy," Rollo said, and he sounded depressed. He was short, dressed all in black, and he was perfectly bald, his head shining brightly beneath the summer moon.

Tommy the Pipe said, "Maybe he left before we got here. It could be that he took her with him, as a hostage."

Linda Cartwright was a woman alone, and Becca knew he'd been in there, with her.

Damn the bright moon, Adam was thinking, it lit them up as clearly as daylight from the front of the farmhouse. But there were thick pine trees crowding the eastern side of the small farmhouse. Folk grew potatoes in this area, and so much of the land was cleared, open, just occasional random clumps of pines and maples dotted here and there, but no place to hide. There was a big mechanical digger sitting in the middle of an open field. There was a small sagging porch in front of the house, a naked lightbulb burning over the front door.

On the eastern side of the house, he could get to within twenty feet of the structure before the pine trees played out. It would have to be good enough. He pulled out his Delta Elite, thoughtfully rubbed his temple with the barrel. Then he said, a feral gleam in his eyes, "I got a plan. Gather round."

"I don't like it," Savich said after Adam had fallen silent. "Too dangerous."

Adam said, "I was thinking that all of us could go in guns blazing, but the woman might still be alive. We can't take the chance he'd pop her then and there and then kill two or three of us, what with all this moonlight."

"All right," Savich said after a moment, "but I'll go with you."

Adam said, "I don't care if you're an FBI agent and your goal in life is to catch bad guys. You're married and you've got a kid. What I need from you and everyone else is good cover. I hear you're a pretty good shot, Savich. Prove it."

"I'm coming with you, Adam," Becca said. "I'll cover your back from right behind you."

He held up his hand. "I'm the professional here. Say some prayers, that's all I ask."

"No," Becca said, and he realized then that if he wanted her to stay put, he'd have to have one of the men tie her down. He didn't like it, but he understood it. It could be dangerous, too dangerous. He didn't know what to do.

"I'm coming," she said, and he knew she was committed. "I have to, Adam, just have to."

He wished he didn't understand, but he did. He nodded. He heard Savich snort. "Becca will cover me from the woods," he said. "No, no arguments, Becca. That's the deal."

Sherlock took the walkie-talkie and spoke to Chuck and Dave at the back of the house, told them what was going to happen.

Becca's heart was pounding hard and fast. The night was chilly but she was sweating. She felt faint nausea in her stomach. This was real and it was scary and she was terrified, not only for Adam and her, but for that poor woman inside the house, that poor woman she prayed was still alive. Sherlock and the men looked calm, alert, ready. Tommy put his pipe back in his pocket and handed Becca a Kevlar vest. "It's the smallest one, after Sherlock's." He shrugged. "Let me help you with it. You're going to stay under cover in the woods, remember. You'll be out of the line of fire, but hey, it always pays to be careful."

Once she was strapped into the vest, she pulled her Coonan, and checked the magazine three times. Adam took one look at her and didn't say a thing, just mouthed at her to stay a bit behind him. Her heart was pounding harder and faster than it had five minutes before. Her hand was shaking, no good, no good. She stuffed her left hand in her pocket. Keep steady, she thought, as she looked down at her right hand, which held her pistol. She looked over at Sherlock, who was frowning at one of the Velcro fastenings on her Kevlar vest. No one was taking any chances at all.

"Showtime," Savich said after he checked his watch. "Go, Adam. Good luck. Becca, you keep down."

Adam, with Becca on his heels, made a wide berth to the east side of the house. He walked slowly, quietly, Becca just as quiet, through the pine trees. When they got to the edge of the woods, Adam pulled up. Twenty feet, he thought, not more than twenty feet. He looked through the window at the other end of those twenty feet, right in front of him. There were curtains, thin, see-through white lace, but they weren't drawn over the single wide window. It was probably a bedroom. He turned to look at Becca, her face as pale as the fat moon overhead. He cupped her neck in his hand and pulled her close. He whispered against her cheek, "I want you to stay right here and keep alert. You stay hidden, do you hear me? You see him, you blow his head off, all right?"

"Yes. Please be careful, Adam. Your vest is on correctly? You're protected?"

"Yeah." He touched his fingertips to her cheek, then dropped his arm. "Stay alert."

It seemed to Adam that it took him near an hour to run those twenty feet. Every step was long and heavy and so loud it shook the earth. It seemed to him that every night sound, from owls to crickets, stopped in those moments. Watching, he thought, they were all watching to see what would happen. Nothing from the house, no movement, no sound, not a single quick shadow. He flattened against the side of the house, his pistol held between both hands, then slowly, slowly, he looked around into a bedroom filled with old white rattan furniture with cheap faded red cushions, a dim-watted bulb shining from an old lava lamp on a nightstand next to a single bed. He saw nothing, no movement, no one. The cover on the twin-size bed barely covered the top of the mattress. He could see that there was nothing beneath the bed except big-time dust balls. No, no one in the room. If anyone was in there, he was in the closet, on the far side, the door closed. He saw that the door to the bedroom was also shut. He quietly tested the window, paused, listened intently. Still nothing. The window wasn't locked. He raised it slowly, the sounds of creaking and scraping against old paint as loud as thunder in his head.

The window was some five feet off the ground. Because he had to, he stuck his pistol in the waistband of his jeans. He'd always hated doing that ever since he'd heard the story some decades back that an agent had stuck his gun in his pants and hit against a car fender in some weird way that pulled the trigger. He shot off the end of his dick. No, he didn't want to do that. He pulled himself up and eased his leg over the windowsill.

He waved back at Becca, motioning for her to stay back and keep hidden. But, of course, she didn't. She trotted right up to the house and stuck out her hand for him to help her through the window.

"Only if you stay hidden in here while I check the rest of the house."

"I promise. Pull me up, hurry. I don't like this, Adam. She was alone here. I know he's done something bad."

A lone owl hooted fifty feet away, from the safety of the woods and a tall tree. The moon glistened down on her face. Adam pulled her over the ledge and she swung her legs to the floor.

She watched him walk toward the closet door, listen intently, then jerk it open. Nothing. Then she watched him walk to the closed bedroom door, staying to the side, never directly facing the door. He slowly turned the knob, then smashed the door open, sending it banging back, and stepped into the hallway, his pistol up. Then he was gone. She stood there shaking, wishing she wasn't, listening to that owl, loud and clear, sounding from the forest.

Where was he? Time passed as slowly as it did in the dentist's office. Maybe even slower.

Finally, she heard him shout, "Becca, go back out the window and tell Savich it's okay for everyone to come in. He's not here."

"No, I want to come out—"

"Out the window, Becca. Please."

When he was sure she was outside, Adam stepped out onto the sagging front porch with its scarred and peeling railing and said, "He's gone. Savich, come here a moment. The rest of you just stay outside and keep watch, okay?"

"Yeah, we'll keep watch, but this is nuts," Tommy said and pulled out his pipe. "No one moved after we got here and we converged on the place not ten minutes after you called, Adam."

Savich said slowly, "Then he knew, of course, that we'd tapped the phone."

"Yes," Adam said. "He knew. In the kitchen, Savich."

"I don't like this," Becca said to Sherlock as she pressed toward the front door. "Why can't we go in the house?"

"Stay there for the moment, Becca."

Several minutes passed. No one said anything, but one by one the men walked into the farmhouse through the open front door.

Becca didn't know what to do. Sherlock, who was standing on the small front porch, her 9mm SIG drawn, sweeping in a wide arc around her, scanning the perimeter, said, "I'll go check. Becca, why don't you wait out here just a while longer?"

Becca stared at her. "Why?"

"Wait," she said, her voice suddenly sharp. "That's an order."

Becca heard the men talking, knew all of them but her were in the house. Why didn't they want her in there? She ran around to the back of the house and slipped in behind one of the men who was standing in the middle of the back door. The kitchen was painfully bright with two-hundred-watt bulbs hanging naked from the ceiling. The kitchen was small, the appliances were harsh white, clean, and very old. There was an old wooden table, scarred, a beautiful old vase holding dead roses in the center. It had been pushed against the wall. Two of the chairs were over-turned on the floor. The refrigerator was humming loudly, like an old train chugging up a hill.

She slipped around the man in the doorway. He tried to hold her back, but she pulled free. Tommy, Savich, and Sherlock were standing in a near circle staring down at the pale green linoleum floor. Adam rose slowly.

And suddenly Becca could see her.

# SEVENTEEN

The woman had no face. Her head looked like a bowl filled with smashed bone, flesh, and teeth. He'd struck her hard, viciously, repeatedly. There were two broken teeth on the floor beside the woman's head. There was dried blood everywhere, congealed and black on her face and on the worn linoleum, streaks of blood, like lightning bolts, down the white wall. Her hair was matted to her head, blood-soaked dark clumps falling away onto the floor. And there was dirt mixed in with the dried bloody hair.

"She's young," she heard a man say, his voice low, calm, detached, but underlying that voice was a thick layer of fury. "Too young. It's Linda Cartwright, isn't it?"

"Yes," Adam said. "He killed her right here in the kitchen."

Linda Cartwright lay on her back on the floor wearing a ratty old chenille bathrobe that had been washed so many times it was nearly white rather than pink, except for the dirt that clung to the robe, dirt everywhere, even on her feet, which were bare, her toenails painted a bright, happy red. Becca eased closer. It was real, it was horrifyingly real, in front of her, and the woman was dead. "Oh, God, no, no."

She watched Savich bend down to unpin a note that was fastened to the front of Linda Cartwright's bathrobe. "Don't let Becca come in here," he said to Sherlock, not looking up as he read the note. "This is too much. Make sure she stays outside."

"I'm already here," Becca said, swallowing again and again against the nausea in her stomach, the vomit rising in her throat. "What is that note?"

"Becca—"

It was Adam and he was turning toward her. She put up her hands. "What is that note?" she asked again. "Read it, please."

Savich paused, then read slowly, his voice firm and clear:

*Hey, Rebecca, you can call her Gleason. Since she didn't look like a dog, I had to smash her up a bit. Now she does. A dead dog. You killed her. You and no one else. Give her a good wake. This is all for you, Rebecca. I'll see you soon and it'll be you and me, from then to eternity.*

*Your Boyfriend*

"He wrote it in black ink, a ballpoint," Savich said, his voice flat, emotionless, as he carefully eased the paper into a plastic bag he pulled out of his pants pocket and closed the zipper. "It's a plain sheet of paper torn out of a notebook. Nothing at all unique about it."

"Do you think he's out of control?" Sherlock said to no one in particular. Her face was pale, the horror clear in her eyes.

"No," Adam said. "I don't think so. I think he's really enjoying himself. I think at last he's discovering who he really is and what he really likes. I can practically hear him thinking, 'I want to scare Rebecca really good, prove to her I'm so bad that when I call her again I won't hear any more cockiness from her. No, I'll hear fear in her voice, helplessness. Now, what can I do to make this happen?'" Adam paused a moment, then said, "And so he decided to kill Linda Cartwright and make her into his fictional dog."

"Yeah," Tommy said, "I think Adam is right. There's nothing but control here. Too much of it."

"I need to make some calls," Savich said, but he didn't move, stared down at the note and at what had been Linda Cartwright.

There was silence in the small, bright kitchen and the harsh breathing of six men and two women, one of them drawing hard on a pipe that wasn't lit. Then Becca broke free, ran out the back door, and fell to her knees, vomiting until her body was jerking and heaving and there was nothing more in her belly. Still she crouched there, holding her arms around herself, shuddering, wanting to die because she'd brought death to Linda Cartwright, as she had to that poor old woman standing outside the Metropolitan Museum, as she'd nearly brought death to the governor of New York. She felt him coming up behind her, knew it was Adam.

"Her face—he obliterated her face, Adam, for a sick joke that only he thought was funny. He murdered her and smashed her face so—"

"I know." Adam fell to his knees behind her, pulling her back against his chest. "I know."

She felt him begin to rock her, back and forth. "I know, Becca."

"I'm responsible for her, Adam. If I hadn't shot him, if I hadn't—"

Adam pulled her around to face him. He handed her a handkerchief, waited for her to wipe her mouth, then said, "Now, you will listen up. If you feel any guilt about that poor woman, I'm going to deck you. None of this is your fault. He's the evil one. This guy will do anything to terrorize you, to hear you whimper, beg, plead with him to stop. Anything."

"He's succeeded."

"Yeah, you've got to stop that as well. You can't let him crawl under your skin. That means he wins. That means he's got the control, he's got the power. Do you understand me?"

She pulled away from him and began kneading his arms with her hands, not even realizing what she was doing. "It's hard, Adam. I know he's evil. I know there must be a reason he's doing all this, a reason that makes perfect sense to him, but in my gut, it feels like I smashed in that poor woman's face. If only I hadn't fired at him, hit him—"

"Stop it," he said and shook her good. "Now, here's the bottom line. We're going to leave her as she is in the kitchen and make an anonymous call. No, don't argue." He lightly tapped his fingers against her mouth. "Listen, I know this is very hard to do, given the fact we're breaking the law and she's not going to get the attention she deserves right away. Even Savich and Sherlock are having a real problem with it.

"Even though they're part of the highest police force in the land, they realize that nothing good would be served if the world suddenly found out that you're here and you're up to your ears in another murder. The cops and the Feds would fight to see who could hold you and question you. On the other hand, you'd be protected, and that's something, but not enough. All of us agree that you would be charged with murder and accessory to murder. It would be a nightmare and it would continue even if they ever let you go. Why? Because he would still be there, waiting, and it would start all over.

"So, Savich and Sherlock have agreed to keep our connection under wraps for a while. He's getting the woman's phone records right now. We'll find out how long he's been here, holding her prisoner. We'll find out who he called besides you. All the guys are going over the house, top to bottom, right now. They're pros. If there's anything to find, they'll find it. If there are fingerprints, and I'm willing to bet there are, they'll pull those up, too. But it's going to take time because we'll have to clean up after ourselves. The last thing we want is to have the police notice some stray fingerprint powder. So we can't call in her murder for another couple of hours."

"He knew the phone was tapped."

"Oh, yes, he knew, and that's why he had the surprise all ready for you. He can't be far away now. He's close. Real close. It's possible he's watching all of us right this instant, hiding in the pine trees, but I don't think even he is that reckless. We'll get him, Becca. You have to believe that. He'll pay for what he did to Linda Cartwright."

She said suddenly, "You're right, Adam, he is watching. Maybe he's a goodly distance away and using binoculars, but I don't think so. I'll bet he's over there, somewhere in those trees, and I think he watched you climb through that window, watched me come out here and puke up my guts. You said he was finally realizing who he is, what he likes, and this is it."

Her eyes went blank, then she said, "He's seen Tyler and Sam. He knows I'm close to them and doesn't that make them targets, too? What if he goes after them?"

"He could, but I doubt it and here's why. He knows we're not fools. He knows there are a lot of us. He wants you. He's made his point. I can't see him veering off course to kill Tyler or Sam. Why? He wants to nail me, but I'm with you, staying with you, taunting him. That's why he wants me. Now, Dave and Chuck will start looking around here when they finish in the house."

"He'll be gone by then."

"Probably."

"Do you think he killed her in those short minutes between when he called me and all the men got here?"

Adam hesitated, then shook his head. "No, she'd been dead for several hours, at least."

"But her face, Adam, her face. It looked—fresh, even though all the blood looked dried and clotted."

"He did that after he called you, after he realized the phone was tapped. She was already dead, Becca."

"How did he kill her?"

Adam didn't want to say anything more about it, but he knew she wasn't going to let it go, she couldn't let it go. "He strangled her."

"Why was there dirt all over her? It was even on her feet, in her hair."

He didn't want to say it but there was no choice. "There was dirt on her because he dug her up to smash her face." There, it was said, and he thought she was going to vomit again. She closed her eyes, her arms fell to her sides, and her head dropped forward against his chest. But she didn't vomit, she cried, making no sound at all, just cried, her hands fists against his Kevlar vest.

He squeezed her hard. "I swear I'll get him, I swear it."

She said nothing for a very long time. His knees were starting to hurt when she finally whispered against his neck, "Not if I can get him first." She shuddered, then he felt her stiffen and slowly, slowly pull back from him. She said, "He was through with her, probably planning on leaving here, and so he killed her and buried her and then decided it would be fun to play this big joke on me."

"Yeah, that's about the size of it."

"He's still here, Adam. He's close. I can feel him. It's like something very black and heavy crawling over my skin."

He said nothing.

"But why? I don't understand why he picked me. Why is he doing this to me?"

Again, Adam said nothing, but he thought, *If Krimakov is really dead, then there isn't a motive, and I don't have the foggiest idea, either, why he picked you.*

BECCA couldn't get Linda Cartwright out of her mind. She kept picturing her, lying there, her face smashed, and no one to take care of her for hour upon hour.

Sherlock handed her a cup of coffee, steam rising from the mug like cigarette smoke. "You only slept a couple of hours, Becca. Here, drink this."

"None of us slept for more than a couple of hours," Becca said. "Where are Adam and Savich?"

"Adam is out talking to Dave and Chuck. They took over outside patrol. He's going to get some other people here, some of his own people, to free up these guys."

"Maybe Hatch is coming." At Sherlock's raised eyebrow, Becca added, "I heard Adam talking to him on the phone. Yeah, I was eavesdropping, so Adam had to tell me. He said Hatch speaks six languages, has lots of contacts, is really smart, and smokes. Adam is always trying to get him to stop smoking by threatening to fire him."

Sherlock laughed and lifted her mug to toast Becca's. "I want to meet this guy. If he dares to light up a cigarette, Savich won't threaten to fire him, he'll take his head off."

"So Adam doesn't work for Thomas?"

"No, not now. They've been friends for a very long time. Adam is sort of like a son to Thomas. No, I won't tell you any more about him."

Becca didn't say anything.

"Listen, Becca, it doesn't matter. Right now, my husband is concerned that the local cops won't be able to do a thing about Linda Cartwright because they're going in completely blind. But we agreed this is the way we'll play it for a while. The cops have been there for a while now, Becca. They're taking care of her. But they won't be able to figure anything out because we're holding back. That really sticks in everyone's craw, probably always will."

"Sherlock, do you know who Krimakov is?"

Sherlock couldn't help it, her eyes gave her away before she could pull down the automatic blinders, and she wanted to kick herself. She shrugged. "Yes, I know. But it would have to be his ghost who killed Linda Cartwright. Evidently, Thomas got information that he was killed in an auto accident a short time ago in Crete, where he supposedly lived. So it's all academic. If he's dead, then he can't have anything to do with this."

"And Thomas has double-checked that this guy is really dead?"

"I would assume so."

"If this Krimakov were alive, and he were behind this terror, why would he be doing it to me in particular? He's what—Russian? What could he possibly have against me? Why would Thomas think it was him?"

"I don't know," Sherlock said, lying cleanly now because she'd had time to slip her mask into place.

"Who is Thomas, Sherlock? Please, you've got to tell me."

"Forget him, Becca," she said over her shoulder. "Drop it. Give it time. Now, I want some more coffee. Can I make you some toast or something?"

"No, nothing." *Who was this Thomas person? Why all the secrecy?* It made no sense to her. She looked over at the single telephone. It was nearly nine o'clock on Thursday morning. Nothing from him. Maybe he was scared now, maybe he knew they were getting close, maybe he would go away. Still, she sat there staring at that black phone like it was a snake about to bite her.

The last person any of them wanted to see arrived midmorning.

"The door looks good," Sheriff Gaffney said when Becca opened it. "What with all this mess, I didn't think you'd worry so much about how your front door looked."

Becca said, "You never know, do you, Sheriff? Would you like to come in? Is there any news about who the skeleton is?"

"Yeah, I'd like to talk to you a moment, Ms. Powell. I believe now that the skeleton that fell out of your basement wall is Melissa Katzen." He rubbed his forehead. "I didn't think old Jacob was that vicious. Bashing a young girl in the face—now that isn't right."

"Sheriff," Adam said, coming up behind Becca, "I was thinking about that. You said she was supposed to elope. Any leads on her boyfriend?"

"Nope, nobody remembers her ever dating. Isn't that weird? Why would she keep it secret? That doesn't make any sense to me or to my wife, Maude. She thinks that a young girl would be really proud to show off a boyfriend."

"Maybe the boyfriend didn't want her to show him off," Becca said. "Maybe he told her to keep quiet."

"But why?"

"I don't know, Sheriff. I wish I did."

"Rachel Ryan remembers her, said she was really nice, nothing new there. She also said that Melissa didn't ever dress in sexy clothes. She was surprised when I told her about the Calvin Klein jeans and that skimpy pink top. She couldn't remember Melissa ever wearing anything suggestive. Maybe you're right, Ms. Powell. Maybe it was her boyfriend. But you know? I can see a cute young girl waltzing over into Jacob Marley's yard, him seeing her and getting all het up. Did he smash her?"

Becca said, "Maybe she was off to meet her boyfriend and coming into Jacob Marley's yard was a shortcut."

"Ain't no shortcut to anywhere," said Sheriff Gaffney. "The back of the Marley property trails off into thick woods and finally stops at the ocean."

"Maybe," Sherlock said, "the jeans and top were her cute traveling clothes. Maybe she did intend to elope, maybe she decided at the last minute that she didn't want to and this boy got mad and killed her."

Sheriff Gaffney said slowly, "Who are you?"

"Oh, sorry, Sheriff," Adam said. "Sherlock and Savich here are friends of mine. They stopped in for a while to visit the town."

"Nice to meet you, ma'am. Now, that's not a bad idea. I guess I'd have to say that for a woman you deduced that real logically, probably better than most other women."

Savich, who heard that, wondered if Sherlock was going to take a flying leap at the sheriff's throat.

"Yeah," Sherlock said thoughtfully, "I'm a lot better than poor Becca here, who can barely find her way to the Food Fort without some guy explaining the poisonous plant streets to her."

"That was sarcasm," Sheriff Gaffney said after a moment. "I know that was sarcasm. I've never believed women should have smart mouths."

Before Sherlock could leap on the sheriff, Adam said, "Are there DNA tests being done?"

The sheriff shook his head. "Still trying to track down her father. No luck yet. Mrs. Ella remembers an aunt, lives in Bangor now. Maybe she read about the skeleton and was the one who made the anonymous call. I've got to track her down." Sheriff Gaffney sighed and patted the gun at his wide leather belt that was really cutting into his gut today. "But we can't count on the skeleton being Melissa, even though I've made up my mind that it is, so we're looking into other things as well." Sheriff Gaffney leaned his considerable weight back on his heels. "Now, folks, the reason I'm here is to ask about these guys I've seen on and off around Riptide. No, don't lie to me. I know they're with you, Mr. Savich. Would you like to tell me what's going on?"

At that moment, the phone in the living room rang.

Tinny, sharp, and too loud, and Becca dropped her coffee cup.

"Becca didn't get much sleep last night," Adam said easily, and picked up the phone. "Hello?"

"Hello, moron. You found my present?"

"Why, yes, I did. Where are you now?"

"I want to speak to Rebecca."

"Sorry, she's not here. It's just me. What do you want?"

The phone went dead.

"It was a salesman," Adam said, all smooth and easy. "The guy wanted to sell Becca some venetian blinds." He shrugged. "What was it you wanted to know, Sheriff?"

The sheriff had not taken his eyes off Savich. "Those guys around town. Who are they, Mr. Savich?"

"You found me out, Sheriff," Savich said. "Actually, my wife and I are here because we're representing a big resort developer who is seriously interested in this section of the Maine coast. It's true Adam is a friend of ours and he, well, he gives us some cover. Now, the guys you're seeing around are supposed to be very discreet, which means you've got a very sharp eye, Sheriff. They're doing all sorts of things, like talking to folk, surveying, checking out soil and other flora and fauna, seeing who owns what and how profitable the businesses are now. This is a lovely section of coastline and Riptide is a real neat little town. A resort not too far away—can you imagine what would happen to your local economy? In any case, we won't be here for much longer, but I would ask you a favor. Could you please keep this under your hat?" Savich said immediately to Sherlock, "I told you the sheriff was too sharp not to catch on to us, honey. I told you he was real smart and he knew everything that went on in his town."

"Yes, Dillon," Sherlock said, "you told me that. I'm sorry I didn't see him as clearly as you did. Yeah, he's pretty smart, all right." She gave the sheriff a brilliant smile.

"So, you want me to keep my mouth shut about this, Mr. Savich?"

"Yes, sir."

"Well, all right, but if any of them cause any trouble, I'll be back. This resort of yours—it wouldn't go spoiling any of the natural beauty around here, would it?"

"No way," Savich said. "That's the prime goal of the group I work with."

Becca eyed Savich after she let the sheriff out the front door, which smelled, he said on his way out, really nice and clean. "You're something, Dillon. I really believed you there for a minute. Goodness, I wanted to ask you the name of the planned resort."

Savich said, "The phone call gave me time to come up with a decent story."

"It was him, wasn't it?" Becca said as she turned to Adam, who was still standing by the phone.

"Yes, it was him. He wanted to speak to you but I told him you weren't here. He always calls you Rebecca, not Becca?" At her nod, Adam said, "He was calling from a public phone booth in Rockland. Again, no cell phone. I wonder why he doesn't seem to use one. Tommy the Pipe tracked it down, so there's nothing we can do."

Sherlock said slowly, studying a bruised knuckle she'd gotten when she'd clipped Tyler McBride's jaw, "We've got to get him back. We've got to set up a meeting somehow."

"Next time I'll speak to him," Becca said. "I'll set one up."

"You won't be bait," Adam said, his voice sharp as a knife. "No way."

"Look, Adam, he wants me. If you made yourself the bait, he'd just shoot you and walk away. But not so with me. He wants me up close and personal. Only me. Help me figure out a way to do this, please."

"I don't like it."

# EIGHTEEN

Hatch, short, built like a young bull, sporting a large mustache, pulled off a tweed Sherlock Holmes hat to show his shaved head. For some reason she couldn't quite fathom, Becca thought he was so impishly cute she wanted to hug him. She thought from the cocky grin on Sherlock's face that she wanted to hug him right along with her.

This guy was potent. He had more charm than a person deserved, she was thinking a few minutes later when Adam held out his hand and said to him, "Give me the pack of cigarettes in your right pocket, Hatch, now, or you're fired."

"Yeah, sure, boss." Hatch obligingly handed Adam a nearly full pack of Marlboros. "Only one, boss, no more, and I didn't inhale much. All I had, just one. I don't want to smoke anywhere near sweet Becca. I wouldn't want to ever take a chance of hurting her lovely lungs. Now, tell me what to do to catch this creep so Becca can go back to writing speeches and smiling a lot." Then he turned those dark brown twinkling eyes on her and said, "Hi."

Becca grinned and pumped his hand. "Hi, Hatch. Listen, I'm ready. The next time he calls—I'm ready. We're going to set a trap for him. I'm going to be the bait."

"Hmmm. I don't think the boss likes that. His jaw is all knotted up."

Adam unknotted his jaw. "No, I don't like it. It's crazy. I don't want her to take this kind of risk. Ah, I can tell by the look on your face, Becca, that you're going to do it regardless of what I think."

"Look, Adam," Savich said, "if I could think of another way, I'd dive on it, but there are enough of us to keep her protected. Now, Hatch, according to Adam, you have a pretty awesome reputation to maintain. Tell us what you've found out."

Hatch took a slim black book out of his jacket pocket, licked his fingers, and ruffled some pages. "Most of this is from Thomas's guys, who've been working their butts off trying to verify Krimakov's death. Now, the CIA has actually spoken to the cop who was the one who poked around his body. Apollo—that's his name—said Krimakov went over a cliff on the eastern end of Crete, near Agios Nikolaos, died instantly, one would suppose from the injuries. It could have been murder, he allowed, but nobody checked into it all that much for the simple fact that no one really cares. Nothing obvious about it, so they closed the case until our agents flew in and spread out and wanted to see and examine everything."

"So he's really dead," Becca said.

Hatch looked up and gave a mournful shake of the head. "Not necessarily. Here's the kicker. Krimakov's body was cremated. You see, for the longest time, our people were stonewalled by the locals, who wouldn't allow them to view the body. It was only after the Greek government got involved that they let it out of the bag that they'd cremated him right away. Why? I don't know, but there was a payoff, somewhere."

No one said a word for a very long time.

"Cremated?" Adam repeated, disbelieving.

"Yes, burned to ashes, poured in an urn. Thing's still sitting on a shelf in the morgue."

Sherlock said, "So there is no definitive proof because there's no body to examine."

"Right," Hatch said. "Now, while we all chew on that, let's go back a bit. Krimakov moved to Crete in the mid-eighties. He showed up and stayed. He was into bad things, but not bad enough so anyone would dig and find out exactly who and what he'd been in Russia. Actually, the impression is they never tried really hard to do any nailing. He probably paid everyone off."

Adam said, "Okay. Now we've got to search his house, top to bottom and under the basement. If he ever was involved in this, there will be something there."

"Our agents have gone over his house, didn't find anything. No clues, no leads, no references at all to Becca. We heard he had an apartment somewhere, but we don't know where it is. That might take a little time. There aren't any official records."

Savich said, "If he had an apartment, I'll find it."

"Just you?" Adam said, an eyebrow raised.

"Didn't Thomas tell you I was good?"

Adam snorted, watching Savich plug in MAX.

Hatch said, "More will be coming about his personal activities. But as yet, there isn't anything out of Russia. It seems that way back when, all Krimakov's records were purged. There's little left. Nothing of interest. The KGB probably ordered it done, then helped him go to ground, in Crete. Again, though, they'll continue searching and probing and questioning all their counterparts in Moscow."

"Krimakov isn't dead," Adam said. And he believed it like he'd never believed anything in his life.

Having said that, Adam sat back and closed his eyes. He was getting a headache.

"Well, yeah, we have something else. I was the one who did all the legwork on this." Hatch licked his fingers again and flipped over a couple more pages. "The Albany cops found a witness not two hours ago who identified the car that ran down Dick McCallum. It's a BMW, black, license number—at least the first three numbers—three-eight-five. A New York plate. I don't have anything on that yet."

"I'll have it run through," Savich said. "It'll be quicker, more complete. I don't want to know how you got that information so quickly."

"She loves my mustache," Hatch said. "Please do call the Bureau, Agent Savich. I didn't have the chance to check back with Thomas and have him do it. Oh yeah, a guy was driving. No clue if it was an old guy or a young guy or in between, really dark windows, like windows on a limo. Fairly unusual for a private car, and that's probably why he stole that particular car."

Savich was on his cell phone in the next ten seconds, nodded and hung up in three more minutes. "Done. We'll have a list of possibles in about five minutes."

Tommy the Pipe knocked lightly on the front door and came in. "We got a guy buying Exxon supreme at a gas station eight miles west of Riptide. The attendant, a young boy about eighteen, said when the guy paid for his gas, he saw dirt and blood on the cuff of his shirt. He wouldn't have thought a thing about it except Rollo was canvassing all the gas stations, asking questions about strangers. It's him."

"Oh, yeah." Adam jumped to his feet. "Please say it, Tommy. Please tell us this kid remembers what the guy looks like, that he remembers the kind of car he was driving."

"The guy had on a green hunting hat with flaps, something like mine but with no style. He also wore very dark glasses. He doesn't know if the guy was young or old, sorry, Adam. Anyone over twenty-five would be old to that kid. But he does remember clearly that the guy spoke well, a real educated voice, all smooth and deep. The car—he thought it was a BMW, dark blue or black. Sorry, no idea about the plate. But you know what? The windows were dark-tinted. How about that?"

"Surely he wouldn't have driven the same car up here that he used to kill Dick McCallum in Albany," Sherlock said.

"Why not?" Savich said. "If it isn't dented, if there isn't blood all over it, then why not?"

Savich's cell phone rang. He stood and walked over to the doorway. They heard him talking, saw him nodding as he listened. He hung up and said, "No go. He stole the license plates. No surprise there. He'd have been an idiot to leave on the original plates. However, those heavily tinted windows, I have everyone checking on New York cars stolen within the past two weeks with those sorts of windows."

Savich's cell phone rang again in eight minutes. He listened and wrote rapidly. When he hung up the phone, he said, "This is something. Like Hatch said, few private cars—domestic or foreign—are built with dark-tinted windows. Three have been stolen. The people are all over the state, two men and one woman."

Becca said with no hesitation, "It's the woman. He stole her car."

Sherlock said. "Let's find out right now."

She called information for Ithaca, New York, and got the phone number for Mrs. Irene Bailey, 112 Huntley Avenue. The phone rang once, twice, three times, then, "Hello?"

"Mrs. Bailey? Mrs. Irene Bailey?"

Silence.

"Are you there? Mrs. Bailey?"

"That's my mother," a woman said. "I'm sorry, but it took me by surprise."

"May I please speak to your mother?"

"You don't know? No, I guess not. My mother was killed two weeks ago."

Sherlock didn't drop the phone, but she felt a great roiling pain through her stomach, up to her throat, and she swallowed convulsively. "Can you give me any details, please?"

"Who are you?"

"I'm Gladys Martin with the Social Security Administration in Washington."

"I know my husband called Social Security. What do you want?"

"We're required to fill out papers, ma'am. Are you her daughter?"

"Yes, I am. What kind of papers?"

"Statistics, nothing more. Is there someone else I can speak to about this? I don't want to upset you."

There was a moment of silence, then, "No, it's all right. Ask the questions. We don't want the government to go away mad."

"Thank you, ma'am. You said your mother was killed? Was this an auto accident?"

"No, someone hit her on the head when she was getting out to her car at the shopping mall. He stole her car."

"Oh, dear, I'm so very sorry. Please tell me that the man who did this has been caught?"

The woman's voice hardened up immediately. "No, he wasn't. The cops put out a description of her car, but no one has reported back with anything as yet. They think he painted the car a different color and changed the license plates. He's gone. Even the New York City cops don't know where he is. She was an old woman, too, so who cares?" The bitterness in the daughter's voice was bone-deep, her pain, disbelief, anger still raw.

"Was there anything distinctive about the car the man stole?"

"Yes, the windows were tinted dark because my mother had very sensitive eyes. Too much sunlight really hurt her."

"I see. What was the color of the car?"

"White with gray interior. There was a small dent above the left rear tire."

"I see. Did you say that there were other than the local cops there?"

"Oh, yes. Of all things, they were from New York City. They should have caught this guy. We don't know why the New York City police are involved. Do you? Is that really why you're calling? You want to pump me for information?"

"No, of course not. This is simply statistical information that we need."

"Are there any more questions, Ms. Martin? I'm sorting through my mother's things and I have to be down at St. Paul's charities in a half hour."

"No, ma'am. I'm very sorry for your loss. I'll take care of everything here." Sherlock turned to see all eyes focused on her. "The killer painted a white car black and stole another license plate. The New York City cops were there. They know. Oh, yeah, the windows are tinted dark because Mrs. Bailey had sensitive eyes."

"Son of a bitch," Hatch said and groped in his pocket for his cigarettes. "How come nobody told me that the cops knew about that car?"

Adam gave him a look and said, "They've got a real lid on that one. My guess is they're keeping it from the Feds, don't want to get aced out. And the victim loses. What the New York cops don't know is that our killer is here in Maine. Shall we tell them?"

Savich said, "Not the New York cops, but I can call Tellie Hawley, the SAC of the New York City office. He'll see it gets to where it needs to go."

"Yeah," Adam said, "why not? Anyone think of a good reason why not?"

"How specific should we be?" Becca asked. She was wringing her hands. Adam frowned.

Savich rolled it around in his brain. "Let's just tell him the guy's been seen on the coast. How's that? It's the truth."

"We've got to get him," Becca said. "If we don't, then we have to call this Thomas person who seems to know everyone and direct everything, and tell him to bring in the Marines."

"HE hasn't called," Becca said, and took a bite of her hot dog. "Why hasn't he called?"

Adam said as he chewed a potato chip, "I think he's going to lie low for a while. He's not stupid. He's going to dig in somewhere else, give you some time to chew your fingernails, then jump back into the game—his game."

They were all eating hot dogs, except Savich, with relish and mustard, the team of guys outside coming in one at a time. Special Agent Rollo Dempsey said to Adam, "I knew your name but I couldn't remember where I'd heard it. Now I do. You saved Senator Dashworth's life last year when that crazy tried to stick a knife in his ribs."

Adam didn't say a word.

"Yeah, it was you. You saved Senator Dashworth's life. Pretty impressive."

"You shouldn't know about that," Adam said finally, frowning at Rollo. "You really shouldn't."

"Yeah, well, I'm an insider, I can't help it if people tell me everything."

"I never heard anything about that," Becca said, her antennae up. "What are you talking about?"

Rollo grinned at her and said, "Did you find out who tried to off him?"

"You don't know about that, too?"

"Hey, I'm an insider, but the spigot was off when it came to the particulars."

Adam shrugged. "Well, who cares now? The guy who wanted the senator dead was his son-in-law. Irving—that's the guy's name—had sent him threats, all the usual anonymous stuff. The senator called me. It turned out Irving had become a heroin addict, didn't have any more money, and wanted the senator's inheritance. The senator managed to keep it from the media, to protect his daughter, and so we got the guy into a sanatorium, where he belonged, where he's still at."

"You run some sort of a bodyguard business?" Becca said, frowning at Adam over a spoonful of baked beans. "I thought you did security consulting."

"I like to keep my hand in a lot of different things," Adam said.

"What I'd like to know," Sherlock said, handing Rollo another hot dog with lots of down-home yellow mustard slathered on it, "is why you didn't find out who it was right away. The guy was an addict? That kind of thing isn't easy to hide."

Adam actually flushed. He played with his fork, didn't meet her eyes. He cleared his throat. "Well, the thing is that the son-in-law wasn't around for those three days I was checking things out. His wife was protecting him, said he had the flu, that he was really contagious, et cetera. She swore to me and to her father that Irving wouldn't even consider doing something like that, no, it had to be a crazy, or a left-wing conspiracy. She was so—well—believable."

"Good thing you were there to deflect the guy's knife," Rollo said.

"That's the truth," Adam said.

Rollo sat down at the kitchen table, squeezing in between Savich and

Becca. Adam said on a deep sigh, "I heard that the wife is trying to get the husband out of there. It could start all over again."

Rollo said, "Not much justice around, is there?"

Then Chuck came in and Rollo, still half a hot dog left, saluted and went back outside.

"It won't be long now," Savich said. "I feel it. Things will happen." He took a last bite of a tofu hot dog, sighed with pleasure, and hugged his wife.

THINGS didn't happen until later.

They were all in the living room drinking coffee and tea, planning, arguing, brainstorming. There was no activity outside. Everything was buttoned down tight, until at exactly ten o'clock a bullet shattered one of the front windows, glass exploded inward, carrying shreds of curtain with it.

"Down!" Savich yelled.

But it wasn't a simple bullet that came through the window to strike the floor molding on the far side of the living room, it was a tear gas bullet. Thick gray smoke gushed out even before it struck the molding.

Adam yelled, "Back into the kitchen. Now!"

Another tear gas bullet exploded through the window. They were coughing, covering their faces, running toward the back of the house.

They heard men's shouts, sporadic gunfire, sharp and loud in the night. The front door burst open and Tommy the Pipe ran in, his face covered with his jacket. "Out, guys, quick. Through the front door, the back's not covered well enough."

"He shot tear gas bullets," Adam said between choking coughs.

"He's probably using a CAR-15, behind our perimeter. Come on out."

They coughed their heads off, tears streaming down their faces. Savich found himself with Becca's nose pressed into his armpit.

"We've got to get him," Adam shouted, coughing, choking, his eyes streaming tears. "Just another minute to get over this and we'll start scouring."

It took another seven minutes before they headed out in the general direction of where the tear gas bullets must have been shot toward the front windows.

They found tire tracks, nothing else, until Adam called out, "Look here."

Everyone gathered around Adam, who was on his haunches. He held up a shell casing that was four inches long and about an inch and a half in diameter. "Tommy the Pipe was right. He used a CAR-15—that's a compact M16," he added to Becca, "stands for carbine automatic rifle."

Savich found the other shell casing and was tossing it back and forth.

"But how can tear gas come from a gun?" Becca said. "I thought they were canisters or something like that. That's what I've always seen in movies and on TV."

"That's real old-hat now," Adam said. "This smaller M16 is real portable, you could carry it under your trench coat. It's got this telescoping collapsible barrel. The SEALs use this stuff. What you do is simply mount an under-barrel tubular grenade launcher and fire away with your tear gas projectiles. It's wicked."

Sherlock said, "He's obviously connected and very well trained. Got all the latest goodies. And where would he get all this stuff?"

And Adam thought: *Krimakov*.

No one said anything.

They got back to the house forty-five minutes later. It was late, and everyone was hyped. Adam said, as he shrugged into his jacket, rechecked his pistol, "I'm going to take one of the first watches."

"Get me up at three o'clock," Savich said.

"I'm outta here," Adam said. He looked over at Becca, saw that she was white-faced and couldn't help himself. He walked to her and pulled her tight against him. He said against her hair, "Sleep well and don't worry. We're going to get him."

Becca didn't think she'd be able to slow her heart down enough even to consider sleeping, but she did, deeply and dreamlessly, until she felt a strange jab in her left arm, above her elbow, like a mosquito bite. She jerked awake, her heart pounding wildly, and she couldn't breathe, just pant and jerk. She was blind, no, it was dark, very dark, the blinds drawn because nobody wanted him to be able to see into the house. She saw a shadowy figure standing over her, gray, indistinct, and she whispered, "What is this? Is it you, Adam? What did you do—?" But he said nothing, merely leaned closer and finally, when her heart was slowing a bit, he whispered right against her face, "I came for you, Rebecca, like I said I would," and he licked her cheek.

"No," she said. "No." Then she fell back, wondering what the silver

light was shining over her face. It seemed to arc toward her, a skinny silver flash, but then it wasn't important. A small flashlight, she thought as
she breathed in very deeply, more deeply than usual for her, and eased
into a soft warm blackness that relaxed her mind and body, and she
didn't know anything more.

# NINETEEN

Her heart beat slow, regular strokes, one after the other, easy, steady, no fright registering in her body. She felt calm, relaxed. She opened her eyes. It was black, no shadows, no hint of movement, just relentless, motionless black. She was swamped with the black, but she forced herself to draw in a deep breath. Her heart wasn't pumping out of her chest now. She still felt relaxed, too relaxed, with no fear grinding through her, at least not yet, but she knew she should be afraid. She was in darkness and he was close by. She knew it, but still she breathed steadily, evenly, waiting, but not afraid. Well, perhaps there was a tincture of fear, indistinct, nibbling at the edges of her mind. She frowned, and it slipped away.

Odd how she remembered perfectly everything that had happened: the jab in her left arm, the instant terror, she remembered all of it—him licking her cheek—with no mental fuzz cloaking the memories.

The nibblings of fear became more focused now, she could nearly grasp it. Her heart speeded up. She blinked, willing herself to know fear, then to control it.

He had gotten her. Somehow he'd gotten into the house, past the guards, and he'd gotten her.

There was suddenly a wispy light, the smell of smoke. He'd lit a candle. He was here, inches from her. She calmed the building fear. It was hard, probably the hardest thing she'd ever had to do, but she knew she had to. She remembered, very suddenly, her mother telling her once that fear was what hurt you because it froze you. "Don't ever give up," her mother had told her. "Never give up." Then her mother had gripped her shoulders and said it one more time: "Never give up."

It was so clear in her mind in that moment, her mother standing over her telling her this. She could even feel her mother's fingers hard on her shoulders. Odd that she couldn't remember what had happened to make her mother tell her this.

"Where are we?"

Was that her voice, all calm and indifferent? Yes, she'd managed it.

"Hello, Rebecca. I came for you, like I said I would."

She laughed, choked, "Please don't lick my cheek again. That was really creepy."

He was dead silent, affronted, she realized, because she was laughing at him.

"You gave me a shot of something. What was it?"

She heard his deep breathing. "Something I picked up in Turkey. I was told that a side effect is a temporary sense of euphoria. You won't feel like laughing for much longer, Rebecca. The effects will fade, and then you'll be heaving with fear, you'll be so scared of me."

"Yeah, yeah, yeah."

He slapped her. She didn't see his hand, it was suddenly there, connecting sharply against her cheek. She tried to leap at him, but she realized she was tied down, her hands over her head, her wrists tied to the slats of the headboard. So she was lying on a bed. Her legs were free. She was still wearing her nightgown, a white cotton nightgown that came up to her chin and went down to her ankles. He'd smoothed it over her legs.

She said with a sneer in her voice, "Hey, I liked the slap better than you licking me. You're really brave, aren't you? Would you like to let my hands free, just for a minute, and then we'll see how brave you are?"

"Shut up!"

He was standing beside her, leaning down, breathing hard. She couldn't see his hands, but she imagined they were fists, ready to bash her.

She said very quietly, "Why did you kill Linda Cartwright?"

"That bitch? She was bothering me, always begging, pleading, whining when she was thirsty or she wanted to pee or she wanted to lie down. I got tired of it."

She said nothing at all, beyond words, wondering what had made him into a madman or had he been born like this? Born evil, nothing to blame but—what?

She could hear him tapping his fingers, *tap, tap, tap*. He wanted her to say something, wanted it badly, but she held quiet.

"Did you like my present to you, Rebecca?"

"No."

"I saw you puking your guts out."

"I thought you probably did. You're sick. You really get off on that?"

"Then I saw that big guy, Adam Carruthers, there with you. He was holding you. Why did you let him hold you like that?"

"I probably would have even leaned against you if I didn't know who you were."

"I'm glad you didn't let him kiss you."

"I had just vomited. That wouldn't be fun for anyone, now would it?"

"No, I guess not."

He didn't sound old, not the age of this Krimakov character. But was he young? She couldn't tell. "Who are you? Are you Krimakov?"

He was silent but only for a moment. Then he laughed softly, deeply, and it froze her. He lightly ran his palm over her cheek, squeezed a bit, made her flinch. "I'm your boyfriend, Rebecca. I saw you and I knew that I would have to be closer to you than your skin. I thought about actually getting under your skin, but that would mean I'd have to skin you and then cover myself, and you're not big enough.

"Then I thought I wanted to be next to your heart, but again, there'd be so much blood, fountains of it. Too many hands ruin the stew, too much blood ruins the clothes. I'm a fastidious man.

"No, don't say it or think it. I'm not crazy, not like that Hannibal character. I said that to make you so afraid you'd start begging and pleading. Already the drug's wearing off. I can see how afraid you are. All I have to do is talk and you're scared shitless."

He was right about that, but she'd give about anything not to show him, not to let him see that she was boiling white hot inside, nearly burned to ashes with fear. "But then when you're all done talking, you'll strangle me like you did Linda Cartwright?"

"Oh no. She wasn't important. She wasn't anything."

"I'll bet she disagreed with that."

"Probably, but who cares?"

"Why me?"

He laughed, and she bet that if she could see his face, he'd be smirking, so pleased with himself. "Not yet, Rebecca. You and I have got lots of things to do before you know who I am and why I chose you."

"There's a reason, naturally, at least in your mind. Why won't you tell me?"

"You'll find out soon enough, or not. We'll see. Now, I'm going to give you another little shot and you'll sleep again."

"No," she said. "I have to go to the bathroom. Let me go to the bathroom."

He cursed—American curses mixed with English-sounding curses, and an odd language thrown in she didn't recognize.

"You try anything and I'll knock you silly. I'll strip the skin off your arm and make it into a pair of gloves. You hear me?"

"Yes, I hear you. I thought you were fastidious."

"I am, about blood. There wouldn't be all those fountains of blood if I just peeled the skin off your arm."

She felt him untie her hands, slowly, and she supposed that the knots must have been complicated. Finally she was free. She brought her arms down and rubbed her wrists. They burned, then eased. She was very stiff. Slowly, she sat up and swung her legs off the bed.

"You try anything and I'll put a knife into your leg, high up on your thigh. I know just the place that won't show much, but the pain will make you wish you were dead it's so bad. There wouldn't be hardly any blood at all. Yeah, forget about skinning your arm. Don't try to see me, Rebecca, or I'll have to kill you right now, and that's the end of it."

She didn't know how she managed to walk, but she did. Then, as the strength came back to her feet and legs, she wanted to run, run so fast she'd be a blur and he'd never catch her, never, never.

But she didn't, of course.

The bathroom was off the bedroom. He'd removed the doorknob. When she was through, she paused to look at herself in the mirror. She looked pale and drawn and gaunt, her hair tangled around her head and down to her shoulders. She looked vague and on the edge, like a woman who had been drugged, knew it, and also realized, at last, that she might very well die.

"Come out now, Rebecca. I know you're through. Come out or you'll regret it."

"I just got here. Give me some time."

There was nothing in the bathroom to use as a weapon, nothing at all. He'd even removed the towel racks, cleared everything from beneath the sink. Nothing.

"Just a moment," she called out. She raced back to the toilet and fell onto her knees. It was old. If the big screw that held the toilet down had

ever had a cap on it, it was long gone. She tried to twist it, and to her utter surprise, it actually moved. It was thick, the grooves deep and sharp.
She was choking, sobbing deep in her throat, praying.

She heard him outside the door. Was he touching the door? Was he
going to push it inward? "Just a second," she yelled. "I'm not feeling too
well. That drug you shot into me, it's making me nauseous. Give me another minute. I don't want to vomit all over myself." *Turn, turn.* Finally,
finally, it came free in her hand. It was thick, about an inch and a half
long, deeply grooved, and those grooves were sharp. What to do with it?
Where to hide it?

"I'm coming," she called out as she gently pulled some thread loose
in the hem of her nightgown. "I feel a bit better. I don't want to vomit,
particularly if you're going to tie my hands again."

If he'd been standing by the bathroom door, he wasn't now. He was
back in the shadows when she came out. She couldn't make out a thing
about him. He said, his voice deep, ageless, "Lie back down on the bed."

She did.

He didn't tie her hands over her head.

"Don't move."

She felt the sting in her left arm, right above her elbow again, before
she could even react. "Coward," she said, her voice already becoming
slurred.

"Filthy coward."

She heard him laugh. And again, he licked her, her ear this time, his
tongue slow, lapping, and she wanted to gag, but she didn't because her
mind was beginning to float now, and it was easy and smooth and the
fear disappeared as she fell away from herself.

No time, she thought, as what she was and what she thought were
slipping away, like grains of sand scattering in a wind. No time, no time to
stab him with that screw. No time to ask him again if he was this Krimakov who'd been cremated. No time for anything.

ADAM stood there in her open bedroom doorway. She was gone, simply
gone. "No," he said, shaking his head. "No! Savich!"

But she was gone, no sign of her, nothing at all.

It was Sherlock who said as she sipped a cup of black coffee, "He used
the tear gas as a diversion. While we were all outside looking for him, he
simply slipped into the house and hid in Becca's bedroom closet. Then he

probably drugged her. How did he get her out? Our guys were back in position by the time we came back inside. Oh, no, get everyone together! We weren't exactly organized when we were looking for him outside. Dillon, who was assigned to the back of the house?"

They found Chuck Ainsley in the bushes twenty feet from the back of the house. He wasn't dead. He'd been struck down from behind, bound and gagged. When they peeled the tape off his mouth, he said, "I let him creep up on me. I didn't hear a thing. He was fast, too fast. What happened? Is everyone all right?"

Savich said matter-of-factly, "He took Becca. Thank God you're not dead. I wonder why he didn't slit your throat, Chuck? Why waste time tying you up?"

Sherlock said, as she hunkered down next to Chuck and untied both his wrists and ankles, "He doesn't want the police here yet. He realized that if he killed one of us, that's what would happen. It would force his hand. He would lose control. We're really glad you're okay, Chuck."

Adam said, "He must have knocked you out before he shot tear gas into the house. We came roaring out, everyone trying to find him, and we didn't miss you. There was too much confusion."

Sherlock gave Chuck a drink of cold water and a couple of aspirin once they got him into the kitchen. "If you don't have a headache, you should," she told him, then hugged him. "Thank goodness you're all right. Since you weren't at the back of the house watching for him, he must have slipped out with Becca over his shoulder."

"We didn't miss you," Adam said slowly. "I can't believe we didn't have the brains to get everyone together and count heads before we settled back into the house for the night. We didn't even think to search the house."

Everyone was rattled as what happened sank in. There was nothing to say, no excuses to make. He'd made fools of them all.

An hour later, Sherlock and Savich found Adam in the kitchen, his head in his hands. Savich lightly laid his hand on his shoulder. "It happened. We've all flagellated ourselves. No thanks to us, Chuck is all right. Now we've got to fix it. Adam, we'll find her."

"I was supposed to keep her safe," Adam said, staring at his clasped hands. "I've got to be the biggest screwup in the world. He's got her, Savich. He's got her and we have no idea where."

"Yes, he's got her," Savich said, "and he's probably going to take her to Washington. That's it, isn't it? He wants her with him when he confronts Thomas? She's his leverage. Thomas would do anything to save her, including giving himself up to this maniac."

"We're talking like Krimakov is alive, like we don't have any doubts about it at all," Sherlock said.

Adam said slowly, "Forget the reports, forget what the operatives said. The body was cremated. That's all I need to know. It's Krimakov. Now, he must not have found out where Thomas is. Thomas owns a house in Chevy Chase, but it's a well-kept secret. The location of his condo in Georgetown is also a secret, but anyone could discover its location if they really wanted to. MAX could probably ferret it out in ten minutes flat. But not the Chevy Chase house. He's very careful. I kid you not, I don't even think the president knows where his house is. So then Krimakov wouldn't know, either. That's why he got Becca. She's his leverage. He'll take her to Washington, to the condo." Adam stopped cold. "We've got to leave now."

Savich said, "I think you should call Thomas first, tell him what's happened. We've put it off long enough, don't you think? He's got to know."

Adam cursed under his breath at the sound of Tyler McBride's angry voice. Tyler came into the kitchen, three agents right behind him, one holding his arm, and yelled, "What is going on here? Every light in the place is on! Who are these guys? Let me go! Where's Becca?"

"Let him go, Tommy," Savich said, nodding to one of Thomas's men who was guarding the front of the house. "He's a neighbor and a friend of Becca's."

"What is going on here, Adam?"

"He took her," Adam said. "We think he's heading to Washington, D.C., with her. We're going to have to clear out soon."

Tyler paled, then yelled, "You were supposed to protect her! You really messed up big-time, didn't you? I wanted to help but you just kissed me off, I was a civilian, of no use at all. What about you? All these big Fed cops, none of you could protect her. None of you were of any help at all!"

Savich said as he closed his fingers around Tyler's arm, "I understand your anger. But all these accusations aren't going to help anyone, particularly Becca. Believe me, we all know what's at stake here."

"You're incompetents," Tyler yelled even louder, "all of you." He jerked away from Savich.

"Tyler," Adam said quietly, "don't go to Sheriff Gaffney. That would be the worst thing you could do."

"Why? How much more could things be screwed up?"

"He might kill her," Adam said. "Don't tell anyone anything."

After Tyler McBride was escorted from the house by three agents, Sherlock said, "Why not tell everyone now?"

Adam shoved his hand through his hair. "Because if some cop happens to see them, then you know our guy would kill her and take off. We can't take the chance. No, we've got to get to Washington, fast."

"First you've got to call Thomas, Adam."

Adam didn't want to, he really didn't.

Savich and Sherlock listened to Adam flail himself on the speakerphone.

There was silence on the other end. Finally, Thomas said, "Get over it, Adam. We've been dealt new cards now, we'll play them. I'm very relieved that Chuck is all right. His wife would roast me alive if he'd been killed. Now, if this is Krimakov, then he at least knows I'm in Washington, probably knows about the condo. I'll stay here. I'll be ready for him. Get back here as quickly as you can, Adam. Savich? Can you and Sherlock stick with us?"

"Yes, Thomas."

"Now, I've got to get myself ready for Krimakov. It's been so many years. Many times I thought he'd finally given it up, but it appears he's been biding his time."

"He could really be dead," Sherlock said.

"No," Thomas said. "Adam, you, Savich, and Sherlock hang around there for a while. Try to get a line on this guy. He's got to be somewhere. He's got to be traceable. Find him. Oh, and Adam?"

"Yes, sir?"

"Stop beating yourself up. Guilt slows down your brain. I want that brain of yours sharp. Get it together and find my daughter."

They finally rang off. Thomas Matlock looked at the phone for a very long time before he slowly eased it back down. Then he leaned his head back against the soft leather of his chair. He closed his eyes to blot out the feeling of helplessness, for only a moment, an instant, but instead, he felt a deep, soul-corroding fear that a man should never have to feel in his life. It was fear for his child, and the knowledge that he was helpless to save her.

It was Krimakov, he knew it, deep in his gut, he knew, and they had cremated the body. No, Krimakov wasn't dead—maybe he'd staged his death, murdered another man who resembled him. He'd somehow found out about Becca and he had begun his reign of terror. There was no doubt at all in Thomas's mind now. Krimakov, a man who had sworn to cut Thomas's heart out even if he had to chase Thomas to hell to do it, had his Becca.

He lowered his face in his hands.

# TWENTY

She was aware of ear-splitting noise—men's and women's voices yelling loudly, car tires screeching, horns blasting, and movement, she could feel the blur of movement everywhere, pounding feet, running fast. She was moving as well, no, she was flying, then she hit hard and the pain ripped through her. She lay on her side, smelling the hot tar of the street, a light overlay of urine, hot and sour, whiffs of food, of too many bodies, feeling the unforgiving cement beneath her. Cement?

People were yelling, coming closer now, and there were men and women shouting, "Stay back! Let us through!"

She tried to open her eyes, but her muscles were too weak, wouldn't obey her, and the pain was boiling up inside her. She was so very tired, nearly blown under with it. Then she felt a hideously sharp stab of pain somewhere in her body, fierce, unrelenting, and she knew tears were leaking out of her eyes.

"Miss! Can you hear me?"

She felt his hand on her shoulder, felt the sun beating down on her, hot on her bare skin—what bare skin? Her legs were bare, that was it. But he was over her, a shadow blocking the sun.

"Miss? Can you hear me? Are you conscious?"

She opened her eyes then because he sounded so very afraid. "Yes," she whispered, "I can hear you. I can see you. Not clearly, but I can see you."

"It's her! It's that Matlock woman!"

More shouting, yelling, some curses, and so much heat, the press of bodies, the running thuds of shoes and boots.

A woman lightly tapped her cheek. "Open your eyes for me. Yes, that's right. Do you know who you are?"

She looked up into Letitia Gordon's grim, incredulous face.

Maybe there was also a touch of worry in those unforgiving eyes.

Becca whispered to that hard face over her, "You're the cop who hates me. How can you be here, right over me, speaking to me? You're in New York, aren't you?"

"Yes, and so are you."

"No, that's not possible. I was in Riptide. You know, I never could figure out why you hated me and believed I was a liar."

The woman's face contorted. Into anger? What?

"He drugged me," she whispered, her mouth so dry she nearly swallowed her tongue. "He drugged me. I hurt so much but I just can't tell where."

"All right. You'll be all right. Hey, Dobbson, is the ambulance here yet? Get off your butt, usher them through. Now!"

Letitia Gordon's face was really close to hers now, her breath minty on her cheek. "We'll find out what's happening here, Ms. Matlock. You rest now."

She felt hands pulling cloth down over her legs. Why were her legs bare? She realized then that there was pain in her legs. But it wasn't as bad as the other pain. Where was she? In New York? But that made no sense. Nothing made sense. Her brain nestled back into the shadows. The pain faded away. Becca sighed deeply and closed down.

SHE heard them speaking, soft, quiet voices not four feet away from her, talking, talking. Then they were closer, much closer, talking above her, which meant what? She opened her eyes. Blinked. She was flat on her back. The people speaking were on the left, and one of the people was Adam.

She wet her lips with her tongue. "Adam?"

He whirled around so fast he nearly lost his balance. Then he was at her side and he lifted her hand and held it hard between his two large ones. She felt the calluses on his palms.

"What's going on? Where are we? I dreamed I saw Detective Gordon, you know, that cop who hates me?"

"Yes, I know. She left a little while ago. She'll be back, but later, when you've got it together again. You're going to be all right, Becca. There's nothing to worry about. Just take it easy and breathe nice shallow, light breaths. That's right. Does your head hurt?"

She thought about that. "No, not really, it's just that I'm all fuzzy. Even you're kind of fuzzy, Adam. I'm so glad to see you. I thought I was going to die, that I'd never see you again. I couldn't bear it. Where are we?"

He lightly touched his fingertip to her cheek. "You're at New York University Hospital. The guy who took you from your bed in Jacob Marley's house, the guy who was holding you, he shoved you out of his car right in front of One Police Plaza."

"It was Krimakov?"

"We believe so. At least it's a strong possibility."

She said, "I asked him if he was Krimakov but he wouldn't answer me. We're in New York City?"

"Yes. You did see Detective Gordon. She was one of the cops who came running. It was early in the afternoon, bunches of people around, lots of cops heading out for lunch. Detective Gordon was there because she had some meetings with the Narcotics Division."

"My lucky day," Becca said.

"I'm sorry, Becca, so sorry. I really messed up and look what happened."

She heard the awful guilt in his voice, the fear, and finally, overlaying all of it, the relief that she was alive. He couldn't be as relieved as she was. "It's okay, Adam, really."

"Hi, Becca."

She smiled up at Sherlock and Savich, one on either side of her hospital bed. "We're sure glad to see you."

"Me, too. I thought you were in Riptide."

"We can move quickly when we have to," Sherlock said, lightly patting Becca's shoulder. "Dillon got a call from Tellie Hawley, the SAC at the New York City office. Tellie told him what happened. We got here three hours later."

"What happened to him? Did they get him?"

Sherlock said, "Unfortunately, no. There was mass confusion. He shoved you out of the car, then jumped out while the car was still rolling and disappeared into the crowd. The car hit three other people before it smashed into a fire hydrant and drenched another fifty people. It was a zoo. We've gotten some descriptions, but no one agrees with anyone else so far."

He was still out there, free. She felt flattened. "So he got away again," she said, and wanted to shriek with the helplessness that flooded her.

Adam was clearing his throat. "We'll get him, Becca. You've got to believe that. Now, there's someone here for you to meet."

Her head came up, fast. "Please, no doctors, Adam. I hate doctors. So did my mother." And she started crying. She didn't know where all the tears came from, but they were there, swamping her, and she was sobbing, tears streaming down her face, and she wanted her mother desperately. "My mom died in a hospital, Adam. She hated it, then she didn't care because she was in a coma. No one could do anything. She died in a hospital like this one." The tears kept coming, she couldn't stop them.

Then suddenly someone was holding her, drawing her close, and a man's dark, smooth voice said next to her ear, "It's all right, my darling girl. It's all right."

And she stilled. Strong arms were around her. She felt his heart pounding rhythmically, powerful and steady against her cheek. "I'm sorry, I don't mean to carry on like this. I miss my mother. I loved her so much and she died. There isn't anyone else for me."

"I miss your mother, too, Becca. It's going to be all right. I swear it to you."

She pulled back a bit and looked up at an older man who looked oddly familiar to her, but that was impossible, wasn't it? She was sure she'd never seen him before in her life. The drugs were still affecting her, holding her brain back, scrambling things, making her cry. "I'm nobody's darling girl," she whispered, and raised her hand to lightly touch her fingers to the man's cheek. He was so handsome, his face lean, his nose thin, straight, his eyes a soft light blue, dreamy eyes. Now that was strange. Her mother had told her that she had dreamy eyes, summer dreamy eyes. "I don't understand," she said, frowning up at the man's face. "Who are you?"

The man looked as if he would cry with her, but he swallowed, several times, and cleared his throat. "I'm your father, Becca. I'm Thomas Matlock. I can't bring your mother back, but I'm here now, and I'll stay."

"You're Thomas? You're the man Adam and Savich are working for?"

"Well, let's say they're helping me out."

She didn't say anything then, frowned a bit, trying to assemble things in her mind, in her memory, to make some sense of them, realizing suddenly that she recognized his eyes because he'd given them to her, realizing— "When he slipped the needle into my arm that second time," she whispered, looking directly into his eyes, "just before I went under, he said right against my ear, 'Tell your daddy hello for me.'"

His face paled and he grew vague, indistinct, his arms loosening. She grabbed his shirt with her fist, trying to pull him closer. "No, don't leave me, please."

"Oh, no, I won't." Thomas looked up at Adam. "I guess that says it all."

"Yes," Adam said. "At least now we know for sure."

"Amen to that," Sherlock said. Then she added, "Why don't we all go out to get a cup of coffee while Thomas gets to know Becca a bit better?"

When she was alone with the man who'd said he was her father, she looked up at him and said, "Why did you leave us? I don't even remember what you looked like I was so young when you left. There is this old photograph of you and Mom, and you looked so young and so handsome. Carefree. It's a wonderful picture."

He held her very close for a long time, then slowly he said, "You were all of three years old when it happened. I was a CIA operative, Becca, and I was very good. There was this other KGB spy—"

"Krimakov."

"Yes. I was sent over to what is now Belarus, to stop him from killing a visiting German industrialist. Krimakov had brought his wife, as if they were there on some sort of vacation. It was in the mountains. There was a gunfight and she tried to save him. I hadn't seen her, hadn't even known she was there." He paused a moment, memory stark and alive in his eyes. He said simply, "I shot her in the head and killed her. Krimakov promised me he would kill not only me but my family. He vowed it. I believed him.

"He managed to escape me. I decided that I would have to kill him to protect you. When I tried, I found out that he'd simply disappeared. There was no trace of him. The KGB helped him, obviously, and he stayed buried until very recently, when I was told he was killed in an auto accident in Crete. You know the rest."

"You left us to protect us?"

"Yes. Your mother and I discussed it. Matlock is a common name. She took you and moved to New York. I saw her four, maybe five times a year. We were always very, very careful. We couldn't tell you. We couldn't put you in danger. It was the hardest thing I've ever had to do in my life, Becca. Believe me."

All of a sudden she had a father. She stared at his face, seeing herself in him, seeing also a stranger. It was too much. She heard him say something, heard Adam arguing with someone inside the door, sharp and loud, then she didn't hear anything at all. That was a good thing, she thought as she slipped away, back where there were no dreams, only seamless darkness, without *him,* no worries or voices to tear her apart. Her father was dead, dead since she was very young. It was impossible that he was here, there was no way. Maybe she was dead, too, and had seen what she wanted to see. Dead. It wasn't bad, truly it wasn't. She heard a sound, like a wounded animal. It had come from her, she realized, but then there was nothing at all.

When she awoke, it was dark in her room except for a small bedside lamp that was turned to its lowest setting. The small hospital room was filled with shadows and quiet voices. There were needles in both of her arms connected to bags of liquid beside both sides of her bed. There were two men sitting in chairs next to the window, in low conversation. One was Adam. The other was her father—oh yes, she believed him now, perhaps even understood a bit—and he'd called her his darling girl. She blinked several times. He didn't fade back into her mind. He remained exactly where he was. She saw him very clearly now, and she could do nothing but stare, breathe him in, settle his face, his features, his expressions, into her mind. He used his hands while he spoke to Adam, just like she did when she was trying to make a point, to convince someone to come around to her way of thinking. He was her father.

She cleared her throat and said, "I know I'm not dead because I would kill for some water. And I don't believe that if someone is dead, she's particularly thirsty. May I please have some water?"

Adam was on his feet in an instant. When he bent the straw into her mouth, she closed her eyes in bliss. She drank nearly the entire glass. She was panting when she finished. "Oh goodness, that was delicious."

He didn't straighten, placed one large hand on either side of her face on that hard hospital pillow. He studied her face, her eyes. "You okay?"

"Yes. I realize I'm not dead, so you must be real. I remember you told me that he threw me out of the car. Is there anything bad wrong with me?"

"No, nothing bad. When he shoved you out of the car yesterday right there at Police Plaza, you were still wearing your nightgown. You got a lot of scrapes, a bruised elbow, but that's it. Now it's just a matter of getting the drug out of your system. They pumped your stomach. Nobody seems to know what the drug was, but it was potent. You should be about clear of it now." He had to close his eyes a moment. He'd never been so afraid in his life, never. But she would live. She would be fine. He said, "Do the scrapes hurt? Would you like a couple of aspirin?"

"No, I'm all right." She licked her lips, looked over into the shadows, clutched his hand, and whispered, "Adam, he really is my father, isn't he? That story he told me, it's the truth? It happened that way?"

"Yes, all of it is true. His name is Thomas Matlock. He never died, Becca. There is probably a whole lot more to tell you—"

"Yes," Thomas said, "a lot more. So many stories to tell you about your mother, Becca."

"My mom said I had dreamy eyes. You do, too. I have your eyes."

Thomas smiled and his eyes twinkled. "I guess maybe you do have my eyes."

Adam said, stroking his chin, "I'm not sure about that. The thing is, Becca, I've never before looked at his eyes in quite the same way I look at yours."

Suddenly, all her attention was on Adam. She said, "Why not?"

"Because—" Adam stopped dead in his tracks. She was actually coming on to him, teasing him. He loved it. He cleared his throat. "Now's not the time. We'll talk about that later, you can count on it. Now, are you up to telling us about this guy who took you?"

"You mean Krimakov."

"Yes."

"A moment, Adam. Sir, you sent Adam to protect me, didn't you?"

"Yes, he did, but I screwed up, big-time."

Becca said, "Sorry, Adam, but you can't take all the credit. What that monster did was very clever. None of us would have ever guessed that he came back to the house while we were out looking for him. How'd he get me out of the house without being seen?"

"Sherlock figured that one out really fast. He knocked out Chuck and tied him up. That's how he escaped with you." He saw the worry in her eyes and quickly added, "He's okay—a headache for a while. I'm sorry, Becca, so sorry. Did he hurt you?" It hurt to say it, but he did: "Did he rape you?"

"No. He licked my face. I told him not to do it again because it was creepy. That made him really mad, but you see, that drug he shot into me, it also calmed me, made me all loose, so when I woke up that first time I wasn't afraid of him. I don't think I was afraid of anything. It was a side effect of the drug, he said, and he didn't like it. He wanted me to be real afraid, he wanted me to beg and plead, like Linda Cartwright did." She shuddered as she said the name. "He said she didn't matter. She was only his present to me."

"Did he tell you his name?"

She shook her head. She said to her father, "I can't even describe him. He never let me see him. When he had me tied down to a bed, he always stood in the shadows, beyond what I could make out. I don't think he was old, but I can't be one hundred percent certain. Was he young? I don't know. But when he cursed, he used a mixture, some American, some British, and some in a language I didn't recognize. Isn't that strange?"

"Yes, but we'll figure it out."

Thomas was standing beside her bed, opposite Adam. He was wearing a dark suit, the dark red tie loosened. He looked tired and worried and, oddly enough, happy. Because of her? Evidently so, and that pleased her very much. He picked up her left hand and held it. His hand was strong, lightly tanned. He was wearing a wedding ring. She stared at that ring, stared and stared, touched her fingers to it, then said finally, "My mother gave you that ring?"

"Yes, when we got married. I wore it all our married lives. I plan to wear it until it finally dissolves off my finger sometime in the distant future. I loved your mother very much, Becca. Like I said, I had to leave both of you so you wouldn't be killed. I know it's all still very confusing. There are lots of facts and details, but the bottom line is exactly what I already told you. I accidentally killed a man's wife and he swore he would kill my family, and then he would kill me, but only after I saw, firsthand, how he had killed everyone I loved. I had no choice. I had to leave my family in order to protect them."

Adam said, "We believe this man who is stalking you, who murdered that old bag lady, who shot the governor, we believe it's Krimakov and somehow he found you and began terrorizing you." He paused for a moment, nodding to Thomas.

Thomas was looking down at this lovely young woman who was his only child. It took him a moment before he said, "Vasili Krimakov was one of the KGB's top agents back in the seventies, as I was for the CIA. Again, there's a whole lot more, but it can wait for a while. Right now, what's important is that we find him, that we neutralize him once and for all."

"You're sure it's Krimakov."

He smiled then. "Oh yes, I'm very sure, particularly after what he told you."

"'Say hello to your daddy.'"

"Yes. No one else would know that."

"My mom wore a ring like yours. When she died—" She couldn't speak, the tears clogged her throat, burned her eyes. He said nothing at all, held her hand, squeezed it a bit more tightly. She swallowed, looked away from him toward the window. It was black out there, no sign of stars from her vantage point. "—I wanted desperately to have something to connect me to her and I almost took that ring, but then I remembered how much she loved you, and I couldn't take it from her.

"Sometimes when she spoke to me of you, she would start crying and I hated you for leaving us, for leaving her, for dying. I remember when I was a teenager I told her she should get married again, that I would be going off to college, and she needed to put you in the past. She needed to find someone else. She was so young and beautiful, I didn't want her to be alone. I remember she'd only smile at me and say she was fine." Then, suddenly, Becca said, "He came after me so he could get to you, didn't he?"

"Yes," Adam said. "That's exactly right. But he didn't know where Thomas was, so he came up with a way to flush Thomas out. He dumped you right in front of One Police Plaza."

"What I don't understand," Thomas said, "is why he didn't simply announce all over the media that he had her, threaten to kill her if I didn't show myself in Times Square. He must have known that I would be there. But he didn't."

Adam said, "Who knows? Maybe a cop saw him, saw an unconscious woman in the backseat, and he was forced to dump Becca in order to escape. However, it's far more likely that he planned this down to the exact spot he'd leave her. I think it's gamesmanship. He wants to prove he's better than you, smarter than all of us, and he wants you to suffer big-time in the process."

"He's succeeded admirably," Thomas said. "He has flushed me out. I guess maybe that's why he didn't let you see him, Becca. He wants to keep playing this insane game. He wants to terrorize you and now he can continue the terror, with me squarely in the game with you."

"And only he knows the rules," Becca said.

"Yes," Adam said. "I wonder if he's been living on Crete all this time."

"Probably so," Thomas said.

"Wait," Becca said, chewing on her bottom lip. "Now I recognize those curses—they were Greek."

"That settles that," Thomas said. "We've got all the proof we need that the ashes in that urn in the Greek morgue aren't Krimakov's."

He leaned down and kissed Becca's forehead. "I won't leave you again. Now we'll find Krimakov, and then you and I have a lot of catching up to do."

"I'd like that," she said. Then she smiled over at Adam, but she didn't say anything.

# TWENTY-ONE

Detective Letitia Gordon and Detective Hector Morales of the NYPD looked over at the woman who lay in that skinny hospital bed, looking pale and wrung-out, IV lines running obscenely into her arms, her eyes shiny with tears.

Detective Gordon cleared her throat and said to the room at large, "Excuse me," and flashed her badge, as did Hector Morales, "but we need to speak to Ms. Matlock. The doctor said it was all right. Everyone out."

Thomas straightened and looked at them, assessing them, quickly, easily, and smiled even as he walked forward, blocking their view of his daughter. "I'm her father, Thomas Matlock, detectives. Now, what can I do for you?"

"We need to speak to her now, Mr. Matlock," Letitia Gordon said, "before the Feds get here and try to big-foot us."

"I am the Feds, Detective Gordon," Thomas said.

Detective Gordon cleared her throat. "It's important, sir. There was a murder committed here in New York, on our turf. It's our case, not yours, and your daughter is involved." Why had she said all that? Because he was a big federal cheese, and that's why she'd tried to excuse herself, tried to justify herself. What was he going to do?

Detective Morales smiled and shook Thomas's outstretched hand. "Hector Morales, Mr. Matlock. And this is Detective Gordon. We didn't realize she had any relatives other than her mother."

"Yes, she does, detectives," Thomas said. "There's still some drug in her system, so she's not really completely back yet, but if you would like to speak to her for a couple of minutes, that probably wouldn't hurt. But you need to keep it low-key. I don't want her upset."

"Look, sir," Detective Gordon said, pumping herself up, knowing that she should be the one giving the orders here, not this man, this stranger who was with the government. "Ms. Matlock ran away. Everyone was looking for her. She is wanted as a material witness in the shooting of Governor Bledsoe of New York."

Thomas Matlock merely arched a very patrician brow at her and looked intimidatingly forbearing. "Fancy that," he said mildly. "I can't imagine why she would ever want to leave New York what with all the protection you offered her."

"Now see here, sir," Detective Gordon said, and tried to shake off Hector Morales's hand on her arm, but he didn't let go, and she looked yet again into that man's face, and she shut up. There were words bubbling inside her, but she wasn't about to say them. He was a Big Feeb, and she saw the power in his eyes, something that flashed red warning lights to her brain, an ineffable something that shouted power, more power than she could imagine, and so she kept her mouth shut.

"There is a lot we do not understand, Mr. Matlock," Detective Morales said, his voice stiff, with a slight accent. "May we please speak to your daughter? Ask her a few questions? She does look very ill. We won't take long."

The thing of it was, Letitia Gordon thought as she walked to the bed where the young woman lay staring at her with dread, her dyed hair tangled and dirty about her face, she wanted to stand very straight in front of that man, perhaps salute and then do exactly what he told her to do. And here was Hector, acting so deferential, like this guy was the president or, more important, the police commissioner. Whatever he was, this man wore power like a second skin.

"Ms. Matlock, in case you don't remember, I'm Detective Gordon and this is Detective Morales."

"I remember both of you very well," Becca said, and concentrated on clearing the sheen of tears out of her eyes. These people couldn't hurt her now, Adam and her father wouldn't let them. And she wouldn't, either. She'd been through enough now that a couple of hard-boiled cops couldn't intimidate her.

"Good," Detective Gordon said, then she caught herself looking over at Mr. Matlock, as if for approval of her approach. She cleared her throat. "Your father said we could ask you a couple of questions."

"All right."

"Why did you run, Ms. Matlock?"

"After my mother died and I'd buried her, there was no reason for me to stay. He found me at the hotel where I was hiding, and I knew he would get me. None of you believed me, and so I didn't think I had a choice. I ran."

"Look, Ms. Matlock," Detective Gordon said, coming closer, "we still aren't certain there was a man after you, calling you, threatening you."

Adam said mildly, knowing until he and Thomas had discussed it, Krimakov's probable identity would remain under wraps to the NYPD, "Then who do you think kicked her out of a moving car at One Police Plaza? A ghost?"

"Maybe it was her accomplice," Detective Gordon said, whirling on Adam, "you know, the guy who shot Governor Bledsoe."

Becca didn't say anything. Thomas saw she was pulling away, even though she hadn't moved a finger, trying to draw into herself. She looked unutterably tired.

"Also," Detective Gordon added, not looking at Mr. Matlock, "our psychiatrist reported that he believed you have big problems, Ms. Matlock, lots of unresolved issues."

Adam raised an eyebrow. "Unresolved issues? I love shrink talk, Detective. Do tell us what that means."

"He believes that she was obsessed with Governor Bledsoe, that she had to have his attention, and that was why she made up these stories about this guy calling her and stalking her, threatening to kill the governor if she didn't stop sleeping with him."

Adam laughed. He actually laughed. "That's amazing."

"I'm sure that old woman who was blown up in front of the Metropolitan Museum didn't think it was funny," Detective Gordon said, her jaw out, not ready to give an inch.

"Let me get this straight," Adam said. "You now think she blew up that old woman to get the governor's attention?"

"I told you the truth," Becca said, cutting in before Letitia Gordon could blast Adam. "I told you he phoned me and told me to look out my window, which happens to face the park and the museum. He killed that poor woman, and you didn't do anything about it."

"Of course we did," Detective Morales said, his voice soothing and low. "There were a lot of conflicting stories coming in."

"Yes," Becca said. "Like the ones Dick McCallum told the cops in Albany that made all of you disbelieve me. This guy probably paid off Dick McCallum to lie about me, and then he murdered him, too. I don't understand why it isn't clear to you now."

Detective Gordon said, "Because you ran, Ms. Matlock. You wouldn't come in and speak to us, you called Detective Morales from wherever you were hiding. You're at the center of all this. You, only you. Tell us what's going on, Ms. Matlock."

"I believe that's enough for the time being," Thomas said, and calmly moved to stand between the two New York detectives and his daughter. "I am very disappointed in both of you. Neither of you is listening. You are not using your brains. Now, let's get this perfectly clear: Since you're having difficulties logically integrating all the facts, I want you to focus on catching the man who kidnapped my daughter and shoved her out of his car right in front of cop headquarters. I trust you people have been trying to find witnesses? Questioning them? Trying to get some sort of composite on this guy?"

"Yes, sir, of course," Detective Morales said. As for Detective Gordon, she wanted to tell him to go hire his daughter a fancy lawyer, that Dick McCallum had been murdered, that she could have had something to do with that, too, maybe revenge, since McCallum had blown the whistle on her. She opened her mouth, all worked up, but Thomas Matlock said quietly, "Actually, detectives, I am a director with the CIA. I am now terminating this conversation. You may leave."

Both detectives were out of there in under five seconds, Detective Gordon leading the way, Morales on her heels, looking both apologetic and scared.

Becca shook her head, back and forth. "They didn't even want to know anything about him. Don't they have to believe me now that Dick McCallum was murdered, too?"

"One would think," Adam said, his eyes narrowed, still looking at the now-empty doorway. "New York's finest aren't shining in this particular instance. Now, not to worry, Becca."

"I think Detective Gordon needs to be pulled off this case," Thomas said. "For whatever reason, she made up her mind about you early on and is now refusing to be objective. I'll make a call."

"I want to leave this place, Adam. I want to go far away, forever."

"I'm sorry, Becca, but there's not going to be any forever yet," Thomas said. "Krimakov got what he wanted. I'm out in the open now. The problem is that you still are, too. Now I'm going to make that call." Thomas walked out of the hospital room, his head down, deep in thought, as he pulled out his cell phone.

The Feds arrived forty-five minutes later.

The first man into the room came to a fast stop and stared. He cleared his throat. He straightened his dark blue tie. He looked as if he wished his wing tips were shinier. "Mr. Matlock, sir, we didn't know you were involved, we had no idea, didn't know she was related to you—"

"No, of course you didn't, Agent Hawley. Do come in, gentlemen, and meet my daughter."

He leaned over her and lightly touched his fingertips to her cheek. "Becca, here are two guys who want to talk to you, not batter you like the NYPD detectives, just talk a bit. You tell them when you're tired and don't want to talk anymore, okay?"

"Yes," she said, her voice so thin Adam swore she was fading away right before his eyes. If he hadn't been worried sick, Adam would have enjoyed watching Thomas turn his power onto the FBI guys, but he didn't. Now Adam wondered how Thomas knew Tellie Hawley, a long-time FBI guy who had a reputation for eating crooks for breakfast. He never cut anyone any slack. He was sometimes very scary, sometimes a rogue, admired by his contemporaries and occasionally distressing to his superiors.

"Hey, Adam," Hawley said. "I guess I'll find out soon enough why you're here. Where's Savich?"

"He and Sherlock will be in a bit later." Adam nodded then to Scratch Cobb, a tough-looking little man who wore elevator shoes that brought him up to Adam's chin. He got his nickname years before, when it was said that he scratched and scratched until he found the answers in a high-profile case. "Scratch, good to see you again. How's tricks?"

"Tricks is good, Adam. How's it going, my boy?"

"I'm surviving." Adam took Becca's hand and lightly squeezed it. He leaned close and whispered in her ear, "The guy standing to the left has hemorrhoids. The big one with the mean eyes, Hawley, will want to cross the line, but he doesn't dare try it, not with your dad here. Actually, he has five dogs and they rule his house. Now, go get 'em, tiger."

*If she were a tiger,* she thought, *she was a very pathetic one, not worthy of the name, but still*— She smiled, she actually smiled. "Hello, gentlemen," she said, and her voice wasn't as paper-thin now. "You wanted to speak to me?"

"Yes," Hawley said, stepping forward. Adam didn't move, smiled a feral smile at him that could make a person's teeth fall out.

"Adam, I'm not going to bite her. I'm a good guy. I work for the U-nited States government. You don't have to stand guard."

"I'm supposed to be protecting the lady, Tellie. The thing is, I screwed up, and the bad guy got her, drugged her, and dumped her right in front of One Police Plaza."

Hawley nodded, then said, "Okay, so you're not going to budge." Hawley continued smoothly, coming one step closer, watching Adam from the corner of his eye. "This guy who kidnapped you and drugged you and put you out of his car, who is he?"

"I don't know, Agent Hawley. If I did, I would have announced it to the world via CNN. You know I reported his stalking me, calling me, threatening to kill the governor. It started in Albany and he followed me to New York. Then he killed that old woman in front of the Metropolitan Museum."

"Yes," Tellie Hawley said, and he shifted from his left foot to his right. "But what we want to know is who this guy is, why he tried to kill the governor. We need to know why and how you're involved in all this—"

Adam said very quietly, "The governor was shot, like the guy threatened to do, and then the aide to Governor Bledsoe turned out to be the one who told the cops that Becca was an obsessed liar. He was murdered. Did you know that, Tellie? Did you know that the guy who killed him ran him down in a car he'd stolen in Ithaca, after he'd murdered the owner? Did you know that the cops have impounded that car with its dark-tinted windows so no one would be able to identify him when he ran down Dick McCallum? Hey, do you and your fed techs realize that you can go crawl all over it right now?"

"Yeah, okay, we know all that."

"Then why are you pretending it didn't happen?"

"We're not pretending it didn't happen," Hawley said, his hands fisted, anger creeping up over his shirt collar to redden his neck. "But there's no reason for him to have picked Ms. Matlock out of the blue, that he targeted someone as unlikely as she is. It only makes sense she must know something, she must be aware of his identity, have some idea who he is and why he's doing this. This is big, bad stuff, Adam, and she's slap-dab in the middle of it. I hear there's all sorts of doings in the CIA, but I can't find out what's going on. I've heard it involves this case, but no one will tell me anything, even my bosses. Let me tell you that it burns my ass to be kept on the outside. Now back off, Adam, or I'll burn your ass before they get mine."

Thomas stepped up. "I wanted to avoid this but now I don't see a choice. I believe it's time for official talks. You people haven't been let in on what's going on here, and it's time."

Thomas raised his hand when all of the men would speak at once. "No more hotdogging, Adam. Agent Hawley, if you like, you and Agent Cobb here can come to Washington. We're going to be meeting with the director of the FBI and the director of the CIA, that is, if I can manage to get the two of them in the same room without bloodshed. I'll have to pick a meeting place where neither of them will get his nose out of joint."

Hawley gaped at him. "Both the CIA and the FBI? But why? I don't understand, Mr. Matlock."

"You will," Thomas said. "Now, go make arrangements to come to Washington, if your bosses want you to stay involved."

"We're New York FBI, Mr. Matlock," said Tellie Hawley. "Of course we'll stay involved. We're the primary players. I've heard there's some really bad stuff going down and Cobb and I want to be part of it."

"Call the director's office in a while and find out when and where."

After the FBI guys had left, champing at the bit to find out what was going down, Thomas closed the hospital door and turned to Becca. "No way will they be allowed to come to Washington, but at least we got rid of them for a while. Now it's time to play with both the big boys, not just Gaylan Woodhouse. I'm hoping he'll see reason and get Bushman at the FBI to work on it. Everyone needs to know what's going on now."

"First thing," Adam said, "is for Savich to find that apartment Krimakov rented. Then we send our own people over to Crete and take the place apart."

"Agreed," Thomas said. "Let's do it. Now, Becca, Tommy the Pipe, Chuck, and Dave will all be here to protect you until we get back."

"No," Becca said, coming up on her elbows. "I'm coming with you."

"You can barely walk," Adam said. "Lie back and calm down. No way our people will let him get near you again."

"No more orders, Adam. Now, sir, there's no way you're going to face this alone." Becca calmly pulled the IV lines from her arms. She pushed back the hospital sheets and swung her legs over the side of the bed. "Give me another drink of water, ask Sherlock to buy me some clothes, and we're out of here. An hour. That's all I need."

"I think," Thomas said slowly, stroking his long fingers over his chin, "that there is perhaps a bit too much of me in you."

Becca grinned at him. "That's what Mom told me, many times."

"Then I'd best clear your leaving town with our local cops," Thomas said, and wanted to pat her cheek, but didn't because she wasn't a little girl anymore and she barely knew him. The thought of that made him clear his throat.


*Washington, D.C.*
*The Eagle Has Landed*

There weren't any leaks. None of them could believe it. Their short flight to Washington, then the drive to Georgetown to a small restaurant called The Eagle Has Landed didn't raise any curious eyebrows. There wasn't a single TV van in front of the restaurant, not a single reporter from the *Washington Post*.

"I don't believe it," Thomas said as he ushered Becca into the foyer of the small British pub. "No flashbulbs."

"Glory be," said Adam.

Andrew Bushman, appointed director of the FBI six months previously after the unexpected retirement of the former director, stood tall even with his rounded shoulders, his gray hair tonsured like a medieval monk's, and beautifully suited, when Thomas walked to the small circular table at the back of the restaurant. Bushman raised an eyebrow. "Mr. Matlock, I presume? You have pulled me away from some very important matters. I came because Gaylan Woodhouse asked me to, told me it had to do with the attempted assassination of the governor of New York. My people are directly involved in this. I will be interested to hear how the CIA could possibly be involved, what they could possibly know that's pertinent."

Gaylan Woodhouse eased around the back of a shoji screen. He was a slight man of sixty-three who had come up through the ranks of the CIA and had been known in the old days as the best spy in the world because no one—absolutely no one—ever noticed him, and still he was paranoid, staying in the shadows until there was no choice but to come out. He had been the director of the CIA for four years now. Thank God, Thomas thought, Gaylan had a long memory and a flexible mind.

"Thank you," Thomas said and shook first the FBI hand and then the CIA hand. "Now, this is my daughter, Becca, who is very closely tied to this matter, and my associate, Adam Carruthers. Gaylan, thank you for putting in a good word for me with Mr. Bushman."

Gaylan Woodhouse merely shrugged. "I know you, Thomas. If you say something is critical, then it's critical. I hope by that you think it's time to bring the FBI up to speed on this thing."

"Yes, it's time," Thomas said.

The two directors eyed each other and managed affable smiles and civil greetings. Andrew Bushman cleared his throat. "Agents Hawley and Cobb won't be joining us today, but I suspect you knew they wouldn't. I will have any information needed by them sent to New York when and if it's appropriate. Now, I need a martini. Then we can nail this thing down."

Becca would have killed for a glass of wine, but she was taking medications that didn't allow it. She would even have accepted Adam's beer. She suffered through approximately four and a half minutes of small talk. Then Gaylan Woodhouse said, "What have you got that's definitive on Krimakov, Thomas?"

Mr. Bushman's eyebrow shot up. "Does this have to do with the attempted assassination of the governor?"

"Indeed it does," Gaylan said. "Thomas?"

Thomas launched into the story of a CIA agent, namely himself, who was playing cat and mouse with a Russian agent in the late-1970s and accidentally killed that agent's wife. And that Russian agent had promised that he would get revenge, that he would kill both Thomas and his family. As Thomas spoke, Becca thought about what her life, her mother's life would have been like if her father hadn't been in that godforsaken place, trying to get the best of a Russian agent named Vasili Krimakov. "Of course, Gaylan knows all of this already. The reason the FBI needs to be involved is because we are trying to prove whether or not Krimakov is still alive and thus was the one who tried to assassinate the governor of New York. Actually, now we're very certain that it's him."

FBI Director Bushman was lounged back in his seat, holding the nearly empty martini glass in his hand. "But this guy is after you. Why would he shoot the governor of New York? I'm not getting something here. Oh, I see, Matlock—you're the Rebecca Matlock, the young woman who escaped the police and went into hiding?"

"Yes, sir, I am."

Andrew Bushman sat forward, his drink forgotten. "All right, Thomas, tell me everything, even stuff that Gaylan doesn't know. I need to have a leg up on him somewhere."

"Krimakov wanted to flush me out. Somehow he found out that I have a daughter—Becca. We don't know how he found out about her, but it appears that he did and he came after her. That's why he's been terrorizing her, that's why he kicked her out of his car in front of One Police Plaza in New York."

"To get you out in the open."

"Yes, that's it exactly. It's not so complicated when you cut right to the chase. He wants to kill me and he wants to kill my daughter. All the rest is window dressing, it's drama, giving him the spotlight, showing the world how brilliant he is, how he's the one in control here." And Thomas thought, *He can't kill Allison because she's dead already, and I wasn't there with her.*

It was Adam who ended things, saying, "So that's it, gentlemen. We found out that Krimakov was cremated, thus leaving doubt that it was indeed he who was killed. However, the man who kidnapped Ms. Matlock whispered in her ear before he shot a drug into her—"

Becca interrupted. "'Say hello to your daddy.'"

"So now there's simply no doubt," Thomas said. "The man cremated wasn't Krimakov."

Gaylan said, "We've been spending hundreds of hours on this because there was the possibility that it could be Vasili Krimakov. Now that we know it's him, you need to stick your oar in, Andrew. Get all those talented people of yours involved in finding this maniac."

"I've got a man trying to track down an apartment we understand Krimakov owns somewhere in Crete, in addition to his house. When we find it, we want agents to go over it."

Gaylan nodded. "As soon as we know, I've got a woman in Athens who can fly down and check it out for us. She's good. She's also got contacts among the local Greek cops. She won't get any problems from them."

"It's Dillon Savich who's finding the apartment," Thomas said.

Andrew Bushman raised an eyebrow. "Why am I not surprised? Savich is one of the best. I gather you're telling me now so that I can cool down before I bust him?"

"That's right," Thomas said. "I knew Savich's father, Buck. I asked the son for help. He and Sherlock have been in the thick of things."

Andrew Bushman sighed and took the last sip of his martini. "All right. Now, I've got lots of stuff to do, meetings to hold, people to assign to get this off and running. What about the NYPD?"

Thomas said, "Why not tell the world? Have Hawley in New York interface with the local cops."

Bushman said, "Hawley is good, very good. He's tough and he deals well with the locals. Talk about bigfoot. He's a Mack truck when he needs to be. All right, gentlemen, we now tell the world."

"Well, then—" Gaylan Woodhouse broke off as his stomach growled. "We forgot to order lunch. I want a hamburger, lots of red meat, something my wife, bless her heart, doesn't allow."

Andrew said even as he was reading the menu, "I want everything to clear through the FBI before it goes to the media. We want our spin on things."

# TWENTY-TWO

The black government car moved smoothly onto the Beltway. It was still too early for rush-hour traffic to gnarl things to the screaming point. It didn't help, though, that the temperature was hovering at about ninety degrees. Inside the big car it was thankfully very cool. Their driver had said nothing at all since picking them up at The Eagle Has Landed. There was still no sign of the media. So far so good, Thomas had said. There would be a media release soon now.

Adam was humming as he flipped off his cell phone. "Thomas, the photo you asked Gaylan Woodhouse to dig out for you is coming over right away. He's sorry that he couldn't immediately put his finger on it."

Thomas turned from studying his daughter's profile to look at Adam. "I'm glad they finally located it. I was afraid I would have to use an artist and re-create him."

Adam said to Becca, "It's a photo of Krimakov from over twenty-five years ago. We'll age it and both can go to the media to plaster everywhere."

"Sir," Becca said, "are you really a CIA director?"

"That's not my title. I used it because it would be familiar to the New York detectives. Actually, I run an adjunct agency that's connected to the CIA. Our primary focus is on terrorism. I'm based here now, though, and don't travel much abroad anymore to the hot spots."

"This photo of Krimakov," Becca said after nodding to her father, "I want to see it, study it. Maybe I'll see something that could help. Did he speak English, sir?"

If Thomas noticed that she hadn't called him Father or Dad, he didn't let on. He had, after all, been a dead memory that had suddenly come alive and was now in her face. He'd also brought terror into her life. He also hadn't been around when her mother was dying, when her mother died. She'd been alone to handle all of it. The pain was sharp and so bitter he thought he'd choke on it. Soon he would tell her how he and her mother had e-mailed each other every day for years. Instead, he managed to say, "Yes, he did. He was quite fluent, educated in England. He even attended Oxford. Quite the *bon vivant* in his younger days." He paused a moment, then added, "How he despised us, the self-indulgent children of the West. That's what he called us. I always enjoyed locking horns with him, outwitting him, at least until that last time when he brought his wife with him to Belarus. The fool was using her as cover—picnics, hikes, pretending it was a vacation, when all the time he planned to kill the West German industrialist Reinhold Kemper."

"Krimakov," she said, as if saying his name aloud would help her remember more clearly, picture him standing in the shadows, "he had a very light sort of English accent, more so on some words than on others. He was fluent in English. I don't think he sounded particularly old, but I can't be certain. Krimakov is your age?"

"A bit older, perhaps five years. He's in his mid-fifties, if he's alive."

"I wish I could say for certain that he was that old but I can't. I'm sorry."

Thomas sighed. "I've always thought it unfair that nothing's easy in this life. He's had years to plan this, years to think through every move, every countermove. He knows me, probably now he knows me better than I knew him back then. When he finally found you—my child—then he was in business."

"I wonder where he is," Becca said. "Do you truly believe he's still in New York?"

"Oh, yes," Adam said, no doubt at all in his voice. "He's in New York, planning how he's going to get to you in the hospital. He's licking his chops, absolutely certain that you'll be there with her, Thomas. He's got to believe he's trapped you now. He's flushed you out and now he's got his best chance to kill both of you."

"It was an excellent idea, Adam," Thomas said, "to let everyone in the media believe that Becca is still at NYU Hospital, recovering from internal injuries and under close guard. I pray he disguises himself and tries to get in."

"I have no doubt he'll want to. I hope he doesn't smell a trap. He's smart, Thomas, you know that. He might have figured we'd do exactly what we have, in fact, done."

"I'm worried about the people at the hospital who are playing us,"

Becca said. "He's—" She paused a moment, trying to find the right words. "He's not normal. There's something very scary about him."

"Don't be worried about the agents," Adam said. "They're professionals to their toes. They're trained, and their collective experience probably exceeds the age of the world. They know what they're doing. They'll be ready for him to make a move. Another smart thing done—the FBI has installed security cameras to record everyone who goes in and out of that room. They've scheduled doctors and nurses to go in there at given hours. Our guys will stay alert. Our undercover agent who's playing you, Becca, Ms. Marlane, won't take any chances if he does show up. She's got a 9mm Sig Sauer under her pillow."

Thomas said, "Then there'll be that black government car pulling up and a guy who looks remarkably like me getting out and going into the hospital."

Adam said, "Yep. Twice a day. I hope Krimakov does try to get in. Wouldn't that be something if it all ended there, in the hospital, in New York?"

Becca said, "He managed to down Chuck with no one the wiser. So far he hasn't failed at anything he's tried."

"She's right, Adam," Thomas said. "Like I said, Vasili is smart; he improvises well. If there aren't any leaks, it's possible he'll sniff out the trap. But even if he's fooled into thinking she's there, perhaps believing that I'm there with her, under guard, for twenty-four hours, it'll give us time to try to come up with some sort of strategy."

Adam nodded and said, "If he doesn't go down in New York, then he'll go down here." He sighed. "Strategy is all well and good, Thomas, but I can't think of anything at the moment that isn't already being done."

Thomas said, "I keep wondering if the agents playing our parts should be told it's a former KGB agent who might come there. Maybe it would make them sharper."

"Knowing a killer is coming is all they need," Adam said. "Besides, they'll know who they're dealing with quick enough. I believe that Krimakov will make a move real soon now. Maybe he'll even make a mistake." Adam looked at Becca, whose hands were fisted in her lap. She was too pale and he didn't like it, but there was nothing he could do about it.

She said, more to herself than to either of them, "If they don't get him, then how do you come up with a strategy to catch a shadow?"

Thirty minutes later, their driver pulled up in front of a white two-story colonial house, set back from the street on a gently sloping grass-covered yard, right in the middle of Bricker Road in the heart of Chevy Chase. It looked like many of its neighbors in this upper-middle-class neighborhood, lots of surrounding land, lots of oak and elm trees, and beautifully landscaped lawns.

"Your house, sir. No one followed us."

"Thank you, Mr. Simms. You took excellent evasive action."

"Yes, sir."

Thomas turned to Becca, who was staring out the car window. He took her hand. "I've lived here for many years. Adam probably told you no one knows about this house. It's a closely guarded secret to protect me. Given Krimakov's actions, he hasn't discovered this house. Don't worry. We'll be safe here." Thomas looked over at the oak tree just to the side of the house. He and Allison had planted it sixteen years before. It was now twenty feet taller than the house, its branches full and laden with green leaves.

"It's lovely," Becca said. "I hope it does all end in New York. I don't ever want him to find out where you live. I don't want him to hurt this house."

"No, I would prefer that he didn't, either," Thomas said. He gently took her hand to help her out of the car.

"Mom and I always lived in an apartment or condo," she said, walking beside her father up the redbrick steps to the wide front porch. "She never wanted a house. I know there was enough money, but she'd always shake her head."

"When your mother and I were able to meet, she usually came here. This was her house, Becca. You'll see her touch everywhere, and I'm sure you'll recognize it as hers."

His voice was low, so filled with pain, with regret, that Adam turned away to focus on the rosebushes that were blooming wildly beside the brick stairs up to the front porch. He saw two agents in a car half a block down the street. He wondered if Thomas would tell his daughter that this house might look like a home-sweet-home, but the security in and around the place was state-of-the-art.

"It'll be dark in about three hours," Adam said, looking up from his watch. "Let's make our phone calls, talk to the guys in New York, get the status on everything, make sure they stay alert. I have this gut feeling that Krimakov is going to try to get into NYU Hospital soon. Now we can tell them exactly who they're up against. As you said, Thomas, there are always leaks. Detective Gordon, for example. I can see her telling everyone in sight. If he doesn't act in the next twenty-four hours, then he won't, because he'll know it's a trap."

Adam looked down at Becca, who was staring intently at the house. He knew she was trying to visualize her mother there, perhaps standing next to her father, smiling at him, laughing. Only she wasn't there, had never been a part of the two of them. He said, "Get rid of that ridiculous hair dye, will you, Becca?"

Thomas turned at his words. "That's right. Your hair is very blond, like your mother's."

"Mom's was more blond than mine," she said. "All right, Adam, but I'll have to go to the store. Who wants to go with me?"

"Me and about three other guys," Adam said. The look on her face had changed, lightened, and he was pleased.

At seven o'clock that evening, Savich and Sherlock, Tommy the Pipe, and Hatch arrived at Thomas's house for pizza and strategy, pizza first. Adam doubted there would be much helpful strategy, but it was good to have everyone together. Who knew what ideas might pop out after hot, cheese-dripping pizza?

Savich was carrying a baby draped over his right shoulder. The kid was wearing only a diaper and a little white T-shirt. Adam looked at Savich, checked out the baby's feet, and said, "You're this little guy's father?"

"Don't act so surprised, Adam." He lightly rubbed his hand over his son's back. "Hey, Sean, you still awake enough to punch this guy in his pretty face?"

The baby sucked his fingers furiously and poked out his butt, making Savich grin.

"He's nearly down for the count," Sherlock said, lightly touching the baby's head, covered with his father's black hair. "He sucks his fingers when he doesn't want to be disturbed and he knows you're talking about him."

"What do you think, Adam? Six-ounce free weights for my boy?"

Adam stared at the big man holding his kid who was madly sucking his fingers, then threw his head back and laughed. "This is not good. I can nearly see him lifting three envelopes in each hand." And he laughed and laughed. "Maybe he can even handle a stamp on each envelope."

There were ten pizzas spread around Thomas Matlock's living room an hour later. Hatch was hovering over the large pepperoni pizza, his shaved head glittering beneath a halogen floor lamp, talking even as he stuffed a big bite into his mouth. "Yipes, this sucker's really hot. Oh boy, delicious. But hot, real hot."

"I hope you burned your tongue," Adam said as he pulled the hot cheese free of a slice of pizza from another box that was closer to him than to anyone else, and reverently lifted it up. "Serves you right for being a pig. I love artichokes and olives."

"Nah, my tongue isn't burned, only a bit of a sting," Hatch said, and pulled up another piece. After he took another big bite, he said, "Now, to make sure everyone's on the same page. All federal agencies are up to date on Krimakov. The New York Bureau guys are going over the car the guy dumped you out of, Becca, with every high-tech scan, every piece of sophisticated equipment they have. Haven't found anything yet. I was really hoping they would find something, but this guy Krimakov is careful, real anal, one of the techs said. He didn't leave anything helpful. Rollo and Dave, who left Riptide yesterday, sent the FBI all the fingerprints we got in Linda Cartwright's house, all the fibers we bagged. No word yet. The woman he killed in Ithaca, and stole her car—they've combed the hills for witnesses but came up empty. All that boils down to nada, nothing, zippo." And then he cursed in some language Becca didn't recognize. She lifted her eyebrow at him. Hatch said, flushing a bit, "That was a bit of Latvian. A nice set of words, full-bodied and pungent, covers a lot of the hind end of a horse and what one could do with it."

There was laughter, lots of it, and it felt so good that Becca looked around at all the people she hadn't even known existed until very recently. People who were friends now. People who would probably remain friends for the rest of her life. She looked over at the baby lying in his carryall, sound asleep, a light blue blanket tucked over him. He was the image of his father.

She looked at Thomas Matlock, who was also looking at the baby and smiling. Her father, who hadn't eaten much pizza because, she knew, he was so worried. About her.

*My* father.

It still felt so very strange. He was real, he was her father, and her brain recognized and accepted it, but it was still too new to accept all the way to the deepest part of her that had no memories, no knowledge of him, nothing tangible, only a couple of photos taken when he and her mother were young, some when they were even younger than she was now, and stories her mother had told her, many, many stories. The stories were secondhand memories, she realized now. Her mother had given them to her, again and again, hoping that she would remember them and, through them, love the father she'd believed was dead.

Her father, alive, always alive, and her mother hadn't told her. Just stories, stupid stories. Her mother had memories, scores of them, and she had stories. *But she kept quiet to protect me*, Becca thought, but the sense of betrayal, the fury of it, roiled deep inside her. They could have told her when she was eighteen or when she was twenty-one. How about when she was twenty-five? Wasn't that adult enough for them? She was an adult, a real live independent adult, and yet they'd never said a thing, and now it was too late. Her mother was dead. Her mother had died without telling her a thing. She could have told her before she fell into that coma. She would never see them together now. She wanted to kill both of them.

She remembered many of those times when her mother had left her for maybe three, four days at a time. Three or four times a year she'd stayed with one of her mother's very good friends and her three children. She'd enjoyed those visits so much she'd never really ever wondered where her mother went, accepting that it was some sort of business trip or an obligation to a friend, or whatever.

She sighed. She still wanted to kill both of them. She wished they were both here so she could hug them and never let them go.

Savich said, "I've got the latest on Krimakov. A CIA operative told me about this computer system in Athens that's pretty top-secret and that maybe MAX could get into. Well, MAX did invite himself to visit the computer system in Athens that keeps data on the whereabouts and business pursuits of all noncitizens residing in Greece. It is top-secret because it also has lists of all Greek agents who are acting clandestinely throughout the world.

"Now, as you can imagine, this includes a lot of rather shady characters that they try to keep tabs on. Remember, there was nothing left in Moscow because the KGB purged everything on Krimakov. But they didn't have anything to do with the Greek records. This is what they had on Krimakov. Now, recognize that we've already learned most of this, that it was pretty common knowledge. However, in this context, it leads to very interesting conclusions." Savich pulled three pages from his jacket pocket and read: "Vasili Krimakov has lived in Agios Nikolaos for eighteen years. He married a Cretan woman in 1986. She died in a swimming accident in 1996. She had two children by a former marriage. Her children are dead. The oldest boy, sixteen, was mountain-climbing when he fell off a cliff. A girl, fifteen, ran into a tree on her motorcycle. They had one child, a boy, eight years old. He was badly burned in some sort of trash fire and is currently in a special burn rehabilitation facility near Lucerne, Switzerland. He's still not out of the woods, but at least he's alive." Savich looked up at all of them in turn. "We've had reports on some of this, but not all of it presented together. Also, they had drawn conclusions, and that's what was really interesting. I know there was more, probably about their plans to act against Krimakov, but I couldn't find any more. What do you think?"

"You mean you have those programs encoded so well you couldn't get in?" Thomas asked.

"No. I mean that someone who knew what he was doing expunged the records. Only the information I read to you was left, nothing more. The wipe was done recently, a little over six months ago."

"How do you know that?" Adam said. "I thought it would be like fingerprints. They'd be there but there was no clue when they were made."

"Nope. I don't know how the Greeks got ahold of it, but this system, the Sentech Y-2002, is first-rate, state-of-the-art. What it does is hard-register and bullet-code every deletion made on any data entered and tagged in preselected programs. It's known as the 'catcher,' and it's favored by high-tech industries because it pinpoints when something unexpected and unwelcome is done to relevant data, and who did it and when."

"How does this hard register and bullet code work?" Becca said.

Savich said, "What the system does is swoop in and retrieve all data the person is trying to delete before it can be deleted. It's funneled through a trapdoor into a disappearing 'secret room.' That means, then, that the data isn't really lost. However, the person who did this was able to do what we call a 'spot burn' on the information he deleted, and so, unfortunately, it's really gone. In other words, there was no opportunity to funnel the deleted data to safety.

"Now, the person who supposedly wiped out the bulk of Krimakov's entries was a middle-level person who would have had no reason to delete anything of this nature, much less even access it. So either someone got to him and paid him to do it or someone stole his password and made him the sacrificial goat in case someone discovered what he had done."

"How long will it take you to find out this person's name, Savich?" Thomas asked.

"Well, MAX already did that. The guy was a thirty-four-year-old computer programmer who was in an accident four months ago. He's dead. Chances are very good that he was set up as the goat. Chances are also good he knew the person who stole his password. I wouldn't be surprised if the guy talked about what he did to someone who took it to Krimakov, who then acted."

"What kind of accident befell this one?" Thomas asked.

"The guy lived in Athens, but he'd gone to Crete on vacation, which is where Krimakov lived. You know the Minoan ruins of Knossos some five miles out of Iráklion? It was reported that he somehow lost his footing and fell headfirst over a low wall into a storage chamber some twelve feet below where he was standing. He broke his neck when his head struck one of the big pots that held olive oil way back when."

Adam said, "I don't suppose Krimakov's former bosses in Moscow have any information at all on this?"

"Not that MAX can discover," Savich said. "If they have any more, and that's quite possible, they're holding it for a trade, since they know we want everything they've got on Krimakov. You know what I think? They've got nothing else useful. There hasn't been a peep out of them in the way of exploratory questions."

"You found out quite a lot, Savich," Thomas said. "All those accidents. Doesn't seem possible, does it? Or very likely."

"Oh, no," Savich said. "Not possible at all. That was the conclusion their agents drew. Krimakov murdered all of them. Hey, wait a minute, when you knew him, there weren't any computers."

"There wasn't much beyond great big suckers, like the IBM mainframes," Thomas said.

Sherlock said, "I wouldn't even want to try to figure out the odds of all those people in one family dying in accidents. They are astronomical, though."

"Krimakov killed all those people," Becca said, then shook her head. "He must have, but how could he kill his own wife, his two stepchildren?

Good grief, he burned his own little boy? No, that would truly make him a monster. What is going on here?"

"He didn't kill his own child," Adam said.

"No, he didn't," Sherlock said. "But the kid won't ever lead any kind of normal life if he survives all the skin grafts and the infections. Was his getting burned an accident?"

Thomas said, "Listen, all of this makes sense, but it's still supposition."

Savich said, "I've put Krimakov's aged photo into the Facial Recognition Algorithm program that's in place now at the Bureau. It matches photos or even drawings to convicted felons. It compares, for example, the length of the nose, its shape, the exact distance between facial bones, the length of the eyes. You get the drift. It'll spit out if there's anyone resembling him who's committed crimes either in Europe or in the United States. The database isn't all that complete yet, but it can't hurt."

"He was a spy," Sherlock said. "Maybe he was a convicted felon, too. It's possible he's done bad stuff other places and got nabbed. If that's so, then there'll be a match and maybe there'll be more information available on Krimakov."

"It's a long shot, but why not," Adam said. "Good work, you guys." Adam paused a moment, then cleared his throat. "Maybe it wasn't such a lame idea for Thomas to bring you on board. Hey, you've even got a cute kid."

The tension eased when they heard Sean sucking his fingers. Sherlock said as she lightly rubbed her son's back, "Hey, Becca, I like your hair back to its natural color."

"I don't think it's quite the right color," Adam said, stroking his fingers thoughtfully over his chin. "It still looks a little fake, a bit on the brassy side."

Becca got him in the belly with her fist, not hard, since he'd eaten at least four slices of pizza covered with olives and artichokes. Of course he was right and she laughed now. "It will grow out. At least it's not a muddy brown anymore."

Thomas thought she looked beautiful, her hair, just like Allison's, straight and shiny to her shoulders, held back from her face with two gold clips.

Becca cleared her throat and said in a short lull in the conversation, "Does anyone know how Krimakov found me?"

The chewing continued, but she could nearly feel the strength of all that IQ power, all that experience, turned to her question.

Her father took a drink of Pellegrino, then set the bottle down on the Japanese coaster at his elbow. "I can't be certain," he said. "But you're more in the public view now, Becca, what with your speechwriting for Governor Bledsoe. I remember several articles about you. Maybe Krimakov read the articles. Naturally he knows the name Matlock very well. He must have checked into it, found out about your mother, seen her travel plans to Washington. He's a very smart man, very focused when he wants to be."

"It makes sense," Sherlock said. "I don't have another more likely scenario."

Sherlock was looking very serious, but one eye was on her small son. Becca remembered Adam saying something about Sherlock taking down an insane psychopath in some sort of maze. It was hard to imagine until she remembered Sherlock clipping Tyler on the jaw with no fuss at all.

"No matter how he finally managed to find out who she was," Adam said, "he did find out and then he set up this elaborate scheme."

"Krimakov was always so straightforward," Thomas said, "back then. No deep, murky games for him." Then he sighed. "People change. It's frightening in this case. He's taken more turns than a byzantine maze."

Hatch, a bit of mozzarella cheese clinging to his chin, rose and said, "I'm going to go out and see what our guys are doing. They were eating their way through three large pizzas the last time I saw them." His pepperoni pizza box was empty, not even a cold thread of cheese left.

"If you smoke out there, Hatch, I'll smell it on you and I'll fire you. I don't care what you've found out, your butt's on the line here."

"No, Adam, I swear I won't smoke." Then Hatch sighed and sat down again.

Adam, satisfied, turned to Becca. "As for you, Becca, eat. Here's my last piece of pizza. I even left three olives on it. I didn't want to, but I looked at your skinny little neck and restrained myself. Eat."

She took the pizza slice and sat there holding it, even as the cheese cooled and hardened. She picked off an olive.

Savich said, smiling at everyone, perhaps preening a bit, "Oh, yeah, I've got something that's not supposition. MAX found Krimakov's apartment. It's a small place in Iráklion. Mr. Woodhouse knows about it. He's sent agents in."

Everyone stared at him a moment, gape-mouthed.

Savich laughed. He was still laughing when the phone rang minutes later. "That's on my public line," Thomas said as he rose. "The tape recorder will automatically kick on and will tell me who's calling." He saw Becca blink and smiled. "Habit," he said as he picked up the phone.

He didn't say a word, but stood there, listening. He was pale as death when he nodded and said to the person on the other end of the line, "Thank you for calling." Becca jumped to her feet to go to him. He held up a hand and said in a very low, contained voice, "The two agents guarding Becca's room are dead. Agent Marlane is dead. The agent posing as me is dead, shot through the head, three times. I shot Krimakov's wife through the head," he added unemotionally. "The security cameras are smashed. There's pandemonium at the hospital. He got away."

# TWENTY-THREE

Adam came into Becca's bedroom just after midnight to see her sitting up in bed, her arms wrapped around her knees, staring blankly at the wall. A single lamp was turned on. In the dim light he could see she was pale, her face strained. She looked over at him and said, guilt weighing heavy in her voice, "I still can't believe it, Adam. Four people dead and it's because of me."

He quietly closed the bedroom door and leaned back against it, his arms crossed over his chest. Her feelings weren't unexpected but it still made him angry. "Don't be a fool, Becca. I'm the one who carries most of the blame because it was my plan in the first place. What no one can figure out is how he managed to walk right up to the guards outside the room, close enough to see the color of their eyes, and shoot them. Of course he used a silencer. Then he waltzes into the hospital room and kills the other two agents before they can react. To top it all off, he shoots out the security camera. And poof—he's gone, escaped, and no one can figure it out.

"Everyone knew he was coming, it was a trap, contingencies all covered, and sure enough he walked right into it, only it didn't stop him. We lost. Whatever his disguise, it must have been something. Four people are dead." He snapped his fingers. "Just like that, they're gone. How did he do it? What did he look like to make them lower their guard?"

She shook her head numbly. "Tellie Hawley still doesn't know anything?"

Adam shook his head. "They've been studying all the security cameras all over the hospital, and they've spotted some men who might be possibles. I told him that didn't make sense. Track down the little old ladies, track the folk on the cameras who no one in his right mind would take for Krimakov." He moved away from the door and walked to the side of her bed. He leaned over and lightly touched his fingers to her cheek. "I came to check on you. I imagined you would be blaming yourself, and I was right. Stop it, Becca. It was a good plan, a solid plan. Any fault for its failure comes right to my door, not yours."

She turned her face into the palm of his hand. She whispered against his skin, "He doesn't seem human, does he?"

"Oh, he's human enough. I want him very badly, Becca. I want to kill him with my bare hands."

"So does my father. I've never seen anyone so enraged, and yet his voice remained calm and controlled. But it was so cold, so deadly. I wanted to shriek and yell and put my fist through a wall, but he didn't."

"Control is very important to your father. It's saved his life on several occasions and other people's lives as well. He's learned not to let emotion cloud his thinking." He cupped her face in his hand. "I haven't learned it yet, but I'm trying. A terrible thing happened, Becca, but please believe me, it wasn't your fault. We'll catch him. We have to catch him. We've both got to get some sleep." He kissed her mouth, then immediately straightened. It was hard because he wanted to kiss her again, and not stop. He wanted to ease her back down and pull up that virginal nightgown of hers and get his mouth on every bit of her he could get naked. He wanted to make both of them forget the horror, for a little while. But he knew he couldn't. He took a step away from the bed. "Good night, Becca. Try to get some sleep, all right?"

She nodded mutely. The pain in her eyes, the awful guilt that was still burrowed deep inside her—he couldn't stand it. He kissed her again, hard and fast, and before he lost his head, he was out of her bedroom in a flash.

In the hallway, he was frowning, rage at Krimakov roiling away in his belly, when he walked straight into Thomas, who was standing there, watching him, a thick dark brow arched.

Adam came to a dead stop. "I didn't touch her."

"No, of course not. I never thought you did. You were in there to ease her guilt, weren't you?"

"Yes, but I doubt I was successful."

"There's enough guilt for all of us to wallow in," Thomas said. "I'm going downstairs for a while. I've got some more thinking to do."

"There isn't any more thinking to do, there's only worrying and second-guessing, all sorts of worthless crap like that. Wait a second—it just occurred to me that he's got to be pissed, rattled. After all, he was expecting to find both you and Becca in that hospital room, but you weren't there. He has to doubt himself now, his judgment, his take on things. He's been meticulous up until now, but this time he wasn't able to be thorough enough. He screwed up big-time. He was wrong. I don't know what he's going to do next, but whatever it is, he might make another mistake. He's also got to contend with the fallout of his cold-blooded murder of four federal agents. They'll mount the biggest manhunt in a decade. He can't believe he's so good he can walk away from this, that he's somehow immune from capture. We're not alone in this anymore. Everyone and his aunt knows about him and what he is."

"I know that, Adam." Thomas shoved his long fingers through his hair. "You know how quick he is, how clever. Look at how he flushed all of you out of that house in Riptide and then snuck in and hid in Becca's closet. That took balls and cunning. And luck. It is possible that you could have missed Chuck when you were all scouring the area for him, possible that you would have found Chuck tied up and gagged, but you didn't. He was lucky there and he got her.

"I hate to say this, but I firmly believe he'll evade capture. He knows I'll be at the center of things, trying to figure out how to get him. He'll come to Washington. He's going to try to find Becca and me. He's got nothing else to do."

"I still can't figure out why he threw Becca out of his car in New York. He had her. He could have announced it and had you knocking on his door to try to save her. But he let her go. Why? I'm making myself crazy. But if he's as smart as you say he is, he won't come down here, at least not yet, not until things cool down a bit."

"There's one thing I am sure about now, Adam. I'm his reason for living, probably his only reason now. That's why he's leaving a trail of death. He doesn't care about himself anymore. He wants me dead. And Becca, too. I'm thinking that Becca should head out to Seattle or maybe even Honolulu."

"Yeah, right. You be the one to convince her of that, okay? She's just found you. You believe for a single second that she'd pull out now, be willing to say *sayonara* to the father she just met?"

"Probably not." Thomas sighed. "She's still so wary of me. It's like she can't make up her mind whether to hug me or slug me for leaving her and her mother."

"I'm thinking she wants to do both. At least now you two are to-gether. The rest will come, Thomas, be patient. She's known you for twenty-four hours."

"You're right, of course. But—never mind. Krimakov went right in there and killed everyone," Thomas said. "Everyone, without hesitation. To flush me out that first time, he released Becca. I can't imagine what he'd do to her now that she's with me. Well, yes I can. He'd kill her with no more remorse than when he killed all the others. And yes, there's no doubt in my mind he believes she's with me now. He had a silencer on the gun, Adam."

"Yes."

"Agent Marlane had six shots pumped into her. He saw that the male agent wasn't me, knew he'd been set up, and went berserk. Dell Carson, the agent playing me, had his gun out, but he didn't have time to fire. Neither did Agent Marlane."

"Yes. I know."

"How did he get away? Hawley had undercover folk stationed all over that floor and the exits."

Adam shook his head. "His disguise must have been something else. Maybe he even dolled himself up as a woman. Who knows? Do you re-member if Krimakov did disguises back then?"

Thomas leaned against the corridor wall, his arms crossed over his chest. "No. But it's been so many years, Adam, too many. What troubles me, and I know I can't let it, is that Becca can't be sure the guy who took her, the guy on the phone to her, was older." Thomas shook his head. "Another thing. Vasili was fluent in English, but I've read the transcripts of the conversations he had with Becca. It sounds so unlike him. And what he wrote, what he said to her, what he did. Calling himself her boy-friend, murdering Linda Cartwright, then digging her up, smashing her face, all as a sick joke to drive Becca over the edge. That's the behavior of a psychopath, Adam. Krimakov wasn't a psychopath. He was supremely arrogant, but as sane as I was."

"Whatever Krimakov was back then, he's changed," Adam said. "Who knows what's happened to him during the past twenty years? Don't forget all those killings: a second wife, two children, the guy whose password he used to get into the computer system to expunge all his personal data, kill-ing someone to fake his own accidental death in that car accident. How many more we don't know about? And that brings up another question.

You said you believe you're now his only focus, his purpose for living. What about his son? He's in that burn clinic in Switzerland. He doesn't care about him anymore? Or maybe that wasn't an accident, either, and he tried to kill him, too?"

"I don't know."

Adam said, "Maybe he was always over the top and he's gotten more so, and maybe that goes to explain why he appears not to be worrying about his son. No, Thomas, don't argue with me. He's now here—in a foreign country to him—no longer in Crete. He's on our turf, and he probably hasn't been here for all that long."

"Listen, Adam, we don't know that. Officially, Vasili Krimakov hasn't come into this country in the past fifteen years. He was here once back in the mid-eighties, checking around, trying to sniff me out. That was when he killed that assistant of mine simply because he'd seen her with me and decided she was my mistress. But I got away that time and he left, returned to Crete. We've learned he went to England a number of times, but he hasn't gone back there recently. Unofficially, he could have bounced in and out of the United States with a dozen different phony passports. Who in Greece would catch on to that? Or if they did, even care?"

"Still, we have to assume that he was in Crete most of the time. He was married. He eventually had a kid with this woman. So he simply can't know his way around here all that well."

Thomas said, "Becca is right. He's a monster, no matter the excuses I make for the man I knew more than twenty years ago. Of course I didn't really know him. He was a target to me, always on the opposite side, the black king to checkmate. Now we're forced to wait, to gnaw our elbows. Krimakov will find us, count on it.

"Oh yeah, Tellie Hawley and Scratch Cobb are coming tomorrow morning to speak to Becca. Maybe that'll be good. I think she liked them both when she met them in New York. Maybe she'll remember more talking to them. They're pretty desperate, as you can well imagine. Hawley is eating himself alive with guilt. They were his agents, all four of them, and now they're dead."

"Yes," Adam said, and streaked his fingers through his hair, sending it on end. "Since Savich found Krimakov's apartment in Iráklion, our people will go in. Maybe they'll find something."

Becca leaned her forehead against the closed door, listening to their voices as they moved off down the hall. She turned then and leaned back against the door, her arms crossed over her chest, just as Adam had done when he'd first come into her room. She closed her eyes.

He'd murdered four more people. Like Thomas, she knew Krimakov would find them. It was as if he were somehow programmed to find Thomas and kill him. And her, too, of course. He would do anything, go anywhere, kill anyone in his way, to gain his objective.

How could he have killed his wife and her two children, his step-children? And his own son was in a burn hospital in Switzerland. Had that one truly been an accident? No, there were no accidents when it came to Krimakov. It was beyond terrifying.

She returned to her bed, curled up, hugging her arms around her knees. It was warm, very warm, but she was cold all the way to her bone marrow. Suddenly, she heard her mother's voice, sharp with impatience, telling her that if she even considered going out with Tim Hardaway— that juvenile delinquent—she would lock her in a closet for a month. Now she smiled with the memory; then, at sixteen, she had believed her life was over. She wondered what her mother would think of Adam. She smiled, then shivered a bit, remembering that hard, fast kiss. Her mother, she thought, would love Adam.

Suddenly, she heard a whispery sound. She jerked up in bed, her heart pounding, and looked toward the window. Again, that whispery brushing sound. Her heart pumping faster and faster now, she walked over and forced herself to look outside. There was an oak tree there, the end of one leaf-laden branch lightly brushing its leaves over the windowpane.

But he was close, she knew that. On her way back to bed, she kept looking over her shoulder out the bedroom window. She didn't want to speak to any more agents. How close was he?

How close?

NOW everyone in the world knew about Krimakov. Adam watched the old photograph of him flash on FOX and all the major networks. Then it was set beside the photograph the CIA artist had aged, showing what Krimakov would probably look like today. It was a fine job. With luck, it matched enough so he could be recognized. Becca hadn't remembered anything more, however, when she'd looked at the photos.

Everyone wanted to interview Becca Matlock, but no one knew where she was.

The New York cops wanted to talk to her, but this time, she didn't have to put up with Letitia Gordon. The FBI had told them to stuff it after the murder of the four FBI agents in NYU Hospital. There was a lot of name-calling, a lot of rancor, but at least she wasn't in the middle of it now. She'd been lost in the shuffle. She was safe.

As for Thomas Matlock, his identity had leaked quickly enough, but at least no one knew where he was, either. If there had been a leak, they knew media vans would be parked in the yard and microphones would be sticking through the windows of the house.

As it was, everything was quiet. The agents posted all around the house and the neighborhood checked in regularly, reporting nothing suspicious.

Ex–KGB agent Vasili Krimakov—who he was exactly, where he was at present, what his motives were, anything and everything that could possibly be tied to him—was discussed fully, exhaustively, on every news show, every talking-head show. Ex–CIA operatives, ex–FBI counter-terrorist agents, and three former presidential aides spoke authoritatively about him. The question was: Why did he want Thomas Matlock so badly? The question remained unanswered until there was some sort of anonymous release from Berlin about how Thomas Matlock had saved Kemper's life and in the process accidentally killed the wife of the Soviet agent, Vasili Krimakov, who'd been sent to present-day Belarus to assassinate Kemper. The press went wild. Larry King interviewed a former aide to President Carter who remembered perfectly and in great detail the incident when CIA Operative Thomas Matlock had a face-off with Krimakov in the faraway land, killed his wife by accident, and the result-ing brouhaha with the Russians. No one else could seem to recall any of it, including President Carter himself, and everyone knew that President Carter remembered everything, including the number of rubber bands in his Oval Office desk drawer.

A United States Marine who had served with Thomas Matlock back in the seventies spoke authoritatively about how Thomas had refused to be intimidated by the enemy. Which enemy? Didn't matter, Thomas would go to hell and back before he'd ever break. This wasn't at all relevant, but nobody really cared. The bottom line was that all the folk interviewed were ex- or former somethings. The current FBI and CIA directors had put a seal on everything. The president and his staff weren't saying a word, at least officially. Everything was working as it had always worked. Speculation was rife, theories were rampant, but nothing could be proved.

As for Rebecca Matlock, the governor of New York was quoted as saying, "She was an excellent speechwriter with a flair for humor and irony. We miss her." And then he'd rubbed his neck where Krimakov had shot him.

NYPD continued with their "No comment" when there was any question from the press about her. There was no more talk about her being an accomplice to the shooting of Governor Bledsoe. Thank goodness, Becca thought, that no one had found out about Letitia Gordon. She'd bet Detective Gordon would be glad to trash-talk her.

Every murder Krimakov had committed was brought out and examined publicly and exhaustively. There was public outrage.

But no one knew where Rebecca Matlock was.

No one knew where or really who Thomas Matlock was, but the world was coming to believe that he was a dashing, quite romantic James Bond sort of guy who had kept the world safe from the Russians and was now being hunted by a former KGB agent who didn't hesitate to murder people to draw him out.

Becca wondered aloud later to Adam about what the United States Marine had said about Thomas on TV. Adam, who was cleaning his Delta Elite at the kitchen table, said, "It means he got paid maybe five hundred bucks to say something so the ratings would spike."

"The guy said Thomas would never break. What does that mean?"

Adam shrugged. "Who cares? I hope Krimakov is watching. Talk about misdirection. Maybe he'll come to believe that Thomas is invincible." Adam snorted, then buffed the handle of his pistol. "We couldn't do it better if we scripted it ourselves."

"I wonder if Detective Gordon still thinks I'm somehow responsible for all of it."

"I think once she makes up her mind, it'd take an avalanche to change it. Yeah, she still thinks you're a big part of it. I spoke to Detective Morales. I could see him shaking his head over the phone. He's depressed, but glad you're safe now."

"It was the murder of Linda Cartwright that got everybody going."

"Yes. She was an innocent. A very nice middle-class woman. Everyone wants him to fry for what he did to her. Don't forget that older woman in Ithaca. Another innocent. Krimakov has a lot to answer for."

"Does anyone know yet how Dick McCallum was involved with him?"

"Yeah. Hatch found out that McCallum's mother had an extra fifty thousand bucks in a checking account."

"That doesn't seem like so much money if you have to die to get it. Did she tell the police or Hatch if Dick told her anything?"

Adam shook his head, lifted his gun, looked at a face that needed a shave in the reflection of the barrel. "Nope. She was upset about it, but he wouldn't tell her anything, except to keep the money quiet, which she did until Hatch tracked her down and got her to talk."

"The FBI are coming soon."

"Yeah. Don't worry, both Thomas and I will be there."

She smiled at him. "That's nice, Adam, but unnecessary. I'm not a child or helpless, you know. And I do know Agents Cobb and Hawley, who's got hemorrhoids."

He grinned up at her. "Nope, it's Cobb with the hemorrhoids. Now, you were helpless, don't try to rewrite the past, and I don't care what you say, I'll be there."

"I should probably go dig out my Coonan and buff it."

"I'd just as soon never see that pistol anywhere near you again."

"Scared you but good, didn't I?"

Thomas appeared in the kitchen doorway, frowning. "This is odd, but a man named Tyler McBride called Gaylan Woodhouse's office with the message that you, Becca, were to call him immediately. Nothing more, only that instruction."

"I don't understand," Becca said, "but of course I'll call him. What's going on?"

Adam was on his feet in an instant. "I don't like this. Why would McBride call the director of the CIA?"

"I'll find out, Adam. He's probably really worried and wants to make sure I'm okay."

Adam said, "I don't want you to call Tyler McBride. I don't want him anywhere near you. I'll call him, find out what he wants. If he wants reassurance, I'll give it to him."

"Look, Adam, you told me he was really scared for me. He wants to hear my voice. I'm not going to tell him where I am. Now, I'm calling him. Let it go."

"Why don't you two stop bickering?" Thomas said. "Call the man, Becca. If something's wrong, Adam, she'll tell us."

"I still don't like it. Another thing: I've been thinking that maybe you would be safer at my house. At least you could stay there some of the time."

Her left eyebrow went up. "Where do you live, Mr. Carruthers?"

"About three miles down the road."

She stared at him. "Then why are you staying here? Why aren't you going home at all?"

"I'm needed here," he said, studiously rubbing the barrel of his Delta Elite to an even higher shine. "Besides, I do go home. Where do you think I get clean clothes?"

"Get over it, Adam," she said, and went to get her small address book.

"Use my private line," Thomas said. "It's untraceable. Adam, your gun looks good."

"You'll like my house," Adam called after her. "It's a showcase, it's the prettiest place you've ever seen. Plants don't like me, but everything else does. I have a housekeeper come in twice a week and she even makes me casseroles."

Becca turned to face him. "What kind?"

"Tuna, ham and sweet potato, whatever. Do you like casseroles?"

"You bet," she said.

He heard her laugh as she walked away.

He wanted to hear what she said to Tyler McBride, he really did, but he didn't move. Neither did Thomas, who stood there leaning against the refrigerator, his arms crossed over his chest.

"I'm giving her privacy," Adam said. "It's tough."

"Yeah, and you want her to think about your house, don't you?"

"It's a very nice house—an old Georgian brick two-story, lovely yard that I pay a big chunk to keep looking good. Remember I told you how my mom talked me into buying the property some four years ago, told me it was a good investment. She was right."

Thomas said, "Parents usually are."

Adam grunted and looked at his reflection in the gun barrel. "McBride wants her, that's why he's called. He wants her to know that he's still laying claim. I don't trust him, Thomas. He'll use Sam if he has to. He can't have her."

Thomas said, grinning now, "I can see the scowl on your face in the barrel of the gun. No, more than a scowl."

Adam grunted. "How about seriously pissed off?"

What was she saying to Tyler McBride? Worse, what was he saying to her?

# TWENTY-FOUR

In her father's study, the door closed, Becca was leaning on the big mahogany desk, so pale, so off balance she felt transparent. She knew that if
she looked in a mirror, she wouldn't see anything at all. "No, Tyler," she
said again. "I can't believe this."

"Becca, it's happened. Sam is gone. Gone from his bed when I looked
in on him this morning. There was this note pinned to his blanket that
said I had to call you, that I could get to you by calling the office of the
CIA director. So I did. And now you've called."

"Sam can't be gone," Becca said, but she knew that he was, she
knew it.

"He wrote in the note that I wasn't to say a word to anyone, not the
local cops, not anyone, only you. He wrote that he'd kill Sam if I said
anything."

She heard his breathing hitch before he said, "Thank God you called,
Becca. What am I going to do?"

Becca heard the awful deadening fear in his voice, the anger, the helplessness.

"Don't call Sheriff Gaffney, Tyler. Don't. Let me think."

He nearly yelled, "Of course I won't call Sheriff Gaffney. Do you
think I'm nuts?" Then he added, more calmly now, "He wrote that you
had to come to Riptide."

She felt a leap of fear, then said, "Wait a second, Tyler, let me get
Adam."

"No!" She nearly dropped the phone he'd yelled so loud. Then she
heard him draw a deep breath. "No, Becca, please, not yet. He says if you
tell anyone—including your father—he'll kill Sam. I didn't even know
you had a father until the media went nuts over you and him. Becca, the

guy's murdered four more people. He's got Sam. Do you hear me? That maniac's got Sam!"

"I know, I know. Read me the entire note, Tyler."

He was breathing hard, and she knew he was trying to get control. Finally, his voice more steady, he read: "'Mr. McBride, you will speak as soon as possible to Rebecca Matlock. To find her, call the office of the director of the CIA. Tell them to inform her that she is to call you immediately, that a life is at stake. Then you will tell her to come to Riptide. You will tell her not to tell anyone, including her father, or else your son is dead. You don't want him to end up like Linda Cartwright. You have twenty-four hours.'"

"How did he sign it?"

"He didn't sign any name at all. What I read to you, that's it. Becca, what am I to do? You know what he did to Linda Cartwright, what he's done to all those other people. Look at what he did to you. All of Maine is up in arms about Cartwright's murder." He waited a beat, then yelled, "Aren't you listening to me? A Russian agent has got my son!"

"I wonder why he doesn't want my father to come? It's my father he's after. It doesn't make any sense."

"I've listened to everything on the news," Tyler said, calmer now. "It doesn't make any sense to me, either. Please, Becca, you've got to come. If you hadn't called me, I don't know what I'd have done."

"If I come, he'll hold me to get my father. Then he'll kill both of us." She didn't add he would also kill Sam. Why wouldn't he? She was afraid that Sam was already dead, but she wasn't about to say it aloud. The thought nearly brought her to her knees. Not Sam, not that precious little boy. No, she couldn't fall apart. Think. There had to be something she could do.

"I know he'd try to kill both of you. Yes, I know that. What are we going to do?"

"I don't know, Tyler."

"Please don't tell that Adam character or your father, please."

"All right. Not yet, anyway. If I do decide to tell them, I'll call you first, warn you. I'll get back to you in three hours, Tyler. I'm so sorry. It's all my fault. I should never have come to Riptide. The man's crazy, obsessed."

He didn't disagree with her, on any of it. "Three hours, Becca. Please, you've got to come. Maybe you and I together can trap him. Somehow."

When Adam came into Thomas's study five minutes later, he saw her standing at the front window, staring out over the fine green lawn. She was rubbing the bridge of her nose with her fingers, her shoulders slumped. She looked defeated, beaten down. He frowned.

"What's going on? Why did McBride have to speak to you?"

She shrugged. "It was just as you thought. He was worried about me, very worried, what with all the stuff on TV."

"I don't believe that's all, is it?"

She turned slowly to face him. "Of course it is. The FBI people have just pulled up." The car was black, the two men were wearing black, their hair was cut short. And Krimakov had taken Sam. He moved fast, too fast, faster than any of them could have imagined. What to do?

"What's wrong, Becca? You look white around the gills."

"Not a thing, Adam. It's Agent Hawley and Agent Cobb. Let's see what they have to say. I suppose they're sworn to secrecy about where they've come from?"

Adam said as he walked toward the front door, "They would be drawn and quartered if they ever opened their mouths."

Adam shook the two men's hands and stepped back. Tellie Hawley said, "It's good to see you again, Adam. Mr. Matlock, Ms. Matlock. Bet you're wondering how we got ourselves assigned to this."

"It did cross my mind," Thomas said, as he waved them toward the living room.

"Boy, it's hot out there," Scratch Cobb said, gave Becca a big smile, and unbuttoned his black suit coat one button. "A very nice house," Scratch added to Thomas as he walked beside him into the living room. He was looking at a particularly lovely old Tabriz carpet.

"Thank you, Agent Cobb," Thomas said. "Won't you be seated?"

After everyone was settled, Agent Hawley said, "Since we were the ones who initially spoke to Ms. Matlock in the hospital, and since I knew you, sir, Mr. Bushman decided we should stay on as the leads. Of course Savich and Sherlock are on it as well, and he approves of that. It doesn't mean, of course, that the folk here at FBI headquarters are sitting on their hands. They're not."

Thomas nodded. "No, they never do. I'm very sorry about the agents Krimakov murdered in New York, Hawley. It's got to be an awful blow."

Tellie Hawley turned pale, then he flushed red with anger. "He killed four more people in cold blood. He waltzed into the hospital—we still don't know how he was disguised—and he killed my agents. How did he get away? We don't know. It's driving everyone nuts. His aged photo is plastered everywhere. We've got dozens of agents walking around a mile radius of NYU Hospital showing everyone his photo. Nothing yet." He stopped and Becca could feel the pain, the guilt, the rage, radiating from him, spilling out in waves. He'd been the one in charge, the one giving orders. She wouldn't want to be in his shoes. She felt guilty enough in her own shoes.

Sam. What to do?

She watched Tellie Hawley get himself together. He cleared his throat, looked directly at her, and said, "Ms. Matlock, we're here to speak to you in detail about your time with him."

"I'm very sorry, Agent Hawley, but I've told you everything I know. I wish there were more but I can't come up with anything else, even irrelevant."

Agent Hawley sat forward in his chair, his hands dangling between his legs. "The mind is a marvelous instrument, Ms. Matlock. It takes in stuff you're not even aware of. We're betting you do know more about Krimakov. You just don't remember it on a conscious level. We're hoping it's lurking in your subconscious. Ah, Agent Cobb here is an expert hypnotist. He'd like to take you under, really get at what this guy was like, maybe even what he looked like. You know, stuff you've blocked out or you're not even aware that you know, stuff you can't bring up to a conscious level."

Agent Cobb handed her the old photo of Krimakov. "You've seen this?"

"Yes, of course. My father showed it to me immediately, the aged photo as well. I've studied and studied it. I'm sorry, but I don't know if it's him. I never saw him. He was always in the shadows."

"Look again at the aged photo."

She took it, studied it yet again. She still saw an older man, whose face was lean and deeply tanned from years of living on the Mediterranean. His hair had receded, leaving two deep slashes of tanned scalp on either side of a spear of gray hair. His eyes were dark, his features Slavic, wide, flat cheekbones. He looked like he could be a very nice grandfather. And she wondered: Is that you? Are you the one who took me from Jacob Marley's house? Did you lick my cheek? She handed Agent Cobb back the photo. "I have thought and thought. I really don't consciously re-member anything more. I'm willing to go under."

"Are you sure, Becca? You don't have to."

She glanced toward her father, who was standing behind a chair, look-ing at her intently. She didn't know that very handsome man with all those expressions on his face that she didn't understand, but then, she realized that she did know him; on a very deep level, she knew him quite well. It was a very strange feeling. "Yes, sir"—her voice was steady—"I'm sure."

"All right, then," Agent Cobb said, looking directly at her. "There's nothing to be concerned about. I don't go for the couch thing. I prefer the traditional face-to-face method.

"Now, there are also many different ways to hypnotize someone. I use the fixation object method." He pulled a shiny pocket watch out of his vest pocket. For a moment he looked embarrassed, then shrugged. "It belonged to my grandfather. I've always worn it, discovered a couple of years ago that it was the perfect object for me to use to relax people. Now, I want you to sit back and look at this watch, Becca. Just listen to the sound of my voice." He started talking, nonsense really, his voice low and smooth and never rising, never falling, always the same. She stared at the watch that was swinging gently back and forth, back and forth. "You will find that your eyelids have a tendency to get heavy," he said in that singsong soft voice. "That's right, just look at the watch. See how it's moving so slowly right before your eyes?"

Agent Cobb continued reciting a familiar litany to everyone in the room. His voice stayed low and smooth and very intimate. That damned watch kept swinging back and forth, shiny, gold, swinging. Adam had to shake his head and look away. He was getting drawn under.

Five minutes later, Becca was still staring at the shiny gold pocket watch, listening to Agent Cobb's voice telling her about how her eyes were going to close now, how she felt good, and comfortable, how she could just let herself drift. But she didn't. She tried desperately to relax, to get with the program, but she couldn't. All she could see was Sam, that sweet little boy, holding out his arms to her, smiling but hardly ever saying anything. Krimakov had him. He would kill him, kill him without hesita-tion, without a qualm of regret, if she didn't do something. An innocent child, it didn't matter to him, any more than Linda Cartwright had mat-tered. She had to—

Agent Cobb knew it wasn't working, but he kept swinging the watch as he said calmly, in an easy, deep voice, "You were sound asleep, right, Becca, the night he took you?"

"Yes, I was," she said, her voice slow, mimicking his. "I remember knowing that I wasn't dreaming, a very good thing. Then I felt this prick in my arm and I jerked awake. It was him."

"But you couldn't make out his features? Could you make out anything? Surmise anything from the way he was standing, the way he held his arms? His body?"

She shook her head. "No, I'm sorry."

"You're not going under, Becca." Scratch sighed. He lowered the beautiful gold watch, slipped it back into his vest pocket. "I don't know why it's not working. Usually someone very intelligent, very creative, like you are, goes under right away. But you didn't."

She knew why. She couldn't tell him, couldn't tell anyone.

He said in that same easy voice, hitting it right on target, "Something's holding you back. Perhaps you know what it is?" When she didn't say anything, he looked over at Thomas Matlock. "No go. For whatever reason."

Tellie Hawley nodded. "Okay, then, we ask questions and you answer as best you can."

She nodded and talked. And there wasn't anything at all new or earthshattering. Except—

"Adam, did anyone find anything in the hem of my nightgown?"

He shook his head.

"Then he must have found it," she said. "He let me go to the bathroom. I knew I had to do something. I managed to unscrew one of those enamel bolts that hold the toilet to the floor. I pulled open the hem in my nightgown and worked it in. He must have found it."

"Yes," said Hawley, "he found it. He left the toilet bolt in the room, on Agent Marlane's bed. The techs found it and I read it on the collected evidence sheet—'one toilet bolt'—and I forgot about it in all the chaos. Actually when the techs found it, they thought some nurse's aide had dropped it and they were laughing about it. Well, it wasn't any joke. That proves conclusively it was the same guy." He shook his head. "A toilet bolt, a stupid toilet bolt."

"He was taunting us," Thomas said. He got to his feet and began pacing the long living room. "I wish to God I knew where he was. I'd put an end to it. Face him, the two of us."

Becca said, her voice overloud, too sharp, "No." And everyone stared at her. "I will not let you face him alone, Father. No way."

They took a break in the kitchen, drinking coffee. Then Thomas took them to his office to see some of his high-tech goodies. When they went back to the living room, Agent Cobb said to Becca, "May we try one more time to put you under?"

She agreed. What else could she do?

This time, though, Agent Cobb handed her a small white pill. "It's a Valium, to help relax you, to keep you from focusing on something else that might be holding you back. Nothing more than that. You game?"

She took the Valium.

And ten minutes later, when Agent Cobb said, "Are you completely relaxed now, Becca?" she answered in an easy, light voice, "Yes, I am."

"You're aware of everything going on here?"

"Yes, Adam is over there staring at me as if he'd like to wrap me into a very small package and hide me inside his coat pocket."

"What is your father doing?"

"It's still hard for me to think of him as my father. He was dead for so very long, you know."

"Yes, I know. But he's here now, with you."

"Yes. He's sitting there wondering if he should let you continue with this. He's afraid for me. I don't know why. This can't hurt me."

"No, it can't."

"She's right," Thomas said. "But I'll deal with it. Continue, Agent Cobb."

Agent Cobb smiled and patted her hand. "Now, Becca, let's go back to that night when you awoke to that prick in your arm."

She moaned, then jerked.

"It's all right," Agent Cobb said quickly. "Listen to me now. He's not here. It's okay, you're safe."

"No, it's not okay. He'll kill him. I know he'll kill him. What am I going to do? It's all my fault. He'll kill him!"

A slight pause, then Agent Cobb said, "You mean that he'll kill you, Becca? You're afraid that he injected some long-waiting poison in your arm?"

"Oh no. He'll kill him. I've got to do something. "

"Do you mean he'll kill your father?"

"No, no. It's Sam. He's got Sam." And then she started crying, deep, tearing sobs that jerked her wide awake. "Oh, no," she said, staring at all the appalled faces. "Oh, no."

"It's all right, Becca," Agent Cobb said. "You'll be fine now."

Thomas said very slowly, "So that's what McBride had to say to you. Krimakov kidnapped Sam and had McBride call the director to find you and have you call him."

"No," she said. "No. I don't know what you're talking about."

Valium, she thought. She had just killed Sam, just killed her father, God knew who else, all because of one Valium.

Adam was on his feet. "Where's your address book? I'm going to call McBride, find out what's going on here."

"No," she said, jumping up to grab his arm. "No, you can't, Adam."

"Why not?"

# TWENTY-FIVE

The room was dead silent.

"No, you can't have my address book."

"Fine. I'll call information." Adam walked toward the phone. "We've got to know exactly what's going on here."

Becca didn't say another word. She ran out of the living room, grabbed her purse from the table in the entryway, and made for the front door.

"Becca! Come back here!"

She heard Adam yelling but didn't pay any attention. She heard her father's voice, then Special Agent Cobb's voice. She didn't slow. She was out on the narrow front porch before Adam reached the entryway.

She heard all of them shouting at her, running after her, but she knew she had to get away. No one else was going to die. Not Sam. Not her father. She had to stop it. She didn't know how she was going to do it yet, but she would think of something. She should have thought of something before—maybe even been a bit on the subtle side. *Yes, you fool, you should have calmly left the living room, pretending to go upstairs or go to the bathroom, whatever.* But no, she'd lost it—here she was running away with people chasing her, FBI agents everywhere. But that didn't matter, either. She had no choice. If she could prevent it, no one else was going to die. She ran.

There were no sidewalks in this very nice neighborhood, just big lawns, thick curbs, and the road. She hit the road. She was fast, always had been since she'd been on the track team in high school. She put her head down, turned off all the voices, and ran. She felt the breath pumping in and out of her lungs, felt herself filling with energy, with power, expanding, moving faster, faster. Her feet in Nikes were unbeatable.

She ran right into Sherlock. Both women went down.

Becca was on her feet in an instant. "Sorry, but I've got to go."

"Stop her!"

Sherlock grabbed her ankle and pulled. Becca went down on the edge of a lawn, hitting her hip on the curb. A shaft of sharp pain went through her, but she ignored it. She was ready to fight, ready to do whatever she had to, but Sherlock had somehow managed to straddle her, how she didn't know, but she'd been fast, too fast, and now she was holding her arms down. How could she be so strong? How did she get her in this position so quickly? Sherlock was leaning over her, her curly red hair bouncing against Becca's face. "What's going on here, Becca?"

"Get off me, Sherlock. Please, you've got to let me go. I don't want to hurt you."

"You can't hurt me, so don't even try. Tell me what's happened."

Becca started struggling, but then it didn't matter, and she stilled because Adam was there, not even panting hard, standing over them, staring down at her, his hands on his hips. "Thanks for bringing her down, Sherlock. That wasn't very smart, Becca."

Sherlock didn't like this one bit. She looked at all the men running to the scene, even the two dark-suited FBI guys who'd been parked discreetly down the street. "What's going on, Adam? Oh yeah, given that I could have hurt Becca dragging her down, I'd really better like the answer." She pulled herself off Becca and slowly got to her feet. She held out her hand.

Becca looked at that white hand that was surely too strong, but she didn't move. She rolled over away from them, grabbed her purse, and was off again. A sharp pain went through her hip but she ignored it.

She got at least ten feet before two arms went around her waist and she was picked up, twirled around, and thrown over a man's shoulder. She hit her chin against his back. "Hold still," he said, and his voice was calm and quiet. Too calm, too quiet.

Sherlock was one thing. Having a big guy haul her over his shoulder was another. It was humiliating. She jerked and pulled and kicked. "All right," he said, and pulled her down. He brought her back up against him, wrapped his arms around her, and held on tight. No matter what she did, she couldn't get free. He'd pinned her arms to her sides but good.

Three hours, she thought. Time was running out. "What time is it?"

"I'll tell you after you promise not to run away again."

She leaned down and bit his hand, hard. He didn't make a single sound, jerked her around to face him and said, "I'm sorry, Becca," and lightly tapped his fist against her jaw. It was the strangest feeling. It didn't really hurt, but she saw a whole skyful of white lights, popping all over her brain, then it was as if someone switched off the lights. Nothing. She slumped against him.

"She's a fighter," he said to Sherlock, who was standing beside him as he picked Becca up in his arms. He looked at the back of his hand. At least he wasn't bleeding, but he could see the row of even teeth marks. That had been close, too close. But now he had her. She was too thin, he thought, as he carried her back. She didn't weigh enough; well, he'd see to that. He'd force food down her gullet if he had to. He frowned as he realized she was a fast runner, very fast. He wasn't certain if he could have caught her if Sherlock hadn't been there. He didn't like that thought, not one bit. He saw Thomas striding toward him, looking frantic.

"What's going on here, Adam?" Suddenly Sherlock was right in his face, and she wasn't going to move. He couldn't very well clip her on the chin. She'd probably flatten him. Since she was married to Savich, he wouldn't be surprised if she had a black belt, maybe two.

He said, "Krimakov kidnapped Sam McBride. Come on back to the house and we'll let everyone know what's happening. She promised McBride she wouldn't tell anyone. However, when Agent Cobb gave her some Valium to relax her so he could hypnotize her, she inadvertently spilled the beans. She did go under. Then it all came out."

"This is insane," said Sherlock. "That maniac kidnapped Sam? Let me get ahold of Savich. I can't believe this. Is that guy everywhere?" She stepped away and pulled the cell phone out of her pocket.

The agents who'd been watching the house were now standing next to Thomas and agents Hawley and Cobb.

They parted from his path and Adam carried Becca back into the house, not saying another word. He hoped no neighbors in this lovely neighborhood had seen this bizarre action and called the cops.

"I hope you didn't hurt her," Thomas said, right on his heels.

"She nearly bit my hand off," Adam said.

"Yeah, but you brought her down."

"No, that was Sherlock. I clamped my arms around her."

"You weren't gentle enough."

"Thomas, what did you want me to do, lie down and let her stomp on me before she ran another four-minute mile?"

"Yeah, Adam," Agent Hawley said. "She got you good, but it's not bleeding. Good straight teeth. Put her down on the couch."

Thomas covered her with an afghan Allison had given him some seven years before. He didn't realize it was quite hot, since they'd left the front door wide open and all the cold air had seeped out.

"I was careful," Adam said, but he was sitting beside her, lightly touching her jaw where he'd hit her. "She shouldn't even bruise. Listen, Thomas, she was going to run and run until we brought her down. She would have fought me until I might have hurt her by accident. She wasn't thinking."

"Yeah, I guess I understand." Thomas raised his eyes to Hawley and Cobb. "We're in deep trouble now."

Becca moaned and opened her eyes. She lurched up only to have two hands push her back down, and Adam's voice close to her face saying, "If you try anything again, I'm going to lock you in your room. If you bite me again, I'll lock you in your closet and feed you moldy bread and water."

Her hair was hanging in her face, her jaw felt swollen and sore, and she was so mad she wanted to spit. More than that, she was desperate. She was tired of failing. All she'd done since Krimakov had come into her life was fail. She raised her head and looked him squarely in the eye. "That wasn't funny."

"No, it wasn't. What I want to do is help you if you'll let me."

The three hours were up, she knew it. She had to do something. She had to do something right this minute. But it didn't matter. It was too late. All of them knew now. She said, trying to control her misery, her deadening fear, "I've got to call Tyler. I promised to call him in three hours. If I don't, I don't know what he'll do, probably go to the media. Don't you understand? Krimakov has Sam. He wants me to come to Riptide, doesn't want me to tell you or Dad. Tyler is desperate."

Adam came down on his knees in front of her. "Becca, look at me."

"I was looking at you. You're trying to lighten things up. You can't. You can't help me. Only I can do something here. I don't want to look at you. It doesn't matter. I've got to call Tyler. You can't help."

"All right." He rose and offered her his hand. A big hand, she thought, and she wished she could bite it again, then flip him over the back of the sofa.

"You all right, sweetheart?" Thomas said, handing her a cup of tea.

Sweetheart? He'd called her sweetheart and it seemed to have come out naturally, not a fake endearment. It nearly made her cry. No one had ever called her sweetheart before. Her mom had always called her honey, or when she was a little girl she'd been Muffin.

She didn't let it touch her. She couldn't, not now at any rate. "I've got to call Tyler, tell him I'm coming right away to Riptide and that none of you are coming with me. Do you understand? Sam dies if anyone comes with me. No, Adam, shut up. I will not let that little boy die."

"But that doesn't make any sense," Thomas said slowly. "He wants you, that's true, but he wants me more. Why doesn't he want both of us to come to Riptide? The package deal he always wanted? What's he up to now?"

Becca said, "I don't know. I agree it doesn't make any sense at all, but that's what he wrote in his note to Tyler. He told Tyler how to contact me, and then when I did call, Tyler was to tell me to come to Riptide alone. Not to tell either of you or Sam would die."

"Note?" Sherlock said. "What note?"

"The kidnapping note," Becca said. "Krimakov left it on Sam's bed after he took him. Told him exactly what to do, told him if I didn't come, he'd kill Sam, just like Linda Cartwright."

"It might not even matter now," Sherlock said, "but if we can get the note, I'll give it to our handwriting experts. Also, they can compare the handwriting to other documents that you have, Thomas, with Krimakov's handwriting on them."

Thomas said, "There are some samples of his handwriting, yes, but what good would it do to analyze it? You're right, it probably doesn't even matter now. We're coming down to the endgame here." Thomas sighed and streaked his fingers through his hair. "I wish I knew what kind of gambit Krimakov was playing."

Sherlock said, "I do, too, but since we don't, we have to keep using the tools we've got. If he gives us the time, if he continues with his delaying tactics, and more distractions, I can get the two samples of his handwriting compared. Maybe they could tell us how far over the edge he's gone, or maybe prove that all he's done is cold manipulation and butchery, and he's as sane as you and I. Our people are good, trust me. There's no reason not to do it."

"I've got to talk to Tyler," Becca said, rising, throwing off the afghan. "Reassure him. Tell him what's going on here."

Sherlock said, "At the very least, if there's still time, the analysis and comparison will let us know what we're up against. Trust me on this. Get that note from Tyler, Becca."

"Yes, she will," Thomas said. "Go make your call, Becca."

Becca nodded and walked to the phone, pulling the small address book out of her purse as she walked. She looked up Tyler McBride's number. She dialed.

After three rings, Tyler answered, his voice frantic. "Becca? Is that you?"

"Yes, Tyler."

"Thank God. Where are you? What are you doing? What's happening?"

"Okay, Tyler, listen to me. Here's the plan. It's the only way to handle this, so don't yell at me. We're all coming up to Riptide, but not together. No, be quiet and listen. We're all going to trickle in. He'll never know there's anyone else but me in Riptide. I'll come directly to your house, we'll speak, he'll see me, then I'll go to Jacob Marley's house. He'll come for me there. You know it. I know it." She drew a deep breath. "He has no reason to kill Sam. He'll have me, so he can keep his word and release him."

"The others will be hiding in Jacob Marley's house?"

"No, but they'll be close by. It will work, Tyler."

She was aware that all of them were staring at her, but she just shook her head at them. It was the only way to go, and all of them knew it. There'd been no reason to flail about and discuss any number of options into the ground. She had to go and she knew no one would let her go alone. Fine. They had a chance now. "Oh yes, Tyler, I need you to give me Krimakov's note. Sherlock wants it. Now, just go about your business. Don't say a word to anyone. We'll be there in under four hours."

Slowly, she lowered the phone into its cradle. She looked up. "Sam's not going to die."

"No," Adam said, walking to her, "no, he won't." Then he couldn't stand it. He pulled her against him and held her there, his hand tight across her back, his other hand fisted in her hair. He felt her heart beating against his chest, hard, fast strokes. He brought her closer. He looked up to see Thomas staring at him, and slowly, he loosened his fingers in her hair, smoothing it down, but he didn't want to let her go.

Thomas said, "Agent Hawley and Agent Cobb, this kidnapping will stay amongst us. It doesn't go to anyone else in the FBI. All right?"

"No problem," said Tellie Hawley. "We're in this thing to the end. That bastard butchered four of my people. I want him as much as you do. If Savich and Sherlock aren't saying anything to the higher-ups, why should we?"

"Let's get rolling," Sherlock said once Thomas had given her several papers with Krimakov's handwriting. "We'll meet at Reagan in an hour?"

"No," Thomas said. "We'll go over to Andrews Air Force Base. I'll have a plane ready for us."

They were nearly out the door when Thomas's private phone rang. He looked undecided, then said, "Hold on. It's got to be important if it's on that phone."

Slowly, because she didn't really want to, Becca forced herself to pull away from Adam. "I'm all right," she said.

"I'm not," he said, and smiled at her. "We'll get through this."

They all followed Thomas back to his study, watched him pick up the phone on the edge of the mahogany desk.

"Yes? . . . Hello, Gaylan."

It was Gaylan Woodhouse, the CIA director. They all watched Thomas's face stiffen, then slowly turn pale and set. "Oh no," he said, his voice bleak. "You're absolutely certain of all this?"

They watched him lower the phone and stare over at them. He looked shaken, dazed. "This is too much," he said. "Just too much."

"What happened?" Adam was at Thomas's side in but a moment.

Thomas shook his head, his eyes dazed. There was a fine tremor in his hands. "You're not going to believe this. CIA Agent Elizabeth Pirounakis was blown up when she went into Vasili Krimakov's apartment in Iráklion. Krimakov must have worked there, left notes there, evidence of his plans.

"The whole building blew up. It's now rubble. Agent Pirounakis is dead, the two other Greek agents with her dead as well. Gaylan isn't certain yet, but given the time of the explosion, thankfully very few people were in the apartment building."

"He did this before he left Crete," Agent Hawley said. "It's not something he's just done."

Adam said, "At least now there has to be an inquiry about the guy they buried. Surely now they can't hang on to the fiction that the man in the car accident was Vasili Krimakov?"

Thomas looked at Adam. "It doesn't much matter now. There's hell to pay over there, but that doesn't help us."

"Time," Adam said. "It's what he hasn't given us."

Thomas nodded, then paused another moment and looked over at his daughter. "You're right. Let's go."

She gave him a smile filled with rage and said, "Yes. Lock and load."

# TWENTY-SIX

It was hot that day in Maine, even by the water. Lobster boats bobbed up and down in the inlets, fishermen, their hats pushed back on their heads, lay in the shade of the awnings on their boats, if they were lucky enough to have awnings.

The white spires of the Riptide churches shone beneath the bright afternoon sun. There wasn't much movement anywhere. It was too hot. The tourists weren't wandering around taking photos of the quaint Maine town, they were holed up in air-conditioned pubs.

The hot weather didn't bother the birds. Osprey dove for fish off the spruce-covered points. Gulls squawked and whirled over the lobster boats. The smell of dead fish left too long in the heat sent out odors that meant you had to take shallow breaths to survive. Cumulus clouds in fantastic shapes dotted the steel blue sky. There was no breeze at all. Still, hot air blanketed the land.

Becca was so scared that all the beauty of the land and ocean, the sound of the birds, the incredible blue of the sky—none of it penetrated her brain. She felt frozen in the near hundred-degree heat.

She'd driven herself in a rented white Toyota from a private airfield near Camden. It had taken her nearly an hour to negotiate the tourist traffic on Highway 1 south to Riptide, below Rockland. Her hands were clammy, her heart slowly thudding in her chest. She tried to think of all that could go wrong, but her mind wouldn't slip into gear.

When a mosquito bit her as she was pumping gas, she was pleased she felt it. She wasn't even aware of being pissed off that the rental agency hadn't filled her car before renting it to her.

When she arrived in Riptide at three o'clock in the afternoon, she drove directly to Tyler's house on Gum Shoe Lane. He was standing in the yard, waiting for her. He was quite alone.

Tyler held her very close, as if she were a lifeline, and so she stood there, his arms locked tightly around her. Finally, she eased back and looked up at him. "Any word at all?"

"Another note from Krimakov."

"Let me see it."

"This is all a huge mess, Becca."

"Yes, I know, and I'm so sorry for it, Tyler. It's all my fault. If I could go back into the past, make the decision not to come here, I swear I would. I'm so sorry. I swear that Sam will be all right. I swear it to you."

He looked at her for a very long time, but he didn't say anything, to either agree or disagree.

"Show me the new note. Then I'll take both of them with me, okay?"

The note was handwritten, big strokes, black ballpoint: *The boy will be all right for another eight hours. If Rebecca isn't here, he's dead.*

She folded both notes, put them in the pocket of her sundress, and left for Jacob Marley's house twenty minutes later. Undoubtedly Krimakov was watching Tyler's house, at least he should be. She would call in another half hour in case Krimakov hadn't been watching. For sure he'd have a trace on Tyler's phone.

She unlocked the front door of Jacob Marley's house. It was still and hot inside, so very silent, nothing moving at all, not a single sound, not even a floorboard. She opened all the windows and switched on the overhead fans. The hot air stirred, nothing more, until fresh air began creeping in. The curtains billowed ever so slightly.

So quiet. It was so very quiet in the house. She went into the kitchen and put on water to boil. She'd make iced tea, there were still bags in the cabinet. She opened the refrigerator, saw that it had been cleaned out, and wondered who had done it. Probably Rachel Ryan, she thought. It was a nice thing for her to do. She had to go to the Food Fort. Good, he could see her driving around, know that she was here, know she was alone. She hoped she wouldn't see Sheriff Gaffney because surely he'd want to talk to her.

When she got into the Toyota, she pulled out the small button on her wristband and said, "I'm heading out to Food Fort now. The cupboard's bare. I'll be back in under an hour. I want to make sure he knows I'm here. I'll leave the notes on the front seat of the car at Food Fort." Then she pushed the button back in.

She was greeted at Food Fort like a celebrity. Everyone knew who she was, impossible for them not to now, what with her photo and her story on every news station in the United States. People peered around corners to look at her, even stare at her, but they really didn't want to get close enough to speak to her. She smiled, nothing more, and put stuff in her shopping cart.

When she was checking out, a woman behind her said, "Well, finally I get to see you. Sheriff Gaffney told me all about you, what a pretty girl you are, how there was this big fellow there at Jacob Marley's house who really wasn't your cousin. He didn't buy that one for a minute. You really lied to him, didn't you, and he couldn't do anything about it. But now everyone knows who you are."

"But I don't know who you are, ma'am."

"I'm Mrs. Ella, his chief assistant."

It was the Mrs. Ella who'd kept her from getting hysterical when she'd called the sheriff's office to report the skeleton falling out of the wall in the basement by telling her about all her dogs, every last one of them. Mrs. Ella, who also shopped at Sherry's Lingerie Boutique. She was a big woman, muscular, with a corded neck and a mustache shadowing her upper lip.

"You're a liar, Ms. Powell. No, you're Ms. Matlock. You made up that name when you came here."

"I had to lie. So nice to speak to you, ma'am."

"Ha, I'll just bet. Why are you back here?"

Becca smiled. "I'm a tourist now, ma'am. I'm going to go out on a lobster boat." And she hefted her two grocery bags and left Food Fort.

"The sheriff will want to speak to you," Mrs. Ella yelled after her. "It's a pity he had to drive to Augusta on O-fficial Business."

She heard Mrs. Ella say behind her, "She's back here to do more bad things, you mark my words, Mrs. Peterson. Here she was all nice and hysterical when she found Melissa Katzen's skeleton in her basement wall, but it was all a lie. If the skeleton hadn't been so old, I would have bet she'd done it."

Becca turned slowly in the half-open door, her arms aching with the heavy bags, and said, "Melissa Katzen was murdered, ma'am, and not by me. That isn't a lie. Does anyone know anything yet?"

"No," called out Mrs. Peterson, the cashier, who had bright red dyed hair. "We're not even one hundred percent sure that it is Melissa Katzen. The DNA tests haven't come back yet. It takes weeks, Sheriff Gaffney said."

"No, I'm the one who told you that," Mrs. Ella said. "Sheriff Gaffney doesn't keep track of DNA sorts of stuff, I do. As for you, Ms. Matlock, I'm going to tell the sheriff you're here again as soon as I can raise him on his cell phone, which he usually doesn't carry because he hates technology."

When Becca got back to the car, the notes in Krimakov's handwriting were gone. She hoped the sheriff wouldn't get to her anytime soon. She hoped that her little trip to Food Fort wouldn't backfire. Surely Krimakov knew she was here now, surely.

Riptide, she thought as she got into the Toyota, her haven once upon a time, with its Food Fort on Poison Oak Circle and Goose's Hardware on West Hemlock. She drove slowly along Poison Ivy Lane, then turned onto Foxglove Avenue, down two blocks to her street, Belladonna Drive. She turned yet again on Gum Shoe Lane, drove past Tyler's house, then turned back onto Belladonna Drive to Jacob Marley's house. It was getting a bit cooler, even though the sun was still high in the summer sky. Maine gave you the earliest sunrise and latest sunset.

She was still wearing the light blue cotton sundress Sherlock had brought back to New York with her, and she wished she had a sweater. Fear seemed to leach the heat right out of her.

The house was cooler. She made iced tea, put together a tuna salad sandwich, and sat out on the wide veranda, watching night slowly fall. She wondered if anyone would slip into Jacob Marley's house. The wristband was one-way.

Odd, but she didn't think about Krimakov. She thought about Adam, his face now clear in her mind.

He'd snuck up on her, just as, she supposed, she'd snuck up on him. She smiled. He was a good man, sexy, which she wouldn't tell him just yet, and he had a streak of honor a mile wide. Even when she'd bitten his hand and cursed him, wanted to kick him into the dirt, she'd known that honor of his was real and wouldn't ever change to suit the circumstance.

And Adam knew her father a lot better than she did. And he'd never said a word. What did that say about this mile-wide honor of his? She'd have to think about that.

She took the last bite of her sandwich and wadded up the napkin. It was nearly dark now. Surely Krimakov would do something soon. Her Coonan was in the pocket of her sundress. She hadn't told anyone about the gun, but she suspected that Adam knew she had it. He'd kept his mouth shut, a smart move, or else she might have bitten him again.

She hadn't seen a soul, at least not a soul who was here especially for her. It would be soon, she felt it. Krimakov was close. Everyone else was close, too. She wasn't alone in this. And she thought of Sam and of Krimakov's note.

She waited and looked up at the sliver of moon in the dark sky. She prayed Sheriff Gaffney had decided not to come see her tonight. Finally, she walked into the house, shut and locked the front door. She closed and locked all the windows. She didn't want to go upstairs to the bedroom where he'd hidden in her closet and stuck a needle in her arm.

She was on the stairs when the phone rang. Her fingers clutched at the oak railing so tightly they turned white. The phone rang again. It had to be Krimakov.

It was. She pushed the small button on the wristband and pressed her wrist close to the phone receiver.

"Hello, Rebecca. It's your boyfriend." His voice was playful, filled with crazy fun. It scared her to death. "Hey, I hope I didn't hurt you too badly when I threw you out of the car in New York?" His voice was still mischievous, but now he'd pitched it lower, maybe even put a handkerchief over the mouthpiece. She wondered if her father would recognize his voice after twenty-something years.

"No, you didn't hurt me too badly, but you already know that, don't you? You killed four people in NYU Hospital to get to me and my father, but we weren't there. You failed, you murdering butcher. Where is Sam? Don't you dare hurt that little boy."

"Why not? He's worth nothing except that he did get you here for me. I'll bet the CIA director got ahold of you really fast. Now you're here and you're alone, I see. You followed my instructions. Hard to believe they let you come here all by yourself, all unprotected."

"I ran away. I'm waiting for you. Come here and bring Sam."

"Now, now, there's no rush, is there?"

He was playing with her, nothing new in that. She drew a deep breath, tried to be calm. "I don't understand why you didn't want my father to come with me. It's him you want to kill, isn't that right?"

"Your father is a very bad man, Rebecca, very bad, indeed. You have no idea what he's done, how many innocent people he's destroyed."

"I know that he shot your wife by accident a long time ago, and that you swore to get revenge. All the rest of it, it's a fabrication of your own crazy mind. I don't think anyone has killed more people than you have. Listen to me, please. Why not stop it all now? My father was devastated when he accidentally shot your wife. He told me you had brought her with you, faking a vacation when you were really there to assassinate that visiting German industrialist. Why did you use your wife like that?"

"You know nothing about it. Shut up."

"Why won't you tell me? Did you really believe that she wouldn't be in any danger if you took her with you?"

"I told you to shut up, Rebecca. Hearing you talk about that wonderful woman dirties her memory. You're from his seed, and that makes you as filthy as he is."

"All right, fine. I'm filthy. Now, why didn't you want my father to come here with me? Don't you still want to kill him?"

"I will, never fear. How and when I do is up to me, isn't it, Rebecca? Everything is always up to me."

"What am I doing here alone? Why did you take Sam if you only wanted me to come here to Riptide?"

"It got you here quickly, didn't it? You'll find out everything in time. Your father was smart. He hid you and your mother very well. It took me a very long time to find you two. Actually, it was you I found first, Rebecca. There was an article about you in the Albany newspaper that was picked up in syndication. It talked about you. I saw your name and got interested. I found out about your mother, your supposedly dead father, and then I learned about your mother's travels each year. It was then I knew. Most of her trips were to Washington, D.C."

He laughed. Her skin crawled. "Hey, I'm real sorry about your mother, Rebecca. I had hoped to get to know her really well, but then she had to go so quickly into the hospital. I suppose I could have gotten into Lenox Hill easily enough and killed her, but why not let the cancer do it? More painful that way. At least I hoped it would be. But as it turned out, your mother didn't have a lick of pain, that's what a nice nurse told me. Then she patted my arm in sympathy. She went away in her mind and stayed there. No pain at all. Even if I had come to her, she wouldn't have known it, so why bother?

"But you're different, Rebecca. I have you now and I will have your father, too. I will kill that bloody murderer." She heard the rage now in his voice, low and bubbling, and it would build and build. She heard his breathing, harsh but more controlled now, and he said finally, "I want you to get in your car and drive to the gym on Night Shade Alley. Do it now, Rebecca. That little boy is depending on you."

"Wait! What do I do when I get there?"

"You'll know what to do. I've missed you. You have a lovely body. I touched you with my hands, ran my tongue all over you. Did you know I left that toilet bolt on that agent's bed at NYU Hospital? It was for you, Rebecca, so you would know I was all over you, looking at you, feeling you, rubbing you. You hoped when you unscrewed that bolt that you could smash it in my eye, didn't you?"

She was shaking with fear and rage, each so powerful alone, but mixed together they quaked through her, making her light-headed.

"You're an old man," she said. "You're a filthy old man. The thought of you even near me makes me want to vomit."

He laughed, a deep laugh that was terrifying. "I'll see you very soon now, Rebecca. And then I'll have a surprise for you. Never forget, this is my game and you will always play by my rules."

He hung up. She knew in her gut that wherever he was hiding this time, there wouldn't have been any way to trace the call, no matter how sophisticated the equipment. All the others knew it, too.

She depressed the button. They'd heard everything. They knew exactly what she knew now.

She didn't take anything with her, except her Coonan. When she got into the Toyota, she again pressed the small button, then started the car. "I'm leaving for the gym now."

Her precious mother, she thought. She'd escaped him by falling into the coma. He'd been in the hospital, asking about her. It was too much, just too much.

She drove to Klondike's Gym in just over eight minutes. It sat right at the very end of Night Shade Alley, a big concrete parking lot in front, trees crowding in all around the rest of the two-story building. There were windows all across the front, lights filling all of them. There were at least two dozen cars in the big concrete lot. She'd been here once with Tyler. That had been in the middle of the day. Not nearly the number of cars there then. Perhaps since it was so hot during the day, the Mainers waited until the evening cool to work out. She drove in, picked a place that had no cars near it, turned off the engine, and sat there. Five minutes passed. Nothing. No sign of Krimakov, no sign of anyone at all.

She depressed the button on the wristband. "I don't see him. I don't see anything out of the ordinary. There are lots of people here."

Everyone should be here by now. They were ready. They all wanted Krimakov. They would do absolutely nothing until they had Krimakov. Everyone had agreed on that.

There was nothing to worry about. "I'm going in now." She got out of the car and walked into the gym. There was a bright-faced young man at the counter, looking like he'd just worked out hard. His clothes were sweated through. "Hi," he said, and looked at her.

She wasn't wearing workout clothes.

She smiled. "I was here once before and I rented a locker in the women's locker room. My clothes are there. I need to pick them up."

"I know you. You've been on TV, on every channel."

"Yes. May I please come in now?"

"That'll be ten dollars. What are you doing here?"

She opened her wallet and pulled out a twenty. "I'm here to pick up my workout clothes." He didn't even look up. She watched him for what seemed like forever as he got her a ten in change. He pressed a buzzer and she went through the turnstile.

The room was large, filled with machines and free weights and mirrors. The lights were very bright, nearly blinding. A radio played loud rock, booming out from the overhead speakers. There were lots of young people here tonight, thus the raucous music. There were at least thirty people throughout the big room. Upstairs were all the aerobic machines. She heard talk, music, groans, the harsh movement of the machines, nothing else.

What was she to do?

She walked back to the women's locker room. There were three women inside, in various stages of undress. No one paid her any attention. Nothing there.

She walked out of the dressing room, and this time she walked slowly, roaming through the big room, looking at all the men. Many of them were young, but there were some older ones as well, all of them different one from the other—fat, thin, in shape, paunchy. So many different sorts of men, all there on this night, working away. Not one of them approached her.

What to do?

A couple of young guys were horsing around, doing fake hits, laughing, insulting each other. One of them accidentally backed into the arm of an old chest machine. The big weighted arms weren't clicked in to a setting. When the young guy hit it, it swung out and hit her squarely on her upper right arm. She stumbled into a big Nautilus machine and lost her balance. She went down.

"I'm sorry. You all right?"

He was helping her up, rubbing her shoulder, her arm, looking at her now with a young male's natural sexual interest. "Hey, talk to me. You okay?"

"Yes, I'm fine, don't worry."

"I haven't seen you here before. You new in town?"

"Yes, sort of."

He was lightly touching her arm now, as if assuring himself that she was okay, and she tried to smile at him, assure him that she was fine. The other young man came up on the other side, vying with the first for her attention.

"Hey, I'm Steve. Would you like to go have a drink with me? I figure I owe you since I knocked you on your butt."

"Or maybe you'd like to go with both of us? I'm Troy."

"No, thank you, guys. I absolve you of all guilt. I have to leave now."

She finally managed to get away from them. She turned once and saw them looking after her, smiling, waving, looking really pleased with themselves now that she'd looked back at them.

Neither of them was more than twenty-five, she thought. Well-built boys. She was twenty-seven. She felt ancient.

Finally, because she couldn't think of anything else to do, she went through the turnstile at the front of the gym. The young guy who'd let her in wasn't there. No one was there. She felt a ripple of alarm. Where had the kid gone? Maybe a shower. Yeah, that was it. He'd really been sweating.

She thought she saw a shadow outside the front door. It was one of the good guys, she thought, it had to be.

Where was Krimakov? He'd said she'd know what to do. He was wrong.

She walked slowly back to the Toyota. The lights weren't bright in this part of the lot and that was why she'd elected to park here. She hadn't wanted to park close by other cars, hadn't wanted to take the risk of Krimakov hurting anyone else. Now she wished she hadn't because no one seemed to be about.

She reached out her hand to the door handle. Suddenly, without warning, she felt a sharp sting in the back of her left shoulder. She gasped, whirled around, but there was nothing, no one. Only the dim light from the lights overhead. No movement. Nothing. She felt herself slipping. That was odd—she was falling, but slowly, sort of sliding down against the door of her car.

# TWENTY-SEVEN

"No," she said into her wristband. "Nobody move. I'm all right. I don't see him. Don't move. Something struck me in the left shoulder, but I'm okay. Stay where you are until he comes out."

She sat on the concrete, the unforgiving hard roughness against her bare legs. She put her head back, listened to her heart pounding, did nothing, unable to do anything. She wanted to cry out but she didn't, she couldn't, Sam's life was at stake, and if she did cry out, she knew Adam would come running. She couldn't allow that. What had he done to her? What kind of drug had he shot into her back? Had he killed her? Would she die here in the concrete parking lot at the gym?

Now she felt only light pain in her shoulder. She pressed back against the door and felt something sharp dig into her flesh. Something was sticking out of her shoulder. She said quietly, because she didn't know if Krimakov was near, "No, don't move. He shot me with something, and now I can feel some sort of dart sticking out of my back. Don't move. I'm all right. There's still no sign of Krimakov." She reached both arms back and managed to grip the narrow shaft. What was going on here? Slowly, because it seemed the only thing to do, she pulled on the shaft. It slipped right out, sliding easily through her flesh, not deep at all, barely piercing the skin. She leaned over, suddenly light-headed. She believed she would faint but she didn't. "I'm all right. Stay hidden. It's some kind of small dart. Just a moment."

She looked at the shaft she'd pulled out of her shoulder. There was something rolled tightly around it. Paper. She pulled it off, unrolled it. Her fingers were clumsy, slow.

She was still alone, still sitting by her car. No one had come out of the gym.

She managed to make out the black printing on the unrolled piece of paper in the dim light. It was in all caps:

GO HOME. YOU'LL FIND THE BOY.

                    YOUR BOYFRIEND

"It says that Sam's at home. Nothing more. He signed it 'Your Boy-friend.'"

What was going on here? She didn't understand, and doubted that any of the others did, either. She wanted to drive like a bat out of hell to get back to Jacob Marley's house, to find Sam, but she couldn't, she was too dizzy. Waves of light-headedness came over her at odd moments. She drove home slowly, watching for other cars, headlights behind her. But nothing seemed out of the ordinary. She knew they had to stay low. No one wanted to risk Sam's life by showing themselves too soon.

She was clearheaded by the time she reached Jacob Marley's house. She turned off the engine, sat there a minute, staring at the house. Every-thing was silent. The sliver of moon shone nearly directly overhead now.

There were lights on only downstairs. She remembered she hadn't even gone upstairs, hadn't wanted to, and then the phone had rung.

Had Sam been locked in her closet upstairs all this time where Kri-makov had hidden himself waiting for her to get into bed?

She was into the house in under three seconds, racing up the stairs, picturing Sam tied up, stuffed in the back of her closet, perhaps uncon-scious, perhaps even dead. She yelled at the wristband, "Is everyone still there? Of course you are! I think you'd better still stay out of sight. I don't know what he's up to. You don't, either. Stay hidden. I'll find Sam if he's here."

She dashed into her bedroom and switched on the light. The room was still, stuffy, closed up for too long. She pulled open the closet door. No Sam. She knew they could hear her footsteps pounding up the stairs, hear her harsh breathing, hear her curse when she didn't find Sam.

She went into every room, opened every closet, searched every bath-room on the second floor.

"No Sam yet. I'm looking."

She called out to him again and again until she was nearly hoarse.

She was in the kitchen, pacing, when she saw the door to the basement. She pulled it open, flipped on the single light switch. The naked hundred-watt bulb flickered, then strengthened.

"Sam!"

He was sitting on the concrete floor, propped against a wall, bound hand and foot, a gag in his mouth. His eyes were wide, dilated with terror. How long had the bastard left him sitting in the dark?

"Sam!" She was on her knees next to him, working the gag loose. "It's all right, honey. I'll have you loose in another second." She got the gag off him. "You okay?"

"Becca?"

A thin little voice, barely there, and she nearly wept. "It's all right," she said again. "Let me get you untied, then we'll go upstairs and I'll make you some hot chocolate and wrap you up in a real warm blanket."

He didn't say anything more, not that she expected him to. She got his ankles and wrists untied and lifted him in her arms. When she got back into the kitchen, she sat down with him and began rubbing the feeling back into his wrists and ankles. "It will be all right now, Sam. Do you hurt anywhere else?"

He shook his head. Then he said, "I was scared, Becca, real scared."

"I know, baby, I know. But you're with me now. I'm not going to let you out of my sight." She carried him into the living room and wrapped him in an afghan. Then she went back to the kitchen, sat him down in a chair, the blanket firmly wrapped around him. "Now some hot chocolate. You hungry, Sam?"

He shook his head. "I want Rachel. My tummy feels weird. She knows what to do."

"Mine would, too, if I'd been through what you have. I'll tell your dad that you want Rachel." While the water heated, she poured the cocoa mix into a cup. Then she held Sam close again, telling him how brave he was, how everything was all right now, how she would call his father. While Sam was drinking the chocolate, Becca, not taking her eyes off him, pulled out her cell phone and called Tyler. "I've got him. He's safe."

"Thank God. Where are you?"

"At home. Krimakov put him in the basement. He's all right, Tyler."

"I'll be right there."

Obviously they'd all heard her but had waited to see if Krimakov was going to show himself. But no longer. Sam was safe. Still, there wasn't a sign of Krimakov. She'd forgotten to tell Tyler to get Rachel.

Adam came through the back door like an avenging angel. Then he saw Sam's white face, saw that the little kid was all wrapped up in a pale green afghan. He wanted to kill Krimakov with his bare hands.

He slowed down, pinned a big smile on his face. He came down on his haunches beside him. "Hi, Sam. You're the youngest hero I've ever known."

Sam stared at him for a minute, then he smiled, a really big smile. "Really?"

Adam was surprised to hear even that one short word out of him. "Really. The youngest. Boy, am I impressed. Do you think you could tell Becca and me what happened?"

Tyler came running through the front door. He stopped cold when he saw the three of them, but his eyes were on Becca first, then slowly he looked at his son.

He didn't say another word, scooped up Sam in his arms and sat down with him. He rocked him back and forth. Becca thought the contact was more for Tyler than to comfort his son. Finally, he raised his head and said quietly, "Tell me what happened."

Becca told him, short, stripped sentences, no emotion in them, stark facts, no details.

"But why did this Krimakov take Sam when all he did was get you here then tell you he was here in the house?"

"I don't know. Adam, did any of you see him? Did you see anything at all?"

Adam shook his head. "We've been looking behind every tree."

She wished then she hadn't reminded Tyler that Adam was here. His eyes narrowed, he hugged Sam more tightly to him. "This is all your fault."

"Get a grip, McBride. Your son is all right. Now, if you don't mind, let's see if Sam can tell us anything about the guy who took him. You know it's important. You don't want Krimakov to get Becca again, do you?"

Tyler said, "Sam rarely says anything, you know that."

"He had a thick sock over his head. I never saw him. He gave me potato chips to eat. I was real hungry, but he told me to be quiet, that Becca would come for me soon enough."

Everyone stared at Sam. He looked quite pleased with himself. He grinned at Becca.

"Sam, that's great." Becca came down on her knees beside him. "I did come for you, didn't I? That's right, sweetie. Take another drink of your hot chocolate. It's good, isn't it? Now, tell us what you were doing when he got you."

But Sam didn't say anything more. He looked once at his father, yawned, and shut down. It was the strangest thing she'd ever seen. Sam shut his eyes and went to sleep, slumping against Tyler's chest. One minute smiling, then gone.

"He's a very brave little kid," Adam said, rising. "If it's okay with you, McBride, can we speak to him in the morning? At least try?"

Tyler looked like he wanted to shoot all of them, but in the end, he slowly nodded. "I'm taking him home now."

Adam looked at Becca. "Nah, forget about us talking to him again. Sam probably doesn't have all that much more to tell us that would be useful. It's done and over. Please don't tell the sheriff about it. We're leaving right now. I guess whatever it was Krimakov wanted, he got."

"But what did he want?"

"I don't know, Tyler," Becca said. She kissed Sam's cheek. "He's a very brave little boy."

"Will you come back to see him again?"

"Yes," she said. "I will. I promise. We have to get all this business resolved first."

When Tyler was out the front door, Adam said suddenly, "Hold it right there, Becca. Your back. With all the excitement, I forgot about your back. He shot you with something. Let me see."

But there wasn't much to see. A bit of blood, a small hole, nothing more. "Why did he do this?"

"I don't know," Becca said to him over her shoulder, "but I promise I feel fine. Here's the dart he shot into my shoulder. You see the rolled paper around it."

Adam unrolled the paper, frowned as he read it. "What is he thinking? What is his plan? I hate this. He's controlling us. All we're doing is reacting to what he initiates. "

"I know. But we'll turn it around. Come on, Adam, let's get out of here. I'm very relieved Sheriff Gaffney hasn't found his way here yet. Where is my father? Sherlock and Savich?"

"Sherlock went back to Washington with the handwriting samples.

Your father, Savich, Hawley, and Cobb are waiting for us. I'll tell them to meet us at the airport; we're out of here."

They were driving away in her rented Toyota when she thought she saw Sheriff Gaffney's car in the distance. She stomped down on the gas.

She looked over at Adam's profile. He looked pissed and very tired. Not physically tired, but defeated tired. She understood because she felt the same way.

Nothing made any sense. He'd gotten her here, he'd shot her with a dart in the shoulder, and delivered Sam. Nothing else.

Where was Krimakov? What was he planning to do now?

DR. Ned Breaker, a physician whose son Savich had gotten back safely after a kidnapping some years before, was waiting at Thomas's house when they arrived.

All the men shook hands, Savich thanked him for coming. "She refused to go to a hospital."

"No one you work with ever does," Dr. Breaker said.

"This is Becca, Thomas's daughter. She's your patient, Ned."

"Dr. Breaker," she said, "I'm really okay, nothing's wrong. Adam already checked me out."

Adam said, "And now it's time for the real doctor to step up and have a look at the wound in your shoulder. We have no idea what was on that shaft Krimakov shot into you. Be quiet, Becca, and do as you're told, for once."

She'd honestly forgotten about her shoulder. It didn't hurt. Adam had washed it with soap and water and put a Band-Aid over it. She was frowning when Thomas said, "Please, Becca."

"All right then." She took off her sweater and lifted her hair out of the way.

"Come into the light," Dr. Breaker said. She felt his fingers on the wound, gently pressing, pushing the flesh together, perhaps to see if any liquid or poison came out. Finally, he said, "This is very strange. You were actually shot with this dart in the parking lot of a gym?"

"That's it."

She felt his fingers probe the area again, then he stepped away. "I'm going to take some blood, make sure there's nothing bad going on inside you. It looks fine, just a shallow puncture wound. Why'd he do it?"

"I think it might have just been to deliver a note to us," Savich said. "There was a note wrapped around the shaft."

"I see. Interesting mail delivery service this guy has. Well, better to be careful." He took a sample of her blood, then left, saying that he'd have results for them in two hours.

"A very good man to have as a friend," Savich said. "I wonder, though, how many more favors he'll believe he owes me."

Thomas said to Savich, but his eyes were on his daughter, "You got his kid back for him. He'll believe he owes you forever."

It was nearly one o'clock in the morning when Dr. Breaker called. Thomas took the call, looked very relieved as he listened. He was smiling when he turned to Becca and Adam. "Everything's okay. Nothing there but your beautiful normal stuff, Becca. He said not to worry."

Becca had rather hoped there might be something, nothing terminal, naturally, but something. Otherwise, they still had not a single clue about anything. Krimakov had kidnapped Sam to get her back to Riptide. Then he'd shot her in the shoulder to deliver that ridiculous note. In the gym parking lot. Nothing made sense.

That night Adam came to her. It was very dark in her room. She was lying there, unable to sleep even though it was very late, staring toward the window, looking at the slice of white moon above the maple treetops. The trees were silhouetted stark and silent against the night, and they were perfectly still, no breeze at all. Thank God the house was air-conditioned. It was cool in her bedroom.

Her door opened, then closed quietly. His voice was soft, pitched low. "Don't be afraid. It's me. And I'm not here to jump you, Becca."

She looked over at him, standing with his back against her closed door.

"Why not?"

He laughed, a painful sound, and walked toward her, tall, strong, and she wanted him.

He said, stopping beside her bed, looking down at her, "You never say what I expect. I want to jump you, at least a dozen times an hour, but no, this is your father's house. One doesn't do that under the parental roof when one isn't married. But don't get me wrong. If I could strip that nightgown off you, I would have it gone in a second flat. But I can't. Not here. I wanted to see how you were doing. Well, hell, that's a big lie. I'm here because I want to kiss you until we're both stupid with pleasure."

He was beside her then, drawing her up and against his chest, and he kissed her, lightly, then with more pressure, and she opened her mouth and didn't want him to stop. His breath was hot and sweet, his scent rich, dark, and that mouth of his was delicious, and she let herself enjoy him fully. She wanted more. It was Adam who pushed her gently back after what seemed like only an instant.

"You're beautiful," he said and streaked his fingers through her hair, pushing it behind her ears. "Even with your hair still a bit brassy."

"I'm not stupid with pleasure yet, Adam."

"I'm not, either, but we've got to stop." He was breathing hard, his hands flexing and unflexing against her back.

"Maybe we could kiss a little bit more?"

"Listen, if we don't stop right now, I'll start crying because I know that sooner or later we'd have to stop. We'll stop now before it kills me."

"All right, then. You be strong and let me mess with you just a bit." She kissed his chin once, then again. She touched her fingers to his cheeks, his nose, his brows, lightly traced over his mouth. She looked at his mouth as she said, "I haven't told you this before, Adam. So much has happened. We haven't known each other all that long, and nothing we've done together has been remotely normal or predictable. But here goes: You're very, very sexy."

He stared at her in the dim light as if he hadn't understood her. "What did you say? You think I'm sexy?"

"Oh, yes, the sexiest man I've ever seen. And finally I've gotten to kiss you. I like it, very much. I kissed your chin because it's sexy, too."

He looked inordinately pleased with himself, and with her. "I guess being sexy is okay. Is that all you think of me, Becca? I'm only a sexy hunk? Isn't there anything else, maybe, you'd like to say to me?"

"What else should I say? Your ego is big enough without my saying more." Then she looked up at him beneath her lashes, a provocative thing to do, and she knew it. For the first time in so very long, actually, longer than she could remember, she allowed herself to enjoy what was happening here.

He didn't say anything, then suddenly he pulled her tightly against him again. He was rubbing his big hands up and down her back. His breathing was sharp, ragged. "I was scared to death when you were in that gym parking lot. When he shot that dart at you, Savich had to just about sit on me. I knew I shouldn't move, shouldn't yell like a banshee, but it was hard staying still, watching you. In fact, it was about the hardest thing I've ever had to do in my blessed life."

He pressed his forehead to hers, holding her loosely now.

His warm breath feathered over her skin. "Oh, yeah, I was married once. It was a long time ago. Her name was Vivie. Everything was okay for a while, then it wasn't. She didn't want kids and I did. But I'm not serious about anyone else. It's only you, Becca. Only you."

"That's nice," she said and yawned against his shoulder. Then she bit his neck, then kissed where she'd bitten him. "I wish you were naked." To his immense credit, he didn't do anything other than shake a bit. "This is very close, Becca. My fingers are actually itching they want to touch you so much. But this is your father's house. We can't. Hey, how would you like to go out in the backyard, maybe we could take a couple of blankets?"

"Out from under the parental roof?"

"That's it. Oh yeah, for sure we could wave to the FBI agents that are scattered around." He sighed deeply, kissed her ear, and sighed again. "My molecules are even turned on."

Becca sighed and rested her hand on his chest. His heart was pounding hard and fast beneath her palm. She arched up and kissed his throat, then eased back in the circle of his arms. "Not fair at all. I mean, the shirt you're wearing is nice but I would love to kiss your chest, maybe even run my hands down over your belly."

He shuddered, drew quickly away from her, and rose. "I've been feeling you against me and it's driving me nuts. Now, since we can't be wicked the way I would like, I've got to get out of here. I can't take any more. I'd like to try but I know it wouldn't work. Good night. I'll see you in the morning. I might be a bit late. I've got to go home and do some stuff." And he was gone, her bedroom door closed very quietly behind him.

She sat there on her bed, hugging her knees. So suddenly her life had changed. And in all this nightmare, she'd found herself a man she hadn't believed could even exist. His first wife, Vivie, had had peas for brains. She hoped that Vivie—silly name—lived as far away as Saint Petersburg, Russia. It was a good enough distance away.

Soon enough, of course, Krimakov intruded. She wanted to shoot him, point a gun at his chest and fire. She wanted him gone, into oblivion, so he couldn't ever hurt anyone again.

\*    \*    \*

THE next day, at precisely noon, when Governor Bledsoe of New York was walking his dog, Jabbers, in his protected garden, a sniper shooting from a distance of about two thousand feet nailed his dog right through the folds of his neck. Jabbers was rushed to the vet and it looked like he would survive, just like his master had.

Thomas turned slowly to his daughter, the two of them alone in the house. "This is over the top. It's too much. He shot the dog in the neck. Unbelievable. At least he isn't here."

"But why did he do it?" Becca said. "Why?"

"To laugh at us," Thomas said. "To make this big joke. He wants us to know how invincible he is, how he can do anything he wants to and get away with it. How he's here and then he's there, and we'll never get him. Yes, he's laughing his head off."

# TWENTY-EIGHT

Gaylan Woodhouse sat at an angle across from Thomas's desk with his face in the shadows, as was his wont, and said, "I don't want you to worry about your daughter, Thomas. Your whereabouts will not be leaked. As you know, the media is still in a frenzy over the shooting of poor Jabbers. The country is primarily amused at his audacity, titillated, glued to their TVs. Everyone wants to know about Krimakov, this man who swore to kill you twenty-some years ago. By shooting that dog, he's turned up the heat. He wants the media to find you for him and then he'll come after you."

"No," Thomas said slowly, shaking his head. "I don't think that was his motive at all. You see, Gaylan, he had me in Riptide. He had to know I would never allow Becca to go up there alone. He could have easily shot me. He proved he was an excellent distance shooter when he shot the governor of New York. From that distance, he could have nailed me with little effort. But he didn't force anything after he kidnapped Sam Mc-Bride, except to shoot Becca in the shoulder with a dart that had a piece of paper rolled around the shaft. No, Gaylan, he shot the governor's dog because he wanted to give me the finger, show me again that it was his decision not to kill me and Becca in Riptide. He wants to show me he doesn't have to do anything until he decides he wants to do it. He wants to prove to me over and over that he's superior to me, that he's the one in control here, that he's the one calling all the shots. It's a cat-and-mouse game and he's proving again and again that he's the cat. Fact is, he is the cat. Adam's right. During all of this, we've only been able to react to what he does."

Gaylan said slowly, "One of my people pointed out that Krimakov certainly managed to get from one place to the next with no difficulty at all, suggested that maybe he has a private plane stashed somewhere. What do you think?"

Thomas said, "Makes you wonder, doesn't it? Heaven knows you can't have much faith in the commercial airlines. But you know, Gaylan, shooting that dog wasn't on a set timetable. You can check it out, but I doubt it."

Gaylan sighed. "We still don't have any leads in New York. His disguise must have been something. The security tapes showed old folk, pregnant women, children—do we track all of them down to question? Still no witnesses. Four good agents dead because of that maniac."

Thomas said, "I've been thinking about that. I'm coming to believe that Krimakov wants Becca and me together, to torment us together, prolong our deaths. But yet he went right to New York University Hospital, shot everyone, then ran. What if Krimakov somehow found out it was a trap? What if he still did it, in fact made a big production of it, all to tell us that he knew about our plan and it didn't matter? Yes, he knew, and he thumbed his nose at us."

"You're making him sound wilier than the Devil," Gaylan said, a brow arched. "More evil, too."

"I would say certifiably insane," Thomas said. "But it doesn't make him stupid. It doesn't really matter what the truth of his motives was, four agents are still dead. Yet it fits into all the things he's done since then. Over the top, frightening."

"Yes," Gaylan said. He looked toward Thomas's bookshelves for a moment. He seemed to shake himself, then took a sip of his coffee. He carefully set the cup back into the saucer. He crossed his legs, then said, "There's another reason I came here, Thomas. The fact is that the president isn't going to sit still much longer. He called me over, paced in front of me for ten minutes, told me all this mess had to come to a close, that the media are totally focused on it to the detriment of what he's trying to accomplish. He's got this new flat tax he's trying to sell to the country, only the media is ignoring him in favor of this. He said he'd even tried to make a joke, but the media was still talking about Jabbers and his sore neck."

"Tell the president if he wants me to go public, challenge Krimakov at high noon, I'll do it."

"No," Gaylan said, "you won't. I won't allow that. He could take you out easily—his shot at the governor was from a distance of at least fifteen hundred feet. You yourself pointed that out to me. He's better than good, Thomas, he's one of the best. He maximized his chances to nail his target." He held up his hand when Thomas would have said something. "No, let me finish. All I'm saying is that we've got to come up with something else. Somehow, we've got to make him dance to our tune."

"A lot of very good minds are working on this, as you know, since some of those minds work for you."

Gaylan nodded, picked up a pen from Thomas's desk, and began rhythmically tapping it against his knee. "Yes, I know. But for now, your whereabouts stay unknown. I'll tell the president that everything will be resolved in a couple more days. Think it's possible?"

"Sure, why not?" And he thought, *How am I supposed to make that come about?*

"All right. We continue the silence. What about that incident with Krimakov in Riptide?"

Thomas said, "Evidently, the media doesn't know about her visit there yet. And Tyler McBride—you know, the man whose son Krimakov kidnapped in Riptide—he isn't saying anything to anyone about Becca. I think he's in love with her and that's why he won't explode sky-high with all this. Becca, however, as much as she cares for his little boy, isn't headed his way." He paused a moment, looking down at the onyx pen set that Allison had given him some five Christmases before. "It's Adam," he said, smiling briefly as he looked at his old friend. "Isn't that nice?"

Gaylan Woodhouse grunted. "I'm too old," he said, then sighed again. "Krimakov won't find you, Thomas. Don't worry. I'll deal with the president. Let's say forty-eight hours, then we'll reassess. Okay?"

"Again, Gaylan, maybe Krimakov needs to find me. Forget the president's political agenda. Maybe Krimakov's reign of terror will continue until he knows where I am. Maybe we should let him know, somehow."

"We'll all think about that, but not yet. Forty-eight hours. Next the guy might try to shoot off the mayor's wig." Gaylan Woodhouse rose, dropped the pen back on top of the desk, shook Thomas's hand, and stepped back through the door, where the shadows were thicker. Three dark-suited men fell in beside and behind him as he left Thomas's house.

Thomas stared after him. Shadows surrounded him. Thomas understood shadows very well. He'd lived in the shadows himself for so long he could see them even as they gathered around him, and wondered if after a while anyone would actually see him or just the shadows.

*Forget shadows,* Thomas thought. Now wasn't the time to wax philosophical. He thought about the meeting. Gaylan was a good friend. He'd hold out against the president about losing the limelight for as long as he could. Forty-eight hours—that was the deal. It wasn't a lot of time and yet it was an eternity. Only Krimakov knew which.

THE next evening, Sherlock and Savich arrived with thick folders of papers, MAX, and Sean, who reared up on Savich's shoulder, staring about sleepily at everyone, a graham cracker clutched in his hand.

Sherlock didn't look happy. "I'm really sorry here, guys, but our handwriting experts turned up something we didn't expect."

"What have you got, Sherlock?" Adam asked, rising slowly, his eyes never leaving her face.

"We were hoping to learn whether or not Krimakov's mental state had deteriorated, at least determine where he was sitting presently on the sanity scale, in order to give us a better chance of dealing with him, predicting what he might do, that sort of thing. That's off now. We have no idea, you see, because the two new samples of handwriting Becca gave me aren't Krimakov's."

Thomas looked like someone had slapped him. He said slowly, "No, that's not possible. Admittedly I just looked at the ones from Riptide briefly, but they looked the same to me. You're sure about this, Sherlock? Absolutely?"

"Oh, yes, completely sure. We're dealing with a very different person here, and this person's mind isn't like yours or mine."

"You mean he's not sane," Thomas said.

"It's possible he's so far over the edge he's holding on by his fingernails. We could throw around labels—psychopath comes readily to mind—but that's just a start. The only thing we're completely certain about—he's obsessed with you, Thomas. He wants to prove to you that you're nowhere near his league, that he's a god and you're dirt. He sees himself as an avenger, the man who will balance the scales of justice, the man who will be your executioner.

"It's been his goal for a very long time; it could at this point even be his only reason for living. He's rather like a missile that's been programmed for one thing and one thing only. He won't stop, ever, until either he's killed you or you've killed him."

"So it was never Krimakov," Adam said slowly. "He really was killed in that auto accident in Crete."

"Probably so. Now, not all of this is from our experts' analysis. Profiling had a hand in it, as well." Sherlock turned back to Thomas. "Like you said, the two different sets of handwriting look close to a layman's eye, which probably means that this guy knew Krimakov, or at least he'd seen his handwriting a goodly number of times. A friend, a former or present colleague, someone like that."

"We're sorry, guys," Savich said. "I know Krimakov's former associates have been checked backwards and forwards, but I guess we're going to have to try to do more. I've already got MAX doing more sniffing around Krimakov's neighbors, business associates, friends in Crete and on mainland Greece, as well. We already know that he had a couple of side businesses in Athens. We'll see where that leads."

"No, all that has already been checked," Thomas said.

Savich shook his head. "We'll have to do more, try anything."

Sherlock said, "We've also inputted everything we know to see what comes out. Remember, the computer can analyze more alternatives more quickly than we can. We'll see."

Thomas said, "All right. What exactly did the profilers have to say, Sherlock?"

"Back to a label. He is psychotic. He has absolutely no remorse, no empathy for any of the people he's killed. None of them mean anything to him. They were detritus to be swept out of his way."

"I wonder why he didn't kill Sam," Becca said.

"We don't know," Savich said. "That's a good question."

"It doesn't seem possible," Adam said. "Why would a colleague or some bloody friend—no matter how close to Krimakov—go on this rampage? Even if he is a psychopath, always has been a psychopath, why wait more than twenty-five years after the fact? Why take over Krimakov's mission as his own?"

No one had an answer to that.

Adam said, "Now we've got to find out who would follow up on Krimakov's vendetta once Krimakov himself was dead. What's his motivation?"

"We don't know," Sherlock said, and she began rubbing Sean's back with her palm. He was cooing against his father's shoulder, the graham cracker very wet but still clutched tightly in his hand.

"There are graham cracker crumbs all over the house," Savich said absently.

Becca didn't say anything. There were few things she'd ever been absolutely sure were true in her life. This was one of them. It simply had to be Krimakov. No matter how infallible the handwriting experts usually were, they were wrong on this one.

But what if they weren't wrong? A psychopath obsessed with finding and killing her father? He'd called himself her boyfriend. He'd blown up that old bag lady in front of the Metropolitan Museum. He'd dug up Linda Cartwright and bashed in her face. No empathy, no remorse, people were detritus, nothing more. It was unthinkable.

She looked over at Adam. He was looking toward Savich, but she didn't think he really saw him. Adam was really looking inward, ah, but his eyes—they were cold and hard and she wouldn't want to have to tangle with him. She heard her father in the other room, speaking to Gaylan Woodhouse on the phone.

Sherlock and Savich left a few minutes later, leaving Adam and Becca in the living room, looking at each other. He said, his hands jiggling change in his pockets, "I've got stuff to do at my house. I want you to stay here with Thomas, under wraps. Don't go anywhere. I'll be back tomorrow."

"Yeah, I want to do some stuff, too," she said, rising. "I'm coming with you."

"No, you'll stay here. It's safe here."

And he was gone.

Her father appeared in the doorway. She said, "I'll see you later, sir. I'm going with Adam." She picked up her purse and ran after him. He was nearly to the road when she caught up with him. "Where are you going?"

"Becca, go back. It's safer here. Go back."

"No. You don't believe any more than I do that some colleague or friend of Krimakov's from the good old days is wreaking all this havoc. I think we're missing something here, something that's been there all the time, staring us in the face."

"What do you mean?" he said slowly. She saw the agents in the car down the street slowly get out and stand, both of them completely alert.

"I mean nothing makes sense unless it's Krimakov. But say that it isn't.

That means we're missing something. Let's go do your stuff together, Adam, and really plug in our brains."

He eyed her a moment, looked around, then waved at the agents. "We've got to walk. It's three miles. You up for it?"

"I'd love to race you. Whatcha say?"

"You're on."

"You're dead meat, boy."

Since they were both wearing sneakers, they could run until they dropped. He grinned at her, felt energy pulse through him. He wanted to run, to race the wind, and he imagined that she wanted to as well. "All right, we're going to my house. I have all my files there, all my notes, everything. I want to scour them. If it is someone who knew Krimakov, then there's got to be a hint of him in there somewhere. Yes, there must be something."

"Let's go."

She nearly had his endurance, but not quite. She slowed in the third mile.

"You're good, Becca," he said, and waved his hand. "This is my house."

She loved it. The house wasn't as large as her father's, but it sat right in the middle of a huge hunk of wooded land, two stories, a white colonial with four thick Doric columns lined up like soldiers along the front. It looked solid, like it would last forever. She cleared her throat. "This is very nice, Adam."

"Thanks. It's about a hundred and fifty years old. It's got three bedrooms upstairs, two bathrooms—I added one. Downstairs is all the regular stuff, including a library, which I use for a study, and a modern kitchen." He looked down at his feet. "I had the kitchen redone a couple years ago. My mom told me no woman would marry me unless the stove would light without having to hold a match to a burner."

She smiled. She nearly had her breathing back to normal.

"I had one of the two upstairs bathrooms redone, too," he said, now looking straight ahead. They climbed the three deep steps to walk across the narrow veranda to the large white front door. He stuck a key in the lock and turned it. "My mom said that no woman wanted to bathe in a claw-footed tub that was so old rust was peeling off the toes."

"That does sound pretty gross. Oh my, Adam, it's lovely."

They stood together in a large entryway, with a ceiling that soared two stories, a chandelier hanging down over their heads and a lovely buffed oak floor. "I know, you redid the floors. Your mom told you no woman would marry you if she had to be carried into a house across a mess of old ratty linoleum."

"How did you know?"

He'd preserved all the original charm of the house—the deeply carved, rich moldings, the high ceilings, the lovely cherry wood carved fireplaces, the incredible set-in windows.

They prepared to hunker down in the library, a light-filled room with built-in bookshelves, beautiful oak floors, a big mahogany desk, and lots of red leather. She looked around at the bookshelves stuffed with all kinds of books—nonfiction, fiction, hardcovers, paperbacks—stuck in indiscriminately.

Adam said as he handed her two folders, "My mom also told me women liked to read all cozied up in deep chairs. It was men, she said, who preferred to read in the bathroom."

"You've even got women's fiction here."

"Yeah, it seems a man can never stack the deck too much in his favor."

"I want to meet your mama," Becca said.

"Undoubtedly you will, real soon." Then he couldn't stand it. He walked to her and pulled her tightly against him. She looked up at him and said, "I want to forget Krimakov for a minute."

"All right."

"Have I told you lately that I think you're really sexy?"

He smiled slowly and kissed her lightly on the mouth. "Not since last night." She wrapped her arms around his neck, stood on her tiptoes, and kissed him back, thoroughly.

"I don't want you to forget it," she said after several minutes had passed. "You've gotten me a bit breathless. I really like it, Adam."

"We're in my house now," he said, and this time he kissed her, really kissed her, no holding back, letting himself crash and burn, letting himself burrow into her. He brought her tightly against him, feeling all of her against him, and he wanted to jerk down her jeans, he wanted to kiss her breasts, touch and kiss every inch of her, and not stop until he was unconscious. And then there was her mouth. He was making himself crazy. It was so good he really didn't want to stop, and why should they stop?

His hands were on the buttons of her jeans when he felt the change not only in himself but in her. It was Krimakov and he was there, just over their shoulders. Waiting. He was close, too close. Krimakov was out there, only it wasn't really Krimakov now. Whoever he was, he was a madman. Adam sighed, kissed her once more, then once again, and said, "I want you very much, but now, at this moment, we've got to solve this thing, Becca."

"I know," she said when she could speak. "I'm getting myself back together. I'm getting myself focused now. You're quite a distraction, Adam, it's hard." She pulled away from him, stiffened her legs. "Okay, I'm ready to think again."

"I promise there'll be more," he said, and gave her one last kiss. "How about a lifetime full of more?"

She gave him a dazzling smile. "Given that gorgeous modern kitchen and how I believe, without a doubt, that you're about the best kisser in the whole world, I think bunches of years might be a wonderful thing." Then she looked at his groin and he nearly expired on the spot.

"Good," he said finally, a slight shiver in his voice, and she loved the way those dark eyes of his were brilliant with pleasure in the afternoon light shining in through the windows. "Now, let's do it."

Two hours, three cups of coffee, and a demolished plate of Wheat Thins and cheddar cheese later, Adam looked up. "I was going over my notes on Krimakov's travel out of Greece over the years. It's been here all the time, staring up at me, and I didn't see it until now." He gave her a mad grin, jumped up, and gathered her beneath her arms and lifted her, then swung her in a circle. He kissed her once, then again, and set her back down. He rubbed his hands together. "Hot damn, Becca, I think I've got the answer."

She was laughing, stroking her hands over his arms, so excited she couldn't hold still. "Come on, Adam. What is it? Spill the beans."

"Krimakov went to England six times. His trips to England stopped about five years ago."

"And?"

"I never stopped to wonder why he went to England all those times, until now. Becca, think about it. Why did he go? To see a former colleague, to see a friend from the good old days? Not a woman, he'd remarried, so no, I don't think so."

She said slowly, "When he moved to Crete, he was alone. No relatives with him. Nobody."

"Yeah, but his files had been purged. Remember, there wasn't even anything about his first wife. It was like she never existed, but she did. So why did the KGB purge her?"

Becca said slowly, "Because she was important, because—" Suddenly, her eyes gleamed. "Sherlock is right. It isn't Krimakov, but neither is it a friend or a former colleague. It's someone a whole lot closer to him."

"Yep. Somebody so close he's nearly wearing his skin. We're nearly there, Becca. The timing of his visits—they're in the early fall or very late spring. Every one of them."

"Like the beginning or the ending of school terms," Becca said slowly. "And then they stop like there's no more school." Then she remembered what had happened in the gym in Riptide, and it all fell together.

When they got back to Thomas's house, only Thomas and Hatch were there, their conversation desultory, both of them looking so depressed that Adam nearly told Hatch to go smoke a cigarette. Becca heard Hatch cursing. It sounded like Paul Hogan and his sexy Aussie accent.

"Cheer up, everyone," Adam said. "Becca and I have a surprise for you. One that will get you dancing on the ceiling. All we've got to do now is have Savich turn on MAX and send him to England. Now we've got a chance." He bent down and kissed Becca, right in front of Thomas. She raised her hand and lightly touched her fingertips to his cheek. "Yes, we do," she said.

The doorbell rang, making everyone suddenly very alert and very focused. It was Dr. Breaker. He nodded to everyone else. "We've found something none of you is going to believe." And he told them about the very slight abnormalities in Becca's blood that a tech had caught. Then he checked Becca's shoulder, and finally he checked her upper arm. It wasn't long before he looked up and said, "I feel something, right here, just beneath her skin. It's small, flexible."

Adam nodded. "The visit to Riptide makes sense now. You know what's in your arm, don't you, Becca?"

"Yes," she said. "Now all of us know." She raised her hand when her father would have begun arguments. "No, I'm not leaving. No more people are going to die in my place, like Agent Marlane. No one is going to be bait in my stead. No, no arguments. I stay here with you. Hey, I've got my Coonan."

\*    \*    \*

FOR the first time in more nights than she could count, Becca wanted to stay awake, stay alert, keep watch. He was close. She wanted to see him with clear eyes and a clear mind and her Coonan in her hand. She wanted to shoot him between the eyes. And she wanted to know why he was doing this. Was he really mad? Psychotic?

She didn't think she'd be able to hang on. She was nearly light-headed she was so tired. She'd been so hyped up the past couple of nights, she'd lain there and blinked at the rising moon outside the bedroom window.

Adam had insisted on tucking her in. She wanted him to stay a little longer, but she knew he couldn't. He kissed her, a nibble on her earlobe, and said against her ear, "No, I don't want another cold shower. But dream of me, Becca, okay? I've got the first watch. It starts soon."

"Be careful, Adam."

"I will, everyone will. Try to sleep, sweetheart. He knows the house. He knows which room is Thomas's. We've got Thomas well guarded." He kissed her once again and rose. "Get some sleep."

She didn't want to. After he eased out of her bedroom door, closing it quietly behind him, she sat up in bed, thinking, remembering, analyzing. She was asleep in under six minutes. She dreamed, but not of the terror that was very close now, not of Adam.

She found herself in a hospital, walking down long, empty corridors. White, so much white, unending, going on and on, forever. She was looking for her mother. She smelled ether fumes, sweet and heavy, the ammonia scent of urine, the stench of vomit. She opened each white door along the corridor. All the beds were empty, the white sheets stretched military tight. No one. Where were the patients?

So long, the hallway went on and on and there were moans coming from behind all those doors, people in pain, but there were no nurses, no doctors, no one at all. She knew the rooms were empty, she'd looked into all of them, yet the moans grew louder and louder.

Where was her mother? She called out for her, then she started running down the corridor, screaming her mother's name. The moans from those empty rooms grew louder and louder until—

"Hello, Rebecca."

# TWENTY-NINE

Becca lurched up in bed, sweaty, breathing hard, her heart pounding. No, it wasn't her mother, no, it was someone else.

Finally he was here. He'd come to her first, not to her father. A surprise, but not a big one, at least to her. She lay very still, gathering herself, her control, her focus.

"Hello, Rebecca," he said again, this time he was even closer to her face, nearly touching her.

"You can't be here," she said aloud. He'd gotten past everyone, but again, that didn't overly surprise her. She wouldn't be surprised if he'd gotten both the house plans and the security system plans. And now he wasn't even six inches from her.

"Of course I can be here. I can be anywhere I want. I'm a cloud of smoke, a sliding shadow, a glimmer of light. I like how frightened you are. Just listen to you, your voice is even trembling with fear. Yes, I like that. Now, you even try to move and I will, very simply, cut your skinny little throat."

She felt the razor-sharp blade against the front of her neck, pressing in ever so slightly.

"We knew you would come," she said.

He laughed quietly, now not even an inch from her ear. She felt his hot breath touch her skin. "Of course you knew I'd find you. I can do anything. Your father is so stupid, Rebecca. I've always known it, always, and now I've proved it the final time. I figured out how to find his lair, and poof—like shimmering smoke—I'm here. You and your bastard father lose now. Soon, you and I are going down the hall to his bedroom. I want him to wake up with me standing over him, you in front of me, a knife digging into your neck. Even with those hotshot FBI guards he's got positioned all around this house, I got through with little effort. There's this great big oak tree that comes almost to the roof of the house. Just a little jump, not more than six feet, and I was on the roof, and then it was easy to pry open that trapdoor into the attic. I took care of the security alarm up there, cut it off for all of the upstairs. No one saw me. It's nice and dark tonight. Stupid, all of you are stupid. Now, get up."

She did as he said. She felt calm. He kept her very close, the knife across her neck as he opened her bedroom door and eased her out into the hallway. "The last door down on the right," he said. "Keep walking and keep quiet, Rebecca."

It was nearly one o'clock in the morning; Becca saw the time on the old grandfather clock that sat in its niche in the corridor.

"Open the door," he said against her ear, "slowly, quietly. That's right."

Her father's bedroom door opened without a sound. There was a night-light on in the connecting bathroom off to the left. All the draperies were open, beams of the scant moonlight coming in through the balcony windows. There was no movement on the bed.

"Wake up, you butcher," he said, one eye on the balcony windows.

There was still no movement on the bed.

She heard his breathing quicken, felt the knife move slightly against her neck. "No, you don't move, Rebecca. One little slice and your blood will spew like a fountain all over the floor." Suddenly, he said, nearly a yell, "Thomas Matlock! Where are you?"

"I'm right here, Krimakov."

He whirled Becca around, facing Thomas, who was standing, fully dressed, in the lighted doorway of the bathroom, his arms crossed over his chest.

"It's about time you got here," Thomas said easily, his eyes on the knife that was pressing into Becca's neck. "Don't hurt her. We've been waiting for you. I was starting to believe you'd lost your nerve, that you'd gotten too scared, that you'd finally run away."

"What do you mean? Of course I got here quickly, at least as quickly as I wanted to. As I told Rebecca, your defenses are laughable."

"Get that knife away from her neck. Let her go. You've got me. Let her go."

"No, not yet. Don't try anything stupid or I'll cut her throat. But I don't want her dead just yet."

Thomas saw he was dressed in black from the ski mask that covered both his face and his head to the black gloves on his hands. "You're the one who's lost," Thomas said, and he saluted him. "There's really no need for you to wear that black mask over your head anymore. We all know who you are. As I said, we've been waiting fourteen hours for you to finally show up."

ADAM spoke quietly into the wristband. "He can't see me. I'm only a shadow at the corner of the balcony door. I can't get him. He's got Becca plastered against the front of him, a knife against her throat. I can't take the risk, even this close. They'll keep him talking. Thomas is good. He'll keep control."

And he prayed with everything that was in him that it would be so.

"Keep alert," Gaylan Woodhouse said. "The minute he makes a move toward Thomas, he'll ease up on her. Then you take him down."

Adam said, "He's pulled a gun out of his jacket pocket. It's small, looks like a Glock subcompact 27. He's pointed it straight at Thomas." And he concentrated, readied himself, saying over and over, *Let Becca go. Just twitch.*

"TURN on the bedside light, Matlock."

Thomas walked slowly into the bedroom, leaned over, and switched on the light. He straightened.

"Now, don't move. Those draperies are open. There's probably a sniper out there, and I don't want him to have a clean shot. He'll get you, Rebecca, if he pulls the trigger."

Thomas said, "I wanted very much for you to be my old enemy, but you aren't. You're something far more deadly than Vasili, something deadly and monstrous that he spawned. Perhaps after he brainwashed you, he realized what he'd produced, realized that he'd unleashed uncontrolled, unrelenting evil, and that's why he kept you away from his new family. He didn't want the evil he'd spawned and nurtured to live in his own house, to be close to all those innocent, pure lives. Pull off the mask, Mikhail, we know who you are."

Stone-dead silence, then, "You can't know, you can't! No one knows anything about me. I don't exist. No records show me as Vasili Krimakov's son. I've covered everything. It isn't possible."

"Oh yes, we know. Even though the KGB tried to erase you, to protect you, we found out all about you."

"Pull those draperies closed, now!"

Thomas pulled them closed, knowing that now Adam was blind to what was going on in the room. He turned and said slowly, "Take off the mask, Mikhail. It really looks rather silly, like a little boy playing hoodlum."

Slowly, his movements jerky, furious, he pulled off the black mask. Then he shoved Becca over toward the bed. Thomas caught her, held her close to his side. But she moved away from him. She sat down on the bed, drew her legs up.

Thomas stared at Vasili Krimakov's son, Mikhail. There was some resemblance to his father in the high, sharp cheekbones, the wide-set eyes, the whiplash-lean body, but the dark, mad eyes, those were surely his mother's eyes. Thomas could still see her eyes, wide, staring up at him.

Becca knew Mikhail had wanted shock, but it was denied him when he realized they knew who he was. Still, he threw back his head and said, "I am my father's son. He loved me. He molded me to be like him. I am here, his avenger."

His dramatic moment got nothing except a laugh from Becca.

"Hi, Troy," she said, giving him a small wave. "Cute, preppy name. Tell me, what if I'd decided to go out with you that night after you planted that little micro homing chip in my upper arm? How would you have gotten out of it?" She said to her father, "I told you how he managed to have the arm of that big old chest machine swing into me as I was walking by, and then he was right there, patting me, making sure I was okay, flirting with me. That was when you planted that little chip in my arm, isn't it, Troy? You were good. I didn't feel a thing, only the sting from that machine arm hitting me. It hurt a little longer than it should have, but who would really notice?"

"No," he said, shaking his head back and forth. "This isn't possible. You couldn't have found that chip. It's plastic mixed with biochemical adhesives, almost immediately becomes one with your skin. After a few minutes, no one could even tell it was there, least of all you. No, you weren't even aware of it. You and everyone else were just worried about that dart in your shoulder. I fooled you, I fooled all of you. You were all so worried about that ridiculous dart in her shoulder, about that stupid note I wrapped around it."

"For a while, that's right," Thomas said. "But actually, it was an analysis of handwriting by some very smart FBI agents that started your downfall. I had samples of your father's handwriting. They compared yours to his. Remember the notes you wrote to Mr. McBride in Riptide? There was no comparison, of course, so it couldn't be Vasili.

"Then Adam remembered that your father had traveled to England quite a number of times. He wondered why, particularly since the visits were always at the beginning of the school term or at the end. He knew your father had remarried, so it probably wasn't a woman he was visiting. He'd purged files, even your mother's name, and we wondered why he would do that. After all, who cared if he had a wife, now dead, or any children?

"It wasn't tough then to track you down, the son whose father had sent him to England to be educated, so that one day he could avenge the murder of his dearest mother. You were at that private boys' school at Sundowns."

Thomas continued, "Your father molded you, taught you to hate me, to hate everything I stood for, programmed you for this."

"I was not programmed. I do this all of my own free will. I am brilliant. I have won. Even though you found out about me, it is I who am standing here in control. It is I who run this show."

Thomas said, "Fine. You run the show. Now tell us how you got into NYU Hospital without being stopped by the FBI agents."

He laughed, preened. "I was a young boy, so sorry-looking in my slouchy clothes, my pants halfway to my knees, and my baseball cap, holding my broken arm, and everyone wanted to help me, to send me here, to send me there, and I came up to those stupid agents, crying about my arm, and then I shot them both. So easy, all of it. In the room when I saw neither of you were there, I just killed them, too, but with the woman, it was very close, too close. But I escaped. I was out of there before anyone realized what had happened."

Thomas said, "Why, Mikhail? What did your father tell you to make you want to do this? What?"

"He didn't make me do anything. He simply told me how you butchered my poor mother, went through her to get to him. You shot her in the head and laughed as my father held her until she died. Then you tried to kill him but he managed to get away. He told me that, and he began teaching me to prepare myself to avenge her. And I'm here now. I'll kill you just as you killed my mother."

"You killed your stepmother, didn't you? And her children?" Becca said.

He laughed, actually laughed. "I hated her as much as she hated me. She didn't want me ever to come back during my vacations. And her spawn—they weren't all that surprised when I killed them because they had guessed I hated them. As for her, she pleaded just like her pathetic daughter."

Becca said, "And your own little brother? Your father's other son?"

"I tried to kill him, burn him out of existence, just to leave ashes, but he survived. My father sent him to Switzerland, to this clinic that specializes in burns. He knew then what I'd done. I called him a coward, told him he'd let that wretched woman, those children, distract him from killing the man who butchered my mother. You know what he said? He said it over and over, tears in his eyes, wringing his hands—it had been an accident, he'd lied to me all those years. I didn't believe him. He wanted it soft and easy—a woman in his bed, children around him—but I wasn't going to let him forget my mother, erase her memory, and turn away like you would turn away.

"Now I've got you both and I'm going to kill you, as you killed my mother. It's justice. It's retribution." He smiled as he raised his gun, aiming right at Thomas.

"No!" Becca yelled. "I won't let you!" She hurled herself in front of her father.

Mikhail Krimakov gave a scream of rage when Thomas shoved Becca to the floor. But he didn't have time to cover her with his own body. Mikhail shot him in the chest, knocking him backward.

Mikhail dropped to the floor, grabbed Becca's ankle, and jerked her hard toward him. He slammed his arm around her neck, and pressed the gun against her ear even as the balcony glass door shattered inward and Adam leapt through the billowing draperies and the broken glass into the bedroom. He stopped dead in his tracks.

Mikhail smiled at him. "You try to kill me and the little bitch is dead. You got that?"

# THIRTY

Mikhail said, the gun pointed in Becca's left ear, "Her father shot my mother in the head. He's paid for it. You move and I'll blow her head off. You won't even recognize what's left."

Adam couldn't believe it, didn't want to accept what he was seeing. "I should never have let you stay here. I should have drugged you, Becca, and hidden you away."

But Becca didn't hear him. Mikhail's arm had tightened until she couldn't breathe, until everything turned black and she heard voices in the distance, but they didn't reach her, not really.

Mikhail eased up on Becca's neck as he waved his gun at Adam. "Drop that gun and do it slowly and very carefully."

Adam let the gun fall to the floor. It came to a stop, he saw, about thirteen inches beyond his left foot.

"I dropped the gun. You've killed Thomas. No one else is near. Let her go, you've already choked her unconscious."

Thomas felt as if his chest was frozen, a good thing, he knew, because soon enough he would be in such pain he probably wouldn't be able to think, much less move. Krimakov's son was pressing a gun against Becca's throat. Adam stood not four feet away, helpless, frozen in place, shattered glass all around him. Thomas knew he was trying desperately to figure out what to do. Becca's eyes were closed, Mikhail's hold against her throat was too strong, far too strong. She'd passed out. He had to do something, anything. He couldn't let her die, not like this, not after she'd hurled herself in front of him, to save him, to take the bullet herself. He felt the pain pulsing deep in his chest, but with it, he felt such an intense surge of love for her that gave him a burst of strength. He managed to ease his hand down to his pants pocket, to the small derringer. A bit more strength, that's all he needed, strength.

Mikhail saw the slight movement from the corner of his eye. "You're supposed to be dead! Don't move!" His hold against her throat lightened and almost immediately he saw that Becca was coming out of it. He clouted her hard on the side of the head, and shoved her away from him. He leaped to his feet, pulled a Zippo lighter from his pocket and set it to the bedding. In an instant, the blanket and sheets burst into flame.

Thomas fired the derringer. Mikhail yelled and grabbed his arm as the bullet punched him backward. He hit the wall but didn't fall. Adam dove for his gun. Thomas fired again, but Mikhail had twisted low and the bullet grazed the side of his head.

Thomas fell back, the derringer falling from his hand. Adam twisted about, his gun raised, but Mikhail was out of the bedroom, and when Adam fired, the bullet hit the door frame. Mikhail slammed the door behind him and the flames gushed higher with the sudden rush of air, igniting the pillows, the thick brocade drapes that were ripped from Adam's run into the bedroom.

Adam shouted, "Becca, are you all right?" He leaned over and slapped her face. "Come on, we've got to get out of here. The drapes are on fire now." He scrambled on his knees to where Thomas lay on his back. He shook him. "Thomas, open your eyes. That's it. Now, can you make it?"

Thomas smiled at him. "No, unfortunately not, Adam. I think this is the end of the line for me. Get Becca out of here. Tell her I love her."

"Don't be a jackass," Adam said. "We're all getting out of here. Come on, you can do it." He wrapped an arm around Thomas and jerked to his feet, pulling Thomas with him. He started to lift him over his shoulder.

"No, not yet," Thomas said, the pain flooding over him now, drawing at his brain, making everything darken, darken. "No, we'll get out of here. Becca, get yourself together! I'm not going to lose you now."

Becca was sitting now, shaking her head, trying to breathe. She heard agents yelling outside, prayed they wouldn't try to come into the burning room, prayed they'd be ready to pump a hundred bullets into Mikhail when he came out of the house. She said, "I'm okay. Give me a second." She stared at her father. "Mother left me. There's no way you're going to leave me now. I'll help you, Adam." Together, one of them on each side of him, they managed to get the door open and drag Thomas into the hallway. The flames were whooshing up high behind them, thick, incredibly hot, smoke gushing out of the room. No time, Adam thought, no time to put it out.

All of them were coughing now from the smoke. "Let's move," Adam said. He pulled the bedroom door closed after him, but it was too late. The fire was already eating away at the hallway carpeting.

"If he isn't dead yet," Adam said, "they'll get him the instant he gets out of the house."

Becca was panting with effort and coughing at the same time. "I had my gun strapped to my leg, but it didn't matter," she said, coughing. "Are you all right, Daddy? Don't you dare talk about dying again. Do you hear me?"

"I hear you, Becca," Thomas said, and his chest was on fire, just as the fire raged around them, it raged inside him. He knew he couldn't last much longer. He didn't want to leave her, not yet, please God, not yet.

"A little farther."

They heard a whoosh of flames behind them. The smoke was dense and black now. "We've got to hurry," Adam said. He picked up Thomas and eased him over his shoulder. "Becca, get downstairs. I'm right behind you."

A shot rang out in the thick smoke. Adam felt the punch in his arm, sharp, hard. He didn't loosen his hold. "Becca, get down, crawl. I don't want him to shoot you."

But Becca had her Coonan in her hand. She stepped behind Adam and fired back through the smoke in the direction of the shot. There were three more shots. Then silence.

"He must be back near the bedroom, Adam." And she fired off another shot. "That'll keep him away. Get my father out of here. The walls are on fire. It's bad, Adam. Hurry! Save my father!"

Adam felt his arm pulsing with raw pain, weakening as he carried Thomas down the front stairs. He felt an instant of dizziness, then shook his head, coughed, and kept moving. He felt a strange pulling in his back, weird, but nothing really. Thomas was now unconscious. He prayed he wasn't dead. He heard another shot, then another, but nothing all that close.

"I'm right behind you, Adam. Go, quickly!"

He didn't realize Becca wasn't with him until he was out the front door and two agents had lifted Thomas from his shoulder. "A chest wound. Get the paramedics over here!"

"The fire department is on the way," Gaylan Woodhouse said, running up, his gun still at the ready. "You're shot, too, Adam. Hey, Hawley, get over here. We need some help." Adam stood there holding his arm, his teeth gritted. And now, of all things, that pulling in his back, it was bringing him down.

"Where is Krimakov?" Savich shouted.

"Becca," Adam said, looking around wildly. "Becca?"

Hatch said, running to Adam, "He got you in the back, boss. Did you know you got shot in the back? Hurry, let's get him down."

"Becca," Adam said, frantic now, and he knew he was barely hanging on. "Where's Becca?" He saw the flames billowing out of the upstairs windows. The beautiful ivy that nearly covered that side of the house was on fire.

"Thomas shot Krimakov," Adam said to Gaylan Woodhouse and Hawley, who were bending over him. "He's got to still be inside. Maybe he's unconscious or dead. Where's Becca? Please, you've got to find her."

The walkie-talkie boomed out, "No one has tried to come out of any windows or the back of the house."

"Get Krimakov," Gaylan shouted. "GET HIM!"

Becca, where was Becca? He wanted to go back into that house to find her. He had to, had to, but he couldn't move. The fire wasn't only in the house now, it was inside him and it was eating its way out. The pain in his back held him utterly locked in place. He couldn't move.

An agent shouted, "Up there!"

"It's Becca," Gaylan Woodhouse whispered. "Oh, no."

Adam did move, suddenly, with a spurt of strength he didn't know he had. He roared to his feet. He followed everyone's eyes to the roof of the house and felt his heart drop to his feet. No, please, no. But it was Becca, on the roof of the burning house.

"Becca!"

There were at least a dozen people standing in the front yard, looking upward. Then everyone was silent, still.

There, highlighted in flames, stood Becca, in her white nightgown, her bare feet spread, holding the Coonan between her hands.

"Becca," Adam shouted, "shoot!"

But she didn't. She stood there, pointing the Coonan at Mikhail Krimakov. He was holding his arm, blood dripping through his fingers. Blood also dripped down his cheek from a head wound. He was leaning over, as it was nearly beyond him to straighten. What had happened to his gun? Adam couldn't believe what he was seeing, would have given five years of his life if he could have changed it, if he could even have moved, at least tried to save her. But there was nothing he could do. He saw an agent raise a rifle. "No," he said, "don't try it. He's off at an angle. Don't take the chance of hitting her. Where are the firemen?"

Flames had caught the roof on fire now, licking out of the balcony off Thomas's bedroom. It wouldn't be long now until the flames ate the roof and sent it crashing into the house, until it was too hot on the roof for her to stand there, barefoot.

He heard her then, speaking loudly, very clearly.

"It's over," Becca said to the young man not eight feet from her. "Finally, it's over. You lost, Mikhail, but the cost was too high. You killed eight people, just because they were there."

"Oh no, I killed many more than that," he said, raising his head, panting with the pain. "They didn't count, any of them. I used them, then of what possible use were they to me?"

"Why didn't you stop when your father died in that car accident?"

He laughed, he actually laughed at her. "It wasn't an accident. I killed him. He wanted me to stop this, said I'd already done enough, that this was too much. He'd turned soft, he'd become a coward. I killed him because he'd become a weakling. He wasn't worthy any longer. He betrayed my beloved mother's memory. Yes, I struck him on the side of the head and drove him in his car over a cliff."

There wasn't a sound from anyone standing below. Then, the sound of sirens in the distance. The flames were licking up over the edge of the roof now. She had to get out of there. Adam stood there, impotent. *Becca, please, please. Get out of there.*

Becca said, her voice still strong, still clear and loud, "It ends here, Mikhail. Since I knew you'd try to escape back through that roof trapdoor, you had to know I wouldn't let you get away. It ends here."

"Yes," he said. "It ends here. I killed the man who murdered my mother—your beloved father. I've done what I promised to do. And I took pleasure along the way, cleaning out the vermin that had invaded my life."

He was standing very still, this handsome young man she'd spoken to in the gym in Riptide. He was slowly straightening now, standing tall.

"My father isn't dead, Mikhail. He'll survive. You failed."

"The roof is going to collapse beneath us, Rebecca. It's getting hotter. You're barefoot. It's got to be burning your feet now, isn't it?"

Fire trucks pulled up to the curb, men jumping out, going into action. Becca heard a man yelling, "We've got a two-story residential fully involved structure fire! What's going on here?"

"There are people standing on the roof! That woman has a gun!"

"We can't ladder the building, it's too late. Get the life net!"

Becca heard them, felt her feet now, the heat burning them, wondered if the roof would collapse under her. "We're going down, Mikhail," she said. "Look, they're bringing one of those safety nets. We'll jump."

"No," he said. "No." Then he pulled the lighter out of his jacket again and lit his sleeve. He rubbed it on his shirt, his pants, even while she watched, so horrified she froze. Then he smiled at her, nearly ablaze now, and ran at her, yelling, "Come away with your boyfriend. Come, let's fly together, Rebecca!"

She pulled the trigger, once, and still he came, a ball of flame now, running toward her, nearly at her, his arms outstretched. She fired again, then again and again, fired until the Coonan was empty.

He fell forward, nearly into her, but she jerked away just in time and he rolled over and over, a flaming ball of fire, off the roof to the ground below.

She heard people yelling. A jet of flame caught the sleeve of her nightgown. She ran quickly to the side of the roof, stood there for just an instant, slapping down the flames on her arm even as the fire inched closer and closer, and at last the firemen had the safety net in place.

Adam yelled, "Jump, Becca!"

And she did, without hesitation, her nightgown billowing out around her, her long legs bare, the white sleeve of her nightgown smoking. She hit the white safety net, her nightgown tangling around her. It closed over her for just an instant, and then a fireman yelled, "We've got her. She's okay!"

He watched her scramble out of the confines of the safety net, shake off the firemen. She ran toward him, and he saw the shock in her face, the blindness in her eyes, but he couldn't think of anything to say to her. Then there was simply nothing. He collapsed where he stood. The last thing he heard before the blackness closed over him was the huge roar of the collapsing roof and Becca's voice, saying his name over and over.

# THIRTY-ONE

He was buried in pain, so deep he wondered if he'd ever climb out, but he knew he could deal with it, even appreciate it, because it meant he was still alive. Finally, after what seemed like beyond forever, he managed to gain a bit of control and forced his eyes to open. He looked up at Becca's face. Ah, but the worry in her eyes, her pallor, it scared him. Was he going to die after all? He felt her fingers lightly touch the line of his eyebrow, his cheek, his chin. Then she leaned down and kissed where her fingers had touched him. Her breath was sweet and warm. His own mouth felt like he'd dived into a box of dried manure.

"Hello, Adam. You'll be fine. I'll bet you're really thirsty, the nurse said you would be. Here's some water to drink. Take it slow, that's it."

He drank. It was the best water he'd ever tasted in his life. He managed to say, "Thomas?"

"He'll live. He told me so himself when he came out of surgery. The doctors say it looks good. He's in great shape, so that's a big help."

"Your arm?"

"My arm is okay. A bit of a burn, nothing serious. We all survived. Except for Mikhail Krimakov. He's very dead. He'll never terrorize anyone again or kill another person. I know you're in bad pain, the bullet went through your back, broke a rib. The other bullet went right through your arm. You'll be okay."

He closed his eyes and said, "It nearly killed me watching you on the roof with him. The flames kept getting closer and closer, the wind whipping your nightgown around your legs, whipping the flames higher. I wanted to do something, but all I could do was stand there yelling at you and I nearly lost what sanity I had left."

"I'm sorry, but I had to go after him, Adam. That's how he got into Thomas's house, from the end of a very long oak branch; then he jumped onto the roof and managed to get the trapdoor open and made it into the attic. When I saw him going down to the end of the hall where those pull-down steps to the attic are, I knew he would escape. I couldn't let him do it. He got in that way, the chances were he'd get out. I had to stop him." She paused a moment, looking inward. "Then he wanted to die. And he wanted me to die with him. But I didn't. We won." She kissed him again, and this time he managed to smile a bit through the pain.

"Now, no more about it. I've done nothing but answer question after question for the FBI. Mr. Woodhouse keeps coming back again and again, but it's mainly to see Dad, not for any more questions. Do you know what Savich is doing? He's sitting in the waiting room, checking out churches on MAX to find one for us to get married in. He said he did that for another FBI agent who'd been shot, and sure enough, the other agent got married on the date and in the church that Savich picked. He said it was a special calling of his."

"My folks?" Adam said. The pain was getting worse, that damned broken rib was digging into him like a sword, dragging him under, and he wanted to howl with it. The novelty of having himself distracted was losing its touch and wearing thin. But he knew he had to hold on, a bit longer. He wanted to look at Becca, look at her, hear her voice, perhaps have her kiss him again. He wanted her to kiss him all over, that would be very nice. He tried to smile up at her but it was a pathetic effort. Thank God she was safe. He wanted to lie very quietly and keep knowing she was safe and she was here and that was her hand on his face.

"But Becca, I have to ask you to marry me before Savich can find a church. What if you say no?"

"You already sort of asked me when we were at your house. But I want the real words now. Ask me, Adam, and see what I say."

"I hurt real bad but will you marry me? I love you, you know."

"Yes, of course I will. I love you, too, more than even I can imagine. Now, Savich has already spoken to both your mother and your father. In fact, the last time I checked in, they were sitting on either side of him. Ah, I like them, Adam, very much. There are brothers and sisters and all sorts of second and third cousins coming in and out. They seem to be on some sort of rotation schedule. Oh yes, everyone is sticking his oar in about church locations and dates. I didn't know you had such a large family."

"Too large. They refuse to mind their own business. Always under-foot." He coughed and it hurt his rib so badly he thought he'd expire on the spot. He couldn't control it any longer. The pain in his rib and in his arm was slicing right through him, pulling him down and down. He was going to sink under and never come up. Then he heard the nurse say, "I'm going to give him some morphine. He'll be okay in a moment. I guess he forgot it was there. Then he needs to rest." He hadn't forgotten, he knew he wouldn't have been able even to push down the button because he was too weak. His arms were limp at his sides. He hated needles and there were two of them sticking out of his arms. He was a mess but he'd be okay. Becca loved him. He said, his voice slurred, "I'm glad you love me. That makes two of us now."

He thought he heard her laugh. He knew he felt her palm against his cheek.

And then he drifted away, the pain pulling back, like a monster's fangs pulling out of his flesh, and it felt blessedly wonderful. Then he was asleep again, deeply asleep, and it was black and dreamless and there was nothing there to hurt him and that was a very good thing.

Becca slowly straightened over him.

The nurse smiled at her from the other side of his bed. "He's doing great. Please don't worry, we're taking really good care of him. I hope he'll sleep now. He should, since the pain has lightened up. You need to get some rest, too, Ms. Matlock."

Becca gave Adam one last long look, a last kiss on his mouth, then walked out of his room, down the corridor to the small sitting room with two windows looking onto the parking lot, pale yellow walls dotted with Impressionist prints. That small room was filled with the latest batch of relatives. There was Adam's mom, Georgia, playing with Sean, while Sherlock and Savich were laughing, taking turns announcing yet another church and yet another possible date for Becca and Adam's wedding, only to have a boo from one relative who had to go salmon fishing in Alaska, or another who had to go to Italy on business, or yet another who had an appointment with her lawyer to cut her husband out of her will. On and on it went.

Becca said from the doorway, "I'm happy to announce that Adam asked me to marry him and I accepted. However, he was hurting a lot. Maybe he won't remember when he wakes up. If he doesn't, why, I'll have to ask him."

"My boy will remember," his father said, a man Adam resembled closely. He grinned at her. "One of the first things Adam told us when he could talk was that he is going to have that second bathroom on the top floor of his house redone so you wouldn't turn him down due to ugly green tile on the counters."

"Well, that certainly shows commitment," she said. "Tell you what, I'll pick out the new tile and then we'll see how fast I can get him to the altar."

She left them laughing, a very nice sound, and now they could do it more easily since their son would be all right. They seemed to like her, which was a relief. His mom was something else. She owned a Volvo dealership in Alexandria and was an auctioneer on the side. His father, she'd been told by one of Adam's older brothers, owned and operated a stud farm in Virginia.

Well, *her* father was alive, but that was all he needed to be, thank you very much. Actually, she wasn't at all certain what he did for a living, but who cared? She thought briefly of his house, where her mother had spent time. Now it was gone, just a shell left. It didn't matter. Her father was alive.

She took the elevator up to the sixth floor, to the ICU. She could make that trip in her sleep, she'd gone back and forth so many times now.

The hospital administration had managed to keep the media away from this area. The doctors and nurses nodded to her. She walked into the huge room with its hissing machines, its ever-present mixture of smells that was overlaid with a sharp antiseptic odor that reminded her of the dentist's office, and the occasional groan from a patient.

An FBI agent sat by her father's room.

"Hello, Agent Austin. Everything all right?"

"No problem," he said and a grin kicked in that was positively evil. "You'll like this. One enterprising reporter managed to get this far, and then I nabbed him. I decked him, stripped him naked, and the nurses and doctors tossed him in a laundry cart and wheeled him down to the emergency room, where they left him, his hands and feet tied with surgical tape, his mouth gagged. Ah, since then, no one else has tried it."

"I heard about that," she said, rolling her eyes. "One of the doctors told me he'd never before been surrounded with such laughter in the emergency room. Well done, Agent. Remind me to stay on your good side."

He was still chuckling when she walked quietly into the glass-windowed room and sat down in the single chair. He was asleep, not unexpected, and it didn't matter. He was on powerful medications and even when he was awake, his mind couldn't focus. "Hello," she said, watching him breathe slowly, in and out through the oxygen tubes in his nostrils. "You're looking wonderful, very handsome. I might have to give your hair a trim though, maybe in a couple of days. Adam will be all right as well, but maybe he's not quite as good-looking as you are. He's sleeping right now. Oh yes, I'm sure you'll be pleased to know that we're going to get married. But you won't be surprised, will you?" White bandages covered his chest. Tubes stuck out of him, and like Adam, he seemed to have a score of needles in his arms. He lay perfectly still, but he was breathing evenly, steady and deep.

"Now, let me tell you again what happened. Mikhail shot you in the chest. You have a collapsed lung. They did what's called a thoracotomy. They cracked open your chest to stop the bleeding and put a chest tube in between your ribs. It's hooked up to suction. That thing's called a pleuravac and you'll hear bubbles in the background. Now, when you wake up the tube will hurt a bit. There are two IVs in place and you'll have this oxygen tube in your nose for a while longer. Other than that, you're just fine."

He was breathing slowly, smoothly. The bubbles sounded in the background. "The house is gone and I'm very sorry about that," she said. "They couldn't save anything. I'm sorry, Dad, but we're alive, and that's what's really important. I just realized that not everything is gone, though. After Mom died, I put all of her things in a storage facility in the Bronx. There are photos there, and a lot of her things. Maybe there are even letters. I don't know, because I couldn't take the time to go through her papers. We'll have those. It's a start."

Did his breathing quicken a bit?

She wasn't sure.

What was important was that he was alive. He would get well.

She laid her cheek against his shoulder. She stayed there for a very long time, listening to the steady sound of his heart beating against her face.

She got the call at the hospital at eight o'clock that evening. She'd just left her father and was going back downstairs to be with Adam when a nurse called out, "Ms. Matlock, telephone for you."

She was surprised. It was the first call she'd gotten, or rather, it was the first call they had put through to her.

It was Tyler and he was talking even before she could say hello. "You're all right. Thank God it's all over, Becca. I've been frantic. They had footage of your father's burning house, with this huge safety net in the front yard.

They said you'd nearly died, up there on that roof with that maniac, that you shot him finally. Are you truly all right?"

"I'm fine, Tyler. Don't worry. I'm spending all my time at the hospital. Both my father and Adam Carruthers were shot, but they'll both survive. The media is outside, waiting, but it will be a long wait. Sherlock is bringing me clothes and stuff so I don't have to try to sneak out of here and take the chance the media might nab me. How's Sam doing?"

There was a bit of silence, then, "He misses you dreadfully. He's really quiet now, won't say a word. I'm worried, Becca, really worried. I keep trying to get him to talk about the man who kidnapped him, to tell me a little bit about him and what he said, but Sam shakes his head. He won't say a word. The TV said that man was dead, that he set himself on fire and hurled himself at you. Is that true?"

"Very true. I think you should take Sam to a child psychiatrist, Tyler."

"Those flimflam bloodsuckers? They'll start psychoanalyzing me, claiming I'm not a fit father, tell me I need to lie on a couch for at least six years and pay them big bucks. They'll say it's about me, not Sam. No way, Becca. No, he wants to see you."

"I'm sorry, but I can't leave here for another week, at least."

Then she heard a little boy wail, "Becca!"

It was Sam and he sounded like he was dying. She didn't know what to do. It was her fault that Sam was having problems, all her fault. "Put Sam on the phone, Tyler. Let me try to talk to him."

He did, but there was only silence. Sam wouldn't say a word.

Tyler said, "It's bad, Becca, really bad."

"Please take him to a child shrink, Tyler. You need help."

"Come back, Becca. You must."

"I will as soon as I can," she said finally, and hung up the phone.

"Problem?" a nurse asked, a thick black brow arched.

"Nothing but," Becca said, and lightly touched her fingers to her right arm. The burns were healing and were itching a bit now.

"Problems are like that," the nurse said. "It rains problems, and then, all of a sudden, it's a sunny day, and the problems have evaporated away."

"I hope you're right," Becca said.

The next day, Adam was much improved, even managed to joke with his nurse, who patted his butt, and her father came down with pneumonia and nearly died.

"It's nuts," Becca said to Agent Austin. "He survives a bullet to the heart and gets pneumonia."

"There's got to be some irony in that," Agent Austin said, shaking his head, "but no matter, it still sucks."

"He'll pull through," the doctor said over and over again to Becca, taking her hands in his. Maybe the doctor didn't like the irony, either, Becca thought, lightly touching her father's shoulder. It was odd, when she touched him—settled her hand on his arm, laid her hand over his, lightly touched his shoulder—his breathing calmed, his whole body seemed to relax, to ease.

And when he was finally awake, his mind alert, and she touched him, he smiled at her, and she saw the pleasure in his eyes, deep and abiding. And when she whispered, "I love you, Dad," he closed his eyes briefly, and she knew she didn't want to see his tears. "I love you," she said again, for good measure, and kissed his cheek. "We're together now. I know you love Adam like a son, but I'm very pleased he isn't your son. If he were, then I couldn't marry him. Now you'll get him anyway."

"If he ever makes you cry, I'll kill him," said her father.

"Nah, I'll do it."

"Becca, thank you for telling me about all your mother's things safely in storage in New York."

He'd heard her, actually heard her speaking to him. And since he'd heard her speaking to him, just maybe her mother had heard her as well, maybe she did have a final connection with her. "You're welcome. As I said then, it's a start."

"Yes," Thomas said, smiling up at his daughter. "It's a very good start."

ADAM was now walking up and down the corridor, ill-tempered, his back throbbing, his arm throbbing, feeling useless, wanting to hit someone because he felt so helpless. At least the catheter was out.

He was carping and carrying on when Becca laughed and said, "All right, you've finally driven me away. My father is doing fine, the pneumonia is kicked, and I'm going to Riptide to see Sam."

"No," he said, leaning against the hospital corridor wall, utterly appalled. He wanted to grab her and tuck her under his arm. "I don't want you going there alone. I don't trust McBride. I don't want you out of my sight. I'd really like it if you would sleep in my bed with me and I could hold on to you all night."

She realized she'd rather like that as well, but she said, "There's no danger, Adam. How could there be? I'm not going to see Tyler. I'm going to see what's going on with Sam. Don't forget, it's my fault that Krimakov even took him, my fault that Sam got traumatized. I've got to fix it. Tyler has nothing to do with it."

"It was Krimakov's fault. Give it another couple of days, Becca, and I'll go with you."

"Adam, you can barely get to the bathroom by yourself now. You'll stay here and concentrate on getting well. Spend time with my father. And maybe you could work on all those church dates as well. None of your family can come to an agreement."

"Well, are you still going to marry me?"

"Is that your final offer?"

He looked both pissed and chagrined. Suddenly he laughed. "I swear I'll change that green tile. Do you mind moving from New York, living down here? We're really close to your dad. Is he going to rebuild?"

"We haven't discussed it yet. Yes, Adam, I'll marry you, particularly if you change that bathroom tile. Consider it a done deal. I have no real ties to Albany. Goodness, there are so many folk around here who need good speechwriters. I'll make a fortune. Now, you can't flirt with any of the hospital staff anymore, you got that? I'm considering that we're now officially engaged.

"Ah, good, here's Hatch. Is that cigarette smoke I smell, Hatch? Adam won't like that. He'll probably take a good strip off you, maybe hit you with his walker."

She watched the two men argue, smiling. Sherlock came up behind her and said, "Everything nearly back to normal, I see. Let's watch FOX. Gaylan Woodhouse is going to be on in about a minute. He's speaking for the president, and you're going to love this spin."

Good grief, she thought, watching the TV, she was now a heroine. Someone, she had no idea who, had somehow taken a photo, very grainy, showing her facing Krimakov on that burning roof, her white nightgown blowing around her legs, her Coonan held in front of her in both hands, pointed straight at Krimakov. Gaylan Woodhouse wouldn't shut up. "Oh dear," Becca said. "Oh dear."

"It's been a long haul, and you came through," Sherlock said, and hugged her tightly. "I'm really glad to have met you, Becca Matlock, and I like your being a heroine. I have this feeling that you, Adam, and your father will be coming to lots of barbecues over at our house, beginning when they get out of this joint. Did I tell you that Savich is a vegetarian? When we barbecue, he eats roasted corn on the cob. We won't know about Sean and his preferences for a while yet. Have you agreed to the date and that marvelous Presbyterian church your in-laws have been members of for years and years?"

"Not yet," Becca said. "Hey, I'm so famous maybe I'll ask if the churches want to place bids for our ceremony."

"You're a writer, you could write a book, make a gazillion bucks."

"She'll have to make it fast," Savich said, coming up and squeezing his wife against his chest, "fame is fleeting nowadays. Another week, Becca, and you'll be a last-page footnote in *People* magazine."

THE next day, Becca flew to Portland, Maine, rented a Ford Escort, and drove up to Riptide. It was cooler this trip, the breeze sharp off the ocean. The first person she saw was Sheriff Gaffney, and he was frowning at her, his thumbs hooked in his wide leather belt.

"Ms. Matlock," he said, and gave her his best intimidating cop look.

"Hi, Sheriff," she said, grinned at him, and went up on her tiptoes. She gave him a big kiss on the cheek. "I'm famous, at least for a week, that's what I was told. Be nice to me."

For the life of him, Sheriff Gaffney couldn't think of a thing to say except "Humph," which he did. "I'll want to speak to you about that skeleton," he called after her. "I'll come to Jacob Marley's house this evening. Will you be there?"

"Certainly, Sheriff, I'll be there."

Then she ran into Bernie Bradstreet, the owner and editor of *The Riptide Independent*. He looked very tired, as if he'd been ill. "My wife's been sick," he said, then he tried to smile at her. "At least all your troubles are over, Ms. Matlock." He didn't mention how she'd lied to him that long-ago night when Tyler had taken her out to dinner at Errol Flynn's Barbecue on Foxglove Avenue. He was a good man, bless him.

And then she was knocking on Tyler's front door just as the sun was setting. The insects were beginning their evening songs. She heard a dog bark from a house farther down on Gum Shoe Lane. She wished she'd brought a cardigan. She shivered, rang the bell again.

Tyler's car wasn't in the driveway.

Where was he? Where was Sam?

She didn't understand it. She'd told him when she'd be here and she was only ten minutes off. She got back in her rental car and cut over to Belladonna, to Jacob Marley's house. She'd paid the rent through the end of the month, so the place was still hers. She planned to use this time to pack up the rest of her things, have the place cleaned, and return the keys to Rachel Ryan. Surely Rachel was spending a lot of time with Sam, helping him. She hoped Rachel was also trying to convince Tyler to take Sam to a child shrink.

She turned the key in the lock and shoved the door open.

"Hello, Becca."

It was Tyler, standing there, Sam in his arms, smiling really big. "We decided to wait for you here. I left the car down the road. We wanted to surprise you. I've got champagne for us and some lemonade for Sam. I even bought a carrot cake; I remembered you liked it. Come in." He set Sam down, and Sam stood there staring at her.

Tyler walked to her and wrapped his arms around her back. He kissed the top of her head. "I like your hair. It's natural again. You're beautiful, Becca." He kissed her again, pulled her more tightly against him. "I thought you were beautiful in college, but you're even more beautiful now."

She tried to ease away from him, but he didn't let her go.

He gently pushed her chin up with his thumb and kissed her. It was a deep kiss, and he wanted to make it deeper, he wanted her to open her mouth. Sam was standing there saying nothing, just looking at them.

"No, Tyler, please, no." She shoved hard against his chest and he quickly stepped back.

He was still smiling, breathing hard, his eyes bright with excitement, with sex, lust. "You're right. Sam is standing right here. He's not a baby anymore. We shouldn't do this in front of him." He turned to smile down at his son. "Well, Sam, here's Becca. What do you have to say to her?"

Sam didn't have anything to say. He stood there, his small face blank of all expression. It scared her to her toes. She walked slowly to him and went down on her knees in front of him. "Hello, Sam," she said, and lightly touched her fingertips to his cheek. "How are you, sweetie? I want you to listen to me now. And believe me because I wouldn't lie to you. That bad man who kidnapped you, who tied you up and put you in the basement, I swear to you that he's gone now, forever. He'll never come back, ever, I can promise you that. I took care of him."

Sam didn't say anything, suffered her touching his face. Slowly, she brought him against her even though his small body was stiff, resistant.

"I've missed you, Sam. I would have come sooner, but my father and Adam—you remember Adam, don't you?—they were both hurt and I had to stay with them in the hospital. But now I'm here."

"Adam."

One word, but it was enough. "Yes," she said, delighted, "Adam."

She turned her head when she heard Tyler say something, but he shook his head at her. "Sam's okay, Becca. I also brought some barbecue from Errol Flynn's for our dinner. All the fixings, too. Would you like to have dinner now?"

And so they drank champagne, Sam drank his lemonade, and everyone ate barbecue pork ribs, baked beans, and coleslaw in Jacob Marley's kitchen. The carrot cake from Myrtle's Sweet Tooth on Venus Flytrap Boulevard stood on the kitchen counter.

After she'd answered countless questions about Krimakov, she said, "What about the skeleton, Tyler? Have the DNA results come in yet? Is it Melissa Katzen?"

Tyler shrugged. "No word yet that I know of. Everyone believes it is. But that's not important now. What's important is us. When do you want to move up here, Becca?"

Becca was handing Sam another rib. Her hand stilled. "Move back here? No, Tyler. I'm here to see Sam and pack up my things."

He nodded and tore meat off the rib he was holding. He chewed, then said, "Well, that's all right. You've just reconnected with your dad, so you need to make sure he's okay, get to know him and all that, but we need to set our wedding date before you go back to see him. Do you think he'll want to move up to be near you after we're married?"

She set down her fork near the coleslaw. Something had gone terribly wrong. She didn't want this, but there was no hiding from it now. She said it slowly, calmly, aware that Sam was now very still again, not eating, listening, but she had no choice. She said, "I'm truly sorry if you've misunderstood, Tyler. You and Sam are my very dear friends. I care about both of you quite a lot. I've appreciated all you've done for me, the support you've given me, the confidence you've had in me, but I can't be your wife. I'm very sorry, but I don't feel about you the way you want me to."

Sam continued to sit there on two thick phone books, still and silent, the half-chewed pork rib clutched in his small fingers.

She forced a smile. "We should probably have this talk after Sam's gone to bed, don't you think?"

"Why? It concerns him. He wants you for his mother, Becca. I told him that was why you were coming back. I told him you were going to fix everything and you'd be here for him forever."

"We should speak of this later, Tyler. This is between us. Please."

Sam looked down at his plate, his small face drawn, pale in the dim kitchen light.

"All right then," Tyler said. "I'm going to put Sam down with a blanket in the living room, on that real comfortable sofa. What do you think, Sam?"

Sam didn't tell them what he thought.

"I'll be right back, Becca."

He scooped Sam up off his phone books and carried him out of the kitchen. She shivered. The house felt uncomfortably cool. She hoped Sam would be warm enough with just one blanket. She hoped Sam had gotten enough to eat. She wished Tyler had wiped Sam's fingers off better.

What was she going to do? Was she the one off base here? Had she given Tyler the wrong impression? She'd known he was jealous of Adam, and that's when she had pulled back from him, even cooling her friendship toward him. But still he'd misunderstood, still he'd come to believe that she wanted to be his wife. How could it be possible? She'd said nothing, done nothing, to give him that idea. And he was using Sam, which was despicable of him.

Sam. What was she going to do? There was something very wrong, triggered, she supposed, by Krimakov's kidnapping of him. She heard Tyler walking back toward the kitchen. She had to clear this up, quickly and cleanly. She had to think what she could do to help Sam.

She'd gotten the name of a really good child psychologist in Bangor from Sherlock. She would start there.

But she didn't have a chance to start anything because Tyler said from the doorway, "I love you, Becca."

# THIRTY-TWO

"No, Tyler, no."

Tyler smiled at her, an intimate smile that chilled her to the bone. "I've loved you from that first time I saw you in Hadley's freshman dorm at Dartmouth. You were looking lost, wondering where to find a bathroom."

She smiled at that, no recollection at all of that meeting. "You didn't love me, Tyler. You dated lots of girls in college. You married Sam's mother, Ann. You loved her."

He came into the kitchen and sat down across from her. "Sure I loved her for a while, but she left me, Becca. She left me and she didn't plan to come back. She was even going to take Sam, but I didn't let her."

What was he talking about? Of course things couldn't have been smooth between them, since Ann had ended up leaving him. They'd faced off about it? There'd been a confrontation? But that didn't concern her now. She said, "I'm really sorry if you've gotten the wrong idea, Tyler. Please believe me. I am your friend and I hope I always will be. I would like to see Sam grow up."

"Since you're going to be his mother, of course you'll see him grow up. You'll make him well again, Becca. He's been silent and withdrawn ever since his mother left."

"Would you like some coffee?"

"Sure, if you're going to make some." He watched her measure the coffee into the machine, then pour in the water. He watched her press the switch, watched it turn red.

"Tell me about Ann," she said, wanting him to remember the woman he'd loved, distract him from her. Why had Ann left him? Had there been another man? Why hadn't she taken Sam with her? So what if Tyler had tried to fight for custody? Sam was still her child, not his. But she had run away without him.

Tyler was still watching the coffeemaker. She watched him breathe in the aroma. Finally, he said, "She was beautiful. She'd been married to a guy who left her the minute he found out she was pregnant. We hooked up kind of by accident. She couldn't get the gasoline cap off her car. I helped her. Then we went to Pollyanna's Restaurant." He shrugged. "We got married a couple months later."

"What happened?"

He said nothing for a very long time. "The coffee's ready."

She poured each of them a cup.

He took a drink, then shrugged. "She was happy and then she wasn't. She left. Nothing more, Becca. Listen, I swear I'll make you happy. You won't ever want to leave. We can have more kids, yours and mine. Sam was Ann's kid anyway."

"I'm going to marry Adam."

He threw the coffee at her. He roared to his feet, sending the wooden chair crashing against the wall, and shouted, "No, you're not! You're mine, do you hear me? You're mine, you bitch!"

The coffee wasn't scalding anymore, but it hurt, splashing on her neck, on the front of her shirt, soaking through to her skin.

He leapt toward her, his hands out.

"No, Tyler." She ran, but he was blocking any escape out the back door. There was no place to go except down to the basement. But she'd be trapped down there. No, wait, there was another small entry on the far side of the basement where long-ago Marleys had had their winter cords of wood dumped. She saw it all in a flash, and ran to the basement door, jerked it open, then pulled it closed behind her. She locked it, flipped on the light, saw the naked bulb dangling from the ceiling by a thin wire, even as she heard him pulling on the knob on the other side, yelling, calling her horrible names, telling her that he would get her, that she wouldn't leave him, not ever.

She ran down the wooden stairs. She looked at the wall where she'd found Sam propped up, bound and gagged, then at the far wall that still gaped open from when the skeleton had fallen out of it after that storm.

She heard the basement door splinter. Then he was on the stairs. She pulled and jerked at the rusted latch that held the small trapdoor down.

It was about chest high. *Move, move,* but she was shrieking it in her mind, not out loud. What was going on with him? It had happened so quickly. He had snapped, turned into a wild man, a crazy man.

She heard his feet clattering to the bottom steps. The latch wouldn't give. She was trapped. She turned to see him running across the concrete floor. He came to a stop. He was panting. He smiled at her.

"I nailed that trapdoor shut last week. It was dangerous. I didn't think we should take the chance that a kid could open it and fall through. Maybe hurt himself. Maybe even kill himself."

"Tyler," she said. *Be calm, be calm.* "What's going on here? Why are you acting like this? Why this rage? At me? Why?"

He said, all calm and serious, and he actually waved his finger at her, like a lecturing teacher, "You're like the others, Becca. I hoped you would be different, I would have wagered everything that you were different, that you weren't like Ann, that faithless bitch who wanted to leave me, wanted to take Sam and go far away from me."

"Why did she want to leave you, Tyler?"

He shrugged. "She thought I was smothering her, but that was in her mind, of course. I loved her, wanted to make her and Sam happy, but she started pulling back. She didn't need all those other friends of hers, they just wasted her time, took her away from me. Then she told me that night that she had to leave me, that she couldn't stand it anymore."

"Stand what?"

"I don't know. I tried to give her everything she wanted, both her and Sam. I just wanted her for myself, wanted her to commit herself only to me, and all I asked was that she stay close to me, that she look to me for everything. And she did for a while, and then she didn't want to anymore."

"She left?"

In that instant, Becca knew that Ann McBride hadn't gone anywhere. She was still here in Riptide.

"Where did you bury her, Tyler?"

"In Jacob Marley's backyard, right under that old elm tree that was around when World War One began. I dug her deep so no animals would dig her up. I even gave her a nice service. She didn't deserve anything, but I gave her all the religious trappings, the sweet and hopeful words. After all, she was my wife." He laughed, remembering now and said with a smirk, "Old Jacob had been dead by then nearly three years so I didn't worry about getting rid of him that time."

He started laughing then. "I killed that ridiculous old dog of his— Miranda—a long time ago. The bitch didn't like me, always growled when I came near. The old man never knew, never."

She remembered the sheriff telling her how much Jacob Marley had loved that dog, how she'd just up and died one day. Her heart was pounding, slowly, painfully. Somehow she had to reach him. She had to try. "Listen to me, Tyler. I didn't betray you. I would never betray you. I came here to Riptide because of what you'd told me about it. I was here to hide out. This was sanctuary for me. You helped me, so very much. You don't know how much I appreciate that." Were his eyes calmer now? Maybe, but he frowned and she tried to still her fear, said quickly, "That madman was trying to kill both me and my father. The last thing I wanted to think about was falling in love with anyone. I never meant for you to believe there was more to it than friendship."

His eyes were darker now, a barely leashed wildness that scared her to her soul. He said, his voice sarcastic, "You didn't want to fall in love, Becca? Then why are you marrying Carruthers?"

For a moment, her brain refused to work. He was right. She had to think, she had to do something. She was alone in the basement with a man who wasn't sane, a man who was somehow twisted, a man who had murdered his wife and buried her in Jacob Marley's backyard. Sheriff Gaffney had been certain that Tyler had murdered his wife. Everyone believed that the skeleton that fell out of the basement wall had been Ann McBride. But it wasn't.

She couldn't bear it, just couldn't. She had to know, all of it. "Tyler, the girl in the wall. Was it Melissa Katzen?"

He said, his voice indifferent, bored, "Yes, of course it was."

"But she was young, not more than eighteen when someone killed her. That was more than twelve years ago. Did you kill her, Tyler?"

He shrugged. "Another faithless bitch, little Melissa. Everyone thought she was so sweet, so giving, so yielding. And she was with me, at first. I gave her attention, small presents—lots of them, all clever, imaginative. I told her how pretty she was and she soaked it up until one day she turned down my latest gift to her. It was a Barbie, all dressed to travel, ready to elope.

"She didn't want to tell anyone about us, and that was okay by me. I was going to laugh my head off when we came back married. She called me that night, asked me to meet her. She gave me back the Barbie, then told me she didn't want to run away with me after all. She whined that she was too young, that her parents would be hurt if she ran off with me. I told her that she had to marry me, that no one else would, that I was the only one who really loved her." He shook his head then, frowning at something he was remembering, at what he was seeing. He said slowly, "She became afraid of me. She tried to get away from me, but I caught her."

She could see him with Melissa in her Calvin Klein white jeans, the cute little pink tank top, see him, hear him trying to convince her, then screaming at her, then killing her. She knew she had to keep him talking. She couldn't let him stop now. When he stopped talking, he would kill her. She didn't want to die. She remembered then that Sheriff Gaffney was coming over, at least he'd told her he was. Sometime during the evening. It was evening, right in the middle of evening. Where was he? What if he left when no one answered the door? She was so afraid, she stuttered. "B-but Jacob Marley was here, wasn't he?"

"True enough." He shrugged. "I put her in the shed out back, and then the next day, I got Jacob Marley out of the house with a phone call. He had a very old sister who lived in Bangor. I called and told him she was dying and asking for him, begging him to come to her. The old jerk left and I dug out the wall and put Melissa behind it. Then I bricked it back up. My dad was in construction before he fell off a building and he taught me a whole lot. I knew all about bricklaying. Then I left. You want to know something funny? Jacob Marley's ancient sister died the very day he showed up at the old folks' home in Bangor. He never even realized that it had been a fake call."

"Tyler, why did you bury Melissa in the basement wall? Why Jacob Marley's house?"

He laughed, and that laugh chilled her. "I was thinking maybe I'd call in an anonymous tip, tell everyone I saw Jacob Marley kill Melissa, then saw him with cement and bricks."

"But you didn't."

"No. Maybe I'd left fingerprints somehow on her. I couldn't take the chance." Then he slashed his hand through the air. His voice lowered, his eyes darkened, became as intense as a preacher's in a revival tent. "I wanted you to marry me, Becca. I would have taken care of you all your life. I would have loved you, protected you, kept you close forever. You could have been Sam's mother. But once you were with me, you wouldn't have spent all that much time with him. Sam would have understood that you were mine first, that he really had no claim on you, not like I did."

She was cold, so cold her teeth would soon be chattering. This lovely man who'd seemed so kind, so gentle—he was crazy, probably he'd been born crazy.

"Melissa was only eighteen, Tyler. Both of you were too young to run off."

"No," he said. "I was ready. I believed she was. She was faithless. She would have left me, just like Ann did."

How many other women had he believed to be faithless? How many others had he killed, then hidden their bodies? Becca looked around for some sort of weapon, anything, but there was nothing. No, she was wrong. There were about half a dozen bricks stacked against the gaping open wall, about six feet away from her.

She took a step sideways.

He said thoughtfully now, "I think I'll bury you close to Ann. Out under that elm tree. But you don't deserve a nice service, Becca, not like the one I did for Ann. She was Sam's mother, after all."

"I don't want to be buried there," she said and took another step. "I don't want to die, Tyler. I haven't done anything to you. I came here to be safe, but I wasn't ever safe, was I? It was all an illusion. You were just waiting, waiting for another woman to love, to possess, to imprison so she'd want out and then you could kill her, do it all over again and again. You need help, Tyler. Let me call someone." She took another step toward the bricks.

He began walking toward her. "I would rather have held you close, Becca. If only—"

There was the sound of a car pulling up outside.

"The sheriff's here," Becca said quickly. "Listen. It's over, Tyler. The sheriff won't let you hurt me now." She took another quick step to the side. Three feet, just another three feet. Tyler looked up and frowned when he heard a car door slam. He cursed even as he ran toward her, his hands outstretched, his fingers curved inward.

Becca leapt toward the pile of bricks, went down on her knees, and grabbed one. He was on her then, his hands around her neck, and she slammed the brick against his shoulder. His fingers tightened, tightened, and his face was blurring above her. She raised the brick again, brought it upward slowly, and he twisted as she heaved it toward him. It struck his face and he howled with agony, and his fingers loosened for just a moment. She gulped in air and struck again. He sent his fist against her head, and she saw blinding flashes of light, felt the pain sear through her head, knew she couldn't hold on. She was losing and she would die because she wasn't strong enough. She tried to raise the brick again but she couldn't.

"You faithless bitch, you're like all the rest of them!" His fingers tightened around her neck.

Sheriff Gaffney yelled, "Let her go, Tyler! Let her go!"

Tyler was heaving now, his fingers strong, so strong, tighter and tighter now and she knew she would die.

Then there was a shot. Tyler jerked over her. His hands fell away. She blinked and saw him turn slowly to face Sheriff Gaffney, standing in a cop's stance, his Ruger P85 pistol held tightly between his hands. "Get away from her, Tyler. Now! MOVE!"

"No," Tyler said and lunged for her again. Another shot rang out. Tyler fell on top of her, his face beside her head. Dead weight, oh God, he was now dead weight.

"Hold on, Ms. Matlock, and I'll get him off you."

Sheriff Gaffney pulled Tyler away. He'd shot him once in the head and once in the back. He gave Becca a hand up. "You okay?"

She was shaking, her teeth chattering, her throat burning, Tyler's blood all over her, and the healing burn on her arm was throbbing fiercely. She smiled up at him. "I think you're the most wonderful man in the whole world," she said. "Thank you for coming in the house. I prayed and prayed that you would see all the lights on and come in."

"I heard little Sam crying," Sheriff Gaffney said.

"Hello?"

A small, thin voice. It was Sam and he was standing at the top of the basement stairs.

"Oh, no," Becca said. "Oh, no."

"I told him to wait in the kitchen for me. Okay, I'll get Rachel over here. Can you pull yourself together, Ms. Matlock? We'll go upstairs and you can take care of Sam until Rachel comes. He loves Rachel a whole lot, you'll see. Keep hanging in there, ma'am." He shook his head, then said, "I knew Tyler killed his wife, knew it in my lawman's gut, you know?

But he also killed poor little Melissa twelve years ago. I wonder how many other women he's killed who rejected him."

Becca didn't want to know.

ADAM was stretched out on the sofa in his living room, a soft pillow under his head, a light afghan pulled to his waist, so relieved that Becca was back safe and sound, staying in his house, her stuff scattered around, all at home now, that all he could do was grin. He didn't want her to leave, not ever. He heard her moving about in his wonderful, fully equipped, very modern kitchen, making him a healthy snack, she'd said.

The house was cool since he'd had the good sense to install central air-conditioning when he'd moved in. Soon, he thought, he'd get that ugly green tile out of that second-floor bathroom. Another four days and his energy would come roaring back and he'd head right down to the tile store. The master bedroom was sort of stark though, with just a big black lacquer bed and a matching black lacquer dresser, a couple of comfortable black and white chairs, and a good-sized closet, nearly walk-in, he'd said to her, lots of room for both of their clothes.

He'd had big plans for the bed the night before, about two hours after she'd gotten back from Riptide, and even though he couldn't move a whole lot and his flexibility was nearly nil, and he'd tended to moan from pain as well as pleasure, it hadn't mattered. She'd simply taken charge. He nearly shook the afghan off now thinking of how she'd looked astride him, her head thrown back when she'd screamed out his name. And then she'd fallen over on him and the pain had nearly made him yell again. But he'd lain there, silent, holding her against him as best he could, stroking her smooth back, and then she'd slowly straightened, frowned at the sight of his rib, all yellow and green now, and said, "I nearly killed you, didn't I? I'm sorry."

"Kill me again," he'd said, and she laughed and kissed him and kissed him again and again, and loved him until he'd yelled again, this time not from any pain in his ribs.

He felt good. He had plans for that bed again today, maybe in about an hour from now. He was stronger today, maybe he'd be able to do a bit more moving around. He hadn't been able to get his hands and mouth everywhere he'd wanted to last night. Ah, but today. His fingers itched, his mouth sort of tingled. And what about tomorrow and the next day?

Maybe he'd keep her in the bedroom until they had to leave for the church to get married, then right back here again. It sounded really fine to him. He wondered what Becca thought about mirrors everywhere.

She brought him some iced tea and a plate of celery stuffed with cream cheese. She sat beside him and fed him between kisses.

He realized suddenly there was something different about her, something he couldn't quite put his finger on. Then he realized what it was—she was hiding something from him. And her eyes, something different there—he realized, finally, that it was shock. Well, he supposed that nearly burning to death on the roof of her father's house would leave its mark. Or realizing a man she'd really liked was in actuality a madman. Or maybe, he thought, his mouth tightening, that madman, Tyler McBride, had, in fact, hurt her or tried to, and she hadn't seen fit to tell him.

He ate another celery stick, eyeing her, then said, his voice all suspicious, his brows lowered, "You swear you didn't lie to me? You swear there was no real trouble up in Riptide?"

She lightly stroked her fingers over his cheek. She loved to touch him. She particularly liked him naked so she could touch all of him, kiss all of him. She leaned down now and kissed his mouth, then straightened again. She said, all easy and blasé, "Nothing that couldn't be handled. Sam's all right. I can't tell you how wonderful Rachel is with him. I knew they were close, but when she came running into the house, Sam left me in a flash and went right to her. I thought she would fall apart, she was so relieved Sam was all right. Sheriff Gaffney told me since there are no relatives, Rachel and her husband would very likely adopt Sam. I called up this morning, and she's already got him an appointment with that child psychologist Sherlock recommended up in Bangor. Oh yeah, I also told Rachel she was probably a very conscientious, great real estate agent, but I would never ever rent another house from her again." His frown was still in place. "Rachel laughed." The frown lightened.

Adam said, "Yeah, I'm relieved about Sam, too. But wait a minute, Becca. Back up here. You're telling me McBride didn't try to hurt you when you told him you didn't love him?"

She stuffed another celery stick in his mouth and kissed him all over his face as he chewed. She whispered in his ear before he could talk again, "Nothing to worry about, really, Adam. It's all over and done with. Hey, you do like the celery sticks?"

"Yeah, they're good. All three dozen that you've stuffed down me.

Now, tell me about how Sheriff Gaffney had to shoot Tyler once he knew the skeleton was that girl Melissa Katzen. I'm not really all that clear on any of it. I want every little detail, Becca. No, no more celery sticks. Yeah, a kiss is all right, but hold off now. You're not going to distract me anymore."

But she kept kissing him until he was nearly heaving himself off the sofa. She said against his ear, "I used low-fat cream cheese, better for your arteries."

"Becca." He grabbed a fist of her hair and pulled her close to his face. "Tell me the truth. What happened up there?"

"Adam, it wasn't all that big a deal. Really, nothing worth mentioning except that Sheriff Gaffney really came through. He was the hero. I've probably forgotten lots of it because it wasn't that memorable. Really, the sheriff had everything under control. I didn't even count. I wasn't even important. Would you please stop your worrying and forget it? I'm home now." He felt her hand on his belly and he nearly lost it, but he didn't. He let her go but his frown deepened. Before he could say anything, Becca smiled and said as she got up from the sofa, "Oh, my, look at the time. Not enough time for me to have my way with you. But I do have a couple of minutes. Do you want me to give you a nice rubdown before I go to the hospital to see Dad?"

He thought about her hand on his belly, moving south, and he nearly went *en pointe*. He said on a big sigh, "No, but how about an apple, Becca? I love apples."

She knew exactly what he was thinking. "I love you, Adam. Maybe when I get back from the hospital, we can play a game of Monopoly, or something, okay? But that means you've got to rest while I'm gone. Now, you sit tight and I'll get you that apple."

The phone rang. Adam stared after Becca, then picked it up. "Hello."

"Is this Mr. Carruthers?"

"It is."

"This is Sheriff Gaffney, from Riptide."

"Hello, Sheriff. What can I do for you?"

"I wanted to speak to Ms. Matlock, make sure she was all right."

"Well," Adam said slowly, staring toward the door, "there's still some shock, you know, from what happened."

The sheriff sighed. "Understandable, of course, poor girl. I don't mind telling you that it was pretty hairy there for a while, Mr. Carruthers. I'm sure it's made your hair stand on end, hearing about her lying on the basement floor with McBride straddling her, choking the life out of her. She was hitting him with a brick, but it wasn't working, she was getting too weak. The guy was strong, really strong. As you know, I had to shoot him, but even that didn't stop him. He was over-the-top, completely whacked out, as my boys say, and all he wanted to do was kill her. I had to shoot him again and the guy fell right on top of her, covered her with blood. But it's over now. All the questions answered. Ms. Matlock didn't get hysterical, thank the good Lord. She's a strong girl. As a man of the law doing my duty, I really appreciated that. And now she's home, and I hear the two of you are going to get married. You're a lucky man."

"Yes, Sheriff. Thank you."

"Any time. Well, do give my best to Ms. Matlock."

"You can be sure that I will, Sheriff." Adam heard her breathing. She was on the line in the kitchen. She'd listened in, heard everything, hadn't said a word. His heart was pounding slow, heavy strokes. He was so furious he couldn't think of anything to say. Then he opened his mouth and shouted into the receiver at the top of his lungs, "BECCA!"

She cleared her throat. "Ah, Adam, I've got to go to the hospital now."

He breathed deeply, got hold of himself, and said, "Not yet. Bring me my apple. I'll even give you a bite before I wash your mouth out with soap for those whoppers you told me."

"Sorry, Adam, the apples aren't ripe enough. You know Sheriff Gaffney, he exaggerates, really, he—"

"After I wash your mouth out, I'm going to maybe shave your head. Then if I'm still pissed off, I'm going to make you change that green tile in the bathroom, then—"

"I'm outta here, Adam. I love you. Er, I'll buy ripe apples while I'm out." She hung up the phone.

"BECCA!"

# HEMLOCK BAY

I wish to thank the following people at FBI headquarters and at Quantico for their generosity and enthusiasm:

William Hayden Matens, *Special Agent, retired*
Thomas B. Locke, *Deputy Assistant Director, Inspection Division*
David R. Knowlton, *Assistant Director, Inspection Division*
Wade M. Jackson, *Unit Chief, Firearms Training Unit*
Gary J. Hutchison, *Agent Instructor*
Alan H. Marshall, *Special Agent, Indoor Range*
Jeffrey Higginbotham, *Assistant Director, Training Division*
Douglas W. Deedrick, *Unit Chief, Information and Evidence Management Unit*
Lester "Wingtips" Davis, *Officer, National Academy Association*
Ruben Garcia, Jr., *Assistant Director, Criminal Investigative Division*
Kenneth McCabe, *Section Chief, Laboratory Division*
Michael J. Perry, *Firearms Instructor*
Sheri A. Farrar, *Deputy Assistant Director, Administrative Services Division*
Royce Curtin, *Special Agent, Hostage Rescue Team*
Stephen R. Band, *Unit Chief, Behavior Sciences Unit*

Lew Elliott, who teaches cops how to fight

I wish to thank my husband, Dr. Anton Pogany, yet again, for his excellent instincts and his eagle eye that never misses a thing—he remains the Editor from Hell.

To Ildiko deAngelis, director of George Washington University Museum Studies Program. She is very smart, very experienced in both law and art history, and has extensive knowledge of museum procedures both in the United States and abroad. She's answered every question I could come up with and provided me valuable insights into a very esoteric world.

She's also the best sister-in-law a body could have. Thank you, Ildi, for your time and for sharing your magnificent brain with me.

—CC

# ONE

It was a chilly day in late October. A stiff wind whipped the last colorful leaves off the trees. The sun was shining down hard and bright on the dilapidated red barn that hadn't been painted in forty years. Streaks of washed-out red were all that was left of the last paint job. There was no charm left, at all.

FBI Special Agent Dillon Savich eased around the side of the barn, his SIG in his right hand. It had taken discipline and practice, but he'd learned to move so quietly that he could sneak up on a mouse. Three agents, one of them his wife, were some twenty feet behind him, covering him, ready to fan out in any direction necessary, all of them wearing Kevlar vests. A dozen more agents were slowly working their way up the other side of the barn, their orders to wait for a signal from Savich. Sheriff Dade of Jedbrough County and three deputies were stationed in the thick stand of maple trees just thirty feet behind them. One of the deputies, a sharpshooter, had his sights trained on the barn.

So far the operation was going smoothly, which, Savich supposed, surprised everyone, although no one spoke of it. He hoped it would continue the way it had been planned, but chances were things would get screwed up. He'd deal with it; there was no choice.

The barn was bigger than Savich liked—there was a big hayloft, and too many shadowy corners for this sort of operation. Too many nooks and crannies for an ambush, plain too many places from which to fire a storm of bullets.

A perfect place for Tommy and Timmy Tuttle—dubbed "the Warlocks" by the media—to hole up. They'd hopscotched across the country, but had dropped out of sight here, in Maryland, with their two latest young teenage boys taken right out of the gym where they'd been playing basketball after school, in Stewartville, some forty miles away. Savich had believed that Maryland was their destination, no sound reason really, but in his gut he felt it. The profilers hadn't said much about that, just that Maryland was, after all, on the Atlantic coast, so they really couldn't go much farther east.

Then MAX, Savich's laptop, had dived into land registry files in Maryland and found that Marilyn Warluski, a first cousin to the Tuttle brothers, and who, MAX had also discovered, had had a baby at the age of seventeen fathered by Tommy Tuttle, happened to own a narrow strip of land near a good-sized maple forest that wasn't far from the serpentine Plum River. And on that sliver of property was a barn, a big ancient barn that had been abandoned for years. Savich had nearly clicked his heels together in excitement.

And now, four hours later, here they were. There'd been no sign of a car, but Savich wasn't worried. The old Honda was probably stashed in the barn. He quieted his breathing and listened. The birds had gone still. The silence was heavy, oppressive, as if even the animals were expecting something to happen and knew instinctively that it wouldn't be good.

Savich was afraid the Tuttle brothers were long gone. All they would find, despite the silence, would be their victims: teenage boys—Donny and Rob Arthur—dead, horribly mutilated, their bodies circumscribed by a large, black circle.

Savich didn't want to smell any more blood. He didn't want to see any more death. Not today. Not ever.

He looked down at his Mickey Mouse watch. It was time to see if the bad guys were in the barn. It was time to get the show on the road.

MAX had found a crude interior plan of the barn, drawn some fifty years before, documented in a computerized county record as having been physically saved and filed. Kept where? was the question. They'd finally turned up the drawing in an old file cabinet in the basement of the county planning building. But the drawing was clear enough. There was a small, narrow entry, down low, here on the west side. He found it behind a straggly naked bush. It was cracked open, wide enough for him to squeeze through.

He looked back, waved his SIG at the three agents peering around the corner of the barn, a signal to hold their positions, and went in on his belly. He pushed the narrow door open an inch at a time. Filth everywhere, some rat carcasses strewn around. He nudged his way in on his elbows, feeling bones crunch beneath him, his SIG steady in his hand.

There was a strange half-light in the barn. Dust motes floated in the narrow spears of light coming through the upper windows, only shards of glass sticking up in some of the frames. He lay there quietly a moment, his eyes adjusting. He saw bales of hay so old they looked petrified, stacked haphazardly, rusted machinery—mainly odd parts—and two ancient wooden troughs.

Then he noticed it. In the far corner was another door not more than twenty feet to the right of the front double barn doors. A tack room, he thought, and it hadn't been shown on the drawing. Then he made out the outline of the Honda, tucked in the shadows at the far end of the barn. The two brothers were in the tack room, no doubt about it. And Donny and Rob Arthur? Please let them still be alive.

He had to know exactly who was where before he called in the other agents. It was still, very still. He got to his feet and ran hunched over toward the tack room door, his gun fanning continuously, his breathing low and steady, his steps silent. He pressed his ear against the rotted wooden door of the tack room.

He heard a male voice, clear and strong, and angry, suddenly louder.

"Listen, you Little Bloods, it's time for you to get in the middle of the circle. The Ghouls want you; they told me to hurry it up. They want to carve you up with their axes and knives—they really like to do that—but this time they want to tuck you away in their carryalls and fly away with you. Hey, maybe you'll end up in Tahiti. Who knows? They haven't wanted to do this before. But it doesn't make any difference to us. Here come the Ghouls!" And he laughed, a young man's laugh, not all that deep, and it sounded quite happily mad. It made Savich's blood run icy.

Then another man's voice, this one deeper. "Yep, almost ready for the Ghouls. We don't want to disappoint them now, do we? Move it, Little Bloods."

He heard them coming toward the door, heard the scuffling of feet, heard the boys' crying, probably beyond reason now, heard curses and prods from the Tuttle brothers. It was then that he saw the huge, crude circle painted with thick, black paint on a cleared-out part of the rotting wooden barn floor.

Zero hour. No time, simply no time now to bring the others in.

Savich barely made it down behind a rotted hay bale before one of them opened the tack room door and shoved a slight, pale boy in front of him. The boy's filthy pants were nearly falling off his butt. It was Donny Arthur. He'd been beaten, probably starved as well. He was terrified. Then a second terrified youth was shoved out of the small tack room next to him. Rob Arthur, only fourteen years old. Savich had never seen such fear on two such young faces in his life.

If Savich ordered the Tuttles to stop now, they could use the boys for shields. No, better to wait. What was all that crazy talk about ghouls? He watched the two men shove the boys forward until they actually kicked them into the center of the circle.

"Don't either of you move or I'll take my knife and shove it right through your arm into the floor, pin you good. Tammy here will do the other with her knife. You got that, Little Bloods?"

*Tammy? Her* knife? No, it was two brothers—Tommy and Timmy Tuttle, more than enough alliteration, even for the media. No, he couldn't have heard right. He was looking at two young men, both in black, long and lean, big, chunky black boots laced up the front to the knees like combat boots. They carried knives and guns.

The boys were huddled together on their knees, crying, clutching each other. Blood caked their faces, but they could move, and that meant no bones were broken.

"Where are the Ghouls?" Tammy Tuttle shouted, and Savich realized in that instant that he hadn't misheard; it wasn't the Tuttle brothers, it was one brother and one sister.

What was all this about the ghouls coming to murder the boys?

"Ghouls," Tammy yelled, her head thrown back, her voice reverberating throughout the ancient barn, "where are you? We've got your two treats for you, just what you like—two really sweet boys! Little Bloods, both of them. Bring your knives and axes! Come here, Ghouls."

It was a chant, growing louder as she repeated herself once, twice, then three times. Each time, her voice was louder, more vicious, the words ridiculous, really, except for the underlying terror they carried.

Tammy Tuttle kicked one of the boys, hard, when he tried to crawl out of the circle. Savich knew he had to act soon. Where were these ghouls?

He heard something, something that was different from the mad human voices, like a high whine, sort of a hissing sound that didn't belong here, maybe didn't belong anywhere. He felt gooseflesh rise on his arms. He felt a shock of cold. He was on the point of leaping out when, to his utter astonishment, the huge front barn doors whooshed inward, blinding light flooded in, and in the middle of that light were dust devils that looked like small tornadoes. The white light faded away, and the dust devils looked more like two whirling, white cones, distinct from each other, spinning and twisting, riding up then dipping down, blending together, then separating—no, no, they were just dust devils, still white because they hadn't sucked up the dirt yet from the barn floor. But what was that sound he heard? Something strange, something he couldn't identify. Laughter? No, that was crazy, but that was what registered in his brain.

The boys saw the dust devils, whirling and spinning far above them, and started screaming. Donny jumped up, grabbed his older brother, and managed to jerk him out of the circle.

Tammy Tuttle, who'd been looking up, turned suddenly, raised her knife, and yelled, "Get back down, Little Bloods! Don't you dare anger the Ghouls. Get back in the circle, now! GET BACK DOWN!"

The boys scrabbled farther away from the circle. Tommy Tuttle was on them in an instant, jerking them back. Tammy Tuttle drew the knife back, aiming toward Donny Arthur, as Savich leaped up from behind the bale of hay and fired. The bullet ripped into her arm at her shoulder. She screamed and fell onto her side, the knife flying out of her hand.

Tommy Tuttle whipped about, no knife in his hand now but a gun, and that gun was aimed not at Savich but at the boys. The boys were screaming as Savich shot Tommy through the center of his forehead.

Tammy Tuttle was moaning on the floor, holding her arm. The boys stood, clutched together, silent now, and all three of them looked up toward those whirling, white cones that danced up and down in the clear light coming through the barn doors. No, not dust devils, two separate things.

One of the boys whispered, "What are they?"

"I don't know, Rob," Savich said and pulled the boys toward him, protecting them as best he could. "Some sort of weird tornado, that's all."

Tammy was yelling curses at Savich as she tried to pull herself up. She fell back. There was a shriek, loud and hollow. One of the cones seemed to leap forward, directly at them. Savich didn't think, just shot it, clean through. It was like shooting through fog. The cone danced upward, then twisted back toward the other cone. They hovered an instant, spinning madly, and in the next instant, they were gone. Simply gone.

Savich grabbed both boys against him again. "It's all right now,

Donny, Rob. You're both all right. I'm very proud of you, and your parents will be, too. Yes, it's okay to be afraid; I know I'm scared out of my mind, too. Stay nice and safe against me. That's it. You're safe now."

The boys were pressed so tightly against him that Savich could feel their hearts pounding as they sobbed, deep, ragged sobs, and he knew there was blessed relief in their sobs, that they finally believed they were going to survive. They clutched at him and he held them as tightly as he could, whispering, "It will be all right. You're going to be home in no time at all. It's okay, Rob, Donny."

He kept them both shielded from Tammy Tuttle, who was no longer moaning. He made no move to see what shape she was in.

"The Ghouls," one of the boys kept saying over and over, his young voice cracking. "They told us all about what the Ghouls did to all the other boys—ate them up whole or if they were already full, then they tore them up, chewed on their bones—"

"I know, I know," Savich said, but he had no idea what his eyes had seen, not really. Whirling dust devils, that was all. There were no hidden axes or knives. Unless they somehow morphed into something more substantial? No, that was crazy. He felt something catch inside him. It was a sense of what was real, what had to be real. It demanded he reject what he'd seen, bury it under a hundred tons of earth, make the Ghouls gone forever, make it so they had never existed. It must have been some kind of natural phenomenon, easily explained, or some kind of an illusion, a waking nightmare, a mad invention of a pair of psychopaths' minds. But whatever they were that the Tuttles had called the Ghouls, he'd seen them, even shot at one of them, and they were embedded in his brain.

Maybe they had been dust devils, playing tricks on his eyes. Maybe.

As he stood holding the two thin bodies to him, talking to them, he was aware that agents, followed by the sheriff and his deputies, were inside the barn now, that one of them was bending over Tammy Tuttle. Soon there were agents everywhere, searching the barn, corner to corner, searching every inch of the tack room.

Everyone was high, excited. They'd gotten the boys back safely. They'd taken down two psychopaths.

Tammy Tuttle was conscious again, screaming, no way to keep the boys from hearing her, though he tried. They held her down on the floor. She was yelling and cursing at Savich as she cradled her arm, yelling that the Ghouls would get him, she would lead them to him, that he was dead meat, and so were those Little Bloods. Savich felt the boys nearly dissolve against him, their terror palpable.

Then one of the agents slammed his fist into her jaw. He looked up, grinning. "Took her out of her pain. Didn't like to see such a fine, up-standing young lady in such misery."

"Thank you," Savich said. "Rob, Donny, she's not going to hurt anyone ever again. I swear it to you." Sherlock came to him, and she looked angry enough to spit nails. She didn't say anything, just put her arms around the two boys.

The paramedics came through with stretchers. Big Bob, the lead, who had a twenty-two-inch neck, looked at the two agents comforting the boys and held up his hand. He said to the three men behind him, "Let's wait here a moment. I think these boys are getting the medicine they need right now. See to that woman. The guy is gone."

Three hours later, the old barn was finally empty again, all evidence, mainly food refuse, pizza boxes, some chains and shackles, a good four dozen candy bar wrappers, carted away. Both Tuttles had been removed, Tammy still alive. The boys were taken immediately to their parents, who were waiting at the sheriff's office in Stewartville, Maryland. From there they'd go on to the local hospital to be checked out. The FBI wouldn't need to speak to them again for at least a couple of days, giving them time to calm down before being questioned.

All the agents drove back to FBI headquarters, to the Criminal Apprehension Unit on the fifth floor, to write up their reports.

Everyone was bouncing off the walls. They'd won. High fives, slaps on the back. No screwups, no false leads. They hadn't been too late to save the boys. "Look at all the testosterone flying around," Sherlock said as she walked into the office. Then she laughed. No one could talk about anything but how Savich had brought them down.

Savich called all the agents who had participated in the raid together.

"When the barn doors swung in, did anyone see anything?"

No one had seen a thing.

"Did anyone see anything strange coming out of the barn, anything at all?"

There wasn't a word spoken around the big conference table. Then Sherlock said, "We didn't see anything, Dillon. The barn doors flew inward; there was some thick dust in the air, but that was it." She looked around at the other agents. No one had seen any more than that. "We didn't see anything coming out of the barn either."

"The Tuttles called them Ghouls," Savich said slowly. "They looked so real I actually shot at one of them. It was then that they seemed to dissipate, to disappear. I'm being as objective as I can. Understand, I didn't want to see anything out of the ordinary. But I did see something. I want to believe that it was some sort of dust devil that broke into two parts, but I don't know, I just don't know. If anyone can come up with an explanation, I'd like to hear it."

There were more questions, more endless speculation, until everyone sat silent. Savich said to Jimmy Maitland, "The boys saw them. They're telling everyone about them. You can bet that Rob and Donny won't call them natural phenomena or dust devils."

Jimmy Maitland said, "No one will believe them. Now, we've got to keep this Ghoul business under wraps. The FBI has enough problems without announcing that we've seen two supernatural cones in a rampaging partnership with two psychopaths."

Later, Savich realized while he was typing his report to Jimmy Maitland that he'd spelled "Ghouls" with a capital G. They weren't general entities to the Tuttles; they were specific.

Sherlock followed Savich into the men's room some thirty minutes later. Ollie Hamish, Savich's second in command, was at the sink washing his hands when they came in.

"Oh, hi, guys. Congratulations again, Savich. Great work. I wish I could have been with you."

"I'm glad to see a man washing his hands," Sherlock said, and poked him in the arm. "In a few minutes I'm going to be washing my hands, too. After I've beaten some sense into my husband here, the jerk. Go away, Ollie, I know you'll want to protect him from me, and I don't want to have to hurt both of you."

"Ah, Sherlock, he's a hero. Why do you want to hurt the hero? He saved those little boys from the Warlocks and the Ghouls."

Savich said, "After what I told you about them, do you spell 'Ghouls' with a capital G in your head?"

"Yeah, sure, you said there were two of them. It's one of those strange things that will stay with you. You sure you weren't smoking something, Savich? Inhaling too much stale hay?"

"I wish I could say yes to that."

"Out, Ollie."

Once they were alone, she didn't take a strip off him, just stepped against him and wrapped her arms around his back. "I can't say that I've never been more frightened in my life, since you and I have managed to get into some bad situations." She kissed his neck and squeezed him even tighter. "But today, at that barn, you were a hot dog, and I was scared spitless, as were your friends."

"There was no time," he said against her curly hair. "No time to bring you in. Truth is, sweetheart, I scared myself, but I had no choice. And then those howling wind things were there. I honestly can't say which scared me more—Tammy Tuttle or whatever it was she called the Ghouls."

She pulled back a bit. "I really don't understand any of that. You described it all so clearly I could almost see them whirling through those barn doors. But Ghouls?"

"That's what the Tuttles called them. It was like they were acolytes to these things. I'd really like to say it was some sort of hallucination, that I was the only one who freaked out, but the boys saw them, too. I know it sounds off the wall, Sherlock, particularly since none of you guys saw a thing."

Because he needed to speak of it more, she held him while he again described what had burst through the barn doors. Then he said, "I don't think there's anything more to do about this, but it was scary, Sherlock, really."

Jimmy Maitland walked into the men's room.

"Hey, where's a man to piddle?"

"Oh, sir, I just wanted to check Dillon out, make sure he was okay."

"And is he?"

"Oh, yes."

"Ollie caught me in the hall on my way to the unit, Savich, said you were getting whaled on in the men's room. We've got a media frenzy cranking up." Jimmy Maitland gave them a big grin. "Guess what? No one's going to pound on us this time—only good news, thank the Lord. Great news. Since you were the one in the middle of it, Savich, we want you front and center. Of course, Director Mueller will be there and do all the talking. They want you to stand there and look like a hero."

"No mention of what we saw?"

"No, not a word about the Ghouls, not even speculation about whirling dust. The last thing we need is to have the media go after us because we claim we were attacked by some weird balls of dust called into the barn by a couple of psychopaths. As for the boys, it doesn't matter what they say. If the media asks us about it, we'll just shake our heads, look distressed and sympathetic. It will be a twenty-four-hour wonder, then it'll be over. And the FBI will be heroes. That sure feels good."

Savich said as he rubbed his hands up and down his wife's back, "But there was something very strange in there, sir, something that made the hair stand up on my head."

"Get a grip, Savich. We've got the Tuttle brothers, or rather we've got one brother dead and one sister whose arm was just amputated at the shoulder. The last thing we need is a dose of the supernatural."

"You could maybe call me Mulder?"

"Yeah, right. Hey, I just realized Sherlock here has red hair, just like Scully."

Savich and Sherlock rolled their eyes and followed their boss from the men's room.

The boys claimed they'd seen the Ghouls, could speak of nothing else but how Agent Savich had put a bullet right in the middle of one and made them whirl out of the barn. But the boys were so tattered and pathetic, very nearly incoherent, that indeed, they weren't believed, even by their parents.

One reporter asked Savich if he'd seen any ghouls and Savich said, "Excuse me, what did you say?"

Jimmy Maitland was right. That was the end of it.

Savich and Sherlock played with Sean for so long that evening that he finally fell asleep in the middle of his favorite finger game, Hide the Camel, a graham cracker smashed in his hand. That night at two o'clock in the morning, the phone rang. Savich picked it up, listened, and said, "We'll be there as soon as we can."

He slowly hung up the phone and looked over at his wife, who'd managed to prop herself up on her elbow.

"It's my sister, Lily. She's in the hospital. It doesn't look good."

# TWO

*Hemlock Bay, California*

Bright sunlight poured through narrow windows. Her bedroom windows were wider, weren't they? Surely they were cleaner than this. No, wait, she wasn't in her bedroom. A vague sort of panic jumped her, then fell away. She didn't feel much of anything now, a bit of confusion that surely wasn't all that important, a slight ache in her left arm at the IV line.

*IV line?*

That meant she was in a hospital. She was breathing; she could feel the oxygen tickling her nose, the tubes irritating her. But it was reassuring. She was alive. But why shouldn't she be alive? Why was she surprised?

Her brain felt numb and empty, and even the emptiness was hazy. Maybe she was dying and that's why they'd left her alone. Where was Tennyson? Oh, yes, he'd gone to Chicago two days before, some sort of medical thing. She'd been glad to see him go, relieved, plain solidly relieved that she wouldn't have to hear his calm, soothing voice that drove her nuts.

A white-coated man with a bald head, a stethoscope around his neck, came into the room. He leaned down right into her face. "Mrs. Frasier, can you hear me?"

"Oh, yes. I can even see the hairs in your nose."

He straightened, laughed. "Oh, that's too close then. Now that my nose hairs aren't in the way, how do you feel? Any pain?"

"No, I can barely feel my brain. I feel vague and stupid."

"That's because of the morphine. You could be shot in the belly, get enough morphine, and you wouldn't even be pissed at your mother-in-law. I'm your surgeon, Dr. Ted Larch. Since I had to remove your spleen—and that's major abdominal surgery—we'll keep you on a nice, steady dose of morphine until this evening. We'll begin to lighten up on it after that. Then we'll get you up to see how you're doing, get your innards working again."

"What else is wrong with me?"

"Let me give you the short version. First, let me promise you that you'll be all right. As for having no spleen, nothing bad should happen in the long run because of that. An adult doesn't really need his spleen. However, you will have all the discomfort of surgery—pain for several days. You'll have to be careful about when and what you eat, and as I said, we'll have to get your system working again.

"You have a concussion, two bruised ribs, some cuts and abrasions, but you'll live. Nothing that should cause any scarring. You're doing splendidly, given what happened."

"What did happen?"

Dr. Larch was silent for a moment, his head tilted a bit to one side. Sun was pouring in through the window and gave his bald head a bright shine. He said slowly, studying her face, "You don't remember?"

She thought and thought until he lightly touched his fingers to her forearm. "No, don't try to force it. You'll give yourself a headache. What is the last thing you do remember, Mrs. Frasier?"

Again she thought, and finally she said slowly, "I remember leaving my house in Hemlock Bay. That's where I live, on Crocodile Bayou Avenue. I remember I was going to drive to Ferndale to deliver some medical slides to a Dr. Baker. I remember I didn't like driving on 211 when it was nearly dark. That road is scary and those redwoods tower over you and surround you and you start feeling like you're being buried alive." She stopped, and he saw frustration building and interrupted her.

"No, that's all right. An interesting metaphor with those redwoods. Now, everything will probably all come back to you in time. You were in an accident, Mrs. Frasier. Your Explorer hit a redwood dead on. Now, I'm going to call in another doctor."

"What is his specialty?"

"He's a psychiatrist."

"Why do I need . . ." Now she frowned. "I don't understand. A psychiatrist? Why?"

"Well, it seems that you possibly could have driven into that redwood on purpose. No, don't panic, don't worry about a thing. Rest and build up your strength. I'll see you later, Mrs. Frasier. If you begin to feel any pain in the next couple of hours, hit your button and you'll get morphine from your IV."

She looked away from him, toward the window, where the sun was shining in so brightly.

"All I remember is last evening. What day is it? What time of day?"

"It's late Thursday morning. You've been going in and out for a while now. Your accident was last evening."

"So much missing time."

"It will be all right, Mrs. Frasier."

"I wonder about that," she said, nothing more, and closed her eyes.

DR. Russell Rossetti stopped for a moment just inside the doorway and looked at the young woman who lay so still on the narrow hospital bed. She looked like a princess who'd kissed the wrong frog and been beaten up, major league. Her blond hair was mixed with flecks of blood and tangled around bandages. She was thin, too thin, and he wondered what she was thinking right now, right this minute.

Dr. Ted Larch, the surgeon who'd removed her spleen, had told him she didn't remember a thing about the accident. He'd also said he didn't think she'd tried to kill herself. She was too "there," he'd said. The meathead.

Ted was a romantic, something weird for a surgeon to be. Of course she'd tried to kill herself. Again. No question. It was classic.

"Mrs. Frasier."

Lily slowly turned her head at the sound of a rather high voice she imagined could whine when he didn't get his way, a voice that was right now trying to sound soothing, all sorts of inviting, but not succeeding.

She said nothing, just looked at the overweight man—on the tall side, very well dressed in a dark, gray suit, with lots of curly black hair, a double chin, and fat, white fingers—who walked into the room. He came to stand too close to the bed.

"Who are you?"

"I'm Dr. Rossetti. Dr. Larch told you I would be coming to see you?"

"You're the psychiatrist?"

"Yes."

"He told me, but I don't want to see you. There is no reason."

Denial, he thought, just splendid. He was bored with the stream of depressed patients who simply started crying and became quickly incoherent and self-pitying, their hands held out for pills to numb them. Although Tennyson had told him Lily wasn't like that, he hadn't been convinced.

He said, all calm and smooth, "Evidently you do need me. You drove your car into a redwood."

Had she? No, it just didn't seem right. She said, "The road to Ferndale is very dangerous. Have you ever driven it at dusk, when it's nearly dark?"

"Yes."

"You didn't find you had to be very careful?"

"Of course. However, I never wrapped my car around a redwood. The Forestry Service is looking at the tree now, to see how badly it's hurt."

"Well, if I'm missing some bark, I'm sure it is, too. I would like you to leave now, Dr. Rossetti."

Instead of leaving, he pulled a chair close to the bed and sat down. He crossed his legs. He weaved his plump, white fingers together. She hated his hands, soft, puffy hands, but she couldn't stop looking at them.

"If you'll give me a minute, Mrs. Frasier. Do you mind if I call you Lily?"

"Yes, I mind. I don't know you. Go away."

He leaned toward her and tried to take her hand, but she pulled it away and stuck it beneath her covers.

"You really should cooperate with me, Lily—"

"My name is Mrs. Frasier."

He frowned. Usually women—any and all women—liked to be called by their first name. It made them feel that he was more of a confidant, someone they could trust. It also made them more vulnerable, more open to him.

He said, "You tried to kill yourself the first time after the death of your child seven months ago."

"She didn't just die. A speeding car hit her and knocked her twenty feet into a ditch. Someone murdered her."

"And you blamed yourself."

"Are you a parent?"

"Yes."

"Wouldn't you blame yourself if your child died and you weren't with her?"

"No, not if I wasn't driving the car that hit her."

"Would your wife blame herself?"

Elaine's face passed before his mind's eye, and he frowned. "Probably not. All she would do is cry. She is a very weak woman, very dependent. But that isn't the point, Mrs. Frasier." It wasn't. He would be free of Elaine very soon now.

"What is the point?"

"You did blame yourself, blamed yourself so much you stuffed a bottle of sleeping pills down your throat. If your housekeeper hadn't found you in time, you would have died."

"That's what I was told," she said, and she swore in that moment that she could taste the same taste in her mouth now as she had then when she'd awakened in the hospital that first time when she'd been so bewildered, so weak she couldn't even raise her hand.

"You don't remember taking the pills?"

"No, not really."

"And now you don't remember driving your car into a redwood. Your speed, it was estimated by the sheriff, was about sixty miles per hour, maybe faster. You were very lucky, Mrs. Frasier. A guy happened to come around a bend to see you drive into the tree, and called an ambulance."

"Do you happen to know his name? I would like to thank him."

"That isn't what's important here, Mrs. Frasier."

"What is important here? Oh, yes, do you happen to have a first name?"

"My name is Russell. Dr. Russell Rossetti."

"Nice alliteration, Russell."

"It would be better if you called me Dr. Rossetti," he said. She saw those plump, white fingers twisting, and she knew he was angry. He thought she was out of line. She was, but she didn't care. She was tired, so very tired, and she wanted to close her eyes and let the morphine mask the pain for a while longer.

"Go away, Dr. Rossetti."

He didn't move for some time.

Lily turned her head away and sought oblivion. She didn't even hear when he finally left the room. She did, however, hear the door close.

When Dr. Larch walked in five minutes later, his very high forehead flushed, she managed to cock an eye open and say, "Dr. Rossetti is a patronizing ass. He has fat hands. Please, I don't want to see him again."

"He doesn't think you're in very good shape."

"On the contrary, I'm in splendid shape, something I can't say about him. He needs to go to the gym very badly."

Dr. Larch laughed, couldn't help himself. "He also said your defensiveness and your rudeness to him were sure signs that you're highly overwrought and in desperate need of help."

"Yeah, right. I'm so overwrought—what with all this painkiller—that I'm ready to nap."

"Ah, your husband is here to see you."

She didn't want to see Tennyson. His voice, so resonant, so confident—it was too much like Dr. Rossetti's voice, as if they'd taken the same Voice Lessons 101 course in shrink school. If she never saw another one of them again, she could leave this earth a happy woman.

She looked past Dr. Larch to see her husband of eleven months standing in the doorway, looking rather pale, his thick eyebrows drawn together, his arms crossed over his chest. Such a nice-looking man he was, all big and solid, his hair light and wavy, lots of hair, not bald like Dr. Larch. He wore aviator glasses, which looked really cool, and now she watched him push them back up, an endearing habit—at least that's what she'd thought when she'd first met him.

"Lily?"

"Yes," she said and wished he'd stay in the doorway. Dr. Larch straightened and turned to him. "Dr. Frasier, as I told you, your wife will be fine, once she recovers from the surgery. However, she does need to rest. I suggest that you visit for only a few minutes."

"I am very tired, Tennyson," she said and hated the small shudder in her voice. "Perhaps we could speak later?"

"Oh, no," he said. And then he waited, saying nothing more until Dr. Larch left the room, fingering his stethoscope. He looked nervous. Lily wondered why. Tennyson closed the door, paused yet again, studying her, then, finally, he walked to stand beside her bed. He gently eased her hand out from under the covers, something she wished he wouldn't do, rubbed his fingers over her palm for several moments before saying in a sad, soft voice, "Why did you do it, Lily? Why?"

He made it sound like it was all over for her. No, she was being ridiculous. She said, "I don't know that I did anything, Tennyson. You see,
I have no memory at all of the accident."

He waved away her words. He had strong hands, confident hands. "I
know and I'm sorry about that. Look, Lily, maybe it was an accident,
maybe somehow you lost control and drove the Explorer into the redwood. One of the nurses told me that the Forest Service has someone on
the spot to see how badly the tree is injured."

"Dr. Rossetti already told me. Poor tree."

"It isn't funny, Lily. Now, you're going to be here for at least another
two or three days, until they're sure your body is functioning well again.
I would like you to speak with Dr. Rossetti. He's a new man with quite an
excellent reputation."

"I've already seen him. I don't wish to see him again, Tennyson."

His voice changed now, became even softer, more gentle, and she
knew she would normally have wanted to cry, to fold into herself, to have
him reassure her, tell her the bogeyman wouldn't come back, but not
now. It was probably the morphine making her feel slightly euphoric,
slightly disconnected. But she also felt rather strong, perhaps even on the
arrogant side, and that, of course, was an illusion to beat all illusions.

"Since you don't remember anything, Lily, you've got to admit that it
wouldn't hurt to cover all the bases. I really want you to see him."

"I don't like him, Tennyson. How can I speak to someone I don't
like?"

"You will see him, Lily, or I'm afraid we'll have to consider an
institution."

"Oh? *We* will consider an institution? What sort of institution?"
Why wasn't she afraid of that word that brought a wealth of dreadful
images with it? But she wasn't afraid. She was looking at him positively
bright-eyed. She loved morphine. She was tiring; she could feel the vague-
ness trying to close her down, eating away at the focus in her brain, but
for this moment, maybe even the next, too, she could deal with anything.

He squeezed her hand. "I'm a doctor, Lily, a psychiatrist, as is Dr.
Rossetti. You know it isn't ethical for me to treat you myself."

"You prescribed the Elavil."

"That's different. That's a very common drug for depression. No, I
couldn't speak with you like Dr. Rossetti can. But you must know that

I want what is best for you. I love you and I've prayed you were getting better. One day at a time, I kept telling myself. And there were some days when I knew you were healing, but I was wrong. Yes, you really must see Dr. Rossetti or I'm afraid I will have no choice but to admit you for evaluation."

"Forgive me for pointing this out, Tennyson, but I don't believe that you can do that. I'm here—I can see, I can talk, I can reason—I do have a say in what happens to me."

"That remains to be seen. Lily, just speak to Dr. Rossetti. Talk to him about your pain, your confusion, your guilt, the fact that you're beginning to accept what your ambition wrought."

Ambition? She had such great ambition that her daughter was killed because of it?

She suddenly wanted to be perfectly clear about this. She said, "What do you mean exactly, Tennyson?"

"You know—Beth's death."

That hit her right between the eyes. Instant guilt, overwhelming her. No, wait, she wasn't going to let that happen. She wouldn't let it happen, not now. Beneath the morphine, beneath all of it, she was still there, hanging on, wanting to be whole, wanting to draw her cartoon strips of No Wrinkles Remus shafting another colleague, wanting . . . Was that the great ambition that had killed her daughter? "I can't deal with this right now, Tennyson. Please go away. I'll be better in the morning."

No, she'd feel like hell when they lessened her pain dosage, she thought, but she wouldn't worry about that now. Now she would sleep; she'd get better, both her brain and her body. She turned her head away from him on the pillow. She had no more words. She knew if she tried to speak more, she wouldn't make sense. She was falling, falling ever so gently into the whale's soft belly, and it would be warm, comforting. Move over, Jonah. She wouldn't have nightmares, not with the morphine lulling her.

She stared at the IV in her arm, upward to the plastic bag filled with fluid above her. Her vision blurred into the lazy flow of liquid that didn't seem to go anywhere, just flowed and flowed. She closed her eyes even as he said, "I will see you later this evening, Lily. Rest well." He leaned down and kissed her cheek. How she used to love his hands on her, his kissing her, but not now. She simply hadn't felt anything for such a very long time.

When she was alone again, she thought, *What am I going to do?* But then she knew, of course. She forced back the haziness, the numbing effect of the morphine. She picked up the phone and dialed her brother's number in Washington, D.C. She heard a series of clicks and then the sound of a person breathing, but nothing happened. She dialed a nine, then the number again. She tried yet again, but didn't get through. Then, suddenly, the line went dead.

She realized vaguely as she let herself be drawn into the ether that there was fear licking at her, from the deepest part of her, fear that she couldn't quite grasp, and it wasn't fear that she'd be institutionalized against her will.

# THREE

Lily awoke to feel the touch of fingers on her eyebrows, stroking as light as a butterfly's wing. She heard a man's voice, a voice she'd loved all her life, deep and low, wonderfully sweet, and she opened to it eagerly.

"Lily, I want you to open your eyes now and look at me and smile. Can you do that, sweetheart? Open your eyes."

And she opened her eyes and looked up at her brother. She smiled. "My big Fed brother. I've worshiped you from the time you showed me how to kick Billy Clapper in the crotch so he wouldn't try to feel me up again. Do you remember that?"

"Yes, I remember. You were twelve and this little jerk, who was all of fourteen at the time, had put his hand up your skirt."

"I really hurt him bad, Dillon. He never tried anything again."

He was smiling, such a beautiful smile, white teeth. "I remember."

"I should have kept kicking guys in the crotch. Then none of this would have happened. I'm so glad you're here."

"I'm here, Lily, so is Sherlock. We left Sean with Mom, who was grinning and singing the 'Hallelujah Chorus' as we drove out of the driveway. We told her you'd been in an accident and that you were okay, that we just wanted to see you. You can call and reassure her later. As for the rest of the family, let Mom do the telling."

"I don't want her to worry. It's true, Dillon, I'll be okay. I miss Sean. It's been so long. I really like all the photos you e-mail me."

"Yes, but it's not the same as being in the room with him, having him gum your fingers, rub his crackers into your sweater, and drool on your neck."

Sherlock said, "You touch any surface in the house and come away with graham cracker crumbs."

Lily smiled, and it was real because she could see that precious little boy dropping wet graham cracker crumbs everywhere, and it pleased her to her very soul. "Mom must be so happy to have her hands on him."

Savich said, "Yes. She always spoils him so rotten that when he comes home, he's a real pain for a good two days."

"He's the cutest little button, Dillon. I miss him."

A tear leaked out of her eye.

Savich wiped the tear away. "I know, so do Sherlock and I and we've only been apart from him for less than a day. How do you feel, Lily?"

"It's dark again."

"Yes. Nearly seven o'clock Thursday evening. Now, sweetheart, talk to me. How do you feel?"

"Like they've already lightened the morphine."

"Yeah, Dr. Larch said he was just beginning to ease up on it now. You're gonna feel rotten for a while, a day or two, but then it'll be less and less pain each day."

"When did you get here?"

"Sherlock and I just got into town. The puddle jumper from San Francisco to Arcata-Eureka was late." He saw her eyes go vague and added, "Sherlock bought Sean a Golden Gate oven mitt at the San Francisco airport."

"I'll show it to you later, Lily," Sherlock said. She was standing on the other side of Lily's bed, smiling down at her, so scared for this lovely young woman who was her sister-in-law that she would have bitten her fingernails if she hadn't stopped some three years before. "It was between an oven mitt with Alcatraz on it and the Golden Gate. Since Sean gums everything, Dillon thought gumming the Golden Gate was healthier than gumming a Federal prison."

Lily laughed. She didn't know where it had come from, but she even laughed again. Pain seared through her side and her ribs, and she gasped.

"No more humor," Sherlock said and lightly kissed her cheek. "We're here and everything's going to be all right now, I promise."

"Who called you?"

"Your father-in-law, about two in the morning, last night."

"I wonder why he called," she said slowly, thinking about the pain that was now coming through and how she would deal with it.

"You wouldn't expect him to?"

"I see now," Lily said, her eyes suddenly narrow and fierce. "He was afraid Mrs. Scruggins would call you and then you would wonder why the family hadn't called. I think he's afraid of you, Dillon. He's always asking me how you're doing and where you are. When you were here before, I think you scared him really good."

"Why would I scare him?"

"Because you're big and you're smart and you're a special agent with the FBI."

Sherlock laughed. "Lots of people don't relax around FBI agents. But Mr. Elcott Frasier? I took one look at him and thought he probably chewed nails for breakfast."

"He could, you know. Everyone thinks that, particularly his son, my husband."

"Maybe he called because he knew we'd want to come here to see you," Savich said. "Maybe he isn't all that much of an iron fist."

"Yes, he is. Tennyson was here earlier." She sighed, tightened a bit from a jab of pain in her bruised ribs, the pulling in her side. "Thank goodness he finally left."

Savich looked over at Sherlock. "What happened, Lily? Talk to us."

"Everyone thinks I tried to kill myself again."

"Fine, let them. It doesn't matter. Talk, Lily."

"I don't know, Dillon, I swear I don't. I remember that I had to drive that gnarly road to Ferndale, you know, 211? And that's all. Everything else is just lost."

Sherlock said, "All right, then. Everyone thinks you tried to kill yourself because of the pills you took right after Beth's death?"

"Yes, I guess so."

"But why?"

"I suppose I haven't been exactly honest with you guys, but I didn't want you to worry. Fact is, I have been depressed. I'll feel lots better and then it's back down again. It's gotten progressively worse the past couple of weeks. Why? I don't know, but it has. And then last night happened."

Savich pulled up a chair and sat down. He took her hand again. "You know, Lily, even when you were a little girl, you'd hit a problem, and I swear you'd worry and work and chew on that problem, never giving up until you had it solved. Dad used to say if he was slow telling you something you really wanted to know, he could just see you gnawing on his trouser leg until you ripped it right off or he talked, whichever came first."

"I miss Dad."

"I do, too. Now, I still don't understand that first time you wanted to die. That wasn't the Lily I knew. But Beth's death—that would knock any parent on his or her butt. But now seven months have passed. You're smart, you're talented, you're not one to be in denial. This depression—that doesn't make a lot of sense to me. What's been happening, Lily?"

She sobered, frowning now. "Nothing's been happening, just more of the same. Like I said, over the past months sometimes I'd feel better, feel like I could conquer the world again, but then it would go away and I'd want to stay in bed all day.

"For whatever reason, yesterday got really bad. Tennyson called me from Chicago and told me to take two of the antidepressant pills. I did. I'll tell you something, the pills sure don't seem to help. And then, when I was driving on that road to Ferndale—well, maybe something did happen. Maybe I did drive into that redwood. I don't remember."

"It's okay. Now, how does your brain feel right now?" Sherlock asked, scooting in a little closer to Lily on the hospital bed.

"Not quite as vague as before. I guess since there's less morphine swimming around up in there, I'm coming back."

"Are you feeling depressed?"

"No. I'm mainly mad because of that idiot shrink they sent by. A dreadful man, trying to be so comforting, so understanding, when really he was a condescending jerk."

"You smart-mouthed him, babe?"

"Maybe. A little bit."

"I'm glad," Sherlock said. "Not enough back-mouthing from you lately, Lily."

"Oh, dear."

"Oh, dear what?"

But Lily didn't say anything, kept looking toward the door.

Savich and Sherlock both turned to see their brother-in-law, Tennyson Frasier, come into the room.

Savich thought, Lily doesn't want to see her husband?

What was going on here? Seven months ago, Lily had come back to Maryland to stay with their mother for several weeks after Beth's funeral. While she'd been there, Savich had done everything he could, turned over every rock he could find, called in every favor, to discover who had struck

Beth and driven off. No luck. Not a clue. But then Lily had wanted to go back to Hemlock Bay, to be with her husband, who loved her and needed her, and yes, she was all right now.

A big mistake to let her come back here, Savich thought, and knew he wouldn't leave her here this time. Not again.

Savich straightened as Tennyson came striding toward him, his hand outstretched. As he pumped Savich's hand, he said, "Boy, am I ever glad to see you guys. Dad told me he called you, in the middle of the night." Then he stopped. He looked at Lily.

Sherlock never moved from her perch on Lily's bed. She said, "Good to see you, Tennyson." Such a handsome man he was, big and in pretty good shape, and at the moment he looked terrified for his wife. Why didn't Lily want to see him?

"Lily, are you all right?" Tennyson walked to her bed, his hand out.

Lily slipped her hand beneath the covers as she said, "I'm fine, Tennyson. Do you know that I tried to call Dillon and Sherlock earlier? And my line went dead. Is it still dead now?"

Sherlock picked up the phone. There was a dial tone. "It's fine now."

"Isn't that strange?"

"Maybe," Tennyson said, leaning down to caress Lily's pale face, kiss her lightly, "with all that morphine in you, you didn't do it right."

"There was a dial tone, then a person's breathing, some clicking sounds, and then nothing."

"Hmmm. I'll check on that, but it's working now, so no harm done." He turned back to Savich. "You and Sherlock got here very quickly."

"She's my sister," Savich said, looking at his brother-in-law closely. "What would you expect?" He'd always liked Tennyson, believed he'd been a solid man, one who was trustworthy, unlike Lily's first husband, Jack Crane. He'd believed Tennyson had been as distraught as Lily when Beth was killed. He had worked with Savich trying to find out who the driver was who'd killed Beth. As for the sheriff, he'd been next to useless. What was wrong? Why didn't Lily want to see him?

Tennyson merely nodded, then kissed Lily again. He said, his voice as soft as a swatch of Bengali silk, "I can't wait to get you out of this place, get you home. You'll be safe with me, Lily, always."

But she hadn't been safe, Sherlock thought. That was the bottom line. She'd run her Explorer into a redwood. Hardly safe. What was wrong with this picture?

"What about that psychiatrist, Tennyson?"

"Dr. Rossetti? I would really like you to see him, Lily. He can help you."

"You said you would institutionalize me if I didn't see him."

Savich nearly went *en pointe*.

Sherlock laughed. "Institutionalize Lily? Come on, Tennyson."

"No, no, all of you misunderstood. Listen, Lily very probably drove into that redwood last night. This is the second time she's tried to end her life. You were both here after the first time. You saw how she was. Her mother saw as well. She's been on medication, but obviously it hasn't helped. I want her to speak to a very excellent psychiatrist, a man I respect very much."

"I don't like him, Tennyson. I don't want to see him again."

Tennyson sighed deeply. "All right, Lily. If you don't like Dr. Rossetti, then I'll find another man who could possibly help you."

"I would prefer a woman."

"Whatever. I don't know of any female psychiatrists who do anything other than family counseling."

Savich said, "I'll have some names for you by tomorrow, Lily. No problem. But we're a bit off the subject here. I want to know the name of the antidepressants Lily's been taking and I want to know why they seem to have the opposite effect on her."

Tennyson said patiently, "It's a very popular drug, Dillon. Elavil. You can ask any doctor."

"I'm sure it is. I suppose there are a certain number of people who simply don't respond appropriately?"

"Unfortunately, yes. I was considering whether or not we should try another drug—Prozac, for example."

Savich said, "Why don't you wait on all the drugs until Lily has seen a new psychiatrist. What happened to Dr. McGill? Weren't you with him for a while, Lily?"

"He died, Dillon, not two weeks after I began seeing him. He was such a sweet man, but he was old and his heart was rotten. He had a heart attack."

Tennyson shrugged. "It happens. Hey, I saw you on TV, Savich, there with all the FBI brass. You got the Warlocks."

"Turns out there was only one warlock, the other was a witch."

"Yes, a brother and a sister. How did everyone miss that?"

"Good question." Savich saw that Lily was listening closely now. She loved hearing about their cases, so he kept talking about it. "Turns out one of them wasn't really a guy, just dressed like one—Timmy was really a she. She even lowered her voice, cropped off her hair, the whole deal. The profilers never saw it and neither did any of my unit. Instead of Tammy, to the world she was Timmy."

"Did the brother and sister sleep together?" Tennyson said.

"Not that we know of."

Lily said, "It was MAX who managed to track down that barn?"

"That's right. Once we knew the Tuttles were back in Maryland, I knew in my gut that this was their final destination, that they'd come home, even though they'd been born and raised in Utah. They kidnapped the boys in Maryland. So where were they? MAX always checks out any and every relative when we know who the suspect is. He dug deep enough to find Marilyn Warluski, a cousin who owned this property. And on the property was this old abandoned barn."

Thank God no one had mentioned anything about the Ghouls.

Lily said, "How many boys did the two of them kill, Sherlock?"

"A dozen, maybe more. All across the country. We'll probably never know unless Tammy decides to tell us, and that's not likely. Her arm was amputated thanks to Dillon's shot. She's not a happy camper. Thank God it's over and the last two boys are all right."

Tennyson asked, "You shot her? Did you kill the brother too?"

"The brother's dead, yes. It was a team effort," Savich said, and nothing more.

"Those poor little boys," Lily said. "Their parents must have been torn apart when they were taken."

"They were, but as I said, everything turned out okay for them."

Nurse Carla Brunswick said from the doorway, "We don't have to worry about crooks while you guys are in town. Now, I get to order the FBI out. Time for Mrs. Frasier's sleeping pills. Say good night—even you, Dr. Frasier. Dr. Larch's orders."

IT wasn't until they were in the hospital parking lot that Tennyson said, "I apologize for not realizing sooner that you'd only just arrived. You will stay with me, won't you?"

"Yes," Savich said. "Thank you, Tennyson. We want to be close."

An hour later, after Savich had called his mother and told her not to worry and had spoken to his son, he climbed into the king-size bed beneath the sloped-ceiling guest room, kissed his wife, tucked her against his side, and said, "Why do you really think Mr. Elcott Frasier called us?"

"The obvious: he was worried about his daughter-in-law and wanted us to know right away. Very thoughtful. He thought it through and didn't call your mom and scare the daylights out of her."

"All right, maybe you're right. After that heavy dose of craziness with the Tuttles, I guess my mind went automatically to the worst possible motive."

Sherlock kissed his neck, then settled back in, her leg over his belly. "I've heard so much psychobabble about Lily. She tries to kill herself because it's the only thing to do if she wants to gain peace. She has to drive her Explorer into a redwood to expiate her guilt. It doesn't sound right. It doesn't sound like Lily. Yes, yes, I remember the first time. But that was then."

"And this is now."

"Yes. Seven months. Lily isn't neurotic, Dillon. I've always thought she was strong, stable. And now I feel guilty because we didn't make an effort to see her over the last months."

"You had a baby, Sherlock, not a week after Beth's funeral."

"And Lily was there for me."

"She wasn't there with you—not like I was. Sherlock, that was the longest day of my life." He squeezed her so hard, she squeaked.

"Yeah, yeah," she said.

"You never curse, but toward the end there you called me more names than I'd ever been called, even by linebackers during football games in college."

She laughed, kissed his shoulder again, and said, "Look, I know Lily's been through a very hard time. She's been understandably depressed. But we've talked to her a lot since Beth died. I simply don't believe she was in a frame of mind to try to kill herself again."

"I don't know," he said. He frowned and turned off the lamp on the bedside table. He pulled Sherlock against him again and held her tight. "It really shakes me up, Sherlock, this happening to Lily. It's so hard to know what to do."

She held him hard. And she was thinking how fragile Lily had been seven months before, so hurt and so very broken, and then she'd taken those pills and nearly died. Savich and their mother had flown out to California for the second time, not more than a week after Beth's funeral, to see Lily lying in that narrow hospital bed, a tube in her nose, an IV line in her arm. But Lily had survived. And she'd been so sorry, so very sorry that she'd frightened everyone. And she'd come back with them to Washington, D.C., to rest and get her bearings. But after three weeks, she'd decided to go back to her husband in Hemlock Bay.

And seven months later, she'd driven her Explorer into a redwood.

She squeezed more tightly against him. "I don't know how I'd handle it if anything happened to Sean. I couldn't bear that, Dillon. I just couldn't. No wonder Lily didn't."

After a long time, he said, "No, I couldn't bear it either, but you know what? You and I would survive it together. Somehow we would. But I think your instincts on this were right. You said something doesn't feel right. What did you mean?"

She nuzzled her nose into his shoulder, hummed a bit, a sure sign she was thinking hard, and said, "Well, last week Lily sent us a *No Wrinkles Remus* strip she'd just finished, her first one since Beth was killed, and she sounded excited. So what happened over the past four days to make her want to try to kill herself again?"

# FOUR

*Hemlock Bay, California*

"I stole the bottle of pills," Savich said when he walked into the kitchen.

Sherlock grinned at her husband, gave him a thumbs-up, and said, "How do we check them out?"

"I called Clark Hoyt in the Eureka field office. I'll messenger them up to him today. He'll get back to me tomorrow. Then we'll know, one way or the other."

"Ah, Dillon, I've got a confession to make." She took a sip of her tea, grinned down at the few tea leaves on the bottom of the cup. "The pills you took, well, they're cold medicine. You see, I'd already stolen the pills and replaced them with Sudafed I found in the medicine cabinet."

Sometimes she bowled him over. He toasted her with his tea. "I'm impressed, Sherlock. When did you switch them?"

"About five A.M. this morning, before anyone was stirring. Oh, yes, Mrs. Scruggins, the housekeeper, should be here soon. We can see what she's got to say about all this."

Mrs. Scruggins responded to Sherlock's questions by sighing a lot. She was a tall woman, nearly as tall as Savich, and she looked very strong, even those long fingers of hers, including her thumbs, each sporting a ring. She had muscles. Sherlock didn't think she'd want to tangle with Mrs. Scruggins. She had to be at least sixty years old. It was amazing. There were pictures of her grandchildren lining the window ledge in the kitchen and she looked like she could take any number of muggers out at one time.

Savich sat back and watched Sherlock work her magic. "An awful thing," Sherlock said, shaking her head, obviously distressed. "We don't understand it. But I'll bet you do, Mrs. Scruggins, here with poor Lily so much of the time. I'll bet you saw things real clearly."

And Mrs. Scruggins said then, her beringed fingers curving gracefully around her coffee cup, "I'd think she was getting better, you know?"

Both Savich and Sherlock nodded.

"Then she'd fall into a funk again and curl up in the fetal position and spend the day in bed. She wouldn't eat, just lie there, barely even blinking. I guess she'd be thinking about little Beth, you know?"

"Yes, we know," Sherlock said, sighed, and moved closer to the edge of her chair, inviting more thoughts, more confidences.

"Every few weeks I'd swear she was getting better, but it wouldn't last long. Last week I thought she was really improving, nearly back to normal. She was in her office and she was laughing. I actually heard her. It was a laugh. She was drawing that cartoon strip of hers, and she was laughing."

"Then what happened?"

"Well, Mrs. Savich, I can't rightly say. Before I left, Dr. Frasier had come home early and I heard them talking. Then she fell back again, the very next day. It was really fast. Laughing one minute, then, not ten hours later, she was so depressed, so quiet. She just walked around the house that day, not really seeing anything, at least that's what I think. Then she'd disappear and I knew later that she'd been crying. It's enough to break your heart, you know?"

"Yes, we know," Sherlock said. "These pills, Mrs. Scruggins, the Elavil, do you refill the prescription for her?"

"Yes, usually. Sometimes Dr. Frasier brings them home for her. They don't seem to do much good, do they?"

"No," said Savich. "Maybe it's best that she be off them for a while."

"Amen to that. Poor little mite, such a hard time she's had." Mrs. Scruggins gave another deep sigh, nearly pulling apart the buttons over her large bosom. "I myself missed little Beth so much I sometimes wanted to lie down and cry and cry and never you mind anything else. And I wasn't her mama, not like Mrs. Frasier."

"What about Dr. Frasier?" Savich asked.

"What do you mean?"

"Was he devastated by Beth's death?"

"Ah, he's a man, Mr. Savich. Sure, he looked glum for a week or so. But you know, men don't take things like that so much to heart, leastwise my own papa didn't when my little sister died. Maybe Dr. Frasier keeps it all inside, but I don't think so. Don't forget, he wasn't Beth's real father. He didn't know little Beth that long, maybe six months in all."

Sherlock said, "But he's been so very worried about Lily, hasn't he?"

Mrs. Scruggins nodded, and the small diamond studs in her ears glittered in the morning sunlight pouring through the window. Diamonds and muscles and rings, Sherlock thought, and wondered. Mrs. Scruggins said, "Poor man, always fretting about her, trying to make her smile, bringing her presents and flowers, but nothing really worked, leastwise in the long term. And now this." Mrs. Scruggins shook her head. She wore her gray hair in a thick chignon. She had lots of hair and there were a lot of bobby pins worked into the roll.

It occurred to Sherlock to wonder if Mrs. Scruggins really cared for Lily, or if it was all an act. Could it be that she was really Lily's companion, or maybe even her guard?

Now where had that thought come from? Hadn't Mrs. Scruggins saved Lily's life that first time Lily had taken the bottle of pills right after Beth's funeral? She was getting paranoid here; she had to watch it.

"I have a little boy, Mrs. Scruggins," Savich said. "I've only had him a bit more than seven months, and you can believe that I would be devastated if anything were to happen to him."

"Well, that's good. Some men are different, aren't they? But my daddy, hard-nosed old bastard he was. Didn't shed a tear when my little sister got hit by that tractor. Ah, well, I'm afraid I have things to do now. When is Mrs. Frasier coming home?"

"Perhaps as soon as tomorrow," Sherlock said. "She's had major surgery and won't be feeling very well for several days."

"I'll take care of her," Mrs. Scruggins said and popped her knuckles.

Sherlock shuddered, shot Savich a look, and thanked the older woman for all her help. She shook Mrs. Scruggins's hand, feeling all those rings grind into her fingers.

Before they left the kitchen, Mrs. Scruggins said, "I'm real glad you're staying here. Being alone isn't good for Mrs. Frasier."

Savich felt a deep shaft of guilt. He remembered he hadn't said very much when Lily had insisted on returning here after recuperating with their mother. She'd seemed fine, wanted to be with her husband again, and he'd thought, *I would want to be with Sherlock, too,* and he'd seen her off at Reagan Airport with the rest of the family. Tennyson Frasier seemed to adore her, and Lily, it seemed then to Savich, had adored him as well.

During the months she was home, she hadn't ever called to complain, to ask for help. Her e-mails were invariably upbeat. And whenever he and Sherlock had called, she'd always sounded cheerful.

And now, all these months later, this happened. He should have done something then, shouldn't have just kissed her and waved her onto the flight to take her three thousand miles away from her family. To take her back to where Beth had been killed.

He looked down to see Sherlock squeezing his hand. There was immense love in her eyes and she said only, "We will fix things, Dillon. This time we'll fix things."

He nodded and said, "I really want to see Lily's in-laws again, don't you, Sherlock? I have this feeling that perhaps we really don't know them at all."

"Agreed. We can check them out after we've seen Lily."

At the Hemlock County Hospital, everything was quiet. When they reached Lily's room, they heard the sound of voices and paused at the door for a moment.

It was Tennyson.

And Elcott Frasier, his father.

Elcott Frasier was saying, his voice all mournful, "Lily, we're so relieved you survived that crash. It was really dicey there for a while, but you managed to pull through. I can't tell you how worried Charlotte has been, crying, wringing her hands, talking about her little Lily dying and how dreadful it would be, particularly such a short time after little Beth died. The Explorer, though, it's totaled."

That, Savich thought, was the strangest declaration of caring he'd ever heard.

"It's very nice of all of you to be concerned," Lily said, and Savich heard the pain in her voice, and something else. Was it fear? Dislike? He didn't know. She said, "I'm very sorry that I wrecked the Explorer."

"I don't want you to worry about it, Lily," Tennyson said and took her hand. It was limp, Savich saw, she wasn't returning any pressure.

"I'll buy you another one. A gift from me to you, my beautiful little daughter-in-law," Elcott said.

"I don't want another Explorer," she said.

"No, of course not," continued Elcott. "Another Explorer would remind you of the accident, wouldn't it? We don't want that. We want you to get well. Oh yes, we'll do anything to get you well again, Lily. Just this morning, Charlotte was telling me how everyone in Hemlock Bay was talking about it, calling her, commiserating. She's very upset by it all."

Savich, quite simply, wanted to throw Elcott Frasier out the window. He knew Frasier was tough as nails, that he was a powerful man, but Savich was surprised that he hadn't been a bit more subtle, not this in-your-face bludgeoning. Why? Why this gratuitous cruelty?

Savich walked into the room like a man bent on violence until he saw his sister's white face, the pain that glazed her eyes, and he calmed immediately. He ignored the men, walked right to the bed, and leaned down, pressed his forehead lightly against hers.

"You hurt, kiddo?"

"A bit," she whispered, as if she were afraid to speak up. "Well, actually a whole lot. It's not too awful if I don't breathe too deeply or laugh or cry."

"More than a bit, I'd say," Savich said. "I'm going to find Dr. Larch and get you some more medication." He nodded to Sherlock and was out the door.

Sherlock smiled brightly at both her brother-in-law and Elcott Frasier. He looked the same as he had the first time she'd met him, eleven months before—tall, a bit of a paunch, a full head of thick, white hair, wavy, quite attractive. His eyes were his son's—light blue, reflective, slightly slanted. She wondered what his vices were, wondered if he really loved Lily and wanted her well. But why wouldn't he? Lily had been his son's wife for eleven months now. She was sweet, loving, very talented, and she'd lost her only child and fallen into a deep well of grief and depression.

She knew Elcott was sixty, but he looked no older than mid-fifties. He'd been a handsome man when he was younger, perhaps as handsome as his only son.

There was a daughter as well. Tansy was her name and she was, what? Twenty-eight? Thirty? Older than Lily, Sherlock thought. Tansy—an odd name, nearly as whimsical as Tennyson. She lived in Seattle, owned one of the ubiquitous coffeehouses near Pioneer Square. Sherlock had gotten the impression from Lily that Tansy didn't come back to Hemlock Bay all that often.

Elcott Frasier walked to Sherlock and grabbed her hand, shook it hard. "Mrs. Savich, what a pleasure." He looked ever so pleased to see her. She wondered how pleased he was to see Dillon, since she knew, right to her toes, that Mr. Elcott Frasier had little respect for women. It was in his eyes, in his very stance—condescending, patronizing.

"Mr. Frasier," she said and gave him her patented, guileless sunny smile. "I wish we could meet again under less trying circumstances." Go ahead, she thought, believe I'm an idiot, worth less than nothing in brain-power.

"Your poor husband is very upset by all this," Mr. Frasier said. "Given all that's happened, I can't say I blame him."

Sherlock said, "Certainly he's upset. It's good to see you again, Tennyson." She went directly to sit on the side of Lily's bed. She lightly stroked her pale hair. Thick, lank strands framed her face. Sherlock saw the pain in her eyes, how stiffly she was holding her body. She wanted to cry. "Dillon will be back in a moment, Lily. You shouldn't have to suffer like this."

"It is about time for a bit more pain medication," a nurse said as she came through the door, Savich at her heels. No one said a word as she injected the painkiller into Lily's IV. She leaned over, checked Lily's pulse, smoothed the thin blanket to her shoulders, then straightened. "The pain will lessen almost immediately. Call if you have too much more discomfort, Mrs. Frasier."

Lily closed her eyes. After a few minutes, she said quietly, "Thank you, Dillon. It was pretty bad, but not now. Thank you." Then, without another word, she was asleep.

"Good," said Savich and motioned for them all to leave. "Let's go to the waiting room. Last time I looked, it was empty."

"My wife and I are grateful to you for being here," Elcott Frasier said. "Tennyson needs all the support he can get. The past seven months have been very hard on him."

"That's just what I was thinking," Savich said. "Lily hitting that redwood gave us the excuse we needed to come here and support Tennyson."

"My father didn't mean it the way it sounded, Dillon," Tennyson said. "It's been difficult—for all of us." He looked down at his watch. "I'm afraid I have patients to see. I will be back to check on Lily in about four hours."

He left them with Elcott Frasier, who asked a passing nurse to fetch him a cup of coffee. She did without hesitation because, Sherlock knew, she wasn't stupid. She recognized the Big Man on the hospital board of directors when she saw him. Sherlock wanted to punch his lights out.

Savich leaned down, kissed Sherlock on the mouth, and said low, "No, don't belt him. Now, I've got all sorts of warning whistles going off in my head. I'm going to look at that car. Grill our brother-in-law's father, okay?"

"No problem," Sherlock said.

When Savich found Sherlock two hours later, she was in the hospital cafeteria eating a Caesar salad and speaking to Dr. Theodore Larch.

"So do you think she was so depressed she decided to end it? Again?"

"I'm a surgeon, Mrs. Savich, not a psychiatrist. I can't speculate."

"Yeah, but you see lots of people in distress, Dr. Larch. What do you think of Lily Frasier's state of mind?"

"I think the surgical pain is masking a lot of her symptoms right now—that is, if she has any symptoms. I haven't seen any myself. But what do I know?"

"What do you think of Dr. Rossetti?"

Dr. Larch wouldn't quite meet her eyes. "He's, ah, rather new here. I don't know him all that well. Dr. Frasier, however, knows him very well. They went to medical school together, I understand. Columbia Presbyterian Medical School, in New York City."

"I didn't know that," Sherlock said and tucked it away. She wanted to meet this Dr. Rossetti, the pompous man Lily didn't like, the man Tennyson appeared to be pushing very hard on his wife.

She smiled at Dr. Larch, took a bite of her salad, which was surprisingly good. "Well, you know, Dr. Larch, if Lily didn't try to kill herself, then that means that perhaps someone is up to no good. What do you think?"

Dr. Ted Larch nearly swallowed the ice cube he was rolling around in his mouth.

"I can't imagine, no, surely not—that's crazy. If she didn't do it on purpose, then it's more likely that something went wrong with the car, an accident, nothing more than a tragic accident."

"Yes, you're probably right. Since I'm a cop, I always leap to the sinister first. Occupational hazard. Hey, I know. She lost control of the car— maybe a raccoon ran in front of the Explorer and she tried not to hit it—and ended up smacking the redwood."

"That sounds more likely than someone trying to kill her, Mrs. Savich."

"Yes, the raccoon theory is always preferable, isn't it?"

Sherlock saw Dillon out of the corner of her eye. She rose, patted Dr. Larch on his shoulder, and said, "Take good care of Lily, Doctor." At least now, she thought, walking quickly toward Dillon, Dr. Larch would keep a very close eye on Lily because he wouldn't forget what she'd said. He would want to dismiss it as nonsense, but he wouldn't be able to, not entirely.

Savich nodded across the cafeteria to Dr. Larch, then smiled down at his wife. Her light blue eyes seemed brighter than when he'd left her, and he knew why. She was up to something. And she was very pleased with herself.

"What about the car?"

"Nothing at all. It's been compacted."

"That was awfully fast, wasn't it?"

"Yeah, sort of like cremating a body before the autopsy could be done."

"Exactly. Dr. Larch thinks Lily is fine, mentally, thank you very much. Actually, I think he has a crush on her. It's Dr. Rossetti he doesn't like, but who knows why? Did you know Dr. Rossetti and Tennyson went to medical school together? Columbia Presbyterian?"

"No. That's interesting. Okay, Sherlock. I know that look. You either want me to haul you to the nearest hot tub, or you've done something. No hot tub? Too bad. All right, then. What have you done?"

"I planted a small bug inside the slat on Lily's hospital bed. I already heard some interesting stuff. Come along and I'll play it back for you. Hmmm. About that hot tub, Dillon . . ."

They went to Lily's room, saw she was still asleep and no one else was there, and Sherlock shut the door. She walked to the window, fiddled with the tiny receiver and recorder, turned on rewind, then play.

"*Dammit, she needs more pain medication.*"

Savich said, "Who's that?"

"Dr. Larch."

"*I cut it back, just like you ordered, but it was too much. Listen, there's no need to make her suffer like this.*"

"*She doesn't react well to pain meds, I've told you that several times. It makes her even crazier than she already is. Keep the pain meds way down. I don't want her hurt anymore.*"

Sherlock pressed the stop button and said, "That was Tennyson Frasier. What do you think it means?"

Sherlock slipped the tiny recorder back into her jacket pocket.

"It could be perfectly innocent," Savich said. "On the other hand, the Explorer has been compacted. The guy at the junked car yard told me Dr. Frasier told him to haul the Explorer in and compact it immediately. Will this thing click on whenever someone's speaking?"

"Yes, it's voice-activated. It turns off when there's more than six seconds of silence. I got it from Dickie in Personnel. He's a gadget freak, owed me one after I busted his sister's boyfriend—you know, the macho drug dealer who was slapping her around."

"Sherlock, have I ever told you that you never cease to amaze and thrill me?"

"Not recently. Well, not since last night, and I don't think you had the same sort of intent then."

He laughed, pulled her against him and kissed her. Her curly hair tickled his cheek. "Let's call Mom and talk to Sean."

# FIVE

*Eureka, California*

Clark Hoyt, SAC of the new Eureka FBI field office, which had opened less than a year before, handed Savich the bottle of pills. "Sorry, Agent Savich. What we've got here is a really common antidepressant, name of Elavil."

"Not good," Savich said and looked out the window toward the small park just to the left of downtown. The trees were bright with fall colors. If he turned his head a bit to the right, he'd see the Old Town section on the waterfront. A beautiful town, Humboldt's county seat, Eureka was filled with countless fine Victorian homes and buildings.

"Something I can help you with, Agent Savich? Sounds like something's happening you don't like."

Savich shook his head. "I wish there was something, but the pills are exactly what they should be. I guess it would have been really easy if they were something different. I told you the Explorer my sister totaled has been compacted. I was really holding out big hopes for those pills. Oh yeah, call me Savich."

"Okay, Hoyt here. Now, the Explorer—that was done awfully fast."

"Yes, maybe too fast, but then again, my life's work is to be suspicious. Maybe it was very straightforward. As of right now, it's all a dead end. However, I think it's time I did a bit of digging on my brother-in-law, Dr. Tennyson Frasier."

Clark Hoyt, who had heard of some of the exploits of Sherlock, Savich, and MAX, Savich's transgender laptop, said, "Don't tell me you didn't do a background search on this guy before he married your sister? Seems to me a brother would have checked out the fillings in his teeth."

"Well, yeah, sure I did. But not a really deep one. He didn't have a record, hadn't ever been in rehab for drugs or alcohol, stuff like that."

"And he wasn't a bigamist?"

"No, I didn't check on that. Lily told me he'd been right up front about the fact that he'd been married before and that his wife had died. You know something, Hoyt? I wonder now what the first wife died of. I wonder how long they were married before she died." His eyes brightened.

"Savich, you don't really think he's trying to kill his wife? The pills were exactly what they were supposed to be."

"They were indeed, and I'm not sure. But you know, information is about the most important thing any cop can have." Savich rubbed his hands together. "MAX is going to love this."

"You know the Frasiers are a really big deal down in Hemlock Bay and the environs. Daddy Frasier has dealings all over the state, I understand."

"Yeah. Before, I didn't see the need to check into Papa's finances and dealings, but now it's time to be thorough."

"Is your sister going to be all right?"

"Yes, she'll be fine."

"I've got the names of some excellent psychiatrists in the area—all women, like you wanted. I hope one of them will be able to help your sister."

"Yeah, me too. But you know—no matter there's no proof of any funny stuff, that it really does look like she drove the Explorer into that redwood on purpose—I simply can't believe that Lily tried to kill herself. No matter what anyone says, I find myself coming back again and again to the fact that it doesn't fit."

"People change, Savich. Even people we love dearly. Sometimes we can't see the change because we're too close."

Savich took another look at that lovely park and said, "When Lily was thirteen, she was running a gambling operation in the neighborhood. She would take bets on anything from the point spread in college football games to who could shoot the most three-point baskets in any pro game. Drove my parents nuts. Since my dad was an FBI agent, the local cops didn't do anything, just snickered a lot. I think they all admired her moxie, but they gave my dad lots of grief about it, called her a chip off the old block.

"When she hit eighteen, she suddenly realized that she liked to draw and she was very good at it. She's an artist, you know, very talented."

"No, I hadn't heard."

"Actually, her talent comes from our grandmother Sarah Elliott."

"Sarah Elliott? Good grief, *the* Sarah Elliott, the artist whose paintings are in all the museums?"

"Yep. Lily's talents lie in a different direction—she's an excellent cartoonist, lots of humor and irony. Have you ever heard of the cartoon strip *No Wrinkles Remus*?"

Agent Hoyt shook his head.

"That's all right. It's political satire and shenanigans, I guess you could say. She hasn't done much for the past seven months, since the death of her daughter. But she will, and once she gets herself back together again, I'm sure she's going to be syndicated in lots of papers across the country."

"She's that good?"

"I think so. Now, given her talent, her background, can you really believe that she would try to kill herself seven months after her daughter was killed?"

"A girl who was the neighborhood bookie, then a cartoon strip artist?" Hoyt sighed. "I'd like to say no, I can't imagine it, Savich, but who knows? Aren't artists supposed to be high-strung? Temperamental? You said she still can't remember a thing about the accident?"

"Not yet."

"What are you going to do?"

"After MAX checks everything out, we'll see. No matter what, I'm taking Lily back to Washington with my wife and me. I think it's been proved that Hemlock Bay isn't healthy for her."

"Everything could be perfectly innocent," Clark Hoyt said. "She could have simply lost control of the car."

"Yeah, but you know something? I saw my brother-in-law differently this time. I saw him through Lily's eyes, maybe. It's not a pretty sight. I want to strangle him. Actually, I wanted to throw his daddy through the hospital window."

Clark Hoyt laughed. "Let me know if there's anything I can do."

"I will, thank you, Hoyt. Count on it. Thanks for the names of the shrinks."

*Hemlock Bay, California*

On the following Sunday afternoon, four days after her surgery, Lily was pronounced well enough to leave the hospital. She suffered only mild discomfort, because Dr. Larch had stopped by her room, looking determined, and given her some pills to keep the worst of the pain at bay. She still walked bent over like an old person, but her eyes were clear, her mood upbeat.

Sherlock had wanted to ask Dr. Larch about lowering Lily's meds temporarily on Dr. Frasier's orders, but Savich said, "Nope, let's hold off on that for a while."

"Nothing else good on the tape," Sherlock said in some disgust as she removed the small bug from beneath Lily's hospital bed while Lily was in the small bathroom bathing. "Not even doctors or nurses gossiping."

Ten minutes later Savich said to his sister as he pushed her wheelchair toward the elevator, "I told Tennyson that Sherlock and I are taking you to see your new shrink. He wasn't happy about that, said he didn't know anything about this woman. She could be a rank charlatan and he'd lose all sorts of money, maybe even get you more depressed. I let him talk on, then gave him my patented smile."

"That smile," Sherlock said, "translates into 'You mess with me, buddy, and even your toenails are gonna hurt.' "

"In any case, at the end of all his ranting, there was nothing he could do about it. He tried to get me to convince you to see Dr. Rossetti. I do wonder why he thinks the guy is so great."

"He's not," Lily said. "He's horrible." She actually shuddered. "He came back again this morning. The nurse had just washed my hair for me, so I looked human and felt well enough to take him on."

"What happened?" Sherlock asked. She was carrying Lily's small overnight bag. Savich pushed her wheelchair onto the elevator, punched the button. No one else was on board.

Lily shuddered yet again. "I think he'd talked to Tennyson some more. He tried to change his tactics. He actually attempted to be ingratiating, at least at first. When he slithered into my room—yes, that's it exactly, he slithered—Nurse Carla Brunswick had just finished blow-drying my hair."

Nurse Brunswick turned toward him and said, "Doctor."

"Leave us alone for a bit, Nurse. Thank you."

Lily said, "I don't want Nurse Brunswick to leave, Dr. Rossetti. I want you to leave."

"Please, Mrs. Frasier, a moment of your time. I fear we got off on the wrong foot when I was here before. You were just out of surgery; it was simply too soon for you to want to hear about anything. Please, just a few minutes of your time."

Nurse Brunswick smiled at Lily, patted her hand, then left the hospital room.

"I see I have little choice here, Russell. What do you want?"

If he was angered at her use of his first name, he didn't let on. He kept smiling, walked to her bed, and stood there, towering over her. She looked at his hands; his plump hands sported a ring this time—a huge diamond on his pinkie. She wished she could throw him out of her room.

"I wanted to speak to you, Mrs. Frasier—Lily. See if perhaps we could deal better with each other, perhaps you could come to trust me, to let me help you."

"No."

"Are you in pain, Lily?"

"Yes, Russell, I am."

"Would you like me to give you a mild antidepressant?"

"My pain is from my ribs and my missing spleen."

"Yes, well, that pain will likely suppress the other, deeper pain for a while longer."

"I hope so."

"Mrs. Frasier—Lily—won't you come to my office, perhaps next Monday? That will give you another week to recuperate."

"No, Russell. Ah, here's Dr. Larch. Hello. Do come in. Dr. Rossetti was just leaving."

Savich looked ready to spit by the time Lily finished, but she laughed. "No need to go pound him, Dillon. He left, didn't say another word, just walked out. Dr. Larch didn't move until he was gone."

"What I don't understand," Sherlock said thoughtfully, "is why both Tennyson and Dr. Rossetti want you as his patient so very much. Isn't that strange? You give Rossetti grief and he still wants you?"

"Yes," Savich said slowly, "it is strange. We'll have to see what MAX has to say about Russell Rossetti. He was ready to give you some antidepressants, right there, on the spot?"

"It seems so."

After Lily was in the car, a pillow over her stomach and ribs, the seat belt as loose as possible over the pillow, Savich said, "I have a psychiatrist for you, Lily. No, not someone to shrink you and give you more medication, but a woman who is very good at hypnosis. What do you think?"

"Hypnosis? Oh, goodness, she'll help me remember what happened?"

"I hope so. It's a start anyway. Maybe it will jump-start your memory. Since it's Sunday, she's coming into her office especially for you."

"Dillon, I think I just gained a whole ton of energy."

Sherlock heard her say under her breath, "I'll know, finally, if I'm really crazy."

"Yes, you'll know, and that's the best thing to happen," Sherlock said and patted her shoulder.

"Then we're off right now to Eureka."

DR. Marlena Chu was a petite Chinese-American woman who looked barely old enough to buy liquor. Lily was tall, nearly five feet eight in her ballet flats, which were what she was wearing today, and she wondered how she could trust someone so small she could easily tuck her beneath her armpit.

Dr. Chu met them in her outer office, since there was no one else there on Sunday. "Your brother has told me what has happened," she said. "This must be very difficult for you, Mrs. Frasier." She took Lily's hands in her own small ones and added, "You need to sit down. I can see that you're still very weak. Would you like a glass of water?"

Her hands felt warm, Lily thought; she didn't want to let them go. And her voice was incredibly soothing. She suddenly felt much calmer, and surely that was odd, but true nonetheless. Also, the nagging pain in her ribs seemed to fade. She smiled at Dr. Chu, hanging on to her hands like a lifeline.

"No, I'm fine. Well, maybe a bit tired."

"All right, then. Come into my office and sit down. I have a very comfortable chair and a nice, high footstool so you won't feel like you're pulling anything. Yes, here we are."

Her inner office was perfectly square with soft blue furnishings and lots of clean, oak parquet floor. Again, Lily felt a wave of peace and calm wash through her.

"Do let me help you sit down, Mrs. Frasier."

"Please, call me Lily."

"Thank you. I'd like that." As soon as Lily was seated, Dr. Chu brought her chair alongside and took Lily's left hand in hers again. Dr. Chu watched Lily's eyelids flutter as warmth and calm flowed through her, and was pleased. She watched Mr. Savich ease the footstool beneath his sister's narrow feet and saw it immediately lessened the pull on her stitches. She studied her patient. Even though she was pale, her eyes were bright. Lovely eyes, a soft light blue that went very nicely with her blond hair. She was a lovely young woman, but that didn't really matter. What was important was that she was in trouble. What was more important was that she was soaking up the strength Dr. Chu was giving her. "Lily is such a romantic name. It sounds like soft music; it's the sort of name to make one dream of fanciful things."

Lily smiled. "It's my grandmother's name. Coincidence, maybe, but she grew the most beautiful lilies."

"It's interesting how some things work out, isn't it?"

"Yes, interesting, but sometimes it's also terrifying."

"True, but there is nothing here to harm you, Lily." She patted Lily's hand again. Dr. Chu knew that Lily Frasier was an artist, and that meant she was creative, probably very bright. Such folk usually went under very easily. She said in her soft voice, "You understand that I'm going to try to help you remember what happened last Wednesday evening. Do you want this?"

"Yes, I want to know very badly what really happened. Tell me what to do. I've never been hypnotized before."

"It's nothing, really. I just want you to relax." She lightly squeezed Lily's hand.

Lily felt more warmth flow through her, all the way to her bones, felt herself becoming utterly calm. Those small hands of Dr. Chu's, how could they make her feel like this?

Savich pulled a chair next to Lily's and took her other hand. A strong hand, she thought, strong fingers. His hand didn't make hers feel warm, but it did make her feel safe. He said nothing at all, was just there beside her, there for her. Sherlock sat on a sofa behind Lily, quiet as could be.

Dr. Chu said, "You will perhaps believe this a bit odd, Lily, but I don't swing a watch in front of your eyes or let you lie on the sofa and chant this and that over and over. No, we'll just sit here and chat. I understand you draw a cartoon strip. *No Wrinkles Remus?* Such an interesting title. What does it mean?"

Lily actually smiled. She felt the familiar pain of Beth's death ease away. "Remus is a United States senator from the state of West Dementia, located in the Midwest. He's very bright, utterly ruthless, completely amoral, has overweening ambition, and loves to pull fast ones on his opponents. He's also known as 'Ept Remus,' as opposed to inept, because he's so fast to come up with a new angle to get what he wants. He's a spin master. He never gives up, ignores what people say because he knows that soon enough they'll forget, ignores what the truth is, and continues until he gets what he wants. What he wants now is the presidency, and he's shafted a friend of his to get it."

Dr. Chu raised a thin, perfectly arched black brow and smiled. "An interesting character study, and not all that unfamiliar."

Lily actually chuckled. "I finished another strip last week. His friend Governor Braveheart isn't taking being shafted well. He's fighting back. Although he's tough, he's got one big problem—he's honest. It's good. At least I hope it is."

"Did you take it to your editor at the paper?"

Lily paused a moment and closed her eyes. "No, I didn't."

"Why not?"

"Because I started feeling bad again."

"What do you mean by 'feeling bad'?"

"Like nothing really mattered. Beth was dead and I was alive, and nothing was worth anything, including me and anything I did."

"You went from feeling great and creative, from smiles and laughter to utter depression?"

"Yes."

"In a day?"

"Yes. Maybe less. I don't remember."

"On the day your husband left for Chicago, how did you feel, Lily?"

"I don't remember feeling much of anything. I was . . . simply there."

"I see. Your husband called you the next day—Wednesday—and he wanted you to take some medical slides to a doctor in Ferndale?"

"That's right."

"And the only road is 211."

"Yes. I hate that road, always have. It's dangerous. And it was dusk.

Driving at that time of day always makes me antsy. I'm always very careful."

"It makes me nervous as well. Now, you took two more antidepressant pills, right?"

"That's right. Then I slept. I had terrible nightmares."

"Tell me what you remember about the nightmares."

Dr. Chu wasn't holding her hand now, but still Lily felt a touch of warmth go through her, felt like it was deep inside her now, so deep it was warming her very soul. "I saw Beth struck by that car, over and over, struck and hurled screaming and screaming, at least twenty feet, crying out my name, over and over. When I awoke, I could still see Beth. I remember lying there and crying and then I felt lethargic, my brain dull."

"You felt leached of hope?"

"Yes, that's it exactly. I felt like nothing was worth anything, particularly me. I wasn't worth anything. Everything was black. Nothing mattered anymore."

"All right, Lily, now you're driving away from your house. You're in your red Explorer. What do you think of your car?"

"Tennyson yells every time I call it a car. I haven't done that for months now. It's an Explorer and nothing else is like it and it isn't a car, so you call it by its name and that's it."

"You don't like the Explorer much, do you?"

"My in-laws gave it to me for my birthday. That was in August. I turned twenty-seven."

Dr. Chu didn't appear to be probing or delving; she was merely speaking with a friend, nothing more, nothing less. She was also lightly stroking Lily's left hand. Then she turned to Savich and nodded.

"Lily."

"Yes, Dillon."

"How do you feel, sweetheart?"

"So warm, Dillon, so very warm. And there's no nagging pain anywhere. It's wonderful. I want to marry Dr. Chu. She's got magic in her hands."

He smiled at that. "I'm glad you feel good. Are you driving on 211 yet?"

"Yes, I just made a right onto the road. I don't mind the beginning of it, but you get into the redwoods and it's so dark and the trees press in on you. I've always thought that some maniac carved that road."

"I agree with you. What are you thinking, Lily?"

"I'm thinking that when it's dark, it will be just like a shroud is thrown over all those thick redwoods. Like Beth was in a shroud and I'm so depressed I want to end it, Dillon, end it and get it over with. It's relentless, this greedy pain. I'm thinking it's settled into my soul and it won't leave me, ever. I can't stand it any longer."

"This pain," Dr. Chu said in her soft voice, holding Lily's hand now, squeezing occasionally, "tell me more about this pain."

"I know the pain wants to be one with me. I want to give over to it. I know that if I become the pain and the pain becomes me, then I'll be able to expiate my guilt."

"You came to the conclusion that you had to kill yourself because it was the only way you could make reparation? To redress the balance?"

"Yes. A life for a life. My life—worth nothing much—for her small, precious life."

Then Lily frowned.

Dr. Chu lightly ran her palm over Lily's forearm, then back to clasp her limp hand. "What are you thinking now, Lily?"

"I just realized that something isn't right. I didn't kill Beth. No, I'd been at the newspaper, giving my cartoon to Boots O'Malley, seeing what he thought, you know?"

"I know. And he laughed, right?"

"Yes. I heard the sheriff say later that Beth's body had been thrown at least twenty feet."

Lily stopped. She squeezed Dr. Chu's hand so tightly her knuckles whitened.

"Stay calm, Lily. Everything is fine. I'm here. Your brother and Mrs. Savich are here. Forget what the sheriff said. Now, you suddenly recognized that you didn't kill Beth."

"That's right," Lily whispered, her eyelids fluttering. "I realize that something is wrong. I suddenly remember taking those sleeping pills that Tennyson put on the bedside table. I took so many of them, felt them stick in my throat and I swallowed and swallowed to get them down, and I sat with that bottle and chanted, more, more, more, and then the bottle was nearly empty and I thought suddenly, *Wait, I don't want to die,* but then it was too late, and I felt so sorry for the loss of Beth and the loss of me."

"I don't understand, Lily," Savich said in that darkly smooth voice of his. "You told me about the pills you took just after Beth's funeral. Why are you thinking about that now, while you're driving?"

"Because I realize that I can't really remember actually taking those pills. Now isn't that odd?"

"It's very odd. Tell us more."

"Well, I realize I didn't want to die then, and I don't want to die now. But why is the guilt eating at me like this? What's inside my brain that's making me want to simply drive the Explorer right into the thick trees that line this horrible road?"

"And did you find an answer, Lily?"

"Yes, I did." She stopped, just stopped and sighed deeply. She was asleep. Her head fell lightly to the side.

"It's all right, Mr. Savich. Let's just let her rest awhile, then I'll wake her and we can carry on. She'll be back with us when she wakes up. We'll see if she needs to go under again.

"You know, Mr. Savich, I'm getting more and more curious about that first time when she took all those sleeping pills. Maybe we should go into that as well."

"Oh, yes," Sherlock said from behind them.

However, they didn't have to wake Lily up. Not more than another minute passed when suddenly Lily opened her eyes, blinked, and said, "I remember everything." She smiled at Dr. Chu, then said to her brother, "I didn't try to kill myself, Dillon, I didn't."

Dr. Chu took both of her hands now and leaned very close. "Tell us exactly what happened, Lily."

"I came back to myself. I felt clear and alert and appalled at what I'd been considering. Then the road twisted, started one of those steep descents. I realized I was going too fast and I pressed down on the brake."

"What happened?" Savich said, leaning toward her.

"Nothing happened."

Sherlock whispered, "I knew it, I just knew it."

Savich said, "Did you pump the brakes the way Dad taught you way back when?"

"Yes, I pumped gently, again and again. Still there was nothing. I was terrified. I yanked up the emergency brake. I know it only works on the rear tires, but I figured it would have to slow me down."

"Don't tell me," Savich said. "The emergency brake didn't work either."

She shook her head, swallowed convulsively. "No, it didn't. I was veering from the center toward the deep ravine on my left. I pulled back, but not too far because the redwoods were directly to my right, thick, impenetrable. I was going too fast, and the downhill grade was becoming even steeper. That stretch twists and wheels back on itself a whole lot before it flattens out at the outskirts of Ferndale."

Sherlock said from behind her, "Did you slam the shift into park?"

"Oh, yes. There was an awful grinding noise, like the transmission was tearing itself up. The Explorer shuddered, screamed, and all the wheels locked up. I went into a skid. I tried to let the side of the Explorer scrape against the redwoods, to slow me down, but then the road twisted again. I knew I was going to die."

Savich pulled her very gently into his arms, settling her on his lap. Dr. Chu never released her left hand. Lily lay against him, her head on his shoulder. She felt Sherlock's fingers lightly stroking her hair. She drew a deep breath and said, "I remember so clearly slamming head-on into that poor redwood, thinking in that split second that the redwood had survived at least a hundred years of violent Pacific storms but it wouldn't survive me.

"I remember hearing the blaring of the horn, so loud, like it was right inside my head. And then there wasn't anything."

She pulled back and smiled, a beautiful smile, clean and filled with self-awareness and hope. "Now, this is a very strange thing, Dillon. The brakes didn't work. Did someone try to kill me?"

Since Dr. Chu was still holding her hand, Lily wasn't frightened. Actually, she felt good all the way to her toes. Her smile didn't fade a bit with those awful words.

"Yeah," Savich said, looking directly into her eyes. "Probably so. Isn't that a kick?"

"Now," Dr. Chu said, "let's go back and see how it happened that you ended up in the hospital with all those sleeping pills in your stomach."

Lily felt peaceful and excited at the same time. "Yes, let's go back."

# SIX

*Hemlock Bay, California*

"All right, MAX, whatcha got?"

Sherlock walked over, looked down at the laptop screen. "Oh, dear, he's not doing anything. You don't think he's becoming MAXINE again so soon, do you, Dillon? He's in a mood?"

"Nah, MAX is still a he, and he's concentrating. He's going to turn up something for us."

"You hope."

"MAX shuddered a bit. That means he's digging deep. Is Lily asleep?"

"Yes, I checked on her. She didn't want a pain pill. Said she didn't need it. Isn't that amazing?"

"Lily told me that a doctor who could make her feel good without hurting her was sure an improvement over a husband who can't. She said she still feels better for having met her."

"Since Dr. Chu didn't hold our hands, we'll have to work out our stress at the gym. Too bad." Then Sherlock laughed. "Remember when she asked Dr. Chu to marry her? That was good, Dillon. She wants out of this mess.

"Now, according to Mrs. Scruggins, Tennyson will be home in about two hours. She told me she's making a vegetarian dinner for you—her special zucchini lasagna, and an apple-onion dish that she assured me would make you hum and help you keep your, er, physique perfect. I think she'd like to see you on a calendar, Dillon. What do you think?"

Savich laughed, then smacked MAX very lightly on his hard drive with the palm of his hand.

"Not going to commit yourself, are you? Okay, she's got a big crush on you, Dillon. I think it struck when she saw you in your T-shirt this morning, your pants zipped up but not fastened. There was lust in her eyes when she said your name. She had her hands clasped on her bosom. That's a sure sign she wants you."

Savich cocked a dark eyebrow at his wife. "Don't go there, Sherlock, it scares me too much."

She thought about how she felt whenever she saw him in a T-shirt—or less—and didn't doubt Mrs. Scruggins's fast-beating heart one bit. She lightly touched her fingertips to the back of his neck and began to knead.

MAX beeped.

"He's jealous."

"No, that was a burp. Well, maybe he's telling me he's distracted, what with you draped all over me."

Sherlock leaned down to kiss the back of his neck, then grinned at him as she did some stretching. "It really is time for the gym. Do you think there's one here in Hemlock Bay?"

"We'll find one. Tomorrow morning, if Lily's still feeling fine, we'll go get the kinks out and lower our stress levels."

She stretched a bit more, rubbing the back of her neck. "You think Tennyson was giving her pills to make her depressed, don't you? You think he changed the pills back, just to be on the safe side since her big brother Fed was here."

"Sounds good to me. After Dr. Chu couldn't get anything conclusive about Lily's so-called attempt to commit suicide right after Beth's funeral, I'm thinking that maybe she never tried to kill herself at all."

"It was strange how Lily sort of remembered, but she didn't really. If she didn't do it, then it had to be Tennyson, and that was the bastard's first try. They'd been married all of four months, Dillon. That's incredibly cold-blooded. It makes me really mad. Let's prove it so we can pound him."

"We'll try, Sherlock. Here we go. Good work, MAX."

Both of them read the small print on the screen, as Savich slowly scrolled. A couple of minutes later, Savich raised his head and looked up into Sherlock's blue eyes.

"Not really all that much of a surprise, is it? So, our Tennyson was married once before, just like he told Lily. Only thing is, he didn't bother to mention that his first wife committed suicide only thirteen months after they'd tied the knot."

Savich hit his palm against his forehead. "I'm an idiot, Sherlock. I

shouldn't have given him the benefit of the doubt, shouldn't have re-
spected his privacy. Some brother I am after that bastard first husband of
hers. After Jack Crane, I should have opened every closet in his house,
checked his bank statements for the past twenty years. You know something else? All I had to do was flat-out ask Tennyson how his first wife
died."

"He probably would have lied."

"It wouldn't have mattered. You know I can tell when someone's lying.
Also, I could have done then what I'm doing now. My holding back, my
respecting Lily's decision, could have cost Lily her life. I want you to flay
me, Sherlock."

Sherlock was twining one curly strand of hair round and round her
finger, a sure sign she was upset. He immediately took her hand between
his two large ones. She said, "I'd just as soon flay myself, Dillon. Do you
think Lily would still have married him if she'd known the first wife
killed herself?"

"We can ask her. You can bet she'll be asking herself the same question, over and over. But the thing is that this is now, and her eyes are wide
open. Eleven months ago she believed she loved him, thought she'd found
a really wonderful father for Beth. If Tennyson had told her, she'd probably have felt sorry for him—poor man—losing his wife like that. She
probably would have married him anyway. If I'd told her, it probably
would have pissed her off, she'd have resented me, and she would have
married him."

"You know, Dillon, sometimes we women do think with our hearts,
not like you men, who think with your . . . well, that's better left unsaid,
isn't it?"

He grinned up at her. "Yep, probably so."

"All of it was an illusion. Look, the first wife—her name was Lynda—
was rich, Dillon, had a nice, fat trust fund from her grandfather. Oh, my,
she was only twenty-five."

"Ah, read this, Sherlock." Savich stroked his fingers over his jaw and
added, disgust thick in his voice, "That immoral bastard. It usually comes
down to money, doesn't it? Daddy got himself into a mess and so his son
tries to bail him out. Or maybe it was both of them in the mess up to
their necks. That sounds more likely."

"It's so mundane, really, just a couple of greedy men trying to get
what they want."

Savich nodded as he read to the end of MAX's information. He sat back a moment, then said, "It seems very likely to me that Tennyson killed his first wife as well as trying to kill Lily. Was Daddy in on it with him? Very likely. Doesn't matter. I don't want to take any more chances. I want Lily out of here. I want you to take her to that very nice bed-and-breakfast we stayed at once in Eureka. What was it?"

"The Mermaid's Tail, off Calistoga Street. It's late fall. Tourist season is over so they'll have room. What will you do?"

"I'm going to have a nice vegetarian dinner with Tennyson. I love lasagna. I'm going to see if I can get him to admit to anything useful. I really want to nail him. I'll join you and Lily later."

He rose and pulled her tightly against him. "Take MAX with you. Keep after him to find out all he can about Daddy Frasier's efforts to get that public road built to the lovely resort spot on the coast he's so hot to build. Without the state legislature passing it, the project would be doomed. He's having trouble. Maybe they ran out of bribery money."

"Don't forget the condos he's planning, too—Golden Sunset."

"Yes, lots of potential profit from those as well. Elcott Frasier has lots and lots of bucks already invested. I wonder if they ran into more roadblocks. Maybe that's why they wanted Lily out of the way. They were in deep financial trouble again. Now, let's get you guys packed up and out of this house."

But Lily didn't cooperate. She was awake, she still didn't hurt very much at all, and she was very clearheaded. She smacked her palm to the side of her head and announced, delight and wonder in her voice, "Would you look at me—I'm not depressed. In fact I can't imagine being depressed. Nope, everything inside there is rattling around clockwise, just as it should be."

They were in the hallway outside her bedroom. Lily was dressed in loose jeans and a baggy sweater, hair pulled back in a ponytail, no makeup, hands on hips, reminding Savich of his once sixteen-year-old sister who stood tall and defiant in front of their parents, who were dressing her down but good for her latest bookie scheme. "No, Dillon, I won't turn tail and leave. I want to read everything MAX has come up with so far. I want to speak to Tennyson, confront him with all this. It's my right to find out if my husband of eleven months married me only to kill me off. Oh, dear. There's a big problem here. Why would he do it? I don't have any money."

"Unfortunately, sweetheart," Savich said, his voice gentle, "you are very rich. All us kids tend to forget what Grandmother left us."

"Oh, my Sarah Elliott paintings. You're right, I forget about them, since they're always on loan to a museum."

"Yes, but they're legally yours, all eight paintings, willed to you. I e-mailed Simon Russo in New York. You remember him, don't you? You met him way back when he and I were in college."

"I remember. That was way back in the dark ages before I started screwing up big time."

"No, you were screwing up then, too," Savich said, lightly punching her arm. "Remember that point spread you had on the Army-Navy game? And Dad found out that you'd gotten twenty dollars off Mr. Hodges next door?"

"I hid out in your room, under your bed, until he calmed down."

They laughed. It sounded especially good to Sherlock, who beamed at both of them. Lily depressed? It was hard, looking at her now, to believe that she'd ever been depressed.

Lily said, "I remember Simon Russo. He was a real pain in the butt and you said yeah, that was true enough, but it didn't matter because he was such a good wide receiver."

"That's Simon. He's neck-deep in the art world, you know. He got back to me right away, said eight Sarah Elliotts are worth in the neighborhood of eight to ten million dollars."

Lily stared at him blank-faced. She was shaking her head. "That's unbelievable. No, you're pulling my leg, aren't you? Please tell me you're kidding, Dillon."

"Nope. The paintings have done nothing but gain in value since Grandmother died seven years ago. Each of the four grandchildren got eight paintings. Each painting is worth about one million dollars right now, more or less, according to Simon."

"That's an enormous responsibility, Dillon."

He nodded. "Like you, I think the rest of us have felt like we're the guardians; it's our responsibility to see that the paintings are kept safe throughout our lifetimes and exhibited so that the public can enjoy them. I remember yours were on loan to the Art Institute of Chicago. Are they still there?"

Lily said slowly, rubbing her palms on the legs of her jeans, "No. When Tennyson and I married he thought they should be here, in a regional museum, close to where we lived. So I moved them to the Eureka Art Museum."

Savich said without missing a beat, "Does Tennyson know anyone who works in the museum?"

Lily said very quietly, "Elcott Frasier is on the board of the museum."

"Bingo," Sherlock said.

WHEN Tennyson Frasier walked through the front door of his house that evening, he saw his wife standing at the foot of the stairs, looking toward him. She watched his eyes fill with love and concern. But it didn't take him long to realize that something was up. He sensed it, like an animal senses danger lying in wait ahead. His step slowed. But when he reached Lily, he said gently, as he took her hands, "Lily, my dear, you are very pale. You must still be in pain. After all, the surgery wasn't long ago at all. Please, sweetheart, let me take you up to bed. You need to rest."

"Actually, I feel fine, Tennyson. You needn't worry. Mrs. Scruggins has made us a superb dinner. Are you hungry?"

"If you're sure you want to eat downstairs, then yes, I'm hungry." He sent a wary look to his brother- and sister-in-law, who had just walked into the entrance hall from the living room. "Hello, Sherlock, Savich."

Savich just nodded.

"Hope you had a good day, Tennyson," Sherlock said and gave him a sunny smile. She hoped he couldn't tell yet that she wanted to strangle him with his own tie.

"No, I didn't actually," Tennyson said. He took a step back from Lily and stuck his hands in his pockets. He didn't take his eyes off his wife. "Old Mr. Daily's medication isn't working anymore. He talked about sticking his rifle in his mouth. He reminded me of you, Lily, that awful hopelessness when the mind can't cope. It was a dreadful day. I didn't even have time to come visit you before you left the hospital. I'm sorry."

"Well, these unpleasant sorts of things occasionally happen, don't they?" Sherlock patted his arm and smiled at the disgusted look he gave her.

Savich winked at her as they walked to the dining room.

Tennyson tenderly seated Lily in her chair in the long dining room. Lily loved this room. When she'd moved in, she had painted it a light yellow and dumped all the heavy furniture. It was very modern now, with a glossy Italian Art Deco table, chairs, and sideboard. On the walls were five Art Deco posters, filled with color and high-living stylized characters.

Tennyson was no sooner seated than Mrs. Scruggins began to serve. Normally, she simply left the food in the oven and went home, but not this evening.

Tennyson said, "Good evening, Mrs. Scruggins. It's very nice of you to stay."

"My pleasure, Dr. Frasier," she said.

Sherlock, who was watching her pile food onto Lily's plate, knew Mrs. Scruggins wasn't about to leave unless she was booted out. "I couldn't very well leave when Mrs. Frasier was coming home, now could I?"

Savich nearly smiled. Mrs. Scruggins wanted to hear everything. She knew the air was hot, even if she didn't know the reason, and would become hotter.

Lily took a small bite of a homemade dinner roll that tasted divine. She said to her husband, "Oh yes, Tennyson, you'll be pleased, I hope, to hear that I didn't try to kill myself by running the Explorer into the redwood. Actually, neither the brakes nor the emergency brake worked. Since I was on that very gnarly part of 211, I didn't stand a chance. Doesn't that relieve your mind?"

Tennyson was silent, frowning a bit over a forkful of lasagna, beautifully flavored, that was nearly to his mouth. He swallowed, then said slowly, his head cocked to the side, "You remembered, Lily?"

"Yes, I remembered."

"Ah, then you mean that you changed your mind? But it was too late because then the brakes failed?"

"That's it exactly. I realized that I didn't want to kill myself, but then it didn't matter, since someone had evidently disabled the brakes."

"Someone? Come on, Lily, that's absurd."

Savich said easily, "Unfortunately, the Explorer was compacted the very next day after the accident, so we can't check it out to see if it is or isn't absurd."

"Perhaps, Lily," Tennyson said very gently, "perhaps you're wanting to remember something different, something that could alleviate the pain of the past seven months."

"I don't think so, Tennyson. You see, I remembered while I was under hypnosis. And then when I came out of it, I remembered the rest of it, all by myself. All of it."

A thick eyebrow went straight up. Savich had never before seen an eyebrow do a vertical lift like that. Tennyson turned to Savich and spoke, his voice low and controlled, but it was obvious to everyone that he was very angry. "You're telling me you took Lily to see a hypnotist? One of those charlatans who plant garbage in their patients' minds?"

"Oh, no," Sherlock said, taking Lily's clenched fist beneath the table. "This doctor didn't plant anything, Tennyson. She simply helped Lily to remember what happened that evening. Both Dillon and I were there the whole time, and he and I are very familiar with hypnotists as part of our work. It was all on the up-and-up. Now, don't you think it's strange that the brakes didn't work? Don't you think it's at least possible that someone disabled them from what Lily said?"

"No, what I think is that Lily disremembers. I'm not sure if she's doing it on purpose or if she's simply confused and wants desperately for it to be this way. Don't you see? She made up the brakes failing so she wouldn't have to face up to what she did. I don't think the brakes failed. I certainly don't think anyone cut the lines. That's beyond what is reasonable, and her saying that, claiming that that's what happened, well, it really worries me. I don't want Lily to even consider such a thing; it could make her lose ground again.

"Listen, I'm a psychiatrist—a real one—one who doesn't use hocus-pocus on people to achieve some sort of preordained result. I am not pleased about this, Savich. I am Lily's husband. I am responsible for her."

Sherlock pointed her fork at him and said, her voice colder than a psychopath's heart, "You haven't been doing such a good job of it, have you?"

# SEVEN

Tennyson looked as if he wanted to throw his plate at Sherlock's head. His breathing was hard and fast.

Sherlock continued after a moment of chewing thoughtfully on a green bean, "I've also wondered at the timing. You remember, don't you, Tennyson? You called to ask Lily to deliver those medical slides to Ferndale, knowing it would be dusk to dark when she was on 211. Then the brakes failed. That sounds remarkably fortuitous, doesn't it?"

"You both went behind my back, did something you knew I wouldn't approve of? Lily is fine now. She no longer needs you here. I repeat, I am her husband. I will take care of her. As for your ridiculous veiled accusations, I won't lower myself to answer them."

"I think you should consider lowering yourself," Sherlock said, and in that moment, Tennyson looked fit to kill.

Savich waited a moment for him to regain some calm, then said, "All right, let's move along. Let's suppose, Tennyson, that Lily does remember everything exactly as it happened. That raises a couple of good questions. Why did the brakes fail? Perhaps it was simply a mechanical problem? But then the emergency brake failed, too. It's rather a difficult stretch to make if there's also a second mechanical problem, don't you think? And that means someone had to have disabled the systems. Who, Tennyson? Who would want Lily dead? Realize, too, that if she had died, why then, everyone would have declared it a clear case of suicide. Who would want that, Tennyson?"

Tennyson rose slowly to his feet. Sherlock could see the pulse pounding in his neck. He was furious, and he was also something more. Frightened? Desperate? She couldn't tell, which disappointed her. He was very good, very controlled.

Tennyson said, the words nearly catching in his throat, "You are a cop. You see bad things. You deal with bad people, evil people. What happened wasn't caused by someone out to kill Lily—other than Lily. She's been very ill. Everyone knows that. Lily knows that; she even accepts it. The most logical explanation is that she simply doesn't remember what happened because she can't bring herself to admit that she really tried to commit suicide again. That's all there is to it. I won't stand for your accusations any longer. This is my home. I want you both to leave. I want you both out of our lives."

Savich said, "All right, Tennyson, Sherlock and I will be delighted to leave. Actually, we'll leave right after dinner. Mrs. Scruggins made it for me, and I don't want to miss any of it. Oh, yes, did I tell you that we know all about Lynda—you remember, don't you? She was your first wife who killed herself only thirteen months after marrying you?"

They hadn't told Lily about Lynda Middleton Frasier. She froze where she sat, her mouth open, utter disbelief scored on her face, any final hope leached out with those words. When her husband had spoken so calmly, so reasonably, she had wondered if it was possible that her mind had altered what really happened, that her mind was so squirrelly that she simply couldn't trust any thought, any reaction. But not any longer. Now she knew she hadn't disremembered anything. Had he killed his first wife? It was horrible, unbelievable. Lily was shaking from the inside out—she couldn't help it.

She said slowly, holding her knife in a death grip, her knuckles white from the strain, "I remember that you told me you'd been married for a very short time, Tennyson, a long time ago."

"A long time ago?" Sherlock said, an eyebrow arched. "Sounds like maybe it was a decade or more, doesn't it? Like he ran away with a girl when he was eighteen? Actually, Lily, Tennyson's first wife, Lynda, killed herself two years ago—eight months before you came to Hemlock Bay and met him." She looked over at Tennyson and said, her voice utterly emotionless, "However, you didn't say a word about your wife having killed herself. Why is that, Tennyson?"

"It was a tragic event in my life," Tennyson said calmly, in control again, as he picked up his wineglass and sipped at the Napa Valley Chardonnay. It was very dry, very woody, just as he preferred. "It is still painful. Why would I wish to speak of it? Not that it was a secret. Lily could have heard it from anyone in town, from my own family even."

Sherlock leaned forward, her food forgotten. The gauntlet was thrown.

This was fascinating. She smiled at Tennyson Frasier. "Still, doesn't it seem like it would be on the relevant side, Tennyson, for her to know, particularly after Lily tried to kill herself seven months ago? Wouldn't you begin to think, Oops, could there be something wrong, maybe, with me? Two wives trying to do away with themselves after they've been married to me only a short time? What are the odds on that, do you think, Tennyson? Two dead wives, one live husband?"

"No, that's all ridiculous. None of it was at all relevant. Lily isn't anything like Lynda. Lily was simply bowled over by her child's death, by her role in her child's death."

"I didn't have a role in Beth's death," Lily said. "I realize that now."

"Do you really believe that, Lily? Think about it, all right? Now, as for Lynda, she had a brain tumor. She was dying."

This was a corker, Savich thought. "A brain tumor?"

"Yes, Savich, she was diagnosed with a brain tumor. It wasn't operable. She knew she was going to die. She didn't want the inevitable pain, the further loss of self, the deterioration of her physical abilities. Her confusion was growing by the day because of the tumor. She hated it. She wanted to be the one to decide her own end, and so she did. She gave herself an injection of potassium chloride. It works very quickly. As for the tumor, I saw to it that it was kept quiet. I saw no reason to tell anyone." He paused for a moment, looked at Savich, then at Sherlock. "There are, of course, records. Check if you want to, I don't care. I'm not lying."

Sherlock said, "So you think it's better for a woman to be known as a suicide for no good reason at all?" She sat back in her chair now, arms crossed over her breasts.

"It was my call and that's what I decided to do at the time."

"Thirteen months," Savich said. "Married the first time only thirteen months. If Lily had managed to die in that accident, then she would have beaten Lynda to the grave by two months. Or, if she had died in her first attempt, right after Beth's death, then she would have really broken the record."

Tennyson Frasier said slowly, looking directly at his wife, "I don't find that amusing, Savich. You have judged me on supposition, on a simple coincidence, no evidence that would stand up anywhere, and surely a cop shouldn't do that. Lily didn't die, thank God, either time. If she had died in that accident, I doubt I would have survived. I love her very much. I want her well."

He was good, Savich thought, very good indeed. Very fluent, very reasoned and logical, and the appeal to gut emotion was surefire. Tennyson was certainly right about one thing—they didn't have any proof. He was right about another thing—Savich had already judged him guilty. Guilty as sin. They had to get proof. MAX had to dig deeper. There would be something; there always was.

Sherlock chewed on a homemade roll that was now cold, swallowed, then said in the mildest voice imaginable, "Where did Lynda get the potassium chloride?"

"From her doctor, the one who diagnosed her in the first place. He was infatuated with her, which is why, I believe, he assisted her. I knew nothing about any of it until she was dead and he told me what had happened, what he had helped her do. I didn't file charges because I'd known she'd wanted to end her life herself, on her own terms. Dr. Cord died only a short while later. It was horrible, all of it."

Lily said, "I heard about Dr. Cord's death from a woman in Casey's Food Market. She said he shot himself while cleaning his rifle, such a terrible accident. She didn't mention anything about your wife."

"The townspeople didn't want to see me hurt any more, I suppose, particularly since I had a new wife, so I guess they kept quiet." He turned to his wife and said, his voice pleading, his hand stretched out toward her, "Lily, when you came to town, just over a year and a half ago, I couldn't believe that someone else could come into my life who would make me complete, who would love me and make me happy, but you did. And you brought precious little Beth with you. I loved her from the first moment I saw her, as I did you. I miss her, Lily, every day I miss her.

"What you've been going through—maybe now it's over. Maybe what happened with the Explorer, maybe that snapped you back. Believe me, dearest, I only want you to get well. I want that more than anything. I want to take you to Maui and lie with you on the beach and know that your biggest worry will be how to keep from getting sunburned. Don't listen to your brother. Please, Lily, don't believe there was anything sinister about Lynda's death. Your brother is a cop. Cops think everyone has ulterior motives, but I don't. I love you. I want you to be happy, with me."

Savich, who'd been finishing off his lasagna during this impassioned speech, looked only mildly interested, as if he were attending a play. He laid down his fork and said, "Tennyson, how long has your dad been on the board of the Eureka Art Museum?"

"What? Oh, I don't know, for years, I suppose. I've never really paid any attention. What does that have to do with anything?"

"You see," Savich continued, "at first we couldn't figure out why you would want to marry Lily if your motive was to kill her. For what? Then we realized you knew about our grandmother's paintings. Lily owns eight Sarah Elliotts, worth a lot of money, as you very well know."

For the first time, Savich felt a mild surge of alarm. Tennyson was a man nearing the edge. He was furious, his face red, his jaw working. He readied himself for an attack.

But what Tennyson did was bang his knife handle on the table, once, twice, then a really hard third time. "I did not marry Lily to get her grandmother's paintings! That's absurd. Get out of my house!"

Lily slowly rose to her feet.

"No, Lily, not you. Please, sit down. Listen to me, you must. My father and I are familiar with the excellent work of the folk at the Eureka Art Museum. They have a splendid reputation. When you told me your grandmother was Sarah Elliott—"

"But you already knew, Tennyson. You knew before you met me that first time. And then you acted so surprised when I told you. You acted so pleased that I had inherited some of her incredible talent. You wanted so much to have her paintings here, in Northern California. You wanted them here so you could be close to them, so you could control them. So that when I was dead, you wouldn't have any difficulty getting your hands on them. Or maybe your father wanted the paintings close? Which, Tennyson?"

"Lily, be quiet, that's not true, none of it. The paintings are great art. Why should the Art Institute of Chicago have them when you live here now? Also, administration of the paintings is much easier when they're exhibited locally."

"What administration?"

Tennyson shrugged. "There are phone calls coming in all the time, questions about loaning the paintings out, about selling them to collectors, the schedule for ongoing minor restoration, about our approval on the replacement of a frame. Endless questions about tax papers. Lots of things."

"There was very little of what you just described before I married you, Tennyson. There was only one contract with the museum to sign every year, nothing else. Why haven't you said anything about any administration to me? You make it sound like an immense amount of work."

Was that sarcasm? Savich wondered, rather hoping that it was.

"You weren't well, Lily. I wasn't about to burden you with any of that."

Suddenly, the strangest thing happened. Lily saw her husband as a grayish shadow, hovering without substance, his mouth moving but nothing really coming out. Not a man, just a shadow, and shadows couldn't hurt you. Lily smiled as she said, "As Dillon said, I'm very rich, Tennyson."

Savich saw that his brother-in-law was trying desperately to keep himself calm, to keep himself logical in his arguments, not to get defensive, not to let Lily see what he really was. It was fascinating. Could a man be that good a liar, that convincing an actor? Savich wished he knew.

Tennyson said, "It's always been my understanding that you simply hold the paintings in a sort of trust. That they aren't yours, that you're merely their guardian until you die and one of your children takes over."

"But you've been in charge of their administration all these months," Lily said. "How could you not know that they were mine, completely mine, no trust involved?"

"I did believe that, I tell you. No one ever said anything different, not even the curator, Mr. Monk. You've met him, Lily, up front, so pleased to have the paintings here."

Savich sipped at the hot tea Mrs. Scruggins had poured into his cup. "None of us hold the paintings in trust," he said. "They're ours, outright." He knew Mrs. Scruggins was listening to everything, forming opinions. He didn't mind it a bit. Maybe she'd have something more to say to him or to Sherlock when this little dinner party was over. "If Lily wants to, she can sell one or two or all of the paintings. They're worth about one million dollars each. Maybe more."

Tennyson looked stunned. "I—I never realized," he said, and now he sounded a bit frantic.

"Difficult not to," Lily said. "You're not a stupid man, Tennyson. Surely Mr. Monk told you what they're worth. When you found out I was Sarah Elliott's granddaughter, it would have been nothing at all for you to find out that she willed them to me. You saw me as the way to get to those paintings. You must have rubbed your hands together. I left everything in my will to Beth, at your urging, Tennyson, if you'll remember, and I named you the executor."

"As it happened," Savich said, "Beth did predecease Lily. Who inherits?"

"Tennyson. My husband." She continued after a moment, so bitter she was nearly choking on it. "How easy I made everything for you. What happened? Big money troubles? You needed me out of the way, fast?"

Tennyson was nearly over the edge now. "No, no, listen to me. I suppose I saw the paintings as your grandmother's, nothing more than that. Valuable things that needed some oversight, particularly after you became so ill. All right, I was willing to do that work. Please, Lily, believe me. When you told me that she was your grandmother, I was very surprised and pleased for you. Then I dismissed it. Lily, I didn't marry you for your grandmother's paintings. I swear to you I didn't. I married you because I love you, I loved Beth. That's it. My father—no, I don't believe there could possibly be anything there. You've got to believe me."

"Tennyson," Lily said, her voice low, soothing, "do you know I've never been depressed in my life until I married you?"

"Before Beth's death, you had no reason to be depressed."

"Well, maybe I did. Didn't I tell you a bit about my first husband?"

"Yes, he was horrible, but you survived him. Lily, it was completely different when your daughter was killed by a hit-and-run driver. It's only natural that you'd be overcome with grief, that you would experience profound depression."

"Even after seven months?"

"The mind is a strange instrument, unpredictable. It doesn't always behave the way we would like it to. I've prayed and prayed for your full recovery. I agree it's been taking you a long time to recover but, Lily, you'll get well now, I know it."

"Yes," she said very slowly and pushed back her chair. "Yes, I know I'll get well now." She felt her stitches pull, a tug that made her want to bend over, but she didn't. "Yes, Tennyson," she said, "I fully intend to get well now. Completely well."

She pressed her palms flat on the table. "I will also love Beth for the rest of my life, and I will know sadness at her loss and grief until I die, but I will come to grips with it. I will bear it. I will pray that it will slowly ease into the past, that I won't fall into that black depression again. I will face life now and I will gain my bearings. Yes, Tennyson, I will get well now because, you see, I'm leaving you. Tonight."

He rose so quickly his chair slammed down to the floor. "No, you can't leave me . . . Lily, no! It's your brother. I wish my father hadn't called him; I wish Savich hadn't come here to ruin everything. He's filled your mind with lies. He's made you turn on me. There's no proof of anything at all. No, none of it's true. Please, Lily, don't leave me."

"Tennyson," Lily said very quietly now, looking directly at him, "what sort of pills have you been feeding me these last seven months?"

He howled, literally howled, a desperate, frightened sound of rage and hopelessness. He was panting hard when he said, "I tried to make you well. I tried, and now you've decided to believe this jerk of a brother and his wife and you're leaving me. I've been giving you Elavil!"

Lily nodded. "Actually, there doesn't seem to be any solid proof to haul you to the sheriff. The sheriff is something of a joke anyway, isn't he? When I remember how he tried so hard to apprehend Beth's killer."

"I know he did the best he could. If you'd been with Beth, maybe you would have made a better witness, but you—"

She ignored his words and said, "If we find proof, then even Sheriff Bozo will have to lock you away, Tennyson—no matter what you or Daddy say, no matter how much money you've put in his pocket, no matter how many votes you got for him—until we manage to get some competent law enforcement in Hemlock Bay. The truth of the matter is, I would leave you even if you didn't kill your first wife, if you hadn't, in truth, tried to kill me, because, Tennyson, you've lied to me; from the very beginning you lied to me. You used Beth's death to make me feel the most profound guilt. You milked it, manipulated me—you're still doing it—and you very likely drugged me to make me depressed, to make me feel even more at fault. I wasn't at fault, Tennyson. Someone killed Beth. I didn't. I realize that now. Were you planning on killing me even as you slid the ring on my finger?"

He was holding his head in his hands, shaking his head back and forth, not looking at anyone now.

"I found myself wondering today, Tennyson—did you kill Beth, too?"

His head came up, fast. "Kill Beth? No!"

"She was my heir. If I died, then the paintings would be hers. No, surely even you couldn't be that evil. Your father could, maybe your mother could, but not you, I don't think. But then again, I've never been good at picking men. Look at my pathetic track record—two tries and just look what happened. Yes, I'm obviously rotten at it. Hey, maybe it's my bookie genes getting in the way of good sense. No, you couldn't have killed or had Beth killed. Maybe we'll find something on your daddy. We'll see.

"Good-bye, Tennyson. I can't begin to tell you what I think of you."

Both Savich and Sherlock remained silent, looking at the man and woman facing each other across the length of the dining table. Tennyson was as white as a bleached shroud, the pulse in his neck pounding wildly. His fingers clutched the edge of the table. He looked like a man beyond himself, beyond all that he knew or understood.

As for Lily, she looked calm, wonderfully calm. She didn't look to be in any particular discomfort. She said, "Dillon and Sherlock will pack all my things while you're at your office tomorrow, Tennyson. Tonight, the three of us are going to stay in Eureka." She turned, felt the mild pulling in her side again, and added, "Please don't destroy my drawing and art supplies, Tennyson, or else I'll have to ask my brother or sister-in-law to break your face. They want to very badly as it is."

She nodded to him, then turned. "Dillon, I'll be ready to leave in ten minutes."

Head up, back straight, as if she didn't have stitches in her side, she left the dining room. Lily saw Mrs. Scruggins standing just inside the kitchen door. Mrs. Scruggins smiled at her as she walked briskly past, saying over her shoulder, "It was an excellent dinner, Mrs. Scruggins. My brother really liked it. Thank you for saving my life seven months ago. I will miss you and your kindness."

# EIGHT

*Eureka, California*
*The Mermaid's Tail*

Lily swallowed a pain pill and looked at herself in the mirror. She'd looked better, no doubt about that. She sighed as she thought back over the months and wondered yet again what had happened to her. Had she looked different when she'd first arrived in Hemlock Bay? She'd been so full of hope, both she and Beth finally free of Jack Crane, on their own, happy. She remembered how they'd walked hand in hand down Main Street, stopping at Scooters Bakery to buy a chocolate croissant for Beth and a raisin scone for herself. She hadn't realized then that she would soon marry another man she'd believe with all her heart loved both her and Beth, and this one would gouge eleven months out of her life.

Fool.

She'd married yet another man who would have rejoiced at her death, who was prepared to bury her with tears running down his face, a stirring eulogy coming out of his mouth, and joy in his heart.

Two husbands down—never, never again would she ever look at a man who appeared even mildly interested in her. Fact was, she was really bad when it came to choosing men. And the question that had begun to gnaw at her surfaced again. Was Tennyson responsible for Beth's death?

Lily didn't think so—she'd been honest the night before about that—but it had happened so quickly and no one had seen anything at all useful. Could Tennyson have been driving that car? And then the awful depression had smashed her, had made her want to lie in a coffin and pull down the lid.

Beth was gone. Forever. Lily pictured her little girl's face—a replica of her father's, but finer, softer—so beautiful, that precious little face she saw now only in her mind. She'd turned six the week before she died. Beth hadn't been evil to the bone like her father. She'd been all that was innocent and loving, always telling her mother any- and everything until . . . Lily raised her head and looked at herself again in the mirror. Until what? She thought back to the week before Beth was killed. She had been different, sort of furtive, wary—maybe even scared.

Scared? Beth? No, that didn't make any sense. But still, Beth had been different before she died.

No, not died. Beth had been killed. By a hit-and-run driver. The pain settled heavily in Lily's heart as she wondered if she would ever know the truth.

She shook her head, drank more water from the tap. Her brother and Sherlock had left, after she'd assured them at least a half dozen times that she still felt calm, didn't hurt at all. She was fine, go, go, pack up her things in Hemlock Bay. She hoped Tennyson hadn't trashed her drawing supplies.

She drew a deep, clean breath. Yes, she wanted her drawing supplies today, as soon as possible. She wanted to hold her #2 red sable brush again, but it would be foolish to buy another one just to use today. No, she'd buy only a small sampler set of pens and pen points, inexpensive ones because it didn't really matter. Maybe she'd get a Speedball cartooning set, like the one her folks had given her when she'd wanted to try cartooning so many years before. Those pens would still feel familiar in her hand. And a bottle of India ink, some standard-size, twenty-pound typing paper, durable paper that would last, no matter how many times it was shoved into envelopes or worked on by her and the editors. Yes, some nice bond paper, not more than a hundred sheets. Usually, since she did political cartoons, she used strips of paper cut from larger sheets of special artist paper, thicker than a postcard—bristol board, it was called, well suited for brushwork. And one bottle of Liquid Paper. She could see herself—not more than an hour from now—drawing those sharp, pale lines that would become the man of the hour, Senator No Wrinkles Remus, the soon-to-be president of the United States, from that fine state of West Dementia, where the good senator has managed to divide his state into halves, to conduct the ultimate experiment with gun control. One half of the state has complete gun control, as strict as in England; the other half of West Dementia has no gun control at all. He gives an impassioned speech to the state legislature, with the blessing of the governor, whom he's blackmailed for taking money from a contractor who is also his nephew: "One year, that's all we ask," Remus says, waving his arms to embrace all of them. "One year and we'll know once and for all what the answer is."

And what happens in the west of West Dementia is that criminals auction off areas to one another since civilians aren't allowed to own any device that shoots a bullet out of a barrel. Criminals break-and-enter at their leisure, whenever the spirit moves them. Houses, banks, gas stations, 7-Elevens, nothing is safe.

In east West Dementia, every sort of gun abounds, from sleek pistols that fire one round a minute to behemoths that kick out eight hundred zillion rounds a second. There are simply no limits at all. Because of the endless supply, guns are really cheap. What happens surprises everyone: robbery stats go down nearly seventy percent after a good dozen would-be robbers are killed breaking in—to homes, banks, filling stations, 7-Elevens.

On the other side of it, killing abounds. Everything that moves, and doesn't move, gets shot—deer, rabbits, cars, people. Some people even take to target-shooting in the rivers. Many trout, it is said, die from gunshot wounds.

There are rumors of payoffs from both the National Rifle Association and the Mafia to No Wrinkles Remus, but like his name, no matter what he does—or people believe he does—that face of his remains smooth and absolutely trustworthy.

Lily was grinning like a madwoman. She rubbed her hands together. She wanted to draw *No Wrinkles Remus*—now, right this minute, as soon as she could get a pen between her fingers. She didn't need a drawing table, the small circular Victorian table in her room would be perfect. The sun was coming in at exactly the right angle.

She didn't want to wait. Lily grabbed her purse, her leather jacket, and headed out of the bed-and-breakfast. Mrs. Blade, standing behind the small counter downstairs, waved her on. Lily didn't know Eureka well, but she knew to go to Wallace Street. A whole bunch of artists lived over in the waterfront section of town, and a couple of them ran art supply stores.

The day was cloudy, nearly cold enough to see your breath, a chilly breeze swirling about in the fallen autumn leaves that strengthened the salty ocean taste when you breathed in. She managed to snag a taxi across the street that was letting off an old man in front of an apartment building.

The driver was Ukrainian, had lived in Eureka for six years, and his high-schooler son liked to doodle, even on toilet paper, he said, which made you wonder what sort of poisoning you could get using that toilet paper. He knew where to go.

It was Sol Arthur's art supply shop. She was in and out in thirty minutes, smiling from ear to ear as she shifted the wrapped packages in her arms. She had maybe eleven dollars left in her purse—goodness, eleven whole dollars left in the world. She wondered what had happened to her credit cards. She would ask Dillon to deal with it.

She stood on the curb looking up and down the street. No way would a taxi magically appear now even though she was ready to part with another four dollars from her stash. No, no taxi. Such good lightning luck didn't strike twice. A bus, she thought, watching one slowly huff toward her. The bed-and-breakfast wasn't all that far from here, and the bus was heading in the right direction. She jaywalked, but not before she was sure that no cars were coming from either direction. There weren't a whole lot of people on the street.

No Wrinkles Remus is looking particularly handsome and wicked, right there, full-blown in her mind again. He looks annoyed when a colleague hits on a staffer Remus himself fancies; he feels absolute joy when he discovers that the wife of a senator cheated on her husband with one of his former senior aides.

She was singing when the bus—twenty years old if not older, belching smoke—lumbered toward her. She saw the driver, an old coot, grinning at her. He had on headphones and was chair-dancing to the music. Maybe she was the only passenger he'd seen in a while.

She climbed on board, banging her packages about as she found change in her wallet. When she turned to find a seat, she saw that the bus was empty.

"Not many folk out today?"

He grinned at her and pulled off his headphones. She repeated her question. He said, "Nah, all of 'em down at the cemetery for the big burying."

"Whose big burying?"

"Ferdy Malloy, the minister at the Baptist church. Kicked it last Friday."

She'd been lying in the hospital last Friday, not feeling so hot.

"Natural causes, I hope?"

"You can think that if you want, but everyone knows that his missus probably booted him to the other side. Tough old broad is Mabel, tougher than Ferdy, and mean. No one dared to ask for an autopsy, and so they're planting Ferdy in the ground right about now."

"Well," Lily said, then couldn't think of another thing. "Oh, yes, I'm at The Mermaid's Tail. Do you go near there?"

"Ain't nobody on board to tell me not to. I'll take you right to the front door. Watch that third step, though, board's rotted."

"Thank you, I'll be careful."

The driver put his headphones back on and began bouncing up and down in the seat. He stopped two blocks down, in front of Rover's Drive-In with the best hamburgers west of the Sillow River, sandwiched next to a storefront that advertised three justices of the peace, who were also notaries, on duty 24/7.

Lily closed her eyes. The bus started up again. No Wrinkles Remus was in her mind again, playing another angle.

"Hey."

She looked up to see a young man swinging into the seat next to her. He simply lifted off the packages, set them on the seat opposite, and sat down.

For a moment, Lily was simply too surprised to think. She stared at the young man, no older than twenty, his black hair long, greasy, and tied back in a ratty ponytail. He had three silver hoops marching up his left ear.

He was wearing opaque sunglasses, an Orioles cap on his head, turned backward, and a roomy black leather jacket.

"My packages," she said, cocking her head to one side. "Why did you put them over there?"

He grinned at her, and she saw a gold tooth toward the back of his mouth.

"You're awful pretty. I wanted to sit next to you. I wanted to get real close to you."

"No, I'm not particularly pretty. I'd like you to move. Lots of seat choice, since the bus is empty."

"Nope, I'm staying right here. Maybe I'll even get a little closer. Like I said, you're real pretty."

Lily looked up at the bus driver, but he was really into his rock 'n' roll, bouncing so heavily on the seat that the bus was swerving a bit to the left, then back to the right.

Lily didn't want trouble, she really didn't. "All right," she said and smiled at him. "I'll move."

"I don't think so," he said, his voice barely a whisper now, and he grabbed her arm to hold her still.

"Let go of me, buster, now."

"I don't think so. You know, I really don't want to hurt you. It's too bad because, like I said, you're real pretty. A shame, but hey, I need money, you know?"

"You want to rob me?"

"Yeah, don't worry I'll do anything else. I just want your wallet." But he pulled a switchblade out of his inside jacket pocket, pressed a small button, and a very sharp blade flew out, long and thin, glittering.

She was afraid now, her heart pumping, bile rising in her throat. "Put the knife away. I'll give you all my money. I don't have much, but I'll give you all I've got."

He didn't answer because he saw that the bus was slowing for the next stop. He said, low, "Sorry, no time for the money."

He was going to kill her. The knife was coming right at her chest. She tightened, felt the stitches straining, but it didn't matter.

"You fool," she said, and drove her elbow right into his Adam's apple, then right under his chin, knocking his head back, cutting off his breath. Still he held the knife, not four inches from her chest.

*Twist left, make yourself a smaller target.*

She turned, then did a right forearm hammer, thumb down smashing the inside of his right forearm.

*Attack the person, not the weapon.*

She grabbed his wrist with her left hand and did a right back forearm hammer to his throat. He grabbed his throat, gagging and wheezing for breath, and she slammed her fist into his chest, right over his heart. She grabbed his wrist and felt the knife slide out of his fingers, heard it thunk hard on the floor of the bus and slide beneath the seat in front of them.

The guy was in big trouble, couldn't breathe, and she said, "Don't you ever come near me again, you bastard." And she smashed the flat of her palm against his ear.

He yelled, but it only came out as a gurgle since he still couldn't draw a decent breath.

Only fifteen seconds had passed.

The bus stopped right in front of The Mermaid's Tail. The driver waved to her in the rearview mirror, still listening to his music, still chair-dancing. She didn't know what to do. Call the cops? Then it was taken out of her hands. The young man lurched up, knowing he was in deep trouble, scooped up his knife, waved it toward the bus driver, who was now staring back at the two of them wide-eyed, no longer dancing. He waved the knife at her once, then ran to the front of the bus, jumped to the ground, and was running fast down the street, turning quickly into an alley.

The bus driver yelled.

"It's okay," Lily said, gathering her bags together. "He was a mugger. I'm all right."

"We need to get the cops."

The last thing Lily wanted was to have to deal with the cops. The guy was gone. She felt suddenly very weak; her heart was pounding hard and loud. But her shoulders were straight. She was taller than she'd been just five minutes before. It hadn't been much more than five minutes when she'd first gotten onto that empty bus, and then the young guy had come on and sat down beside her.

It didn't matter that she felt like all her stitches were pulling, that her ribs ached and there were jabs of pain. She'd done it. She'd saved herself. She'd flattened the guy with the knife. She hadn't forgotten all the moves her brother had taught her after she'd finally told him about Jack and what he'd done.

Dillon had said, squeezing her so hard she thought her ribs would cave in, "Lily, I'm not about to let you ever be helpless again. No more victim, ever." And he'd taught her how to fight, with two-year-old Beth shrieking and clapping as she looked on, swinging her teddy bear by its leg.

But he hadn't been able to teach her for real—how to handle the bubbling fear that pulsed through her body when that knife was a finger-length away. But she'd dealt with the fear, the brain-numbing shutdown. She'd done it.

She walked, straight and tall, her stitches pulling a bit now, into The Mermaid's Tail.

"Hello," she called out, smiling at Mrs. Blade, who was working a crossword puzzle behind the counter.

"You look like you won the lottery, Mrs. Frasier. Hey, do you know a five-letter word for a monster assassin?"

"Hmmm. It could be me, you know, but Lily is only four letters. Sorry, Mrs. Blade." Lily laughed and hauled her packages up the stairs.

"I've got it," Mrs. Blade called out. "The monster assassin is a 'slayer.' You know, *Buffy the Vampire Slayer*."

"That's six letters, Mrs. Blade."

"Well, drat."

Upstairs in her room, Lily arranged the small Victorian table at just the right angle to the bright sun. She carefully unwrapped all her supplies and arranged them. She knew she was on an adrenaline high, but it didn't matter. She felt wonderful. Then she stopped cold.

Her Sarah Elliott paintings. She had to go right now to the Eureka Art Museum and make sure the paintings, all eight of them, were still there. How could she have thought only of drawing Remus?

No, she was being ridiculous. She could simply call Mr. Monk, ask him about her paintings. But what if he wasn't trustworthy—no one else had proved the least trustworthy to date—he could lie to her.

Tennyson or his father could have stolen them last night after they'd left the house. Mr. Monk could have helped them.

No, someone would have notified her if the paintings were gone. Or maybe they would call Elcott Frasier or Tennyson. They were her paintings, but she was sick, wasn't she? Another suicide attempt. Incapable of dealing with something so stressful.

She was out the door again in three minutes.

# NINE

The Eureka Art Museum took up an entire block on West Clayton Street. It was a splendid old Victorian mansion surrounded by scores of ancient, fat oak trees madly dropping their fall leaves in the chilly morning breeze. What with all the budget cuts, the leaves rested undisturbed, a thick red, yellow, and gold blanket spread all around the museum and sidewalks.

Lily paid the taxi driver five dollars including a good tip because the guy had frayed cuffs on his shirt, hoping she had enough cash left for admission. The old gentleman at the entrance told her they didn't charge anything, but any contributions would be gracefully accepted. "Not gratefully?"

"Maybe both," he said and gave her a big grin. All she had to give him in return was a grin to match and a request he tell Mr. Monk that Mrs. Frasier was here.

She'd seen the paintings here only once, during a brief visit, before the special room was built, right after she'd married Tennyson. She'd met Mr. Monk, the curator, who had gorgeous black eyes and looked intense and hungry, and two young staffers, both with PhDs, who'd just shrugged and said there were no jobs in any of the prestigious museums, so what could you do but move to Eureka? At least, they said, big smiles on their faces, the Sarah Elliott paintings gave the place class and respectability.

It wasn't a large museum, but nonetheless, they had fashioned an entirely separate room for Sarah Elliott's eight paintings, and they'd done it well. White walls, perfect lighting, highly polished oak floor, cushion-covered benches in the center of the room to sit on and appreciate.

Lily stood there for a very long time in the middle of the room, turning slowly to look at each painting. She'd been overwhelmed when her grandmother's executor had sent them to her where she was waiting for them in the office of the director of the Art Institute of Chicago. Finally, she'd actually touched each one, held each one in her hands. Every one of them was special to her, each a painting she'd mentioned to her grandmother that she loved especially, and her grandmother hadn't forgotten. Her favorite, she discovered, was still *The Swan Song*—a soft, pale wash of colors, lightly veiling an old man lying in the middle of a very neat bed, his hands folded over his chest. He had little hair left on his head and little flesh as well, stretched so taut you could see the blood vessels beneath it. The look on his face was beatific. He was smiling and singing to a young girl, slight, ethereal, who stood beside the bed, her head cocked to one side. Lily felt gooseflesh rise on her arms. She felt tears start to her eyes.

She loved this painting. She knew it belonged in a museum, but she also knew that it was hers—hers—and she decided in that moment that she wanted to see it every day of her life, to be reminded of the endless pulse of life with its sorrowful endings, its joyous beginnings, the joining of the two. This one would stay with her, if she could make that happen. The value of each of the paintings still overwhelmed her.

She wiped her eyes.

"Is it you, Mrs. Frasier? Oh my, we heard that you had been in an accident, that you were in serious condition in the hospital. You're all right? So soon? You look a bit pale. Would you like to sit down? May I get you a glass of water?"

She turned slowly to see Mr. Monk standing in the doorway of the small Sarah Elliott room, with its elegant painted sign over the oak door. He looked so intense, like a taut bowstring, he seemed ready to hum with it. He was dressed in a lovely charcoal gray wool suit, a white shirt, and a dark blue tie.

"Mr. Monk, it's good to see you again." She grinned at him, her tears dried now, and said, "Actually, the rumors of my condition were exaggerated. I'm fine; you don't have to do a thing for me."

"Ah, I'm delighted to hear it. You're here. Is Dr. Frasier here as well? Is there some problem?"

Lily said, "No, Mr. Monk, there's no problem. The past months have been difficult, but everything is all right now. Oh, yes, which of these paintings is your favorite?"

"*The Decision*," Mr. Monk said without hesitation.

"I like that one very much as well," Lily said. "But don't you find it the least bit depressing?"

"Depressing? Certainly not. I don't get depressed, Mrs. Frasier."

Lily said, "I remember I told my grandmother I loved that one when I'd just lost a lot of money on a point spread between the Giants and Dallas. I was sixteen at the time, and I do remember that I was despondent. She laughed and loaned me ten dollars. I've never forgotten that. Oh, yes, I paid her back the next week when a whole bunch of fools bet New Orleans would beat San Francisco by twelve."

"Are you talking about some sort of sporting events, Mrs. Frasier?"

"Well, yes. Football, actually." She smiled at him. "I am here to tell you I will be leaving the area, Mr. Monk, moving back to Washington, D.C. I will be taking the Sarah Elliott paintings with me."

He looked at her like she was mad. He fanned his hands in front of him, as if to ward her off. "But surely, Mrs. Frasier, you're pleased with their display, how we're taking such good care of them; and the restoration work is minor and nothing to concern you—"

She lightly laid her fingers on his forearm. "No, Mr. Monk, it looks to me like you've done a splendid job. But I'm moving, and the paintings go where I go."

"But Washington, D.C., doesn't need any more beautiful art! They have so many beautiful things that they're sinking in it, beautiful things that are stuck in basements, never seen. They don't need any more!"

"I'm very sorry, Mr. Monk."

Those gorgeous dark eyes of his glittered. "Very well, Mrs. Frasier, but it's obvious to me that you haven't discussed this with Dr. Frasier. I'm sorry but I cannot release any of the paintings to you. He is their administrator."

"What does that mean? You know very well the paintings are mine."

"Well, yes, but it's Dr. Frasier who's made all the decisions, who's directed every detail. Also, Mrs. Frasier, it's common knowledge here that you haven't been well—"

"Lily, what are you doing out of bed? Why are you here?"

Dillon and Sherlock stood behind Mr. Monk, and neither of them looked very pleased.

She smiled, saying only, "I'm here to tell Mr. Monk that the paintings go where I go, and in this case, it's all the way to Washington, D.C. Unfortunately, he says that everyone knows I'm crazy and that Dr. Frasier is the one who controls everything to do with the paintings—and so Mr. Monk won't release them to me."

"Now, Mrs. Frasier, I didn't quite mean that."

Savich lightly tapped him on the shoulder, and when Mr. Monk turned, in utter confusion, he said, "The paintings can't be released to my sister? Would you care to explain that to us, Mr. Monk? I'm Dillon Savich, Mrs. Frasier's brother, and this is my wife. Now, what is all this about?"

Mr. Monk looked desperate. He took a step back. "You don't understand. Mrs. Frasier isn't mentally competent, that's what I was told, and thus the paintings are all controlled by Dr. Frasier. Appropriate, naturally, since he is her husband. When we heard she'd been in an accident, an accident that she herself caused, there were some who thought she was dying and thus Dr. Frasier would inherit the paintings and then they would never leave the museum."

"I'm not dead, Mr. Monk."

"I can see that you're not, Mrs. Frasier, but the fact is that you aren't as well as you should be to have charge of such expensive and unique paintings."

Savich said, "I assure you that Mrs. Frasier is mentally competent and is legally entitled to do whatever she wishes to with the paintings. Unless you have some court order to the contrary?"

Mr. Monk looked momentarily flummoxed, then, "A court order! Yes, that's it, a court order is what's required."

"Why?" said Savich.

"Well, a court could decide whether she's capable of making decisions of this magnitude."

Sherlock patted his shoulder. "Hmm, nice suit. I'm sorry, Mr. Monk, as this seems to be quite upsetting to you, but she is under no such obligation to you. I suppose you could try to get her declared incompetent, but you would lose, and I'm sure it would create quite a stir in the local papers."

"Oh, no, I wouldn't do that. What I mean is that I suppose then that everything is all right, but you understand, I have to call Dr. Frasier. He has been dealing with everything. I haven't spoken to Mrs. Frasier even once over all the months the paintings have been here."

Savich pulled out his wallet, showed Mr. Monk his ID, and said, "Why don't we go to your office and make that phone call?"

Of course Savich had shown Mr. Monk his FBI shield. He swallowed, looked at Lily like he wanted to shoot her, and said, "Yes, of course."

"Good," Savich said. "We can also discuss all the details of how they'll be shipped, the insurance, the crating, all those pesky little details Dr. Frasier doesn't have to deal with anymore. By the way, Mr. Monk, I do know what I'm doing since I also own eight Sarah Elliott paintings myself."

"Would you like to go now, Mr. Savich?"

Savich nodded, then said over his shoulder as he escorted Mr. Monk from that small, perfect room, "Sherlock, you stay here with Lily, make sure she sits down and rests. Mr. Monk and I will finalize matters. Come along, sir."

"I hope the poor man doesn't cry," Lily said. "They built this special room, did a fine job of exhibiting the paintings. I think that Elcott and Charlotte Frasier donated the money to build the room. Wasn't that kind of them?"

"Yes. You know, Lily, many people have enjoyed the paintings over the past year. Now people in Washington can enjoy them for a while. You need to think about where you want the paintings housed. But we can take our time there, no rush, let people convince you they're the best.

"Oh, Lily, don't feel guilty. There are a whole lot of people there who have never seen these particular Sarah Elliott paintings."

"Truth be told, I'm mighty relieved they're all present and accounted for and I'm not standing here looking at blank walls because someone stole the paintings. That's why I came, Sherlock. I realized that since Tennyson married me for the paintings, maybe they were already gone."

Sherlock patted a cushion and waited until Lily eased carefully down beside her. "We didn't want to wait either." She paused to look around. "Such beauty. And it's in your genes, Lily, both yours and Dillon's. You're very lucky. You draw cartoons that give people great pleasure, and Dillon whittles the most exquisite pieces. He whittled Sean, newly born, in the softest rosewood. Whenever I look at that piece, touch it, I feel the most profound gratitude that Dillon is in my life.

"Now, I'm going to get all emotional and that won't help anything. Did I have a point to make? Oh yes, such different aspects of those splendid talent genes from your grandmother."

"What about your talent, Sherlock? You play the piano beautifully.

You could have been a concert pianist, if it hadn't been for your sister's death. I want to listen to you play when we get back to Washington."

"Yes, I'll play for you." Sherlock added, without pause, "You know, Lily, I was very afraid that Tennyson and his father had stolen the paintings as well, and you hadn't been notified because you'd been too ill to deal with it."

"I suppose they had other plans. All of this happened very quickly."

"Yes, they did have time, but don't you see? If the paintings were suddenly gone, they would have looked so guilty San Quentin would have opened its doors and ushered them right on in. I suppose they were waiting to sell them off when you were dead and they legally belonged to Tennyson."

"Dead." Lily said the word again, then once more, sounding it out. "It isn't easy to believe that someone wants you dead so they can have what you own. That's really low."

"Yes, it is."

"I feel shock that Tennyson betrayed me, probably his father as well, but I don't want to wring my hands and cry about it. Nope, what I really want to do is belt Tennyson in the nose, maybe kick him hard in his ribs, too."

Sherlock hugged her, very lightly. "Good for you. Now, how do you feel, really?"

"Calm, a bit of pain, nothing debilitating. I believed I loved him, Sherlock, believed I wanted to spend the rest of my life with him. I trusted him, and I trusted him with Beth."

"I know, Lily. I know."

Lily got ahold of herself, tried to smile. "Oh yes, I've got something amazing to tell you. Remus was dancing in my head this morning, yelling at me so loud that I went out and bought art supplies. Then, strange thing, I get on this empty city bus to go back to The Mermaid's Tail and this young guy tries to mug me."

Sherlock blinked, her mouth open.

Lily laughed. "Finally I've managed to surprise you so much you can't think of anything to say."

"I don't like this, Lily. Tell me exactly what happened."

But Mr. Monk appeared in the doorway. "I will contact our lawyers and have them prepare papers for your signature. I've detailed to Mr. Savich how the paintings will be packed and crated in preparation to be

shipped to Washington. You will need to inform us of their destination so
that we can make arrangements with the people at the other end. There
will be two guards as well for the trip. It's quite an elaborate process,
necessary to keep them completely safe. I will phone you when the papers
are ready. Did you plan to leave the area soon?"

"Fairly soon, Mr. Monk." Lily rose slowly, her stitches pulling, aching
more now, and took his hand. "I'm sorry, but I really can't leave them here."

"It's a pity. Dr. Frasier said on the phone that you were divorcing him
and that he had no more say in anything."

"I'm relieved he didn't try anything underhanded," Lily said.

Mr. Monk looked profoundly uncomfortable at that. "He's a fine
man, and so are his esteemed father and mother."

"I understand that many people think that. Yes, we're divorcing, Mr.
Monk."

"Ah, such a pity. You've been married such a short time. And you lost
your little girl a few months ago. I do hope you're making this decision
with a clear head."

"You still think my mental condition is in question, Mr. Monk?"

Mr. Monk seemed to pump himself up. He swallowed and said, "Well,
I think that maybe you're acting in haste, not really thinking things through.
And here you are divorcing poor Dr. Frasier, who seems to love you and
wants only the best for you. Of course, Mrs. Frasier, this is a very bad thing
for me and for the museum."

"Well, these things happen, don't they? And I'd have to say that Dr.
Frasier loves my paintings, sir, not me. I'm staying at The Mermaid's Tail
here in Eureka. Please call when I can finalize all this."

Lily's last view of Mr. Monk was of him standing in the doorway to
the Sarah Elliott room, hunched in on himself, looking like he'd just lost
all his money in a poker game. The museum had run fine before Sarah Elliott's paintings had arrived, and it would do so after they went away.

When they were walking down the stone steps of the museum, Savich
on one side of Lily, her arm resting heavily on his, Sherlock on the other,
Savich said, not looking at her, "I was wondering if Tennyson would be
obstructive when we called him up. To be honest, if it had been you,
Lily—by yourself on the phone—he would have been, no doubt in my
mind about that. But he couldn't this time, not with two of us federal
agents and one of them your brother."

He stopped abruptly, turned, and grasped Lily's shoulders in his big hands. "I'm not pleased with you, Lily. You should have let Sherlock and me take care of all this. I'll bet you pulled your stitches and now your belly aches like you've been punched."

"Yes," Sherlock said, "Dillon's right. You look like you're ready to fall over."

Lily smiled at her sister-in-law—tall, fine-boned, strong, capable. She had curly hair, a fire of autumn color, and the sweetest smile. Lily bet she could take down a guy three times her size. And she played the piano beautifully. She'd known from the moment they'd first met at her and Dillon's wedding that Sherlock's love for Dillon was steady and absolute. Beth had been three years old at the time, so excited to see her uncle Dillon, and so proud of her new patent-leather shoes. Lily swallowed, got herself together. She said, "Do you know that you and Dillon could finish each other's sentences? Now, don't fret, either of you. I am feeling a bit on the shaky side, but I can hold on until we get back to the inn." She hugged him tight, then stepped back. "You know what, Dillon? I've decided I'm going to check into my own credit card situation."

"What does that mean?"

Lily smiled. He helped her into the backseat, gently placed the pillow over her stomach, and fastened her seat belt. She lightly touched her fingertips to his cheek. "I'm glad you came to the museum. I don't think I had enough money to pay for a taxi back to the B-and-B."

Savich shook his head at her as he slipped his hand beneath the seat belt to make sure it wouldn't press too hard against her middle, got in the driver's seat, and drove off.

"Now then, Lily," Sherlock said, turning in her seat. "You can't put it off any longer. Dillon will want to hear all about this, too. I want you to tell us about the mugger who attacked you on that empty bus this morning. No more than two hours ago."

Savich nearly drove into a fire hydrant.

THEY were eating lunch in a small Mexican restaurant, The Toasted Taco, on Chambers Street, down the block from The Mermaid's Tail, Lily having decided she was starving more than she was aching.

"Good salsa," Lily said and dipped in another tortilla chip and stuffed it in her mouth. "That's a sure sign that the food will be okay. Goodness, I don't think I've ever been so hungry in my life."

Savich said, "Talk."

She told them about the bus driver who'd explained to her the bus was empty because of the big burying and was having a fine time chair-dancing while he drove, headphones turned up high, and about the young man with three earrings in his left ear, the switchblade that was sharp and silver and nearly went into her heart.

Savich blew out a big breath, picked up a tortilla chip, and absently chewed on it. "I suppose it's occurred to you it may not have been a mugger."

"He talked like one, maybe, I'm not sure since I've never been mugged before. Then he ruined it by pulling this switchblade knife. One thing I'm absolutely sure of—there was death in his eyes. And you know what? I knew all the way to my stomach lining it was the end of the line. But then I went after him, Dillon, wrecked him good—all the moves you taught me. I could hear your voice telling me things, 'Make yourself as small as possible,' stuff like that. I hammered him—my hand a tight fist and whap! Then I hammered him hard against his chest, then polished him off by slamming my palm against his ear. Unfortunately, he got himself together and jumped off the bus, got away. Hey, I smashed him, Dillon, really smashed him."

She looked so proud of herself that Dillon wanted to hug her until she squeaked, but he was too scared. She could have been killed so very easily.

He cleared his throat. "Did you call the police?"

Lily shook her head. "To be honest, all I wanted to do was get back to the B-and-B. Then I thought of the paintings and got to the museum as fast as I could. Why don't you think it was a mugger?"

Savich was still shaking with reaction. "I'm upset about this, Lily, really upset. He most certainly wasn't a mugger. Listen, an empty bus, a guy starts with a throwaway line about taking your wallet to keep things real calm, then he brings out the knife? A mugger? No, Lily, I don't think so."

"The question is," Sherlock said, chewing on a chip that she'd liberally dipped in salsa, her right hand near her glass of iced tea, "who found him, got him up to speed and moving so fast? You only told Tennyson last night that you were leaving him. Talk about fast action—that really surprises me. Tennyson, his father, whoever else is involved in this—they're not pros, yet they got this guy after you very quickly. He must have been watching the B-and-B, then followed you to the art supply shop, got ahead of you and on the bus at the next stop. It was well planned, well executed, except he failed."

"Yeah, they didn't know what Dillon had taught me." She actually rubbed her hands together, realized she'd gotten salsa all over herself, and laughed. "Can we have another basket of chips?" she called out to the young Mexican waitress, then, "I saved myself, Dillon, and it felt really good."

Savich understood then, of course. Her life had been out of control for so very long, but no longer. He patted her back. "I wonder if it would help to check hospitals. Did you hurt him that bad?"

"Maybe. Good idea, I didn't think of that."

"He's paid to think of things like that," Sherlock said and got out her cell phone. She looked up at them after a moment, "We've got a lot of possibilities here."

Savich said, "You know, I was going to call the cops. But now that I think about it, I don't think the local constabulary is what we need just yet. What I want is Clark Hoyt from the FBI field office right here in Eureka. If he knows the local cops, thinks they could help with this, then we can bring them into it. But for the time being, let's use our own guys."

Sherlock said, as she called information, "Great idea, Dillon. I'm sure glad they opened up this field office last year. The one in Portland wouldn't be able to help us with much. Clark can get all the hospitals checked in no time. Now, Lily, tell me where you hit this guy. Be as specific as you can."

"Yeah, I can do that, and then hand me a napkin so I can draw the guy for you."

# TEN

*Eureka, California*
*The Mermaid's Tail*

Savich flipped open his cell phone, which was softly beeping the theme song from *The Lion King,* listened, and said, "Simon Russo? Is this the knuckle-head who shot himself in the foot with my SIG?" Then he laughed and listened some more. Then he talked. Savich realized quickly enough that Simon didn't like what he had been hearing, didn't like it at all. What was going on here? He listened as Simon said slowly, "Listen, Savich, get your grandmother's paintings safely back to Washington. Do it right away, don't dither or let the museum curator put you off. Don't take any shortcuts with their safety, but move quickly. I'll be down to Washington as soon as the paintings get there. I want to see them. It's very important that I see them. Don't take any chances."

Savich frowned into his cell phone. What was this all about? "I know you like my grandmother's paintings, Simon. She gave you your favorite when you graduated from MIT, but you don't have to come down to Washington to see them right away."

"Yes," Simon said, "trust me on this, I do." And he hung up.

Sherlock was standing on the far side of the bedroom, her own cell phone dangling from her hand. "Sweetheart," he called out to her, "strang-est thing. Simon is all hot under the collar to see Lily's eight Sarah Elliott paintings. He's being mysterious, won't tell me a thing, insists he has to see the paintings as soon as they arrive in Washington."

Sherlock didn't say anything. Savich felt a sharp point of fear. She looked shell-shocked, no, beyond that. She looked drop-dead frightened, her pupils dilated, her skin as pale as ice. He was at her side in an instant. He gathered her against him, felt that she was as cold as ice as well, and held on to her tightly. "What's wrong? Tell me what's wrong. It's Sean, isn't it? Something's happened to our boy?"

She shook her head hard, but still no words.

He pulled back, saw the shock of fear still deep in her eyes, and shook her lightly. "Please tell me, Sherlock, talk to me. What's going on? What happened?"

She swallowed, and managed finally to get the words out. "Sean's all right. I checked in at the office. I heard Ollie yell in the background that he had to speak to us. Dillon, Ollie said that Tammy Tuttle just up and walked out of the jail wing of Patterson-Wright Hospital."

"No," Savich said, shaking his head in utter disbelief, "you've got to be kidding me." Things like that didn't happen. She was very dangerous, and everyone at the hospital knew it. He continued to stare down at his wife, wanting to see some flicker of doubt that wasn't there. "That can't be possible," he went on slowly. The panic of it was nearly under control, but he didn't want to believe it, to accept it. "She was in the jail ward. She was well guarded. The woman is nuts. Everyone knows what she's done. She couldn't walk out."

"They were going to put her in restraints tomorrow or the next day, when they thought she was well enough to be a danger to them. Then there was a screwup in the scheduling of the guards. Evidently, she was ready for something to give her a chance. When she got her break, she snagged a nurse, knocked her out cold, and took her white pantsuit. At least she didn't kill her. But she walked out."

"It hasn't been even a week since they amputated her arm. How could she have the strength to take down a nurse? They're used to violent patients; they're trained. She's got only one arm."

"Obviously no one thought she had the strength or the ability, and that's why when there was the scheduling foul-up, no one was really concerned. And that's why no one even discovered she was gone until a nurse went in to give her a shot and found another nurse tied up naked in the closet. They figure she got herself at least a two-hour window."

Savich shook himself. His brain was back in gear, finally. "All right. Where would she go? Do they have any leads?"

"Ollie says there are more cops looking for her than the hunt for Marlin and Erasmus Jones. Everyone knows she's really scary, that she's truly dangerous. No one wants her free again." Sherlock cleared her throat. "There's the question of those things you saw in the barn, Dillon—the Ghouls."

He squeezed her again and said against her temple, her curly hair tickling his nose, "I know what I want to do right this minute. I want to talk to Sean and listen to him gurgle. That little guy is so sane, and that's what we need right now, a big dose of normalcy." He didn't add that he wanted to know for sure, all the way to his soul, that his little boy was all right. As for the Ghouls . . . if they were real—and Savich knew to his bones that they were—then it was possible there was more danger than anyone could begin to imagine. Would the FBI let all the people looking for Tammy Tuttle know that she could have accomplices? Or were they going to ignore everything he'd told them?

They took turns gurgling with their son, who was busy gnawing a banana, not a graham cracker. Then they called Ollie back to see if there was any news yet.

"Yes," Ollie Hamish said, "but not good." Sherlock could see him leaning back in his chair, spinning it just a bit, because he was nervous and scared. "Tammy Tuttle murdered a teenage boy a block outside of Chevy Chase, Maryland. She left a note on the body. Well, actually, she didn't leave it *on* the body, she left it attached to the body. It's addressed to you, Savich."

"Read it, Ollie."

"Here goes: 'I'll get you and I'll rip your arm off and then I'll cut your head off, you murdering bastard. Then I'll give you to the Ghouls.'"

"That's real cheery," Savich said. "Was it addressed specifically to me?"

"Yeah, which means she knows your name. How? Everyone thinks she probably heard people talking about you in the hospital. She left her fingerprints all over the paper and envelope, obviously didn't care. Oh yes, at the murder scene, there was also a black-painted circle, and the boy was inside it. She's loose, Savich. Everyone is shaken to their toes. It was a really gruesome crime scene. That poor kid, he was only thirteen years old."

"Black-painted circle," Savich said. "Tammy called to the Ghouls to come get the boys in the circle."

"I was hoping maybe you really hadn't seen anything, Savich, that maybe you'd experienced a temporary vision distortion. Since the boy's body was a mess, maybe more of a mess than a single one-armed sick woman could have done, then maybe these things—these Ghoul characters—were somehow involved. Jimmy Maitland brought it up. And the bosses even had a big meeting about it. They've all decided that what you saw in that barn were dust devils."

Savich said finally, "Mr. Maitland has my number here if he wants to talk about it. Now, here's something to do. Bring in Marilyn Warluski."

"We already went looking. She's long gone, no one knows where."

"MAX found out she has an ex-boyfriend in Bar Harbor, Maine, name of Tony Fallon. Check there. Maybe she'll be with him and know something. Tammy has to go somewhere, and Marilyn loaned her and her brother that barn for their use. Did Tammy steal any money?"

"Not at the hospital, but elsewhere? We haven't heard of anything yet. Also, there have been a dozen reports of stolen vehicles. We're checking all those out as well."

"Okay. Find Marilyn and wring her out, Ollie. I think you should be the one in direct contact with her. You know more than the others."

"Okay. Let me take a deep breath here. I'm very glad you aren't listed in the phone book and your phone number's private. It's unlikely she could find you where you are, but I want you to be careful, Savich, really careful."

"You can count on that, Ollie."

"Okay. How are things going out there with Lily?"

Savich said, "She managed to hurt a guy who tried to kill her on an empty bus a couple of hours ago. Clark Hoyt in the new Eureka field office is checking all the hospitals. No word yet. Lily drew a picture of him and we just heard from a Lieutenant Dobbs at the Eureka Police Department that the guy's a local hood-for-hire, a freelancer, who would kill his own mom for the right price. Name of Morrie Jones. Everyone's looking for him. He's a kid, only twenty."

Savich could see Ollie shaking his head back and forth as he said, "Big troubles on both coasts. Ain't nothing easy anywhere in this world, is there?"

LILY slept for three hours—no nightmares, thank God—and awoke to see her brother seated on a big wing chair pulled near her lovely Victorian canopied bed, a gooseneck lamp beaming light over his right shoulder, reading through a sheaf of papers.

He looked up immediately.

"You're fast. I opened one eye and you knew I was awake."

"Sean got both Sherlock and me trained in a matter of days. He yawns or grunts, and we're ready to move."

She managed a smile, but truth be told, the day's events had caught up with her. She'd gone from being euphoric about drawing Remus again, to nearly being murdered, to getting back her paintings. At least she'd had a great Mexican lunch and it hadn't made her sick to her stomach.

But now, even after a very long sleep, she still felt wrung out. Her side ached something fierce, and her head sat heavy and dull on her shoulders. "No, Dillon, don't get up. What are you reading?"

"Articles and reports MAX found for me on weird phenomena. I'm trying to find other reported crimes with similarities to the Tuttles' rampage and the Ghouls."

"You told me a little bit about the Tuttles and these Ghoul things, Dillon. Tell me more."

"There were two of them, two distinct white cones that sometimes came together. You can imagine how the two boys—Tammy and Timmy Tuttle called them 'Little Bloods'—were reacting. I've never seen such terror. I nearly swallowed my own tongue I was so afraid. Then Tammy Tuttle called to the Ghouls, yelled for them to bring their axes and knives, their 'treats' were ready for them. The boys wanted out of that circle and Tammy pulled her knife. She was going to nail them to the barn floor, inside that circle. That's when I shot her, and the bullet nearly tore her arm off. Timmy pulled his gun then, but he wasn't going to shoot me, no, he was aiming at the boys, so I had to kill him clean and quick, no choice. Then one of those white cones was coming at us, and I shot it. Did the bullet hurt it? I have no idea. I pulled the boys out of that circle and then both of the white cones whooshed out of there. No one outside the barn saw them. So it was the two boys, me, and Tammy, who had called them."

"That's scary."

"More than you can imagine."

Lily said, "I wonder, did their victims have to be inside that circle?"

"Good question. Since I was there and saw all of it, I think they did have to have their victims inside the circle. Or maybe it was a ritual that they themselves had developed over time, a ceremony that gave the Tuttles more of a kick out of what they were doing. However, I didn't see that the

Ghouls had any knives or axes, so why did they say that?" He paused a moment, thinking back. "You know, Tammy had a knife but I didn't see any axes anywhere."

"Maybe she was speaking dramatically."

Savich thought about the teenage boy, his body mutilated. "Maybe. I don't think so."

"What sorts of things has MAX dug up?"

He paused for a moment, then gave a slight shake of his head as he said, "You'd be surprised what's turned up over the years."

"Yeah, I bet I would, only you're not going to tell me anything, are you?"

There was a knock on the door.

Sherlock's voice. "Quick, Dillon. Open up!"

She was carrying three covered trays, stacked on top of one another. "From Mrs. Blade, downstairs," she said and handed them to Savich. "Besides doing crossword puzzles, she likes to cook. She insisted that if we couldn't come down to the dining room, she was sending this up."

Two huge plates of spaghetti with meatballs, one huge plate without the meatballs for Savich, lots of Parmesan cheese in a big bowl on the side, eight slices of garlic bread, and three large bowls of Caesar salad.

No one said a word for at least seven minutes, just groaned with pleasure and chewed. Finally, Lily sat back, patted her stomach, and sighed. "That garlic bread makes your back teeth sing the Italian anthem. Goodness, that was nearly as good as our Mexican lunch."

Sherlock wanted to laugh, but her mouth was full of spaghetti. Savich said, "Nah, Lily, give me a salty tortilla and salsa hot enough to burn the rubber off my soles any day. I wonder which one of your in-laws is going to pay us a visit this evening?"

Lily turned a bit pale. "But why would any of them want to see me again?"

Sherlock took the tray off her lap and said matter-of-factly, "Because their pigeon is bent on flying out of the coop. You survived the attack on the city bus this morning. No more attacks since Dillon and I have been with you. Nope, now they've got to visit you and try to convince you that Tennyson can't live without you."

"A final shot," Lily said.

"Yes, that's right," Sherlock said.

Savich smiled. "Only thing is, they also know that their little pigeon has two big crows guarding her. We'll see exactly what tack they take. Ah, look at that dessert Sherlock was hiding from us. Chocolate mousse, one of my favorites."

Tennyson and his mother showed up an hour later, at precisely eight o'clock.

Charlotte Frasier had come to the hospital only once, stood by Lily's bed, and told her at least three times that she desperately needed to see dear Dr. Rossetti, a fine doctor, an excellent man who would help her. She was so worried about her dear Lily, everyone was. No one wanted her to try to kill herself again. To which Lily had simply stared at her, not a single word coming to mind after that outrageous speech. This evening, she was beautifully dressed in a dark wine-colored wool suit, a pale pink silk blouse beneath. Her thick black hair, not a hint of white, was cut short and tousled in loose curls and waves around her face. It was a very young style, but it didn't look ridiculous at all. Her teeth were white and straight, her lipstick bloodred. Charlotte looked good; she always had.

As for Tennyson, he paid no attention to either Savich or Sherlock, just marched directly to Lily's bed, grabbed her hand, and held on tightly.

"Come home with me, Lily. I need you."

"Hello, Tennyson. Hello, Charlotte. What more could we possibly have to say to each other? Dillon thought you would come by this evening, but I have to admit I'm very surprised." Lily finally got her hand back and asked, "Oh yes, where is your father? Isn't he well?"

Savich said easily, "Maybe they don't think they need him. They're hopeful they can talk you around by themselves."

Lily said to her husband, "You can't."

Charlotte said in her rich-as-sin Savannah-smooth voice, "Elcott wanted to come tonight, but he had a slight indigestion. Now, listen to me for a moment, Lily. My son loves you very much. Since he's a man, it's difficult for him to speak from his heart—that's a woman sort of thing to do, so I am telling you for him that he really does need you."

"Actually, Charlotte, Tennyson can speak very eloquently. However, I don't think his heart has anything to do with it. No, Charlotte, what Tennyson really needs is my Sarah Elliott paintings."

"That's not true." Tennyson whirled about to face Savich. "You have filled her head with suspicions, doubts, with lies about me and my family and my motives. I don't have any ulterior motives! I love my wife, do you hear me? Yes, that is from my bruised and bleeding heart! I wouldn't do anything to harm her. She's precious to me. Why don't you and your wife go back to Washington and fight criminals, you know, people who have really done bad things, not innocent people you've taken a dislike to. That's what you're paid to do, not rip apart a loving family! Leave us alone!"

"That was a very impassioned speech," Sherlock said, smiling and nodding in approval. She knew from the furious pulse pounding in Tennyson's neck that he would cheerfully murder her.

Charlotte's voice was still as silky and soft as gently flowing honey. "Now, now, my dears, all of you need to calm down. Lily dearest, you're a grown woman. My Tennyson is as protective of his own younger sister as your brother is of you. But your brother and his wife have gone over the line. They dislike my son, for whatever reasons I'm sure I can't say. But there can simply be no proof to any of their accusations, not a shred. Mad accusations, all of them. Lily, how could you possibly believe such things of my son?"

Sherlock said, "I wouldn't call them particularly 'mad accusations,' but, yes, ma'am, you're right about proof. If we had proof, we'd haul his butt to jail."

Charlotte said, "So, then, why are you continuing to poison poor Lily's mind? You're doing her a disservice. She's really not well, you know, and you're pushing her farther down a road none of us want her to travel."

"Mother—"

"No, it's true, Tennyson. Lily is mentally ill. She needs to come home so we can take care of her."

Lily said in a loud, clear voice that brought everyone's eyes back to her, "A young guy tried to murder me this morning."

"What? Oh, no!" Tennyson nearly jerked her up into his arms, but Lily managed to press herself against the headboard and hold firm. Even as she was struggling, she said, "No, Tennyson, I'm quite all right. He didn't succeed, as you can see. Actually, I beat the stuffing out of him. The cops know who he is. Do back away now before my sister-in-law bites you."

Sherlock laughed.

"That's right," Savich said. "His name is Morrie Jones. Ring a bell, Tennyson? Charlotte? No? Well, you certainly got to him quickly enough, set everything in motion with nary a wasted moment. The cops will catch him anytime now and he'll spill his guts to them, and then we'll have our proof."

Tennyson said, "It's another lie, Lily. The guy must have mistaken you for someone else; that, or more likely, the guy was just a mugger. Where did it happen?"

"That's right, you couldn't have known where he'd find me, could you? He got on a local city bus that was empty except for me and the bus driver, because of the funeral."

"Yes," Charlotte said. "Dear old Ferdy Malloy died, probably poisoned by his wife. Everybody knows it, but no one was about to insist on an autopsy, least of all the coroner."

"Yes, yes, but that's not important, Mother. Someone tried to hurt Lily."

"A sharp knife probably meant he was planning to do more than hurt me," Lily said. "Lucky for me that Dillon had taught me how to protect myself."

"Maybe," Tennyson said now, his voice all soft and gentle, his patented shrink's voice, "maybe there was this young guy who came on to you, maybe even asked you out. I know Dr. Rossetti believes that a young woman, vulnerable like you are, uncertain, her mind clouded, can imagine many different things to disguise her sickness—"

Lily, who'd been staring at him like he had sprouted a TV antenna from his head, said, "Why did I ever think I loved you? You're the biggest jerk."

"I'm not, I'm just trying to understand you, to make you face things. Besides, that's what Dr. Rossetti thinks."

Lily began laughing, rich, deep laughter that didn't stop for a good, long time. Finally, wiping her eyes, she said, "You're really good, Tennyson, both you and Dr. Rossetti. You combined all your shrink analysis with some pills to drive me over the edge, and no wonder I wanted to do away with myself. So I made the guy up to assuage my guilt. Do you know what, Tennyson? I think I'm just about over blaming myself."

Charlotte said, "Lily dearest, I'm glad to hear you say that, actually—"

Lily interrupted her mother-in-law. She was waving Tennyson away even as she said, her voice light, amused, "Please go now, both of you. I hope that I'm lucky enough never to see either of you again."

Sherlock said, "Oh, I hope we do see them again, Lily. In a courtroom."

Savich said suddenly, "Your first wife, Tennyson. I don't suppose Lynda's fondest wish was to be cremated?"

Tennyson was shaking so much from rage, Sherlock was sure he was going to go after her husband, a singularly stupid thing for him even to consider. She stepped quickly to him, laid her hand on his forearm and said, "Don't even think about it. You couldn't take me and I'm half your size. Even five days after surgery, I doubt you could take Lily either. So please leave, Tennyson, and take your mother with you."

"I am appalled that you have relatives who are so very close-minded and obnoxious, Lily," Charlotte Frasier said, her words smooth out of her mouth. They left, not another word out of either mouth, but Tennyson did pause to give Lily a tormented look over his shoulder.

Sherlock said thoughtfully, "He was trying to reproduce a patented Heathcliff look there, all down-in-the-mouth and pathetic. He didn't do it well, but he tried."

Lily said, "Did you notice that lovely black turtleneck sweater Tennyson was wearing? I gave it to him for Christmas."

"You know what I think, Lily?" Savich asked, shaking his head at her. "I think the next time a guy appeals to you, red lights need to flash in your brain. Then we need to take him in for questioning."

"I was thinking about that this morning. Maybe I'm too gullible. Okay, no more good-looking men; actually, no more men at all, Dillon, or I'll kick myself from here to Boston. Nothing but nerds with pocket protectors for me in the future, and they'll just be friends."

That was going overboard, Sherlock was thinking, but for the time being, not a bad way for Lily to think about the opposite sex.

Lily said, "I wish I had a beer so I could drink to that."

Savich said, "No beer. Here's more iced tea."

"Thanks." Lily sipped the tea and laid her head back against the pillow. "I wonder where my father-in-law was. You think they really thought he'd be a liability?"

"Evidently so," Savich said. "What amazes me is they don't seem to realize what a liability the both of them are."

"I've never heard such a charming Southern accent," Sherlock said. She sat down on the bed beside Lily and lightly rubbed her arm. "Talk about candy coating."

"She frightened me more than Tennyson." She gave both of them a fat smile. "I held up," she said, gave a deep sigh, and said again, "I held up. He never guessed I was scared."

Savich felt her pain in his gut. He gathered her against him, very careful with her stitches. He kissed the top of her head. "Oh no, sweetheart, there isn't a reason for you to be afraid of him, ever again. I was proud of you. You held up great."

"Yes, you did, Lily, so no more talk about being scared. Remember, you've got your two bulldogs right here. You know something? I don't know what they thought they could gain by coming here. They didn't try to be very conciliatory. Are they stupid or was there some method to their approach?"

"I surely hope not," Lily said and closed her eyes.

Savich's cell phone rang.

# ELEVEN

"You go to bed now, Lily. No arguments. You look like a ghost out of *A Christmas Carol*."

Lily managed a small smile and did as she was told. She was still weak, and the long plane trip back east had knocked her flat. She awoke an hour later to hear Dillon and Sherlock talking to Sean. They cuddled, hugged, and kissed him until finally he was so exhausted he hollered big-time for about two minutes. Then he was out like the proverbial light. His nursery was right next to the guest room, where she lay quietly in the dim light. She didn't realize she was crying until a tear itched her cheek. She wiped it away.

She closed her eyes when she heard her door open slightly. No, she wasn't ready to see anyone yet, although she loved them both dearly for caring about her so very much. She pretended to be asleep. When she heard them go downstairs, she got up and went into the baby's room. Sean was sleeping on his knees, his butt in the air, two fingers in his mouth, his precious face turned toward her. He looked like his father, dark hair, dark eyes. She lightly rubbed her fingers over his back. So small, so very perfect.

She cried for the beauty of this little boy and for the loss of Beth.

Late that evening, over a good-sized helping of Dillon's lasagna, she said, "Have you checked back with your office? Did they find Marilyn Warluski?"

Savich said, "Not yet. They found the boyfriend, Tony Fallon, but he claims she hasn't contacted him. But there were a couple of folk in Bar Harbor who identified a photo of her, said they'd seen her recently. They're going back to put his feet to the coals. We'll know something soon."

"We hope," Sherlock said. Then she smiled. "You should have seen Dillon's mother when we picked up Sean—she didn't want us to take him. She said we'd promised her at least a week with him all to herself, but we'd lied; it was barely a week. She was shouting 'Foul' even as we were pulling out of her driveway."

Savich shook his head. "Now he'll be so spoiled that we'll actually have to say no to him a couple of times to get him grounded back into reality."

"I bet Mom would love to babysit him on a regular basis," Lily said.

"Well," Savich said, "she's got her own life. She's his treat; two or three times a week he gets big doses of Grandma. It works well that way. Our nanny, Gabriella Henderson, is the best. She's young, so she's got the energy and stamina to keep up with him. Believe me, he can wear you down very fast."

Lily was laughing, looking over at Sean, who was seated in his walker, a nifty contraption that let him scoot all over the downstairs. If he ran into something, he just changed directions.

Savich said, "Those wheels are bad for the floor, but Sherlock and I decided we'd have them refinished when he moves on to crawling and walking."

Lily said slowly, "Isn't it strange? I never imagined you with a kid, Dillon."

Savich smiled and helped her down on his big stuffed chair. "I didn't either, but here came Sherlock, blasted right into my comfortable life, and it seemed like the right thing. We're very lucky, Lily. Now, sweetheart, we've been traveling all day and you're jet-lagged, probably really bad what with the surgery a week ago. I want you to sleep at least ten hours before you face the world here in Washington tomorrow."

"You and Sherlock have to be jet-lagged too. Even though you travel a lot and you are FBI agents, you—"

The front doorbell rang.

Savich walked around Sean, who was speeding toward the front door. It was Simon Russo. Savich knew him as a man of immense energy and focus, a man who just didn't quit. And now Simon was looking beyond him to the living room.

"Simon, it's good to see you. What are you doing here?"

Simon grinned at his friend, shook his hand, and said, "Yeah, good to see you, Savich. I came to see the paintings. Where are they? Not here, I hope. You don't have the kind of security to keep the paintings here, even overnight."

"No we don't. Come on in. No, the paintings are in the vault in the Beezler-Wexler Gallery, safe as can be."

"Good, good. I'd like you to arrange for me to see them, Savich."

"So you said. First, however, you need a cup of tea and a slice of apple pie. My mom made it."

"Oh, not your blasted tea. Coffee, please, Savich, I'm begging you. Coffee, black. Then we can see the paintings."

"Simon, come on in and say hello to Sherlock and meet my sister, Lily. You can see the paintings tomorrow."

Simon shook his head and asked, "Not until tomorrow? How early?"

"Get a grip, Simon. Come on in. Hey, guys, look who flew through our front door? Simon Russo."

Lily's first impression of Simon Russo was that he was too good-looking, that he was a man who looked like a Raphaelesque angel, hair black and thick and a bit too long. Yeah, the angel Gabriel, probably, the head angel, the big kahuna. He was taller than her brother, long and lean, his eyes brighter and bluer than a winter sky over San Francisco Bay, and he looked distracted. He hadn't shaved. He was wearing blue jeans, sneakers, a white dress shirt, a yellow and red tie, and a tweed jacket. He looked like a gangster academic, an odd combination, but it was true. Or maybe a nerd gangster, what with a name like Simon. He also looked like he knew things, maybe dangerous things. Lily was sure all the way to her bones that she wouldn't trust him if he pledged his name in blood.

Red lights flashed in her brain. No, she wouldn't let herself even see him as a man. He was an expert who wanted to see her Sarah Elliott paintings for some reason. He was Dillon's friend. She wouldn't have to worry about him. Still, she found herself drawing back into the big chair.

"Simon!" Sherlock was across the living room in under three seconds, her arms thrown around him, laughing and squeezing him. He was hugging her, kissing her bouncing hair. She pulled back finally, kissed his scratchy cheek, and said, "Goodness, you're here in a hurry. Yes, I know it isn't us you want to see, it's those paintings. Well, you'll have to wait until morning."

Lily watched him hug her sister-in-law close once again, kiss her hair once again, and say, "I love you, Sherlock, I'd love to keep kissing you, but Dillon can kill me in a fair fight. The only time I ever beat him up, he was sick with the flu, and even then it was close. He also fights dirty. I don't want him to mess up my perfect teeth." He lifted her over his head, then slowly lowered her.

Savich said, crossing his arms over his chest, "You kiss her hair again and I'll have to see about those teeth."

Simon said, "Okay, I'll stay focused on the paintings, but, Sherlock, I want you to know that I wanted you first." He started to kiss her again, then sighed deeply.

Then he turned those dark blue eyes on Lily, and he smiled at her, far too nice a smile, and she wished she could stand up and walk out of the room. He was dangerous.

"Why," she said, not moving out of her chair, actually pressing her back against the cushions, "are you so hot to see my paintings?"

Savich frowned at her, his head cocked to one side. She sounded mad, like she wanted to kick Simon through a window. He said easily, "Lily, sweetheart, this is Simon Russo. You've heard me talk about him over the years. Remember, we roomed together our senior year at MIT?"

"Maybe," Lily said. "But what does he want with my paintings?"

"I don't know yet. He's a big-time dealer in the art world. He's the one I called to ask how much Grandmother's paintings are worth in to-day's market."

"I remember you," she said to Simon. "I was sixteen when you came home with Dillon on Christmas your senior year. Why do you want to see my paintings so badly?"

Simon remembered her, only she was all grown up now, not the wily, fast-talking teenager who'd tried to con him out of a hundred bucks. He didn't remember the scheme—some bet, maybe, but he did remember that she would have gotten it out of him, too, if her father hadn't warned him away and told him to keep his money in his wallet.

Simon wasn't deaf. He heard wariness, maybe even distrust in her voice. Why would she dislike him? She didn't even know him, hadn't seen him in years. She didn't look much like that teenager, either. She still looked like a fairy princess, but this grown-up fairy princess looked ground under—alarmingly pale, shadows beneath her eyes. Her hair was pulled back in a ratty ponytail and badly needed to be washed. She also needed to gain some weight to fill out her clothes. Antipathy was pouring off her in waves, a tsunami of dislike to drown him. Why?

"Are you in pain?" he asked, taking a step toward her.

Lily blinked at him, drawing herself in even more. "What?"

"Are you in pain? I know you had surgery last week. That's got to be tough."

"No," she said, still looking as though she was ready to gut him. Then Lily realized that she had no reason at all to dislike this man. He was her brother's friend, nothing more, no reason to be wary of him. The only problem was that he was good-looking, and surely she could overlook that flaw. He was here to see her paintings.

The good Lord save her from good-looking men who wanted her paintings. Two had been more than enough.

She tried to smile at him to get that puzzled look off his face.

Now what was this? Simon wondered, but he didn't get an answer, of course. He didn't say anything more. He turned on his heel and walked to where Sean had come to a halt in his walker and was staring up at him, a sodden graham cracker clutched in his left hand. Crumbs covered his mouth and chin and shirt.

"Hi, champ," Simon said and came down on his haunches in front of Sean's walker.

Sean waved the remains of the graham cracker at him.

"Let me pass on that." He looked over his shoulder. "He's still teething?"

Sherlock said, "Yep, for a while yet. Don't let Sean touch you, Simon, or you'll regret it. That jacket you're wearing is much too nice to have wet graham cracker crumbs and spit all over it."

Simon merely smiled and stuck out two fingers. Sean looked at those two fingers, gummed his graham cracker faster, then shoved off with his feet. The walker flew into Simon. He was so startled, he fell back on his butt.

He laughed, got back onto his knees, and lightly ran his fingers over Sean's black hair. "You're going to be a real bruiser, aren't you, champ? You're already a tough guy, mowed me right down." He turned on his heel to say to Lily, "Are you the changeling or is Savich?"

Savich laughed and gave Simon a hand up. "She's the changeling in our immediate family. However, she looks like Aunt Peggy, who married a wealthy businessman and lives like a princess in Brazil."

"Okay, then," Simon said, "let's see if she tries to bite my hand off." He stuck out his hand toward Lily Frasier. "A pleasure to meet another Savich."

Good manners won out, and she gave him her hand. A soft hand, smooth and white, but there were calluses on her fingertips. He frowned as he felt them. "I remember now, you're an artist, like Savich here."

"Yes, I told you about her, Simon. She draws *No Wrinkles Remus,* a political cartoon strip that—"

"Yes, of course I remember. I've read the strip, but it's been a while now. It was in the *Chicago Tribune,* if I remember correctly."

"That's right. It ran there for about a year. Then I left town. I'm surprised you remember it."

He said, "It's very biting and cynical, but hilarious. I don't think it matters if the reader is a Democrat or a Republican, all the political shenanigans ring so true it doesn't matter. Will the world see more of Remus?"

"Yes," Lily said. "As soon as I'm settled in my own place, I'm going to begin again. Now, why are you so anxious to see my paintings?"

Sean dropped the graham cracker, looked directly at his mother, and yelled.

Sherlock laughed as she lifted him out of the walker. "You ready for a bath, sweetie? Goodness, and a change, too. It's late, so let's go do it. Dillon, why don't you make Lily and Simon some coffee. I'll be back with the little prince in a while."

"Some apple pie would be nice," Simon said. "I haven't had dinner yet; it would fill in the cracks."

"You got it," Savich said, gave Lily the once-over to make sure she was okay, and went to the kitchen.

"Why do you want to see my paintings so badly?" Lily asked again.

"I'd as soon not say until I actually see them, Mrs. Frasier."

"Very well. What do you do in the art world, Mr. Russo?"

"I'm an art broker."

"And how do you do that, exactly?"

"A client wants to buy, say, a particular painting. A Picasso. I locate it, if I don't know where it is already—which I do know most of the time—see if it's for sale. If it is, I procure it for the client."

"What if it's in a museum?"

"I speak to the folk at the museum, see if there's another painting, of similar value, that they'd barter for the one my client wants. It happens that way, successfully sometimes, if the museum wants what I have to barter more than the painting they have. Naturally, I try to keep up with the wants and needs of all the major museums, the major collectors as well." He smiled. "Usually, though, a museum isn't all that eager to part with a Picasso."

"You know all about the illegal market, then."

Her voice was flat, no real accusation in it, but he knew to his toes she was very wary of him. Why? Ah, yes, her paintings, that was it. She didn't trust him because she was afraid for her paintings. Okay, he could deal with that.

He sat down on the sofa across from her, picked up the afghan, and held it out to her.

Lily said, "Thanks, I am a bit cold. No, no, just toss it to me."

But he didn't. He spread it over her, aware that she didn't want him near her, frowned, then sat down again and said, "Of course I know about the illegal market. I know all of the main players involved, from the thieves to the most immoral dealers, to the best forgers and the collectors who, many of them, are totally obsessed if there is a piece of art they badly want. 'Obsession' is many times the operative word in the business. Is there anything you want to know about it, Mrs. Frasier?"

"You know the crooks who acquire the paintings for the collectors."

"Yes, some of them, but I'm not one of them. I'm strictly on the up-and-up. You can believe that because your brother trusts me. No one's tougher than Savich when it comes to trust."

"You've known each other for a very long time. Maybe trust just starts between kids and doesn't end, particularly if you rarely see each other."

"Whatever that means," Simon said. "Look, Mrs. Frasier, I've been in the business for nearly fifteen years. I'm sorry if you've had some bad experiences with people in the art world, but I'm honest, and I don't dance over the line. You can take that to the bank. Of course I know about the underside of the business or I wouldn't be very successful, now would I?"

"How many of my grandmother's paintings have you dealt with?"

"Over the years, probably a good dozen, maybe more. Some of my clients are museums themselves. If the painting is owned by a collector—legally, of course—and a museum wants to acquire it, then I try to buy it from the collector. Since I know what all the main collectors own and accumulate, I will try to barter with them. It cuts both ways, Mrs. Frasier."

"I'm divorcing him, Mr. Russo. Please don't call me that again."

"All right. 'Frasier' is a rather common sort of name anyway, doesn't have much interest. What would you like to be called, ma'am?"

"I think I'll go back to my maiden name. You can call me Ms. Savich. Yes, I'll be Lily Savich again."

Her brother said from the doorway, "I like it, sweetheart. Let's wipe out all reminders of Tennyson."

"Tennyson? What sort of name is that?"

Lily actually smiled. If it wasn't exactly at him, it was still in his vicinity. "His father told me that Lord or Alfred wouldn't do, so he had to go with Tennyson. He was my father-in-law's favorite poet. Odd, but my mother-in-law hates the poet."

"Perhaps Tennyson, the poet—not your nearly ex-husband—is a bit on the 'pedantic' side."

"You've never read Tennyson in your life," Lily said.

He gave her the most charming smile and nodded. "You're right. I guess 'pedantic' isn't quite right?"

"I don't know. I haven't read him either."

"Here's coffee and apple pie," Savich said, then cocked his head, looking upward. He said, "I hear Sherlock singing to Sean. He loves a good, rousing Christmas carol in the bathtub. I think she's singing 'Hark! The Herald Angels Sing.' You guys try to get along while I join the singalong. You can trust him, Lily."

When they were alone again, Lily heard the light slap of rain on the windows for the first time. Not a hard, drenching rain. An introduction, maybe, to the winter rains that were coming. It had been overcast when they'd landed in Washington, and there was a stiff wind.

Simon sipped Savich's rich black coffee, sighed deeply, and sat back, closing his eyes. "Savich makes the best coffee in the known world. And he rarely drinks it."

"His body is a temple," she said. "I guess his brain is, too."

"Nah, no way. Your brother is a good man, sharp, steady, but he ain't no temple. I bet Savich would fall over in shock if he heard you say that about him."

"Probably so, but it's true nonetheless. Our dad taught all of us kids how to make the very best coffee. He said if he was ever in an old-age home, at least he'd know he could count on us for that. Our mom taught Dillon how to cook before he moved to Boston to go to MIT."

"Did she teach all of you?"

"No, only Dillon." She stopped, listening to the two voices singing upstairs. "They've moved on to 'Silent Night.' It's my favorite."

"They do the harmony well. However, what Savich does best is country and western. Have you ever heard him at the Bonhomie Club?"

She shook her head, drank a bit of coffee, and knew her stomach would rebel if she had any more.

"Maybe if you're feeling recovered enough, we could all go hear him sing at the club."

She didn't say anything.

"Why do you distrust me, Ms. Savich? Or dislike me? Whatever it is."

She looked at him for a good, long time, took a small bite of apple pie, and said finally, "You really don't want to know, Mr. Russo. And I've decided that if Dillon trusts you, why, then, I can, too."

# TWELVE

Raleigh Beezler, co-owner of the Beezler-Wexler Gallery of Georgetown, New York City, and Rome, gave Lily the most sorrowful look she'd seen in a very long time, at least as hangdog as Mr. Monk's at the Eureka museum.

He kissed his fingers toward the paintings. "Ah, Mrs. Frasier, they are so incredible, so unique. No, no, don't say it. Your brother already told me that they cannot remain here. Yes, I know that and I weep. They must make their way to a museum so the great unwashed masses can stand in their wrinkled walking shorts and gawk at them. But it brings tears to my eyes, clogs my throat, you understand."

"I understand, Mr. Beezler," Lily said and patted his arm. "But I truly believe they belong in a museum."

Savich heard a familiar voice speaking to Dyrlana, the gorgeous twenty-two-year-old gallery facilitator, hired, Raleigh admitted readily, to make the gentlemen customers looser with their wallets. Savich turned and called out, "Hey, Simon, come on back here."

Lily looked through the open doorway of the vault and watched Simon Russo run the distance to the large gallery vault in under two seconds. He skidded to a stop, sucked in his breath at the display of the eight Sarah Elliott paintings, each lovingly positioned against soft black velvet on eight easels, and said, "Incredible," and nothing else.

He walked slowly from painting to painting, pausing to look closely at many of them, and said finally, "You remember, Savich, your grandmother gave me *The Last Rites* for my graduation present. It was my favorite then and I believe it still is. But this one—*The Maiden Voyage*—it's magnificent. This is the first time I've seen it. Would you look at the play of light on the water, the lace of shadows, like veils. Only Sarah Elliott can achieve that effect."

"For me," Lily said, "it's the people's faces. I've always loved to stare at the expressions, all of them so different from each other, so telling. You know which man owns the ship by the look on his face. And his mother— that look of superior complacency at what he's achieved, mixed with the love she holds so deeply for her son and the ship he's built."

"Yes, but it's how Sarah Elliott uses light and shadow that puts her head and shoulders above any other modern artist."

"No, I disagree with you. It's the people, their faces, you see simply everything in their expressions. You feel like you know them, know what makes them tick." She saw he would object again and rolled right over him. "But this one has always been my favorite." She lightly touched her fingertips to the frame on *The Swan Song*. "I really hate to see it go to a museum."

"Keep it with you then," Savich said. "I've kept *The Soldier's Watch*. The insurance costs a bundle as well as the alarm system, but very few people know about it, and that's what you'll have to do. Keep it close and keep it quiet."

Simon looked up from his study of another painting. "I have *The Last Rites* hung in a friend's gallery near my house. I see it nearly every day."

"That's an excellent idea," Raleigh Beezler said and beamed at Lily, seeing hope. "Do you know, Mrs. Frasier, that there is an exquisite town house for sale not two blocks from my very safe, very beautiful, very hassle-free gallery that would accord you every amenity? What do you say I call the broker and you can have a look at it? I understand you're a cartoonist. There is this one room that is simply filled with light, perfect for you."

That was well done, Lily thought. She had to admire Mr. Beezler. "And I could leave some of my paintings here, in your gallery, on permanent display?"

"An excellent idea, no?"

"I'd like to see the town house, sir, but the price is very important. I don't have much money. Perhaps you and I could come to a mutually satisfying financial arrangement. My painting displayed right here for a monthly stipend, a very healthy one, given that this house sits in the middle of Georgetown and I'd have to afford to live here. What do you think?"

Raleigh Beezler was practically rubbing his hands together. There was the light of the negotiator in his dark eyes.

Simon cleared his throat. He'd continued studying the rest of the paintings, and now he turned slowly to say, "I think that's a very good idea, Ms. Savich, Mr. Beezler. Unfortunately, there is a huge problem."

Lily turned to frown at him. "I can't see any problem if Mr. Beezler is willing to pay me a sufficient amount to keep up mortgage payments, at least until I can get an ongoing paycheck for *No Wrinkles Remus*, maybe even get it syndicated . . ."

Simon shook his head. "I'm sorry, but it's not possible."

"What's wrong, Simon?" Because he knew Simon, knew that tone of voice, Savich automatically took Lily's hand. "All right, the floor's yours. You really wanted to see the paintings. You've seen them. I've watched you studying them. What's wrong?"

"No easy way to say this," Simon said. "Four of them are fakes, including *The Swan Song*. Excellent fakes, but there it is."

"No," Lily said. "No. I would know if it weren't real. You're wrong, Mr. Russo."

"I'm sorry, Ms. Savich, but I'm very sure. Like I said, the way Sarah Elliott uses light and shadows makes her unique. It's the special blend of shades that she mixed herself and the extraordinary brush strokes she used; no one's really managed to copy them exactly.

"Over the years I've become an expert on her paintings. Still, if I hadn't also heard some rumors floating around New York that one of the big collectors had gotten ahold of some Sarah Elliott paintings in the last six months, I wouldn't have come rushing down here."

Savich said, "I'm sorry, Lily, but Simon is an expert. If he says they're fake, then it's true."

"I'm sorry," Simon said. "Also, there were no Sarah Elliotts for sale that I knew of. When I heard *The Swan Song* as one of the paintings acquired, I knew something was wrong. I immediately put out feelers to get more substantial information. With any luck, I'll find out what's going on soon. Unfortunately, I haven't yet heard a thing about what happened to the fourth painting. Since I knew that you, Ms. Savich, owned them, and they'd been moved from the Art Institute of Chicago to the Eureka Art Museum eleven months ago, I didn't want to believe it—there are always wild rumors floating through the art world. I couldn't be sure until I'd actually seen them. I'm sorry, they are fakes."

"Well," Sherlock said, her face nearly as red as her hair, "shit."

Savich stared at his wife and said slowly, "You really cursed, Sherlock? You didn't even curse when you were in labor, at least you didn't until the end."

"I apologize for that, but I am so mad I want to chew nails. This is very bad. I'm really ready to go over the edge here. Those bastards— those officious, murdering bastards. There, I don't have to curse anymore. I'm sorry, Dillon, but this really is too much. This is so awful, Lily, but at least we have a good idea who's responsible."

Lily said, "Tennyson and his father."

Sherlock said, "And Mr. Monk, the curator of the Eureka museum. He had to be in on it. No wonder he was near tears when you told him you were taking the paintings. He knew the jig would be up sooner or later. He had to know that in Washington, D.C., experts would be viewing the paintings and one of them would spot the fakes."

"So did Tennyson," Savich said.

Lily said, "Probably my father-in-law as well. Maybe the whole family was in on this. But they couldn't have known we would find out the very day after we got here." She turned to Simon Russo. "I'm madder than Sherlock. Thank you, Mr. Russo, for being on top of this and getting to us so quickly."

Simon turned to Savich. "There is one positive thing here. At least Tennyson Frasier didn't have time to have all eight of them forged. Now that I know for certain that we've got four forgeries, I can find out the name of the forger. It won't be difficult. You see, it's likely to be one of three or four people in the world—the only ones with enough technique to capture the essence of Sarah Elliott and fool everyone except an expert who's been prepared for the possibility."

Lily said, "Would you have known they were fakes if you hadn't heard about them being sold to a collector?"

"Maybe not, but after the second or third viewing, I probably would have realized something was off. They really are very well done. When I find out who forged them, I'll pay a visit to the artist."

"Don't forget, Simon, we need proof," Savich said, "to nail Tennyson. And his family, and Mr. Monk at the Eureka museum."

Sherlock said, "No wonder that guy tried to murder you on the bus, Lily. They knew they had to move quickly and they did. It's just that you're no wuss and you creamed the guy. I wanna lock them all up, Dillon. Maybe stomp on them first."

Simon, who had been studying *The Maiden Voyage*, looked up. "What do you mean she creamed the guy? Someone attacked you? But you were only days out of surgery."

"Sorry, I forgot to mention that," Savich said.

Lily said, "There was no reason to tell him. But yes, I'd been five or six days out of surgery. I was okay, thanks to a psychiatrist who—well, never mind about that. But I was feeling fine. A young guy got on an empty bus, sat beside me, and pulled out this really scary switchblade. He was lucky to get away." And Lily gave him a big smile, the first one he'd gotten from her. He smiled back.

"Very good. Your brother taught you?"

"Yes, after Jack—No, never mind that."

"You have a lot of never minds, Ms. Savich."

"You may have to get used to it." But she saw him file Jack's name away in that brain of his.

Simon said, "As for the fourth painting, *Effigy*, I thought it was fine at first, but then I realized that the same forger who did the other three did that one as well. No leads yet on *Effigy*, but we'll track it down. It probably went to the same collector."

Mr. Beezler, shaken, wiped a beautiful linen handkerchief over his brow and said, "This would be a catastrophe to a museum, Mr. Savich, like a stick of dynamite stuck in the tailpipe of my Mercedes. You, Mr. Russo, you are, I gather, in a position to perhaps get the original paintings back?"

"Yes," said Simon, "I am. Keep the black velvet warm, Mr. Beezler."

Savich said, "I'll speak to the guys in the art fraud section, see what recommendations they have. The FBI doesn't do full-blown stolen art investigations at this time, so our best bet is Simon finding out who acquired the paintings."

Simon said, "First thing, I'll do some digging around, hit up my informants to get verification on who our collector is, find the artist, and squeeze him. The instant our collector hears I'm digging—and he'd hear about it real quick—he'll react, either go to ground, hide the paintings, or maybe something else, but it won't matter."

"What do you mean 'something else'?" Lily asked.

Savich gave him a frown, and Simon said quickly, shrugging, "Nothing, really. But since I plan to stir things up, I'll be really careful who's at my back. Oh yeah, Savich, I'm relieved you didn't use the shippers that Mr. Monk wanted you to use."

Savich said, "No, I used Bryerson. I know them and trust them. There's no way Mr. Monk or Tennyson or any of the rest of them could know, at least for a while, where the paintings ended up. However, I will call Teddy Bryerson and have him let me know if he gets any calls about the paintings. Simon, do you think anyone will realize these four paintings are fakes if they're out in the open for all to see?"

"Sooner or later someone would notice and ask questions."

Lily said to Mr. Beezler, "I can't very well let a museum hang the four fakes. What do you think about hanging all of them here for a while, Mr. Beezler, and we can see what happens?"

"Yes, I will hang them," said Raleigh, "with great pleasure."

Lily said to Simon, "Do you really think you can get the paintings back?"

Simon Russo rubbed his hands together. His eyes were fierce, and he looked as eager as a boy with his first train set. "Oh, yes."

She imagined him dressed all in black, even black camouflage paint on his face, swinging down a rope to hover above an alarmed floor.

Savich said, "One thing, Simon. When you find out who bought the paintings, I go with you."

Sherlock blinked at her husband. "You mean that you, an FBI special agent, unit chief, want to go steal four paintings?"

"Steal back," Savich said, giving her a kiss on her open mouth. "Bring home. Return to their rightful owner."

Lily said, "I'll be working with Mr. Russo to find the person who forged them and the name of the collector who bought them. And then we'll have proof to nail Tennyson."

"Oh no," Savich said. "I'm not letting you out of my sight, Lily."

"No way," Sherlock said. "No way am I letting you out of my sight either. Sean wants his auntie to hang out with him for a while."

Simon Russo looked at Lily Savich and slowly nodded. He knew to his bones that when this woman made up her mind, it would take more than an offering of a dozen chocolate cakes to change it. "Okay, you can work with me. But first you need to get yourself back to one-hundred-percent healthy."

"I'll be ready by Monday," Lily said. She raised her hand, palm out, to her brother before he could get out his objection. "You guys have lots to worry about—this Tammy Tuttle person. She's scary, Dillon. You've got to focus on catching her. This is nothing, in comparison, just some work to track these paintings, maybe talking to these artists. I know artists. I know what to say to them. It won't be any big deal. I can tell Mr. Russo exactly how to do it."

"Right," said Simon.

Sherlock was pulling on a hank of curly hair, something, Savich knew, she did when she was stressed or worried. She said, "She's right, Dillon, but that doesn't mean I like it." She sighed. "And it's not only Tammy Tuttle. Oh well, I'll spit it out. Ollie phoned just before we left the house this morning."

"He did?" Savich turned the full force of his personality on his wife, a dark brow raised. "And you didn't see fit to mention it to me?"

"It's Friday morning, Gabriella was at the dentist and running late; she's our nanny," Sherlock added to Simon. "Besides, you'd already told Ollie and Jimmy Maitland that you wouldn't be in until late morning. I was going to tell you on the way in."

"I know I don't want to hear this, but out with it, Sherlock. I can take it."

"Besides worrying about Tammy Tuttle, there's been a triple murder in a small town called Flowers, Texas. The governor called the FBI and demanded that we come in, and so we will. Both the ATF and the FBI are involved. There's this cult down there that they suspect is responsible for the murder of the local sheriff and his two deputies who'd gone out to their compound to check things out. Their bodies were found in a ditch outside of town."

"That's nuts," Simon said.

"Yes," Sherlock said, "it is. Ah, Raleigh, would you mind visiting with Dyrlana for a moment? All this stuff is sort of under wraps."

Raleigh looked profoundly disappointed, but he left them in the vault. At the doorway, he said, "What about your sister and Mr. Russo? They're civilians, too."

"I know, but I can control what they say," Savich said. "I really couldn't get away with busting your chops."

They heard him chuckling as he called out, "Dyrlana! Where is my gumpoc tea?"

"One problem is," Sherlock said, "that the cult has cleared out, split up into a dozen or more splinter groups and left town in every direction.

Nobody knows where the leader is. They've pulled in a few of the cult members, but these folks shake their heads and claim they don't know anything about it. The only good thing is that we have a witness, of sorts. It seems that one of the women is pregnant by the guru. Lureen was rather angry when she found him seducing another cult member, actually at least three or four other cult members. She slipped away and told the town mayor about it."

Savich said, "A witness, then. Did she identify the guru as the guy who ordered the murders?"

"Not yet. She's still thinking about it. She's afraid she'd screw up her child's karma if she identified the father as a murderer."

"Great," Savich said and sighed. "Like Ollie said, there doesn't seem to be anything in this life that's easy. Do we have some sort of name on this guy?"

"Oh, sure, that's no secret," Sherlock said. "Wilbur Wright. Lureen wouldn't say his name out loud, but everybody knows it, since he was around town for a couple of months."

"Isn't that clever?" Savich rubbed the back of his neck, nodded to Simon, grabbed his wife's hand, and walked out of the vault. He said over his shoulder, "It's settled then. Lily, you rest and recuperate. Simon, you can stay at the house. I'd feel better if you did. Sherlock and I will call you guys later. Oh yes, don't spoil Sean. Gabriella is besotted with him already; she doesn't need any more help. Holler if you want MAX to check anything out for you, Simon."

"Will do."

"Oh, yes, there's one other thing," Sherlock said to Savich once they were out of the vault and in the gallery itself, alone and beyond the hearing of Lily or Simon. She glanced at Raleigh and Dyrlana, who were drinking gumpoc tea over by the front glass doors.

Savich knew he didn't want to hear this. He merely looked at her, nodding slowly.

"The guru. He had the hearts cut out of the sheriff and his two deputies."

"So this is why the Texas governor wants us involved. This guy has probably done something this sick before in other states. Ah, Sherlock, I knew it couldn't be as straightforward as you presented it. So, is Behavioral Sciences also involved?"

"Yes. I didn't want Lily to have to hear that."

"You're right. All right, love, let's go track down Tammy Tuttle and Wilbur Wright."

Lily Savich and Simon Russo stood in the silent vault, neither of them saying a word. She walked to one of the paintings that was real, not forged—*Midnight Shadows*. She said, "I wonder why he tried to kill me when he did? What was the hurry? He had four more paintings to have forged. Why now?"

Savich had told Simon most of what had happened to his sister the previous evening, after she'd gone to bed, looking pale and, truth be told, wrung out. All except for the murder attempt on the city bus in Eureka. What had happened to her—what was still happening—was tragic and evil, and it all came on top of the death of her daughter.

But perhaps they could recover the paintings. He sure wanted to. He said, "That's a good question. I don't know why they cut the brake lines. My guess is that something must have happened to worry them, something to make them move up the timetable."

"But why not kill me off right away? Surely it would have been easier for Tennyson to simply inherit the paintings, to own them himself. Then he wouldn't have had to go to all the trouble and risk of finding a first-class forger and then collectors who would want to buy the paintings."

"Count on Mr. Monk to help with all that. I bet you Mr. Monk doesn't have all that sterling a reputation. I'll check into that right away."

"Yes," Lily continued, her head cocked to one side, still thinking. "He could have killed me immediately, and then he would have owned the paintings. He could then have sold them legally, right up front, with no risk that someone would turn on him, betray him. Probably he would have made more money that way, you know, in auctions."

"First of all, Lily, killing you off would have brought Savich down on their heads, with all the power of the FBI at his back. Never underestimate your brother's determination or the depths of his rage if something had happened to you. As for legal auctions for the paintings, you're wrong there. Collectors involved in illegal art deals pay top dollar, many times outrageous amounts because they want something no one else on the face of the earth owns. The stronger the obsession, the more they'll pay. Going this route was certainly more risky, but the payoff was probably greater, even figuring in the cost of the forgery. It was trying to kill you that was the real risk. As I said, something very threatening must have happened. I don't know what, but we'll probably find out. Now, you ready to go have some lunch before you go home to bed?"

Lily thought about how tired she was, how she could simply sit down and sleep, then she smiled. "Can I have Mexican?"

# THIRTEEN

*Quantico, Virginia*
*FBI Academy*

Savich was seated in his small office in the Jefferson dorm at the FBI Academy when two agents ushered in Marilyn Warluski, who'd borne a child by her cousin Tommy Tuttle, now deceased, the child's whereabouts unknown. They'd nabbed her getting on a Greyhound bus in Bar Harbor, Maine, headed for Nova Scotia. Since she'd been designated a material witness, and Savich wanted to keep her stashed away, they'd brought her in an FBI Black Bell Jet to Quantico.

He'd never met her, but he'd seen her photo, knew she was poorly educated, and guessed that she was not very bright. He saw that she looked, oddly, even younger than in her photo, that she'd gained at least twenty pounds, and that her hair, cropped short in the photo, was longer and hung in oily hanks to her shoulders. She looked more tired than scared. No, he was wrong. What she looked was defeated, all hope quashed.

"Ms. Warluski," he said in his deep, easy voice, waving her to a chair as he said her name. The two agents left the office, closing the door behind them. Savich gently pressed a button on the inside of the middle desk drawer, and in the next room, two profilers sitting quietly could also hear them speak.

"My name is Dillon Savich. I'm with the FBI."

"I don't know nothin'," Marilyn Warluski said.

Savich smiled at her and seated himself again behind the desk.

He was silent for several moments, watched her fidget in that long silence. She said finally, her voice jumpy, high with nerves, "Just because you're good-lookin' doesn't mean I'm gonna tell you anythin', mister."

This was a kick. "Hey, my wife thinks I'm good-looking, but I'm wondering, since you said it, if you're trying to butter me up."

"No," she said, shaking her head, "you're good-lookin' all right, and I heard one of the lady cops on the airplane say you're a hunk. They were thinkin' that a sexy guy will make me talk, so they got you."

"Well," Savich said, "maybe that's so." He paused a fraction of a second, then said, his voice unexpectedly hard, "Have you ever seen the Ghouls, Marilyn?"

He thought she'd keel over in her chair. So she knew about the Ghouls. She paled to a sickly white, looked ready to bolt.

"They're not here, Marilyn."

She shook her head back and forth, back and forth, whispering, "There's no way you could know about the Ghouls. No way at all. Ghouls are bad, real bad."

"Didn't Tammy tell you that I was there in the barn, that I saw them, even shot at them?"

"No, she didn't tell me . . . I don't know nothin', you hear me?"

"Okay, she didn't tell you I saw them and she didn't tell you my name, which is interesting since she knows it. But she did tell you she wanted to have at me, didn't she?"

Marilyn's lips were seamed tight. She shook her head and said, "Oh, yeah, and she will. She called you that creepy FBI jerk. I don't know why she didn't tell me that you saw the Ghouls."

"Maybe she doesn't trust you."

"Oh, yeah, Tammy trusts me. She doesn't have anybody else now. She'll get you, mister, she will."

"Just so you know, Marilyn, I'm the one who shot her, the one who killed Tommy. I didn't want to, but they left me no choice. They had two kids there, and they were going to kill them. Young boys, Marilyn, and they were terrified. Tommy and Tammy had kidnapped them, beaten them, and they were going to murder them, like they've murdered many young boys all across the country. Did you know that? Did you know your cousins were murderers?"

Marilyn shrugged. Savich saw a rip beneath the right arm of her brown, cracked leather jacket. "They're my kin. I could miss Tommy—seein' as how he's dead now—but he killed our baby, cracked its poor little head right open, so I was really mad at him for a long time. Tommy was hard, real hard. He was always doin' things you didn't expect, mean things, things to make you scream. You killed him. He was one of a kind, Tommy was."

Savich didn't respond, only nodded, waiting.

"You shouldn't have shot Tammy like you did, tearing her arm all up so they had to saw it off. You shouldn't have been there in my barn in the first place. It wasn't none of your business."

He smiled at her, sat forward, his palms flat on his desk. "Of course it's my business. I'm a cop, Marilyn. You know, if I had killed her in the barn then she wouldn't have killed that little boy outside Chevy Chase. Either she did it or the Ghouls did it. Maybe the Ghouls did kill the boy, since there was a circle. Do the Ghouls have to have a circle, Marilyn? You don't know? Were you with her when she took that boy? Did you help her murder him?"

Marilyn shrugged her shoulders again. "Nope, I didn't even know what she was going to do, not really. She left me at this grungy motel on the highway and told me to stay put or she'd bang me up real bad. She looked real happy when she got back. There was lots of blood on her nurse's uniform; she said she'd have to find somethin' else to wear. She thought it was neat there was blood on the uniform, said it was a-pro-pos or somethin' like that. Now, I'm not goin' to say any more. I already said too much. I want to leave now."

"You know, Marilyn, your cousin's very dangerous. She could turn on you, like this." He snapped his fingers, saw her cower in the chair, saw her shudder. He said, "How would you like to be ripped apart?"

"She wouldn't turn on me. She's known me all my life. I'm her cousin, her ma and mine were sisters, at least half sisters. They wasn't real sure since their pa was always cattin' around."

"Why did Tammy pretend to be Timmy?"

Marilyn focused her eyes on the pile of books along the side wall of the office and didn't answer. Savich started to leave it for the moment since it obviously upset her, when she burst out, "She wanted me, you know, but she weren't no dyke and so she played with me only when she was dressed like Timmy, but never when she was Tammy."

For an instant, Savich was too startled to say a word. What a wild twist. He said finally, "Okay then, tell me what kind of shape Tammy is in right now."

That brought Marilyn up straight in her chair. "No thanks to you she's going to be okay, at least she kept telling me that. But she hurts real bad and her shoulder looks all raw and swollen. She went to a pharmacy late one night, just when they was closing, and got the guy to give her some antibiotics and pain pills. He nearly puked when he saw her shoulder."

"I didn't hear about any robbery in a pharmacy," Savich said slowly. They'd been looking, but hadn't gotten any news as yet.

"That's because Tammy whacked the guy after she got the medicine from him, tore the place up. She said that'd make the cops go after the local druggies."

"Where was this, Marilyn?"

"In northern New Jersey somewhere. I don't remember the name of that crummy little town."

Local law enforcement hadn't connected the pharmacist's murder to the Tammy Tuttle bulletin the FBI had circulated all over the eastern seaboard. Well, at least now they'd find out everything the local cops had on the murder. He said, "Where did Tammy go after you went off to Bar Harbor?"

"She said she wanted some sun so's it would heal her shoulder. She was going down to the Caribbean to get herself well. No, I don't know where; she wouldn't tell me. She said there were lots of islands down there and she'd find the one that was best for her. Of course she didn't have enough money, so she robbed this guy and his wife in a real fancy house in Connecticut. Got three thousand and change. That's when she told me she'd be all right and I could take off."

"Naturally she's going to call you, let you know how she's doing?"

Marilyn nodded.

"Where will she call you?"

"At my boyfriend's, in Bar Harbor. But I'm not there anymore, am I? My boyfriend will tell her that the cops came around and I left."

That was true enough, Savich thought, no hope for it. He hoped Tammy wouldn't call until they'd found out where she was in the Caribbean.

Marilyn said, "I'll bet she really wants to kill you bad because of what you done to her. She'll come back when she's really well, and she'll take you down. Tammy's the meanest female in the world. She beat the crap out of me every time I saw her when we was growin' up. She'll get you, Dillon Savich. You're nuthin' compared to Tammy."

"What are the Ghouls, Marilyn?"

Marilyn Warluski seemed to grow smaller right in front of him. She was pressed against the back of her chair, her shoulders hunched forward. "They're bad, Mr. Savich. They're really bad."

"But what are they?"

"Tammy said she found them when she and Tommy were hiding out in some caves in the Ozarks a couple years ago. That's in Arkansas, you know. It was real dark, she told me, real dark in that stinkin' cave, smelled real bad, and Tommy was out takin' a leak, and she was alone and then, all of a sudden, the cave filled with weird white light and then the Ghouls came."

"They didn't hurt her?"

Marilyn shook her head.

"What else did she say?"

"Said she knew they were the Ghouls, knew somehow they'd got inside her head and told her their name, then told her that they needed blood, lots of young blood, and then they laughed and told her they were counting on her, and then they winked out. That's what Tammy said: they laughed, spoke in her head, and just 'winked out.' "

"But what are they, Marilyn? Do you have any idea?"

She was silent for the longest time, then she whispered, "Tammy told me a couple of days ago the Ghouls were pissed off at her because she and Tommy hadn't given them their young blood in the barn, that if Tommy was still alive, they'd eat him right up."

"Do you think that's why Tammy got that kid? So the Ghouls could have their young blood?"

She didn't say anything, just looked at him and slowly nodded. Then she started crying, hunched over, her bowed head in her hands.

"Do you know anything else, Marilyn?"

She shook her head. Savich believed her. He also understood why she was shivering. He was close to shivering himself. He had goose bumps on his arms.

Two FBI agents escorted Marilyn Warluski out of Savich's office. She would remain here at Quantico, a material witness and the FBI's guest until Savich and Justice made a decision about what to do with her.

He was standing by his desk, deep in thought, looking out the window toward Hogan's Alley, the all-American town the FBI Academy had created and used to train their agents in confronting and catching criminals, when Steve Jeffers, a profiler in the Behavioral Sciences, housed three floors down here at Quantico, said in his slow, Alabama drawl even before he cleared the doorway, "This is about the strangest shared delusion I've ever heard, Savich. But what are the things to them? How do they interact with Tammy Tuttle? Marilyn said Tammy told her the Ghouls got in her head and told her to do things."

"What we've got to do is predict what Tammy Tuttle will do next given this belief of hers in the Ghouls," said Jane Bitt, a senior profiler who'd lasted nearly five years without burning out.

Jane Bitt came around Jeffers and leaned against the wall, her arms crossed over her chest. "Lots of other monsters but not anything like this. Tammy Tuttle is a monster. She's got monsters inside her—monsters within a monster. The problem is that we don't have any markers, any clues to give us even a glimmer of an idea of what we're working with here. We're faced with something we've never seen before."

"That's right," said Jeffers, the two words so drawn out in his accent that Savich wanted to say them for him, that or just pull them out of his mouth. "How do we get her, Agent Savich? I sure want to hear what she has to say about the Ghouls."

Savich said, "You heard Marilyn say that Tammy went to the Caribbean, to an island 'right' for her. She couldn't have walked there, and she sure can't be hard to spot. Let me call Jimmy Maitland. They can get on that right away." He placed the phone call, listened, and when he finally hung up, he said, "Mr. Maitland was nearly whistling. He's sure they'll get her now. What else do you guys think from listening to her?"

"Well," Jane said as she sat down, crossing her legs and leaning forward, "it seems to be some sort of induced hallucination. Marilyn seems to think they're real, and both you and the boys saw *something* unusual in that barn, isn't that right, Agent Savich?"

"Yes," Savich said.

"Maybe Tommy and Tammy have some sort of ability to alter what you see and feel, some sort of hypnotic ability."

Savich said to Jeffers, "You did a profile on Timmy Tuttle before he turned out to be Tammy."

"Savich is right, Jane," Jeffers said. "We ain't got nothing useful that fits a psychotic cross-dresser who may have hypnotic skills."

Savich laughed, said, "You know what I want to try? I want to talk Marilyn into letting us hypnotize her. Maybe if you're right about this, she can tell us a lot more when she's under."

Jeffers laughed. "Hey, maybe the Ghouls are real, maybe they're entities, aliens from outer space. What do you think, Jane?"

"I like the sound of that, Jeffers. It'd perk up our boring lives a bit, add some color to our humdrum files. White cones whirling around black circles—maybe they're from Mars, you think?"

Savich said, "Actually, I've been reading articles, studies on various phenomena involved in past crimes."

"Found anything?" Jeffers asked.

"Nothing like this," Savich said. "Not a thing like this." He added as he stood, "Joke all you want, but don't do it in front of the media."

"Not a chance," Jane said. "I don't want to get committed." She rose, shook Savich's hand. "Marilyn told you Tammy met up with the Ghouls in a cave. My husband is really into speleology and we usually go spelunking on our vacations. In fact, we were planning on visiting some of the caves in the Ozarks this summer. No matter how much I can laugh about this, I might want to rethink that plan."

*Washington, D.C.*

Lily was leaning over her drawing table, looking at her work. No Wrinkles Remus was emerging clear and strong and outrageous from the tip of her beloved sable brush. The brush was getting a bit gnarly, but it was good for another few weeks, maybe.

*First panel:* Remus is sitting at his desk, a huge, impressive affair, looking smug as he says to someone who looks like Sam Donaldson, "Here's a photo of you without your wig. You're really bald, Sam. I'm going to show this photo to the world if you don't give me what I want."

*Second panel:* Sam Donaldson clearly isn't happy. He grabs the photo, says, "I'm not bald, Remus, and I don't wear a wig. This photo is a fake. You can't blackmail me."

*Third panel:* Remus is gloating. "Why don't you call Jessie Ventura? Ask him what I did to him."

*Fourth panel:* Sam Donaldson, angry, defeated, says, "What do you want?"

*Fifth panel:* Remus says, "I want Cokie Roberts. You're going to fix it so I can have dinner with her. I want her and I'm going to have her."

Lily was grinning when she turned to see Simon Russo standing in the doorway.

He looked fit, healthy, and tanned. She felt suddenly puny and weak, still bowed over a bit. She wished he'd go away, but she said, "Yes?"

"Sorry to bother you, but you should be in bed. I spoke to Savich, and he said to check on you. He knew you wouldn't be following orders. You've got a strip nearly ready?"

"Yep. It's not the final version yet, but close. Remus is in fine form. He's blackmailing Sam Donaldson."

Simon wandered over to look down at the panels. He laughed. "I've missed Remus, the amoral bastard. Glad to see him back."

"Now I've got to see if the *Washington Post* would like to take me and *Remus* in. Keep your fingers crossed they'll agree. I won't get rich anytime soon, but it's a start."

Simon said after a moment, looking down at the *Remus* strip, "I know a cartoonist doesn't make much money until he or she is syndicated. Hey, I happen to know Rick Bowes. He runs the desk. How about I give him a call, go to lunch, show him the strips?"

Lily didn't like it, obvious enough, so he didn't say anything more until she shook her head. "All right, then, you bring some of these strips to show him and I'll take you both to a Mexican restaurant."

"Well," she said, "maybe that would be okay."

"Will you take a nap now, Lily? You should take some of your meds, too."

Sean hollered from the nursery down the hall. They heard Gabriella telling him that if he'd stop chewing his knuckles as well as hers, she'd get him a graham cracker and they'd go for a walk in the park. Sean let out one more yell, then burbled. Gabriella laughed. "Let's go get that cracker, champ."

Lily heard Sean cooing as Gabriella carried him down the hall. She tried to swallow the tears, but it wasn't possible. She stood there, not making a sound, tears rolling down her cheeks.

Simon knew about tragedy, knew about the soul-deep pain that dulled over time but never went away. He didn't say a word, just very slowly pulled her against him and pressed her face to his shoulder.

When the phone rang a minute later, Lily pulled away, wouldn't look him straight in the eye, and answered it.

She handed it to him. "It's for you."

# FOURTEEN

*New York City*

It was nearly ten o'clock Sunday night. Simon was back in New York and had just finished a hard workout at his gym. He felt both exhausted and energized, as always. He toweled off his face, wiped the sweat off the back machine, stretched, and headed for the showers. There were at least a dozen guys in the men's locker room, all in various stages of undress—cracking jokes, bragging about their dates, and complaining about injured body parts.

Simon stripped and nabbed the only free shower. It was late when he finally stepped out and grabbed up his towel. Only two guys were left, one of them blow-drying his hair, the other peeling a Band-Aid off his knee. Then, not three minutes later, they were gone. Simon had on his boxer shorts when the lights went out.

He grabbed for his pants. He remembered the circuit breaker was outside the men's locker room, right there on the left wall.

He heard something, a light whisper of sound. It was the last thing he remembered. The blow over his right ear knocked him out cold. He fell flat to the locker room floor.

"Hey, man, wake up! Oh God, please, man, don't be dead. I'd lose my job for sure. Please, man, open your eyes!"

Simon cracked open an eye to see an acne-ridden face, a very young face that was scared to death, staring down at him. The young guy was shaking his shoulder.

"Yeah, yeah, I'm not dead. Stop shaking me." Simon raised his hand and felt the lump behind his right ear. The skin was broken, and he felt the smear of his own blood. He looked up at the kid and said, "Someone turned out the lights and hit me with something very hard."

"Oh, man," the kid said, "Mr. Duke is going to blame me for sure. I'm supposed to take care of this place, and I've only been here a week and he's going to fire me. I'm roadkill." He began wringing his hands, looking around wildly, as if expecting to see Mr. Duke, the manager, at any minute.

"The guy who hit me—I guess you didn't see him?"

"Nah, I didn't see any guy."

"All right. Don't worry, chances are he's long gone. Help me up, I've got to check my wallet." Once on his feet, Simon opened his locker door and reached for his ancient black bomber jacket that had seen its best days at MIT a dozen years before. His wallet was gone.

A robber trips the circuit breaker, then comes into the gym locker room to steal a wallet? He must have known only one guy was left, which meant that he'd had to look in, to check. A mugger in a men's locker room?

"Sorry, kid, but we should call the cops. Can't hurt. Maybe they'll turn up something."

Simon canceled his credit cards while he waited for the cops to show up. The police, two young patrolmen, took a statement, looked around the gym and in the locker room, but—

Simon waited to call Savich until he was back at his brownstone on East Seventy-ninth Street.

Savich said, "What's happening?"

Simon said, "I had a bit of trouble a while ago."

Savich said, "You leave my house this afternoon after you get a phone call, don't call me to tell me what's going on, and you're telling me you've already landed into trouble?"

"Yeah, that's about the size of it. Is Lily better?"

"Lily is indeed better, and she wants to slug you. She said tomorrow is Monday, her stitches are out in the morning, and she's coming up to New York, no matter what kind of excuses you try to pawn off on her."

"I'll have to think about that," Simon said.

"All right, tell me what happened."

After Simon had finished, Savich said, "Go to the hospital. Have a doctor check out your head."

"Nah, it's nothing, Savich, the skin's barely split. Don't worry about that. Thing is my wallet was taken, and I really don't know what to make of it all."

Savich said slowly, "You think some people know you're after my grandmother's paintings?"

"Could be. Thing is, when I got that phone call at your house, I wasn't exactly truthful with Lily. It wasn't an emergency with a client here in New York. It was from an art world weasel I do business with occasionally. I'd called him from your house earlier and he said he'd heard some things, too, and now he's put out some feelers for me on the Sarah Elliott paintings. He was expecting some solid results soon, would have something to show me, and he needed me up here in New York. I was supposed to meet him tonight, but he called earlier and said he didn't have everything together yet. So it's on for tomorrow night, at the Plaza Hotel, the Oak Room Bar, one of his favorite places. The guy's good, really knows what he's doing, so I'm hopeful."

"All right, sounds promising. Now, in case you were wondering how good a liar you are, Lily didn't believe you for a minute. Your mugging, Simon, maybe it was just a mugging or maybe it was a warning. They didn't hurt you seriously, and they could have. I'll bet you a big one that your wallet is in a Dumpster somewhere near the gym. So take a look."

Simon could picture Savich pacing up and down that beautiful living room with its magnificent skylights.

"How's Sean?"

"Asleep."

"Is Lily asleep, too?"

"Nope. She's here, knows it's you on the phone, and wants to lay into you. I can't stop her from coming up, Simon."

Simon said, "Okay, give her my address, tell her to take a shuttle up here. I'll meet her unless there's a problem. I wish you could keep her with you longer, Savich."

"No can do."

Simon said, "I changed my mind, Savich. It may be turning dangerous, real fast. I really don't want Lily involved in this. She's a civilian. She's your sister. I take it all back. Tie her to a chair; don't let her come up here."

"Do you happen to have any suggestions about what I should do, other than tying her up?"

"Put her on the phone. I want to talk to her."

"Sure. She's about to rip the phone away from me in any case. Good luck, Simon."

A moment later, Lily said, "I'm here. I don't care what you have to say. Be quiet, go to the hospital, get a good night's sleep, and meet my plane tomorrow. I'll take the two-o'clock United shuttle to JFK. Then we can handle things. Good night, Simon."

"But Lily—"

She was gone.

Then Savich's voice came on. "Simon?"

"Yeah, Savich. Well, I'd have to say it was a nonstarter."

Savich laughed. "Lily's my sister. She's smart, and they are her paintings. Let her help with it, Simon, but keep her safe."

Simon bowed to the inevitable. "I'll try."

He took two aspirins and went back to his gym. There was a Dumpster half a block away. Lying on the top was his wallet, with only the cash gone. He looked up to see two young guys staring at him.

When one of them yelled an obscenity at him, Simon started forward. They didn't waste time and swaggered away, then turned when they figured they were far enough away from him and gave him the finger.

Simon smiled and waved.

HE was waiting for her, arms crossed, looking pissed.

Lily smiled, said even before she got to him, "I didn't want to carry much because of my missing spleen. I've got a bag down on carousel four."

"I've decided you're going back to Washington to draw your cartoons."

"While you find my paintings? Doesn't look like you started out very well, Mr. Russo. You don't look so hot. I think I did better on that bus than you did in your men's locker room last night. And I want to find my grandmother's paintings worse than you do."

And she walked past him to follow the signs to Baggage Claim.

Simon didn't own a car, had never felt the need to, so they took a taxi to East Seventy-ninth, between First and Second. He assisted her out of the cab, took her purse and suitcase, grunted because it had to weigh seventy pounds, and said, "This is it. I've got a nice guest room with its own bath. You should be comfortable until you wise up and go back home. How are they doing on that cult case in Texas? They got him yet? Wilbur Wright?"

"Not yet. What Dillon does is feed all the pertinent information into protocols he developed for the CAU—Criminal Apprehension Unit. Put that eyebrow back down. So you already know what he does and how he does it."

"I should have asked, has MAX got Wilbur yet?"

"MAX found out that Wilbur Wright is Canadian, that he attended McGill University, that he's a real whiz at cellular biology, and that his real name is Anthony Carpelli—ancestry, Sicily. Oh my, Simon, this is very lovely."

Lily stepped into a beautifully marbled entryway, and felt like she'd stepped back into the 1930s. The feel was all Art Deco—rich dark wood paneling, lamps in geometric shapes, a rich Tabriz carpet on the floor, furniture right out of the Poirot series on PBS.

"I bought it four years ago, after I got a really healthy commission. I knew the old guy who'd owned it for well nigh on to fifty years, and he gave me a good deal. Most of the furnishings were his. I begged and he finally sold me most of them. Neat, huh?"

"Very," she said, a vast understatement. "I want to see everything."

There was even a small library, bookshelves to the ceiling with one of those special library ladders. Wainscoting, leather furniture, rich Persian carpets on the dark walnut floor. He didn't show her his bedroom, but guided her directly to a large bedroom at the end of the hall. All of the furniture was a rich Italian Art Deco, trimmed with glossy black lacquer. Posters from the 1930s covered the walls. He put her suitcase on the bed and turned. She said, shaking her head, "You are so modern, yet here you are in this museum of a place that actually looks lived in. This is a beautiful room."

"Wait till you see the bathroom."

He didn't tell her that he was leaving until he had the key in his hand that evening at 10:30.

"I'm meeting a guy with information. No, you're not coming with me."

"All right."

He distrusted her, she could see it, and she smiled. "Look, Simon, I'm not lying. I'm not going to sneak out after you and follow you like some sort of idiot. I'm really tired. You can go hear what your informant has to say. Be careful. When you get back, I'll still be awake. Tell me what you find out, okay?"

He nodded and was at the Plaza Hotel by ten minutes to eleven.

LouLou was there, pacing back and forth along the park side of the Plaza, beautifully dressed, looking like a Mafia don. The uniformed Plaza doormen paid him little attention.

He nodded to Simon, motioned to the entrance to the Plaza's Oak Room Bar. It was dark and rich, filled with people and conversation. They found a small table, ordered two beers. Simon leaned back, crossing his arms over his chest. "How's it going, LouLou?"

"Can't complain. Hey, this beer on you? Drinks aren't cheap here, you know?"

"Since we're in New York, I figured the Oak Room would be our venue. Yeah, I'm paying for the beer. Now, what have you got for me?"

"I found out that Abe Turkle did the Elliotts. Talk is he had a contract to do eight of them. Do you know anything about which eight?"

"Yeah, I do, but you don't need to know any more. I would have visited Abe Turkle second. You sure it's not Billy Gross?"

"He's sick—his lungs—probably cancer. He's always smoked way too much. Anyway, he took all his money and went off to Italy. He's down living on the Amalfi Coast, nearly dead. So it's Abe who's your guy."

"And where can I find him?"

"In California, of all places."

"Eureka, by any chance?"

"Don't know. He's in a little town called Hemlock Bay, on the ocean. Don't know where it is. Whoever's paying him wants him close by where he is."

"You're good, LouLou. I don't suppose you'll tell me where you heard this?"

"You know better, Simon." He drank the rest of his beer in one long pull, wiped his mouth gently on a napkin, then said, "Abe's a mean sucker, Simon, unlike most artists. When you hook up with him, you take care, okay?"

"Yeah, I'll be real careful. Any word at all on who our likely collectors are?"

LouLou fiddled with a cigarette he couldn't light, even here in a bar. "Word is that it might be Olaf Jorgenson."

This was a surprise, a big surprise, to Simon. He wouldn't have put Olaf in the mix. "The richest Swede alive, huge in shipping. But I heard that he's nearly blind, nearly dead, that his collecting days are over."

LouLou said, "Yeah, that's the word out. Why buy a painting if you're blind as a bat and can't even see it? But, hey, that's what I heard from my inside gal at the Met. She's one of the curators, has an ear that soaks up everything. She's been right before. I trust her information."

"Olaf Jorgenson," Simon said slowly, taking a pull on his Coors. "He's got to be well past eighty now. Been collecting mainly European art for the past fifty years, medieval up through the nineteenth century. After World War Two, I heard he got his hands on a couple of private collections of stolen art from France and Italy. Far as I know, he's never bought a piece of art legally in his life. The guy's certifiable about his art, has all his paintings in climate-controlled vaults, and he's the only one who's got the key. I didn't know he'd begun collecting modern painters, like Sarah Elliott. I never would have put him on my list."

LouLou shrugged. "Like you said, Simon, the guy's a nut. Maybe nuts crack different ways when they get up near the century mark. His son seems to be just as crazy, always out on his yacht, lives there most of the time. His name's Ian—the old guy married a Scotswoman and that's how he got his name. Anyway, the son now runs all the shipping business. From the damned yacht."

Simon gave a very slight shake of his head to a very pretty woman seated at the bar who'd been staring at him for the past couple of minutes. He moved closer to LouLou to show that he was in very heavy conversation and not interested. "LouLou, how sure are you that it's Olaf who bought the paintings?"

"Besides my gal at the Met, I went out of my way to get it verified. You know my little art world birdies that are always singing, Simon. I spread a little seed, and they sing louder and I heard three songs, all with the same words. One hundred percent? Nope, but it's a start. Cost me a cool thousand bucks to get them to sing to me."

"Okay, you done good, LouLou." Simon handed him an envelope that contained five thousand dollars. LouLou didn't count it, just slipped the fat envelope inside his cashmere jacket pocket. "Hey, you know what the name of Ian Jorgenson's yacht is?"

Simon shook his head.

"*Night Watch.*"

Simon said slowly, "That's the name of a painting by Rembrandt. That particular painting is hanging in the Rijksmuseum in Amsterdam. I saw it there a couple of years ago."

LouLou cocked his head to one side, his hairpiece not moving a bit because it was expensive and well made, and gave Simon a cynical smile. "Who knows? Just maybe *Night Watch* is hanging in Ian's stateroom, right over his bed. I've often wondered how many real paintings there are left in the museums and not beautifully executed fakes."

"Actually, LouLou, I don't want to know the answer to that question."

"Since Sarah Elliott died only some seven years ago, all her materials—the paints, the brushes—still exist. You take a superb talent with an inherent bent toward her sort of technique and visualization, and what you get is so close to the real thing, most people wouldn't even care if you told them."

"I hate that."

"I do, too," LouLou said. "I need another beer."

Simon ordered them another round, ate a couple of peanuts out of the bowl on their table, and said, "Remember that forger Eric Hebborn, who wrote that book telling would-be forgers exactly how to do it—what inks, papers, pens, colors, signatures, all of it? Then he up and dies in ninety-six. The cops said it was under mysterious circumstances. I heard it was a private collector who killed Hebborn because a dealer friend had sold him an original Rubens that turned out to be a fake that Hebborn himself had done. Supposedly the dealer died shortly thereafter in a car accident."

LouLou said, "Yeah, I met old Eric back in the early eighties. Smart as a whip, that guy, and so talented it made you cry. You wondering if it was Olaf Jorgenson who popped him? Hey, Simon, there's a whole bunch of collectors who'd cut off hands to have a certain medal or stamp or train or painting. They've got to have it or life loses its meaning for them. Look, Simon, when you get down to it, they're the people who keep us in business."

"I wonder if Olaf ordered all eight paintings. I wonder what he's paying for them."

"Huge bucks, my man, huge, count on it. All eight Sarah Elliotts? Don't know. I haven't heard any other names floated around. Simon, I heard those eight paintings are owned privately by a member of the Elliott family?"

"Yes, Lily Savich owns them. And therein lies a very long, convoluted tale." Simon rose, putting a fifty-dollar bill on the table. "LouLou, thank you. You know where to find me. I think I'll be heading out to California soon to track down one of the major players—Abraham Turkle. He's English, right?"

"Half Greek. Weird guy. Very eccentric, said to eat only snails that he raises himself." LouLou shuddered. "You take care around him, Simon. Abe killed a guy who tried to rip him off with his bare hands, just a couple of years ago. So have a care. Hey, this Lily Savich hire you?"

Simon paused, cocked his head to the side. "Not exactly, but that's about it. I want to get those four paintings back."

"I hope the others are safe."

"Much safer than the snails in Abe's garden. Take care, LouLou."

"Why are you going after Abe?"

Simon said, "I want to see if I can shake something loose. It's not only the art scam. There are other folk involved in this deal who have done very bad things, and I want to nail them. Maybe Abe can help me do that."

"He won't help you do squat."

"We'll see. His forging days in Hemlock Bay are over. I want to catch him before he takes off to parts unknown. Who knows what I can get out of him."

"Good luck shaking the wasp nest. You know, I've always liked the name Lily," LouLou said and gave Simon a small salute. Then, when Simon left, LouLou turned his attention to that very pretty lady at the bar who'd kept looking over at them.

# FIFTEEN

Dr. Hicks said quietly, "Marilyn, tell me, how did Tammy look when she came back to the motel?"

"She had on a coat and she just ripped it apart and showed me her nurse's uniform. It was soaked with blood."

"Did she seem pleased?"

"Oh yes. She was crazy happy that she got away. She kept laughing and rubbing her bloody hand against herself. She loves the feel of fresh blood."

"How did she get back to the motel? You said her hand was all bloody. Wouldn't somebody have noticed?"

"I don't know." Marilyn looked worried, shaking her head.

"No, no, that's okay. It's not important. Now, you said she was wearing a coat. Do you know where she got the coat?"

"I don't know. When she came to get me, she was wearing it. It was too big for her, but it covered her arm where she didn't have one, you know?"

"Yes, I know. Mr. Savich would like to ask you some questions now. Is that all right, Marilyn?"

"Yes. He was nice to me. He's sexy. I'm kinda sorry Tammy's gonna kill him."

Dr. Hicks raised a thick brow at Savich, no look of shock on his face since he'd heard it all. He just shook his head as Savich eased his chair nearer to Marilyn's.

"She's well under, Savich. You know what to do."

Savich nodded. "Marilyn, how are you feeling about Tammy right now?"

She was silent, her forehead creased in a frown, then she shook her head, said slowly, "I think I love her; I'm supposed to since she's my cousin, but she scares me. I never know what she's going to do. I think she'd kill me, laugh while she rubbed my blood all over the only hand she's got left, if she was in the mood, you know?"

"Yes, I know."

"She's going to kill you."

"She might try, you told me. How do you think she contacts the Ghouls?" Savich ignored Dr. Hicks, who didn't have a clue who or what the Ghouls were. He shook his head and repeated the question. "Marilyn?"

"I've thought about that, Mr. Savich. I know they were there when she killed that little boy. Maybe, from what she said, she thinks about them and they come. Or maybe they follow her around and she says that to prove how powerful she is. Do you know what the Ghouls are?"

"No, I don't have any idea, Marilyn. You don't either, do you?"

She shook her head. She was sitting in a comfortable chair, her head leaning back against the cushion, her eyes closed. She'd been staying in a room at the Jefferson dormitory at the FBI complex, watched over by female agents. She'd washed her hair, and they'd given her a clean skirt and sweater. Even hypnotized, she looked pale and frightened, her fingers continually twitching and jerking. He wondered what would happen to her. She had no other family, no education to speak of, and there was Tammy, in the Caribbean, who'd scared her all of her life. He hoped the FBI would find her soon and Marilyn wouldn't have to be scared of her anymore.

He said, "Has Tammy been to the Caribbean before?"

"Yeah. She and Tommy visited the Bahamas a couple years ago. In the spring, I think."

"Did they take the Ghouls with them?"

Marilyn frowned and shook her head.

"You don't know if they killed anyone while they were there?"

"I asked Tommy, and he laughed and laughed. That was right before he got me pregnant."

Savich made a note to check to see if there'd been any particularly vicious, unsolved killings during their stay.

"Has Tammy ever talked about the Caribbean, other than the Bahamas? Any islands she'd like to visit?"

She shook her head.

"Think, Marilyn. That's right, just relax, lean your head back, and think about that. Remember back over the times you've seen her."

There was a long silence, and then Marilyn said, "She said once—it was Halloween and she was dressed like a vampire—that she wanted to go to Barbados and scare the crap out of the kids there. Then she laughed. I never liked that laugh, Mr. Savich. It was the same kind of laugh that Tommy had after the Bahamas."

"Did she ever talk about what the Ghouls did to those kids?"

"Once, when she was being Timmy, she said they just gobbled them right up."

"But the Ghouls don't just gobble them up, do they? They maybe take an arm, a leg?"

"Oh, Mr. Savich, they only do that when they're full and aren't interested in anything but a taste. But I can't be sure because both Tommy and Tammy never really told me."

Savich felt sick. Did she really mean what he thought she meant? That there were young boys who'd simply disappeared and would never be found because the Tuttles had eaten them? Were they cannibals? He unconsciously rubbed his arms at a sudden chill.

He looked at Dr. Hicks. His face was red, and he looked ready to be ill himself.

Savich lightly touched her forearm. "Thank you, Marilyn, you've been a big help. If you could choose right now, what would you like to do with your life?"

She didn't hesitate for a second. "I want to be a carpenter. We lived for about five years in this one place and the neighbor was a carpenter. He built desks and tables and chairs, all sorts of stuff. He spent lots of time with me, taught me everything. 'Course I paid him like he wanted, and he liked that a lot. In high school they told me I was a girl and girls couldn't do that, and then Tommy got me pregnant and killed the baby."

"One more question. Was Tammy planning to contact you from the Caribbean?" He'd asked her this before. He wanted to see if she added anything under hypnosis because now he had a plan.

"Yeah. She didn't say when, just that she would, sometime."

"How would she find you?"

"She would call my boyfriend, Tony, up in Bar Harbor. I don't think he likes me anymore. He said if the cops were after me, then he was out of there."

Savich hoped that Tony wouldn't take off too soon. He was still there, working as a mechanic at Ed's European Motors. He'd check in again with the agents in Bar Harbor, keep an eye on him, maybe some wiretaps. Now they had something solid. A call from Tammy.

"Thank you, Marilyn." Savich rose and went to stand by the door. He watched as Dr. Hicks brought her gently back. He listened as he spoke quietly to her, reassuring her, until he nodded to Savich, who led her from the room, holding her shoulder.

Savich said, "It's time for lunch, Marilyn. We'll eat in the Boardroom, not the big cafeteria. It's down the hall on this floor."

"I'd really like a pizza, Mr. Savich, with lots of pepperoni."

"You've got it. The Boardroom is known for its pizza."


*Eureka, California*

Simon was pissed. He'd sent Lily back to Washington. She'd been as pissed as he was now, but she'd finally given up, seen reason, and slid her butt into the taxi he'd called for her. Only she hadn't gone back to Washington. She'd simply taken the same plane he had to San Francisco, keeping out of sight in the back, then managed to make an earlier connection from San Francisco to Arcata-Eureka Airport. She'd waltzed right up to him at the damned baggage carousel and said in a chirpy voice, "I never thought I'd be traveling back to Hemlock Bay only two weeks after I finally managed to escape it."

And now they were sitting side by side in a rental car, and Simon was still pissed.

"You shouldn't have pulled that little sneaking act, Lily. Some bad stuff could happen. We're in their neck of the woods again, and I—"

"We're in this together, Russo, don't forget it," she said. She gave him a long look, then glanced out the back window of their rental car to study the three cars behind them. None appeared to be following them. She said, "You're acting like I've cut off your ego. This isn't your show, Russo. They're my paintings. Back off."

"I promised your brother I wouldn't let you get hurt."

"Fine. Okay, keep your promise. Where are we going? I was thinking it would be to Abe Turkle. You said maybe you could get something out of him, not about the collector he was working for, but maybe about the Frasiers. Since he's here, that pretty well proves he's involved with them, doesn't it?"

"That's right."

"You said Abraham Turkle is staying in a beach house just up the coast from Hemlock Bay. Do we know who owns it? Don't tell me it's my soon-to-be-ex-husband."

Simon gave it up. He turned to her as he said, "No, it's not Tennyson Frasier. It's close, but no, the cottage is in Daddy Frasier's name."

"Why didn't you tell me that sooner? That really nails it, doesn't it? Isn't that enough proof?"

"Not yet. Be patient. Everything will come together. Highway 211 is a very gnarly road, like you told me. Are we going to be passing the place where you lost your brakes and plowed into that redwood?"

"Yes, just ahead." But Lily didn't look at the tree as they passed it. The events of that night were growing more faint, the terror fading a bit, but it was still too close to her.

Simon said, "Turns out Abraham Turkle has no bank account, no visible means of support. So the Frasiers must be paying him in cash."

"I still can't get over their going to all this trouble," Lily said.

"After we verify that Mr. Olaf Jorgenson of Sweden now has three in his possession—no, we want him to have all four of the paintings, it'd keep things simple—we may be able to find out how much he's paid for them. I'm thinking in the neighborhood of two to three million per painting. Maybe higher. Depends on how obsessed he is. From what I hear, he's single-minded when he wants a certain painting."

"Three million? That's a whole lot of money. But to go to all this trouble—"

"I can tell you stories you don't want to hear about how far some collectors will go. There was one German guy who collected rare stamps. He found out his mother had one that he'd wanted for years, only she wanted to keep it for herself. He hit her over the head with a large bag of coins, killed her. Does that give you an idea of how completely obsessed some of these folk are?"

Lily could only stare at him. "It's hard to believe. This Olaf Jorgenson—you told me he's very old and nearly blind in the bargain."

"It is amazing that he can't control his obsession, not even for something as incidental as, say, going blind. I guess it won't stop until he's dead."

"Do you think his son Ian has the real *Night Watch* aboard his yacht?"

"I wouldn't be at all surprised."

"Are you going to tell the people at the Rijksmuseum?"

"Yeah, but trust me on this, they won't want to hear it. They'll have a couple of experts examine the painting on the sly. If the experts agree that it's a forgery, they'll try to get it back, but will they announce it? Doubtful.

"We've been checking out Mr. Monk, the curator of the Eureka Art Museum. He does have a PhD from George Washington, and a pedigree as long as your arm. If something's off there, Savich hasn't found it yet. We're going deeper on that, got some feelers out to a couple of museums where he worked. You keep looking back there. Is anyone following us?"

Lily shifted in her seat to face his profile. "No, no one's back there. I can't help it. To me, this is enemy territory."

"You're entitled. You had a very bad experience here. You met Mr. Monk, didn't you?"

"Oh yes."

"Tell me about him."

Lily said slowly, "When I first met Mr. Monk, I thought he had the most intense black eyes, quite beautiful really, 'bedroom eyes' I guess you could call them. But he looked hungry. Isn't that odd?"

Simon said, "He has beautiful eyes? Bedroom eyes? You women think and say the strangest things."

"Like men don't? If it were Mrs. Monk, you'd probably go on about her cleavage."

"Well, yeah, maybe. And your point would be?"

"You'd probably never even get to her face. You men are all one-celled."

"You think? Really?"

She laughed, she just couldn't help it. He pushed his sunglasses up his nose, and she saw that he was grinning at her. He said with a good deal of satisfaction, "You're feeling better. You've got a nice laugh, Lily. I like hearing it. Mind you, I'm still mad because you followed me out here, but I will admit this is the first time I've seen you that you don't look like you want to curl up and take a long nap."

"Get over it, Simon. We must be nearly to Abraham Turkle's cottage. Up ahead, Highway 211 turns left to go to Hemlock Bay. To the right there's this asphalt one-lane track that goes the mile out to the ocean. That's where the cottage is?"

"Yes, those were my directions. You've never been out to the ocean on that road?"

"I don't think so," she said.

"Okay now, listen up. Abe has a bad reputation. He's got a real mean side, so we want to be careful with him."

They came to the fork. Simon turned right, onto the narrow asphalt road. "This is it," Simon said. "There's no sign and there's no other road. Let's try it."

The ocean came into view almost immediately, when they were just atop a slight rise. Blue and calm as far as you could see, white clouds dotting the sky, a perfect day.

"Look at this view," Lily said. "I always get a catch in my throat when I see the ocean."

They reached the end of the road very quickly. Abe Turkle's cottage was a small gray clapboard, weathered, perched right at the end of a promontory towering out over the ocean. There were two hemlock trees, one on either side of the cottage, just a bit protected from the fierce ocean storms. They were so gnarly and bent, though, that you wondered why they even bothered to continue standing.

There was no road, only a dirt driveway that forked off the narrow asphalt. In front of the cottage sat a black Kawasaki 650 motorcycle.

Simon switched off the ignition and turned to Lily. She held up both hands. "No, don't say it. I'm coming with you. I can't wait to meet Abe Turkle."

Simon came around to open her car door. "Abe only eats snails and he grows them himself."

"I'm still coming in with you."

She carefully removed the seat belt, laid the small pillow on the backseat, and took his hand. "Stop looking like I'm going to fall over. I'm better every day. Getting out of a car is still a little rough." He watched her swing her legs over and straighten, slowly.

Simon said, "I want you to follow my lead. No reason to let him know who we are yet."

When he reached the single door, so weathered it had nearly lost all its gray paint, he listened for a moment. "I don't hear any movement inside."

He knocked.

There was no answer at first, and then a furious yell. "Who the hell is that and what the hell do you want?"

"The artist is apparently home," Simon said, cocking a dark eyebrow at Lily, and opened the door. He kept her behind him and walked into the cottage to see Abraham Turkle, a brush between his teeth, another brush in his right hand, standing behind an easel, glaring over the top toward them.

There was no furniture in the small front room, only painting supplies everywhere, at least twenty canvases stacked against the walls. The place smelled of paint and turpentine and french fries and something else—maybe fried snails. There was a kitchen separated from the living room by a bar, and a small hallway that probably led to a bedroom and a bathroom.

The man, face bearded, was indeed Abe Turkle; Simon had seen many photos of him.

"Hi," Simon said and stuck out his hand.

Abe Turkle ignored the outstretched hand. "Who the hell are you? Who is she? Why the hell is she standing behind you? She afraid of me or something?"

Lily stepped around Simon and extended her hand. "I like snails. I hear you do, too."

Abraham Turkle smiled, a huge smile that showed off three gold back teeth. He had big shoulders and hands the size of boxing gloves. He didn't look much like an artist, Simon thought. Abraham Turkle looked like a lumberjack. He was wearing a flannel shirt and blue jeans and big boots that were laced halfway to his knees. There were, however, paint splotches all over him, including his tangled dark beard and grizzled hair.

"So," Abe said, and he put down the brushes, wiped the back of his hand over his mouth to get off the bit of turpentine, and shook Lily's hand. "The little gal here likes snails, which means she knows about me, but I don't know who the hell you are, fella."

"I'm Sully Jones, and this is my wife, Zelda. We're on our honeymoon, just meandering up the coast, and we heard in Hemlock Bay that you were an artist and that you liked snails. Zelda loves art and snails, and we thought we'd stop by and see if you had anything to sell."

Lily said, "We don't know yet if we like what you paint, Mr. Turkle, but could you show us something? I hope you're not too expensive."

Abraham Turkle said, "Yep, I'm real expensive. You guys aren't rich?"

Simon said, "I'm in used cars. I'm not really rich."

"Sorry, you won't want to buy any of my stuff." He looked at Lily.

"Aw, hell. Wait here." Abe Turkle picked up a towel and wiped his hands. He walked past them to the far wall, where there were about ten canvases piled together. He went through them, making a rude noise here, sighing there, and then he thrust a painting into Lily's hand. "Here, it's a little thing I did just the other day. It's the Old Town in Eureka. For your honeymoon, little gal."

Lily held the small canvas up to the light and stared at it. She said finally, "Why, thank you, Mr. Turkle. It's beautiful. You're a very fine artist."

"One of the best in the world actually."

Simon frowned. "I'm sure sorry we haven't heard of you."

"You're a used-car salesman. Why would you have heard of me?"

"I was an art history major," Lily said. "I'm sorry, but I haven't heard of you either. But I can see how talented you are, sir."

"Well, maybe I'm more famous with certain people than with the common public."

"What does that mean?" Simon asked.

Abe's big chest expanded even bigger. "It means, used-car salesman, that I reproduce great paintings for a living. Only the artists themselves would realize they hadn't painted them."

"I don't understand," Lily said.

"It ain't so hard if you think about it. I reproduce paintings for very rich people."

Simon looked astonished. "You mean you forge famous paintings?"

"Hey, I don't like that word. What do you know, fella, you're nothing but a punk who sells heaps of metal; the lady could do a lot better than you."

"No, you misunderstand me," Simon said. "To be able to paint like you do, for whatever purpose, I'm really impressed."

"Hold it," Abe said suddenly. "Yeah, wait a minute. You aren't a used-car salesman, are you? What's your deal, man? Come on, what's going on here?"

"I'm Simon Russo."

That brought Abe to a stop. "Yeah, I recognize you now. Dammit, you're that dealer guy . . . Russo, yeah, you're him. You're Simon Russo, you son of a bitch. You'd better not be here to cause me any trouble. What the hell are you doing here?"

"Mr. Turkle, we—"

"Dammit, give me back that painting! You aren't on any honeymoon now, are you? You lied to me. As for you, Russo, I'm going to have to wring your scrawny neck."

# SIXTEEN

Lily didn't think. She assumed a martial arts position Dillon had shown her, the painting still clutched in her right hand.

She looked both ridiculous and defiant, and it stopped Abe Turkle in his tracks. He stared at her. "You want to fight me? You going to try to karate chop me with my own painting?"

She moved back and forth, flexed her arms, her fists. "I won't hurt your bloody painting. Listen, pal, I don't want to fight you, but I can probably take you. You're big but I'll bet you're slow. So go ahead, if you want, let's see how tough you are."

"Lily, please don't," Simon said as he prepared to simply lift her beneath her armpits and move her behind him. To Simon's surprise, Abe Turkle began shaking his head. He laughed, and then he laughed some more.

"You're something, little lady."

Abe made to grab the painting from Lily's hand, and she said quickly, whipping it behind her back, "Please let me keep it, Mr. Turkle. It really is beautiful. I'll treasure it always."

"Oh, hell, keep the stupid thing. I don't want to fight you either. It's obvious to me you're real tough. I might never get over being scared of you. All right, now. Let's get it over with. What do you want, Simon Russo? And who is the little gal here?"

"I'm here to see which Sarah Elliott you're working on now."

Abe Turkle glanced back at his easel, and his face blotched red as he said, "Listen to me, Russo, I barely heard of the broad. You want to look?"

"Okay." Simon smiled and walked toward Abe.

Abe held up a huge hand still stained with daubs of red, gold, and white paint. "You try it and I'll break your head off at your neck. Even the little lady here won't be able to hold me off."

Simon stopped. "Okay. Since there were no paintings missing from the Eureka Art Museum, you must be having trouble working from photographs they brought to you. Which one is it? Maybe *The Maiden Voyage* or *Wheat Field*? If I were selecting the next one, it would be either of those two."

"Go to hell, boyo."

"Or maybe you had to stop with the Sarah Elliotts altogether now they're gone from the museum? So you're doing something else now?"

"I'd break your head for you right this minute, right here, but not with my new stuff around. You want to come outside?"

"You were right about the lady," Simon said. "She isn't my wife. She's Lily Savich, Sarah Elliott's granddaughter. The eight paintings that were in the museum, including the four you've already copied, belong to her."

"Are you finishing a fifth one, Mr. Turkle? If you are, it's too bad because you won't get paid for it. The real one is back in my possession so there won't be any chance to switch it."

Simon said, "Actually, I'm surprised you're still here in residence since the paintings have flown the coop. They're hoping they'll get them back? No chance.

"To be honest, Abe, the real reason we're here is that we want to know who commissioned you. Not the collector, but the local people who are paying you and keeping you here."

"Yes," Lily said. "Please, Mr. Turkle, tell us who set this up."

Abe Turkle gave a big sigh. He looked at Lily and his fierce expression softened, just a bit. "Little gal, why don't you marry me and then I could look at those paintings for the rest of my life. I swear I'd never forge anything again."

"I'm sorry, but I'm still married to Tennyson Frasier."

"Not for long. I heard all about how you walked out on him."

"That's right. But even so, the paintings belong in a museum, Mr. Turkle, not in a private collection somewhere, locked away, to be enjoyed by only one person."

"They're the ones with all the money. They call the shots."

Simon said, "Abe, she's divorcing Tennyson. She wants to fry that bastard's butt, not yours. You'd do yourself a favor if you helped us."

Abe said slowly, one eyebrow arched up a good inch, "You've got to be joking, boyo."

Lily stepped forward and laid her hand on Abe Turkle's massive shoulder. "We're not joking. You could be in danger. Listen, Tennyson tried to kill me, and I wondered, Why now? Do you know? Did something happen to make him realize I was a threat to him, before you'd finished copying all the paintings? Please, Mr. Turkle, tell us who hired you to copy my paintings. We'll help you stay safe."

"That really so? Your old man tried to kill you? I'm sorry about that, but I don't have a clue what you're talking about. Both of you need to get out of here now."

He was standing with his legs spread, his big arms crossed over his chest. "I'm sorry you were almost killed, but it doesn't have anything to do with me."

"We know," Simon said, "that this cottage is owned by the Frasiers. You're staying here. It isn't a stretch to figure it out."

"I don't have anything to say about that. Maybe when this is over, the little gal will share some lunch with me, I'll marinate up some snails, then broil them. That's the best, you know."

Lily shook her head, then walked to the easel. Abe didn't get in her way, didn't try to block her. She stopped and sucked in her breath. On the easel was a magnificent painting nearly finished—it was Diego Velázquez's *Toilet of Venus,* oil on canvas.

"It's incredible. Please, Mr. Turkle, don't let some collector take the original. Please."

Abe shrugged. "I'm painting it for the fun of it. I'm in between jobs right now. No, you don't want to say it's because you took all the Sarah Elliott paintings away from the museum. Nah, don't say that. There's nothing going on here so I'm just having me some fun."

Simon came around and looked at the nearly completed painting. "The original is in the National Gallery in London. I hope your compatriots elect to leave it there, Abe."

"Like I said, this is for fun. A guy's got to keep practicing, you know what I mean? Look, I painted this from a series of photos. If I were in it for bucks, I wouldn't have let her see it. I'd be in London, too."

Lily couldn't give up, not yet. "Won't you tell us the truth, Mr. Turkle? Tennyson Frasier married me only to get his hands on the paintings. Then he tried to kill me. Did he tell you that, Mr. Turkle? It's possible that he murdered my child as well, I don't know for sure. Please, we won't involve you. Please tell us."

Abe Turkle looked back and forth between the two of them. He slowly shook his head.

"I wish you hadn't found me, Russo," Abe Turkle said, shaking his big head. "I really wish you hadn't." He turned then and walked out the cottage door.

"Wait!" Lily started after him.

Simon grabbed her sleeve and pulled her back. "Let him go, Lily."

They watched from the doorway as the big, black Kawasaki scattered rocks and dirt as it picked up speed. Then he was gone.

"We screwed up," Simon said.

"I wish he'd stayed and fought me," Lily said.

Simon looked down at her, remembering the image of her in a fighting position, with that painting in her right hand. He grinned. He lightly touched his hand to her hair. "You're all blond and blue-eyed, you're skinny as a post, your pants are hanging off your butt, and knowing you for just a short time, I know you've got more guts than brains. I swear to you, when I tell Savich how his little sister was ready to take on Abe Turkle, he'll— No, better not tell him how I nearly got you into a fight."

Lily punched him in the gut. "You jerk. I didn't see you trying to do anything."

Simon grunted, rubbed his palm over his belly, and grinned down at her. "I hope you didn't pull anything loose when you hit me. Not in me, in you."

"I might have, no thanks to you."

She didn't speak to him until they were back in the car and headed down to Hemlock Bay.

"We're going to see Tennyson?"

"Nope, we've got other fish to fry."

*Washington, D.C.*
*The Hoover Building*
*Fifth Floor, The Criminal*
*Apprehension Unit*

It was one o'clock in the afternoon. Empty sandwich wrappers were strewn on the conference table, leaving the vague smell of tuna fish with an overlay of roast beef, and at least a dozen soda cans stood empty. They'd just finished their daily update meeting. Savich's second in charge, Ollie Hamish, said to the assembled agents around the CAU conference table, "I'm going to Kitty Hawk, North Carolina, in the morning. Our research says that he not only took the real Wilbur's name, he's spent a lot of time in Wright's hometown. Chances are, though, that he's not going to Dayton, since everyone's looking for him there, but to Kitty Hawk. I've gotten all the data over to Behavioral Sciences, to Jane Bitt. We'll see what she's got to add, but that's it, so far.

"I'm going to our office down there, fill them all in, and get things set up for when he turns up."

Savich nodded. "Sounds good, Ollie. No more supposed sightings of the guru in Texas?"

"Oh, yeah," Ollie said, "but we're letting the agents there deal with them. Our people here believe guru Wilbur is already heading across country, due east to North Carolina. Our offices across the South are all alerted. Maybe we can get him before he hits Kitty Hawk. It might be that Kitty Hawk will be his last stand. We don't want him to bring real havoc when he gets there. We'll see if Jane Bitt agrees."

Sherlock said, "Have we got photos?"

"The only photo we've got is old and fuzzy, unfortunately. We're looking at getting more."

Special Agent Dane Carver, newly assigned to the unit, said, "Why don't you give me the photo, Ollie, and let me work on it. Maybe we can clean it up in the lab."

"You got it."

Savich looked around the conference table. "Everyone on track now?"

There were grunts, nods, and groans.

Shirley, the CAU secretary, said, "What about Tammy, Dillon? Any sightings? Any word at all yet?"

"Not a thing as yet. It's only been a day since I spoke to Marilyn Warluski at Quantico. Our people are staying with Tony, Marilyn's boyfriend, in Bar Harbor. His phone's covered. If Tammy calls, we'll hear it all. He's cooperating." Savich paused a moment, then shrugged. "It's frustrating. She's not in good shape, yet no one's seen her. Chances are very good she did indeed murder a pharmacist in Souterville, New Jersey. The other pharmacist checked and said someone had rifled through the supplies. Vicodin, a medication to control moderate pain, and Keflex, an oral antibiotic, a good three or four days' supply, were missing. Evidently she killed the guy because he refused to give her anything.

"As you know, we alerted police on all islands to Tammy's possible presence. Now they also know to keep a close eye on doctors and pharmacies, and why."

Ollie said, sitting forward, his hands clasped, "Look, Savich, she threatened you. I read you the note. She means it. We've all been talking about it, and we think you should have some protection. We think Jimmy Maitland should assign you some guards."

Savich thought about it a minute, then looked down the table to Sherlock. He realized she was thinking about Tammy finding out where they lived and coming to the house. She was thinking about Sean. He said to Ollie, "I think that's a great idea. I'll speak to Mr. Maitland this afternoon. Thanks, Ollie, I really hadn't thought it through."

He called a halt, scheduled a meeting with his boss, Jimmy Maitland, within the hour, and kissed Sherlock behind a door. Then he went to his office and punched in Simon's cell phone.

Simon answered on the third ring. "Yo."

"Savich here. Is Lily all right? What's going on?"

"Yes, she's fine." Simon then told him about their meeting with Abe Turkle, omitting Lily's challenge to beat the crap out of Abe. Then he told him about their much shorter meeting in Hemlock Bay with Daddy Frasier. "That old guy's really something, Savich. The guy hates Lily, you can see it in his eyes, colder than a snake's, and in his body language. I think he would have threatened her if I hadn't been there."

Savich wanted details, and so Simon told him exactly what had happened.

They'd gone to Elcott Frasier's office because they wanted to get in the old man's face, scare the bejesus out of him, let him know that everyone was on to him. Since he was the president and big cheese of the Hemlock National Bank, he had the shiny corner office on the second floor, all windows, a panoramic view of both the ocean and the town. Simon had wondered if Frasier would see them. His administrative assistant, Ms. Loralee Carmichael, at least twenty-one years old, and so beautiful it made your teeth ache to look at her, left them to kick up their heels for only twelve minutes, acceptable, Simon decided, since they'd caught the old man off guard and he'd probably want to get himself and his stories together. But Simon was worried about Lily. He'd have given anything to put her on a plane back to Washington, D.C., where she'd be safe. She looked nearly flattened, her face pale and set. If there'd been a bed nearby, he'd have tied her down in it. She moved slowly, but she had that lockjaw determined look, and so he kept his mouth shut.

Elcott Frasier welcomed them into his office, patted Lily's shoulder, his hand a bit on the heavy side, and said, "Lily, dear. May I say that you don't look well."

"Mr. Frasier." She immediately moved away from him. "Since you've already said it, I don't suppose there's anything I can do about it." She gave him a smile as cold as his own. "This is Mr. Russo. He's a dealer of art. He's the one who verified that four of my Sarah Elliott paintings are forgeries."

Elcott Frasier nodded to Simon and motioned to them to be seated. "Well, this comes as quite a surprise. You say you're an art dealer, Mr. Russo. I don't know many art dealers who can spot forgeries. Are you quite sure about this?"

"I'm not exactly an art dealer, Mr. Frasier, as in running a gallery. I'm more a dealer/broker. I bring buyers and sellers together. Occasionally I track down forgeries and return them to their rightful owners. Since I own a Sarah Elliott and know her work intimately, I was able to spot the fakes among the eight paintings that Lily owns, particularly since I knew which four had been forged."

Simon paused a moment, wondering how much to tell Frasier and if it would frighten the man. He'd known, of course, about the forgeries, didn't even try to act shocked. Why not push it all the way, since he had a pretty good idea of how it had gone down? It would have to make him act. He hadn't told Lily this and hoped she wouldn't act surprised. He smiled toward her, then added, "I originally thought that you initiated the whole deal. But then I got to thinking that you're really a very small man, with no contacts at all. There's a collector, a Swede named Olaf Jorgenson, who isn't a small man. He's very powerful, actually. When he wants something, he goes after it, no obstacle too great. I believe that it was Jorgenson who instigated the whole thing. It went this way: Olaf wanted the Sarah Elliott paintings when they were in the Art Institute of Chicago, but he couldn't pull it off and had to wait. He knew exactly when Lily Savich left Chicago to move to Hemlock Bay, California. He put out feelers and found you very quickly, and your son, Tennyson, who was the right age. Then you all cut a deal. Actually, I heard Olaf had only three of the paintings. I don't know where the fourth one is as of yet. Hopefully, he has it as well. It makes everything cleaner, easier." Simon snapped his fingers right in Frasier's face. "We'll get them back fast as that. So, Mr. Frasier, did I get it all right?"

Elcott Frasier didn't bat an eye. He looked faintly bored. Lily, though, who knew him well, saw the slight tic in his left eye, there only when he was stressed out or angry. He could be either or both at this moment in time. She was surprised initially at what Simon had said but realized that it had probably happened just as Simon had said. She said, "Jorgenson is indeed powerful, Elcott. He isn't a small man at all, not like you."

Simon thought her father-in-law would belt her. He was ready for it, but Frasier managed to hold himself in. He said, dismissively and as smoothly as a politician accepting a bribe for a pardon, "That's quite a scenario, Mr. Russo. I'm sorry to hear four of the paintings were forged. No matter what you say, it must have happened while they were at the Art Institute of Chicago. All this elaborate plot by this fellow Olaf Jorgenson sounds like a bad movie. However, none of this has anything to do with me or my family. I really don't know why you came here to accuse me of it."

He turned to Lily and there was a good deal of anger in those eyes of his. "As for you, Lily, you left my son. I fear for his health. He is not doing well. All he talks about is you. He says that your brother and sister-in-law slandered him, and none of it's true. He wants to see you, although if I were him, and I've told him this countless times, I'd just as soon see the back of you for good. You weren't a good wife to him. You gave him nothing, and then you just up and left him. His mother is also very concerned. The mere idea that he would marry you to get ahold of some paintings, it's beyond absurd."

"I don't think it's absurd at all, Elcott. It could have happened the way Mr. Russo said. Or maybe it was Mr. Monk who found Mr. Jorgenson. Either way, four of my paintings are fakes and you are the one responsible.

"Now, if Tennyson isn't doing well, I recommend that he pay a visit to Dr. Rossetti, the psychiatrist he very badly wanted me to see when I was still in the hospital. One wonders what he had to do with all this." Lily paused a moment, shrugged, then continued. "But of course you would know about that. How much did you pay Morrie Jones to kill me?"

"I didn't pay him a—" She'd snagged him, caught him completely off guard. He'd burst right out with it, then cut off like a spigot, but too late. Simon was impressed.

The tic was very pronounced now, and added to it was a face turning red with outrage.

"You're quite a bitch, you know that, Lily? I can see why you brought your bodyguard with you. This painting business, I don't know what you've done, but you can't lay it on me. I'm not to blame for anything."

Simon wanted, quite simply, to stand, reach over Mr. Frasier's desk, and yank the man up by his expensive shirt collar and smash him in the jaw. It surprised him, the intense wish to do this man physical damage. But when he spoke, he was calm, utterly measured. "Trust me, Mr. Frasier, Lily isn't a bitch. As for your precious son, what he is isn't in much doubt. Would you like to tell us why Abe Turkle is staying at your cottage?" Simon sat slightly forward in his chair, the soul of polite interest.

"I don't know who that is or why he's there. The real estate agent handles rentals."

"Naturally Abe knows you, Mr. Frasier, knows everything, since he's forged the paintings for you. I do know that he's expensive. Or perhaps Olaf is handling his payments as part of the deal?"

Mr. Frasier got to his feet. The pulse was pounding in his heavy neck. He was nearly beyond control, his hands shaking. Almost there, Simon thought. Elcott Frasier pointed to the door and yelled, "I don't know any damned Olaf! Now, get out, both of you. Lily, I don't wish to see you again. It's a pity that the mugger didn't teach you a lesson."

Simon said, "We'll return for a very nice visit, along with the FBI, when we have our proof. Not much longer. Consider this a reality check. You might want to consider cutting a deal right now, with us. If you don't, just think of all those big, mean prisoners in the federal lockups; they like vulnerable old guys like you."

"Get out or I'll call the sheriff!"

Lily laughed, couldn't help it. "Sheriff Bozo?"

Elcott Frasier yelled, "His name is Scanlan, not Bozo!" Then he nearly ran to the door, jerked it open, and left them staring after him. Simon said to Lily as he helped her to her feet, "It's been quite a morning, first Abe and now your soon-to-be-ex-father-in-law, both of them leaving us in their lairs and stalking off. But everyone is shook up now, Lily. We've stirred the pot as much as we can. Now we wait to see who does what. Maybe old man Frasier will decide to cut a deal. Now, you ready for a light lunch, maybe Mexican?"

"There isn't a Mexican restaurant in Hemlock Bay. We'll have to go to Ferndale."

Loralee Carmichael looked them over very carefully as they left the reception area. Simon wiggled his fingers in good-bye to her. There was no sign of Elcott Frasier.

He said carefully, as he walked slowly beside her to the elevator, "I want you to consider leaving the rest of this to me. Can I talk you into going back to Washington?"

"No, don't even try, Simon."

"I had to try. When bad men are afraid, Lily, they do things that aren't necessarily smart, but are, many times, deadly."

"Yes. We will be very careful."

He sighed and gave it up. "Over tacos we can discuss our next foray."

"Do you really think Olaf Jorgenson set this whole thing up?"

"When you think about it, he's the one with all the contacts and the expertise, unless our Mr. Monk knows more about the illegal side of the business than we're aware of yet. I'm sure Frasier will be speaking to Mr. Monk if he hasn't already. I can't wait to hear what this guy with his bedroom eyes has to say."

SIMON paused a moment, switched his cell phone to his other ear, then said, "That's all of it, Savich, every gnarly detail."

He waited for Savich to ask him questions, but Savich didn't say anything. Simon could practically hear him sorting through possible scenarios.

Simon said, "Lily did really good, Savich. She's tired, but she's hanging in. I've tried to talk her into going back to Washington, but she won't hear of it. I swear I'll keep her safe."

"I know you will," Savich said finally. "Just to let you know, Clark Hoyt, the SAC in the Eureka FBI office, is going to provide you backup. I figured you guys would stir everything up and that could be very dangerous. I don't want you to be on your own. If you happen to see a couple of guys following you, they're there to keep you safe. If you have any concerns, give Clark Hoyt a call. Now, you make Lily rest. How many tacos did she get down?"

"Three ground beef tacos, a basketful of chips, and an entire bowl of hot salsa. We're going to hole up now, then see Mr. Monk in the morning.

By then, they'll all have spoken together, examined their options, made plans. I can't wait to see what they'll do. Give my love to Sherlock, and let Sean teethe on your thumb. Any word on Tammy Tuttle?"

"No."

"I'll call you after we've seen Mr. Monk tomorrow."

"Clark told me they've got a line on Morrie Jones. It shouldn't be long before he's in the local jail."

"I'll call the cops in Eureka and find out." He paused, then added, "I'm not planning on letting Lily out of my sight."

# SEVENTEEN

*Eureka, California*
*The Mermaid's Tail*

Lily was deeply asleep, dreaming, and in that dream, she was terrified. There was something wrong, but she didn't know what. Then she saw her daughter, and she knew Beth was crying, sobbing, but Lily didn't know why. Suddenly, Beth was far away, her sobs still loud, but Lily couldn't get to her. She called and called, and then Beth simply wasn't there and Lily was alone, only she wasn't really. She knew there was something wrong, but she didn't know what.

Lily jerked up in bed, drenched with sweat, and groaned with the sharp ache the abrupt movement brought to her belly. She grabbed her stomach and tried to breathe in deeply.

When she did, she smelled smoke. Yes, it was smoke and it was in her room. That was what was wrong, what had brought her out of the nightmare. The smell of smoke, acrid, stronger now than just a moment before. Then she saw it billowing up around the curtains in the window, black and thick, the curtains just catching fire.

Dear God, the bed-and-breakfast was on fire. She hauled herself out of the high tester bed with its drapey gauze hangings and hit the floor running.

Her door was locked. Where was the key? Not in the door, not on the dresser. She ran to the bathroom, wet a towel, and pressed it against her face.

She ran to the phone, dialed 911. The phone was dead. Someone had set the fire and cut the phone lines. Or had the fire knocked out the lines? Didn't matter, she had to get out. Flames now, in the bedroom, licking up around the edges of the rug beneath that window with its light and gauzy draperies. She raced, bowed over, to the wall and began banging on it. "Simon! Simon!"

She heard him then, shouting back to her. "Lily, get the hell out of there, now!"

"My door's locked. I can't get it open!"

"I'm coming! Stay low to the floor."

But Lily couldn't just lie down and wait to be rescued. She was too scared. She ran back to the door and pulled and tugged the doorknob. She picked up a chair and smashed it hard into the door. The chair nearly bounced off it. It didn't matter, anything to loosen it from its frame. The door did shudder a bit. She realized the door wasn't hollow. It was old-fashioned and solid wood. She heard Simon jerk his door open, heard him knocking on doors, yelling. Thank God he hadn't been locked in like she was.

Then he was at her door, and she quickly moved back. She heard him kick it, saw it shudder. Then he kicked it hard again, and the door slammed inward. "You okay?"

"Yes. We've got to warn everyone." She began coughing, doubled over, and he didn't hesitate. He picked her up in his arms and carried her down the wide mahogany staircase.

Mrs. Blade was in the lobby, and she was helping out a very old lady who was sobbing quietly.

"It's Mrs. Nast. She's a permanent resident. I tried to call nine-one-one but the line's dead, of all things. There are people on the third floor, Mr. Russo. Please get them."

"I've already called nine-one-one on my cell phone. They're on their way." Simon set Lily down and ran back up the stairs. He heard her hacking cough as he ran.

He didn't get to the top of the stairs alone. Beside him at the last minute were firemen, all garbed up and yelling for him to get back downstairs and out of the building.

He nodded, then saw a young woman struggling with two children, coughing, trying to pull them down the corridor. The two firemen had their hands full with other guests. Simon simply grabbed all three of them up in his arms and carried them downstairs. They were all coughing by the time they got out the front door, the kids crying and the mother holding herself together, comforting them, thanking him again and again until he put his hand over her mouth. "It's okay. Take care of your kids."

They saved a lot of The Mermaid's Tail, and all of the ten people staying there. No serious injuries, only some smoke inhalation.

Colin Smith, the agent sent over by Clark Hoyt to maintain an overnight watch on the bed-and-breakfast, told them he'd seen two men sneaking around, followed and lost them, turned back to see the smoke billowing up, and immediately called the fire department. That was why most of The Mermaid's Tail was still standing.

Agent Smith left them, after making certain they were okay, to repeat his story to the fire chief and the arson investigator, who'd just arrived.

Simon was holding Lily close to him. She was barefoot, wearing a long white flannel nightgown that came to her ankles, and her hair was straggling around her shoulders. He'd managed to scramble into jeans and a sweater and sneakers before he'd left his bedroom. He blew out, but didn't see his breath. It was cold, probably just below fifty degrees, and the firemen were distributing coats and blankets to all the victims. Neighbors were coming out with more blankets and coffee, even some rolls to eat.

Simon said, "You okay, Lily?"

She nodded. "We're alive. That's all that matters. The bastards. I can't believe they set the entire place on fire. So many people could have been hurt, even killed."

"Your brother realized before I did they'd probably try something. You met Agent Colin Smith. Your brother got the SAC here in Eureka to send him to watch over us."

She sighed. She was exhausted, doubted that any part of her would move, even if she begged. "Yeah, I realized he was a guard for us. I sure wish he'd caught them before they set the fire."

"He does, too. He's really beating himself up. He was calling in his boss, Clark Hoyt, last time I saw him. Hoyt will probably be here soon. I'll bet you he's already called Savich."

"At four o'clock in the morning?"

"Good point."

"It's really cold, Simon."

He was sitting on a lawn chair that a neighbor had brought over. He pulled her onto his lap, wrapping the blankets around both of them. "Better?"

She nodded against his shoulder and whispered, "This really sucks."
He laughed.

"You know, Simon, even Remus wouldn't go so far as to do this sort
of thing. Someone so desperate, so malevolent, they don't care how many
people they kill? That's really scary."

"Yes," he said slowly, "it is. I didn't expect anything like this."

"You got mugged in New York so soon after you left Washington.
These people work really fast. I'm beginning to think it's Olaf Jorgenson
behind all this, not the Frasiers, like you said. How would the Frasiers
have even known about you or where you were?"

"I agree. But you know, the guy didn't try to kill me, at least I don't
think he did."

"Probably a warning."

"I guess. This wasn't a warning. This was for real. We're in pretty
deep now, Lily. I'll bet you Clark Hoyt isn't going to let us out of his sight
for as long as we're in his neck of the woods."

"At this point I'm glad. No, Simon, don't say it. I'm not about to leave
you alone now." She fell silent, and for a little while he thought she'd finally given out. Then she said, "Simon, did I ever tell you that Jeff Mac-
Nelly was my biggest influence for Remus?"

Who was Jeff MacNelly? He shook his head slowly, fascinated.

"Yes, he was. I admired him tremendously." When she realized he
didn't have a clue, she added, "Jeff MacNelly was a very famous and talented cartoonist. He won three Pulitzer Prizes skewering politicos. But he
never once said that they were evil. He died in June of 2000. I really miss
him. It upsets me that I never told him how much he meant to me, and to
Remus."

"I'm sorry to hear that, Lily." He realized then she was teetering on
the edge of shock, so he pulled another blanket around her. It was too
much even for her. Her life had flown out of control when she'd married
Tennyson Frasier. He couldn't imagine what she'd gone through when
her daughter had been killed and she'd managed to survive months of
depression. And then all this.

Lily said, "Jeff MacNelly said that 'when it comes to humor, there's
no substitute for reality and politicians.' I don't like this reality part, Simon, I really don't."

"I don't either."

*Washington, D.C.*
*Hoover Building*

Savich slowly hung up the phone, stared out his window a moment, then lowered his face to his hands.

He heard Sherlock say, "What is it, Dillon? What's happened?" Her competent hands were massaging his shoulders, her breath was warm on his temple.

He raised his head to look up at her. "I should have killed her, Sherlock, should have shot her cleanly in the head, like I did Tommy Tuttle. This is all my fault—that boy's death in Chevy Chase, and now this."

"She's killed again?"

He nodded, and she hated the despair in his eyes, the pain that radiated from him. "In Road Town, Tortola, in the British Virgin Islands."

"Tell me."

"That was Jimmy Maitland. He said the police commissioner received all our reports, alerted his local officers, waited, and then a local pharmacist was murdered, his throat cut. The place was trashed, impossible to tell what drugs were taken, but we know what was stolen—pain meds and antibiotics. They don't have any leads, but they're combing the island for a one-armed woman who's not in good shape. No sign of her yet. Not even a whiff. Tortola isn't like Saint Thomas. It's far more primitive, less populated, more places to hide, and the bottom line is there's no way to get to and from the island except by boat."

"I'm very sorry it happened. You know she's gotten ahold of a boat. By now she's probably long gone from Tortola, to another island."

"It's hard to believe that no one's reported a boat stolen."

"It's late," Sherlock said. "E-mail all the other islands, then let it go for a while. Let's go home, play with Sean, then head over to the gym. You need a really hard workout, Dillon."

He rose slowly. "Okay, first I've got to talk to all the local cops down there, make sure they know what's happened on Tortola, tell them again how dangerous she is." He kissed her, hugged her tightly, and said against her temple, "Go home and start playing with Sean. I'll be there in a while. Have him gum some graham crackers for me."

*Quantico, Virginia*
*FBI Academy*

Special Agent Virginia Cosgrove cocked her head to one side and said, "Marilyn, it's for you. A woman, says she's with Dillon Savich's unit at headquarters. I'll be listening on the other line, okay?"

Marilyn Warluski, who was folding the last of her new clothes into the suitcase provided by the FBI, nodded, a puzzled look on her face. She was staying in the Jefferson dorm with two women agents, just starting to get used to things. What did Mr. Savich want from her now? She took the phone from Agent Cosgrove and said, "Hello?"

"Hi, sweet chops. It's Timmy. You hot for me, baby?"

Marilyn closed her eyes tight against the shock, against the disbelief. "Tammy," she whispered. "Is it really you?"

"No, it's Timmy. Listen up, sweetie, I need to see you. I want you to fly down here, to Antigua, tomorrow; that's when I'll be there. I'll be at the Reed Airport, waiting for you. Don't disappoint me, baby, okay?"

Marilyn looked frantically over at Virginia.

Virginia quickly wrote on a pad of paper, then handed it to Marilyn. "Okay, I can do it, but it'll be late."

"They treating you all right at that cop academy? Do you want me to come up with the Ghouls and level the place?"

"No, no, Tammy, don't do that. I'll fly down late tomorrow. Are you all right?"

"Sure. Had to get me some more medicine on Tortola. Lousy place, dry and boring, no action at all. Can't wait to get out of here. See you tomorrow evening, baby. Bye."

Marilyn slowly placed the phone in its cradle. She looked blankly at Virginia Cosgrove. "How did she know where I was? I need to call Dillon Savich, but it's really late."

Assistant Director Jimmy Maitland called Dillon Savich to mobilize the necessary agents. He got it done in two hours and set himself up to coordinate the group leaving for Antigua.

Maitland called in the SWAT team at the Washington, D.C., field office because they were bringing this all down very possibly in an airport, and there could always be trouble. He told Savich, "Yeah, I threw them some meat and they agreed to come out and play. We got one team, six really good guys."

Vincent Arbus, point man for the team, built like a bull, bald as a Q-tip, and many times too smart for his own good, looked at Savich, then at Sherlock, who was standing at his side, and said in his rough, low voice, "Call me Vinny, guys. I have a feeling that we're going to be getting tight before this is all over.

"Now, how did this crazy one-armed woman know that Marilyn Warluski was holed up in Jefferson dorm at Quantico? How did she get her number?"

"Well," Savich said slowly, not looking at Sherlock, "I sort of let it be known. Actually, I set the whole thing up."

# EIGHTEEN

*Eureka, California*

Mr. Monk was gone, his office left looking as if he would be returning the next day. There were no notes, no messages, no telltale appointments listed in his date book, which sat in the middle of his desk. There was no clue at all as to where he'd gone.

Nor was he at his big bay-windowed apartment on Oak Street. He hadn't cleaned out his stuff, had apparently taken off without a word to anyone.

Hoyt said to Simon when he opened his hotel room door, "He's gone. I stood in the middle of that empty living room with its fine paintings by Jason Argot on the white walls, with its own specialized lighting, and I tell you, Russo, I wanted to kick myself. I knew we should have covered his place, but I didn't. I'm an idiot. Kick me. There's got to be a clue somewhere in there about where his bolt-hole is. Or maybe not, but I haven't found a bloody thing. Really, Russo, kick my ribs in."

"Nah," Simon said as he zipped the fly on his new jeans and threaded his new belt. He waved Hoyt into his deluxe room with its king-size bed that took up nearly three-quarters of the space. Lily was right through the adjoining door. They were staying at the Warm Creek Lodge, both with an ocean view from one window and an Old Town view from the other. "I appreciate your checking him out for us first thing, since Lily and I didn't have any clothes at all. Though I wouldn't have minded paying the jerk a visit myself. Good thing I left my wallet in my jeans pocket last night or we'd be in really deep trouble. Actually, if the credit card companies hadn't sent me replacement credit cards after my wallet was stolen in New York, we'd still be in deep trouble. We're all outfitted now, real spiffy. What about Monk's car? Any sign of it?"

"We've got an APB out on it—a Jeep Grand Cherokee, 'ninety-eight, dark green. And we're covering the Arcata airport. We've sent out alerts as far down as SFO, though I don't think he could have gotten that far."

"Problem is, we don't know when he bolted. Don't you think it would be better if you issued a tri-state airport alert?"

"Yeah, good idea. I'm thinking he probably got scared. I doubt he has a fake ID or a passport. If he tries to take a flight, we'll nail him."

Simon nodded. "Would you like a cup of coffee? Room service just sent some up with croissants."

Clark Hoyt looked like he would cry. He didn't say another word until he'd downed two cups of coffee and eaten a croissant, smeared with a real butter pat and sugarless apricot jam.

When Lily came in a few minutes later, Simon smiled at the sight. She looked even better than he'd imagined. She was wearing black stretch jeans, a black turtleneck sweater, and black boots. She looked like a fairy princess who was also a cat burglar on her nights off. Clark Hoyt, when he rose to greet her, said, "Quite a change from how you looked early this morning. I like all the black."

Lily thanked him, poured herself a cup of coffee, and watched him eat a second croissant. He filled Lily in on what they hadn't found so far.

Hoyt said, "I called Savich back at Disneyland East and filled him in. He made me swear on the head of my schnauzer, Gilda, that you guys didn't have a single singed hair on your heads. It was arson, all right, but no idea yet who the perps were or who hired them."

"Disneyland East?" Lily asked, an eyebrow up.

"Yep, just another loving name for FBI headquarters. Hey, thanks for breakfast. You guys still smell like smoke. It's really tough to get it all out. I should know, I was overenthusiastic with my barbeque last summer and lost my eyebrows, although my face was so black you couldn't tell. Lay low; keep out of sight until I get some news for you, okay?"

IT was early afternoon when Hoyt came to get them from the lodge. Mr. Monk hadn't tried to fly out of harm's way. Actually, he hadn't flown anywhere. He was quite dead, head pressed against the steering wheel, three bullets through his back. The Jeep was in a sparse stand of redwood trees, and some hikers, poking around, had found him.

Lieutenant Larry Dobbs of the Eureka Police Department knew the situation was dicey, that it involved a whole lot more than this one body, and even the FBI was involved. He agreed to let Clark Hoyt bring out the two civilians, after the crime scene had been gone over.

Simon and Lily stood looking at the Jeep. "They didn't really try to hide him," she said. "On the other hand, it could have been a long time before someone accidentally came upon him. God bless hikers."

"The medical examiner estimates he's been dead about seven hours, give or take," said Clark Hoyt. "He'll know a lot more after the autopsy. Our lab guys will crawl all over that Jeep to see what's what. Ah, here comes Lieutenant Dobbs. You've met, haven't you?"

"We've spoken on the phone," Simon said and shook Dobbs's hand. Simon saw quickly enough that the lieutenant was impressed with how Clark Hoyt deferred to him.

"Do you think he was with someone?" Lily asked both men. "And that someone killed him and then moved his body to the driver's side?"

Lieutenant Dobbs said, "No. From the trajectory of the bullets, there was someone, the shooter, riding in the backseat, behind Monk. Maybe someone else riding in the passenger seat. I don't know. Maybe Monk knew they were taking him out to kill him. But if so, why did he calmly pull over? Again, I don't know. But the fact is he did pull off the road into the redwoods, and the guy in the backseat shot him."

Simon and Lily were given permission to walk over the area. They looked everywhere, but there wasn't anything to see. The hikers had made a mess of things in their initial panic. There were five cop cars and two FBI cars adding to the chaos. There weren't any tire tracks except the Jeep's, which meant that the other car must have stayed parked on the paved road.

Lieutenant Dobbs eyed Simon and Lily and said, "Agent Hoyt tells me you guys are involved in this up to your eyeballs. Let me tell you, you two have brought me more woes than I've had for the last ten years, beginning with that jerk who attacked you on the public bus, Mrs. Frasier. Oh, yeah, Officer Tucker found Morrie Jones a couple of hours ago, holed up in a fleabag hotel down on Conduit Street."

"Keep him safe, Lieutenant," Lily said. "He was part of this, too, as was Mr. Monk. And look what happened to him."

"You got it." Lieutenant Dobbs said then, "You know, it hasn't been all bad. I've met Hoyt here, a real federal agent and all, and I haven't had to watch *Wheel of Fortune* with my wife. I haven't had a single bored minute since I got that first call from you guys. Only bad thing is this body over there. A body's never good." He sighed and waved to one of the other officers. He said over his shoulder, "Clark, try to keep these two out of more mischief, all right? Oh, yes, I'm going to be interviewing all the Frasiers, including your husband, Mr. Tennyson Frasier. Maybe it'll scare them, make them do something else stupid. I understand you've already tried, got them all riled up. Now let's see how they handle the law." He waved toward the body bag containing Mr. Monk. "This wasn't a bright thing to do."

"Don't forget Charlotte Frasier, Lieutenant," Lily said, "and don't be fooled by that syrupy accent. She's terrifying."

Hoyt said, "Then I'm going to wait until the lieutenant is through with them, wait until they're nice and comfortable at their homes in Hemlock Bay again, and then I'm going to pay them a little visit and grill them but good. Savich has sent me lots of stuff. I've been speaking to some of our representatives in Sacramento, checking real close into El-cott Frasier's financial situation. Lots of conflicting info so far, but there's been a lot of flow in and out of his accounts there. Something will shake loose; it usually does. Oh, yeah, I heard that Elcott Frasier has hired Mr. Bradley Abbott, one of the very best criminal lawyers on the West Coast, to represent him and his family." Hoyt rubbed his hands together. "This is going to be really interesting."

As they drove back to Eureka, Simon was brooding. Lily recognized the signs. He looked single-minded as he drove, looking neither right nor left, saying nothing to Lily, who was hungry and wanted to go to the bathroom.

"Stop it, Simon."

That jerked him around to stare at her. "Stop what?"

"You've got a look that says you're far away, like maybe the Delta Quadrant."

"Yeah, I was thinking. About Abe Turkle. He's a loose end, Lily, like Mr. Monk. So is Morrie Jones, but he's in jail, and hopefully safe there. The lieutenant is going to put a guard on him."

Lily said, "I forgot to tell you, when you and Hoyt were talking back there, Lieutenant Dobbs told me Morrie claims he doesn't know a thing, that a couple of thugs hurt him when he was minding his own in a bar. He claimed no broad could ever hurt him. Oh yes, Morrie's got a big-time lawyer. I wonder how much money Morrie's being paid to keep his mouth shut."

Simon said, "Can Lieutenant Dobbs find out who hired the lawyer?"

"I asked him if he knew. He said he'd sniff around. Now, Simon, you're brooding because you think Abe Turkle might be in danger." In that instant, Lily forgot she was hungry, forgot she needed to go to the bathroom. "You've just made my stomach drop to my knees. Let's go see Abe, Simon."

He grinned over at her, braked, and did a wide U-turn.

"Hey," she said, "not bad driving. Won't this piece of garbage go any faster?"

Simon laughed. "You're the best, Lily, do you know that? Hey, I see someone doing another U-turn behind us. Must be our protection."

"Good. Hope he can keep up with us."

Simon laughed.

"My dad, Buck Savich, used to tell me that if I decided to become a professional bookie, I'd be the best in the business. Except for one thing."

"What's that?"

"He'd say my eyes changed color whenever I lied, and if anyone noticed that, my days as a bookie would be over."

"Your eyes are blue right now. What color do they go to when you lie?"

"I don't know. I've never looked at myself in the mirror and lied to it."

"I'll keep that in mind, though, and let you know."

Simon turned his attention back to the road. He saw big Abe Turkle in his mind, a paintbrush between his teeth, ready to beat the crap out of him. Then Abe's smile when he looked at Lily. The man was a crook, but he was an excellent artist. Simon didn't want him to get killed.

He sped up to sixty because his gut was crawling. Bad things, bad things. But he said in a smooth, amused voice, "You probably remember that I met your dad when Dillon and I were in our senior year at MIT. He was something else."

"Yes," she said. "He was the best. I miss him very much. All us kids do. As for Mom, she was a mess for a long time. She met this guy, a congressman from Missouri, just last year, still claims they're only friends, but she's a lot happier, smiles a lot more, just plain gets out and does more things. She adores Sean, too. He's the only grandkid close by."

"What did your mom think of all the legends about Buck Savich? There were so many colorful ones floating about long before he died."

"She'd shake her head, grin like a bandit, and say she didn't think the tales were exaggerations at all. Then, I swear it to you, she'd blush. I think she was talking about intimate things, and it always freaked us kids out. You can't think of your parents in that way, you know what I mean?"

"Yeah, I do. I guess, on the other side of the coin, our parents look at us and see little kids who will be virgins for the rest of their lives."

Lily laughed. "What about your parents? Where do they live?"

"My folks have been divorced for a very long time. My dad's a lawyer, remarried to a woman half his age. They live in Boston. No little half brothers or half sisters. My mom didn't remarry, lives in Los Angeles, runs her own makeover consulting firm. If they ever had any liking for each other, it was over before I could remember it. My sisters, both older than I am, told me they'd never seen anything resembling affection either." He paused a moment, slowed a bit for a particularly gnarly turn, then sped up again. "You know, Lily, I have a hard time seeing you as a bookie. Did you make some money for college?"

She gave him a shark's grin, all white teeth, ready to bite. "You bet. Thing was, though, Mom decided it was better that Dad not know exactly what my earnings totaled from age sixteen to eighteen, especially since I hadn't paid any taxes."

"It boggles the mind." He looked at her then, saying nothing, just looking. "Do you know that you're looking more like a fairy princess again? I like you in all that black. How's your scar doing?"

"My innards are fine; the scar itches just a bit. It's no wonder you like all black since you bought all my clothes. You want me to look like Batgirl, Simon?"

"I always did like to watch her move." He grinned at her. "Truth is, I saw the black pants and knew it would have to be black all the way." He gave her a sideways look. "I don't mean to be indelicate, but did all the underwear fit?"

"Too well," she said, "and I don't like to think about it, so stop looking at me."

"Okay." For a couple of seconds, Simon kept his eyes on the road. Then he said, chuckling, "As I said, when I saw the black, I knew it was you. But you know, I think the biggest change was your getting all that ash and soot washed out of your hair and off your face."

Every stitch she was wearing was black, even the boot socks. She said, not intending to, "Why haven't you ever married?"

"I was married, a very long time ago."

"Tell me."

He gave her another sideways look, saw that she really wanted to know, and said, "Well, I was twenty-two years old, in overwhelming lust, as was Janice, and so we got married, divorced within six months, and both of us joined the army."

"That was a long time ago. Where is Janice now?"

"She stayed in the army. She's a two-star general, stationed in Washington, D.C. I heard she's gorgeous as a general. She's married to a four-star. Hey, maybe someday she'll be chief of staff."

"I wonder why Dillon didn't tell me."

"He would have been my best man in the normal course of things, but we eloped and he was off in Europe that summer, living on a shoestring, so I knew he didn't have the money to fly home, then back to Europe again." Simon shrugged. "It was just as well. Who was your first husband? Beth's father?"

"His name was Jack Crane. He was a stockbroker for Phlidick, Dammerleigh and Pierson. He was a big wheeler-dealer at the Chicago Stock Exchange."

"Why'd you split up?"

She tried to shrug it off, give him a throwaway smile, but it wasn't possible. She drew a deep breath and said, "I don't want to talk about that."

"Okay, for now. Here we are. Keep your eyes open, Lily, I really have a bad feeling about this." He turned right onto the narrow asphalt road that led to the cottage, looked back, and saw their protection turning in behind them.

No motorcycle.

Simon did a quick scan, didn't see a thing. "I really don't like this."

"Maybe he just went into town to get some barbeque sauce to go with his snails."

Simon didn't think so, but he didn't argue as they walked up to the cottage. The door wasn't locked. He didn't say a word, picked Lily up under her armpits and moved her behind him. He opened the door slowly.

It was gloomy inside, all the blinds pulled down. The room was completely empty—no stacked paintings against the walls, no easel, no palette, not even a drop of paint anywhere or the smell of turpentine.

"Check the kitchen, Lily. I'm going to look in the bedroom." They met back in the empty living room five minutes later.

Agent Colin Smith stood in the open doorway. "No sign of Abe Turkle?"

Simon shook his head and said, "Nope. All that's left is a box of Puffed Wheat, a bit of milk, not soured, and a couple of apples, still edible, so he hasn't been gone long."

Lily said, "He's packed up and left. All his clothes, suitcase, everything gone, even his toothpaste."

"Do you think he went to London with that painting he was finishing?"

"I hope not. It was really very good, too good."

Colin Smith asked, "You were afraid he was dead, weren't you? Murdered. Like Mr. Monk."

Simon nodded. "I had a bad feeling there for a while. Let's tell Lieutenant Dobbs about this. Agent Smith, if you'll call Clark Hoyt, fill him in. You know, Abe had lots of stuff—at least thirty paintings leaning against the walls. All he had was a motorcycle. Maybe he rented a U-Haul to carry everything away."

"Or maybe one of the Frasiers loaned him a truck."

"Maybe. Now then, Agent Smith, Lily and I are off to pay a visit to Morrie Jones. I need to speak to Lieutenant Dobbs and the DA, get their okay. I've got an offer for Morrie he can't refuse."

Lily held up a hand. "No, I don't want to know. Maybe by now they know who's paying his lawyer." Simon closed the cottage door and waved to Agent Smith.

"Don't count on it," Simon said as he set the pillow gently over Lily's stomach and fastened the seat belt.

# NINETEEN

*Saint John's, Antigua*
*Public Administration Building*
*Near Reed Airport*

"It's so bright and hot and blue," Sherlock said, scratching her arm. Then she sighed. "You know, Sean would really like this place. We could strip him down and play in that sand, build a castle with him, even a moat. I can see him rolling over on the castle, flattening it, laughing all the while."

For the first time in as long as she could remember, Sherlock realized Dillon wasn't listening. She could only imagine what was going through his mind, all the ifs and buts. It was his show, and naturally he was worried, impossible not to be. They were working through the American Consular Agent with the Royal Police Force at Police Headquarters located on, strangely enough, American Road. But they were still in a foreign country, dealing with locals who were both bewildered by the extreme reaction of the United States federal cops—all fifty of them—to one woman, who only had one arm and was supposedly coming to their airport. But they were cooperating, really serious now after Savich had shown the entire group photos of her victims, including the latest one on Tortola. That one really brought it home.

Tammy couldn't have gotten to Antigua before late morning, no way, even with a fast boat. Tortola was too far away. The weather had been calm, no high winds or waves. She couldn't have gotten here ahead of them, except by plane, and they'd been checking air traffic from Tortola and nearby islands. And there was no indication at all that she knew how to fly. They'd had time to get everything set up, to get everyone in position.

Sherlock gave him a clear look. "We have time. Stop worrying. Marilyn will be here in about two hours. We'll go over everything with her, step by step."

"What if Tammy isn't alone? What if Tammy has been traveling around as Timmy this whole time? Remember, it was Timmy who called Marilyn at Quantico."

Sherlock had never before seen him so questioning of what he was doing.

When she spoke, Sherlock's voice was as calm as the incredible blue water not one hundred yards away, "One arm is one arm, despite anything else. No one on any of the islands has reported anyone jiggering about with one arm. The odds are stacked way against her. You know all the local police in both the British Virgin Islands and the U.S. Virgin Islands are on full alert. The Antiguan authorities aren't used to mayhem like this, so you can bet they're very concerned, probably more hyper than we are, particularly after those crime-scene photos. Dillon, everyone is taking this very seriously."

"So you think I should chill out?"

"No, that's impossible. But you're very smart, top drawer. Stop trying to second-guess yourself. You've done everything to prepare. If we have to deal with something other than just Tammy, we will."

The local cops, of which there weren't many, had converged on the airport. They were trying to look inconspicuous and failing, but they were trying, a couple of them even joking with tourists. All of them were used to dealing with locals who occasionally smoked too much local product or drank too much rum, or an occasional tourist who tried to steal something from a duty-free store. Nothing like this. This was beyond their experience.

Savich couldn't help himself. He checked and rechecked with Vinny Arbus on the status of the SWAT team. If Tammy Tuttle managed to grab a civilian, they were ready. Marksmen were set up, six of them, in strategic spots around the airport as well as inside. Half the marksmen were dressed like tourists, the other half, like airport personnel. They blended right in.

Would Tammy come in by plane? Would she simply walk in? No one knew. All hotels and rooming houses had been checked, rechecked. Jimmy Maitland was seated in the police commissioner's office with its overhead fan, boiling alive in his nice fall suit.

There were nearly fifty FBI personnel involved in the operation, now named Tripod. Special Agent Dane Carver had picked the name because the perp had only one arm and two legs, so Tuttle was the tripod.

A couple of hours later, Marilyn Warluski, scared to the soles of her new Nike running shoes, pressed close to Agent Virginia Cosgrove, her lifeline. Cosgrove was jittery, too, but too new an agent to be as scared as she should be. As she saw it, she was the most important agent present. It was to her that Tammy Tuttle would come. She was an excellent shot. She would protect Marilyn Warluski. She was ready.

"She's coming, Mr. Savich," Marilyn said, her voice dull and flat when he checked in with her again at six o'clock that evening. She was standing by the Information Desk in the airport, the Caribbean Airlines counter off to the left.

"It will be all right, Marilyn," Virginia said, her voice more excited than soothing, and patted her hand for at least the thirtieth time. "Agent Savich won't let anything happen, you'll see. We'll nail Tammy."

"I told you it was Timmy who called me. When she's Timmy, she can do anything."

"I thought she could do anything when she was Tammy, too," Savich said.

"She can. He can. If they're both here, not just Timmy, then there'll be real trouble."

Savich felt a twist of fear in his guts. He said slowly, his voice deep and calm, "Marilyn, what do you mean if they're both here? You mean both Tammy and Timmy? I don't understand."

Marilyn shrugged. "I didn't think to tell you, but I saw it happen once, back a couple of years ago. We were in that dolled-up tourist town, Oak Bluffs. You know, on Martha's Vineyard. I saw Tammy comin' out of this really pretty pink Victorian house where we were all stayin' and she suddenly turned several times, you know, real fast, like Lynda Carter did whenever she was goin' to change into Wonder Woman. Same thing. Tammy turned into Timmy, like they were blended together somehow, and it was the scariest thing I'd ever seen until Tammy walked into that motel room all covered in that little boy's blood."

Savich knew this was nuts. Tammy couldn't change from a woman into a man. That was impossible, but evidently Marilyn believed it. He said, carefully, "It seemed to you that Tammy and Timmy somehow coalesced into one person?"

"Yeah, that's it. She whirled around several times and then there was Timmy, all horny and smart-mouthed."

"When Tammy turned into Timmy, what did he look like?"

"Like Tammy but like a guy, you know?"

Virginia Cosgrove looked thoroughly confused. She started to say something, but Savich shook his head at her. Savich wanted to ask Marilyn to describe Timmy. Marilyn was suddenly standing perfectly still. She seemed to sniff the air like an animal scenting danger. She whispered, "I can feel Timmy close, Mr. Savich. He's real close now. Oh, God, I'm scared. He's going to wring my neck like a chicken's for helping you."

"I don't understand any of this." Virginia Cosgrove whispered low, like Marilyn had. "So Tammy is really a guy?"

"I guess we'll find out, Agent Cosgrove. Don't dwell on it. Your priority is Marilyn. Just protect Marilyn."

Marilyn leaned close and took Virginia's hand. "You won't let him take me, will you, Agent Cosgrove?"

"No, Marilyn, I won't even let him get close to you." She said to Savich, "You can count on me. I'll guard her with my life."

It was seven o'clock in the evening, an hour later. Since it was fall, the sun had set much earlier, and it was dark now, the sky filling with stars and a half-moon. It was beautiful and warm. The cicadas and the coquis were playing a symphony if anyone was inclined to listen.

The airport looked fairly normal except it was probably a bit too crowded for this time of day, something Savich hoped Tammy Tuttle wouldn't realize. But he knew she would notice because the local cops looked jumpy, too ill at ease for her not to notice. Or for Timmy to notice. Or whichever one of them showed.

Savich drew a deep breath as he watched the crowd. He said, "Timmy is close, Sherlock, that's what Marilyn said. She said she could feel him. That was an hour ago. I think she's even more scared than I am. She also firmly believes—no doubt at all in her mind—that Tammy can change into a guy at will, into this Timmy."

Sherlock said, "If a Timmy shows up, then I'll check us both into Bellevue."

"You got that right."

There weren't that many tourists in the airport now, real tourists at least. The major flights from the States had arrived, passengers dispersed, and a few island-to-island flights were going out in the evening. This was both good and bad. There was less cover, but also less chance that a civilian would be harmed.

When it happened, it was so quick that no one had a chance to stop it. A short, rangy man, pale as death itself, with close-cropped black hair, except for some curls on top of his head, seemed suddenly to simply appear behind Agent Virginia Cosgrove. He said against her ear, "Move, sweetie, make any movement at all to alert all the Feds hanging around here and I'll slice your throat from ear to ear. What'll be fun is that you'll live long enough to see your blood gush out in a bright red fountain."

Virginia heard Marilyn whimper. How had he gotten behind her? Why hadn't someone alerted her? Why hadn't someone seen him? Yes, it sounded like a man, like this Timmy Tuttle Marilyn had talked about. What was going on here? She had to be calm, wait for her chance. She slowly nodded. "I won't make a move. I won't do anything."

"Good," the man said and sliced her throat. Blood gushed out. Virginia had only a brief moment to cry out, but even then it wasn't a cry, it was only a low, blurred gurgling sound.

He turned to Marilyn, smiled, and said, "Let's go, baby. I've missed my little darlin'. You ready, baby?"

Marilyn whispered, "Yes, Timmy, I'm ready."

He took her hand in his bloody one, and with his other hand, he raised the knife to her throat. At that moment, Savich, who'd been in low conversation with Vinny Arbus, saw the blood spurting out of Virginia Cosgrove's neck. He'd been looking at her just a moment before. How was it possible? Then he saw a guy dragging Marilyn with him, a knife at her throat. A dozen other agents and at least a dozen civilians saw Virginia fall, her blood splattering everywhere, and saw a pale-as-death man dragging Marilyn Warluski.

It was pandemonium, people screaming, running, frozen in terror, or dropping to the floor and folding their arms over their heads. But what was the most potent, what everyone would remember with stark clarity, was the smell of blood. It filled the air, filled their lungs.

It was a hostage situation, but it wasn't a bystander who was the hostage. It was Marilyn Warluski.

Savich spotted the man, finally free of screaming civilians, and he'd recognize that face anywhere. It was Tammy Tuttle's face—only it wasn't quite. No, not possible. But Savich would go to his grave swearing that it was a man with the knife held to Marilyn's throat, and he had two arms, that man, because Savich saw two hands with his own eyes. It had to be someone else, not Tammy Tuttle dressed up like a man. Someone who looked enough like Tammy to fool him. But how had that crazy-looking man gotten so close to Virginia and Marilyn so quickly, and no one had even noticed? Suddenly nothing made sense.

Agents grabbed tourists who were still standing and pushed them to the floor, clearing the way to get to the man and his hostage.

A local police officer, a very young man with a mustache, closed with them first. He shouted at the man to stop and fired a warning shot in the air.

The man calmly turned in the officer's direction, pulled a SIG from his pocket so fast it was a blur, and shot him in the forehead. Then he turned around and it seemed he saw Savich, who was at least fifty feet from him. He yelled, "Hey, it's me, Timmy Tuttle! Hell-ooooo, everyone!"

Savich tuned him out. He had to or he couldn't function. He knew that the marksmen stationed inside the terminal had Tuttle in their sights. Soon now, very soon, it would be over.

He moved around the perimeter, slid behind the Caribbean Airlines counter with half a dozen agents behind him, and kept moving toward Timmy Tuttle.

Three shots rang out simultaneously. Loud, clear, sharp. It was the marksmen, and they wouldn't have fired without a clear shot at Timmy Tuttle.

Savich raised his head. He knew he couldn't be more than twenty feet from Timmy Tuttle. He couldn't see him. Could they have missed?

Then there were half a dozen more shots, screaming, and deep and ugly moans wrung out of people's throats from terror.

Savich felt something, something strong and sour, and he turned quickly. He saw Sherlock some ten feet away, just off to his left, with three other agents, rising from her kneeling position, her SIG aimed toward where Timmy Tuttle and Marilyn had been moments before. She looked as confused as he felt. It took everything in him not to shout for her to stay back, please God, just stay back, he didn't want her hurt. And what would hurt her? A man who really wasn't a man, but an image in whole cloth spun from Tammy Tuttle's crazy brain?

Savich saw a flash of cloth, smelled the scent of blood, and he simply knew it was Timmy Tuttle. He ran as fast as he could toward a conference room, the only place Timmy could have taken Marilyn. He kicked open the door.

He stopped cold, his gun steady, ready to fire. There was a big rectangular table in the center and twelve chairs, an overhead projector, a fax, and two or three telephones.

There wasn't anyone in the room. It was empty. But even in here he smelled Virginia's blood; he could swear that he smelled her blood, rich, coppery, sickening. He swallowed convulsively as he took in every inch of the room.

So Timmy hadn't come in here. Another room then. Agents on his heels, he ran across the hall to see his wife, gun held in front of her, pushing open a door with SECURITY stenciled on the glass.

He was across that hall and into the room in an instant. He saw Sherlock standing in the middle of the room, the three agents fanned out behind her, all of them searching the room. But Sherlock wasn't doing anything. She was standing there staring silently at the single large window that gave onto the outside.

She turned slowly to see him in the open doorway, agents at his back, staring at her, shock and panic alive in his eyes. She cocked her head to one side in silent question, then simply closed her eyes and fell over onto the floor.

"Sherlock!"

"Is she shot?"

"What happened?"

The other three agents converged.

Savich knew he couldn't stop, but it was the hardest thing he'd ever done in his life. He yelled, "Make sure she's all right! Conners, check everyone out! Deevers, Conlin, Marks, Abrams, you're with me!"

He heard one of the agents shout after him, "She's breathing, can't see anything wrong with her. The guy wasn't in here, Savich. We don't know where he went."

The window, he thought, Sherlock had been staring at that window. He picked up a chair and smashed it into the huge glass window.

When they managed to climb out the window they'd cleared of glass, they knew, logically, that Timmy Tuttle and Marilyn Warluski couldn't have come this way since the glass hadn't been broken. But it didn't matter. Where else could Timmy Tuttle have gone? They covered every inch of ground, looked into all the buildings, even went onto the tarmac where one American 757 sat waiting, calling up to the pilot. But Tammy or Timmy Tuttle was gone, and Marilyn as well. As if they'd just vanished into thin air, with nothing left to prove they'd even been there except for Virginia Cosgrove's body, bloodless now, lying on her side, covered with several blankets, local technicians working over her. And the one local officer Timmy Tuttle had shot through the head.

He'd used his right hand when he'd shot that officer.

Savich had shot Tammy Tuttle through her right arm in that barn in Maryland, near the Plum River.

At the hospital, they'd amputated her right arm.

He wondered if they were all going mad.

No, no, there was an explanation.

Somehow a man had gotten into the airport, killed Virginia Cosgrove, and grabbed Marilyn. And no one had seen him until he had Marilyn by the neck and was dragging her away.

No one much wanted to talk. Everyone who had been in the airport appeared confused and looked, strangely, hungover.

Savich and his team went back to the security room. Sherlock was still unconscious, covered with blankets, a local physician sitting on the floor beside her.

No one had much to say. Jimmy Maitland was sitting in a chair near Sherlock.

Savich picked up his wife, carried her to a chair, and sat down with her in his arms. He rocked her, never looking away from her face.

"It's as if she's asleep," the physician said, standing now beside him. "Just asleep. She should wake up soon and tell us what happened."

Jimmy Maitland said, "We've put out an island-wide alert for Timmy Tuttle, with description, and Marilyn Warluski, with description. The three agents with Sherlock didn't see a single blessed thing. Nada."

Savich nodded, touched his wife's hair. He didn't think he'd be surprised by anything ever again.

A few minutes later, Sherlock opened her eyes. She looked up and, surprisingly, smiled. "You're holding me, Dillon. Why? What happened?"

"You don't remember?" He spoke very slowly, the words not really wanting to speak themselves, probably because he didn't want an answer.

She closed her eyes for a moment, frowned, then said, "I remember I ran into this room, three other agents behind me. No one was here." She frowned. "No, I'm not sure. There was something—a light maybe—something. I can't remember."

"When I came in, you were standing perfectly still, staring out that big window. The other agents were searching the room. But you didn't move, didn't twitch or anything, and then you just fell over."

Jimmy Maitland said, "Did you see anything of Timmy Tuttle or Marilyn?"

Sherlock said, "Timmy Tuttle—yes, that crazy-looking guy who was as pale as an apocalypse horseman—yes, I remember. He was holding Marilyn around her neck—a knife, yes, he had a knife. I was terrified when I saw Dillon go in after him into that conference room."

"You saw Timmy go into the conference room?"

"I think so. But that can't be right. Didn't he come in here?"

"We don't know. None of the agents saw him in here," Savich said. "No, Sherlock, that's okay. You rest now. You'll probably remember more once you get yourself together. Does your head ache?"

"A bit, why?"

"You feel maybe a bit like you're hungover?"

"Well, yes, that's right."

Savich looked up at Jimmy Maitland and nodded. "Everyone I've spoken to, agents and civilians alike, everyone feels like that."

"Sherlock," Maitland said, crouching down beside her. "Why was it you who collapsed? You must have seen something."

"I'm thinking, sir, as hard as I can."

Dillon slowly eased her up until she was sitting on his lap. She started shaking. Savich nearly lost it. He pulled her hard against him, protecting her, from what, he didn't know. He didn't want her hurt, no more hurt, no more monsters from the unknown.

Then she said, pulling away from him, her voice firm and steady, "Dillon, I'm all right. I promise. I've got stuff to think about. Something really weird happened, didn't it?"

"Yes."

"It's there, in the back of my brain, and I'll get it out."

# TWENTY

*Eureka, California*

Morrie Jones stared at the young woman who had taken him down, hurt him, curse her eyes, before he could get away from her. He couldn't believe it. She was skinny, looked like a damned little debutante with her blond hair and blue eyes and innocent face, like the prototypical little WASP. That idiot lawyer of his had even told him that she'd been recovering from surgery and she'd still stomped his ass. He really wanted to hurt her. He'd even do it for free, this time.

He said to Simon, "You claimed I didn't need my lawyer, that you only wanted to talk to me, that you had something to offer that I couldn't refuse. You from the DA's office?"

Simon said, "No, but I have her approval. I see you remember Ms. Savich."

"Nah, I heard her name was Frasier. I know that's right because that's the name of the broad I'm going to sue for attacking me."

Lily gave him a big smile. "You go ahead and sue me, boyo, and I'll just smack your face off again. What do you think?" She cracked her knuckles, a sound Morrie Jones had hated since he was a kid and his old man did it whenever he was drunk.

"Stop that," Morrie said, staring at her hands. "Why'd the cops let you two in here?"

She cracked her knuckles again, something she'd rarely done since she was a bookie and some kid from another neighborhood had threatened to horn in on her territory. "What's the matter, Morrie? I still scare you?"

"Shut up, you bitch."

"Call me a bitch again and I'll make you eat your tongue." She gave him a sweet smile, with one dimple.

Simon said, "All right, Lily, don't scare the boy. Listen up, Morrie. We want you to tell us who hired you. It could save your life."

Morrie started whistling "Old Man River."

Lily laughed. "Come on, Morrie, spare us. You got a brain? Use it. Herman Monk is dead, shot three times in the back."

"I don't know no Herman Monk. Sounds like a geek. Don't know him."

That could be true. Simon said, "Monk was a loose end. He's dead. You're a loose end, too, Morrie. Think about your lawyer for a moment. Who is he? Who sent him? Who's paying his bill? Do you really think he's going to try to get *you* off?"

"I hired him. He's a real good friend, a drinking buddy. We watch the fights together down at Sam's Sports Bar, you know, over on Cliff Street."

Lily said, as she tapped her fingers on the Formica surface, split down the middle by bars, with Simon and Lily on one side, Morrie on the other, "He's setting you up, Morrie. You too stupid to use your brain? You know he told the sheriff that he took your case pro bono?"

"I want a cigarette."

"Don't be a moron. You want to die, hacking up your lungs? He said he took you on for free, out of the goodness of his heart. I want you to think about all this. What did your lawyer promise you?"

"He said I was getting out of here, today."

"Yeah, we heard," Simon said, and it was true, according to Lieutenant Dobbs. The judge had called and was prepared to set bail. "You know what's going to happen then?"

"Yeah, I'm going to go get me a beer."

"That's possible," Lily said. "I hope you really enjoy it, Morrie, because you're going to be dead by morning. These people really hate loose ends."

Morrie said, "Who did you say this Monk geek was?"

Lily said, "He was the curator of the museum where my grandmother's paintings were displayed. He was part of the group who had four of the paintings copied, the originals replaced with the fakes. When it all came out, when it was obvious that things were unraveling, he was shot in the back. That's why they wanted you to kill me. They want my paintings and here I am doing what they knew I'd do—stirring things up until I find out who stole my paintings. I wonder how long before they shoot you, Morrie."

"I'm leaving town, first thing."

"Good idea," Simon said. "But I see two big problems for you. The first is that you're still in jail. Your lawyer said he was going to get you out? Who's going to pay the bail, Morrie, and that's your second problem. Your pro bono lawyer? That's possible, what with all the money from the people who hired you in the first place. So, let's say you walk out of here, what are you going to do? Hide out in an alley and wait for them to kill you?"

Morrie believed him, Simon knew it in that moment. Simon waited a beat, then said, "Turns out I can solve both problems for you."

"How?"

"Ms. Savich here will drop charges against you, we'll get you out of here without your lawyer knowing about it. To sweeten the deal, I'll give you five hundred bucks. That'll get you far away from these creeps, give you a new start. In return you give me the name of who hired you."

Morrie said, "Look, I'm going to sue her the minute I get out of here. Five hundred bucks? I'm gonna gag."

Simon's gut was good. He knew he was going to get Morrie. One more nudge. He turned on the recorder in his jacket pocket. "You know, Morrie, Lieutenant Dobbs and the DA don't really want me to cut any deal with you. I had to talk them into it. They want to take you to trial and throw your butt in jail for a long time. Since Lily hurt you pretty good, it's more than your word against hers. You'd be dead meat, Morrie."

It took only three more minutes of negotiation. Simon agreed to give Morrie Jones eight hundred dollars, Lily agreed to drop the charges, and Morrie agreed to give them a name.

"I want to see her sign papers and I want to see the money before I do anything."

Lieutenant Dobbs and the DA weren't pleased, but knew that Morrie was incidental compared to the person who'd hired him.

Lily, in the presence of Lieutenant Dobbs, an assistant DA, a detective, and two officers, signed that she was dropping the charges against one Morrie Jones, age twenty.

Once they were alone again, Morrie said, slouching back in his chair, "Now, big shot, give me the money before I say another word."

Simon rose, pulled his wallet out of his back pocket, and laid out the entire wad. There were eight one-hundred-dollar bills and a single twenty. "Glad you didn't wipe me out completely, Morrie. I appreciate it. That twenty will buy Lily and me a couple of tacos."

Morrie smirked as Simon started to slide the hundred-dollar bills through the space beneath the bars. "Tell me a story, Morrie."

"I don't exactly have a name. Hey, no, don't take the money back. I got as good as a name. Look, she called me. It was this woman and she had this real thick accent, real Southern, you know? Smooth and real slow. She didn't give me her name, just Lily Frasier's name. She described her, told me where she was staying and to get it done fast.

"I went right over to the bank, picked up the money, then I went to work." He slid his eyes toward Lily. "It didn't quite work out the way I wanted."

"That's because you're a wimp, Morrie."

Morrie half rose out of his chair. The jail guard standing against the wall immediately straightened. Simon raised a hand. "How much did this woman pay you to kill Lily?"

"She gave me a thousand for a down payment. Then she was to have five thousand to me when it was done and on the news."

"This is not a good business, Simon." She stared at Morrie. "I was only worth six thousand dollars?"

Morrie actually smiled. "That's all. You know, I would have done it for less if I'd known you then."

Simon realized that Lily was enjoying herself. She was having a really fine pissing contest with this young thug. He pressed his knee against her leg.

But she had one more line. "What I did to you I did for nothing."

Simon shook his head at her. "Morrie, which bank?"

"Give me the money first."

Simon slid the money all the way through. Morrie's hand slid over it, presto. He closed his young eyes for a moment, feeling the money like it was a lover's flesh. "Wells Fargo," he said, "the one over on First Street and Pine. The money was there in my name."

"You didn't ask who had left the money waiting there for you?"

Morrie shook his head.

"Thanks, Morrie," Lily said as she rose. "Lieutenant Dobbs thinks you'll be out sometime this afternoon. He's agreed not to tell your lawyer. My advice to you—get out of Dodge. This time you don't have to be afraid of me. The woman who hired you—chances are good she wants you dead, and she's capable of doing it herself."

"You know who she is?"

Lily said, "Oh yeah, we know. She'd eat you with her poached eggs for breakfast. Hey, what happened to the thousand bucks she gave you?"

Morrie's eyes slid away. "None of your business."

Lily laughed, shook her finger at him. "You pissed it away in a poker game, didn't you?"

"No, dammit. It was pool."

Clark Hoyt was waiting for them in Lieutenant Dobbs's office. His arms were folded over his chest. He looked very odd. "I got a call from Savich. He was calling from Saint John's, in Antigua, of all places, said to tell you that all hell will break loose in the media really soon now, but that he and Sherlock are okay. It seems Tammy Tuttle got ahold of Marilyn Warluski and they're gone. There was a big situation there at the airport. Savich called it a fiasco."

"Antigua?" Simon said. "I guess he couldn't tell us he was there."

Lily said, shaking her head, "Dillon will not be a happy camper about this."

Hoyt himself wondered what had happened, but he said only, "Savich didn't give me any details, said he'd call again this evening. I told him where you guys are staying now. Okay, tell me who hired Morrie."

"Yeah," Lieutenant Dobbs said as he came into his own office to see the two civilians and the Fed. "Who was it?"

"It was my mother-in-law," Lily said. "No doubt at all that it was Charlotte. She didn't give Morrie her name, but that accent of hers—it has so much syrup in it, you could sweeten a rock."

Lieutenant Dobbs shook his head. "So now you know, but there's still no case. Both Hoyt and I interviewed the Frasiers—all three of them—separately. In all three cases, their lawyer, Bradley Abbott, a real hardnose, was present. The Frasiers refused to answer any questions. Abbott read a statement to us. In the statement, the Frasiers claim all of this is nonsense. They are sorry about Mr. Monk, but it has nothing to do with them, and this is a waste of everyone's time. Oh yeah, then their lawyer told us that you were nuts, Lily, that you'd do anything to get back at them, for what reason they don't know, but no one should believe a single word you say. We need more evidence before we can bring them to the station and put them in an interview room again."

Hoyt said to Simon and Lily, "We'll have two agents on Morrie

Jones. Lieutenant Dobbs hasn't got a problem with that, especially since he's short officers right now. We won't let the little twerp out of our sight."

"Good," said Lieutenant Dobbs. "All right, listen up. I've got a murder to solve. As for you, Lily, you're only an attempted murder, so I guess I can let you slide a bit. I understand this thing is more complicated than a Greek knot, and that all of it ties together."

Simon said, "If it's okay with you, Lieutenant, I'd like to go to Wells Fargo to see if there's a record of who gave Morrie a thousand dollars for the hit on Lily. That'd be too easy, but it's worth a shot."

Lieutenant Dobbs said, "She paid that little dip just a thousand bucks to off Lily?"

"Oh, no," Lily said. "I'm worth lots more than that. There was another five thousand bucks when the job was done."

Simon said, "Okay, then, let's get cracking."

On the way out the door, Lily looked at Simon for a moment, at his too-long, very dark hair, and realized she hadn't really noticed before how it curled at his neck. "Those little curls—they're cute," she said and patted his nape.

Simon rolled his eyes.

Hoyt, who was walking behind them, laughed.

Since Hoyt was along, they got instant cooperation at Wells Fargo. One of the vice presidents, who seemed more numerous than tellers at the windows, hustled onto the computer and punched up the money transfer transactions for the very morning Morrie had attacked Lily on the city bus.

Mr. Trempani raised his head, looked at each of them in turn. "This is very strange. The money was wired in care of Mr. Morrie Jones by a company called Tri-Light Investments. Any of you ever heard of them?"

"Tri-Light," Lily said. "I don't think Tennyson ever mentioned that company."

"Who are they?" Hoyt asked.

"All we have is an account number in Zurich, Switzerland. It simply lists Tri-Light Investments and the Habib Bank AG at 59 Weinbergstrasse."

"Curiouser and curiouser," Simon said.

Hoyt said, "I'll call Interpol and get someone to check this out. But don't count on finding anything out. The Swiss have duct tape over their mouths." He paused for a moment. "You suspect someone, don't you, Simon? And not just the Frasiers. Who?"

"If the owner of this Tri-Light Investments is a Swede by the name of Olaf Jorgenson, then we're confirming lots of things," Simon said.

"Makes sense," Hoyt said. "He's the collector, isn't he? That's how it all ties into Ms. Savich's paintings. You guys think he's the one who commissioned them."

"It's possible," Simon said.

Lily punched Simon in the ribs. "It's more than possible, Clark. Call us on the cell phone as soon as you know, okay?"

Hoyt said, "You promised no hotdogging. That means you don't go see Charlotte Frasier without having at least me along."


*Hemlock Bay, California*

Lily pointed to the Bullock Pharmacy, and Simon pulled into an open parking spot in front of Spores Dry Cleaners next door. An old man was staring out at them from the large glass windows that held three hanging Persian carpets, presumably just cleaned.

Ten minutes later, Lily came out of the Bullock Pharmacy carrying a small paper bag. She eased into the passenger seat and drew a deep breath. "It's such a beautiful town," she said. "I always thought so. You can smell the ocean, feel that light sheen of salt on your skin. It's incredible."

"Okay, I agree, lovely town, lovely smell in the air. What happened?"

"I had a real epiphany going into that pharmacy." And then she told him what had happened. There'd been about ten people in the store, and all of them, after they saw her, were talking about her behind their hands. They stepped away if she came near them, didn't say anything if she said hello to them. Lily was frankly relieved when Mr. Bullock senior, at least eighty years old, nodded to her at the checkout line. Evidently he was the spokesperson. He looked at her straight in the eye before he rang up her aspirin and said, "Everyone is real sorry you tried to kill yourself again, Mrs. Frasier."

"I didn't, Mr. Bullock."

"We heard you blamed it on Dr. Frasier and left him."

"Is that what everyone believes?"

"We've known the Frasiers a long time, ma'am. Lots longer than we've known you."

"Actually, Mr. Bullock, it's very far from the truth. Someone has tried to kill me three times now."

He shook his head at her, waved the bottle of aspirin, and said, "You need something stronger than these, Mrs. Frasier. Something lots stronger. You'll never live to be as old as I am if you don't see to it now."

"Why don't you talk to Lieutenant Dobbs in Eureka?"

He looked at her, saying nothing more. Lily didn't feel like standing there arguing with the old man to change his mind, with the dozen other people in the store likely listening, so she paid and left, knowing those people were thinking she was one sick puppy, no doubt about it.

"That's it. Nothing much, really." She waved the bottle of aspirin. "Thanks, Simon." He handed her a bottle of diet Dr Pepper, and she took two of the tablets.

"Isn't it interesting no one wanted to speak to me," she said, "except Mr. Bullock. They were all content to hang back and listen."

"It's still a beautiful town. Tennyson, Mom, and Dad have been busy," Simon said. "How about some lunch?"

After a light lunch at a diner that sat right on the main pier, Lily said, "I want to visit my daughter, Simon."

For a moment, he didn't understand. She saw it and said, even as tears stung her eyes, "The cemetery. After I leave, I know I won't be back for a while. I want to say good-bye."

He wasn't about to let her go by herself. It was too dangerous. When he told her that, she simply nodded. They stopped at a small florist shop at the end of Whipple Avenue, Molly Ann's Blooms.

"Hilda Gaddis owns Molly Ann's. She sent a beautiful bouquet of yellow roses to Beth's funeral."

"The daffodils are lovely."

"Yes. Beth loved daffodils." She said nothing more as they drove the seven minutes to the cemetery set near the Presbyterian church. It was lovely, in a pocket nestled by hemlock and spruce trees, protected from the winds off the ocean.

He walked with her up a narrow pathway that forked to the right. There was a beautiful etched white marble stone, an angel carved on top, her arms spread wide. Beth's name was beneath, the date of her birth, the date of her death, and beneath, the words *She Gave Me Infinite Joy.*

Lily was crying, but made no sound. Simon watched her go down on her knees and arrange the daffodils against the headstone.

He wanted to comfort her but realized in those moments that she needed to be alone. He turned away and went back to the rental car. His cell phone rang.

It was Clark Hoyt, and he was excited.

# TWENTY-ONE

*Saint John's, Antigua*

There was nothing more for Savich to do in Antigua. Timmy Tuttle, with two healthy arms, had Marilyn, and Savich didn't want to even think of what he was doing to her.

Or maybe two different people had her, one wild-eyed man with black hair and two arms, and a woman with one arm and madness and rage in her eyes.

Savich couldn't stand himself. He'd set up Marilyn, gotten an FBI agent killed, along with a local police officer, and left chaos in his wake. He knew he'd see Virginia Cosgrove's sightless eyes for a very long time, and that long red gash that had slit her throat open.

Jimmy Maitland had taken his arm, trying to calm him down. "Batten down the guilt, Savich. I approved everything you did. We faced something or someone that shouldn't have been there. It happened. You've got to prepare to move on."

Maitland shook his head, ran fingers through his gray hair, making it stand on end. "I'm losing it. There's nothing more we can do here. We're going home. I'm leaving Vinny Arbus and his SWAT team in charge. They'll keep looking for Marilyn and coordinate with local law enforcement. This confusion, Savich, it will unravel in time. There's an explanation, there has to be."

Savich didn't let Sherlock out of his sight. He realized soon enough she was different—more quiet, her attention not on any of them, and he'd look at her and know she was thinking about what had happened, her eyes focused, yet somehow far away.

There was so much cleanup, so many explanations to give, most omitting the inexplicable things because they didn't help anyone to know the sorts of things that could drive you mad. And most important, there was no sign of the man who'd taken Marilyn Warluski from the Saint John's airport.

When they got back to Washington, Savich left immediately for the gym and worked out until he was panting for breath, his body so exhausted it was ready to rebel.

When he walked in the front door, feeling so exhausted each step was a chore, his son was there to greet him, crawling for all he was worth right up to Savich's feet, grabbing onto his pants leg. Savich started to reach down to pick him up when he heard Sherlock say, "No, wait a second."

Sean yanked hard on his father's pants, got a good hold, braced himself, and managed to pull himself up. Then he grinned up at his father and lifted one leg, then the other.

All the miserable unanswerable questions, all the deadening sense of failure, fell away. Savich whooped, picked up his son, and tossed him into the air, again and again, until Sean was both yelling and laughing, one and then the other.

It was Savich who wrote Sean's accomplishment in his baby book that evening. "An almost giant step for kid-kind." Then "The leg lift, one at a time—he's getting ready to walk, amazing. His grandmother says I started walking early, too."

In bed that night, Sherlock nuzzled her head into Savich's neck, lightly laid her palm over his heart, and said, "Sean brings back focus, doesn't he?"

"Yes. I was ready to fall over from working out so hard when I walked in the house, and then he crawls over to me and pulls himself up. Then he lifts each leg, testing them out, nearly ready to take off. I didn't think I had any laughter left in me, but I guess I do."

"Don't feel guilty about it. You should have seen Gabriella. She was so tickled when I got home, so proud of both herself and Sean that she couldn't wait to show off what he could do. Those leg lifts, I haven't read about that in any baby books. Gabriella got some video of him doing that with me. I swear she didn't want to leave this afternoon. I expect her husband to call me and complain about what demanding employers we are."

Savich settled his hand on her hip, kneaded her for a moment, thinking she'd dropped weight, kissed her forehead, then turned on his back to stare up at the dark ceiling.

"Dillon?"

"Hmm?"

"I waited until Sean was in bed and we were lying here, all relaxed."

"Waited for what, sweetheart?"

She took a deep breath. "I've remembered some stuff that happened in that room at the airport."


*Hemlock Bay*

Hoyt said, "You'll never believe this, Simon!"

"Yeah, yeah, what, Clark?"

"Lieutenant Dobbs, he's got—"

Simon heard the slight shifting in sound, perhaps a small movement in the backseat of the car, but just as he knew something was different, he felt something very hard come down over his right temple. He slumped forward on the steering wheel, his forehead striking the horn.

It blared.

"Simon? Simon, where are you? What happened?"

Lily heard the horn. Their rental car? But Simon was there, surely. Then she realized something was very wrong. She was on her feet in a second, racing down those beautifully manicured paths to the visitors' parking lot. She heard the man running behind her, just one man; she heard the deep crunching of gravel beneath his feet.

She ran faster, veering away from the parking lot, running back into the thick stand of hemlock and spruce trees. She was fast, always had been.

She heard the man shout, but not at her. He was shouting at his accomplice. What had happened to Simon? The horn was still blaring, but it was more distant now. And then she realized that he must have fallen on the horn. Was he dead? No, no, he couldn't be, he just couldn't.

She was through the trees, out the back, and there was the damned cliff, miles and miles of it, running north and south. She had been here before, and there wasn't any escape this way. What to do?

She ran along the edge of the cliff, searching for a way down, and found one, some yards ahead just before the cliff curved inward, probably from sliding and erosion over the years. There was a skinny, snaking trail, and she took it without hesitation. There was nothing ahead except empty land dotted with trees and gullies. They'd get her for sure, that or shoot her down. Maybe there was something there on the beach. Anything was better than staying up here and being an easy target.

The path was steep, and she had to slow way down. Still she tripped a couple of times, and the last time, she had to grab a bush that grew beside the trail to halt her fall. It had thorns, and she felt them score her hands and fingers.

She vaguely heard birds calling overhead.

She knew the men had to be nearly at the top of the trail now. They'd come after her. What was down here except more beach? There had to be someplace to hide, some cover, a cave, anything.

Her breath was spurting out of her, broken, tight. A stitch ripped through her side. She ignored it. She had to be calm, keep herself in control.

She kept her eyes on the winding trail. Wouldn't it ever stop? She heard the men now, yelling from the top for her to come back up, they weren't going to hurt her.

She managed three more steps, then there was a shot, then an instant ricochet off a rock one foot to her right, scattering chips in all directions. A chip hit her in the leg, but it didn't go through her jeans.

She hunkered down as much as she could, twisting to the left, then the right, going down until at last her feet hit the hard sand on the beach. She chanced a look back up to the top and saw one of the men start down after her. The other man was aiming his gun at her. It was a handgun, not accurate enough at this distance, she hoped.

It wasn't. He shot at her three more times, but none of the bullets seemed to strike close to her.

She stumbled over a gnarly piece of driftwood and went flying. She landed on her stomach, her hands in front of her face. She saw wet sand, driftwood, kelp, and even one frantic sand crab not six inches from her nose.

She lay there for a moment, drawing in deep breaths, feeling the stitch in her side lessen. Then she was up again. She saw the man coming down the trail, but he wasn't being as careful as she'd been. He was a big guy, not in the best of shape. He was wearing those opaque wraparound sunglasses, so she couldn't really make out his features. He had thick, light brown hair and a gun in his right hand. She watched him stumble, wildly clutching at the air to regain his balance, but he didn't. He tumbled head over heels down the trail and landed hard at the bottom, not moving. His gun. His gun was her only chance. She'd seen it flying. She ran to his side in an instant. She picked up a big piece of driftwood, realized it was soggy and not heavy enough, and grabbed up a rock instead. She leaned over him and brought the rock down on his head as hard as she could. She slipped her hand inside his coat and pulled out his wallet. She shoved it into her pocket, then saw the gun some six feet back up the trail, just off to the side, lying on top of a pile of rocks.

The man on top was yelling, firing, but she ignored him. She got the gun, turned, and ran for all she was worth down the beach.

*Washington, D.C.*

Savich felt his heart pound faster beneath his wife's palm. He shot up, turned on the bedside lamp, then faced her. "Tell me."

"I remember being scared for you when I saw you go into that conference room. Then I'm sure I saw Timmy Tuttle dragging Marilyn into that security room across the hall. I ran into the room, the three other agents behind me. The room was empty. At least that's what I thought at first.

"I saw this bright light, Dillon. It nearly blinded me, and I swear to you, for some reason I just couldn't move. The light was right in front of that big window, and I know I saw Timmy and Marilyn in the middle of that light.

"I could hear the other agents yelling at each other. I realized they weren't seeing what I was. Still I couldn't move. I was nailed to the spot looking at that white light. Then Timmy Tuttle grabbed Marilyn tight around her neck, and . . ."

"And what?"

"Dillon, I'm not crazy, I swear."

He pulled her against him. "I know."

"They disappeared. It was like they were right in front of me, then they were in front of the window, and the window was bathed in the white light. Then they receded through that white light until they were gone. Then everything seemed to close down. That's all I remember."

Savich said, "That's fine, Sherlock. Well done. It fits right into the rest of it. It seems logical to everyone that Tammy Tuttle used some sort of mass hypnosis. You know how David Copperfield walked through the

Great Wall of China? How he got sawed in half with millions of people watching, most of them on TV?"

"Yes. You think Tammy has this skill?"

"It makes sense. There she or he was with Marilyn, and then she or he just wasn't there. I think the whole thing was this big performance she worked out to show us we're dealing with a master. You know what else I think? I think Tammy knew I was trying to trap her and using Marilyn as bait. She knew we'd be at the airport waiting for her. She was ready for us. I also think she really wants us to believe that everything we saw was supernatural, beyond our meager brains. But it's not. She's just very, very good. She wanted to scare us all to death, paralyze us. I do wonder, though, why she didn't try to kill me."

Sherlock pulled away, stroked her fingers over his jaw, and said, "I think it's because she couldn't get close enough to you. I've given this a lot of thought, Dillon, and I think you're one of the few people Tammy's ever met she can't hypnotize or perform an illusion for when she's up close to you. And if she can't get close to you without your seeing exactly what she is, then she can't kill you."

"You mean if I had been close to her, I wouldn't have seen Timmy, I'd have really seen Tammy?"

"Yes, it sounds reasonable. If she can't get close enough to you without your seeing her exactly as she is, then she knows she's at a disadvantage. When you were in the barn in Maryland with her, how far away were you standing from her?"

"Maybe two dozen feet."

"And she was always just what she was? Tammy Tuttle?"

"Yes. She called the Ghouls, but she didn't change. When I shot her, I saw the bullet nearly rip her arm from her body. I saw her fall, heard her yells of pain. She remained exactly what she was and who she was."

Sherlock said, "Then at the airport, she just couldn't get close enough to you to kill you. And she realized, too, that she couldn't get too close or you'd see her as she really is and kill her. She's being really careful after what you did to her at the barn."

Savich said, "Jimmy Maitland called me at the gym, told me Jane Bitt in Behavioral Sciences allowed that maybe it's possible Tammy is a strong telepath in addition to all her illusion skills. She won't swear to it, says she doesn't want to get mocked out, but we should consider it, given the incredible control Tammy was able to exert at the airport."

Sherlock said, "So maybe she's got both this talent and skill in creating illusions. I think you were right. Tammy knew that you were setting her up. She also knew you would bring Marilyn. For whatever reason, she wanted Marilyn back. I'm just hoping that she didn't want her back to kill her. Maybe she really is fond of Marilyn. Maybe Marilyn feeds her ego, makes her feel powerful because she's so very malleable and suggestible. Tammy can make Marilyn see, make her believe anything she tells her to believe. Didn't you tell me that Marilyn firmly believes everything Tammy says?"

"Oh, yes, and it's genuine, Sherlock. Even under hypnosis, Marilyn was frightened of Tammy and she believed everything she said to Dr. Hicks and to me. She remembered it as fact, for heaven's sake, so she had to have believed it."

Savich threw back the covers and jumped to his feet. He grabbed a pair of jeans as an afterthought and pulled them on. "I'm going to do some research on this with MAX."

He walked back to the bed, grinned down at his wife, pulled her up tightly against him, and kissed her until she wanted to ask him to wait until morning to visit MAX. But she knew that brain of his was working again, asking questions, wanting to know everything, and fast.

"I won't be gone too long."

She lay back down in bed, shut off the table lamp, pulled the covers to her chin, and smiled into the darkness when she heard Dillon speaking to MAX down the hall in his study. She heard him laugh.

# TWENTY-TWO

*Hemlock Bay, California*

There weren't any caves, not even one indentation in the rock where she could squeeze in and wait them out, only a beach that went on and on, driftwood piled all over it, and slimy trails of kelp, dangerous when you were running.

But she had a gun. It was small and ugly, but she wasn't defenseless. From what she knew about guns, which wasn't much, it was a close-range gun, useless at a distance, but if you got near enough, it could kill a person quite easily.

The temperature dropped as the sun went behind gathering clouds, whirling rain clouds. Any minute now rain would pour down. Would that help her or not? She didn't know.

Had there been three men? One staying with Simon and the other two after her? Maybe there were only two men and Simon could get away and call for help. They'd been idiots—telling their FBI protectors they were going to the cemetery and wanted to be private, they'd meet them back in Hemlock Bay.

She stopped, bending over, her hands on her thighs, so tired her breath was catching and she was wheezing with the effort to breathe. She flattened herself in the shadow of the cliff and looked back.

Then, suddenly, she heard one of the men cup his hands around his mouth and shout, "Lily Frasier! We have Simon Russo. Come out now or we will kill him. That is a promise. Then we will call our friends to come at you from the other end of the beach. We will trap you, and you won't like what will happen to you then."

The man's words brought her breath back, straightened her right up. The man's voice was also thick with an accent—stilted, unnatural. Swedish. It seemed Olaf Jorgenson himself had come, or sent his friends. She ran again, until she rounded a slight promontory and looked up. She had found her way out. Another narrow trail snaked up the cliff, much like the one she'd taken down. Two miles back up the beach? Three miles? She didn't make a sound, just shot up that trail, using her hands on rocks and scrubs, anything to keep her steady, knowing they couldn't see her until they came around the promontory themselves.

They couldn't kill Simon. They'd left him alone in the car. If there was a third man watching him, well then, they couldn't contact him. Unless they had a cell phone. Everybody had a cell phone. Oh, God, please, no. It had to be a bluff, it had to be.

She slipped once, saw pebbles and small rocks gushing out from the cliff and pounding their way back down to the beach. She held still, then started up again. She was up to the top of the cliff in no time and running. The men would realize soon enough where she'd gone.

Hurry, she had to hurry. She hurt, really bad, but she thought of Simon, of his hair curling at his neck, and she knew nothing could happen to him. She wouldn't let it. Too much loss in her life, she couldn't bear any more. She came into the back of the cemetery, climbed the wrought-iron fence, and ran down the path toward the visitors' parking lot.

The horn wasn't blaring anymore.

Nearly there, she was nearly there. She saw their rental car, but didn't see Simon. She got to the car. He was stretched out on the front seat, unconscious. Or dead.

She pulled the driver's side door open. "Simon! Wake up!"

He moaned, struggled to a sitting position. He blinked, finally focusing on her face.

"They're after us, two men, both with guns. I got away from them but we don't have much time. Scoot over, we're getting out of here. I'm going to drive us right to jail and have Lieutenant Dobbs lock us in. It's the only safe place in the world. No lawyers allowed. Only Lieutenant Dobbs. He can bring our food. We'll get Dillon and Sherlock out here. They'll figure this all out, and we can get out of here."

As she spoke, she managed to shove his feet off the seat and push him toward the passenger door. "It will be all right. You don't have to do anything, see, I can drive now. Just rest, Simon."

"No, Lily, no more driving. You're not going anywhere, not anymore."

Lily turned slowly at that syrupy voice and stared up at Charlotte Frasier, who was pointing a long-barreled gun at her. "You've given us too much trouble. If I hadn't decided to oversee this myself, you would have escaped yet again. I always believed three times was a charm, and so it is. Get out of the car, Lily. Now."

Lily wasn't surprised, not really. Not Elcott, but Charlotte. Then she almost smiled. Charlotte didn't know she had a gun, too. Would Charlotte take the chance of killing them here, in the cemetery parking lot? She believed all the way to her gut Charlotte was capable of anything. She was still free, and Mr. Monk had been dead for three days now.

Then she saw the men running toward them. She had to hurry, had to do something. She opened the door, lifting one arm, hiding the other hand slightly behind her.

"Where's Elcott?" she said, wanting to distract Charlotte, just for an instant. "And that marvelous son of yours? Who loves me so much he'd like nothing more than to bury me? Aren't they hanging back there, waiting for you to tell them what to do?"

"Don't you dare speak of my husband and my son like that—"

Lily was clear. She raised the gun and fired.


*Washington, D.C.*
*FBI Headquarters*


Ollie Hamish came running into Savich's office. "We got him! We got Anthony Carpelli, a.k.a. Wilbur Wright. He was right there in Kitty Hawk on the Outer Banks. He was kneeling in front of the monument at Kitty Hawk and we came up on him and he folded down like a tent and gave it all up."

For an instant, Savich was so distracted he didn't know what Ollie was talking about. Then he remembered, the guru from Texas who'd had his followers murder the two deputies and the sheriff, the Sicilian Canadian who'd attended McGill University and had an advanced degree in cellular biology. Savich said slowly, "Sit down, Ollie. You said he was kneeling at the monument? As in worshiping?"

"Maybe so. All the agents were so relieved at how easily it went down, they were celebrating, drinking beers at eleven o'clock in the morning. We got him, Savich. He'll go back to Texas and fry, probably."

"Probably not," Savich said. "Remember that he isn't tied directly to those killings, just hearsay from a woman who was pissed off."

"Yes, Lureen. Evidently they're holding her as a material witness. They've also picked up two more of Wilbur's people who were in the cult. Everyone thinks his own people will finally nail him. At least we got him and he's not going to be killing anybody else.

"Hey, Savich, you should be really pleased. After all, it was you and MAX who predicted he'd probably go back to Kitty Hawk."

Savich realized he was so caught up with Tammy Tuttle that he didn't feel much of anything about Wilbur Wright. And it was a victory, a very clean win. Everyone would be very pleased. He smiled at Ollie. "I am pleased. MAX discovered sixteen more killings throughout the Southwestern U.S. that sound like the work of Wilbur. So there's lots of other crimes to tie in to this one; local law enforcement should be brought up to speed and get with the program. Dane Carver is heading that up. Now that you've got Wilbur Wright, you can get our doctors on him and see what makes him tick."

"I really don't want to know."

"Unfortunately a jury will demand to know. Meet with Dane and go over all the other cases, then head down to interview Wilbur."

"When we caught him, I looked at him, Savich. You know, I don't think I've ever seen such dead eyes, and I've seen lots of bad folk up close and personal; but Wilbur, he was flat-out scary. You wonder what exactly he's seeing with those dead eyes. It won't be long before they extradite him back to Texas with more than enough evidence to fry his butt."

"You can bet the lawyers will fight extradition."

"Yeah, they'd prefer a state where there's no death penalty, but if we get enough evidence, it won't matter."

"We done good, Ollie. Now you and Dane sew it up, okay?"

"You got it." Agent Ollie Hamish leaned forward in his chair, clasping his hands between his legs. "I've heard all sorts of things, Savich, about what happened in Antigua. How's that going?"

Savich told him all of it. "We've got people working on where she learned her illusion skills so we can get a better handle on what she's capable of. There are more people scouring the airport in Antigua trying to find out how she managed to get away, questioning everyone in the area, searching all boats, all private charters."

Ollie said, "She's still got only one arm and, physically, she's in bad shape, right?"

"I don't know how bad it still is. Her surgeon said if she has an infection, she could be dead within a week without antibiotics. But if she doesn't have an infection, she could make it through fine. He said she responded superbly to the surgery. I asked the doctor if anyone had ever reported seeing someone other than Tammy Tuttle or seeing her where she shouldn't be."

"Did he even understand what you meant?"

"Yes," Savich said slowly, "he did. He said that an orderly told him he'd seen Tammy up and walking to the bathroom the day after surgery. When he went to check her, she was lying strapped down to the bed. Nobody believed the orderly. Then she escaped and no one could figure that out, either. Anyway, Ollie, how are Maria and Josh? He just turned two, right?"

"Yeah. He's running all over the house, opening every drawer, banging every pot. He yells 'no' at least fifty times a day, and he's cuter than the new puppy we just got, who peed on the shirt I was going to wear this morning."

Savich laughed. It felt good. He nodded Ollie out, then turned back to MAX.

A call came in an hour later. Tammy Tuttle had been spotted in Bar Harbor, Maine, where agents had showed her photo all over town, along with Marilyn's, and left phone numbers. A local photo shop owner had called the Bar Harbor Police Department to say she'd left film and was going to come back.

"I've got to get close to her," Savich said to Sherlock. He kissed her nose and left the unit, nearly on a run, shouting over his shoulder, "I've got to see Tammy with one arm, and not something she wants me to see."

"Please, not too close," Sherlock called out, but she didn't think he heard her.

It took very little time for Savich and six other agents to board a Sabreliner at Andrews Air Force Base for a flight to Bar Harbor.

He spent the entire flight telling the agents everything he could think of. It was time, Savich decided, feeling a weight lift off his shoulders, to let everyone know exactly what they were dealing with.

A psychopathic killer who is an illusionist, possibly a telepath. He had never seen anything like it, and he hoped he never would again.

He'd just finished telling all the agents about the Ghouls, detailing what Marilyn had told him and what he himself had seen. If they didn't believe him, they were cool enough to keep it to themselves.

One agent, a friend of Virginia Cosgrove's, didn't doubt a single word. As they were debarking from the jet in Bar Harbor, she said, "Virginia told me some things Marilyn Warluski had told her. It was terrifying, Mr. Savich."

"Just Savich, Ms. Rodriguez. I'm very sorry about Agent Cosgrove."

"We all are, sir." Then she managed a grin. "Just Lois, Savich."

"You got it."

"The thing is, guys," he said a few minutes later to all of them, "if you see her or him again"—he waved the artist's drawing under all their noses—"don't play any games. Don't even think about trying to take her alive. Don't trust anything you see happen, fire without hesitation, and shoot to kill. Now, I'm going to the photo shop, make sure there's no confusion. Then we'll get together at the local police department and get everything set up."

He wondered if the Ghouls would be with her, with Tammy as their head acolyte, their priestess of death.

He was becoming melodramatic. All he really knew as he walked into the photo shop, Hamlet's Pics, on Wescott Avenue, was that he was glad to his soul that Sherlock wasn't here, that she was at home, safe with Sean.

He spoke to the photo shop employee, Teddi Tyler—spelled with an "i" he was told—to verify what he'd said to the local police. Teddi repeated that the woman whose photo Savich was showing him had indeed been in the shop, just yesterday, late afternoon. He'd called the police right away.

"What did she want?"

"She had some film she wanted developed."

Savich felt his heart pound, deep and slow, and it was all he could do to remain calm and smooth. They were so close now. "Did you develop the film, Mr. Tyler?"

"Yes, sir, Agent Savich. The police told me to go ahead and develop it and hold the photos for the FBI."

"When did she say she wanted to pick the photos up?"

"This afternoon, at two o'clock. I told her that would be fine."

"Did she look like she was in good health, Mr. Tyler?"

"She was sort of pale, but looked good other than that. It was pretty cold yesterday so she was all bundled up in a thick coat, a big scarf around her neck and a wool ski cap, but I still recognized her, no problem."

"Did you make any comment to her about how she looked familiar?"

"Oh, no, Agent Savich. I was really cool."

Yeah, I bet, Savich thought, praying that he'd been cool enough not to alert Tammy he was on to her. One thing—Teddi Tyler was still alive, and that meant Tammy hadn't felt threatened, he hoped. Everything he'd told Savich so far was exactly what he'd told the local cops.

"I want you to think carefully now, Mr. Tyler. When she handed you the film, which hand did she use?"

Teddi frowned, furrowing his forehead into three deep lines. "Her left hand," he said at last. "Yes, it was her left hand. She had her purse on a long strap hanging over her left shoulder. It was kind of clumsy."

"Did you ever see her right hand?"

Again Teddi went into a big frown. "I'm sorry, Agent Savich," he said finally, shaking his head, "I don't remember. All I'm sure about is that she stayed all bundled up—again no surprise, since it was so cold."

"Thank you, Mr. Tyler. Now, a special agent will take your place behind the counter. Agent Briggs will be in soon and you can go over procedures with him." Savich raised his hand, seeing that Teddi Tyler wanted to argue. "There's no way you are going to face this woman again, Mr. Tyler. She's very dangerous, even to us. Now, show me those photos."

Savich took the photo envelope from Teddi and moved away from the counter to the glass front windows. The sun was shining brightly for a November day. It didn't look like it was forty degrees outside. He slowly opened the envelope and pulled out the glossy 4x6 photos. There were only six of them.

He looked at one after the other, and then looked again. He didn't understand. All of them were beach shots, undoubtedly taken in the Caribbean. Two were taken in the early morning, two when the sun was high, and two at sunset. None of them was very well done—well, that made sense since she had only one arm—but what was the point? All beach shots, no people in any of them. What was this about?

He held the photos up to Teddi. "Did she say anything about the photos? What they were? Anything at all?"

"Yeah, she said they were vacation photos she wanted to show her roommate. Said her roommate didn't believe her when she'd said how beautiful it was down in the Caribbean. She had to prove it."

If Tammy hadn't lied, then Marilyn was alive. She wanted Marilyn to admire the beaches in the Caribbean.

He told Teddi Tyler to take off as soon as Agent Briggs arrived. As for Briggs, he was a natural retailer, experienced in undercover jobs. He was fast, a good judge of people's behavior. Savich trusted him. Briggs knew how dangerous Tammy was, knew everything Savich knew.

They had three hours to get it all set up. There were three agents undercover near Marilyn's boyfriend's house just off Newport Drive. He doubted they would see either Marilyn or Tammy at the boyfriend's house. Of course not, Savich thought, that would be too easy.

Savich left, drew the salty air deep into his lungs, and called Simon Russo on his way to the meet with the other agents. He hadn't spoken to Russo or Lily in nearly thirty hours. He knew they were all right; otherwise Hoyt would have yelled out. Still, he wanted to know what was happening. He was worried about Lily, just couldn't help it. He knew Simon would protect her with his life, knew Hoyt and the Eureka police were with them all the way. But still, she was his sister, and he loved her deeply. He didn't want anything to happen to her. When he thought of what she'd already endured, he felt rage in his gut.

The more he thought about it, the more Savich worried.

He pulled his leather jacket collar up around his ears and dialed. Simon's cell phone didn't answer. Savich wasn't about to second-guess himself and try to believe that the battery was dead. He immediately put in a call to Clark Hoyt.

# TWENTY-THREE

*Bar Harbor, Maine*

Clark Hoyt answered his cell phone on the third ring. "Savich? Good thing you called. We can't find Simon or Lily. Our guys have been sticking close to them, but when Lily wanted to go to the cemetery, everyone decided they'd be safe there, and so we agreed to give them some privacy. Savich, they went after them in the cemetery!

"When they didn't show up in an hour at Bender's Café in Hemlock Bay, my agents called me, then drove to the cemetery. We found Simon's rental car and one of the Frasiers' cars in the parking lot. There weren't any other cars around. We know Lily visited her daughter's grave because the daffodils she'd bought were there."

Hoyt paused.

"What is it, Clark? What else did you find?"

"Some blood on the front seats, Savich, just a trace, but there was blood on the parking lot cement, a good bit more. We're testing it. We screwed up, Savich. I'm sorry. We'll find them, I swear it to you."

Savich felt fear twisting in his belly, but when he spoke, his voice was controlled. "The fact that you found the Frasiers' car there as well as Simon's—were the Frasiers taken, too? Or were the Frasiers a part of it and just left their car there? If they plan to come back, then why would they leave their car next to Simon's—that's a sure giveaway that they were involved."

"That's what we think."

"At least you didn't find them dead. They've been taken. By whom?"

"We're trying to track down the Frasiers, but nothing yet. They must be with Simon and Lily. Lieutenant Dobbs and I went to the hospital to see Tennyson Frasier. He claimed he didn't know where his parents were. Seemed to me that he really didn't care one way or the other. When we told him Lily was gone, I thought he'd go nuts. This Dr. Rossetti—you remember, the shrink who wanted to treat Lily when she was still in the hospital after the accident? The guy Lily didn't like? Well, he was there with Tennyson. He got all huffy, said Tennyson was a fine man, a great doctor, and his wife was a bitch and didn't deserve him. He then gave Tennyson three happy pills while we were watching. I'll tell you, Savich, I think Tennyson really doesn't know anything about the disappearance."

Savich was hearing everything, but he wasn't thinking a whole lot in that instant. He was flat-out scared. He wanted to leave Bar Harbor and fly immediately out to California, but he couldn't. He simply couldn't leave. It was that simple and that final. He said, "I'm not sure what I think right at this moment, Clark. And I can't break free. I'm up to my eyeballs right now." He drew a deep breath. "Actually, we're about to confront a psychopathic killer right here in Bar Harbor, Maine, and I'm in charge."

"Look, Savich, there are a whole bunch of us on this. We'll find out who took them."

Yeah, yeah, Savich thought, then said, "If this Olaf Jorgenson is behind this, we're talking about a lot of resources, like a private Gulfstream jet here, with flight plans out of the country. It won't be hard to find them."

"We're already on that. I'll call you when we get something. Ah, good luck in Bar Harbor."

"Thank you. Keep me posted."

"Yes, I will. Look, Savich, I'm sorry. I was supposed to keep them covered, keep them safe. I'll do everything I can with this. I'll call you every hour."

"No, Hoyt, call me only if it's an emergency for the next three hours. Otherwise, I'll get back to you when I can." Clark Hoyt didn't know what nuts was, Savich thought, as he punched off his cell phone. He had to call Sherlock, tell her what was going on. Thank God she was home and safe. He didn't want her to hear about Simon and Lily from Hoyt or Lieutenant Dobbs. He had two hours and forty minutes left to set up the operation. He walked over to Firefly Lane to the Bar Harbor Police Department. He knew he simply had to try to stop thinking about Lily and Simon now. He had to concentrate on killing Tammy Tuttle.

He wanted to press his fingers against the pulse point in her neck and not feel a thing.

LILY heard moaning, then a series of gasping curses that seemed to go on forever. Those curses sounded strange, long and drawn out. Then she heard crying. Crying?

No, she wasn't crying. Nor was she cursing. She felt movement, but it wasn't tossing her around; it was just there, all around her, subtle, faintly pulsing.

Simon. Where was Simon?

She opened her eyes slowly, not really wanting to because her head already hurt and she feared it would crack open when she opened her eyes.

There was a woman moaning again. Crying, then more of those soft, slurred curses.

It was Charlotte. Lily remembered now. She'd shot Charlotte, but she was still alive. And hurting. Lily at least felt some satisfaction. If her head hadn't hurt quite so badly, she would have smiled. She hadn't saved herself or Simon, but she had managed to inflict some damage.

She moved her head a little bit. There was a brief whack of pain, but she could handle it. She saw that she was sprawled in a wide leather seat, some sort of belt strapping her in. It cut into her belly and didn't hurt much, just a little tug, and that was a relief.

She saw Simon was seated next to her. He was strapped in, too. She realized then that he was holding her hand on top of his leg. He was looking toward Charlotte.

"Simon."

He made no sudden movement, just slowly turned his head to look down at her. He smiled, actually smiled, and said, "I knew I should have left you at home."

"And miss all this excitement? No way. I'm so glad you're alive. Where are we?"

"We're about thirty thousand miles up, a private jet, I'd say. How are you doing, sweetie?"

"I don't feel much like a sweetie right now. We're in an airplane? So that's that funny feeling, like we're in some sort of moving cocoon. Oh, dear, I guess maybe we're on our way to Sweden?"

"I guess it's possible, but why did you say it like you already knew."

"When those guys were chasing me down the beach, they shouted to me. They're foreign, very stilted English, Swedish, I think. I thought then that Mr. Olaf Jorgenson had gotten tired of waiting to have things done for him."

"You're right about their being Swedish." He was silent for a moment, then said, "You said you were running down the beach to get away from them?"

She told him what had happened, finding the trail back up, finding him unconscious, and then about Charlotte.

"If Charlotte hadn't been there, we would have gotten away and I would have moved us to the Eureka jail, no visitors allowed."

He picked up her hand and held it. "That crying and cursing—it's Charlotte Frasier. The pilot, who also seems to be a medic, has been working on her. You shot her through her right arm. Pity, but she'll be all right. Before you came awake, she was screaming that you were an ingrate, after all she'd done for you. She said she was going to kill you herself." He didn't add that she'd punctuated everything she said with the foulest language he'd heard in a long time.

She was thoughtful for a long moment, then said, "Are you all right?"

"Yes, just a slight headache now. How's your head?"

"Hurts."

"Ah, they see we're awake. Here comes Mr. Alpo Viljo. No, I'm not making it up, his name is Alpo. Sounds Swedish to me. He's an enforcer, a bodyguard maybe. I've never run into a real Swedish badass before. From what I've heard, he's the one who smacked his pistol butt against your head."

Alpo Viljo was indeed one of the men who'd chased her on the beach near the cemetery. He was even bigger up close, but really out of shape, his belly hanging over his belt, unlike most of the Scandinavian people she'd met. At least he was blond and blue-eyed. Had to be some Viking blood in there somewhere.

He didn't say anything, just stood there, his arms crossed over his chest, staring down at her.

Lily said, "What's your partner's name?"

He started, as if he wasn't sure he understood her, then said in his stilted, perfectly understandable English, "His name is Nikki. He's a mean man. Do not do anything to piss him off."

"Where are we going, Mr. Viljo?"

"That is none of your business."

"Why is Mr. Olaf Jorgenson bringing us to Sweden?"

He shook his head at her, grunted, turned, and walked back to the front of the cabin, where Charlotte Frasier was still muttering a curse every little while.

"You got that, Lily? No pissing off Nikki. As for Alpo, I think he likes you. You do look like a princess, and maybe Alpo's a romantic man. But don't count on it, okay?"

She had to grin, even though it hurt her head to move her mouth. She looked out the window at the mountains and canyons of white clouds. She said as she turned back to face him, "Simon, I really do like your hair. Even messed up, it's cool the way it curls at your neck. Long, but not too long. Sexy."

"Lily," he said, leaning closer, his voice very low, "you're not thinking straight at the moment. I want you to close your eyes and try to sleep."

"I think that's probably a very good idea. All right. Maybe I could have some aspirins first?"

Simon called out to Alpo Viljo, and soon Lily was downing a couple of aspirin and a very large glass of water. She gave him a silly grin as her eyes closed.

And in that exact moment, Simon knew it was all over for him. He'd met a woman to trust, a woman loyal to her bones. She sent his feelings right off the scale. His princess, all delicate and soft and pale as milk—well, not right now, since she was still damp from the rain, her clothes torn and splattered with mud, and that hair of hers, all limp and tangled around her head; it was his opinion that she looked superb.

What was a man to do?

He eased a small airplane pillow between her belly and the seat belt. He leaned back against the seat and closed his own eyes.

Lily awoke thinking of her brother, knowing he must be frantic. Surely Hoyt and Dillon knew they'd been taken. But did they have any idea where? And, for that matter, why had they been kept alive at all?

She looked over at Simon's seat. It was empty. He was gone. But where?

She heard a man's deep voice say in halting English right next to her ear, "You eat now."

Nikki eased himself down into Simon's seat. He was holding a tray on his lap. It was the man who'd shouted to her on the beach, the man Alpo had said was mean.

"Where's Simon?"

The big man just shook his head. "Not your worry. Eat now."

She said very slowly, very deliberately, "No, I won't do anything until I see Simon Russo."

Nikki cupped his big hand around the back of her neck and dragged her head back. He picked up a glass of something that looked like iced coffee without the ice and forced her to drink it. She struggled, choked, the liquid spilling down her chin and onto her clothes, soaking in, smelling like coffee and something else. Something like pills went down her throat. She felt dizzy even before Nikki let go of her neck. "Why did you do that?"

"We land soon. Officials here. We want you quiet. Too bad you did not eat. Too thin."

"Where's Simon, you son of a bitch?" But she knew the words didn't sound right coming out of her mouth. She wished she'd eaten, too. She heard her stomach growl even as she fell away into a very empty blankness.

wooden and it creaked. The place was really old. It was dead quiet, not even any rats around. He swept over the room, hurrying because he didn't believe she'd stayed in here, no, she'd go through the door at the far end of the storeroom. It wasn't in Tammy's nature to hide and wait.

He opened the door and stared into a bright, sunlit dining room filled with a late-lunch crowd. He saw a kitchen behind a tall counter on the far side of the dining room, smoke from the range rising into the vents, exits to the left leading to bathrooms, and a single front door that led out to the sidewalk. He stepped into the room. He smelled roast beef and garlic. And fresh bread.

Slowly the conversations thinned out, then stopped completely, everyone gaping at the man who was in a cop stance, swinging a gun slowly around the room, looking desperate, looking like he wanted to kill someone. A woman screamed. A man yelled, "Here, now!"

"What's going on here?"

This last was from a huge man with crew-cut white hair, a white apron stained with spaghetti sauce, coming around the kitchen counter to Savich's left, carrying a long, curved knife. The smell of onions wafted off the knife blade.

"Hey, fellow, is this a holdup?"

Savich slowly lowered his gun. He couldn't believe what he was seeing, couldn't believe he'd come through a dank storeroom into a café and scared a good twenty people nearly to death. Slowly, he reholstered his gun. He pulled out his FBI shield, walked to the man with the knife, stopped three feet away, and showed it to him. He said in a loud voice, "I'm sorry to frighten everyone. I'm looking for a woman." He raised his voice so every diner in the big room could hear. "She's mid-twenties, tall, light hair, very pale. She has only one arm. Did she come in here? Through the storeroom door, like I did?"

There were no takers. Savich checked the bathrooms, then realized Tammy was long gone. She might have remained hidden in the storeroom, knowing he'd feel such urgency he'd burst into the café. He apologized to the owner and walked out the front door.

In that moment, standing on the Bar Harbor sidewalk, Savich could swear that he heard a laugh—a low, vicious laugh that made the hair on his arms stand up. There was no one there, naturally. He felt so impotent, so completely lost that he was hearing her in his mind.

Savich walked slowly back to Hamlet's Pics. When he got there, he

# TWENTY-FOUR

*Bar Harbor, Maine*

Special Agent Aaron Briggs, neck size roughly twenty-one inches, biceps to match, a gold tooth shining like a beacon in his habitual big smile, nodded from behind the counter at agents Lowell and Possner. Both agents were dressed casually in jeans, sweaters, and jackets, trying to appear like ordinary customers looking at frames and photo albums.

It was two o'clock, on the dot.

Savich was in the back. Aaron knew he had his SIG ready, knew he wanted Tammy Tuttle so bad he could taste it. Aaron wanted her, too. Dead was what Tammy Tuttle needed to be, for the sake of human beings everywhere, particularly young teenage boys. He'd listened to every word Dillon Savich had said on the flight up here. He knew agents who'd seen the wild-eyed guy in Antigua who'd slit Virginia Cosgrove's throat, agents who couldn't explain what they'd seen and heard. He felt a ripple of fear in his belly, but he told himself that soon she'd be dead, all that inexplicable stuff he'd heard she'd done down in the airport in Antigua would then be gone with her.

The bell over the shop door sounded as the door opened. In walked Tammy Tuttle, wrapped up in a thick, unbelted wool coat that hung loose on her. Aaron put out his big smile with its shining gold tooth and watched her walk toward him. He could feel the utter focus of agents Possner and Lowell from where he stood, his SIG not six inches from his right hand, beneath the counter.

She was pale, too pale, no makeup on her face, and there was something about her that jarred, something that wasn't quite right.

Aaron was the best retail undercover agent in the Bureau, bar none, with the reputation that he could sell a terrorist a used olive green

Chevy Chevette, and he turned on all his charm. He said, "Hi, may I help you, miss?"

Tammy was nearly leaning against the counter now. She wasn't very tall. She bent toward him and his eyes never left her face as she said, "Where's the other guy? You know, that little twerp who spells Teddi with an 'i'?"

"Yea, ain't that a hoot? Teddi with an 'i.' Well, Teddi said he had a bellyache—he's said that before—and called me to cover for him. Me, I think he drank too much last night at the Night Cave Tavern. You ever been there? Over on Snow Street?"

"No. Get my photos, now."

"Your name, miss?"

"Teresa Tanner."

"No problem," Aaron said and slowly turned to look in the built-in panels, sectioned off by letter of the alphabet. Under *T*, he found Teresa Tanner's envelope third in the slot, which was exactly where he'd placed it himself an hour before. He picked up the envelope with her name on it, was slowly turning back to her, knowing Savich was ready for him to drop to the floor so he'd have a clear shot at her, when suddenly he heard a hissing sound, loud, right in his ear, and he froze. Yes, a hiss, like a snake, right next to him, too close, too close, right next to his neck, and its fangs would sink deep into his skin and . . .

No, his imagination was going nuts on him, but there it was again. Aaron forgot to fall to the floor so Savich could have his shot. He grabbed his SIG from beneath the counter, brought it up fast, just like he knew Possner and Lowell were doing, and whipped around. The photo envelope was suddenly in her hand; he didn't know how she'd gotten it, but there it was, and then both Tammy Tuttle and the envelope were gone. Just gone.

He heard Savich yell, "Get out of the way, Aaron! Move!"

But he couldn't. It was like he was nailed to the spot. Savich was trying to shove him aside, but he resisted, he simply had to resist, not let him by. He saw a harsh, bright glow of fire in the corner of the shop, smelled burning plastic, harsh and foul, and heard Agent Possner scream. Oh God, the place was on fire; no, it was mainly Agent Possner. She was on fire— her hair, her eyebrows, her jacket, and she was screaming, slapping at herself. Flames filled her hair, bright and hot and orange as a summer sun.

Agent Aaron Briggs shoved Savich aside and started running, yelling as he ran toward Possner.

Agent Lowell was turning to Possner, not understanding, and when he saw the flames, he tackled her. They fell to the floor of the shop, knocking over a big frame display, and he was slapping at her burning hair with his hands. Aaron jerked off his sweater as he ran toward them, knocking frame and album displays out of the way.

Savich was around the counter, running toward the door, his gun drawn. Aaron saw him but didn't understand. Didn't he care that Possner was on fire? He heard a gunshot, a high, single pop, then nothing. Suddenly the flames were out. Possner was sobbing, in the fetal position on the floor, Lowell's shirt wrapped around her head, and Aaron saw Lowell was all right, no burns that Aaron could see. He had his cell phone out, calling for backup, calling for an ambulance. And Aaron realized that his fingers looked normal. He thought he'd seen them burned, just like he'd seen Possner burned.

SAVICH was running, searching through the streets. There weren't that many folk around, no tourists at all, it being fall and much too chilly for beach walks in Bar Harbor. He held his SIG at his side and made a grid in his mind. He'd studied the street layout. Where would she go? Where had she come from?

Then he saw her long, dark blue wool coat, thick and heavy, flapping around a corner half a block up Wescott. He nearly ran down an old man, apologized but didn't slow. He ran, holding his SIG against his side, hearing only his own breathing. He ran around the corner and stopped dead in his tracks. The alley was empty except for that thick wool coat, lay in a collapsed pile against a brick wall at the back of the alley.

Where was she? He saw the narrow, wooden door, nearly invisi along the alley wall. When he got to it, he realized it was locked. He ra his SIG and fired into the lock. Two bullets dead on and the lock s tered. He was inside, crouched low, his gun steady, sweeping the spa was very dim, one of the naked bulbs overhead, burned out. He blin adjust his vision and knew he was in grave danger. If Tammy was in here, she could easily see his silhouette against the streetlight him and nail him.

He realized he was in a storeroom. There were barrels li walls, shelves filled with boxes and cans, paper goods. The f

stood a moment outside the shop, incredulous. There'd been mayhem when he'd burst out of there. But now there were no cop cars, no ambulance, no fire engines. Everything was quiet, nothing seemed to be out of the ordinary.

He walked into the photo shop. There were three agents standing on the far side of the shop talking quietly among themselves.

Agent Possner wasn't burned. There was no sign that there had ever been a fire in Hamlet's Pics. Agents Briggs, Lowell, and Possner stared back at him.

Savich walked out. He sat down on a wooden bench on the sidewalk just outside the photo shop and put his head in his hands.

For the first time, he thought the FBI needed to assign someone else to catch this monster. He'd failed. Twice now, he'd failed.

He felt a hand on his shoulder and slowly raised his head to see Teddi Tyler standing over him. "I'm sorry, man. She must really be something to get past you guys."

"Yeah," Savich said, and he felt a shade better. "She's something. We'll get her, Teddi. I just don't know how as of yet."

She was still somewhere in Bar Harbor with Marilyn, she had to be. He got slowly to his feet. He had to get a huge manhunt organized.

In that instant, he realized that even if they didn't find her, she had every intention of finding him. She would hunt him down, not the other way around. And the good Lord knew, he was much easier to find.

*Gothenburg, Sweden*

It was cold, so bloody cold Lily didn't think she could stand it. Strange thing was that she knew she wasn't really conscious, that she didn't really know what was happening or where she was, but her body just kept shuddering, convulsing with the cold. The cold was penetrating her bones, and she felt every shake, every shudder.

Then, suddenly, she felt Simon near her, no doubt it was him because she knew his scent. She already knew his damned scent, a good scent, as sexy as his hair curling at his neck. His arms were suddenly around her, and he hugged her hard against him, pulling her so close she was breathing against his neck, feeling his heart beat steady and strong against hers.

He was breathing deeply, and cursing. Really bad words that Savich had never said even when he was pissed off, which had been quite often when they were growing up. What a long time ago. Sometimes, like now, she thought as she shivered, being an adult really sucked. She pressed closer, feeling his warmth all the way to her belly. The convulsive jerks lessened, her brain began to function again.

She said against his collarbone, "Where are we, Simon? Why is it so cold? Did they leave us beside a fjord?"

His hands were going up and down her back, big hands that covered a lot of territory, and he rolled her under him so he could cover more of her.

"I guess we're in Sweden. It's sure too cold in this room for us to be in the Mediterranean near Ian's yacht. I woke up a while ago. They drugged us. Do you remember?"

"Yes, Nikki forced something down my throat. I guess you were already under. How much time has passed?"

"A couple of hours. We're in a bedroom, and there isn't even a heater working. The door is locked, and the bed is stripped, so we have no blankets or sheets. I didn't realize you were so cold until just a minute ago. Are you warming up now?"

"Oh yes," she said, against his neck, "definitely better."

He was silent for a long time, listening to her breathe, feeling her relax as she grew warmer. He cleared his throat and said, "Lily, I know this is an awfully unusual place and perhaps even a somewhat strange time to mention this, but I have to be honest here. You didn't do well picking your first two husbands. I'm thinking that you need a sort of consultant who could help you develop a whole new set of criteria before you try a third husband."

She raised her head, saw his bristly chin in the dim light, and said only, "Maybe, but I'm still married to the second one."

"Not for much longer. Tennyson is soon to be only another very bad chapter in your history. Then he'll be a memory, and you'll be ready to begin work with your consultant."

"He's scary, Simon. He married me to get to my paintings. He fed me depressants. He probably tried to kill me by cutting the brake lines in the Explorer. He's a very bad chapter, maybe the biggest, baddest yet, and my history isn't all that long. It's not particularly good for the soul to have both Jack Crane and Tennyson Frasier in your life."

"You'll divorce Tennyson just like you did Jack Crane. Then we'll figure out these new criteria together."

"You want to be my marriage consultant?"

"Well, why not?"

"I don't even know your educational background or your experience in this area."

"We can discuss that later. Tell me about your first husband."

"All right. His name is Jack Crane. He knocked me around when I was pregnant with Beth. The first and last time. I called Dillon and he was there in a flash, and he beat Jack senseless. Loosened three of his perfect white teeth. Cracked two ribs. Two black eyes and a swollen jaw. Then Dillon taught me how to fight so if he ever came around again, I could take care of him myself."

"Did he ever come around after you divorced him so you could beat him up?"

"No, dammit, he didn't. I don't think he was scared of me. He was scared Dillon would get every FBI agent in Chicago on him and he'd be dead meat. You know, Simon, I don't think having a consultant to select new criteria would help. You can be sure I thought long and hard about Tennyson, given Jack was a wife beater."

"You didn't think long enough or hard enough. You have trouble with criteria, Lily, and that's why you need a consultant, to keep your head screwed on straight, to see things properly."

"Nope, it's more than that. I'm simply rotten at picking men. Your counseling me wouldn't work, Simon. Besides that, I don't need you. I've decided that I'm never going to get married again. So I don't need to consult you or anyone else about it."

"A whole lot of men aren't anything like your first or second husbands. Look at Savich. Do you think Sherlock ever has any doubts about him?"

He felt her shrug. "Dillon is rare. There are no criteria that fit him. He's just wonderful, and that's all there is to it. He was born that way. Sherlock is the luckiest woman in the world. She knows it; she told me so."

She was quiet for a moment, and he could feel her relaxing, warming up, and it was driving him nuts. He couldn't believe what he was saying to her.

She said into his neck, "You know, I'm beginning to think that once I marry a man, he turns into Mr. Hyde. He sinks real low real fast. But I guess you'll tell me it's because of my lousy criteria, again."

"Are you saying that all guys would turn into a Mr. Hyde?"

"Could be, all except for Dillon. But you see my point here, Simon. Don't be obtuse. With both Jack and Tennyson, I didn't believe either of them was anything but what I believed them to be when I married them. I loved them, I believed they loved me, admired me, even admired my Remus cartoons. Both Jack and Tennyson would go on and on about how talented I was, how proud they were of me. And so I married them. I was happy, at least for maybe a month or two. About Jack—he did give me Beth, and because of that I will never regret marrying him." Her voice caught over her daughter's name. Just saying her name brought back horrible memories, painful memories she'd lived with for so very long. It had been so needless, so quick, and then her little girl was gone. She had to stop it, cut it off. It was in the past, it had to stay there. She pictured Beth in her mind, decked out in her Easter dress of the year before, and she'd been so cute. She'd just met Tennyson. She sighed. So much had happened and now poor Simon was caught up in all of it. And he suddenly wanted her?

She said, "You can't possibly want to consult with me on this, Simon. I think you could say we've got a situation here; we might die at any minute—no, don't try to reassure me, don't try it. You know it's very possible, and you're trying to take my mind off it, but talking about Jack and Tennyson isn't helping."

He kept holding her and said finally, nodding against her hair, "I understand."

"Stop using that soothing voice on me. You know you're not thinking straight. You know what? I think God created me, decided He'd let me screw up twice, and then He'd keep me safe from further humiliations and mistakes."

"Lily, you may look like a princess—well, usually—but what you just said, that was nuts. I intend to make use of some proper criteria. You'll choose really well next time."

"Forget it, Simon. I'm the worst matrimonial bet on the planet. I'm warm now, so you can get off me."

He didn't really want to, but he rolled off and came up on his elbow beside her. "This bare mattress smells new. I can make out more of the room now. It's nice, Lily, very nice."

"We're at Olaf's house, somewhere in Sweden."

"Probably."

"Why did . . ."

She let the words die in her mouth when the bedroom door opened, sending in a thick slice of bright sunlight. Alpo walked in, Nikki behind him. "You are awake now?"

"Yes," Simon said, coming up to sit on the side of the bed. "Don't you guys believe in heat? Is Olaf trying to economize?"

"You are soft. Shut up."

Lily said, "Well, we don't have your body fat; maybe that's the difference."

Nikki shouldered Alpo out of the way and strode to where Simon was sitting. "You get up now. You, too," he said to Lily. "A woman does not speak like that. I am not fat; I am strong. Mr. Jorgenson is waiting for you."

"Ah," Lily said, "at last we get to meet the Grand Pooh-Bah."

"What is that?" Nikki asked as he stepped back so they could get up.

"The guy who controls everything, the one who believes he's the big cheese," Simon said.

Alpo looked thoughtful for a moment, then nodded. "We will go see the Grand Pooh-Bah now." He said to Lily, "He will like you. He may want to paint you before he kills you."

Not a happy thought.

# TWENTY-FIVE

*Bar Harbor, Maine*

It had been nearly a whole day, and there was no sign of Tammy Tuttle or Marilyn Warluski. There'd been dozens of calls about possible sightings, all of which had to be investigated, but so far, nothing. It was the biggest manhunt in Maine's history, with more than two hundred law enforcement people involved. And always there in Savich's mind was Lily and where she was. Whether she was alive. He couldn't bear it and there was nothing he could do.

He was nearly ready to shoot himself when Jimmy Maitland called from Washington.

"Come home, Savich," he said. "You're needed here in Washington. We'll get word on Tammy sooner or later. There's nothing more you can do up there."

"She'll kill again, sir, you know it, I know it, and that's when we'll get word. She's probably already killed Marilyn."

Jimmy Maitland was silent, a thick, depressed silence. Then he said, "Yes, you're right. I also know that for the moment there's nothing more we can do about it. As for you, Savich, you're too close now. Come home."

"Is that an order, sir?"

"Yes." He didn't add that he was calling from Savich's house in Georgetown, sitting in Savich's favorite chair, bouncing Sean on his knee, Sherlock not two feet away, holding out a whiskey, neat, in one hand and a graham cracker in the other. Jimmy hoped the cracker wasn't intended for him. He needed the whiskey.

Savich sighed. "All right. I'll be back in a few hours."

If Sean had decided to talk while his father was on the phone, Jimmy would have been busted, but the kid had been quiet, just grinning at him and rubbing his knuckles over his gums. Jimmy hung up the phone, handed Sean to Sherlock, and said as she handed him the whiskey, "This is a royal mess, but at least Savich will be home sometime this evening. He's really upset, Sherlock."

"I know, I know. We'll think of something. We always do." She gave Sean the graham cracker.

Jimmy said, "Savich feels guilty, like he's the one who's failed, like the murders of all those people, including our own Virginia Cosgrove, are his fault."

"He always will. It's the way he is."

Jimmy looked over at the baby, who was happily gumming the graham cracker. He said, "Sean reminds me of my second to oldest, Landry. He was a pistol, that one, gave me every gray hair I've got on my head. If you ever get tired of this little champ, give me a call."

He downed his whiskey and stared for a moment at the marvelous Sarah Elliott painting hanging over the fireplace. "I've always wondered about the soldier in that painting, wondered what he was thinking at that moment when he was frozen for all time. I wonder if there was someone at home who would grieve if he died."

"Yes, it's excellent. Has Dillon kept you in the loop about Lily and Simon?"

"He told me earlier Agent Hoyt found the flight plan for a private Gulfstream jet owned by the Waldemarsudde Corporation that took off from Arcata airport bound for Gothenburg, Sweden. The CEO is Ian Jorgenson, son of Olaf Jorgenson, the collector we believe is involved in all this."

Sherlock nodded and said, "Did he also tell you that we think his son is a collector as well?"

"Yes," Jimmy said. "Interesting, isn't it, that Charlotte and Elcott Frasier were also taken? Or maybe they went willingly because the jig was almost up for them here. Tennyson is still in Hemlock Bay. There's not a shred of evidence yet to connect him to the attempts on Lily's life or Mr. Monk's murder, or any of the rest of it. Seems to me Lily's husband is his parents' dupe."

"Maybe so," Sherlock said. "It doesn't matter. Lily's divorcing him. Oh yes, Dillon has already called two cop friends he has in Stockholm and Uppsala. We know Jorgenson has a huge estate in Gothenburg called Slottsskogen, or Castle Wood. It's about halfway up the coast of Sweden on the western side. Dillon said that one of his friends, Petter Tuomo, has two brothers in the Gothenburg police. They're on it. We haven't heard anything back yet."

Jimmy said, "Good, things are moving. Does Savich have friends all over the world?"

"Just about." She sighed, kissed Sean, who was wriggling to get down, and shook her head. "Everywhere we look, there's something horrible ready to fall on our heads. We're terrified about Lily and Simon. We're praying Olaf Jorgenson hasn't killed them."

"I can't see why he'd bother to kidnap them if he wanted them dead, Sherlock. There's got to be more going on here than we know."


*Gothenburg, Sweden*

An hour later, bathed, warm, and in fresh clothes, Lily and Simon preceded Alpo and Nikki down a massive oak staircase that could accommodate six well-fed people at a time. They were led to the other side of an entrance hall that was a huge chessboard, black-and-white square slabs of marble, with three-foot-tall classic carved black-and-white marble chess pieces lined up along the walls.

They walked down a long hall, through big mahogany double doors into a room that was two stories high, every wall covered from floor to ceiling with books. There were a good half dozen library ladders. A fire burned in an exquisite white marble fireplace with an ornately carved mantel that was at least two feet wide and covered with exquisite Chinese figures. There was a large desk set at an angle in the corner. Behind the desk was a man not much older than fifty, tall, blond and blue-eyed, fit as his Viking ancestors. He was tanned, probably from days spent on the ski slopes. The man rose as Simon and Lily were brought in. He looked at them, his expression gentle and sympathetic. She drew herself up. That was nonsense, and she wouldn't underestimate him. The man nodded, and both Alpo and Nikki remained by the door.

"Welcome to Slottsskogen, Mr. Russo, Mrs. Frasier. Ah, that means Castle Wood. Our city's largest park was named after this estate many years ago. Won't you sit down?"

"What is the city?"

"Sit down. Good. I'm Ian Jorgenson. My father asked me to greet you. You both look better than you did when you arrived."

"I'm sure that's true," Lily said.

"Your English is fluent," Simon said.

"I attended Princeton University. My degree, as you might imagine, is in art history. And, of course, business."

Lily said, "Why are we here?"

"Ah, here is my father. Nikki, bring him very close so he can see Mrs. Frasier."

Lily tensed in her chair as Nikki pushed a wheelchair toward them. In the chair sat an impossibly old man, with a few tufts of white hair sticking straight up. He looked frail, but when he raised his head, she saw brilliant blue eyes, and they were cold and sharp with intelligence. The brain in that head was not frail or fading.

"Closer," the old man said.

Nikki brought him to within inches of Lily. The old man reached out his hand and touched his fingertips to her face. Lily started to draw back, then stilled.

"I am Olaf Jorgenson, and you are Lily. I speak beautiful English because, like my son, I also attended Princeton University. Ah, you are wearing the white gown, just as I instructed. It is lovely, as I hoped it would be. Perfect." He ran his fingers down her arm, over the soft white silk, to her wrist. "I want you to be painted in this white dress. I am pleased those American buffoons failed to execute you and Mr. Russo."

"So are we," Lily said. "Why did they want to kill us so badly, Mr. Jorgenson?"

"Well, you see, it was my intention to let the Frasiers deal with you. I understand they bungled the job several times, for which I am now grateful. I hadn't realized what you looked like, Lily. When Ian showed me your picture, I ordered the Frasiers to stay away from you. I sent Alpo and Nikki to California to fetch you back to me. They were clumsy also, but it turned out not to matter because you, my dear, are here at last."

Lily said slowly, "I don't look like anyone special. I'm just myself." But she knew she must look like someone who mattered to him, and so she waited, holding her breath, keeping still as his fingers stroked her arm, up to her shoulder. She saw that his nails were dark and unhealthy-looking.

The old man said finally, "You look exactly like Sarah Jameson when I first met her in Paris a very long time ago, before the Great War, when the artistic community in Paris broke free and flourished. Ah yes, we enraged the staid French bourgeoisie with our endless and outrageous play, our limitless daring and debauchery. I remember the hours we spent with Gertrude Stein. Ah, what an intelligence that one had, her wit sharper than Nikki's favorite knife, and such noble and impossible ideas. And there was the clever and cruel Picasso—he painted her, worshiped her. And Matisse, so quiet until he drank absinthe, and then he would sing the most obscene songs imaginable as he painted. I remember all the French neighbors cursing through the walls when he sang.

"I saw Hemingway wagering against Braque and Sherwood—it was a spitting contest at a cuspidor some eight feet away. Your grandmother kept moving the cuspidor. Ah, such laughter and brilliance. It was the most flamboyant, the most vivid time in all of history, all the major talent of the world in that one place. It was like a zoo with only the most beautiful, the wildest and most dangerous specimens congregated together. They gave the world the greatest art ever known."

"I didn't know you were a writer or an artist," Simon said.

"I'm neither, unfortunately, but I did try to paint, studied countless hours with great masters and wasted many canvases. So many of my young friends wanted to paint or to write. We were in Paris to worship the great ones, to see if perhaps their vision, their immense talent, would rub off, just a bit. Some of those old friends did become great; others returned to their homes to make furniture or sell stamps in a post office. Ah, but Sarah Jameson, she was the greatest of them all. Stein corresponded with her until her death right after World War Two."

"How well did you know my grandmother, Mr. Jorgenson?"

Olaf Jorgenson's soft voice was filled with shadows and faded memories that still fisted around his heart, memories he could still see clearly. "Sarah was a bit older than I, but so beautiful, so exquisitely talented, so utterly without restraint, as hot and wild as a sirocco blowing up from the Libyan desert. She loved vodka and opium, both as pure as she could get. The first time I saw her, another young artist, her lover, was painting her nude body, covering it with phalluses, all of them ejaculating.

"She was everything I wanted, and I grew to love her very much. But she met a man, a damned American who was simply visiting Paris, a businessman, ridiculous in his pale gray flannels, but she wanted him more than me. She left me, went back to America with him."

"That was my grandfather, Emerson Elliott. She married him in the mid-1930s, in New York."

"Yes, she left me. And I never saw her again. I began collecting her paintings during the fifties. It wasn't well known for some time that she'd willed paintings to her grandchildren, such a private family matter. Yes, she willed eight beautiful paintings to each child. I knew I wanted them all for my collection. You are the first; it is unfortunate, but we managed to gain only four of the originals before the Frasiers became convinced that you were going to leave their son, despite the drugs they were feeding you. They knew you'd take the paintings with you, so they decided to kill you, particularly since your husband was your beneficiary after your daughter's death."

"But I didn't die."

"No, you did not, but not for their lack of trying."

"You're telling me that my husband was not part of this plot?"

"No, Tennyson Frasier was their pawn. His parents' great hopes for him were dashed, but he did manage to make you his wife. It's possible he even fell in love with you, at least enough to marry you, as his parents wished."

She'd been so certain that Tennyson had been part of the plot. She asked, "Why didn't you just offer me money?"

"I knew you would turn me down, as would your siblings. You were the most vulnerable, particularly after your divorce from Jack Crane, and so I selected you."

"That's crazy. You invent this convoluted plan just to bilk me out of my grandmother's paintings?"

"Sarah's paintings belong with me, for I am the only one who can really appreciate them, know them beyond their visual message and impact, because I knew her, you see, knew her to her soul. She would talk to me about her work, what each one meant to her, what she was thinking when she was painting each one. I fed her opium, and we talked for hours. I never tired of watching her paint, of listening to her voice. She was the only woman I ever wanted in my life, the only one." He paused for a moment, frowning, and she saw pain etched into the deep wrinkles in his face. From the loss of her grandmother or from illness?

He said, his voice once again brisk, "Yes, Lily, I selected you because you were the most vulnerable, the most easily manipulated. Most important, you were alone. When you moved to Hemlock Bay, I had Ian approach the Frasiers. Tell them, Ian."

"I played matchmaker," Ian Jorgenson said and laughed. "It was infinitely satisfying when it all came together. I bought the Frasiers—simple as that. You married Tennyson, just as we planned, and his parents told him to convince you to have your Sarah Elliott paintings moved from Chicago to the Eureka Art Museum. And there our greedy Mr. Monk quickly fell in with our plans."

Simon said to the old man, "You managed to have four of them forged before I got wind of it."

Those brilliant blue eyes swung to Simon, but he sensed the old man couldn't see him all that clearly. "You meddled, Mr. Russo. You were the one who brought us down. You found out through your sources, all that valuable information sold to them by an expatriate friend of mine who betrayed me, and then it was sold to you. But that is not your concern. If she had not betrayed me, then I would have all your paintings now, and you, Lily, would be dead. I am not certain that would have been best."

"But now you'll never get the other four," Lily said. "They're out of your reach. You won't be hanging onto those you do have very long. Surely you know that."

"You think not, my dear?" The old man laughed, then said, still wheezing, "Come, I have something to show you."

Three long corridors and five minutes later, Lily and Simon stood motionless in a climate-controlled room, staring at fourteen-foot-high walls that were covered with Sarah Elliott paintings. The collection held at least a hundred fifty paintings, maybe more.

Simon said as he stared at the paintings, slowly taking in their magnificence, "You couldn't have bought this many Sarah Elliott paintings legally. You must have looted the museums of the world."

"When necessary. Not all that difficult, most of them. Imagination and perseverance. It's taken me years, but I am a patient man. Just look at the results."

"And money," Simon said.

"Naturally," Ian Jorgenson said.

"But you can't see them," Lily said as she turned to look at Olaf Jorgenson. "You stole them because you have some sort of obsession with my grandmother, and you can't even see them!"

"I could see them all very well until about five years ago. Even now, though, I can see the graceful sweeps of her brush, shadows and sprays of color, the movement in the air itself. Her gift is unparalleled. I know each one as if I had painted it myself. I know how the subjects feel, the texture of the expressions on their faces. I can touch my fingers to a sky and feel the warmth of the sun and the wind caressing my hand. I know all of them. They are old friends. I live inside them; I am a part of them and they of me. I have been collecting them over forty years now. Since I want all of them before I die, it was time to turn to you, Lily. If I'd only known at the beginning that you were so like my Sarah, I wouldn't have allowed those fools to try to kill you. Because you are resourceful, you saved yourself. I am grateful for that."

Lily looked down at the old man sitting in his wheelchair, a beautiful hand-knitted blue blanket covering his legs. He looked like a harmless old gentleman, in his pale blue cashmere sweater over a white silk shirt with a darker blue tie. She didn't say anything. What was there to say, after all? It was crazy, all of it. And rather sad, she supposed, if one discounted the fact that he was perfectly willing to murder people who got in his way.

She looked at the walls filled with so many of her grandmother's paintings. All of them perfectly hung, grouped by the period in which they were painted. She had never seen such beauty in one room before in her life. It was her grandmother's work as she had never seen it.

She watched Simon walk slowly around the large room, studying each of the paintings, lightly touching his fingertips to some of them until he came to one that belonged to Lily. It was *The Swan Song*, Lily's own favorite. The old man lying in the bed, that beatific smile on his face, the young girl staring at him.

Olaf said, "That was the first one of yours I had copied, my dear. It was always my favorite. I knew it was at the Art Institute of Chicago, but I couldn't get to it. It was frustrating."

Simon said, "So it was the first one you stole from the Eureka Museum."

"Nothing so dramatic," Ian Jorgenson said, coming forward. He laid his hand lightly on his father's shoulder. "Mr. Monk, the curator, was quite willing to have the painting copied. He simply gave it to our artist, replacing it with a rather poor, quickly executed copy until the real copy was finished. Then they were simply switched. No one noticed, of course. You know, Mr. Russo, I had hopes for you, at least initially. You yourself own a Sarah Elliott painting. I had hoped to convince you to join me, perhaps even to sell me your painting in return for a generous price and my offer of a financially rewarding partnership in some of my business ventures."

Ian looked toward Simon and his eyes narrowed, but when he spoke, his voice was perfectly pleasant. "My father realized you wouldn't agree after Nikki and Alpo described your behavior on the long trip over here. You were in no way conciliatory, Mr. Russo. Actually, my father's desire to make use of you in his organization was the only reason we bothered to bring you to Sweden. My father wanted to test you."

"Give me a test," Simon said. "Let's just see what I would say."

"Actually, I was going to ask you to give me your Sarah Elliott painting, *The Last Rites;* it is one I greatly admire. In exchange, I would offer you your life and a chance to prove your value to me."

"I accept your offer, if, in return, you give Lily and me our freedom."

"It is as I feared," Olaf said and sighed. He nodded to his son.

Ian looked at his hands, strong hands, and lightly buffed his finger-nails on his cashmere sleeve. He said to Simon, "I look forward to killing you, Mr. Russo. I knew you could never be brought to our side, that you could never be trusted. You have interfered mightily."

Simon said, "You had your chance to get *The Last Rites,* Mr. Jorgen-son. Freedom for Lily and me, but you turned it down. Let me promise you that you will never get that painting. When I die, it goes to the Met-ropolitan Museum of Art."

Olaf said, "I do detest making mistakes in a person's character. It is a pity, Mr. Russo."

Lily said to Ian, "Is it true you have Rembrandt's *Night Watch* aboard your yacht?"

Ian Jorgenson raised a blond brow. "My, my, Mr. Russo has many tentacles, doesn't he? Yes, my dear, I had it gently removed from the Rijksmuseum some ten years ago. It was rather difficult, actually, since it's quite large. It was a gift to my wife, who died later that year. She was so pleased to look at it in her last days."

The old man laughed, then coughed. Nikki handed him a handker-chief, and he coughed into it. Lily thought she saw blood.

Ian said, "As my father said, the Art Institute of Chicago is a difficult place, more difficult than even I wished to deal with. In the past ten years they've added many security measures that make removal of art pieces very challenging. But most important, my only contact, a curator there, lost his job five years ago. It was a pity. I didn't know what to do until you moved to that ridiculous little town on the coast of California. This Hemlock Bay."

Olaf said, "My son and I spent many hours coming up with the right plan for you, Lily. Ian traveled to California, to Hemlock Bay. What a quaint and clever name. It was such a simple little town, generous and friendly to newcomers, such as you and your daughter, was it not? He liked the fresh salt air, the serenity of the endless stretches of beach and forest, the magnificent redwoods, and all those clever little roads and houses blended into the landscape. Who could imagine it would be so simple to find such perfect tools? The Frasiers—greedy, ambitious people—and here they had a son who would be perfect for you."

"Did they murder my daughter?"

# TWENTY-SIX

"You think the Frasiers killed your daughter?" Ian Jorgenson repeated, his voice indifferent. He shrugged. "Not that I know of." Lily suddenly hated him.

Olaf said, "I know you felt sorrow over your daughter's death. But what does it matter to you now who is responsible?"

"Whoever struck her down deserves to die for it."

"Killing them won't bring back your little girl," Ian said, frowning at her. "We, in Sweden, actually in most of Europe, do not believe in putting people to death. It is barbaric."

What is wrong with this picture? Simon wondered, staring at Ian Jorgenson.

"No," Lily said, "it won't bring Beth back, but it would avenge her. No one who kills in cold blood should be allowed to continue breathing the same air I breathe."

"You are harsh," said Olaf Jorgenson.

"You are not harsh, sir? You, who order people murdered?"

Olaf Jorgenson laughed, a low, wheezy sound thick with phlegm, perhaps with blood.

"No, I always do only what is necessary, nothing more. Vengeance is for amateurs. Now, you do not have to wonder again if the Frasiers killed your daughter. They did not. They told me that they'd been concerned because your daughter, by ill chance, had seen some e-mails on Mr. Frasier's computer, communications that she shouldn't have seen. They, of course, assured the child that the messages were nonsense, nothing important, nothing to even think about."

So that was why Beth had been moody, withdrawn, that last week.

Why hadn't her daughter come to her, told her, at least asked her about what she had seen? But she hadn't, and then she'd been killed.

Olaf Jorgenson continued, "I understand it was an accident, one of your American drunk drivers who was too afraid to stop and see what he'd done."

Lily felt tears clog her throat. She'd happily left Chicago and Jack Crane and moved to a charming coastal town. She couldn't believe what it had brought them.

Simon took her hand, squeezed her fingers. He knew she was feeling swamped with the memories of her loss and despair. She raised her head to look at Olaf Jorgenson and said, "What do you intend to do with us?"

"You, my dear, I will have painted by a very talented artist whom I've worked well with over the years. As for Mr. Russo here, as I said, I hold no hope now of bringing him into my fold. He is much too inflexible in his moral code. It is not worth the risk. Also, he seems taken with you, and I can't have that. Isn't that interesting? You've known each other for such a short time."

"He just wants to be my consultant," Lily said.

Simon smiled.

"He wants you in bed," Ian said. "Or maybe you're already lovers and that's why he's helping you."

"Don't be crude," Olaf said, frowning toward his son, then added, "Yes, I fear Mr. Russo must take a nice, long boat ride with Alpo and Nikki here. We still have two lovely canals left from those built back in the early seventeenth century by our magnificent Gustav. Yes, Mr. Russo, you and my men here will visit one of the canals this very night. It's getting cold now, not many people will be about at midnight."

Simon said, "I can't say I find that an appealing way to spend the evening. What do you intend to do with the Frasiers?"

Olaf Jorgenson said to Lily, not to Simon, "At the moment they are my honored guests. They accompanied you here since they knew they could not remain in California. Your law enforcement, and so on. They expect to receive a lot of money from me. In addition, Mr. Frasier already has very nice bank accounts in Switzerland. They are prepared to spend the rest of their lives living very nicely in the south of France, I believe they said."

Lily said, "After you've painted me, then what will happen?"

He smiled then, showing her his very beautiful white teeth, likely false. "Yes, yes, I know I am an old man, but I do not have much longer to live. I want you with me until it is my time. I was hoping, perhaps, that you would see some advantage in marrying me."

"Oh, is that why I'm wearing white? To put me in the mood?"

"You want manners," Ian said. He was angry, she could see it as he stepped toward her only to stop when he felt his father's hand on his forearm. Ian shook off his father's hand and said, "She is disrespectful. She needs to see what an honor it would be to be your wife!"

Olaf only shook his head. He even smiled again as he said to Lily, "No, my dear, you are wearing white because that is a copy of the dress I last saw your grandmother wearing in Paris. It was the day she left with Emerson Elliott. The day I believed my world had collapsed."

"You are good at copies, aren't you?" Lily said. "I am not my grandmother, you foolish old man."

Ian struck her across the face. Simon didn't say a word, hurled himself at Ian Jorgenson, slammed his fist into his jaw, then whirled back and kicked him in the kidney.

"Stop!" It was Nikki and he'd pulled a gun, which was aimed at Simon.

Simon gave him a brief bow, straightened his shirt, and walked away.

Ian slowly raised himself to his feet, grimacing in pain. "I will go with Nikki and Alpo this evening. I will be the one to kill you."

"All this," Simon said, marveling as he turned to Olaf Jorgenson, "and you raised a coward, too."

Lily lightly placed her hand on Simon's arm. She was terrified.

She said to Olaf, "Even if I found you remotely acceptable in matrimonial terms, sir, I couldn't marry you. I'm married to Tennyson Frasier."

The old man was silent.

"I don't ever wish to marry again, at least until I've seriously reconsidered my criteria. I don't think there's any way in the world that you would ever fit them. I'm married anyway, so it doesn't matter, does it?"

Still the old man was silent, thoughtfully looking at her. Then he slowly nodded. He said, "I will be back shortly."

"What are you going to do, Father?"

"I do not believe in bigamy. It is immoral. I'm going to make Lily a widow. Nikki, take me to my library." As Nikki wheeled him out of the huge room, Lily and Simon saw him pull a small, thick black book from his sweater pocket. They watched him thumb through it as he disappeared from their view.

"He's completely mad," Lily whispered.

*Washington, D.C.*

Savich walked through the front door of his home, hugged his wife, kissed her, and said, "Where's Sean?"

"At your mom's house—babbling, gumming everything in sight, and happy. I left your mom a two-box supply of graham crackers."

Savich was too tired, too depressed to smile. He raised an eyebrow in question.

She said, without preamble, "Both the Bureau and I agree with your plan. Tammy wants you, Dillon. She's focused on you. There's no doubt in anyone's mind she will come here. I took Sean to your mother's because we don't want him in harm's way.

"Right before you got home, Jimmy Maitland issued a statement to the media that you were no longer the lead investigator in the manhunt for Tammy Tuttle. Aaron Briggs has replaced you as the lead. He said you were urgently needed to gather vital evidence in the Wilbur Wright case, the cult leader responsible for the heinous murders of a sheriff and two deputies in Flowers, Texas. You're traveling to Texas on Friday to begin working with local law enforcement."

He hugged her close and said against her hair, "You and Mr. Maitland got it done really fast. So I'm to leave on Friday? Today is Tuesday."

"Yes. It gives Tammy plenty of time to get here."

"Yes, it does." Savich streaked his fingers through his hair, making it stand straight up. "Have you got Gabriella safely stashed away?"

"Actually, she's at your mom's house during the day. Both of them are safe. She said she doesn't want to miss a single step that Sean takes."

But Sean's parents were missing his first steps, Savich thought. He felt brittle with rage, bowed with his failure.

He said finally, knowing that she wouldn't like or accept it, "She's scary, Sherlock. I don't want her near you, either."

She nodded slowly as she stepped against him, pressing her face to his neck. "I know, Dillon, but I couldn't think of anything else. Jimmy Maitland told me you'd balk because of me and Sean, and I knew I couldn't allow that. Now we've gotten both Gabriella and Sean to safety. Don't even think you can send me away. We're in this together, we always have been, and we're going to get her. We have the advantage here because we control the scene. We can act and plan, we can be ready for her, not just wait to react to something she does."

He held her tightly. He wondered if she could smell his fear, there was such a huge well of it. Savich kissed her and hugged her until she squeaked. "We've got to be ready for her, Sherlock, and I've got some ideas about that. I've been thinking about this for a good while now."

"Like what?" she asked, pulling back, looking up at him.

"She has the power to create illusions, to make people see what she wants them to see. Whether it's some kind of magician's trick or a strange ability that's inside her sick brain, the end result is the same."

He let her go and began pacing. He looked at his grandmother's painting over the fireplace, then turned and said, "You believe she can't fool me if I'm close enough to her. If we can get her here in the house, I'll be close enough."

He came back to her, smiled down at her while he ran his fingers through her curly hair.

"Kiss me, Dillon."

"Can I do more than kiss you?"

"Oh yes."

"Good. Dinner can wait."

All the world can wait, Sherlock thought, as she held him to her. "After dinner, I want us to go to the gym. It'll relieve all the stress."

"You got it. But if you have much stress after I'm through with you, I'll have to reassess my program."

And he laughed, actually laughed.

*Gothenburg, Sweden*

Bloated clouds hung low, blotting out the moon and stars. They would bring rain, perhaps even snow, before the night was over.

Simon was sitting low in a small boat, his hands tied behind him.

Alpo was rowing and Nikki was beside him, the gun pressed against his side. In a boat trailing them were Ian Jorgenson and a small man Simon hadn't seen before who was rowing.

The canal was wide, the town of Gothenburg on either side casting ghostly shadows in the dark light. There was only the rippling of the oars going through the water, smooth and nearly soundless.

The canal twisted to the right, and the buildings became fewer. There were no people that Simon could see.

He very nearly had the knot on his hands pulled loose. A few more minutes and his hands would be free, and a little more time after that to get circulation back into his hands and fingers.

If he had a bit more time, he had a chance. But the buildings were thinning out too much. They could kill him at any time without worry.

He worked the knot, rubbing his wrists raw, but that didn't matter. His blood helped loosen the strands of hemp.

"Stop!"

It was Ian Jorgenson. His small boat pulled up beside theirs.

"Here. This is fine. Give me the gun, Nikki, I want to put a bullet through this bastard. Then you can put him in that bag and sink him to the bottom."

Simon could feel Nikki leaning toward Ian to give him the gun. It was his last chance. Simon jumped up, slammed against Alpo, and dove at the small man in the other boat. Both boats careened wildly, the men shouting and cursing. As Simon hit the water, he heard a splash behind him, then another.

There was nothing colder on earth than this damned water. What did he expect? He was in Sweden in November. He wondered how long he had before hypothermia set in and he died. He didn't fight it, let himself sink, quickly, quietly, trying not to think of how cold he was, how numb his legs felt. He had to get free or he would die, from the frigid water or from a bullet, it didn't matter. He worked his hands until he hit the bottom of the canal, twisted away from where he thought the other men were. He swam as best he could with only his feet in the opposite direction, back down the canal, veering toward the side, back to where there was more shelter and a way to climb out of the water.

He was running out of breath and he was freezing. There wasn't much more time. There was no hope for it. He kicked upward until his head broke the surface. He saw Nikki and Ian both in the water, speaking, but softly, listening for him. His hands weren't free yet.

He heard a shout. They'd spotted him. He saw Alpo rowing frantically toward him. He didn't stop to get Ian or Nikki out of the water, just came straight toward Simon.

At last his hands slipped free from the frayed hemp. He felt his blood slimy on his wrists, mixing with the water. It should have stung but he didn't feel much of anything. His hands were numb.

He dove as he saw Alpo raise a gun and fire. The frigid water splashed up in Simon's face, close. Too close. He dove at least ten feet down and swam with all his strength toward the side of the canal.

When he came up, his lungs on fire, the boat was nearly on him. The second boat was behind him and now all the men were in it, searching the black water for a sign of him.

Ian shouted, "There he is! Get him!"

Gunshots split the water around him.

Then he heard sirens, at least three of them.

He went under again, deeper this time, and changed direction to swim toward the sound of those sirens. It was so cold his teeth hurt.

When he couldn't hold his breath for another second, simply couldn't bear the water any longer, he came up as slowly as he could, his head quietly breaking the surface.

He couldn't believe what he was seeing. A half dozen police cars screeched to a stop on the edge of the canal, not ten feet from him. Guns were drawn, men were shouting in Swedish, flashing lights on Ian and his crew.

A man reached out his hand and pulled Simon out of the canal. "Mr. Russo, I believe?"

# TWENTY-SEVEN

Lily walked beside Olaf's wheelchair back to the main entrance hall with its huge black-and-white marble chessboard, its three-foot-tall pieces lining opposite sides of the board, in correct position, ready to be moved.

He motioned for a manservant to leave his chair right in the middle of the chessboard, squarely on the white king five square. He looked at Lily, who stood beside the white king, then glanced down at the watch on his veined wrist and said, "You didn't eat much dinner, Lily."

"No," she said.

"He's dead by now. Accept it."

Lily looked down at the white queen. She wondered how heavy the chess piece was. Could she heft it up and hurl it at that evil old man? She looked toward the silent manservant, dressed all in white like a hospital orderly, and said, "Why don't you get an electric wheelchair? It's ridiculous for him to push you everywhere."

Olaf said again, his voice sharper now, not quite so gentle, "He's dead, Lily."

She looked at him now and said, "No, I don't believe he is, but you soon will be, won't you?"

"When you speak like that, I know you aren't at all like your grandmother, despite your look of her. Don't be disrespectful and mean-spirited, Lily. I don't like it. I'm quite willing to present you the Frasiers' heads on platters. What more can I offer you?"

"You can let Simon and me leave with my grandmother's paintings."

"Don't be a child. Listen to me, for this is important. In a wife I require obedience. Ian, I'm sure, will help me teach you manners, teach you to curb your tongue."

"It's a new millennium, Olaf, and you're a very old man. Even if you died within the week, I would refuse to remain here."

He banged his fist on the wheelchair hard, making it lurch. "You will do what you're told. Do you need to see your lover's body before you will let go of him? Before you accept that he really is dead?"

"He's not my lover. He just wants to be my consultant."

"Not your lover? I don't believe you. You spoke of him as if he were some sort of hero, able to overcome any obstacle. That is nonsense."

"Not in Simon's case." She wished that she really did believe him capable of just about anything, even if it was nonsense. But she was hoping frantically that Simon wasn't dead. He'd promised her, and he wouldn't break his word. When they'd taken him but two hours before, he'd lightly cupped her face in his hands and whispered, "I will be all right. Count on it, Lily."

And she'd licked her dry lips, felt fear for him moving deep and hard inside her, and whispered back, "I've been thinking about those new criteria, Simon. I admit I sure do need help when it comes to men."

He patted her cheek. "You got it."

She'd watched the three men take him out of that beautiful grand mansion, watched the door close behind them, heard the smooth wheels of Olaf Jorgenson's chair across the huge chessboard foyer.

Olaf brought her back, saying, "You will forget him. I will see to it."

She glanced at the two bodyguards, standing utterly silent. They'd both come with them from the dining room.

"Do you know I have an incredible brother? His name is Dillon Savich. He doesn't paint like our grandmother; he whittles. He creates beautiful pieces."

"A boy's hobby, not worth much of anything to anyone with sophistication and discrimination. And you spend your time drawing cartoons. What is the name? Remus?"

"Yes, I draw political cartoons. His name is No Wrinkles Remus. He's utterly immoral, like you, but I've never yet seen him want to murder someone." She paused for a moment, smiled at the motionless manservant. "I'm really quite good at cartooning. Isn't it interesting the way Grandmother's talent found new ways to come out in us, her grandchildren?"

"Sarah Elliott was unique. There will never be another like her."

"I agree. There will never be another cartoonist like me either. I'm unique, too. And what are you, Olaf? Other than an obsessed old man who has had too much money and power for far too long? Tell me, have you ever done anything worthwhile in your blighted life?"

His face turned red; his breathing became labored. The manservant looked frightened. The two bodyguards stood straighter and tensed, their eyes darting from Lily to their boss.

She couldn't stop herself. Rage and impotence roiled inside her, and she hated this wretched monster. Yes, let him burst a vessel with his rage; let him stroke out. It was payback for all that he'd done to her, to Simon. "I know what you are—you're one of those artists manqué, one of those pathetically sad people who were just never good enough, who could only be hangers-on, always on the outside looking in. You weren't even good enough to be a pale imitation, were you? I'll bet my grandmother thought you were pitiful, yes, pathetic. I'll bet she told you what she thought of you, didn't she?"

"Shut up!" He began cursing her, but it was in Swedish and she couldn't understand. The bodyguards were even more on edge now, surprised at what the old man, their boss, was yelling, the spittle spewing out of his mouth.

Lily didn't shut up. She talked over him, yelled louder than he was yelling, "What did she say to you that last day when she left with my grandfather? Because you went to her, didn't you? Begged her to marry you instead of Emerson, but she refused, didn't she? Did she laugh at you? Did she tell you she would even take that woman-hating Picasso before you? That you had the talent of a slug and you disgusted her, all your pretenses, your affectations? What did she say to you, Olaf?"

"She said I was a spoiled little boy who had too much money and would always be a shallow, selfish man!" He was wheezing, nearly incoherent, flinging himself from side to side.

Lily stared at him. "You even remember the exact words my grandmother said to you? That was more than sixty-five years ago! You were pathetic then, and you're beyond that now. You're frightening."

"Shut up!" Olaf seemed feverish now, his frail, veined hands clutching the arms of the wheelchair, his bent and twisted fingers showing white from the strain.

The manservant was leaning over him now, speaking urgently in his ear. She could hear the words, but he spoke in Swedish.

Olaf ignored him, shook him off. Lily said, smiling, "Do you know that Sarah loved Emerson so much she was always painting him? That there are six of his portraits in our mother's private collection?"

"I knew," he screamed at her, "of course I knew! You think I would ever want a portrait of that philistine? That damned fool knew nothing of what she was. He couldn't have understood or appreciated what she was! I could, but she left me. I begged her, on my knees in front of her, but it didn't matter—she left me!"

He was trembling so badly she thought he would fall from his wheelchair.

Suddenly, Olaf yelled something in Swedish to his manservant. The man grabbed the handles and began pushing the wheelchair across the huge chessboard.

"Hey, Olaf, why are you running away from me? Don't you like hearing what I have to say? I'll bet it's only the second time anyone's told you the truth. Don't you want to marry me anymore?"

She heard him yelling, but she couldn't make out the words; they were garbled, incoherent, some English, some Swedish. He sounded like a mad old man, beyond control. What was he going to do? Why had he left? She stood on the king one square, leaning against the beautifully carved heavy piece, shuddering with reaction, wondering what she'd driven him to with her contempt, her ridicule. She couldn't run because she didn't doubt the two bodyguards would stop her.

Where was the manservant taking him? What had he said to him? The two bodyguards were speaking low, so she couldn't really hear them. They stared at her again, and she saw bewilderment in their eyes. She wouldn't get three steps before they were on her.

Lily's rage wilted away and was replaced with a god-awful fear. But she'd held her own. She thought of her grandmother and wondered how like her she was. They'd both faced down this man, and she was proud of what they'd done.

She stood there, her brain squirreling madly about, wondering what to do now. She didn't have time to think about it. She heard the smooth wheelchair wheels rolling across the marble floor and saw Olaf coming toward her. This time he was pushing himself, his gnarled, trembling hands on the cushioned wheel pads. His two bodyguards took a step forward. He shook his head, not even looking at them. He was staring at Lily, and there was memory in his eyes, memory of that other woman, painfully clear and vivid. She knew that what had happened that day had struck him to his very soul, maimed him, destroyed what he'd seen himself as being and becoming. And now he saw what he had become after that day so very long ago.

Lily saw madness in his eyes; it was beyond hatred, and it was aimed at her. At her and her grandmother, who was dead and beyond his vengeance. Everything that had driven him, the decades of obsession with her grandmother as the single perfect woman, all of it had exploded when Lily had pushed him to remember the events as they'd really happened, forced him to see the truth of that day Sarah Elliott told him she was leaving with another man.

He came up to within six feet of her and stopped pushing the wheels. She wondered if he could make out her outline. Or was she a vague shadow?

He spoke, his voice low and steady as he said, "I've decided I won't marry you. I have seen clearly now that you don't deserve my devotion or my admiration. You are nothing like Sarah, nothing at all." He lifted a small derringer from his lap and pointed it at her.

"The Frasiers are dead. They weren't worth anything to me alive. And now, you aren't either."

The bodyguards took a step forward, in unison.

He'd had the Frasiers killed?

Lily ran at the wheelchair, smashed into it as hard as she could and sent it over onto its side, scraping against the marble floor. Olaf was flung from the chair.

Lily didn't hesitate. She ran as fast as she could, to fall flat behind the white king. She heard two rapid shots. The king's head shattered and fragments of marble flew everywhere.

She heard Olaf yell at the bodyguards, heard their loud running steps. She stayed flat on the floor. Several shards of marble had struck her, and she felt pricks of pain, felt the sticky flow of blood down her arm, rolling beneath her bra, staining the white dress.

She heard Olaf cursing, still helpless on the floor. He was screaming at his bodyguards to tell him if he'd killed her yet.

The bodyguards shouted something, but again it was in Swedish so she didn't understand. They didn't come after her, evidently because he wanted to have this pleasure all for himself, and they knew it.

She began moving on her elbows, behind the queen now, toward the great front door, behind the bishop. She looked out toward Olaf. One of his bodyguards was bending over him, handing him his own gun.

The bodyguard picked Olaf up and set him again in his wheelchair, then turned the chair toward her. And now Olaf aimed that gun right at her.

She rolled behind the knight. She wasn't any farther than ten feet from the front doors.

"I like this game," Olaf shouted and fired. The bishop toppled, shattering as it fell, falling over her ankles. She felt a stab of pain, but she could still move her feet. She moved solidly behind the knight and stilled.

Olaf shouted again. Then he laughed. Another shot, obscenely loud in the silence, and she saw a huge chunk of marble floor, not three feet from her, spew in all directions. He fired again and again, sending the white king careening into the queen.

Lily was on her knees behind the rook now, close to the front door.

Another shot whistled past her ear, and she flattened herself. One of the bodyguards yelled and ran toward her. Why?

Then she heard more shots, at least six of them, but they weren't from Olaf or the bodyguard; they were coming through the front door. She heard yelling, men's voices, and pounding on the door until it crashed inward.

Olaf and the bodyguards were shooting toward the door.

Lily lurched to her feet, lifted a huge shard of the bishop's white miter, ran toward Olaf, and hurled it at his wheelchair.

It hit him. Olaf, his gun firing wildly, straight up now, went over backward. His bodyguards ran as policemen fired at them from the open front door.

More gunfire. So much shouting, so much noise, too much. Simon was there, just behind the third policeman. He was alive.

There was sudden silence. The gun storm was over. Lily ran to Simon, hurled herself against him. His arms tightened around her.

She raised her head and smiled up at him. "I'm glad you came when you did. It was pretty dicey there for a while."

She heard Olaf screaming, spewing profanity. Then he was quiet.

Simon said in her ear, "It's over, Lily, all over. Olaf isn't going anywhere. It's time to worry about yourself. You're bleeding a little. I want you to hold still; there's an ambulance coming."

"I'm all right. It's just cuts from the flying marble. You're wet, Simon," she said. "Why are you wet?"

"I was careless. Be still."

"No, tell me. How did you get away from them? What happened?"

He realized she couldn't let it go, and he slowed himself, keeping his voice calm and low. "I dove into the canal to get away, but I couldn't.

Then there were all sorts of cops there to pull me out of the canal and take care of Alpo, Nikki, and Ian. Nobody was killed. They're all in the local lockup. It was your brother, Lily. He called a friend in Stockholm who happened to have two brothers living here in Gothenburg. The police were watching the mansion, saw Ian and the boys stuff me in the car, called backup, and followed."

"I want to meet those brothers," she said. For the first time, she felt like smiling, and so she did, a lovely smile that was filled with hope.

# TWENTY-EIGHT

*Washington, D.C.*

Late Saturday night, it was colder in Washington than it had been in Stockholm. The temperature had plummeted early in the day and the skies had opened up and sprinkled a dusting of snow all over the East Coast. Lily was finally in bed, her shoulder and back no longer throbbing from the shards of marble that had struck her. "Nothing important here—all surface pain," the Swedish doctor had said, and she'd wanted to slug him. Now she would probably have more scars.

When she'd said this on a sigh to Simon, he'd said, as he'd eased some pillows around her on the roomy first-class seat, that he liked banged-up women. The scars showed character.

"No," Lily had said as she let him ease a thin airplane blanket to her chin, "what it shows is that the woman has bad judgment."

He'd laughed as he'd kissed her. Then he'd smoothed the hair off her forehead and kissed her again, not laughing this time.

Then Simon had cupped her face in his palm and said very quietly, since the movie was over and everyone was trying to sleep in the dimly lit cabin, "I think we're going to make a fine team, Lily. You, me, and No Wrinkles Remus."

Lily snuggled down under the comforter. She hoped Simon was doing better than she was. Like her, he'd been ready to fall flat on his face from exhaustion. She hoped he was sleeping.

Actually, Simon was turning slowly over in the too-short cot, not wanting to roll himself accidentally off onto the floor. He had managed to get the blanket carefully wrapped around his feet, no easy thing, since his feet were off the cot and on the big side. He'd taken up temporary residence in Sean's room, down the hall from Lily, since the baby was still with Mrs. Savich. A precaution, Dillon had said as he'd helped Dane Carver, a new special agent in his unit, carry in the narrow army cot that would be Simon's bed. He'd announced to both men that he didn't care if he had to fit himself into Sean's crib, if that's what it took to get to sleep.

Simon knew she was okay, just down the hall. Not near enough to him for the time being, but Simon had plans to change that. He could easily picture her in his brownstone, could picture how he'd redo one of those large upstairs bedrooms to make it her workroom. Great light in that room, exactly right for her.

Simon was smiling as he breathed in the scent of Sean. Nice scent, but he would have preferred to be in the guest room with Lily, in her bed. He'd always been a patient man, which, he supposed, was a good thing, since he'd only known Lily for a little more than two weeks.

As for Lily, she didn't know why she couldn't sleep. It was after midnight in Washington, morning in Sweden. But she and Simon had been in Sweden such a short time, her body had no clue what time of day it was. She was beyond exhaustion, yet she couldn't sleep.

She was still very worried about her brother. Tammy Tuttle hadn't shown up, hadn't come after Dillon, and both her brother and Sherlock were frustrated and on edge, at their wits' end.

On Friday afternoon, as announced, Dillon had taken a taxi to the airport and checked in for a flight to Texas. Then, at the last minute, he'd deplaned and slipped back into the house in Georgetown.

Now it was Saturday night, well beyond the deadline, and Lily knew there were still agents covering the house. Jimmy Maitland wasn't taking any chances, and the very sophisticated house alarm was set.

Lily hoped Dillon and Sherlock were sleeping better than she was. She knew they missed Sean. When they'd all come up to bed, they'd automatically turned to go to Sean's room.

She rolled onto her side and sucked in her breath at a sudden jab of pain. She didn't want to take any more pain pills. She closed her eyes and saw that huge room again, its walls covered with her grandmother's paintings. So many to be returned to museums all over the world. Olaf Jorgenson and his son would not be able to stop it. Ian would be in jail for a very long time. Olaf was in the hospital, in very bad shape.

After a good deal of time, she was finally floating toward sleep, when her brain clicked on full alert and her eyes flew open. She'd heard something. Not Simon or Dillon or Sherlock moving around, something that wasn't right.

Maybe it was nothing at all, a phantom whisper from her exhausted brain or only a puff of wind that had sent a branch sweeping against the bedroom window. Yes, the sound was outside, not in her bedroom. Maybe it was in Simon's bedroom. Had he awakened?

Lily continued to wait, gritty eyes staring around the dark room, listening.

She started to relax again when she heard a creak. A slight pressure on the oak floor could cause a creak, but it was there and it was close. In the air, no longer heard, but she still felt it. Lily waited, straining to hear, her heart pounding now.

The scattered carpets covering the oak floors would mask any creaks, make someone walking hard to hear.

Lily lurched upright, straining to see. Too late, she saw a shadow, moving fast, and something coming down at her. She felt a deadening pain like a sharp knife driving into her skull.

She fell back onto the pillow. Before she passed out, she saw a face over her, a woman's face, and she knew whose face it was. The mouth whispered, "Hi, little sister."

SHERLOCK couldn't sleep. Dillon's arm was heavy over her chest, and he was close and warm, his familiar scent in the air she breathed, but it didn't help. Her brain wouldn't turn off; it just kept moving, going over and over what they knew about Tammy, what they imagined but didn't know.

When she couldn't stand it anymore, Sherlock eased away from him, got out of bed, and pulled on her old blue wool robe. She wore socks to keep her feet warm against the oak floor.

She had to check the house again, though she'd already checked it three times, and Dillon had checked probably another three. She had to be sure. It was early Sunday morning, it was snowing, and Sean was at his grandmother's, safe. When would she feel secure enough to bring him home? Ever? It had to end. Tammy had to do something; it had to end, sometime.

She hoped the four agents outside weren't freezing their butts off. At least she knew they had hot coffee; she'd taken them a huge thermos about ten o'clock.

She got to the end of the hall and paused for a moment, feeling the house warm around her, breathing in its comforting smells. It took a moment, but Sherlock realized that something was different.

It was quiet in a way she wasn't used to. Too quiet. She realized that the alarm was off, the very low hum you could barely hear wasn't there. Panic lurched up into her throat.

She turned to look down the beautifully carved oak staircase. She saw dim light pooling at the bottom from the glass arch above the front door, snowflakes drifting lazily down. She took one step, then another, when a hand hit her square in the middle of the back. She screamed, or at least she thought she did, as she went head over heels down the stairs. Someone passed by her as she lay there facedown on a thick Persian carpet, the breath knocked out of her, barely hanging on to consciousness. She'd struck her head, struck everything on her body, and she could hardly move.

She thought she heard a moan, and then the figure was gone. The front door opened as she stared at it, yes, she was sure it was open, now fully open, because she felt a slice of cold air reach her face, and she shivered.

The front door stayed open. Only an instant passed before she realized what had happened. Someone had shoved her down the stairs. Someone had just gone out through the front door.

She managed to stagger to her feet, fear swamping her. Tammy Tuttle, it had to be her, but how? How had she gotten past the agents and into the house? Why hadn't Sherlock seen her?

She threw back her head and yelled, "Dillon! Oh God, Dillon, come quickly!"

Savich and Simon appeared at the top of the stairs at the same time, both wearing only boxer shorts. A light went on.

"Sherlock!"

Savich was beside her, holding her tightly against him, then gently pushing her down, afraid that he was hurting her.

Sherlock came back up, grabbed his arms. "No, no, Dillon, I'm okay. Tammy—she was here; she shoved me down the stairs. The alarm was off and I was just coming downstairs to check. I heard a woman's moan. It wasn't me. Where's Lily? Dear God, check Lily."

Simon was back up the stairs, taking them two, three at a time. They heard him yell, "She's gone!"

Dillon grabbed his cell phone to call the agents outside.

Simon turned on all the lights as Dillon spoke to the agents. The front door was open and there was no sign of Lily. Somehow, Tammy had taken her out without Sherlock seeing anything.

Savich stood on his front porch in his boxer shorts, straining to see through the snow falling like a thin, white curtain in front of him, into the darkness beyond.

JIMMY Maitland said as he sipped his coffee, so blessedly hot it nearly burned his tongue, "What do the folk in Behavioral Sciences have to say?"

Savich said, "Jane Bitt is guessing, she freely admits it, but as far as she knows, no one has ever before encountered anything like Tammy Tuttle. She may have some sort of genetic gift, be able to project what she wants you to see. What's amazing is the scope. She had everyone in that airport in Antigua believing she was a man, and this is what makes her so unique. Jane said even given that, we shouldn't focus exclusively on it— there's no percentage to it. She says there's no beating her that way. We should focus on a woman with one arm who's twenty-three years old. What would she do? If we can predict that, she's vulnerable."

"But we don't know what she'll do, where she'd take Lily," Sherlock said.

"She was supposed to come after *me* here, not Lily—to tear my head off," Savich said slowly, staring at his hands, which were clasped tightly together around Sherlock's waist.

Simon was on his feet, pacing in front of the two of them. He was wearing only wrinkled black wool slacks, no shirt, even his feet were bare.

"Listen, Savich, you know she took Lily because she figured it was better revenge than killing you. Now, think. Where would Tammy Tuttle take Lily?"

It was nearly four o'clock in the morning, snow still falling lightly. No one said a word. Savich sat in his favorite chair, leaned his head back, and closed his eyes. He felt Sherlock leaning against him.

Then Sherlock said very softly, "I think I know where she might have taken Lily."

# TWENTY-NINE

Lily was colder than when she'd been lying on that naked mattress in Gothenburg. Her wrists and ankles were bound together loosely, with duct tape. She was lying on her side in a dark room, and it smelled funny. It wasn't unpleasant, but she didn't recognize it.

She was all right. She felt a dull throb on the side of her head, but it wasn't bad, and her side hurt, but that wouldn't kill her. No, it was the insane woman who had brought her here who could kill her.

Did she hear someone laugh? She couldn't be sure.

She gritted her teeth and tried working at her wrists. There was a little bit of movement; the tape wasn't all that tight. She kept pulling and twisting, working the duct tape.

Where was she? Where had Tammy Tuttle taken her? She knew Tammy was utterly mad and smart, since up to now she'd managed to evade Lily's brother. She'd taken Lily because she was Dillon's sister. She thought it was better revenge against Dillon than killing him. She wanted to make him suffer.

Lily knew she was right about that. Dillon was probably driving himself mad with guilt. She kept working the duct tape.

What was that smell that permeated the air? Then she knew. She was in some sort of barn. She smelled old hay, linseed oil, yes, that was it, at least it was some kind of oil, and the very faint odor of ancient dried manure.

A barn somewhere. She remembered Simon asking Dillon where they'd first caught up with the Tuttle brother and sister, and he'd said it was at a barn on Marilyn Warluski's property near the Plum River in Maryland.

Maybe that was where she was. At least Dillon and Sherlock knew about this place. Was this Marilyn Warluski here with her as well? Was she still alive?

Dull, gray light was coming through the filthy glass behind her. It was dawn. Soon it would be morning.

Lily kept working the duct tape. She didn't want to think about how in all the years she'd used duct tape it had never broken or slipped off. But it was looser than before, she knew it.

Lily needed to go to the bathroom. She was hungry. Her side and shoulder were thudding with pain. Just surface pain, that damned doctor had assured her. She wished now she had slugged him. Let him feel some surface pain for a while, the jerk.

There was more light, dull, flat light, and she could see now that she was in a small tack room. There was an ancient desk shoved against the opposite wall, two old chairs near it. A torn bridle with only one rein was dangling from a nail on the wooden-slatted wall.

It was cold. She couldn't stop shivering. Now that she could see around her, see the cracks in the wooden walls that gave directly to the outside, she was even colder. She was wearing only her nightgown. At least it was a long-sleeve flannel number that came to her neck and down to her ankles.

But it wasn't enough.

She turned her head when she heard the door slowly open.

She saw a woman standing in the dim light. "Hello, little sister. How are you doing with the duct tape? Loosen it up a bit yet?"

Lily said, "I'm not your little sister."

"No, you're Dillon Savich's little sister and that's more than close enough. That's just dandy." Tammy walked into the small room, sniffed the air, frowned for just a moment, then pulled one of the rickety chairs away from the desk and sat down. She crossed her legs. She was wearing huge-heeled black boots.

"I'm very cold," Lily said.

"Yeah, I figured."

"I also have to go to the bathroom."

"Okay, I don't care if you're cold, but I wouldn't make you lie there on your side and pee on yourself. That would be gross. I'm going to unfasten your feet so you can walk. You can go out in the barn and pick your corner. Here, I'll put the duct tape around your wrists in front of you. I wouldn't want you to pee on yourself." Lily didn't have a chance to fight her. Her ankles were bound. She could do nothing, just wait for the duct tape to go around her wrists again. At least they were in front of her now, even for a short time.

"Here's a couple of Kleenex."

Lily walked ahead of Tammy into the large barn. It was a mess—overflowing rotting hay, random pieces of rusted equipment, boards hanging loose, letting in snow and frigid air. She quickly saw the big, black-painted circle. It was starkly clean. That was where Tammy and her brother had forced the two boys to stay while Tammy called her Ghouls.

"How about the corner over there? Hurry up now, you and I have lots to do. I don't trust you not to be stupid but it won't matter if you are. Move, little sister."

Lily relieved herself, then turned to face Tammy, who'd been watching her.

"How did you get into the house? The alarm system is one of the best made."

Tammy smiled at her. Lily saw her very clearly now in the shaft of strong morning light that speared through a wide slash in the wall. She was wearing black jeans over those black boots, and a long-sleeve black turtleneck sweater. One sleeve dangled where her arm should have been. She wasn't ugly or beautiful. She looked normal, average even. She didn't look particularly scary, even with her moussed, spiked-up dark hair. Her eyes were very dark, darker than her hair, in sharp contrast to her face, which was very pale, probably made more pale with white powder, and her mouth was painted a deep plum color. She was thin, and her single hand was long and narrow, the fingernails capped with the same plum color that was on her mouth. Even thin, she gave the overwhelming impression she was as strong as a bull.

"I'll bet your brother and that little redheaded wife of his were chewing off their fingernails waiting for me. But I didn't come when they wanted me to. That announcement the FBI character made on TV, I didn't believe it, not for an instant. I knew it was a trap, and that was okay. I took my time, found out all about the alarm, how to disarm it. It wasn't hard. Sit down, little sister."

Lily sat on a bale of hay so old it cracked beneath her. "I don't think you could have done that alarm yourself, alone. It would require quite some expertise."

"You're right. People always underestimate me because they think I'm a hick." Tammy grinned down at her, then began pacing in front of her, every once in a while looking down at her empty sleeve, where her other hand should have been. Lily watched her and saw the look of panic, then bone-deep hatred, cross her face.

"What are you going to do with me?"

Tammy laughed. "Why, I'm going to put you in the circle and I'm going to call the Ghouls. They'll come and tear you apart, and that's what I'll deliver back to your brother—a body he'd rather not see." Tammy paused for a moment, cocked her head to one side. "They're close now, I can hear them."

Lily listened. She could hear the faint rustling of tree branches, probably from the constant fall of snow, the movement of the wind. But nothing else, not even early-morning birds, no animal sounds at all. "I don't hear anything."

"You will," said Tammy. "You will. We're going to walk over to that black circle. You're going to sit down in the middle of it. I won't even tie your hands behind you. Now, move it, little sister." Tammy pulled out a gun and aimed it at Lily.

"No, I'm not going anywhere," Lily said. "Will the Ghouls still want me if I'm not in the circle? What if you've already killed me with that gun of yours? Will they still want me then?"

"We'll have to see, won't we?" Tammy raised the gun and aimed it at Lily's face.

SIMON wished he were on his motorcycle, weaving in and out of the heavy, early-morning traffic. Why didn't Savich have a siren? Why were there so many people at this hour?

When there was finally a break in the traffic, Savich pressed his foot hard on the accelerator. Simon looked out the back window, saw six black FBI cars, one after the other, coming fast, keeping pace with them.

"Tell me, Sherlock," he said, his heart thudding fast, hard beats. "We'll be there soon. Tell me about Tammy."

SLOWLY, Tammy lowered the gun. "You think you're pretty cute, don't you?"

Lily slowly shook her head, so relieved she was nearly sick. She'd been ready to feel a bullet go right through her heart, to be gone, and that was it. Sudden and final and she was dead. But she was still here, still alive, with Tammy, who was still holding that ugly gun.

The circle—it appeared Tammy wanted her in that circle, still alive. "Where is Marilyn? She's your cousin, isn't she?"

"You want to know about my sweet little cousin? I'm not real happy with her right now. See, she told your brother everything about me. Then he used her for bait. That was ruthless of him. I like that in a guy. She was waiting for me right there in the open, in that airport, standing next to that stupid agent who was supposed to be guarding her. From me. What a joke that was. I cut the agent's throat, and everyone saw a crazy young man do it. Everyone believed it, but it was really me.

"You want to know why I hate your brother? It's not hard. He killed my brother, shot my arm off, just left it dangling by a few strips of muscle, and I saw it hanging there and I thought I was going to die. And they strapped me down to this bed because your brother told them I was bad trouble, and then they cut the rest of it right off in the hospital and I nearly died. All because of your damned brother."

Then Tammy let loose, screamed to the rafters, "One damned arm! Look at me—my sleeve is empty! I nearly died from the infection, damn him to hell. He shot my arm off! After I set the Ghouls on you, after they've gnawed you to a bloody mess, I'm going to get him, *get him*, GET HIM!"

Lily kept her mouth shut, tried to pull herself together enough to work on the duct tape. She wished she could raise her hands and use her teeth, but Tammy would notice that for sure. At least her hands were still bound in front of her; that might give her some chance.

Tammy drew a deep breath as she slowly lowered the gun. Her eyes focused again, on Lily. "You're like him—stubborn."

"How did you get past all the agents guarding the house?"

"Stupid buggers, all of them. It was easy. There's hardly any challenge anymore. I didn't let them see me."

Lily didn't want to believe anything that outrageous, but she said, "And they couldn't see me either?"

"Oh yes. Nothing to it. I dragged you out, wearing that cute little nightgown—sorry I didn't get you a coat. But I figured after you realized what was going to happen to you, you'd want to feel the cold, better than being dead and not feeling anything at all. Now, little sister, move into the circle."

"No."

Tammy raised the gun and fired. Lily cried out, unable to help herself. She threw herself to the right, off the bale of hay, felt the hot whoosh of the bullet not an inch from her cheek, and rolled and kept rolling, pulling and twisting at the tape on her wrists. Another bullet hit a pile of moldering hay and spewed it upward.

Then Tammy stopped shooting. She walked over to Lily and stood still, staring down at her, the gun pointed at her chest. Lily looked up, frozen, afraid to move, afraid even to breathe.

Lily said, finally, "You have a problem, don't you, Tammy? The Ghouls won't come if I'm not staked like a tethered goat in that black circle, right? So get used to it. I'm not going anywhere."

Tammy didn't say a thing to that, just turned and walked away, her strides in those heavy, black boots long and solid. Lily watched her disappear into the tack room and close the door behind her, hard.

It was so silent Lily could hear the barn groan as the rising wind hit it. Then Lily heard a scream, a woman's scream, Tammy's scream and two gunshots, loud, sharp.

Dillon ran out of the tack room toward her, his SIG in his hand, yelling, "Lily! Are you all right, sweetheart? Everything's okay. I got into the tack room, shot her before she saw me. Are you hit?"

She felt such relief she thought she'd choke on it. She yelled, "Dillon, you came! I kept her talking, knew I had to keep her talking. She's so scary. Then she started shooting at me and I thought it was all over—"

Lily stopped cold. Dillon was nearly to her, not more than six feet away, when suddenly Lily didn't see her brother anymore. She saw Tammy. She wasn't holding Dillon's SIG; she was holding that same little ugly gun that was hers. Her brain froze. Simply froze. She couldn't accept what she was seeing, what was right in front of her, she simply couldn't.

"Honey, are you okay?"

It was Tammy's voice, no longer Dillon's.

Then Lily realized it really was Tammy. She thought she'd seen Dillon because she wanted to so much, and Tammy wanted her to. And Tammy thought it was working.

Lily said, "I'm okay. I'm so glad you're here, Dillon, so glad."

Tammy dropped to her knees beside Lily and turned her onto her side. "Let me get that tape off you, sweetheart. There, let me slip the knife under the tape. Good, you've already loosened it. You could have gotten yourself free and away, couldn't you?" Then Tammy Tuttle pulled Lily against her and hugged her, kissed her hair. Stroked her single hand down her back. Lily felt Tammy's slight breasts against hers.

Tammy had laid the gun on the ground, a hand's length away from her, not more than six inches. "Hold me, Dillon. I was so scared. I'm so glad you came so quickly."

She cried, sobbed her heart out, felt Tammy squeeze her and kiss her hair again. Lily's hand moved slowly toward the gun, slowly, until her fingers touched the butt.

Tammy swept up the gun, tucked it into her waistband, and said, "Let me help you up, honey. That's right. You're okay now. Sherlock is outside with the other agents. Let's go see them."

Tammy was holding her tightly against her side, walking toward the barn doors. No, not really toward the doors. She was swerving to the left now, toward that big black circle.

Just as Tammy flung her onto her back and into the circle, Lily grabbed the gun from Tammy's waistband, raising it at her.

Tammy didn't seem to notice that Lily had her gun, that she was pointing it at her. She'd turned toward the barn doors, raised her head, and yelled, "Ghouls! No young bloods for you this time, but a soft, sweet morsel, a female. Bring your axes, bring your knives, and hack her apart! Come here, Ghouls!"

The barn doors blew inward. Lily saw whirling snow blowing in, and something else in that snow. A dust devil, that was it. That was what Dillon had seen as well, wasn't it?

The snow seemed to coalesce into two distinct formations, like tornadoes, whirling and dipping, coming toward her. But they were white, twisting this way and that, in constant motion, coming closer and closer. Lily felt frozen in place, just stared at those white cones coming closer, not more than a dozen feet away now, nearly to the black circle now. She had to move, had to.

Tammy saw that something was wrong. She pulled a knife out of her boot leg, a long, vicious knife. She raised that knife and ran toward Lily.

Lily didn't think, just raised the gun and yelled, "No, Tammy, it's over. Yes, I see you. The minute you got close, I saw you, not my brother. The Ghouls won't help you."

Just as Tammy leaped at her, the knife raised, the blade gleaming cold, Lily pulled the trigger.

Tammy yelled and kept coming. Lily pulled the trigger again and again, and Tammy Tuttle was kicked off her feet and hurled a good six feet by the force of the bullets. She sprawled on her back, gaping holes in her chest. Her one arm was flung out, the empty sleeve flat on the ground.

But Lily didn't trust her. She ran to her, breathing hard and fast, nearly beyond herself, and she aimed and fired the last bullet not a foot from Tammy's body. Her body lurched up with the bullet's impact. She fired again, but there was only a click. The gun was empty, but Tammy was still alive, her eyes on Lily's face, and Lily couldn't stop. She pulled the trigger, like an automaton, again and again, until, finally, only hollow clicks filled the silence.

Tammy lay on her back, covered with blood, her one hand still clenched at her side. Even her throat was ripped through by a bullet. Lily had fired six shots into her. Lily dropped to her knees, put her fingertips to Tammy's bloody neck.

No pulse.

But her eyes were looking up at Lily, looking into her. Tammy was still there, still clinging to what she was. Her lips moved, but there was no sound. Slowly, ever so slowly, her eyes went blank. She was dead now, her eyes no longer wild and mad, no longer seeing anything at all.

There was utter silence.

Lily looked up, but the Ghouls were gone. They were gone with Tammy.

# THIRTY

*Washington, D.C.*

FBI specialists from the evidence labs went over every inch of the barn at the Plum River in Maryland.

They found candy wrappers—more than three dozen—but no clothing, no bedding, no sign that Tammy Tuttle had been there for any time at all.

There was no sign of Marilyn Warluski.

"She's dead," Savich said, and Sherlock hated the deadening guilt in his voice.

"We can't be sure of anything when it comes to that family," Sherlock said matter-of-factly, but she'd moved closer, put her hand on his shoulder.

*Two Days Later*

It was late afternoon, and the snow had stopped falling. Washington was covered with a blanket of pristine white, and a brilliant sun was overhead. People were out and about on this cold, crystalline Sunday even as the national media announced the shooting death of the fugitive killer Tammy Tuttle in a barn in Maryland.

Lily came into the living room, a cup of hot tea in her hand. "I called Agent Clark Hoyt in Eureka. He said Hemlock Bay was rife with gossip over the deaths of Elcott and Charlotte. The mayor, the city council, and the local Methodist church are holding meetings to plan a big memorial service. No one, he said, really wants to delve too deeply into why they were killed, but it's possible the floating rumors could even exceed the truth."

Lily paused for a moment, then added, "I also called Tennyson. He's very saddened by his parents' death. It's difficult for him to accept what they did, that they used him—used both of us—to gain their ends. He said he knows now his parents were feeding me depressants all those months and they had been the ones to arrange for my brakes to fail when I was driving to Ferndale."

"But how did they know what you would be doing?" Sherlock asked.

"Tennyson said he called them from Chicago, just happened to mention that he'd asked me to drive to Ferndale, and when. I feel very bad for him, but I wonder how he could have been so blind to what his own parents were."

"They fooled you as well," Savich said. "At least enough. No one wants to see evil; no one wants to admit it exists."

Lily said, "I've decided to fly to California for the memorial service. I'm going for Tennyson. He's been hurt terribly. I feel that I must show him my support now, show everyone that I believe he was innocent of everything that happened. He knows I'm not coming back to him, as his wife, and he accepts it." She sighed. "He said he was leaving Hemlock Bay. He never wants to see the place again."

"I can't say I blame him," Simon said.

Savich said, "Please tell Tennyson for us that we are very sorry about what happened."

"I will." Lily raised her head, listened, and smiled. "Sean's awake from his nap."

Both Savich and Sherlock were up the stairs, side by side, their hands clasped.

Simon smiled at Lily, sipped his coffee. Savich had made it, so it was excellent. He sighed with pleasure.

"So, Lily, as your new consultant, I think it's very good for you to go back for his parents' memorial service. It will put closure on things. It will be over. Then you will begin to move forward. Now, I've been thinking hard about this."

"And what did you decide, Mr. Russo?"

"I think the first step is for you to move to New York. It's never wise for a client to be any distance at all from her consultant."

Lily walked across the living room, gently placed her teacup on an end table, and sat down on Simon's lap. She took his face between her hands and kissed him.

Simon sighed, set down his own cup, and pulled her close. "That's very nice, Lily."

"Yes, it is. Actually it's better than just nice." She kissed his neck, then settled herself against him. "I want to tell you you're the best, Simon. I can't believe it's all really over—that I'm even going to get all my paintings back. But you know what? I want to stay in Washington for a while. I want to settle down, let the past sort itself out, and when I'm ready for the future, I want it to be with a clean slate, no excess baggage dragging along with me. I want to launch *No Wrinkles Remus* again. I want to be my own boss for a while."

She thought for a moment he'd argue with her, but he didn't. He rubbed his hands up and down her back and said, "Our time together hasn't had many normal moments, like this. I think the consultant will need frequent visits, lots of contact, and both of us can think about things looking forward, not back."

She kissed him again, pressed her forehead to his. "Deal," she said.

Simon settled back and wrapped his arms around her, her cheek pressed against his neck. He said, "I forgot to tell you. An art dealer friend e-mailed me, said Abe Turkle is in Las Vegas gambling, and winning. He said Abe looked and acted like some big lumberjack; no one would believe for an instant he's one of the top forgers in the world."

"I wish I could remember what happened to that painting he gave me at his cottage."

The doorbell rang.

Dillon and Sherlock were still upstairs playing with Sean. Lily pulled herself off Simon's lap and went to answer the door. When she opened it, a FedEx man stood there, holding out an envelope. "For Dillon Savich," he said. Lily signed the overnight receipt and brought the envelope back into the living room.

She called out to Dillon. Shortly, Savich, carrying Sean over his shoulder, Sherlock at his side, came downstairs.

Dillon patted his sister's cheek. "What have you got, babe?"

"An overnight envelope for you, Dillon."

Savich handed Sean to Sherlock and took the envelope. He looked down at it, bemused, and said, "It's from the Beach Hotel in Aruba." He opened the envelope, pulled out a sheaf of color photos. Slowly, he looked at each of them.

"Come on, Dillon, what is it?"

He raised his head and said to Sherlock, "These are the photos that Tammy took in the Caribbean to show to Marilyn." There was a white sheet of paper behind the last photo, a few lines written on it. He read aloud.

"Mr. Savich, Tammy was right, the beaches here are very beautiful. I'm glad she didn't kill you."

MARILYN WARLUSKI

# TWENTY-FOUR

*Bar Harbor, Maine*

Special Agent Aaron Briggs, neck size roughly twenty-one inches, biceps to match, a gold tooth shining like a beacon in his habitual big smile, nodded from behind the counter at agents Lowell and Possner. Both agents were dressed casually in jeans, sweaters, and jackets, trying to appear like ordinary customers looking at frames and photo albums.

It was two o'clock, on the dot.

Savich was in the back. Aaron knew he had his SIG ready, knew he wanted Tammy Tuttle so bad he could taste it. Aaron wanted her, too. Dead was what Tammy Tuttle needed to be, for the sake of human beings everywhere, particularly young teenage boys. He'd listened to every word Dillon Savich had said on the flight up here. He knew agents who'd seen the wild-eyed guy in Antigua who'd slit Virginia Cosgrove's throat, agents who couldn't explain what they'd seen and heard. He felt a ripple of fear in his belly, but he told himself that soon she'd be dead, all that inexplicable stuff he'd heard she'd done down in the airport in Antigua would then be gone with her.

The bell over the shop door sounded as the door opened. In walked Tammy Tuttle, wrapped up in a thick, unbelted wool coat that hung loose on her. Aaron put out his big smile with its shining gold tooth and watched her walk toward him. He could feel the utter focus of agents Possner and Lowell from where he stood, his SIG not six inches from his right hand, beneath the counter.

She was pale, too pale, no makeup on her face, and there was something about her that jarred, something that wasn't quite right.

Aaron was the best retail undercover agent in the Bureau, bar none, with the reputation that he could sell a terrorist a used olive green

Chevy Chevette, and he turned on all his charm. He said, "Hi, may I help you, miss?"

Tammy was nearly leaning against the counter now. She wasn't very tall. She bent toward him and his eyes never left her face as she said, "Where's the other guy? You know, that little twerp who spells Teddi with an 'i'?"

"Yea, ain't that a hoot? Teddi with an 'i.' Well, Teddi said he had a bellyache—he's said that before—and called me to cover for him. Me, I think he drank too much last night at the Night Cave Tavern. You ever been there? Over on Snow Street?"

"No. Get my photos, now."

"Your name, miss?"

"Teresa Tanner."

"No problem," Aaron said and slowly turned to look in the built-in panels, sectioned off by letter of the alphabet. Under *T,* he found Teresa Tanner's envelope third in the slot, which was exactly where he'd placed it himself an hour before. He picked up the envelope with her name on it, was slowly turning back to her, knowing Savich was ready for him to drop to the floor so he'd have a clear shot at her, when suddenly he heard a hissing sound, loud, right in his ear, and he froze. Yes, a hiss, like a snake, right next to him, too close, too close, right next to his neck, and its fangs would sink deep into his skin and . . .

No, his imagination was going nuts on him, but there it was again. Aaron forgot to fall to the floor so Savich could have his shot. He grabbed his SIG from beneath the counter, brought it up fast, just like he knew Possner and Lowell were doing, and whipped around. The photo envelope was suddenly in her hand; he didn't know how she'd gotten it, but there it was, and then both Tammy Tuttle and the envelope were gone. Just gone.

He heard Savich yell, "Get out of the way, Aaron! Move!"

But he couldn't. It was like he was nailed to the spot. Savich was trying to shove him aside, but he resisted, he simply had to resist, not let him by. He saw a harsh, bright glow of fire in the corner of the shop, smelled burning plastic, harsh and foul, and heard Agent Possner scream. Oh God, the place was on fire; no, it was mainly Agent Possner. She was on fire— her hair, her eyebrows, her jacket, and she was screaming, slapping at herself. Flames filled her hair, bright and hot and orange as a summer sun.

Agent Aaron Briggs shoved Savich aside and started running, yelling as he ran toward Possner.

Agent Lowell was turning to Possner, not understanding, and when he saw the flames, he tackled her. They fell to the floor of the shop, knocking over a big frame display, and he was slapping at her burning hair with his hands. Aaron jerked off his sweater as he ran toward them, knocking frame and album displays out of the way.

Savich was around the counter, running toward the door, his gun drawn. Aaron saw him but didn't understand. Didn't he care that Possner was on fire? He heard a gunshot, a high, single pop, then nothing. Suddenly the flames were out. Possner was sobbing, in the fetal position on the floor, Lowell's shirt wrapped around her head, and Aaron saw Lowell was all right, no burns that Aaron could see. He had his cell phone out, calling for backup, calling for an ambulance. And Aaron realized that his fingers looked normal. He thought he'd seen them burned, just like he'd seen Possner burned.

SAVICH was running, searching through the streets. There weren't that many folk around, no tourists at all, it being fall and much too chilly for beach walks in Bar Harbor. He held his SIG at his side and made a grid in his mind. He'd studied the street layout. Where would she go? Where had she come from?

Then he saw her long, dark blue wool coat, thick and heavy, flapping around a corner half a block up Wescott. He nearly ran down an old man, apologized but didn't slow. He ran, holding his SIG against his side, hearing only his own breathing. He ran around the corner and stopped dead in his tracks. The alley was empty except for that thick wool coat. It lay in a collapsed pile against a brick wall at the back of the alley.

Where was she? He saw the narrow, wooden door, nearly invisible along the alley wall. When he got to it, he realized it was locked. He raised his SIG and fired into the lock. Two bullets dead on and the lock shattered. He was inside, crouched low, his gun steady, sweeping the space. It was very dim, one of the naked bulbs overhead, burned out. He blinked to adjust his vision and knew he was in grave danger. If Tammy was hidden in here, she could easily see his silhouette against the streetlight behind him and nail him.

He realized he was in a storeroom. There were barrels lining the walls, shelves filled with boxes and cans, paper goods. The floor was wooden and it creaked. The place was really old. It was dead quiet, not even any rats around. He swept over the room, hurrying because he didn't believe she'd stayed in here, no, she'd go through the door at the far end of the storeroom. It wasn't in Tammy's nature to hide and wait.

He opened the door and stared into a bright, sunlit dining room filled with a late-lunch crowd. He saw a kitchen behind a tall counter on the far side of the dining room, smoke from the range rising into the vents, exits to the left leading to bathrooms, and a single front door that led out to the sidewalk. He stepped into the room. He smelled roast beef and garlic. And fresh bread.

Slowly the conversations thinned out, then stopped completely, everyone gaping at the man who was in a cop stance, swinging a gun slowly around the room, looking desperate, looking like he wanted to kill someone. A woman screamed. A man yelled, "Here, now!"

"What's going on here?"

This last was from a huge man with crew-cut white hair, a white apron stained with spaghetti sauce, coming around the kitchen counter to Savich's left, carrying a long, curved knife. The smell of onions wafted off the knife blade.

"Hey, fellow, is this a holdup?"

Savich slowly lowered his gun. He couldn't believe what he was seeing, couldn't believe he'd come through a dank storeroom into a café and scared a good twenty people nearly to death. Slowly, he reholstered his gun. He pulled out his FBI shield, walked to the man with the knife, stopped three feet away, and showed it to him. He said in a loud voice, "I'm sorry to frighten everyone. I'm looking for a woman." He raised his voice so every diner in the big room could hear. "She's mid-twenties, tall, light hair, very pale. She has only one arm. Did she come in here? Through the storeroom door, like I did?"

There were no takers. Savich checked the bathrooms, then realized Tammy was long gone. She might have remained hidden in the storeroom, knowing he'd feel such urgency he'd burst into the café. He apologized to the owner and walked out the front door.

In that moment, standing on the Bar Harbor sidewalk, Savich could swear that he heard a laugh—a low, vicious laugh that made the hair on his arms stand up. There was no one there, naturally. He felt so impotent, so completely lost that he was hearing her in his mind.

Savich walked slowly back to Hamlet's Pics. When he got there, he